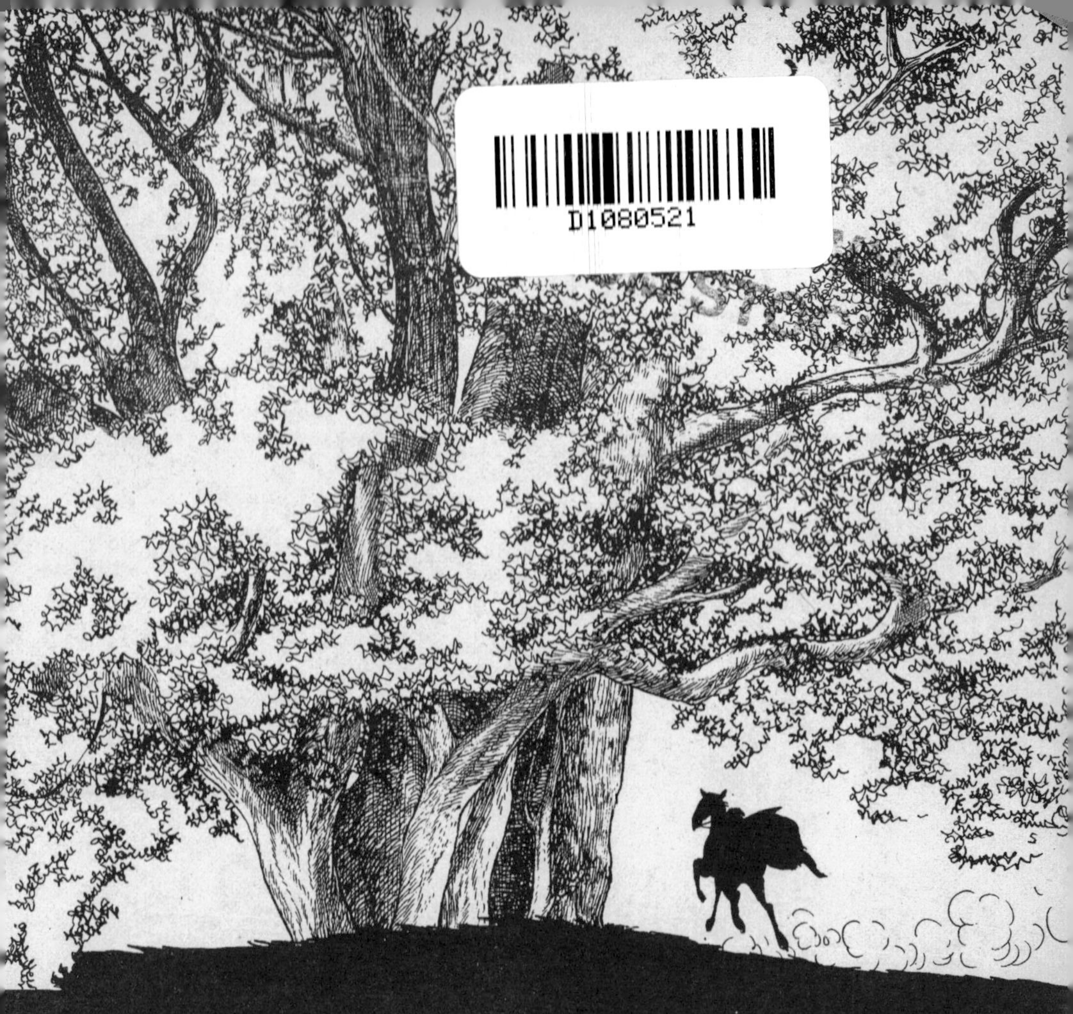

BUDDHA

OSAMU TEZUKA

5: Deer Park

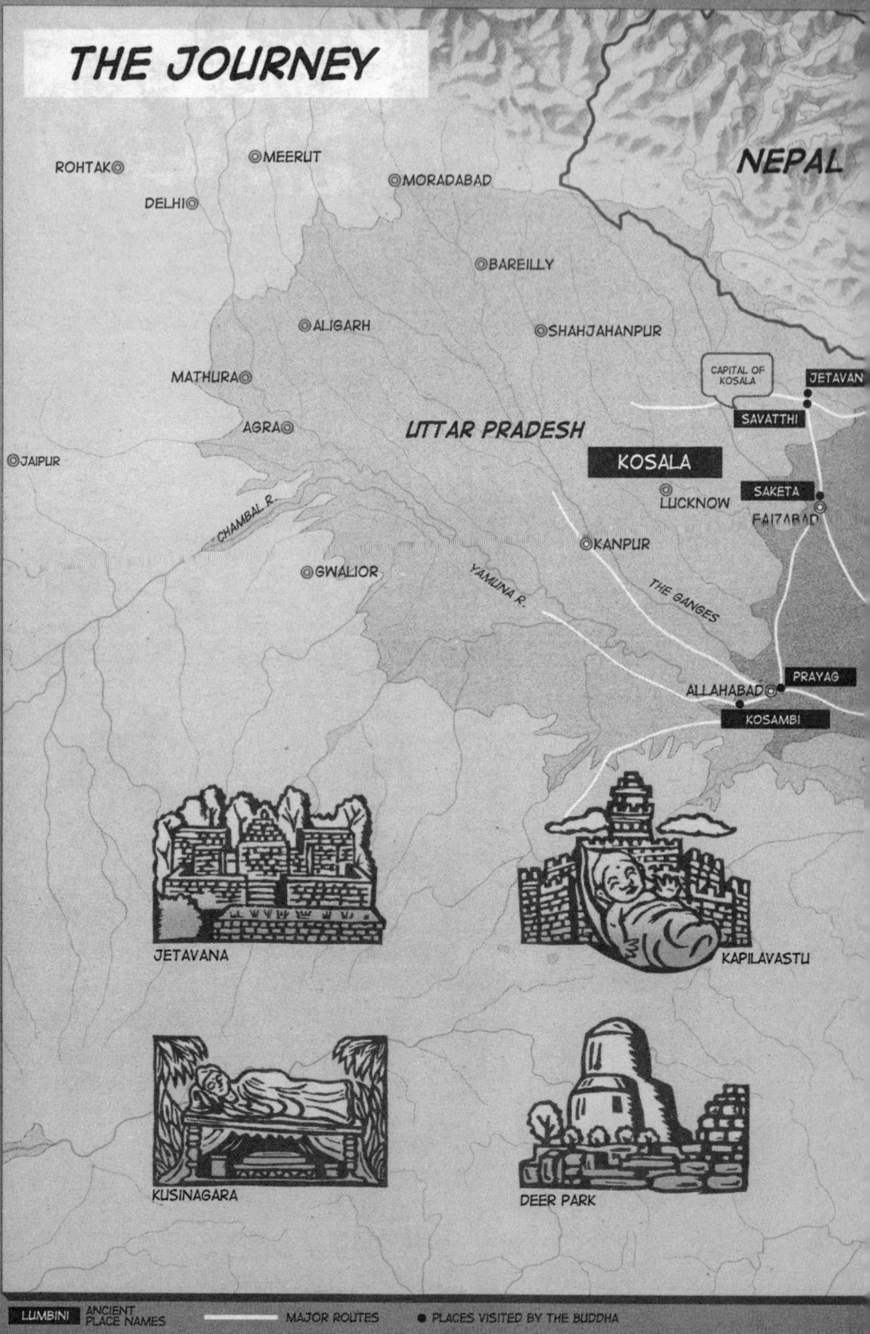

THE JOURNEY
NEPAL
ROHTAK
MEERUT
MORADABAD
DELHI
BAREILLY
ALIGARH
SHAHJAHANPUR
CAPITAL OF KOSALA
JETAVAN
MATHURA
SAVATTHI
AGRA
UTTAR PRADESH
JAIPUR
KOSALA
SAKETA
LUCKNOW
FAIZABAD
CHAMBAL R.
KANPUR
GWALIOR
YAMUNA R.
THE GANGES
PRAYAG
ALLAHABAD
KOSAMBI
JETAVANA
KAPILAVASTU
KUSINAGARA
DEER PARK
LUMBINI
ANCIENT PLACE NAMES
MAJOR ROUTES
PLACES VISITED BY THE BUDDHA

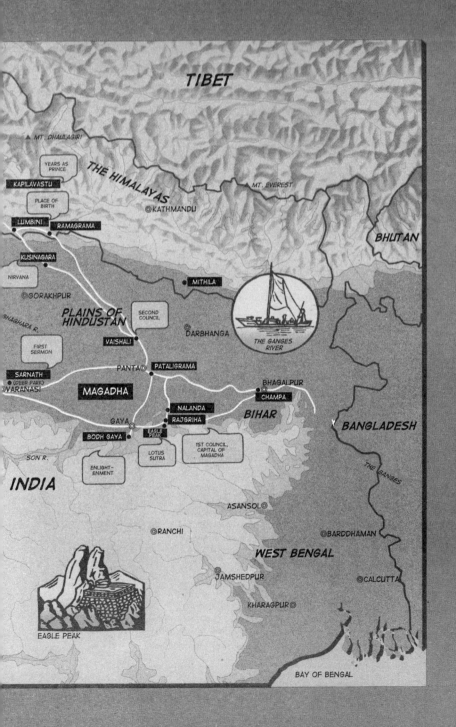

TIBET

▲ MT. DHAULAGIRI

THE HIMALAYAS

YEARS AS PRINCE

KAPILAVASTU

MT. EVEREST

PLACE OF BIRTH

◎KATHMANDU

LUMBINI   RAMAGRAMA

BHUTAN

KUSINAGARA

NIRVANA

MITHILA

◎GORAKHPUR

PLAINS OF HINDUSTAN

SECOND COUNCIL.

SHAGHARA R.

FIRST SERMON

VAISHALI

◎DARBHANGA

THE GANGES RIVER

SARNATH

(DEER PARK)

◎VARANASI

PANTA◎   PATALIGRAMA

BHAGALPUR

MAGADHA

CHAMPA

NALANDA

GAYA   RAJGRIHA

BIHAR

BODH GAYA

EAGLE PEAK

BANGLADESH

LOTUS SUTRA

1ST COUNCIL, CAPITAL OF MAGADHA

ENLIGHT-ENMENT

THE GANGES

INDIA

SON R.

ASANSOL◎

◎RANCHI

◎BARDDHAMAN

WEST BENGAL

◎JAMSHEDPUR

◎CALCUTTA

EAGLE PEAK

KHARAGPUR◎

BAY OF BENGAL

HarperCollins*Publishers*
77–85 Fulham Palace Road,
Hammersmith, London W6 8JB

www.harpercollins.co.uk

Published by HarperCollins*Publishers* 2006

1

Copyright © Tezuka Productions 2005
Translation Copyright © Vertical Inc. 2005

A catalogue record for this book
is available from the British Library

ISBN-13 978-0-00-722455-5
ISBN-10 0-00-722455-9

The artwork of the original has been produced as a mirror image
in order to conform with English language.
This work of fiction contains characters and episodes
that are not part of the historical record.

Printed and bound in Great Britain by
Clays Limited, St Ives PLC

CONTENTS

PART FOUR

PART FOUR

CHAPTER ONE

THE SWORDSMAN
AND
THE DRIFTER

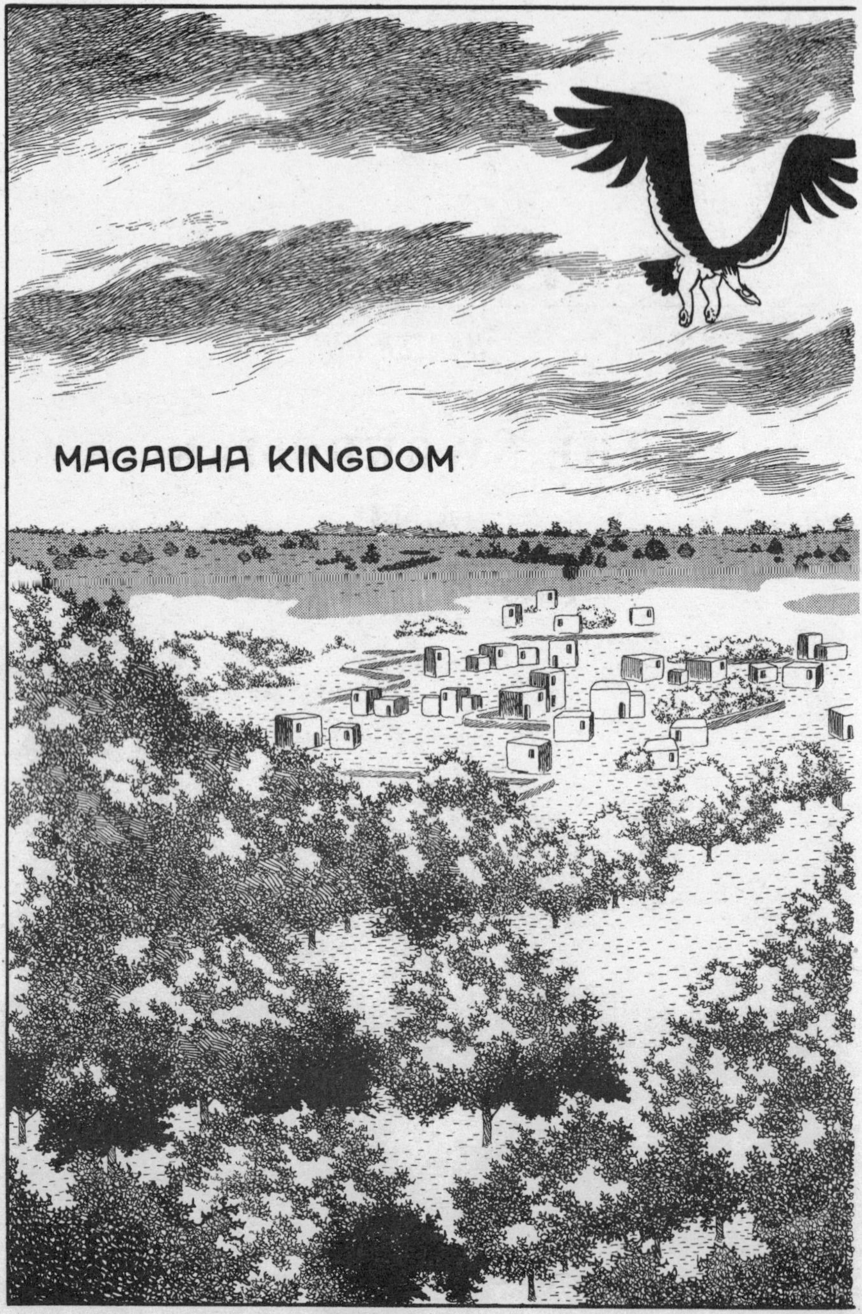
MAGADHA KINGDOM

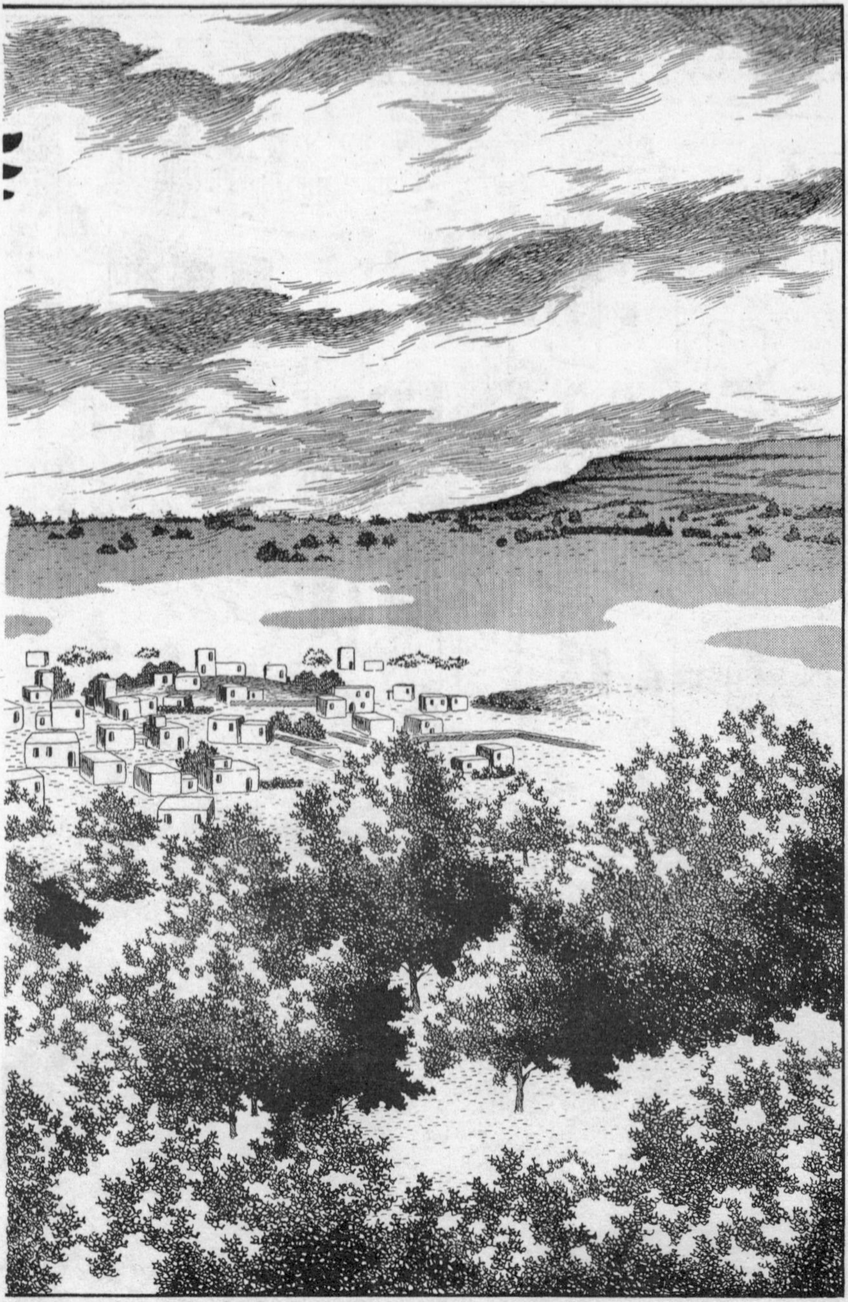

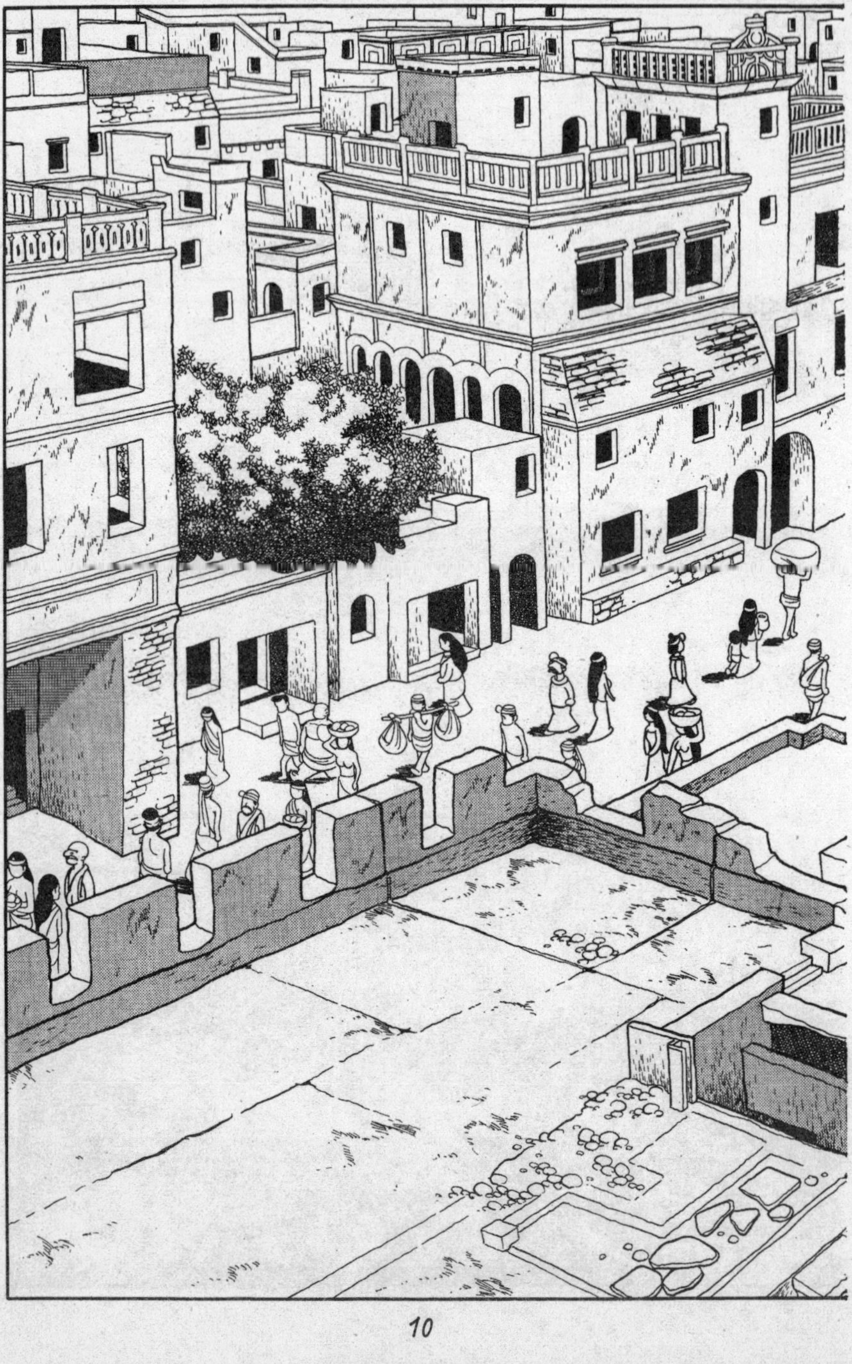

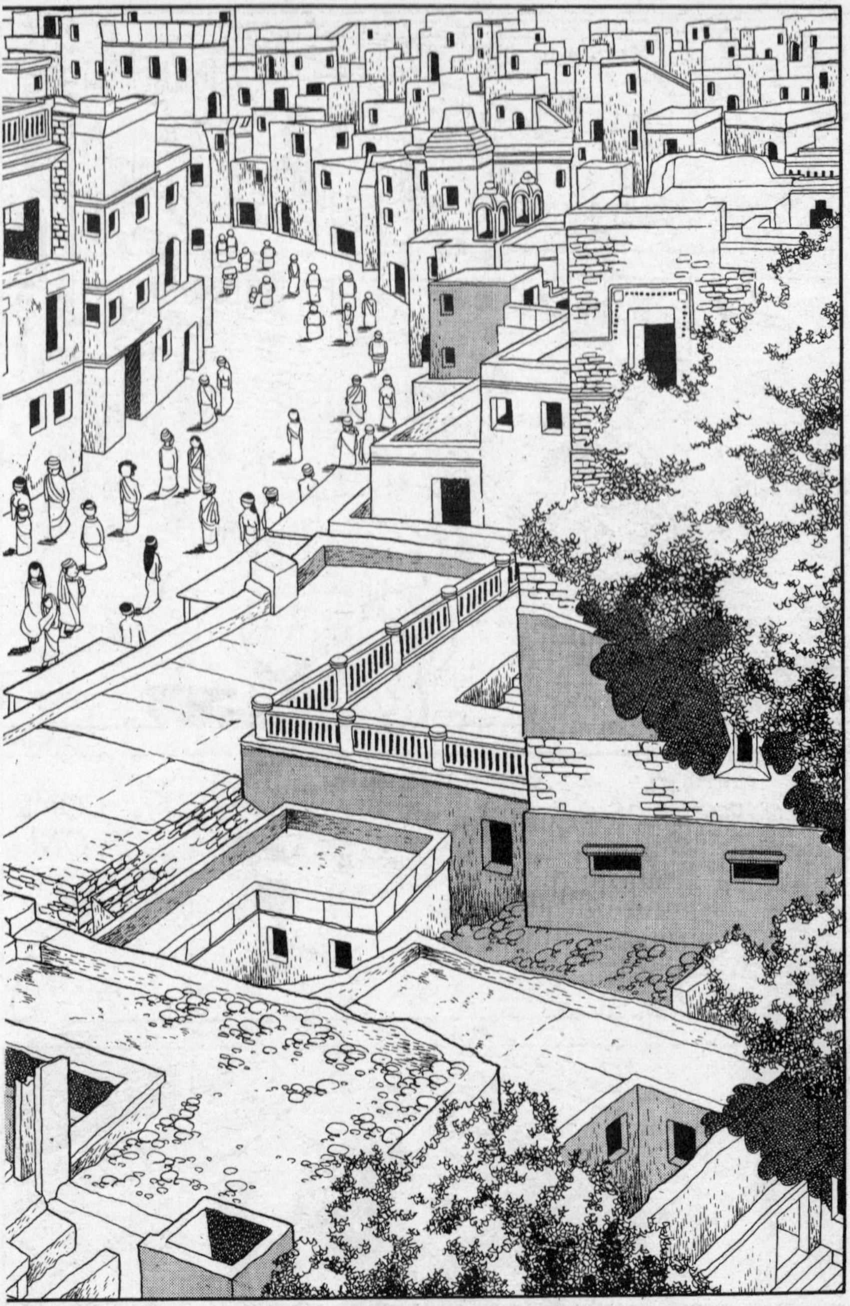

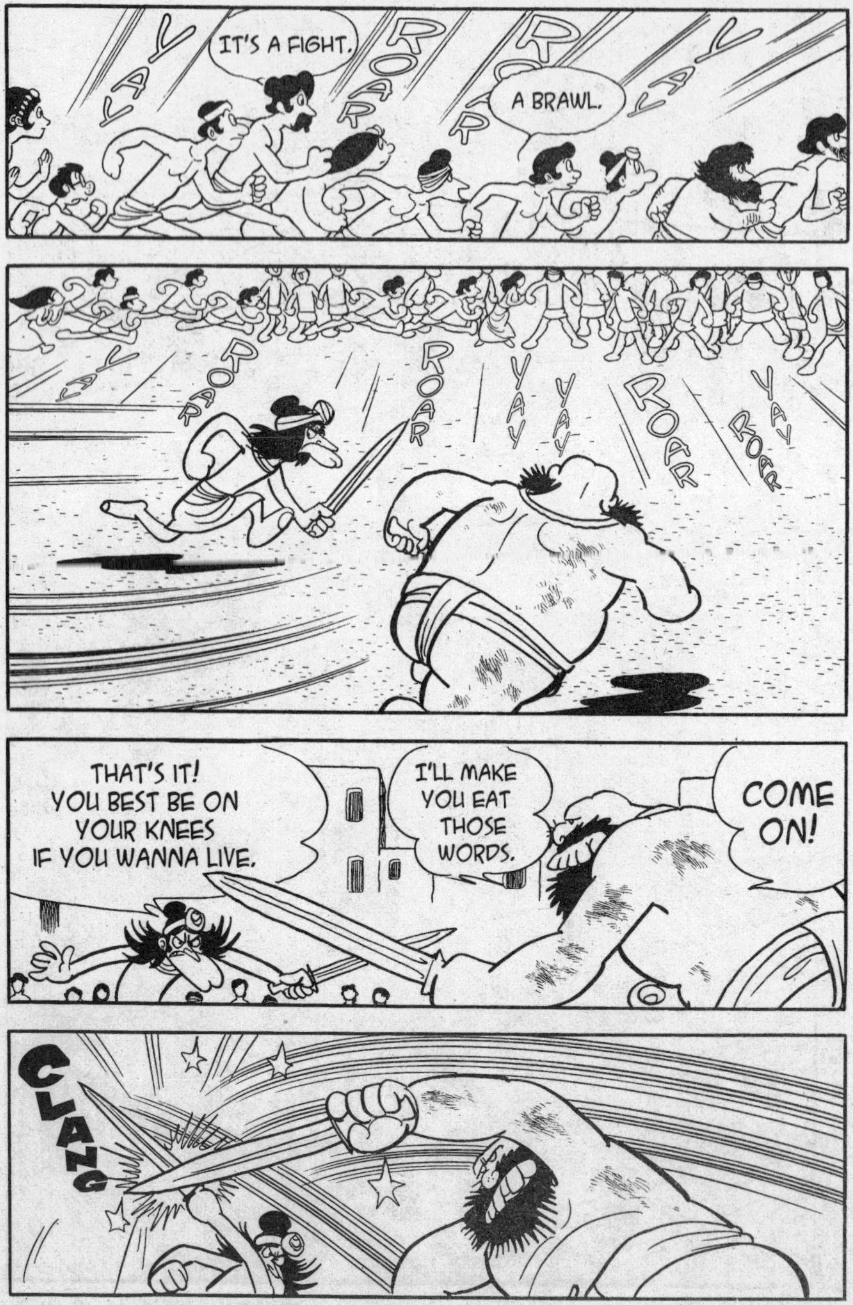
YAY
IT'S A FIGHT.
ROAR
ROAR
A BRAWL.
YAY
YAY
ROAR
ROAR
YAY
YAY
ROAR
ROAR
YAY
THAT'S IT! YOU BEST BE ON YOUR KNEES IF YOU WANNA LIVE.
I'LL MAKE YOU EAT THOSE WORDS.
COME ON!
CLANG

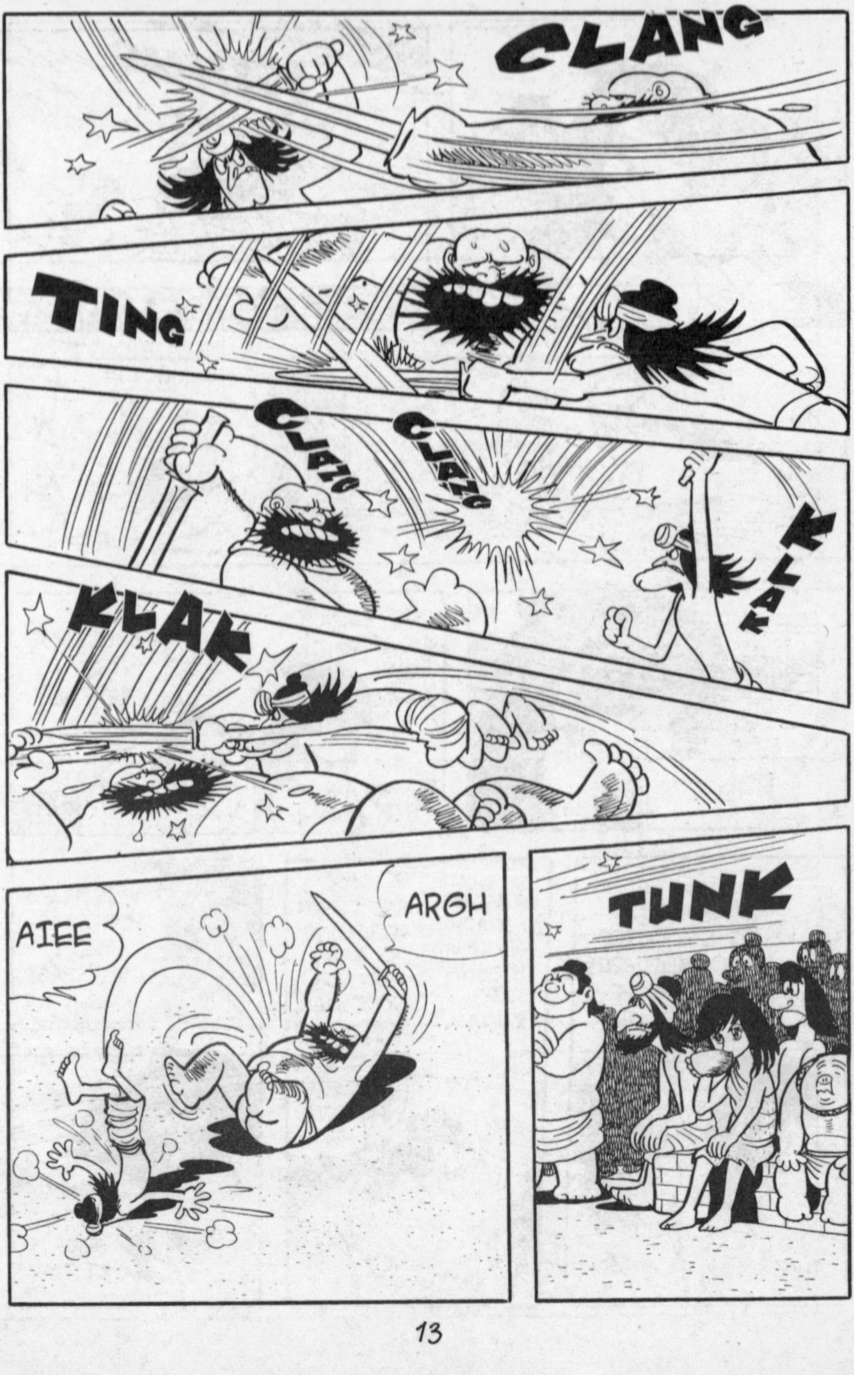
CLANG
TING
CLANG
CLANG
KLAK
KLAK
AIEE
ARGH
TUNK

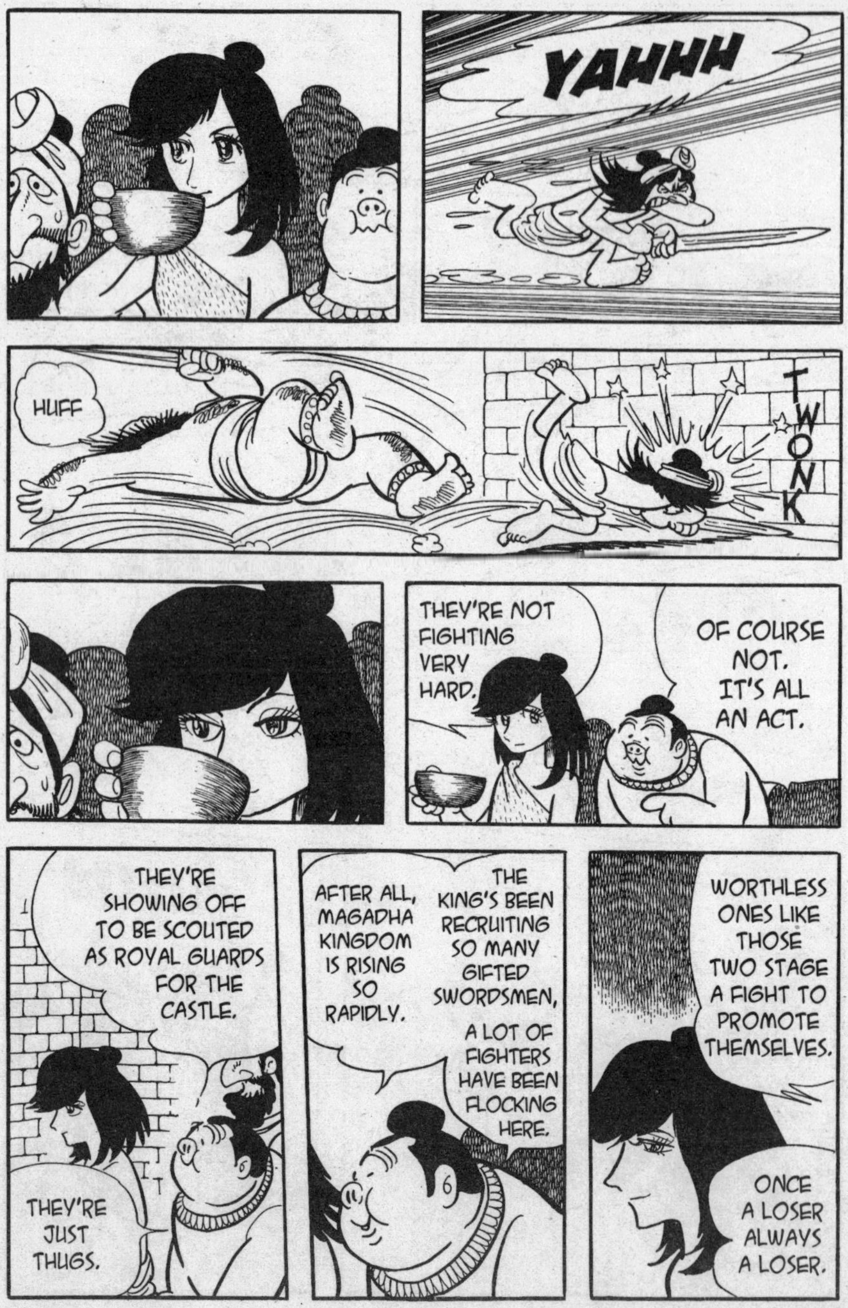
YAHHH
HUFF
TWONK
THEY'RE NOT FIGHTING VERY HARD.
OF COURSE NOT. IT'S ALL AN ACT.
THEY'RE SHOWING OFF TO BE SCOUTED AS ROYAL GUARDS FOR THE CASTLE.
THEY'RE JUST THUGS.
AFTER ALL, MAGADHA KINGDOM IS RISING SO RAPIDLY.
THE KING'S BEEN RECRUITING SO MANY GIFTED SWORDSMEN,
A LOT OF FIGHTERS HAVE BEEN FLOCKING HERE.
WORTHLESS ONES LIKE THOSE TWO STAGE A FIGHT TO PROMOTE THEMSELVES.
ONCE A LOSER ALWAYS A LOSER.

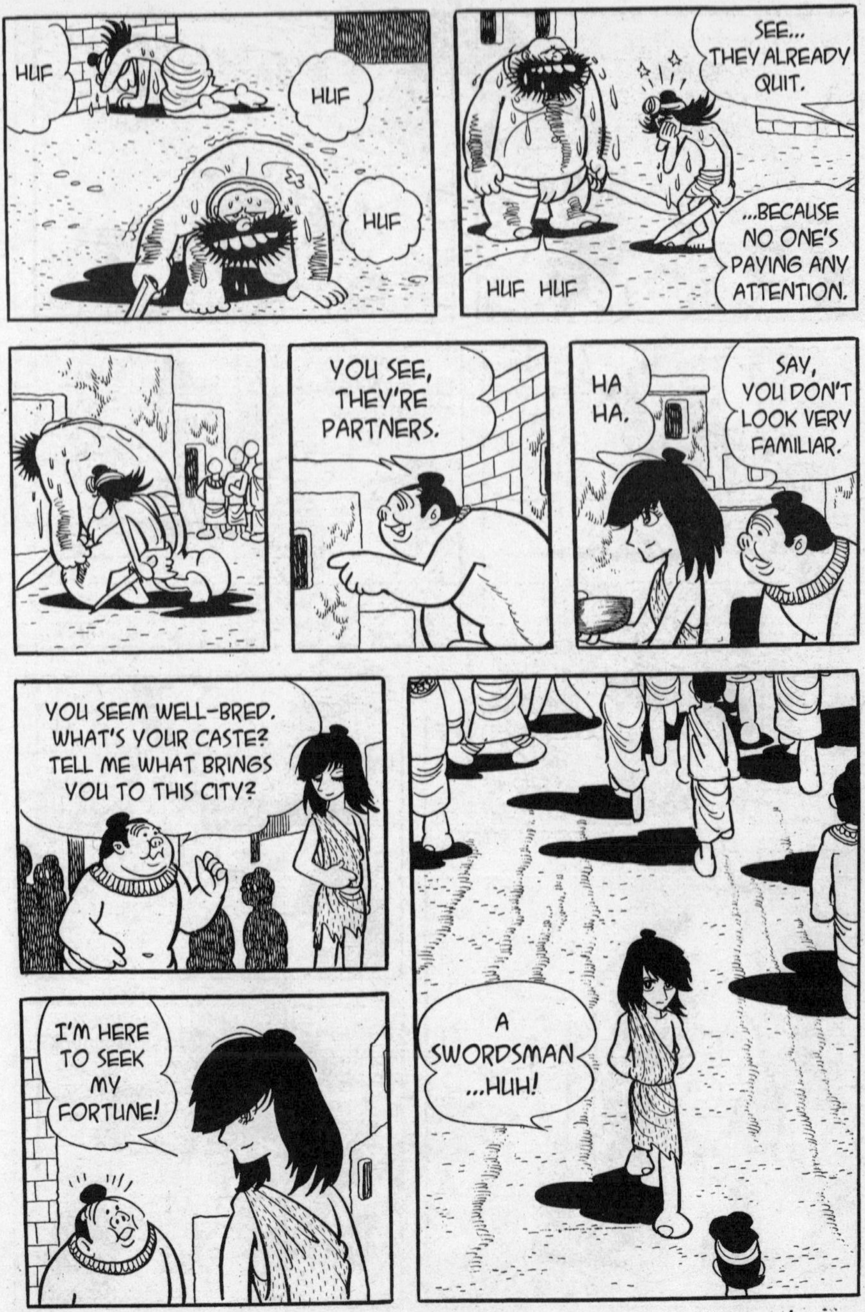
HUF
HUF
HUF
SEE... THEY ALREADY QUIT.
...BECAUSE NO ONE'S PAYING ANY ATTENTION.
HUF HUF
YOU SEE, THEY'RE PARTNERS.
HA HA.
SAY, YOU DON'T LOOK VERY FAMILIAR.
YOU SEEM WELL-BRED. WHAT'S YOUR CASTE? TELL ME WHAT BRINGS YOU TO THIS CITY?
I'M HERE TO SEEK MY FORTUNE!
A SWORDSMAN ...HUH!

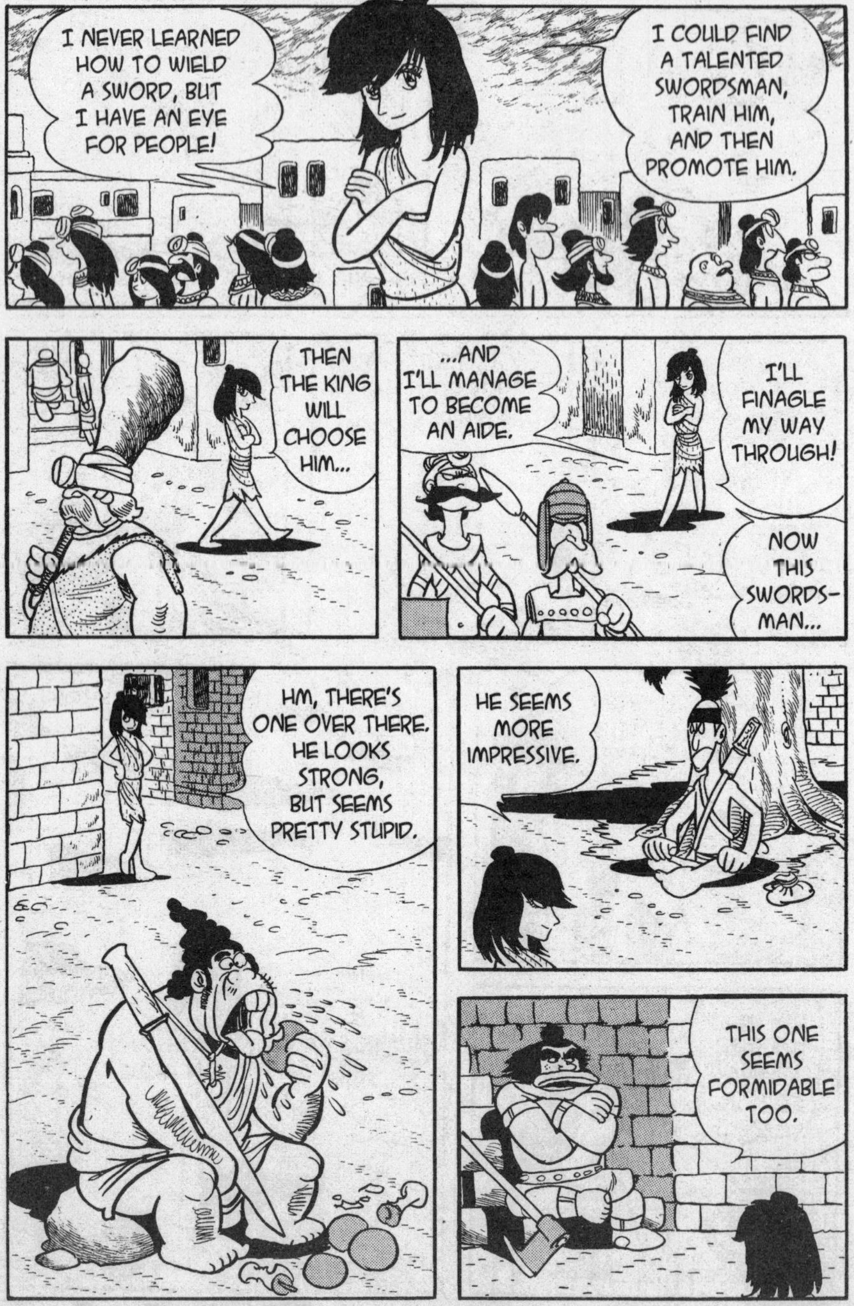
I NEVER LEARNED HOW TO WIELD A SWORD, BUT I HAVE AN EYE FOR PEOPLE!
I COULD FIND A TALENTED SWORDSMAN, TRAIN HIM, AND THEN PROMOTE HIM.
THEN THE KING WILL CHOOSE HIM...
...AND I'LL MANAGE TO BECOME AN AIDE.
I'LL FINAGLE MY WAY THROUGH!
NOW THIS SWORDS-MAN...
HM, THERE'S ONE OVER THERE. HE LOOKS STRONG, BUT SEEMS PRETTY STUPID.
HE SEEMS MORE IMPRESSIVE.
THIS ONE SEEMS FORMIDABLE TOO.

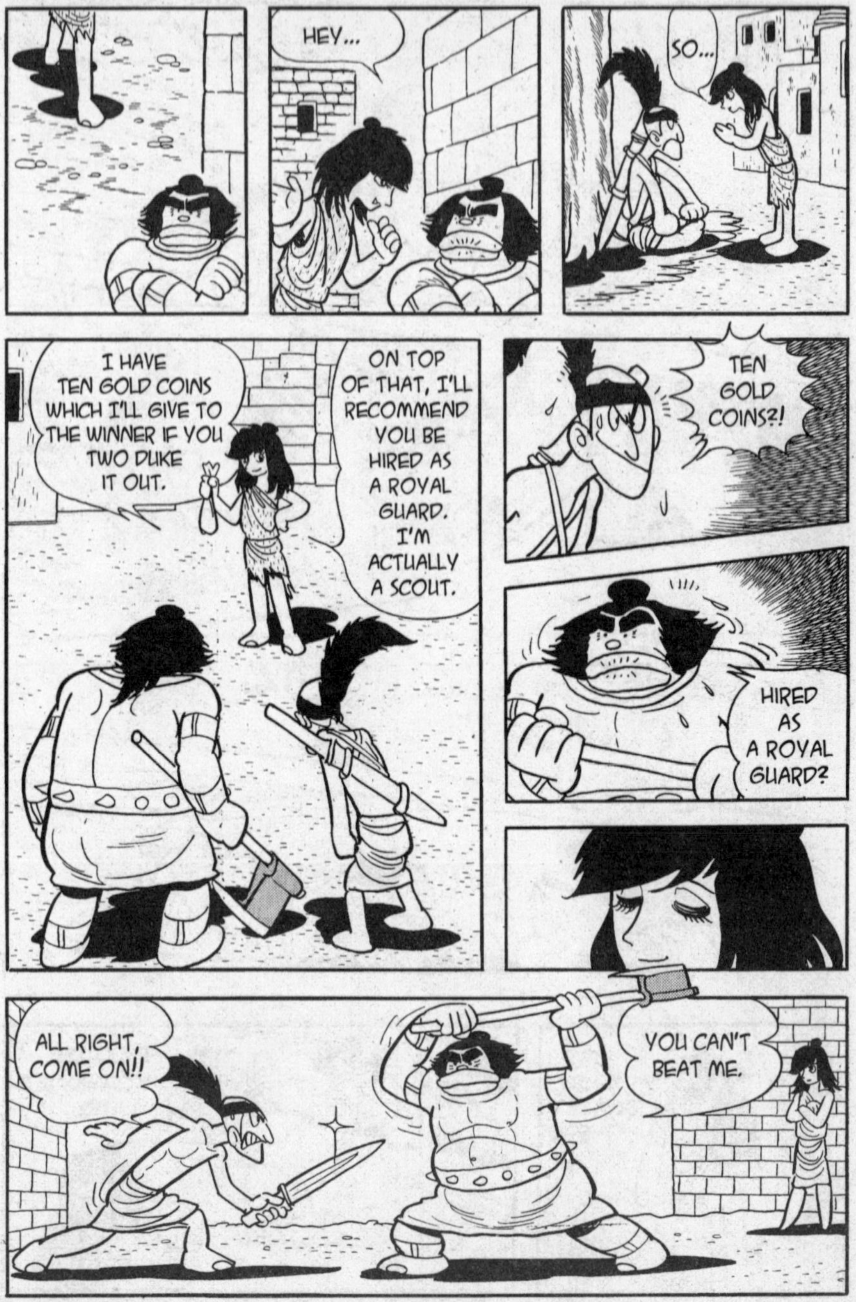
HEY...
SO...
I HAVE TEN GOLD COINS WHICH I'LL GIVE TO THE WINNER IF YOU TWO DUKE IT OUT.
ON TOP OF THAT, I'LL RECOMMEND YOU BE HIRED AS A ROYAL GUARD. I'M ACTUALLY A SCOUT.
TEN GOLD COINS?!
HIRED AS A ROYAL GUARD?
ALL RIGHT, COME ON!!
YOU CAN'T BEAT ME.

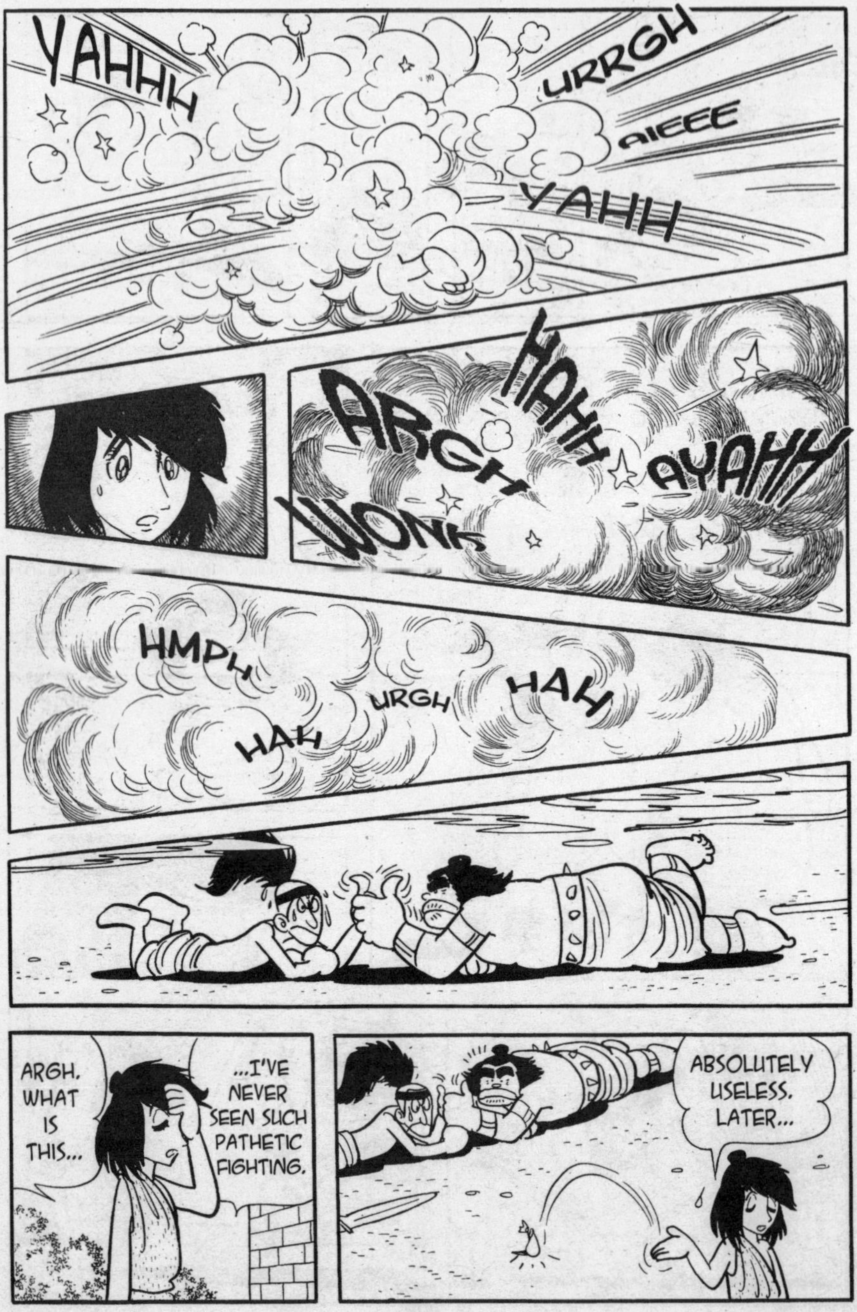
YAHHH
URRGH
AIEEE
YAHH
HAHH
ARGH
AYAHH
WONK
HMPH
URGH
HAH
HAH
ARGH. WHAT IS THIS...
...I'VE NEVER SEEN SUCH PATHETIC FIGHTING.
ABSOLUTELY USELESS. LATER...

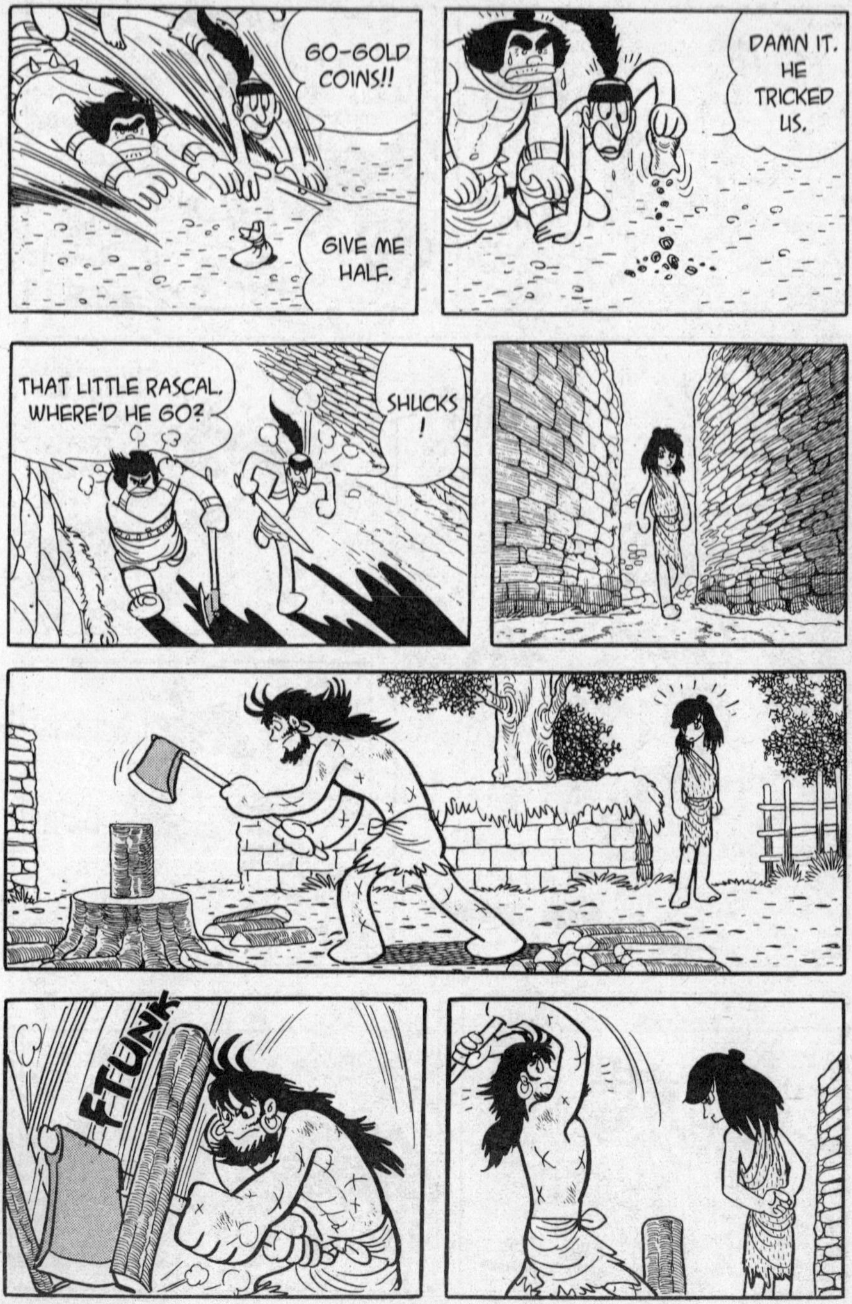
GO-GOLD COINS!!
GIVE ME HALF.
DAMN IT. HE TRICKED US.
THAT LITTLE RASCAL. WHERE'D HE GO?
SHUCKS !
FTUNK

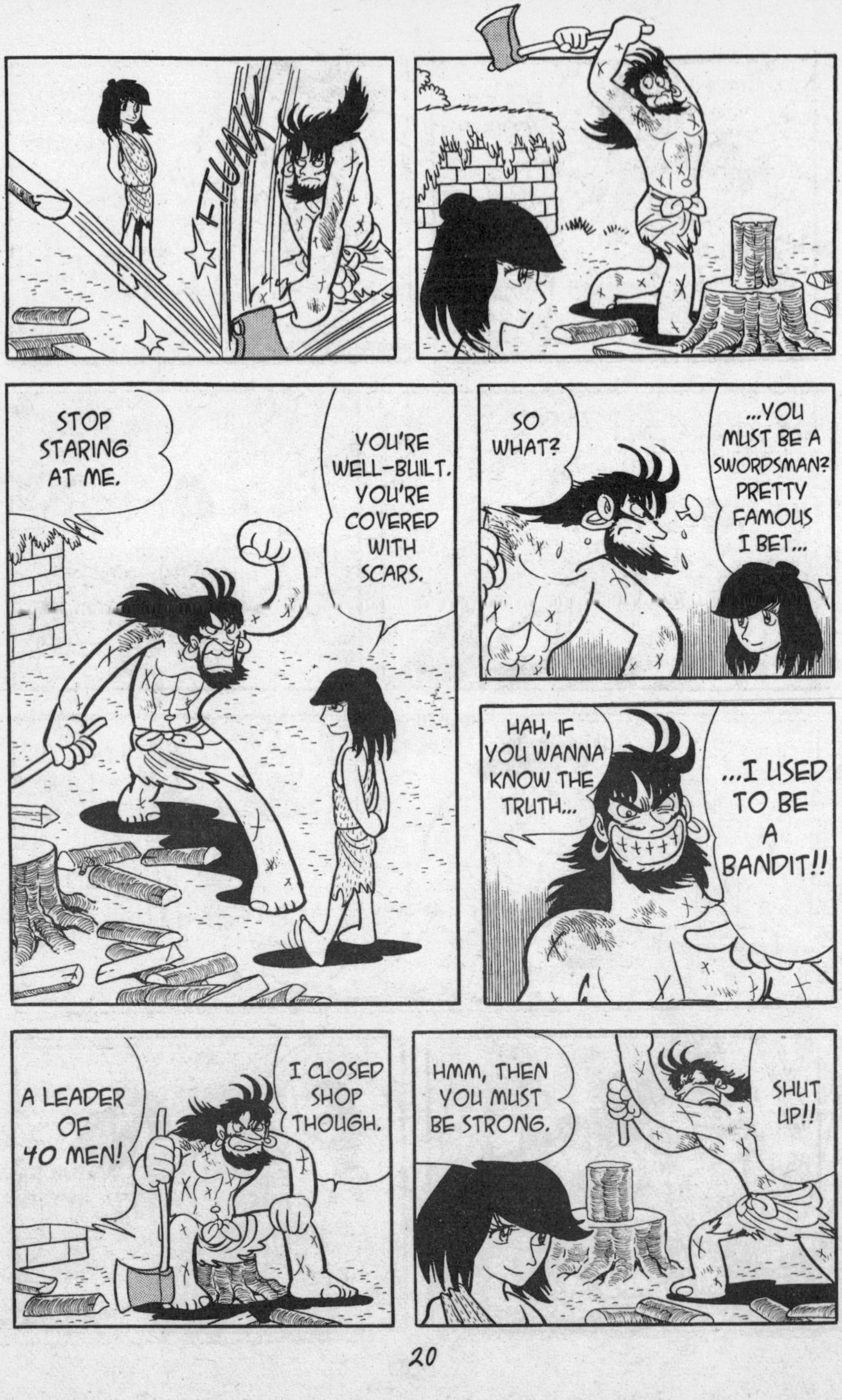
FTUNK
STOP STARING AT ME.
YOU'RE WELL-BUILT. YOU'RE COVERED WITH SCARS.
SO WHAT?
...YOU MUST BE A SWORDSMAN? PRETTY FAMOUS I BET...
HAH, IF YOU WANNA KNOW THE TRUTH...
...I USED TO BE A BANDIT!!
A LEADER OF 40 MEN!
I CLOSED SHOP THOUGH.
HMM, THEN YOU MUST BE STRONG.
SHUT UP!!

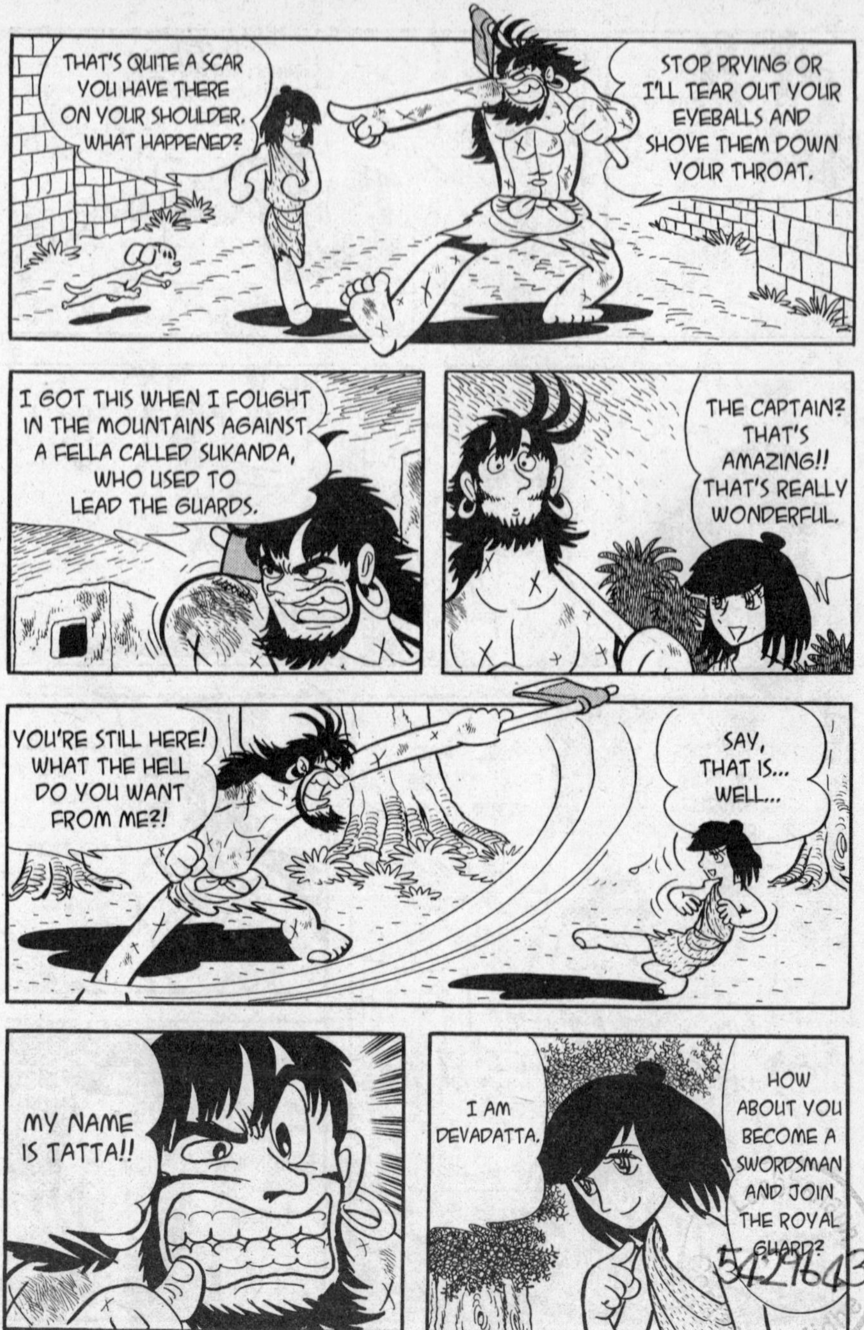
THAT'S QUITE A SCAR YOU HAVE THERE ON YOUR SHOULDER. WHAT HAPPENED?
STOP PRYING OR I'LL TEAR OUT YOUR EYEBALLS AND SHOVE THEM DOWN YOUR THROAT.
I GOT THIS WHEN I FOUGHT IN THE MOUNTAINS AGAINST A FELLA CALLED SUKANDA, WHO USED TO LEAD THE GUARDS.
THE CAPTAIN? THAT'S AMAZING!! THAT'S REALLY WONDERFUL.
YOU'RE STILL HERE! WHAT THE HELL DO YOU WANT FROM ME?!
SAY, THAT IS... WELL...
MY NAME IS TATTA!!
I AM DEVADATTA.
HOW ABOUT YOU BECOME A SWORDSMAN AND JOIN THE ROYAL GUARD?

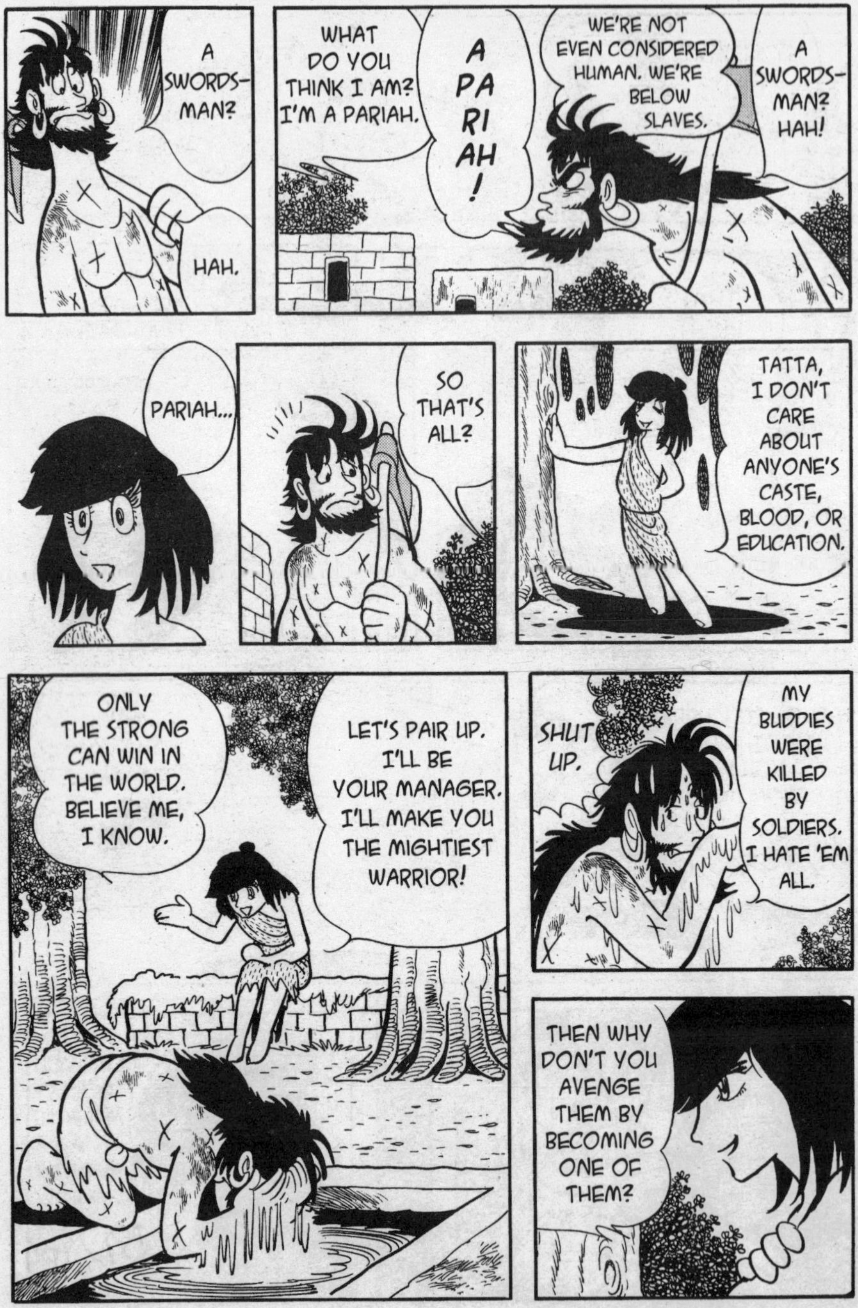

A SWORDS-MAN?
HAH.
WHAT DO YOU THINK I AM? I'M A PARIAH.
A PARIAH!
WE'RE NOT EVEN CONSIDERED HUMAN. WE'RE BELOW SLAVES.
A SWORDS-MAN? HAH!
PARIAH...
SO THAT'S ALL?
TATTA, I DON'T CARE ABOUT ANYONE'S CASTE, BLOOD, OR EDUCATION.
ONLY THE STRONG CAN WIN IN THE WORLD. BELIEVE ME, I KNOW.
LET'S PAIR UP. I'LL BE YOUR MANAGER. I'LL MAKE YOU THE MIGHTIEST WARRIOR!
SHUT UP.
MY BUDDIES WERE KILLED BY SOLDIERS. I HATE 'EM ALL.
THEN WHY DON'T YOU AVENGE THEM BY BECOMING ONE OF THEM?

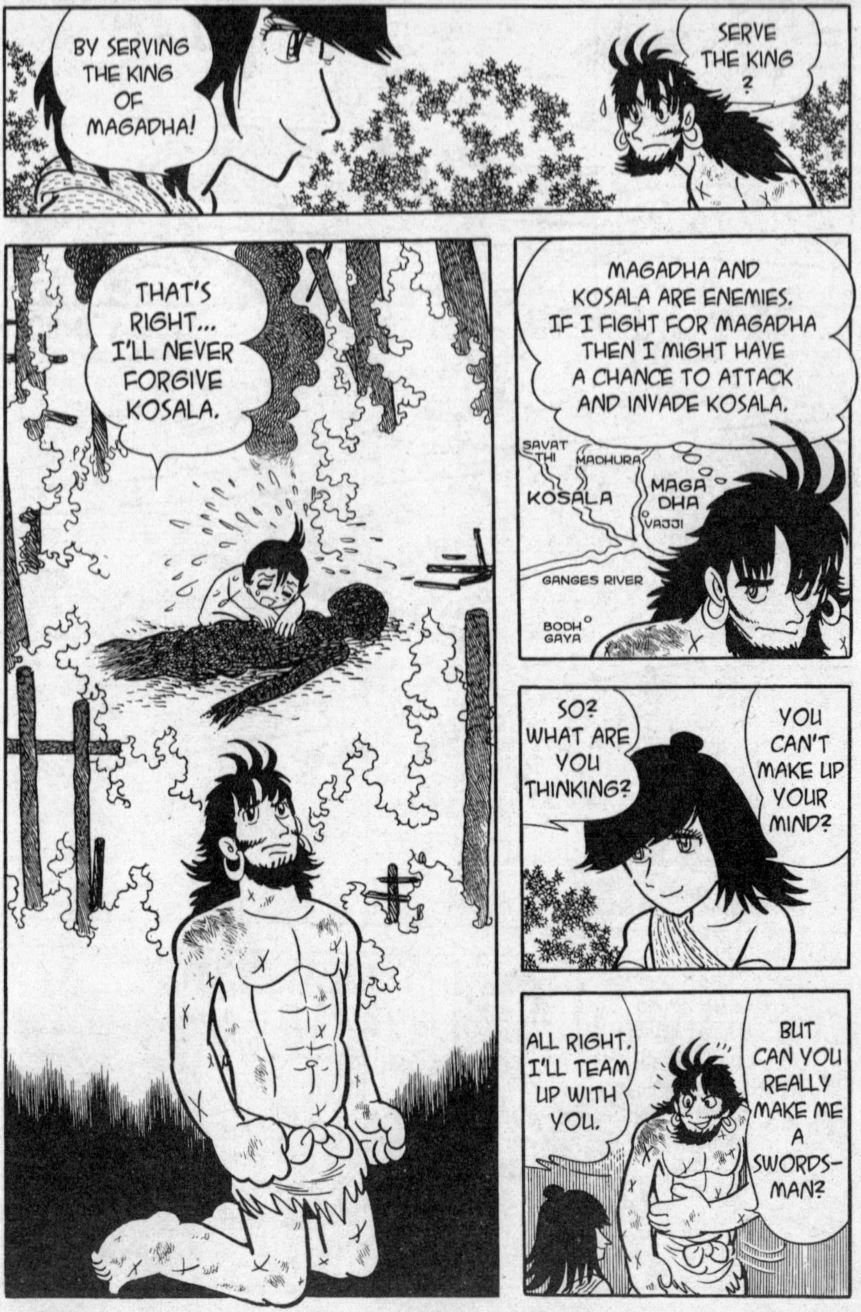
BY SERVING THE KING OF MAGADHA!
SERVE THE KING ?
THAT'S RIGHT... I'LL NEVER FORGIVE KOSALA.
MAGADHA AND KOSALA ARE ENEMIES. IF I FIGHT FOR MAGADHA THEN I MIGHT HAVE A CHANCE TO ATTACK AND INVADE KOSALA.
SAVAT THI
MADHURA
KOSALA
MAGA DHA
VAJJI
GANGES RIVER
BODH GAYA
SO? WHAT ARE YOU THINKING?
YOU CAN'T MAKE UP YOUR MIND?
ALL RIGHT. I'LL TEAM UP WITH YOU.
BUT CAN YOU REALLY MAKE ME A SWORDS-MAN?

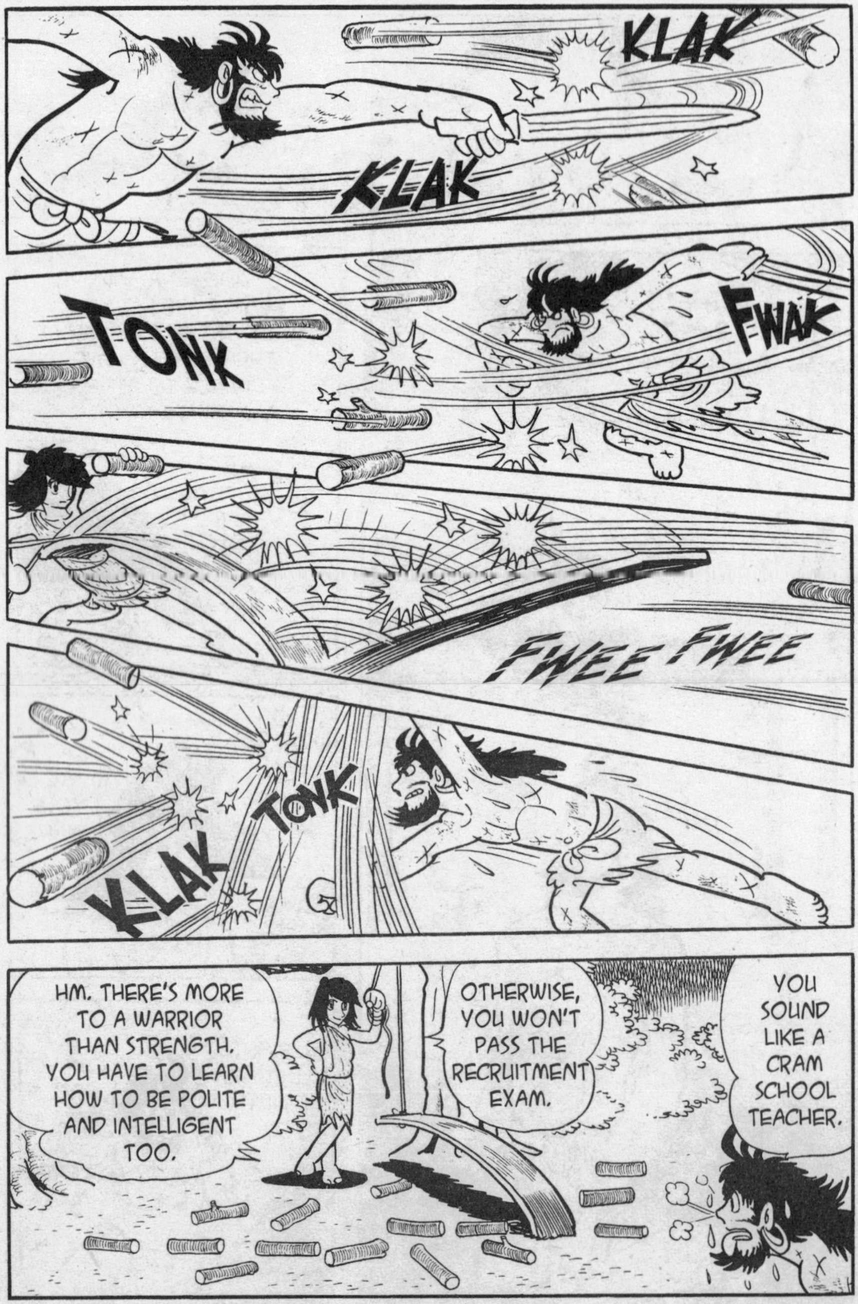
KLAK
KLAK
TONK
FWAK
FWEE FWEE
TONK
KLAK
HM. THERE'S MORE TO A WARRIOR THAN STRENGTH. YOU HAVE TO LEARN HOW TO BE POLITE AND INTELLIGENT TOO.
OTHERWISE, YOU WON'T PASS THE RECRUITMENT EXAM.
YOU SOUND LIKE A CRAM SCHOOL TEACHER.

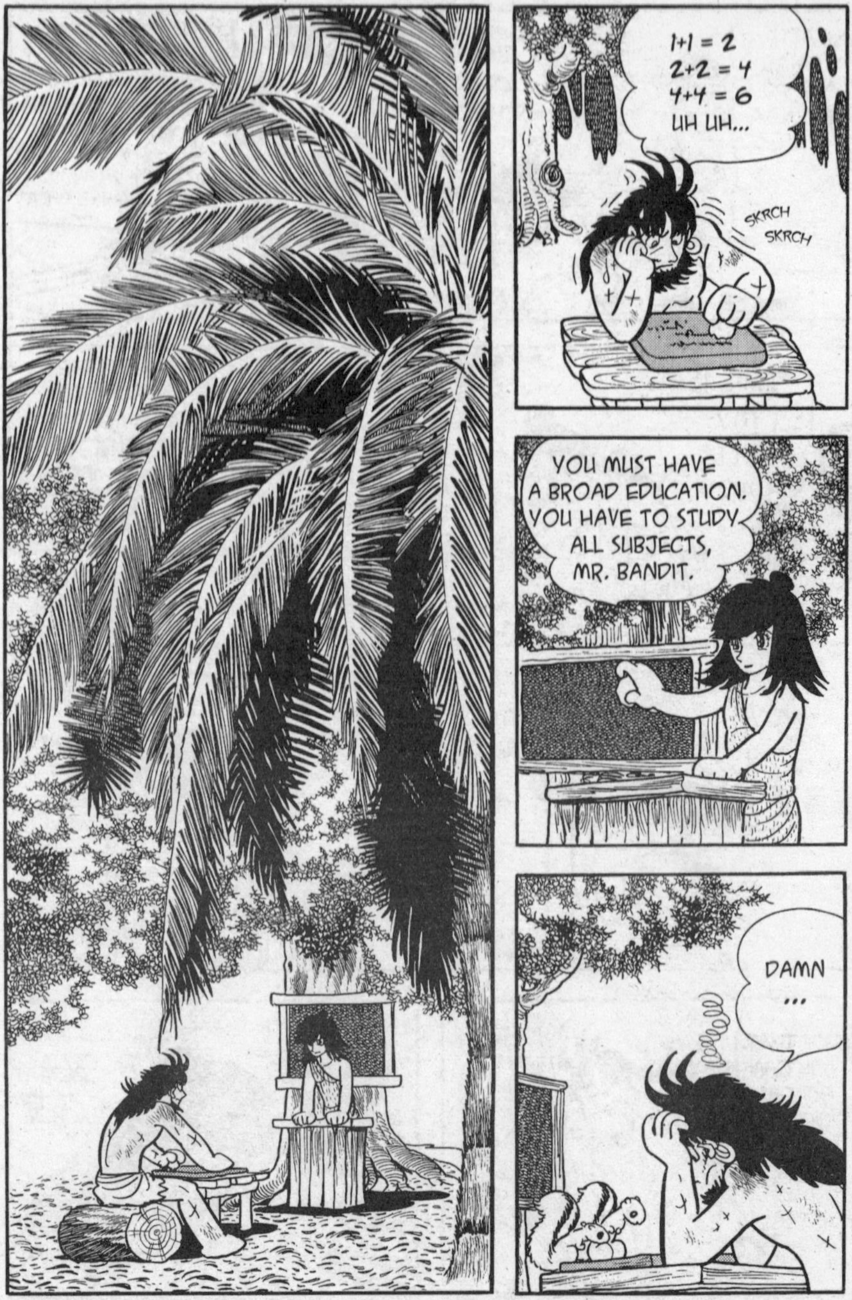

1+1 = 2
2+2 = 4
4+4 = 6
UH UH...
SKRCH SKRCH
YOU MUST HAVE A BROAD EDUCATION. YOU HAVE TO STUDY ALL SUBJECTS, MR. BANDIT.
DAMN ...

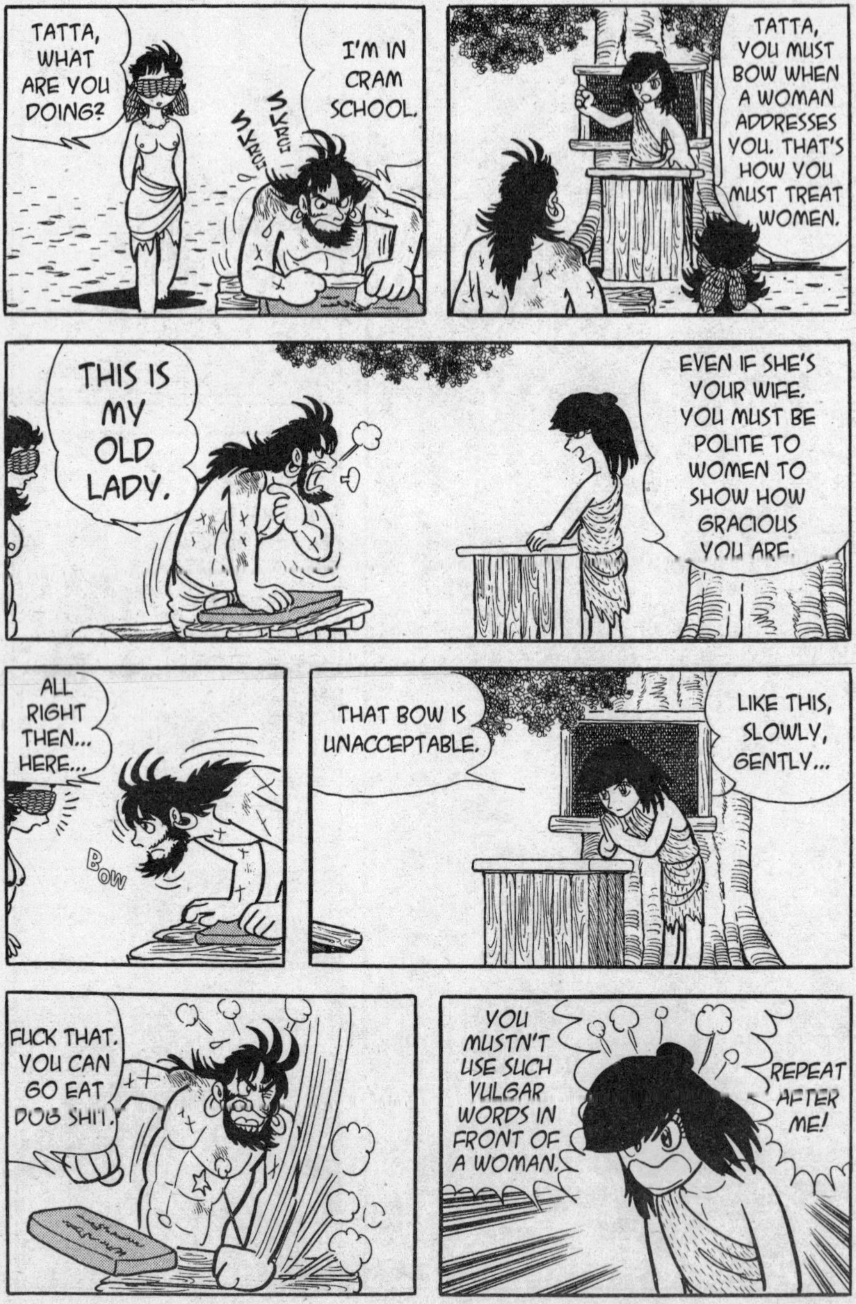
TATTA, WHAT ARE YOU DOING?
I'M IN CRAM SCHOOL.
SKRCH SKRCH
TATTA, YOU MUST BOW WHEN A WOMAN ADDRESSES YOU. THAT'S HOW YOU MUST TREAT WOMEN.
THIS IS MY OLD LADY.
EVEN IF SHE'S YOUR WIFE, YOU MUST BE POLITE TO WOMEN TO SHOW HOW GRACIOUS YOU ARE.
ALL RIGHT THEN... HERE...
BOW
THAT BOW IS UNACCEPTABLE.
LIKE THIS, SLOWLY, GENTLY...
FUCK THAT. YOU CAN GO EAT DOG SHIT.
YOU MUSTN'T USE SUCH VULGAR WORDS IN FRONT OF A WOMAN.
REPEAT AFTER ME!

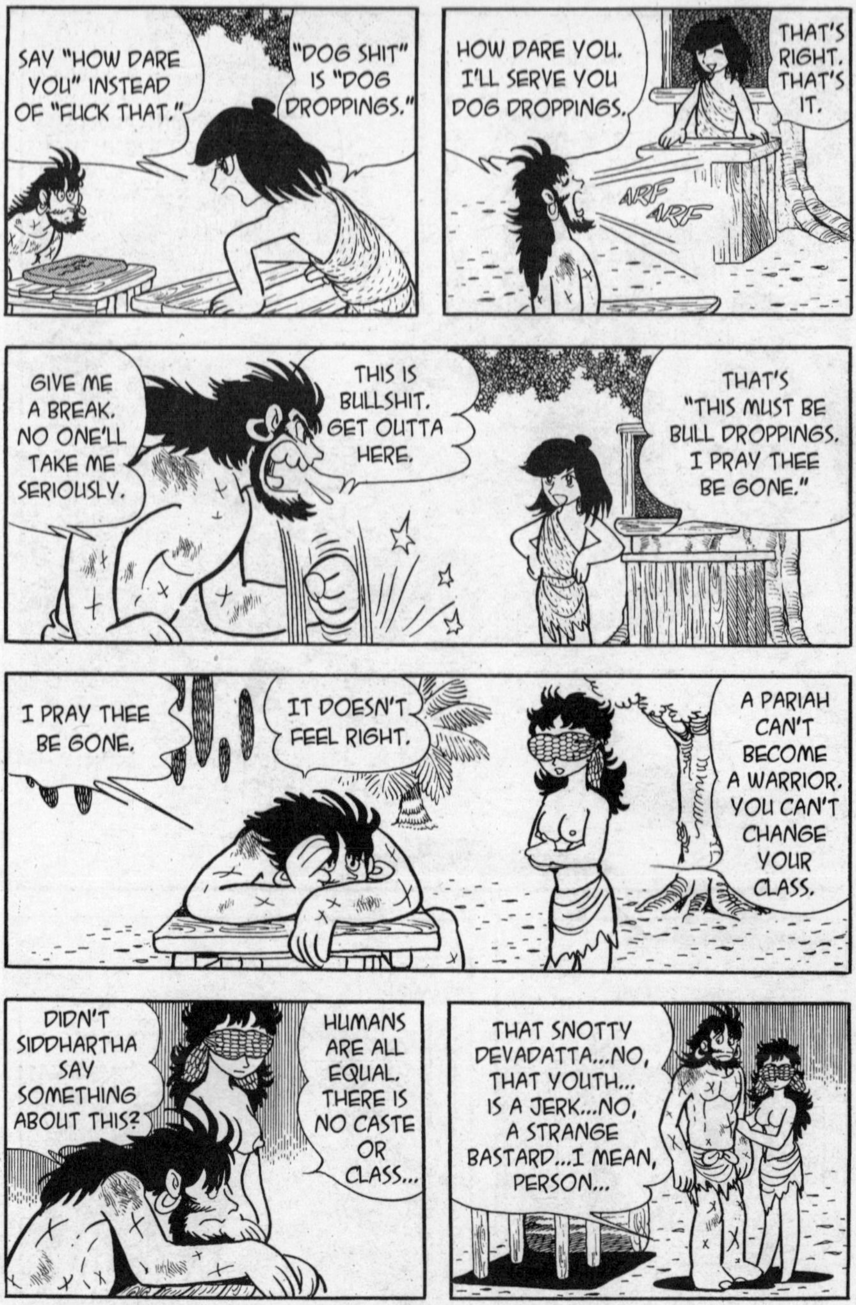
SAY "HOW DARE YOU" INSTEAD OF "FUCK THAT."
"DOG SHIT" IS "DOG DROPPINGS."
HOW DARE YOU. I'LL SERVE YOU DOG DROPPINGS.
THAT'S RIGHT. THAT'S IT.
ARF ARF
GIVE ME A BREAK. NO ONE'LL TAKE ME SERIOUSLY.
THIS IS BULLSHIT. GET OUTTA HERE.
THAT'S "THIS MUST BE BULL DROPPINGS. I PRAY THEE BE GONE."
I PRAY THEE BE GONE.
IT DOESN'T FEEL RIGHT.
A PARIAH CAN'T BECOME A WARRIOR. YOU CAN'T CHANGE YOUR CLASS.
DIDN'T SIDDHARTHA SAY SOMETHING ABOUT THIS?
HUMANS ARE ALL EQUAL. THERE IS NO CASTE OR CLASS...
THAT SNOTTY DEVADATTA...NO, THAT YOUTH... IS A JERK...NO, A STRANGE BASTARD...I MEAN, PERSON...

DON'T GAWK AROUND ONCE WE ENTER THE CASTLE. LOOK STRAIGHT AHEAD AND STRIDE FORWARD.
ONCE THE KING APPEARS...YOU ARE TO BOW AS I INSTRUCTED YOU TO.
YES, SIR !
HELLO THERE!
TUMP TUMP

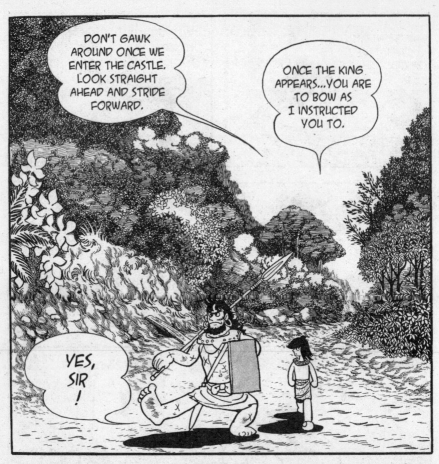

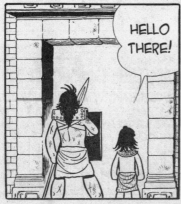

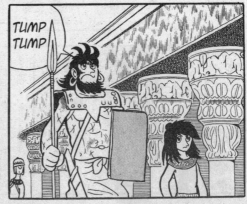

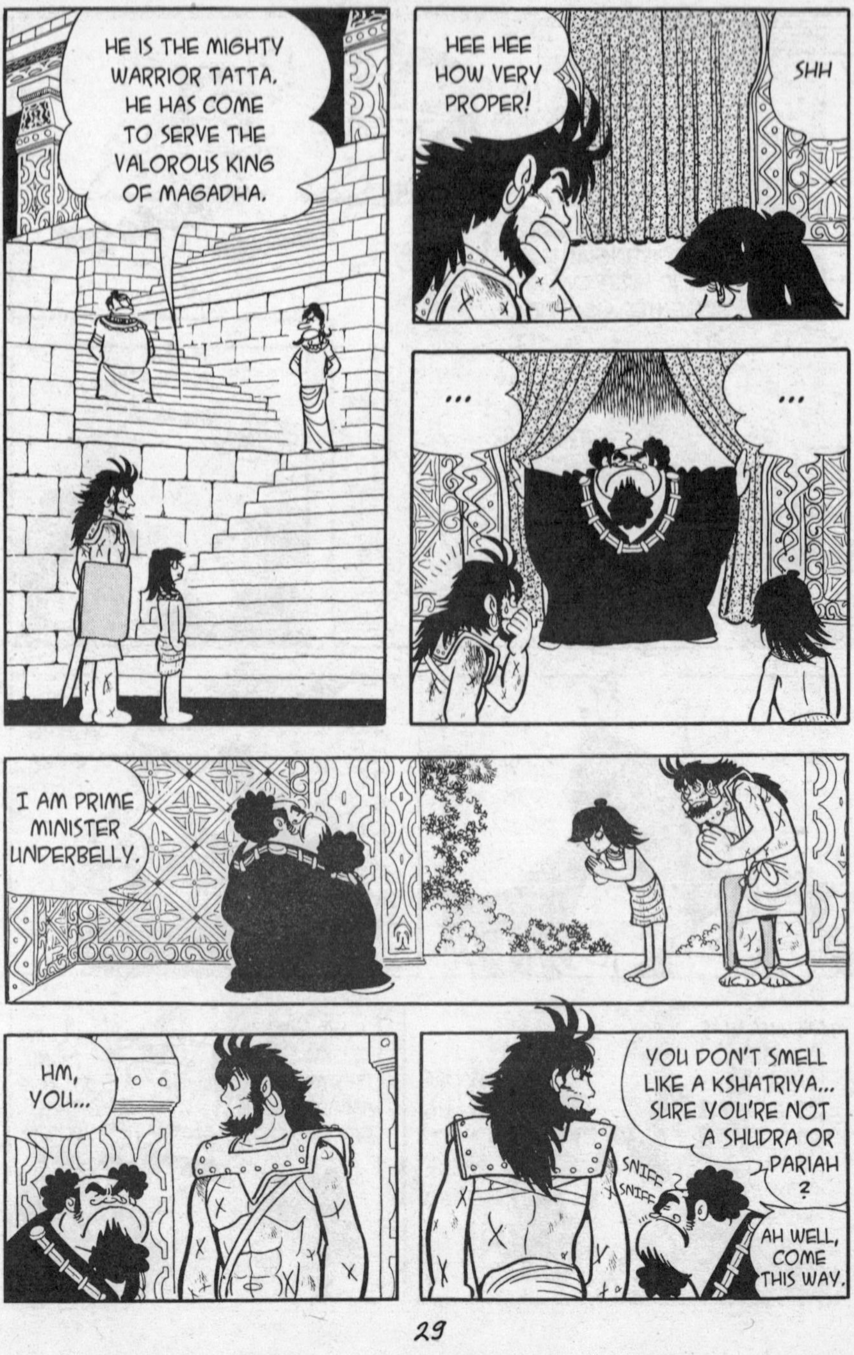
HE IS THE MIGHTY WARRIOR TATTA. HE HAS COME TO SERVE THE VALOROUS KING OF MAGADHA.
HEE HEE HOW VERY PROPER!
SHH
...
...
I AM PRIME MINISTER UNDERBELLY.
HM, YOU...
YOU DON'T SMELL LIKE A KSHATRIYA... SURE YOU'RE NOT A SHUDRA OR PARIAH ?
SNIFF SNIFF
AH WELL, COME THIS WAY.

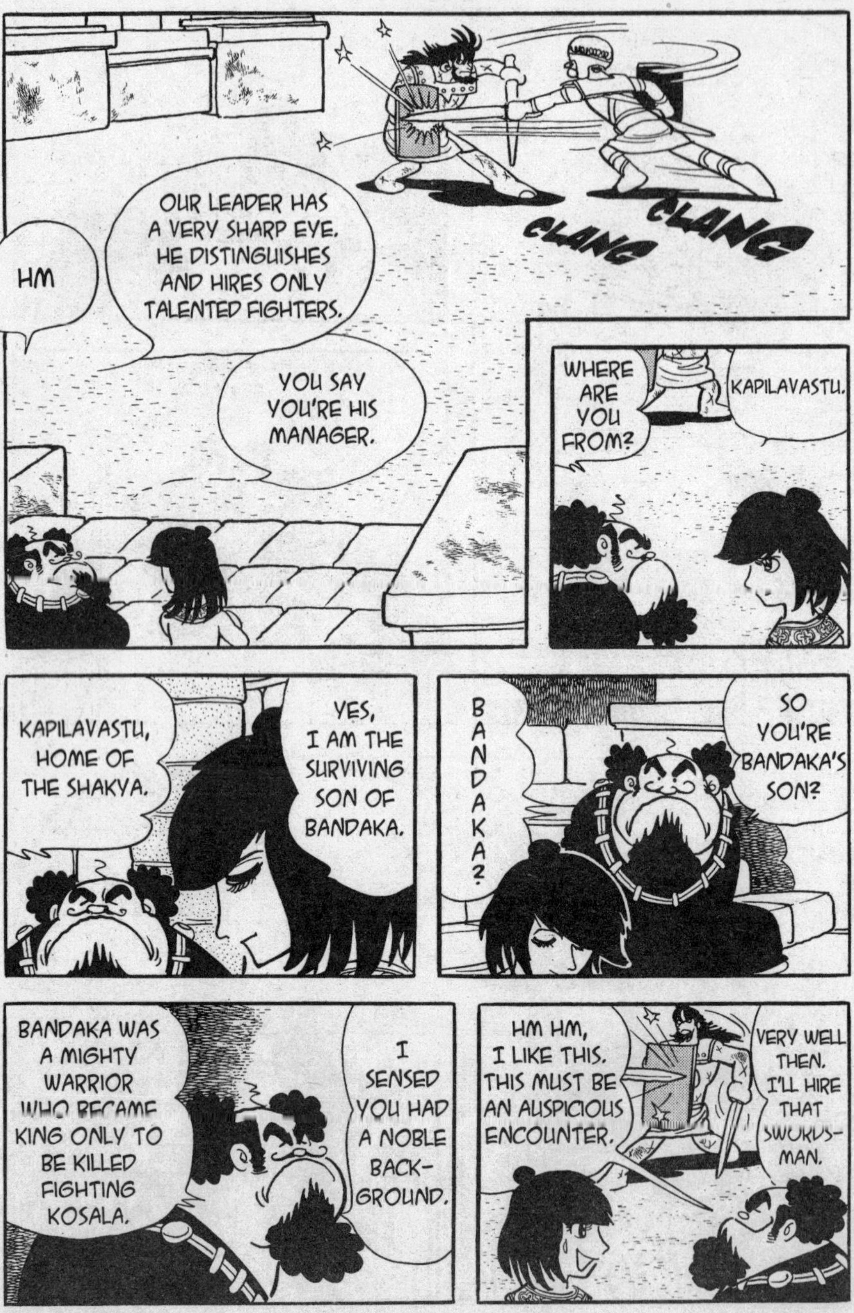

CLANG
CLANG
HM
OUR LEADER HAS A VERY SHARP EYE. HE DISTINGUISHES AND HIRES ONLY TALENTED FIGHTERS.
YOU SAY YOU'RE HIS MANAGER.
WHERE ARE YOU FROM?
KAPILAVASTU.
KAPILAVASTU, HOME OF THE SHAKYA.
YES, I AM THE SURVIVING SON OF BANDAKA.
BANDAKA?
SO YOU'RE BANDAKA'S SON?
BANDAKA WAS A MIGHTY WARRIOR WHO BECAME KING ONLY TO BE KILLED FIGHTING KOSALA.
I SENSED YOU HAD A NOBLE BACK-GROUND.
HM HM, I LIKE THIS. THIS MUST BE AN AUSPICIOUS ENCOUNTER.
VERY WELL THEN. I'LL HIRE THAT SWORDS-MAN.

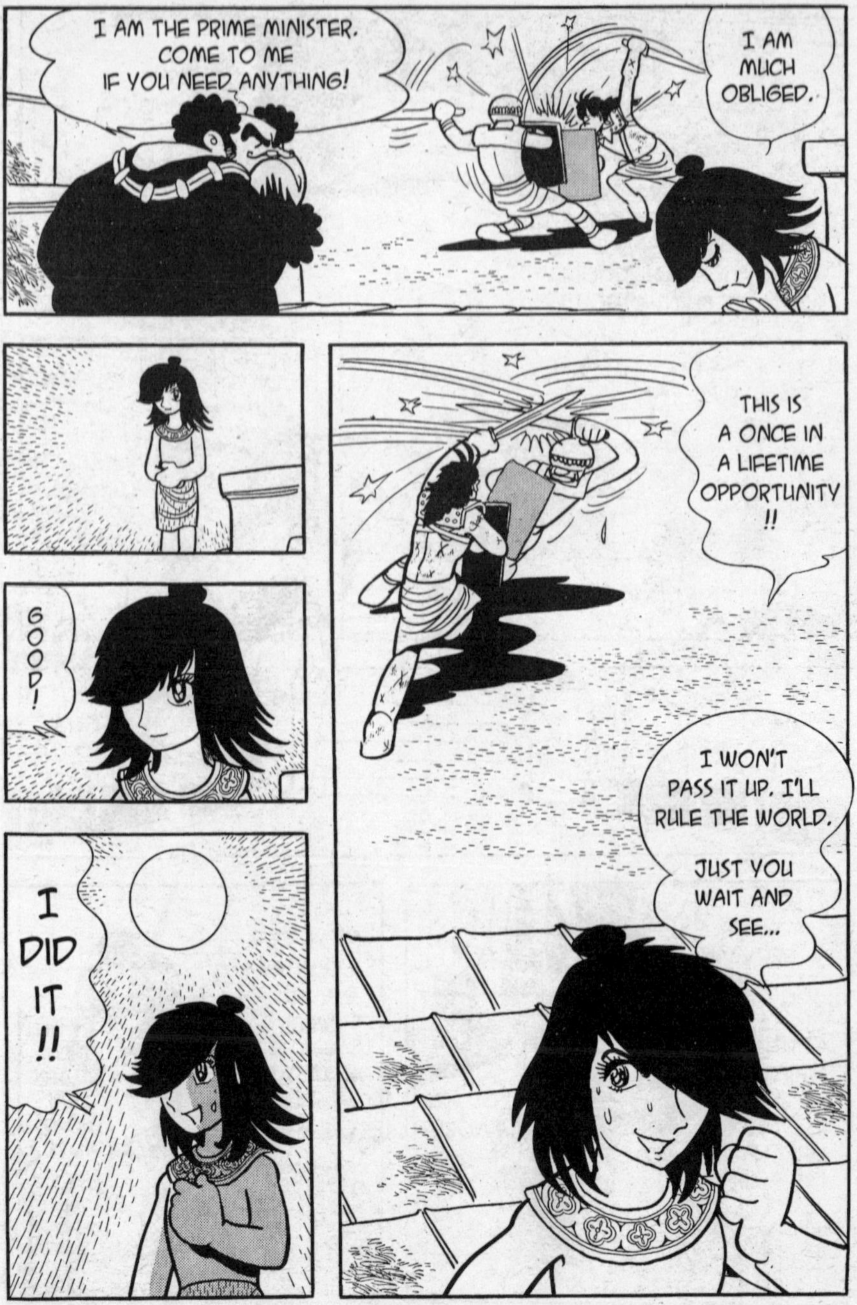
I AM THE PRIME MINISTER. COME TO ME IF YOU NEED ANYTHING!
I AM MUCH OBLIGED.
THIS IS A ONCE IN A LIFETIME OPPORTUNITY !!
GOOD!
I WON'T PASS IT UP. I'LL RULE THE WORLD.
JUST YOU WAIT AND SEE...
I DID IT !!

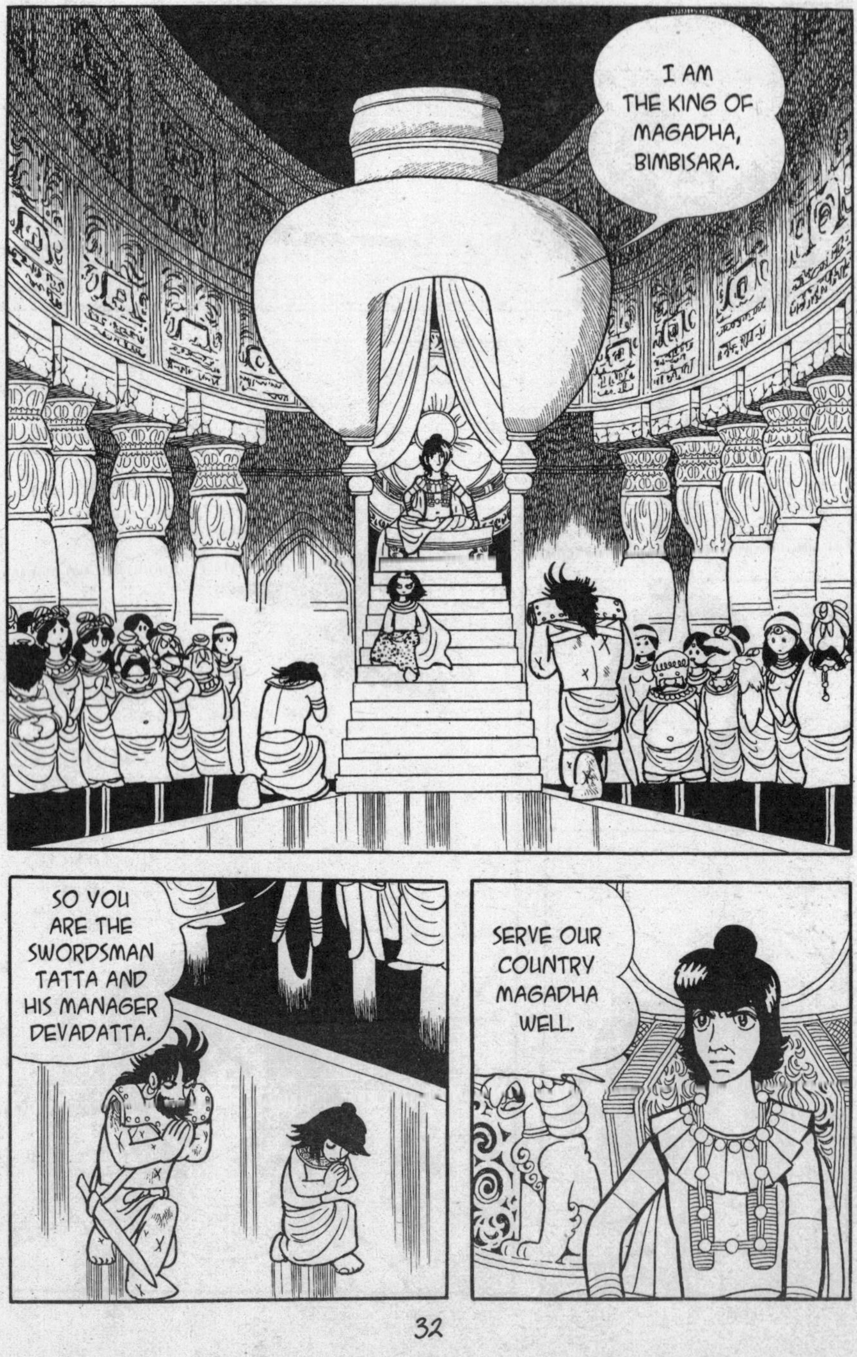
I AM THE KING OF MAGADHA, BIMBISARA.
SO YOU ARE THE SWORDSMAN TATTA AND HIS MANAGER DEVADATTA.
SERVE OUR COUNTRY MAGADHA WELL.

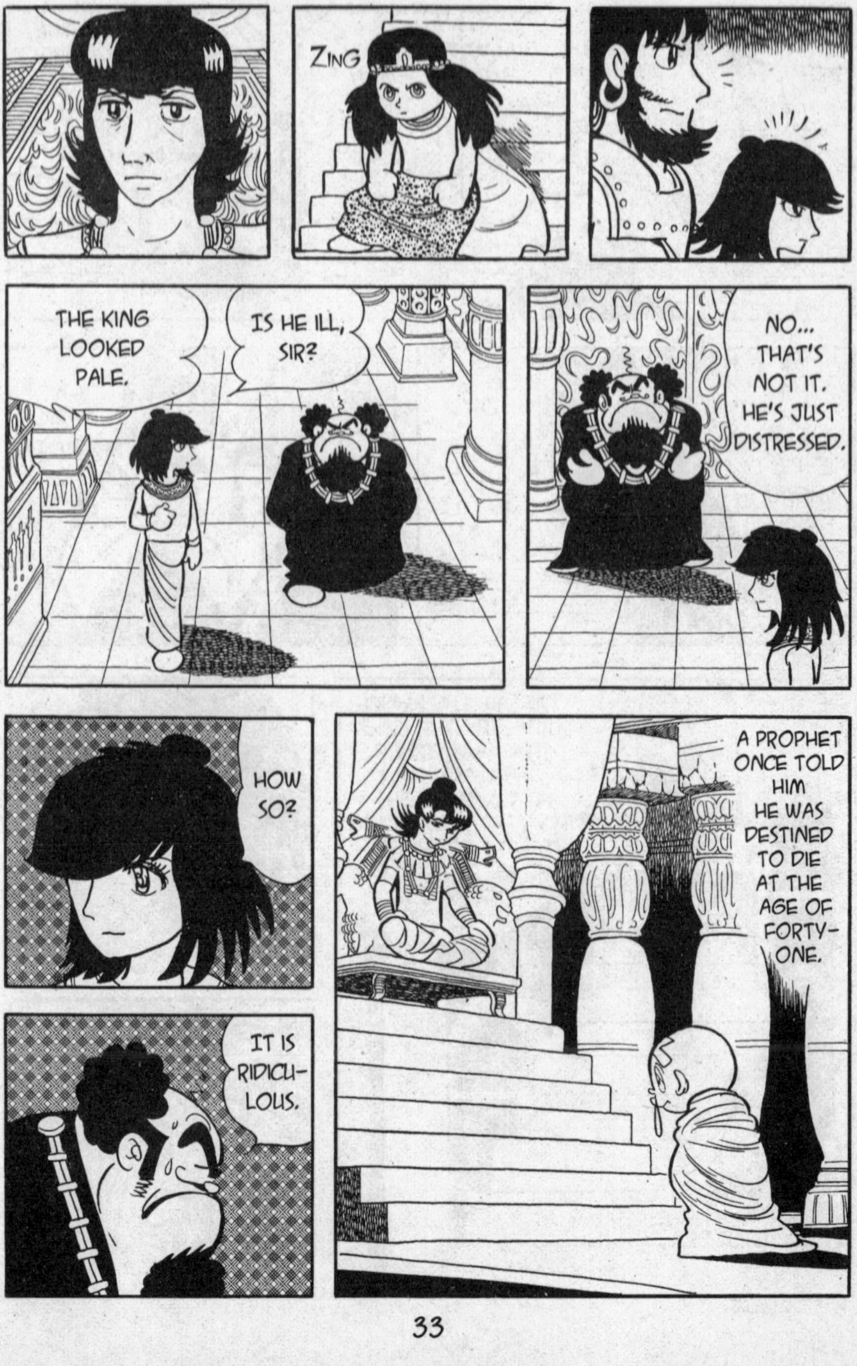
ZING
THE KING LOOKED PALE.
IS HE ILL, SIR?
NO... THAT'S NOT IT. HE'S JUST DISTRESSED.
HOW SO?
A PROPHET ONCE TOLD HIM HE WAS DESTINED TO DIE AT THE AGE OF FORTY-ONE.
IT IS RIDICULOUS.

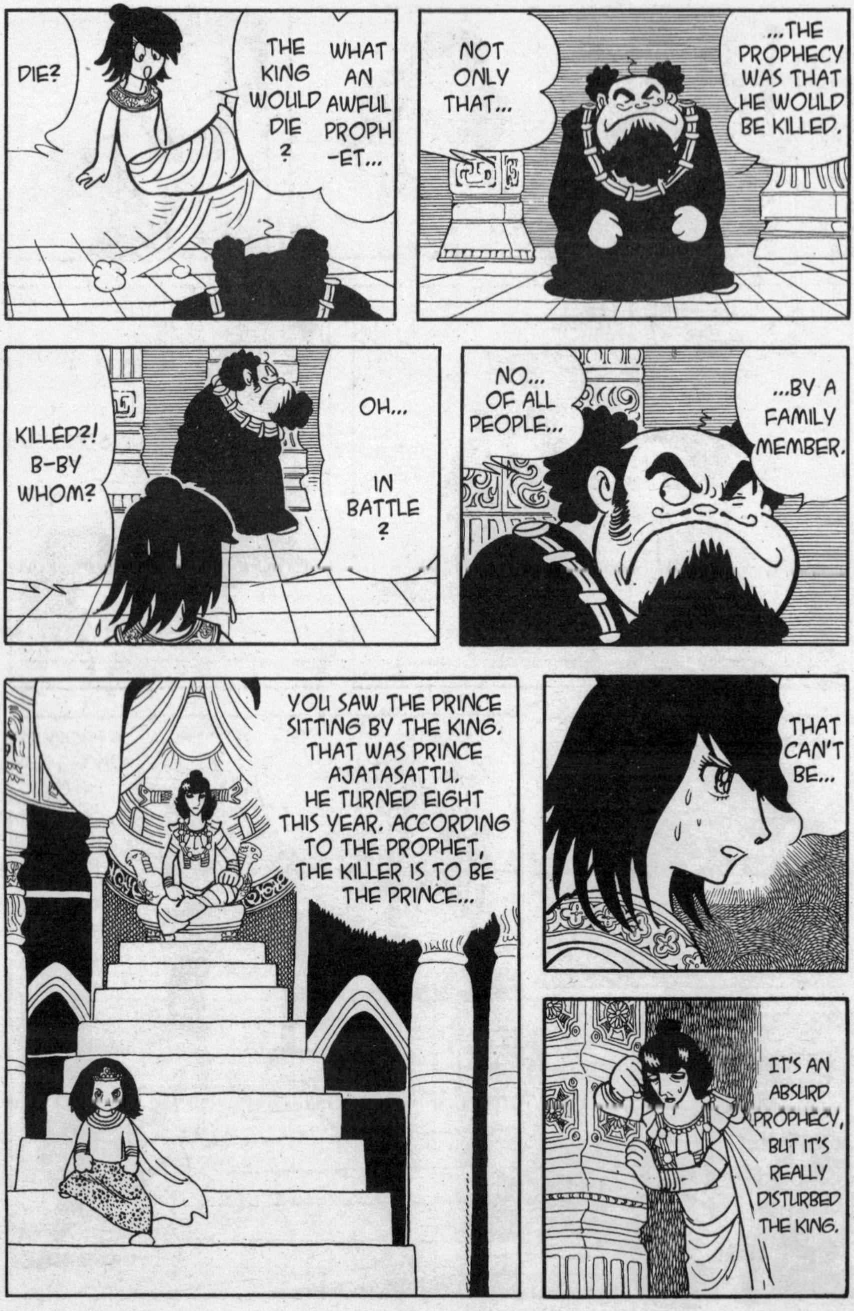

DIE?
WHAT AN AWFUL PROPH-ET...
THE KING WOULD DIE?
...THE PROPHECY WAS THAT HE WOULD BE KILLED.
NOT ONLY THAT...
OH... IN BATTLE?
KILLED?! B-BY WHOM?
...BY A FAMILY MEMBER.
NO... OF ALL PEOPLE...
YOU SAW THE PRINCE SITTING BY THE KING. THAT WAS PRINCE AJATASATTU. HE TURNED EIGHT THIS YEAR. ACCORDING TO THE PROPHET, THE KILLER IS TO BE THE PRINCE...
THAT CAN'T BE...
IT'S AN ABSURD PROPHECY, BUT IT'S REALLY DISTURBED THE KING.

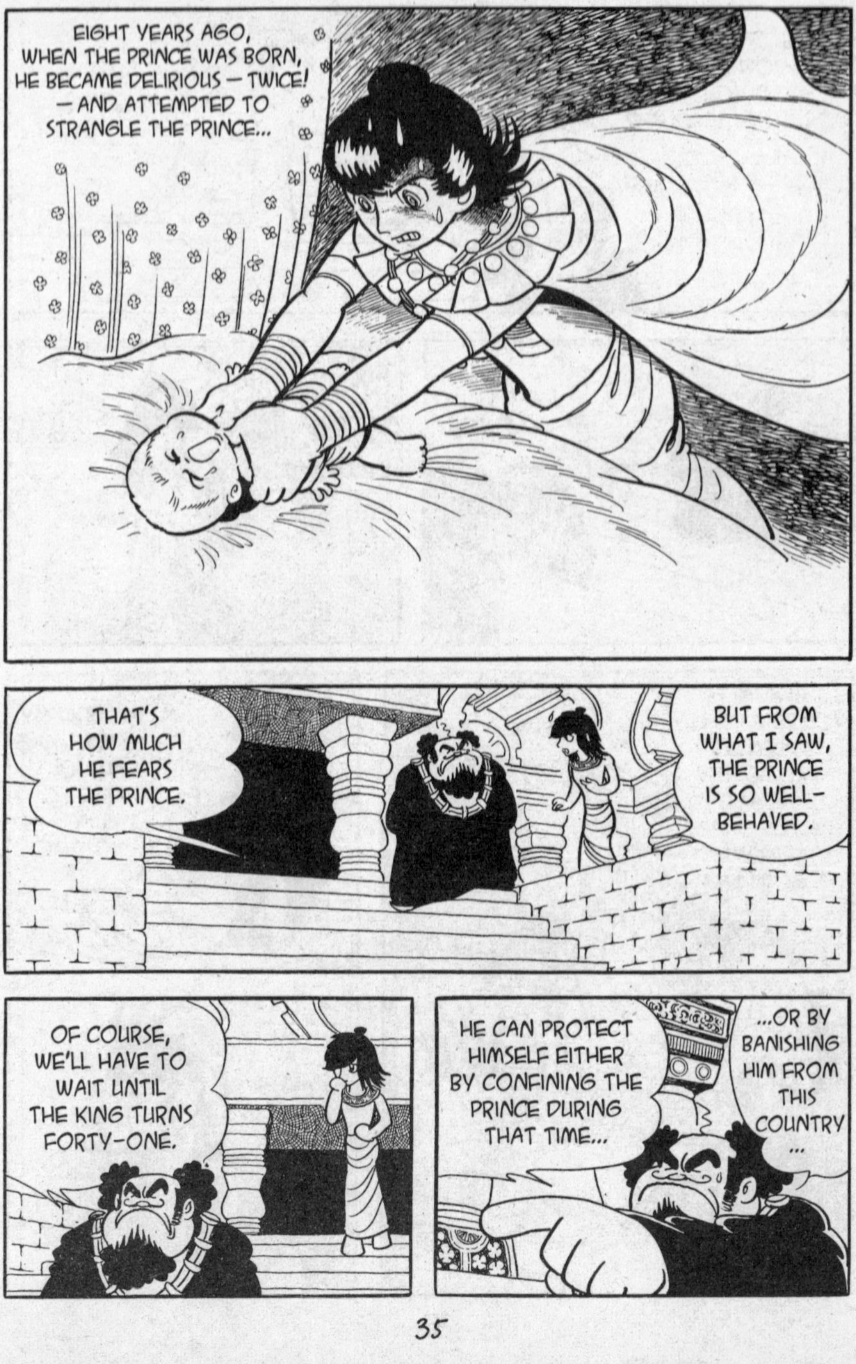
EIGHT YEARS AGO, WHEN THE PRINCE WAS BORN, HE BECAME DELIRIOUS — TWICE! — AND ATTEMPTED TO STRANGLE THE PRINCE...
THAT'S HOW MUCH HE FEARS THE PRINCE.
BUT FROM WHAT I SAW, THE PRINCE IS SO WELL-BEHAVED.
OF COURSE, WE'LL HAVE TO WAIT UNTIL THE KING TURNS FORTY-ONE.
HE CAN PROTECT HIMSELF EITHER BY CONFINING THE PRINCE DURING THAT TIME...
...OR BY BANISHING HIM FROM THIS COUNTRY ...

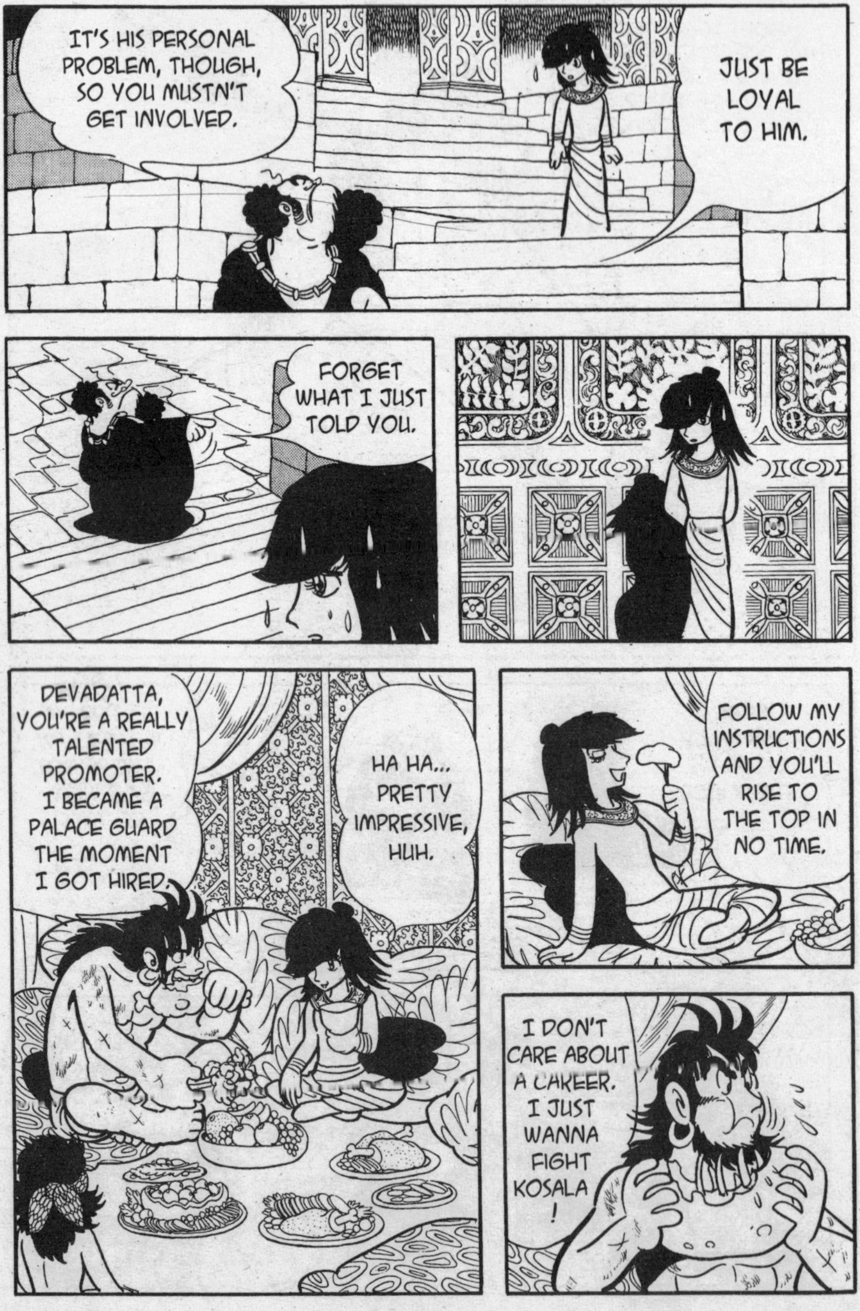
IT'S HIS PERSONAL PROBLEM, THOUGH, SO YOU MUSTN'T GET INVOLVED.
JUST BE LOYAL TO HIM.
FORGET WHAT I JUST TOLD YOU.
DEVADATTA, YOU'RE A REALLY TALENTED PROMOTER. I BECAME A PALACE GUARD THE MOMENT I GOT HIRED.
HA HA... PRETTY IMPRESSIVE, HUH.
FOLLOW MY INSTRUCTIONS AND YOU'LL RISE TO THE TOP IN NO TIME.
I DON'T CARE ABOUT A CAREER. I JUST WANNA FIGHT KOSALA!

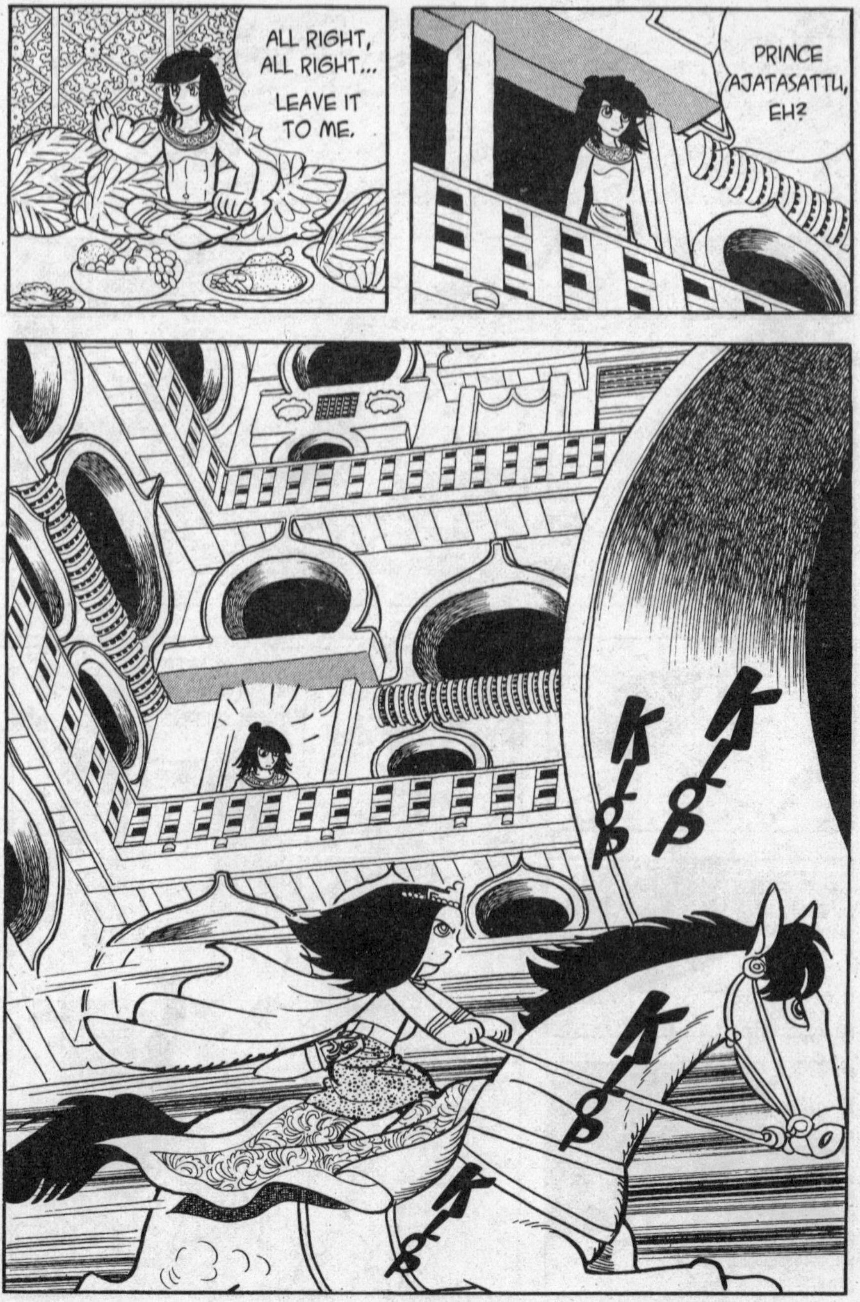
ALL RIGHT, ALL RIGHT...
LEAVE IT TO ME.
PRINCE AJATASATTU, EH?
KLOP
KLOP
KLOP
KLOP

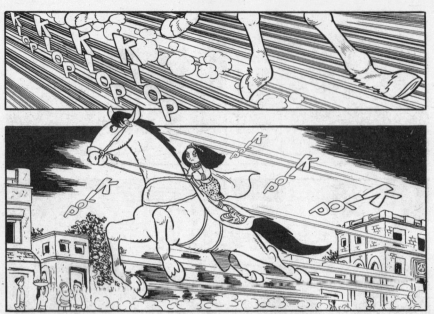

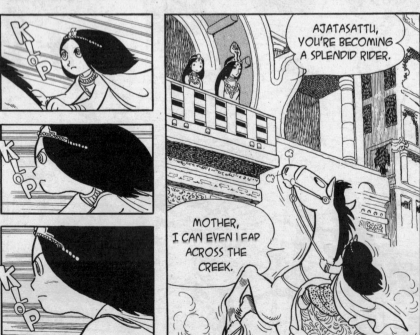

KLOP
KLOP
KLOP
KLOP
KLOP
KLOP
KLOP
KLOP
KLOP
KLOP
KLOP
AJATASATTU, YOU'RE BECOMING A SPLENDID RIDER.
MOTHER, I CAN EVEN LEAP ACROSS THE CREEK.

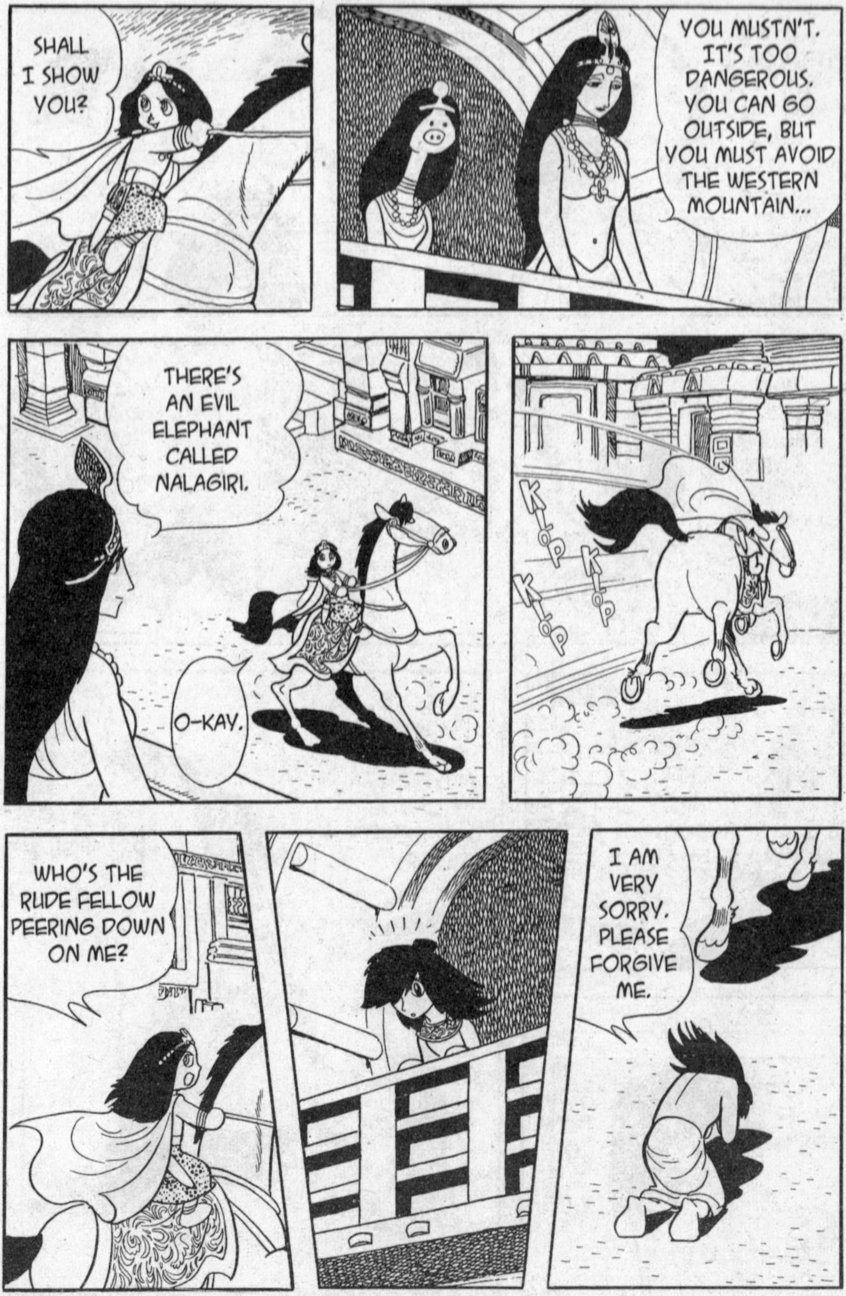

SHALL I SHOW YOU?
YOU MUSTN'T. IT'S TOO DANGEROUS. YOU CAN GO OUTSIDE, BUT YOU MUST AVOID THE WESTERN MOUNTAIN...
THERE'S AN EVIL ELEPHANT CALLED NALAGIRI.
O-KAY.
KLOP KLOP KLOP
WHO'S THE RUDE FELLOW PEERING DOWN ON ME?
I AM VERY SORRY. PLEASE FORGIVE ME.

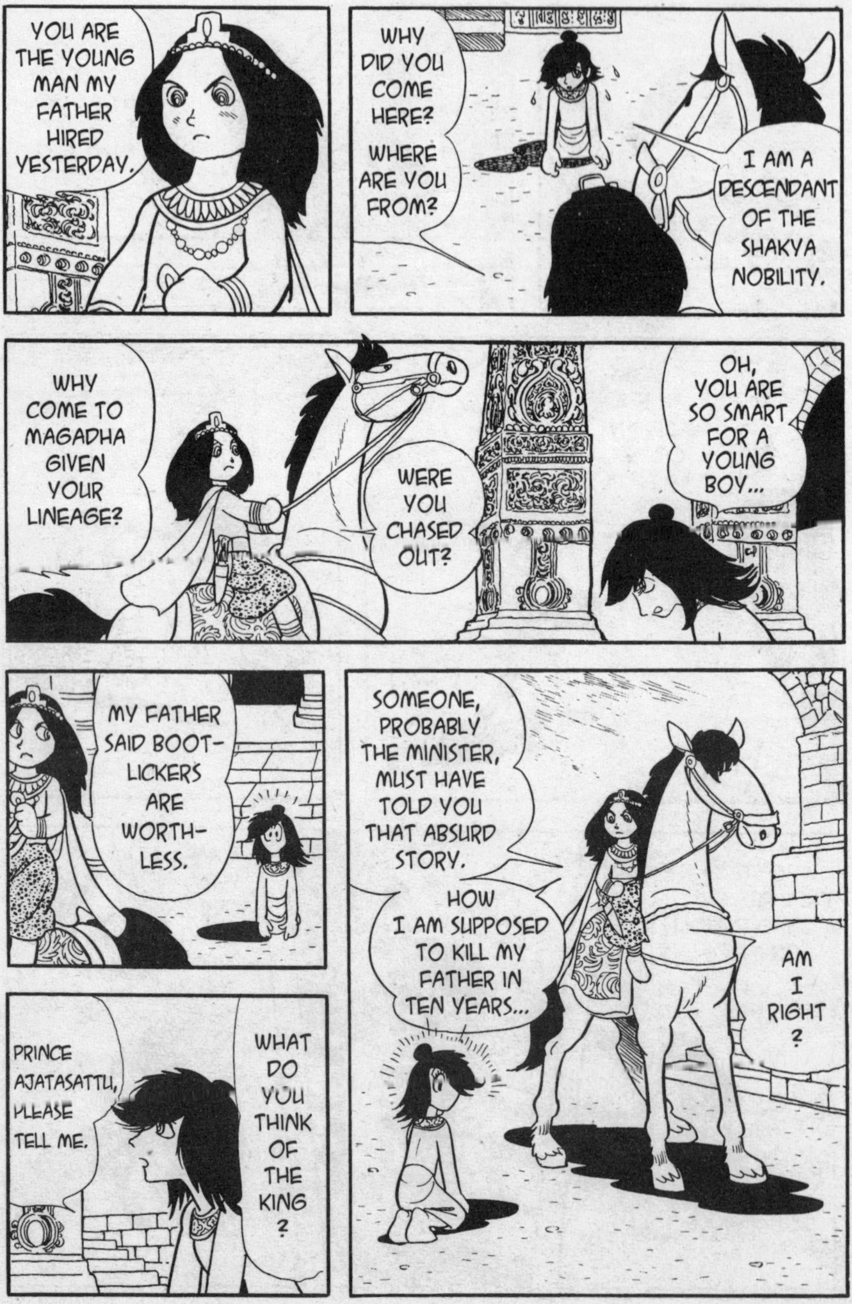

YOU ARE THE YOUNG MAN MY FATHER HIRED YESTERDAY.
WHY DID YOU COME HERE?
WHERE ARE YOU FROM?
I AM A DESCENDANT OF THE SHAKYA NOBILITY.
WHY COME TO MAGADHA GIVEN YOUR LINEAGE?
WERE YOU CHASED OUT?
OH, YOU ARE SO SMART FOR A YOUNG BOY...
MY FATHER SAID BOOT-LICKERS ARE WORTH-LESS.
PRINCE AJATASATTU, PLEASE TELL ME.
WHAT DO YOU THINK OF THE KING?
SOMEONE, PROBABLY THE MINISTER, MUST HAVE TOLD YOU THAT ABSURD STORY.
HOW I AM SUPPOSED TO KILL MY FATHER IN TEN YEARS...
AM I RIGHT?

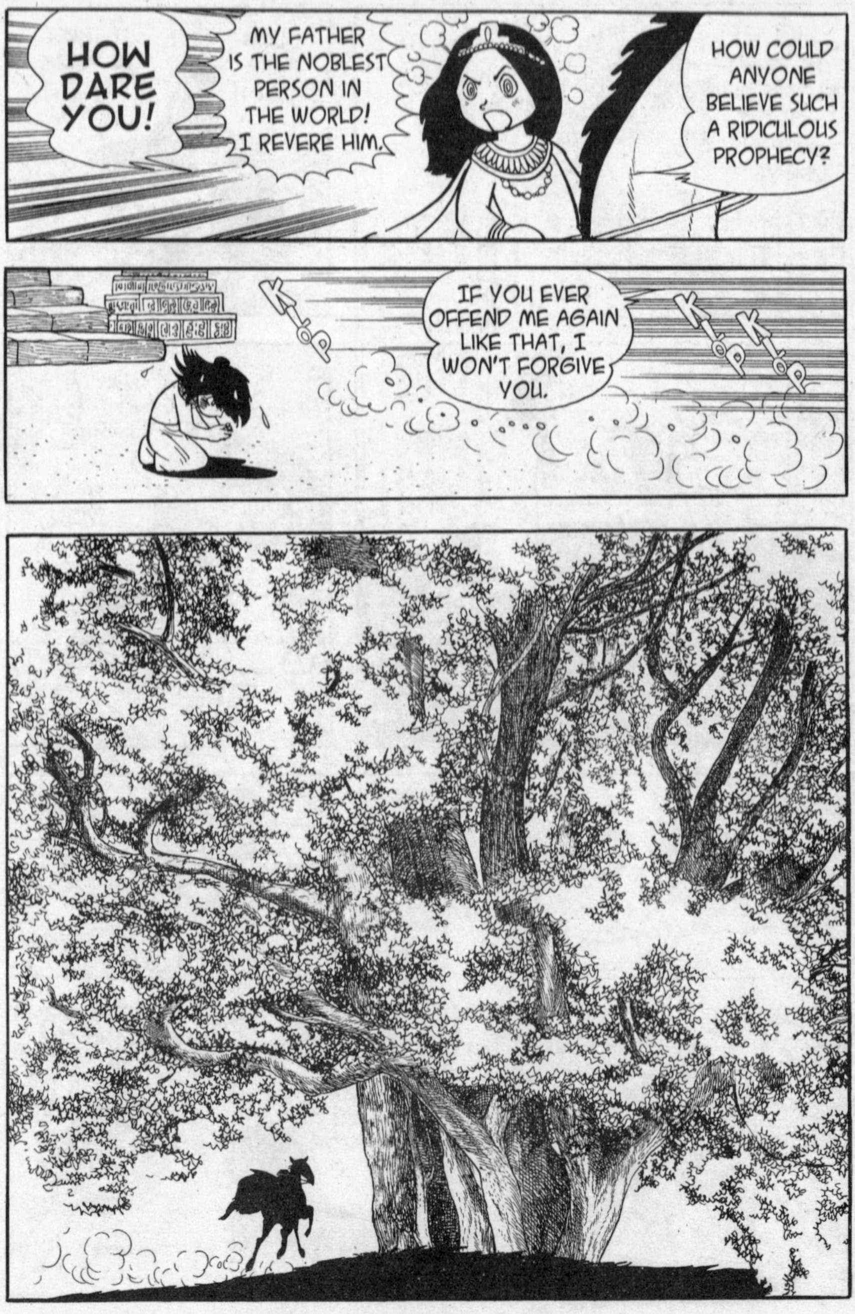
HOW DARE YOU!
MY FATHER IS THE NOBLEST PERSON IN THE WORLD! I REVERE HIM.
HOW COULD ANYONE BELIEVE SUCH A RIDICULOUS PROPHECY?
KLOP
IF YOU EVER OFFEND ME AGAIN LIKE THAT, I WON'T FORGIVE YOU.
KLOP KLOP

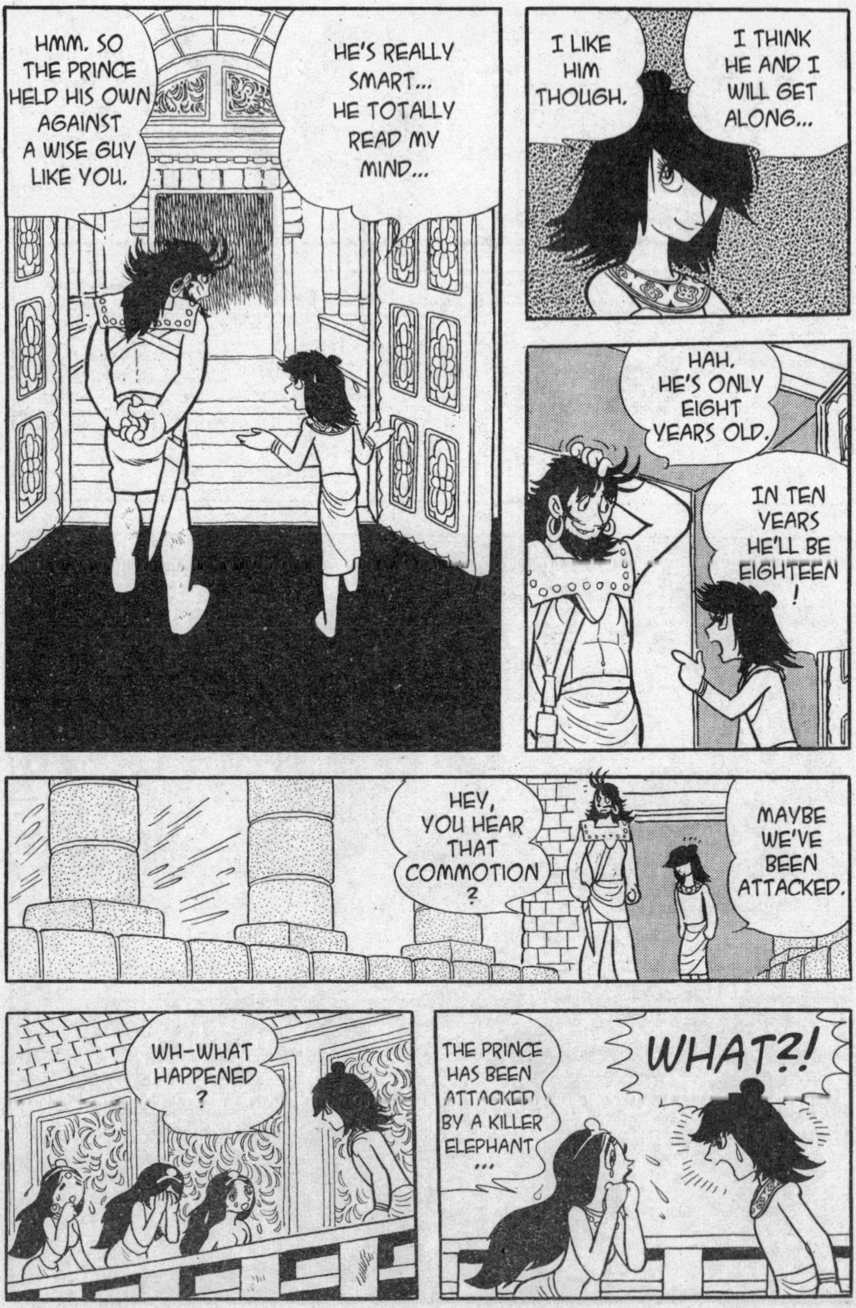
HMM. SO THE PRINCE HELD HIS OWN AGAINST A WISE GUY LIKE YOU.
HE'S REALLY SMART... HE TOTALLY READ MY MIND...
I LIKE HIM THOUGH.
I THINK HE AND I WILL GET ALONG...
HAH. HE'S ONLY EIGHT YEARS OLD.
IN TEN YEARS HE'LL BE EIGHTEEN!
HEY, YOU HEAR THAT COMMOTION?
MAYBE WE'VE BEEN ATTACKED.
WH-WHAT HAPPENED?
THE PRINCE HAS BEEN ATTACKED BY A KILLER ELEPHANT...
WHAT?!

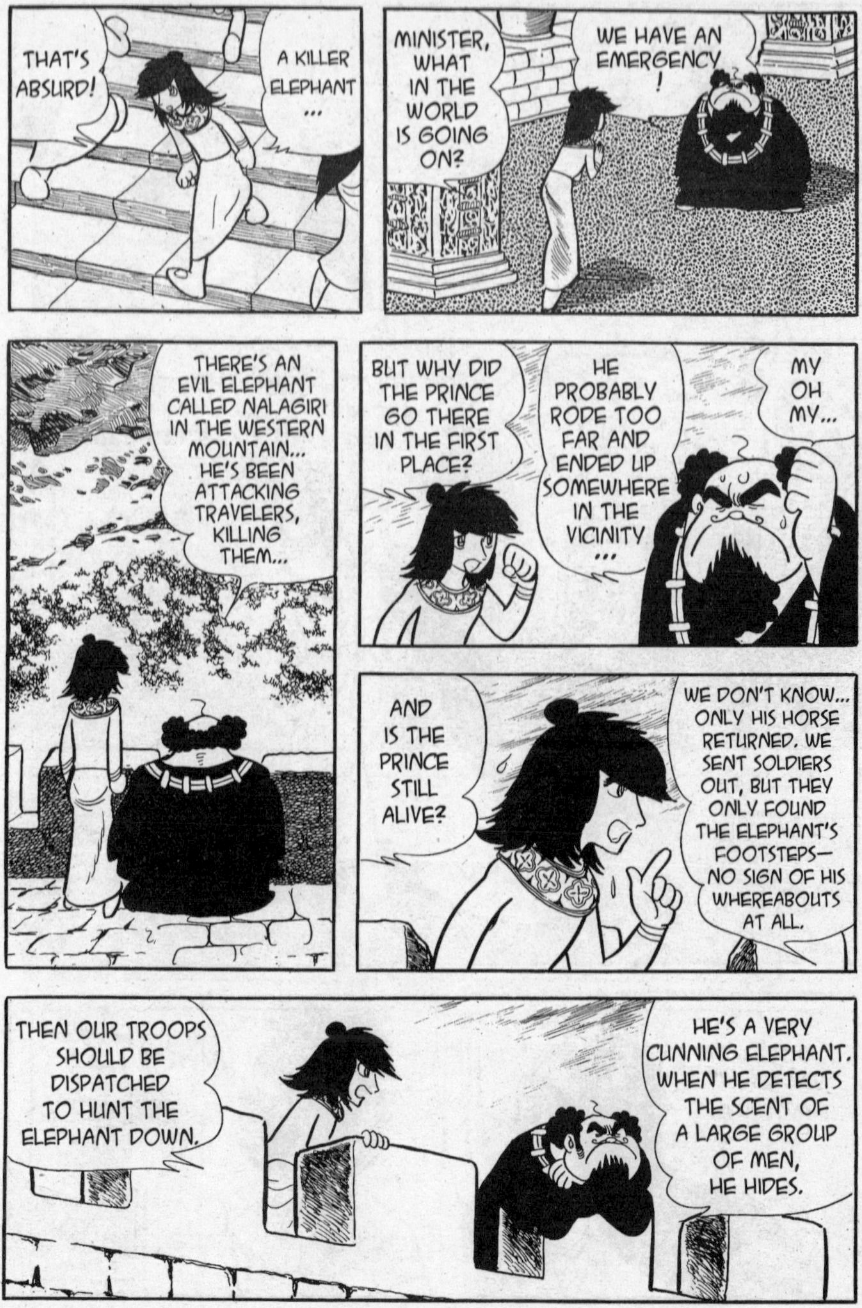
THAT'S ABSURD!
A KILLER ELEPHANT ...
MINISTER, WHAT IN THE WORLD IS GOING ON?
WE HAVE AN EMERGENCY !
THERE'S AN EVIL ELEPHANT CALLED NALAGIRI IN THE WESTERN MOUNTAIN... HE'S BEEN ATTACKING TRAVELERS, KILLING THEM...
BUT WHY DID THE PRINCE GO THERE IN THE FIRST PLACE?
HE PROBABLY RODE TOO FAR AND ENDED UP SOMEWHERE IN THE VICINITY ...
MY OH MY...
AND IS THE PRINCE STILL ALIVE?
WE DON'T KNOW... ONLY HIS HORSE RETURNED. WE SENT SOLDIERS OUT, BUT THEY ONLY FOUND THE ELEPHANT'S FOOTSTEPS— NO SIGN OF HIS WHEREABOUTS AT ALL.
THEN OUR TROOPS SHOULD BE DISPATCHED TO HUNT THE ELEPHANT DOWN.
HE'S A VERY CUNNING ELEPHANT. WHEN HE DETECTS THE SCENT OF A LARGE GROUP OF MEN, HE HIDES.

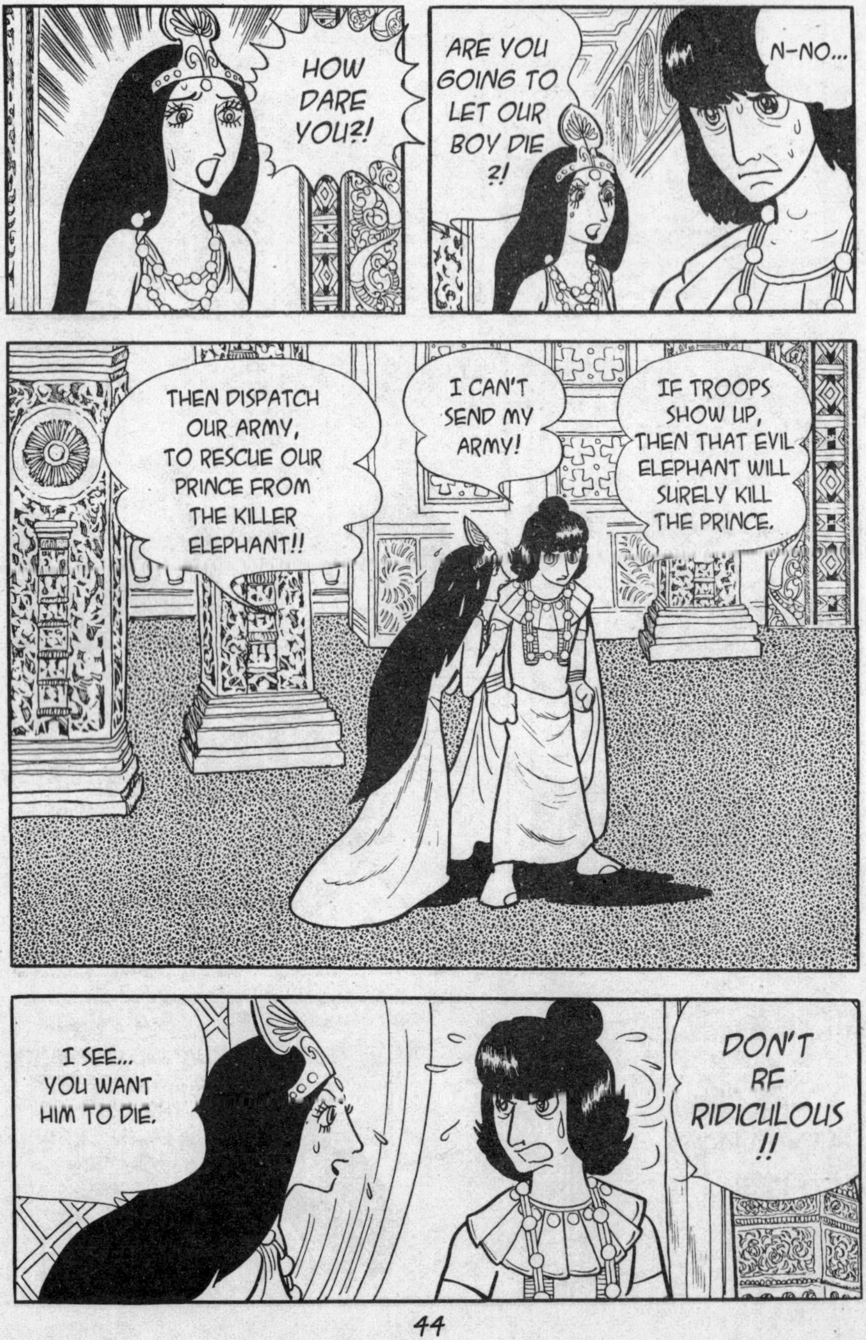
HOW DARE YOU?!
ARE YOU GOING TO LET OUR BOY DIE ?!
N-NO...
THEN DISPATCH OUR ARMY, TO RESCUE OUR PRINCE FROM THE KILLER ELEPHANT!!
I CAN'T SEND MY ARMY!
IF TROOPS SHOW UP, THEN THAT EVIL ELEPHANT WILL SURELY KILL THE PRINCE.
I SEE... YOU WANT HIM TO DIE.
DON'T BE RIDICULOUS !!

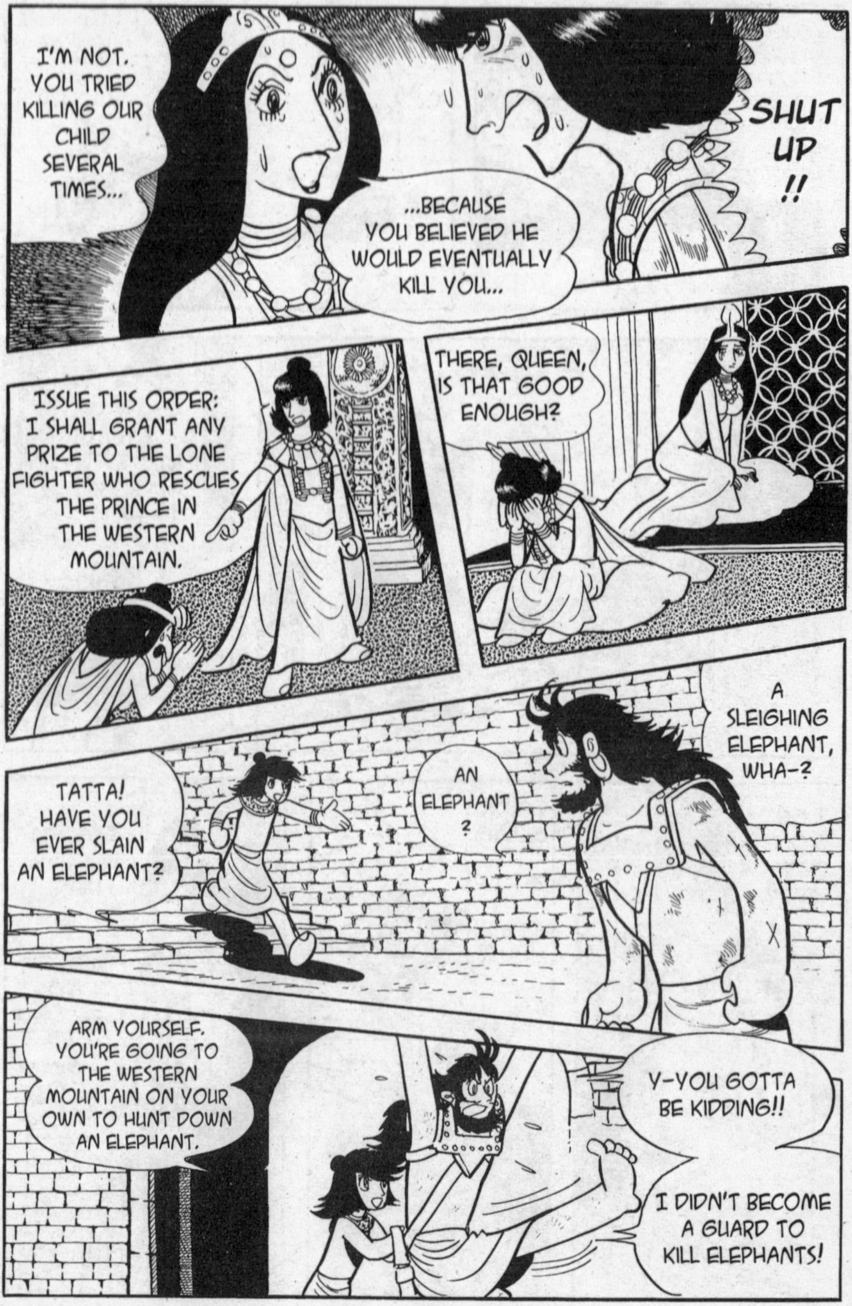
I'M NOT. YOU TRIED KILLING OUR CHILD SEVERAL TIMES...
...BECAUSE YOU BELIEVED HE WOULD EVENTUALLY KILL YOU...
SHUT UP !!
ISSUE THIS ORDER: I SHALL GRANT ANY PRIZE TO THE LONE FIGHTER WHO RESCUES THE PRINCE IN THE WESTERN MOUNTAIN.
THERE, QUEEN, IS THAT GOOD ENOUGH?
TATTA! HAVE YOU EVER SLAIN AN ELEPHANT?
AN ELEPHANT ?
A SLEIGHING ELEPHANT, WHA-?
ARM YOURSELF. YOU'RE GOING TO THE WESTERN MOUNTAIN ON YOUR OWN TO HUNT DOWN AN ELEPHANT.
Y-YOU GOTTA BE KIDDING!!
I DIDN'T BECOME A GUARD TO KILL ELEPHANTS!

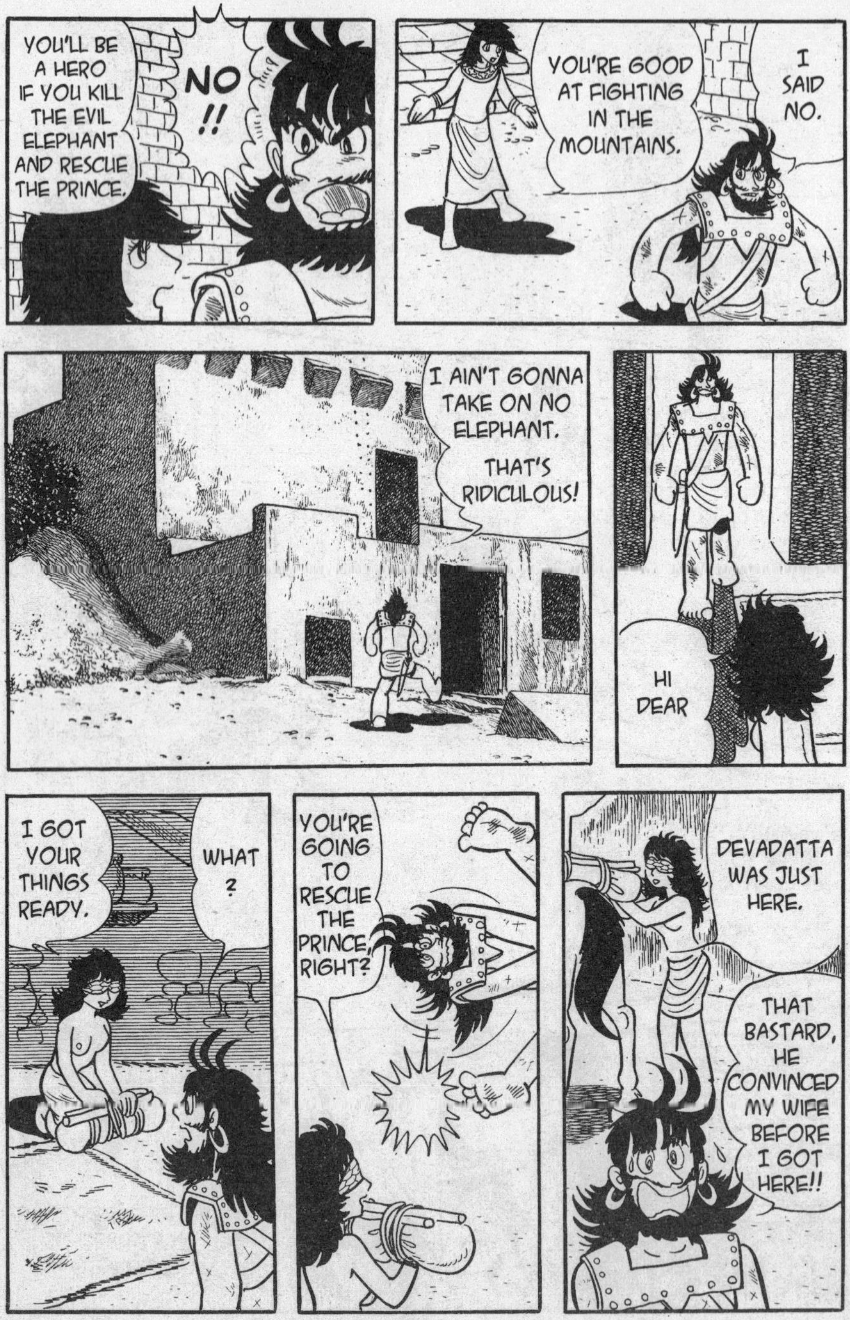
YOU'LL BE A HERO IF YOU KILL THE EVIL ELEPHANT AND RESCUE THE PRINCE.
NO !!
YOU'RE GOOD AT FIGHTING IN THE MOUNTAINS.
I SAID NO.
I AIN'T GONNA TAKE ON NO ELEPHANT.
THAT'S RIDICULOUS!
HI DEAR
I GOT YOUR THINGS READY.
WHAT ?
YOU'RE GOING TO RESCUE THE PRINCE, RIGHT?
DEVADATTA WAS JUST HERE.
THAT BASTARD, HE CONVINCED MY WIFE BEFORE I GOT HERE!!

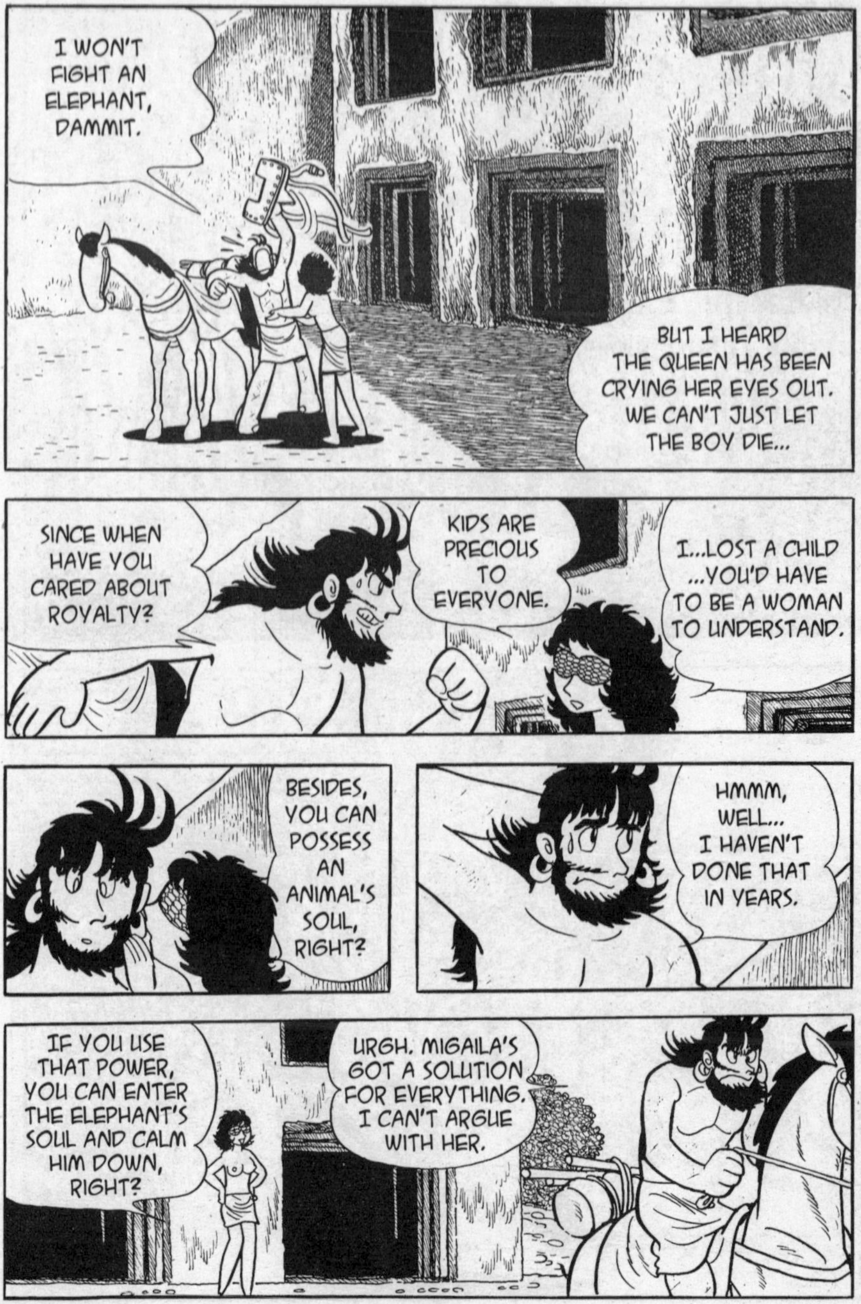
I WON'T FIGHT AN ELEPHANT, DAMMIT.
BUT I HEARD THE QUEEN HAS BEEN CRYING HER EYES OUT. WE CAN'T JUST LET THE BOY DIE...
SINCE WHEN HAVE YOU CARED ABOUT ROYALTY?
KIDS ARE PRECIOUS TO EVERYONE.
I...LOST A CHILD ...YOU'D HAVE TO BE A WOMAN TO UNDERSTAND.
BESIDES, YOU CAN POSSESS AN ANIMAL'S SOUL, RIGHT?
HMMM, WELL... I HAVEN'T DONE THAT IN YEARS.
IF YOU USE THAT POWER, YOU CAN ENTER THE ELEPHANT'S SOUL AND CALM HIM DOWN, RIGHT?
URGH. MIGAILA'S GOT A SOLUTION FOR EVERYTHING. I CAN'T ARGUE WITH HER.

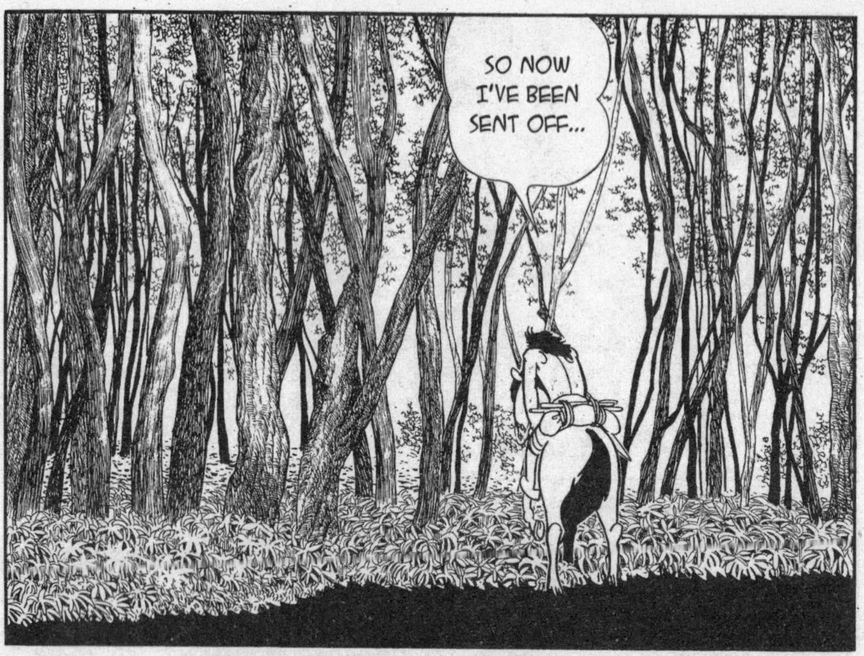
SO NOW I'VE BEEN SENT OFF...

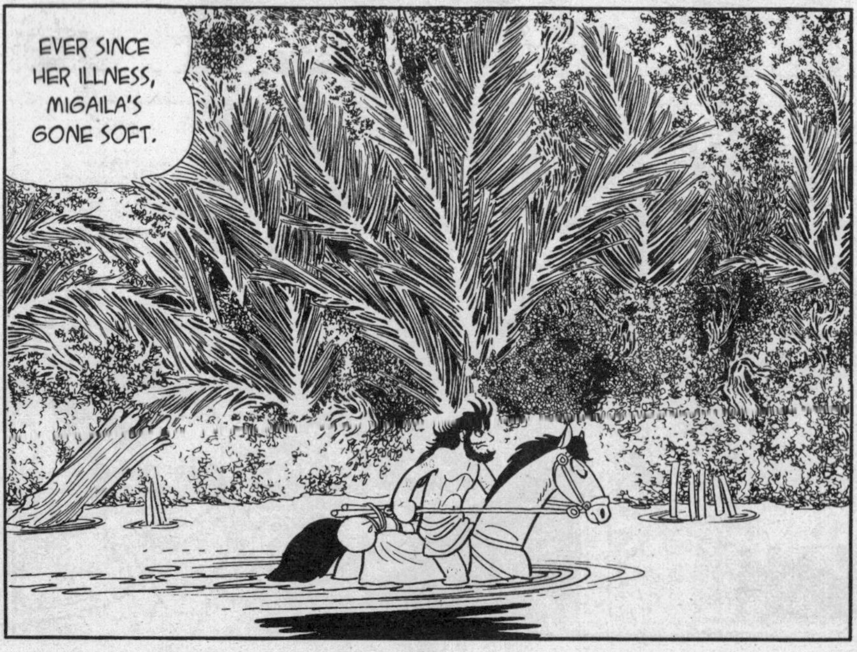
EVER SINCE HER ILLNESS, MIGAILA'S GONE SOFT.

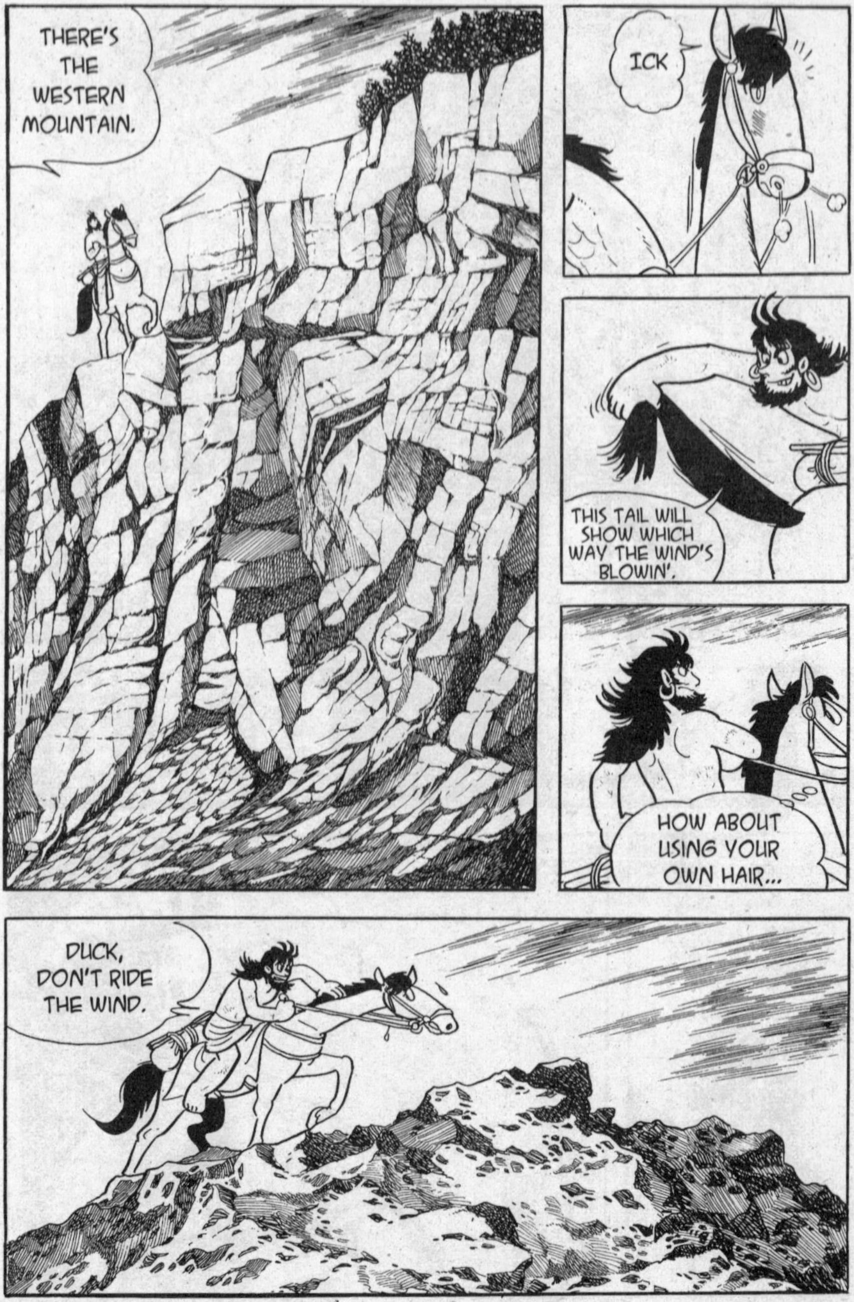
THERE'S THE WESTERN MOUNTAIN.
ICK
THIS TAIL WILL SHOW WHICH WAY THE WIND'S BLOWIN'.
HOW ABOUT USING YOUR OWN HAIR...
DUCK, DON'T RIDE THE WIND.

THERE HE IS...

HE'S HUGE...!!

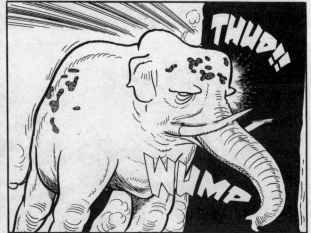

THUD!!

WHUMP

50

THUMP!

AIEE
AIEE
AIEE

HEY... SOMEONE OVER THERE... IT MUST BE THE PRINCE!

THUD THUD THUD

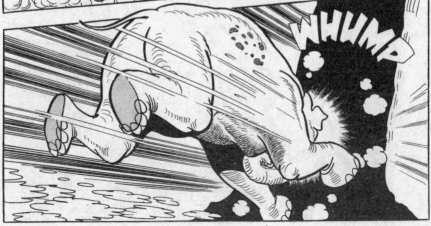

WHUMP

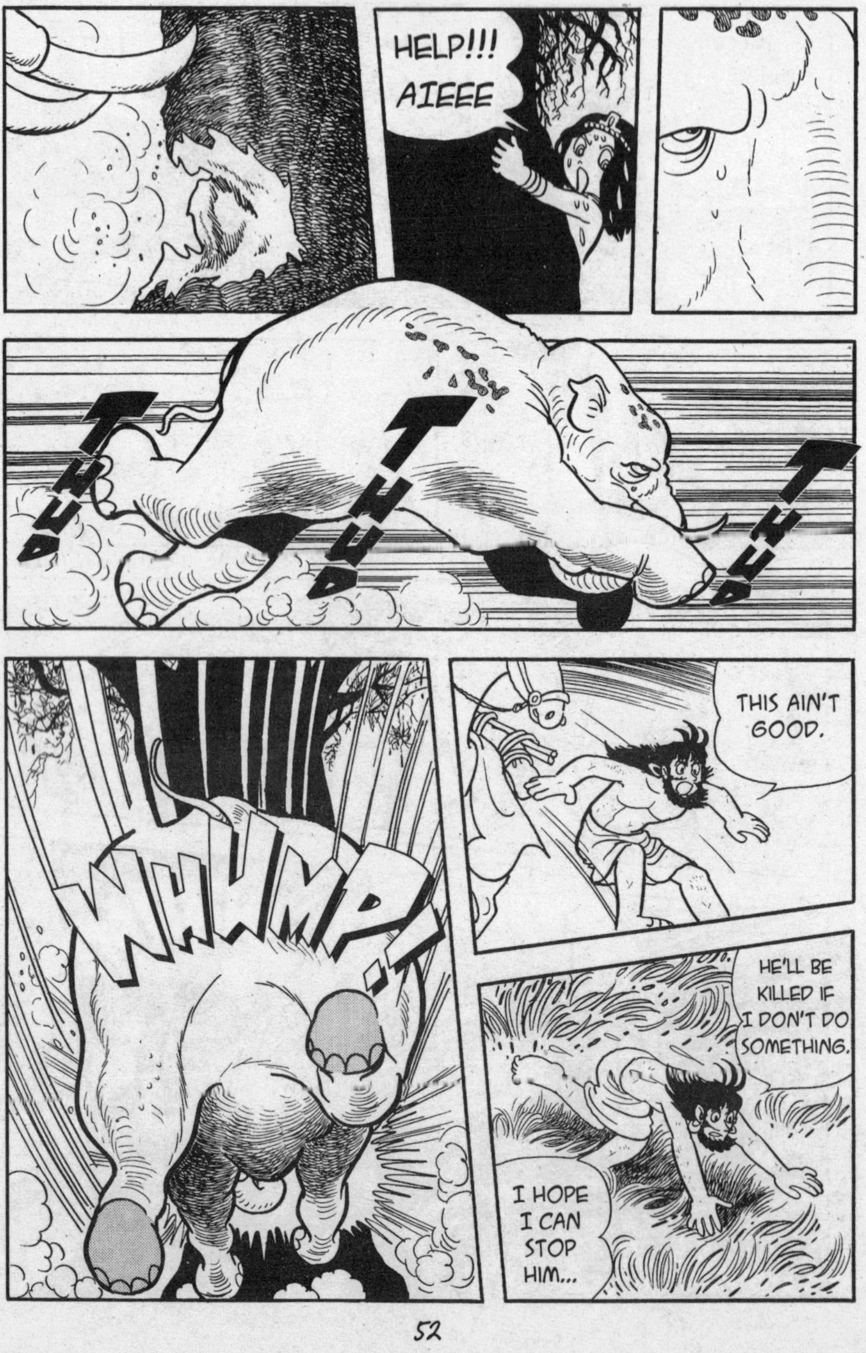
HELP!!!
AIEEE
THUD
THUD
THUD
WHUMP!!
THIS AIN'T GOOD.
HE'LL BE KILLED IF I DON'T DO SOMETHING.
I HOPE I CAN STOP HIM...

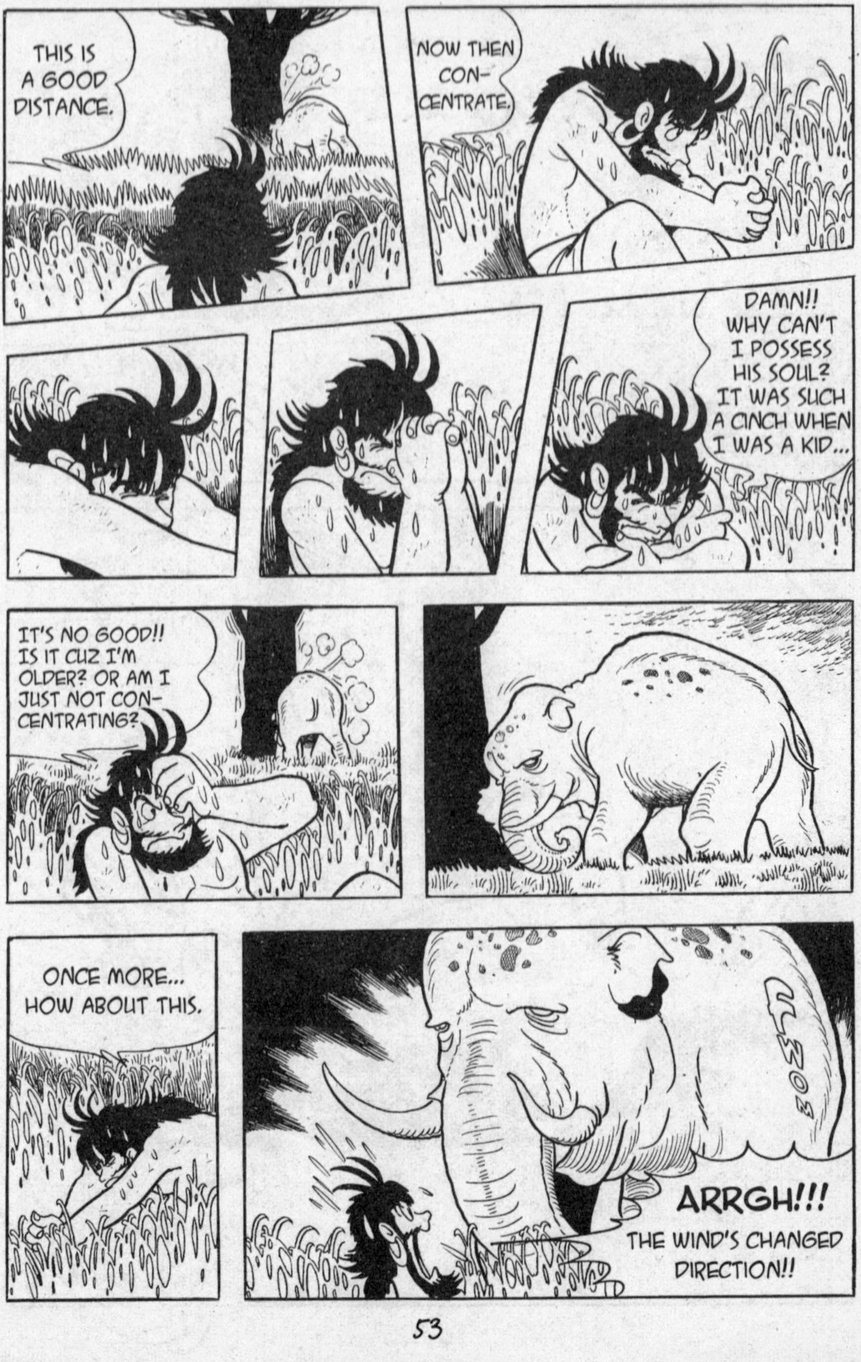
THIS IS A GOOD DISTANCE.
NOW THEN CON-CENTRATE.
DAMN!! WHY CAN'T I POSSESS HIS SOUL? IT WAS SUCH A CINCH WHEN I WAS A KID...
IT'S NO GOOD!! IS IT CUZ I'M OLDER? OR AM I JUST NOT CON-CENTRATING?
ONCE MORE... HOW ABOUT THIS.
FWOM
ARRGH!!!
THE WIND'S CHANGED DIRECTION!!

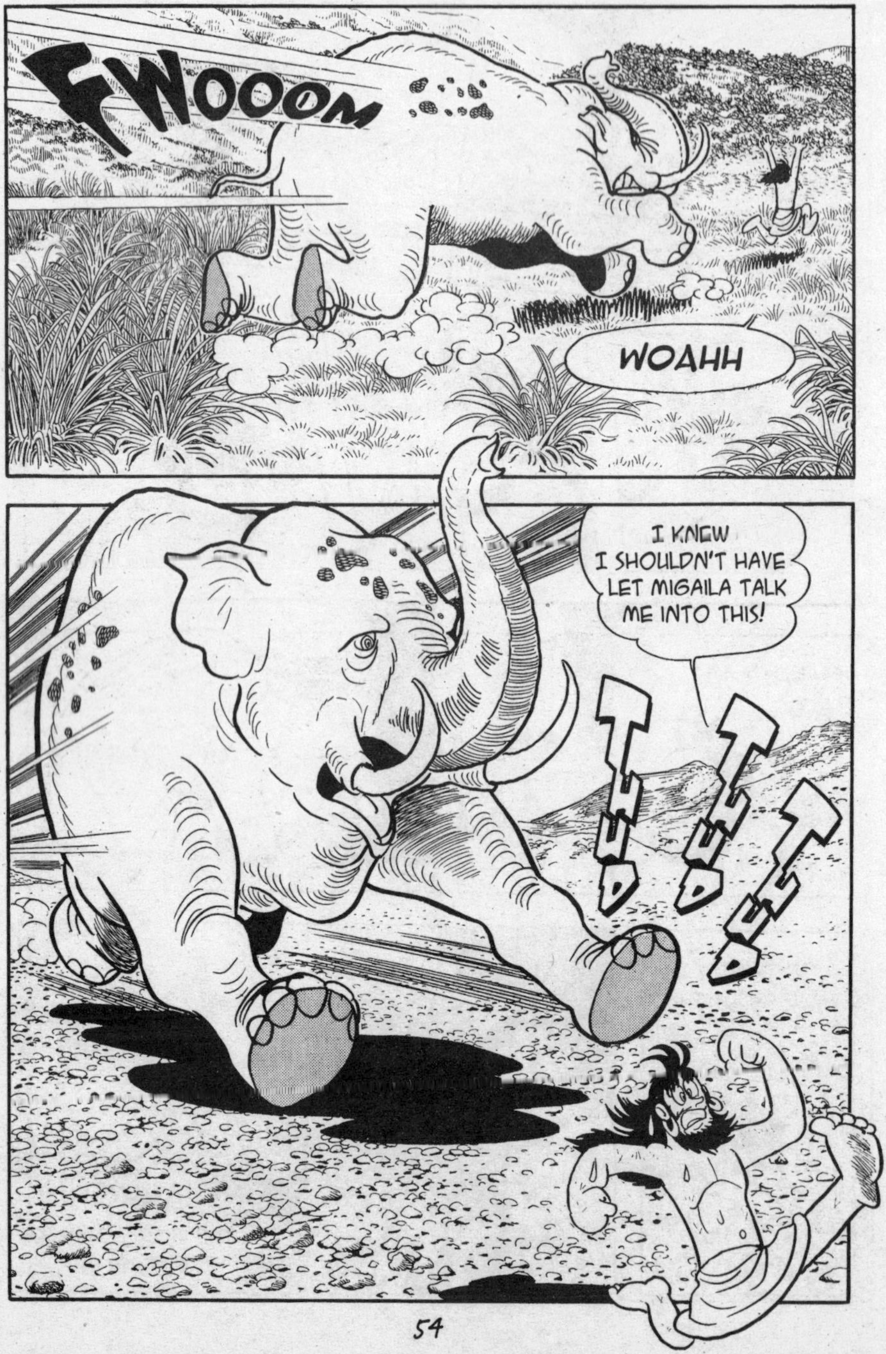
FWOOOM
WOAHH
I KNEW I SHOULDN'T HAVE LET MIGAILA TALK ME INTO THIS!
THUD
THUD
THUD

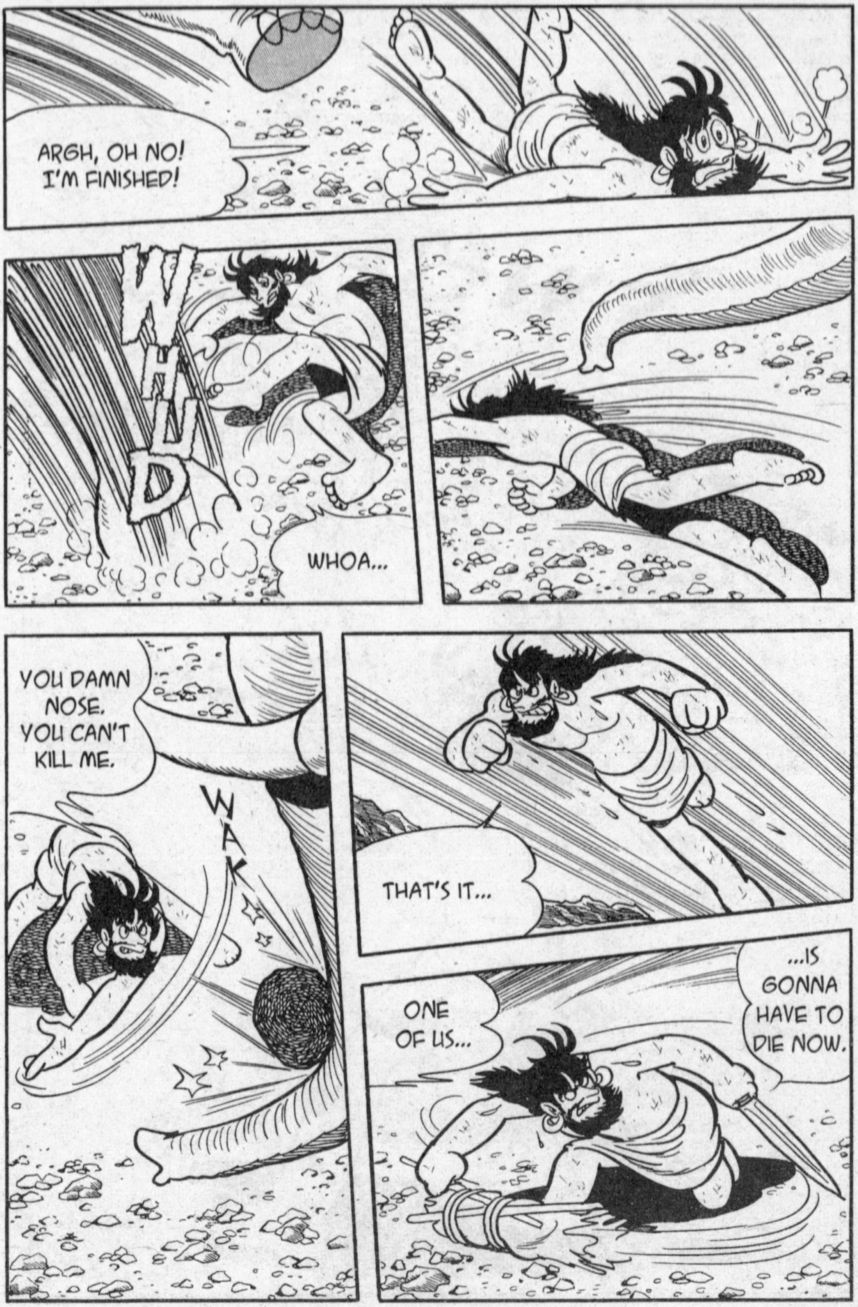
ARGH, OH NO! I'M FINISHED!
WHUD
WHOA...
YOU DAMN NOSE. YOU CAN'T KILL ME.
WAK
THAT'S IT...
ONE OF US...
...IS GONNA HAVE TO DIE NOW.

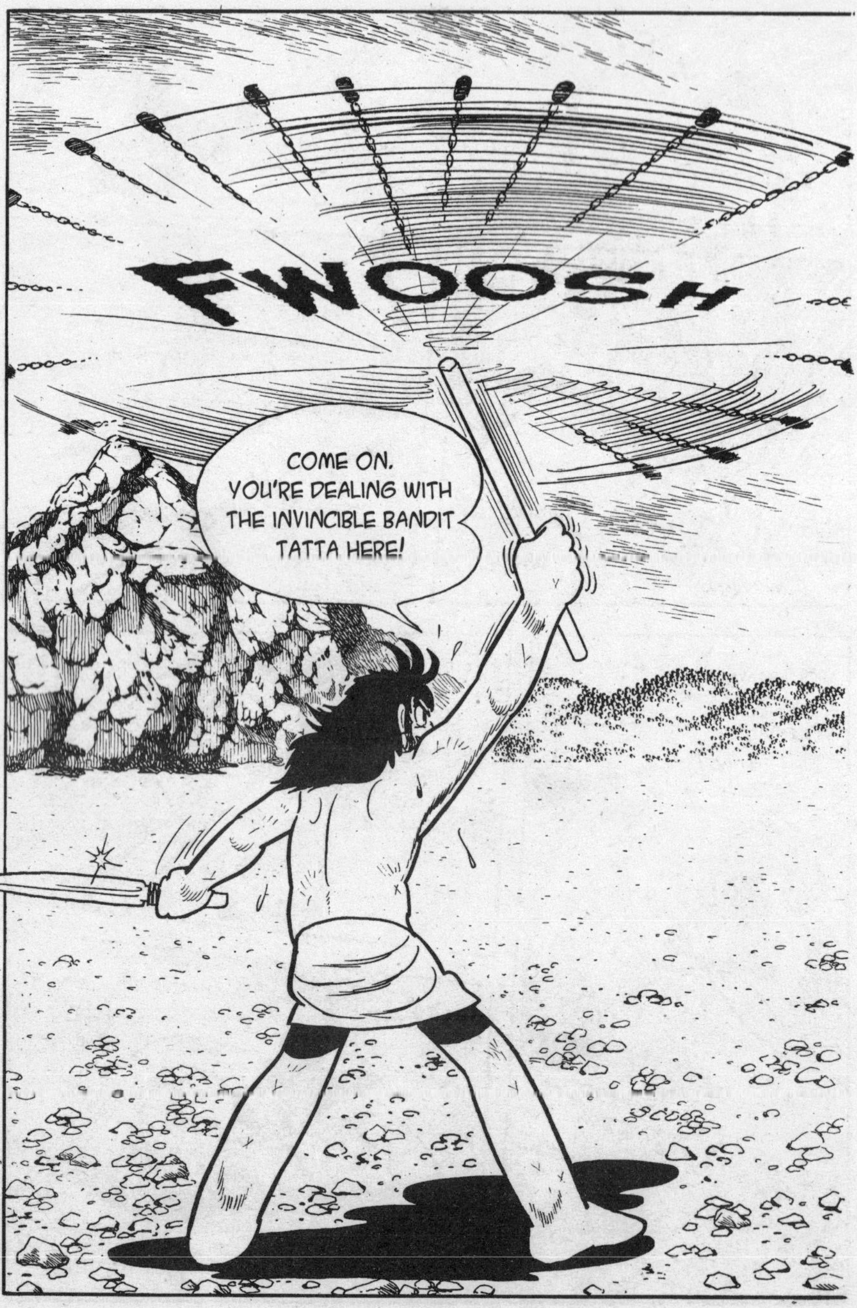
FWOOSH
COME ON. YOU'RE DEALING WITH THE INVINCIBLE BANDIT TATTA HERE!

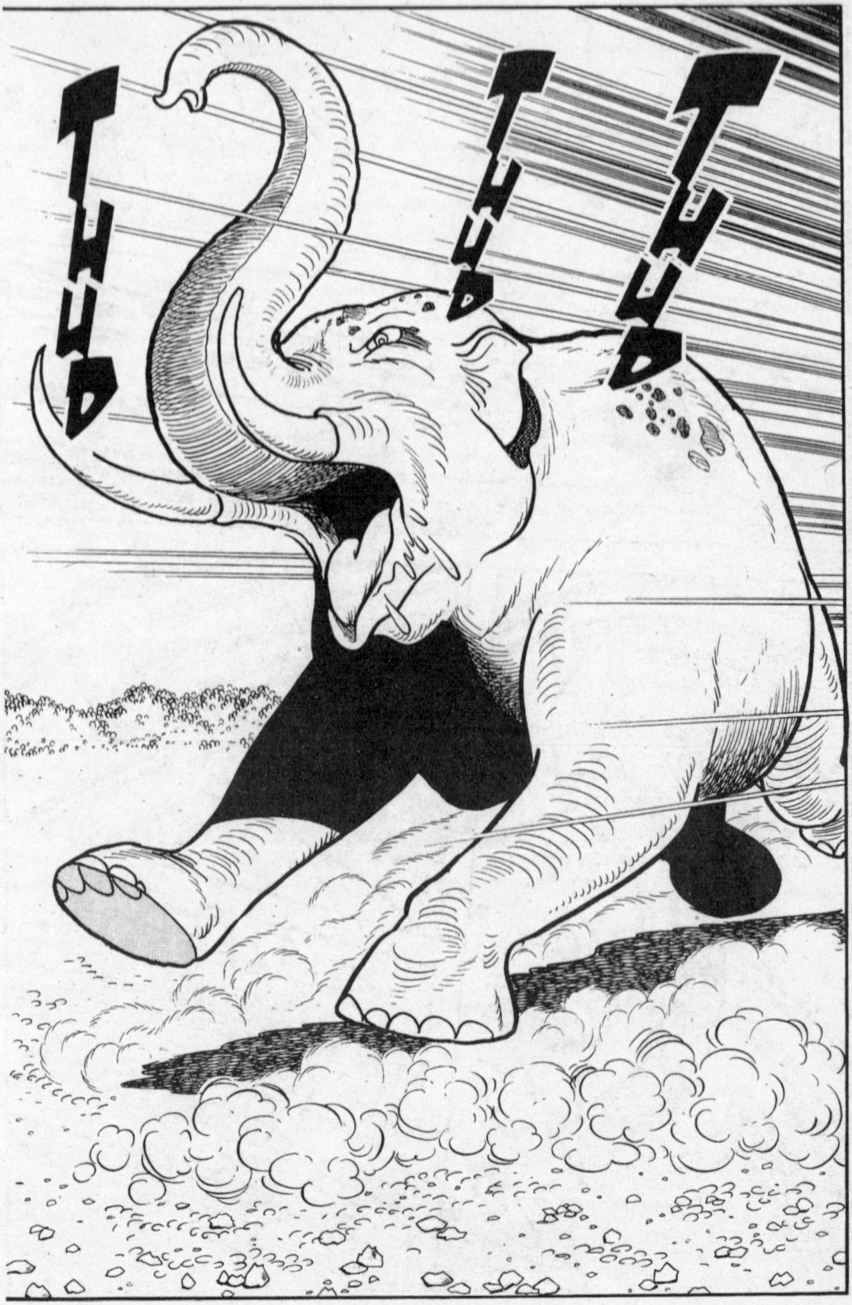
THUD
THUD
THUD

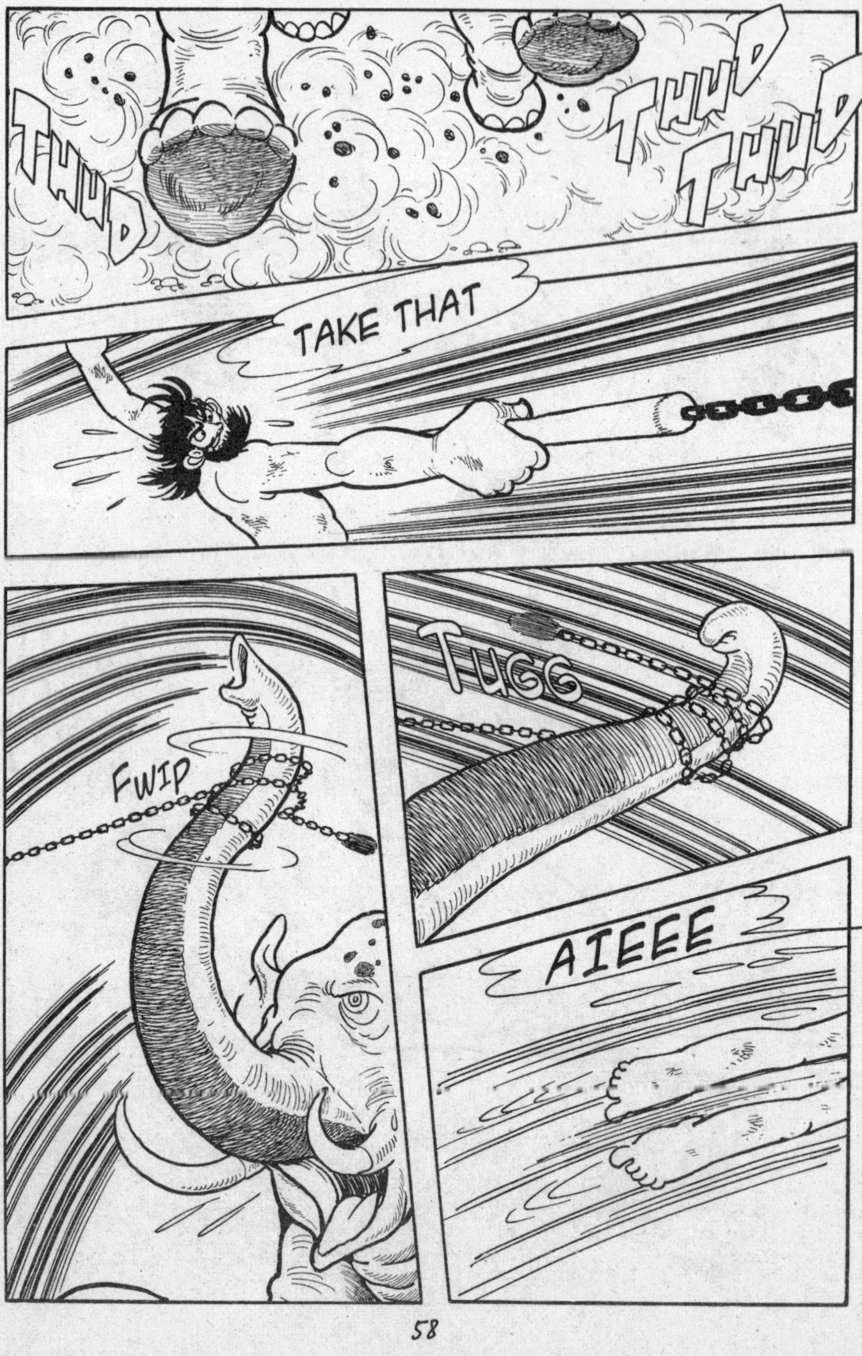
THUD
THUD
THUD
TAKE THAT
Fwip
Tugg
AIEEE

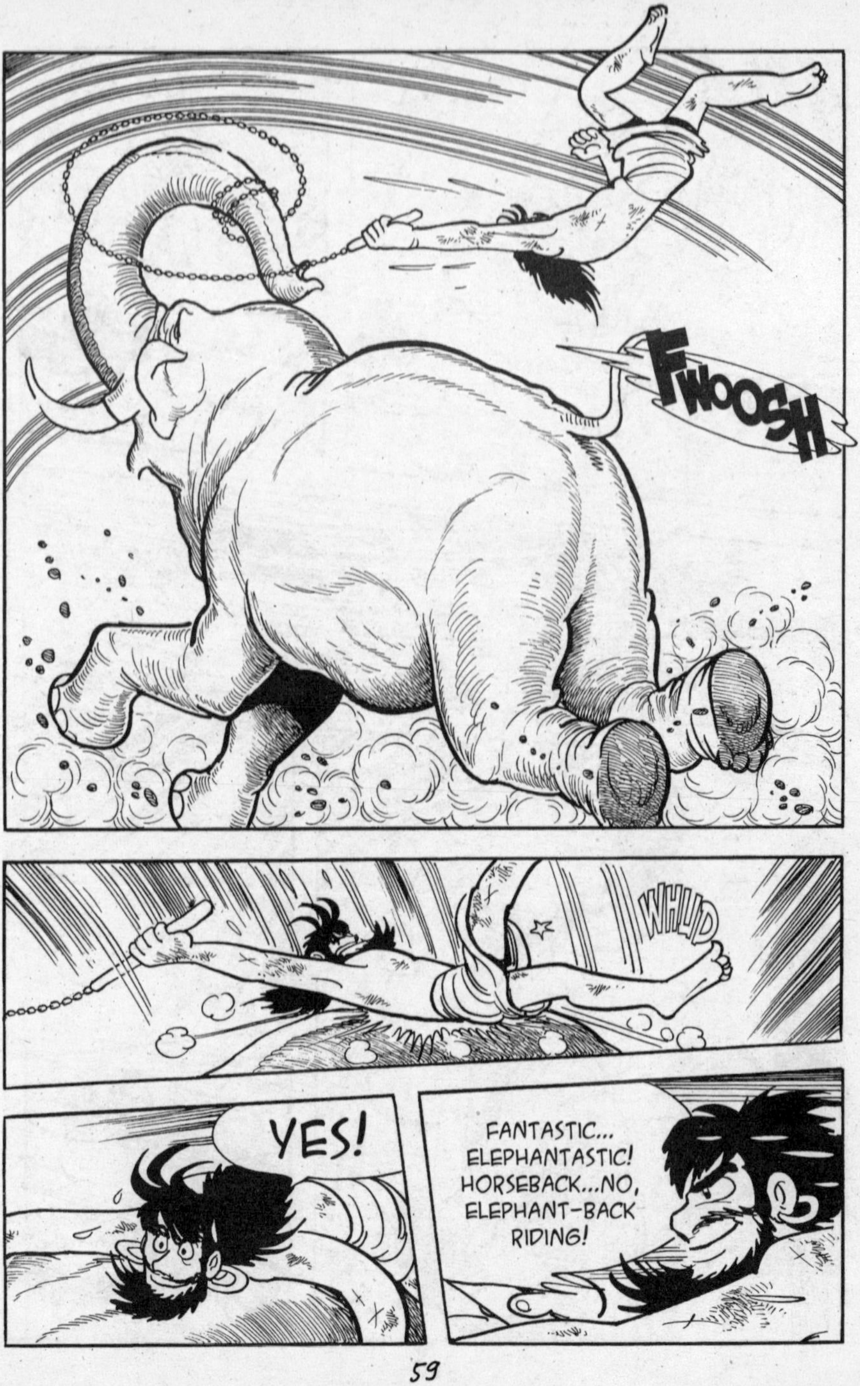
FWOOSH
WHUD
YES!
FANTASTIC... ELEPHANTASTIC! HORSEBACK...NO, ELEPHANT-BACK RIDING!

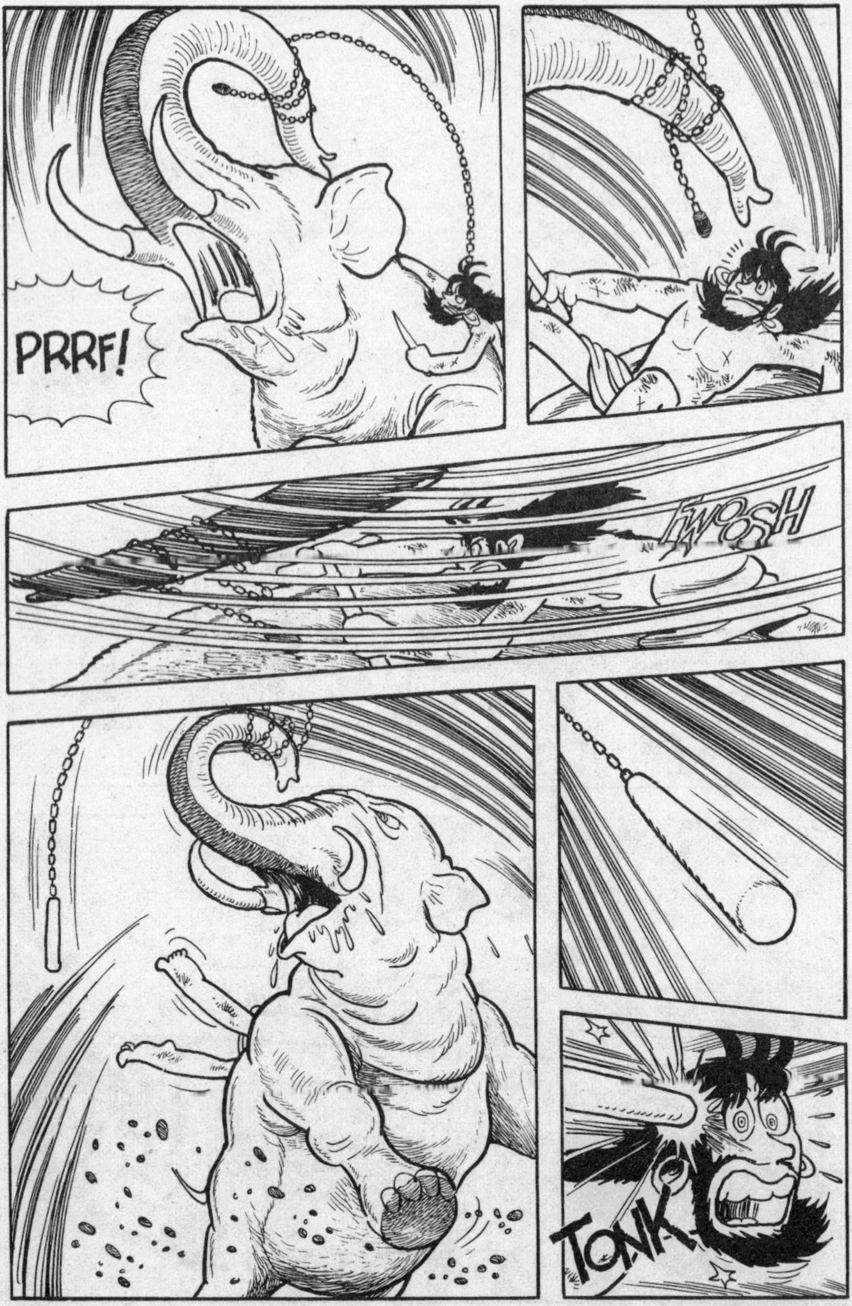
PRRF!
FWOOSH
TONK

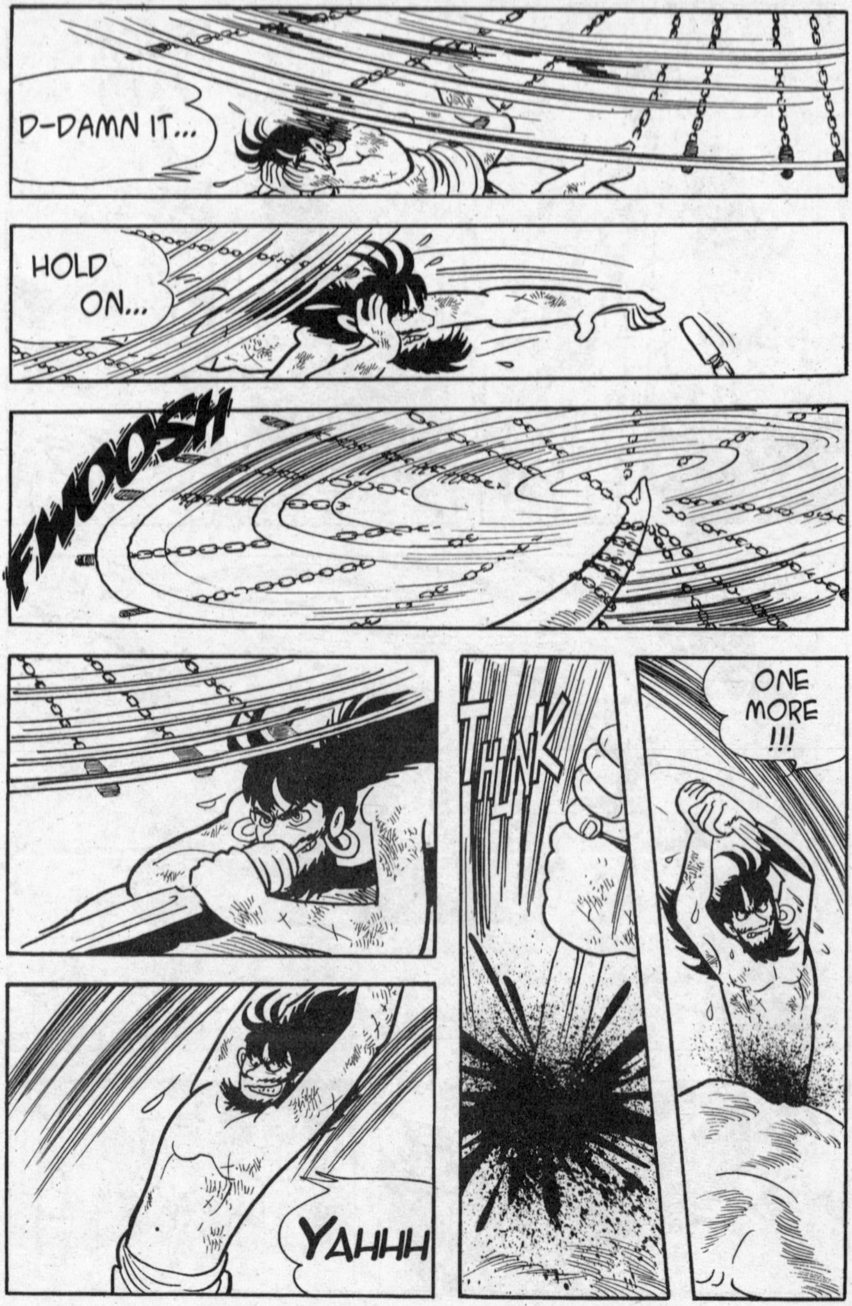
D-DAMN IT...
HOLD ON...
FWOOSH
YAHHH
THUNK
ONE MORE !!!

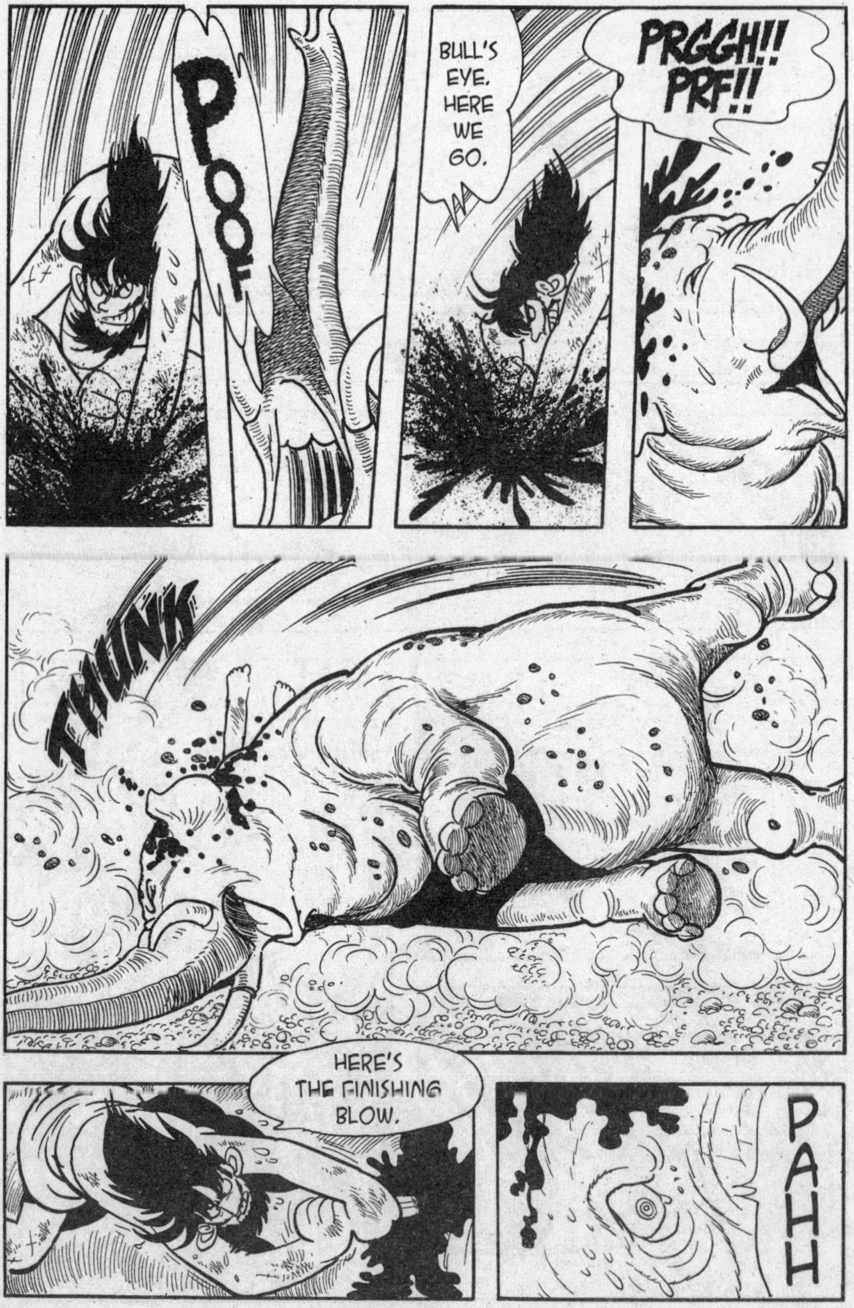
POOF
BULL'S EYE. HERE WE GO.
PRGGH!! PRF!!
THUNK
HERE'S THE FINISHING BLOW.
PAHH

WHUD

UNGH!!

OWW OUCH...

PRRGH

ARR ARR

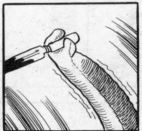

HRF

HRF

OH...

WHOA...

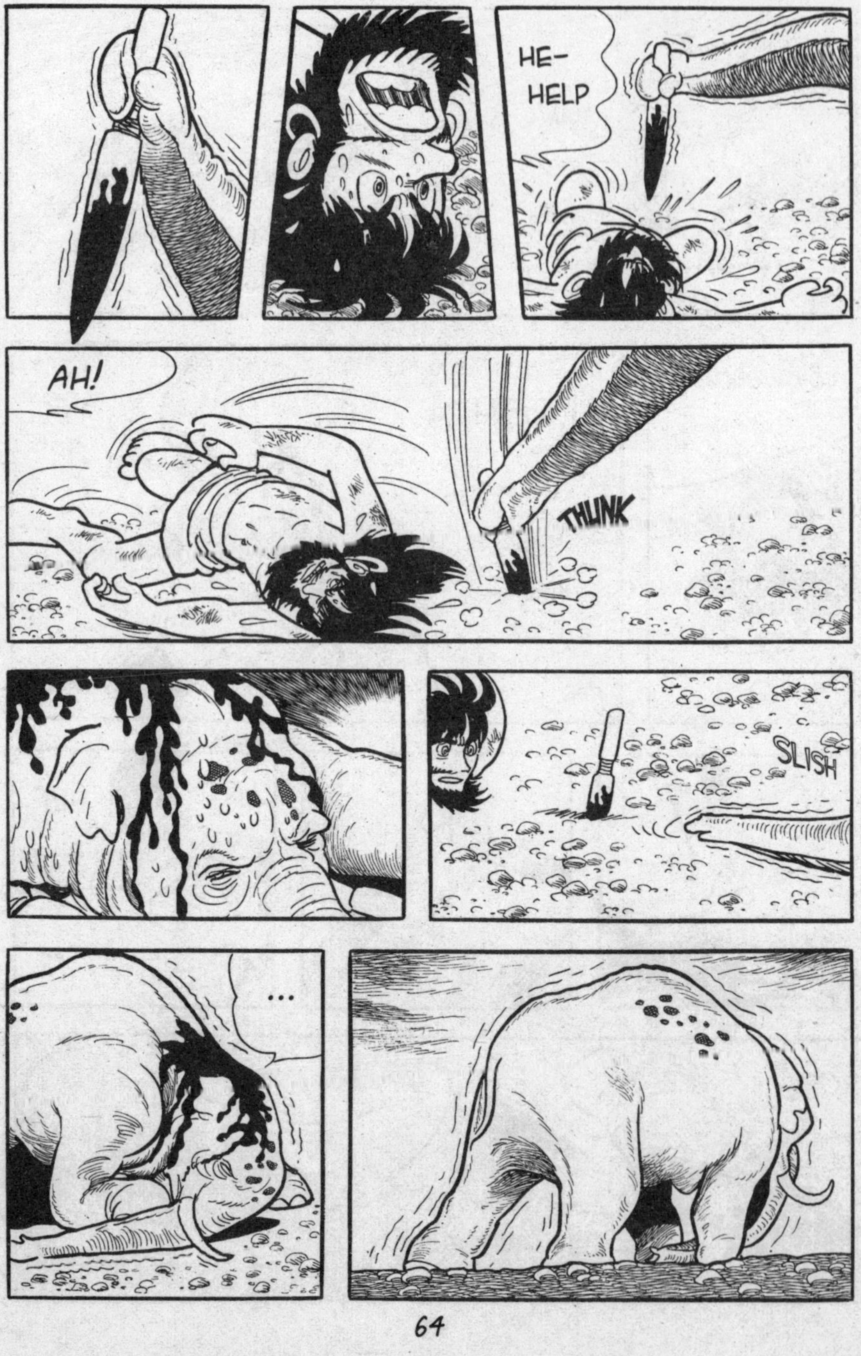
HE-
HELP
AH!
THUNK
SLISH
...

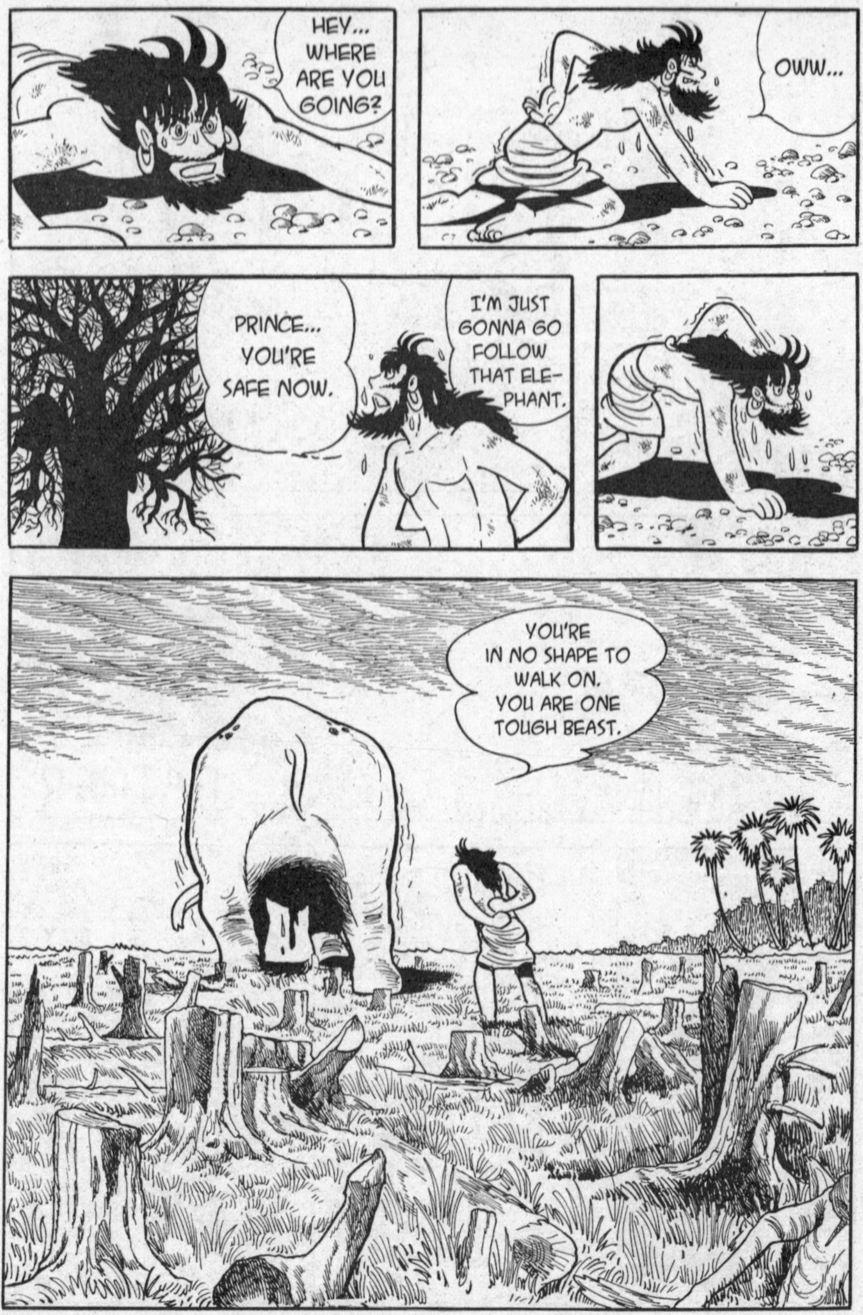
HEY... WHERE ARE YOU GOING?
OWW...
I'M JUST GONNA GO FOLLOW THAT ELE-PHANT.
PRINCE... YOU'RE SAFE NOW.
YOU'RE IN NO SHAPE TO WALK ON. YOU ARE ONE TOUGH BEAST.

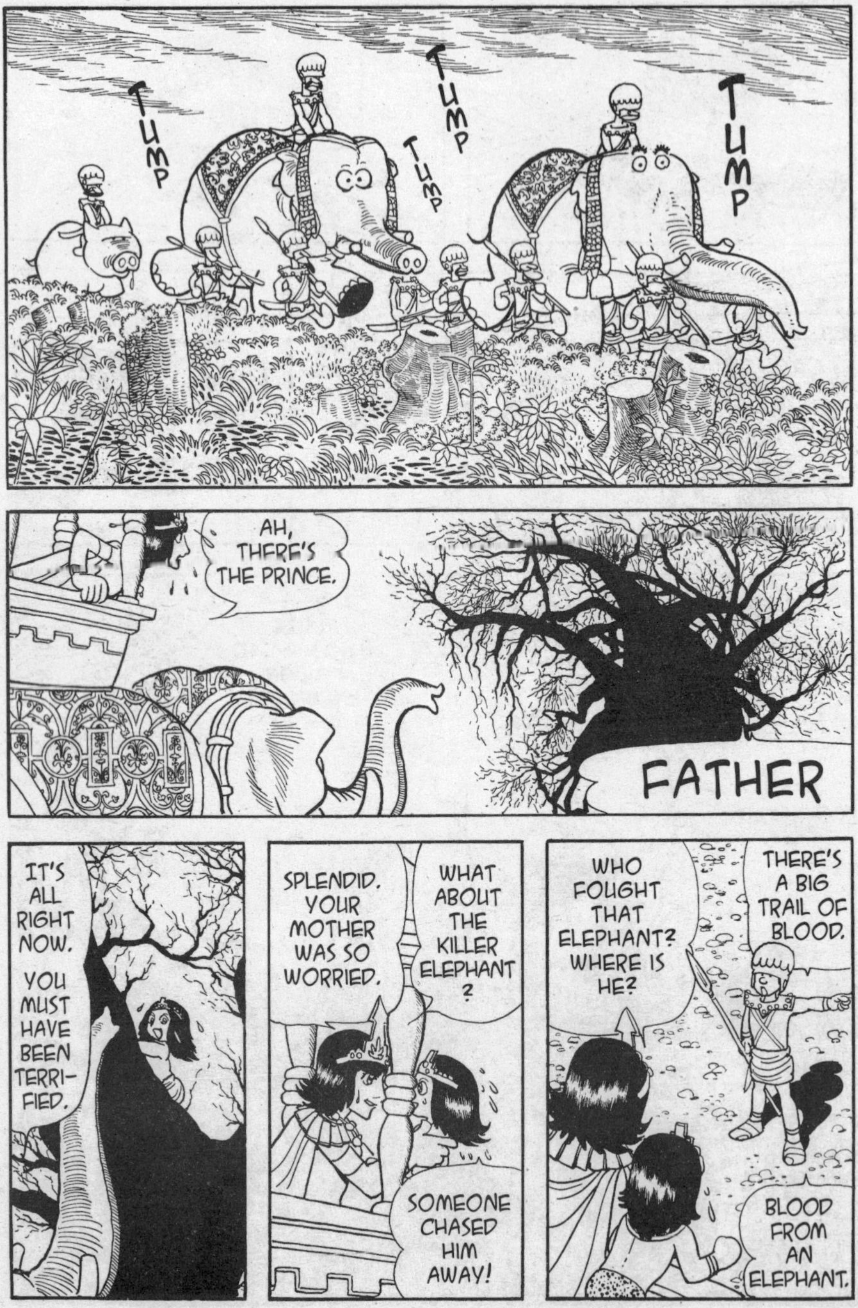
TUMP
TUMP
TUMP
TUMP
AH, THERE'S THE PRINCE.
FATHER
IT'S ALL RIGHT NOW.
YOU MUST HAVE BEEN TERRI-FIED.
SPLENDID. YOUR MOTHER WAS SO WORRIED.
WHAT ABOUT THE KILLER ELEPHANT?
SOMEONE CHASED HIM AWAY!
WHO FOUGHT THAT ELEPHANT? WHERE IS HE?
THERE'S A BIG TRAIL OF BLOOD.
BLOOD FROM AN ELEPHANT.

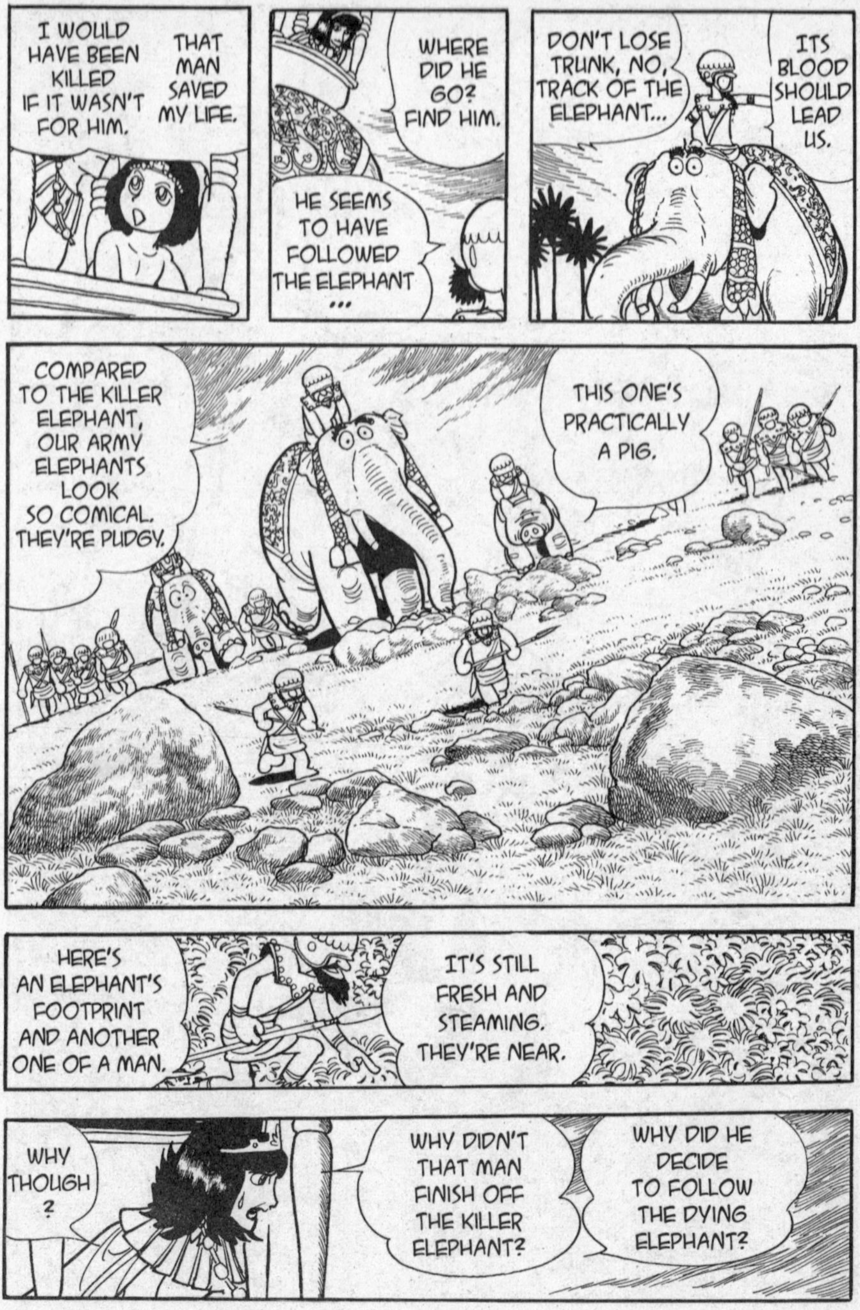
I WOULD HAVE BEEN KILLED IF IT WASN'T FOR HIM.
THAT MAN SAVED MY LIFE.
WHERE DID HE GO? FIND HIM.
HE SEEMS TO HAVE FOLLOWED THE ELEPHANT ...
DON'T LOSE TRUNK, NO, TRACK OF THE ELEPHANT...
ITS BLOOD SHOULD LEAD US.
COMPARED TO THE KILLER ELEPHANT, OUR ARMY ELEPHANTS LOOK SO COMICAL. THEY'RE PUDGY.
THIS ONE'S PRACTICALLY A PIG.
HERE'S AN ELEPHANT'S FOOTPRINT AND ANOTHER ONE OF A MAN.
IT'S STILL FRESH AND STEAMING. THEY'RE NEAR.
WHY THOUGH ?
WHY DIDN'T THAT MAN FINISH OFF THE KILLER ELEPHANT?
WHY DID HE DECIDE TO FOLLOW THE DYING ELEPHANT?

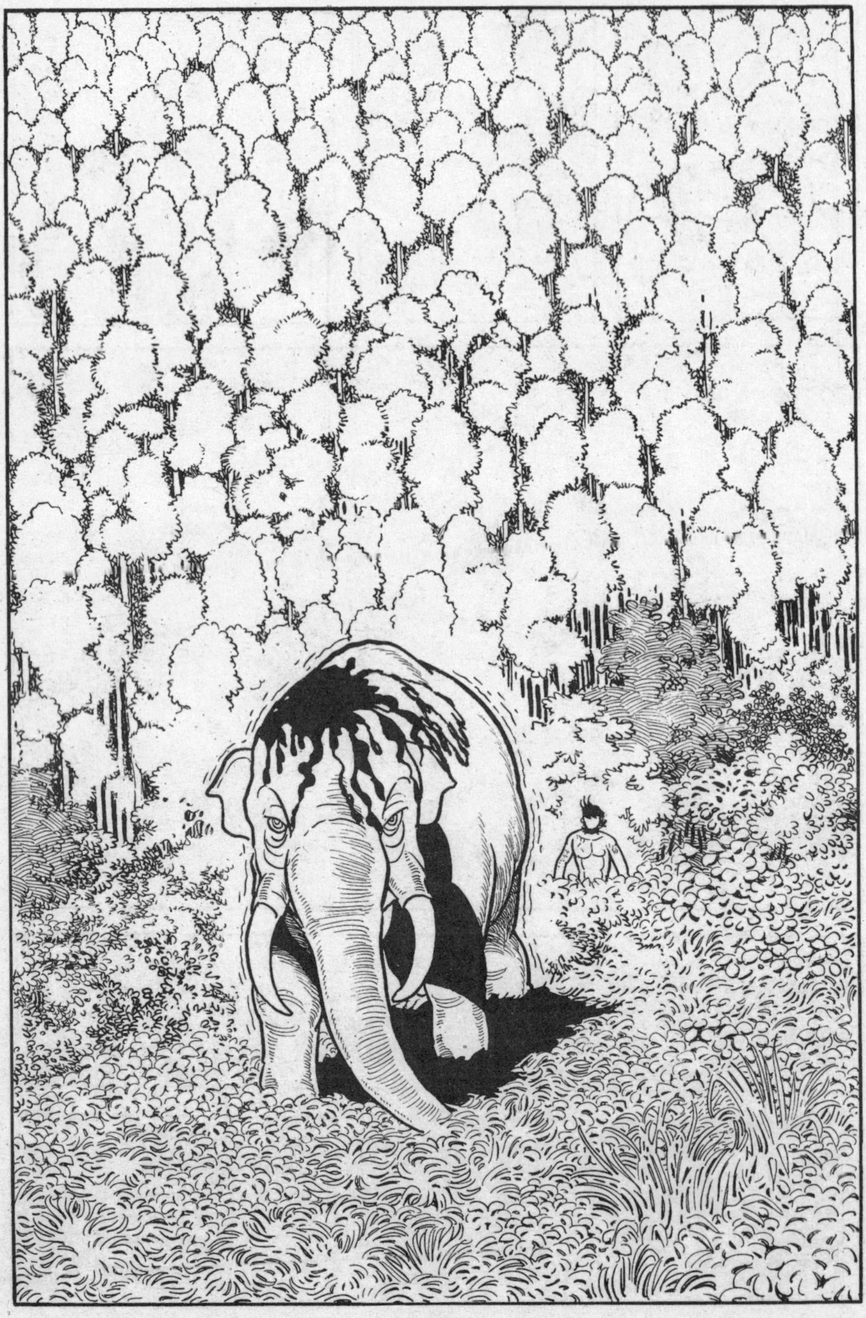

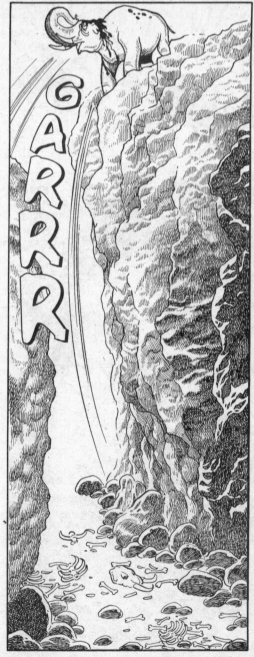

GARRR

WHAT A SIGHT.

THE ELEPHANTS' GRAVEYARD YOU HEAR ABOUT.

I'VE HEARD THAT ELEPHANTS GO AWAY WHEN THEY'RE ABOUT TO DIE. SO IT'S TRUE.

69

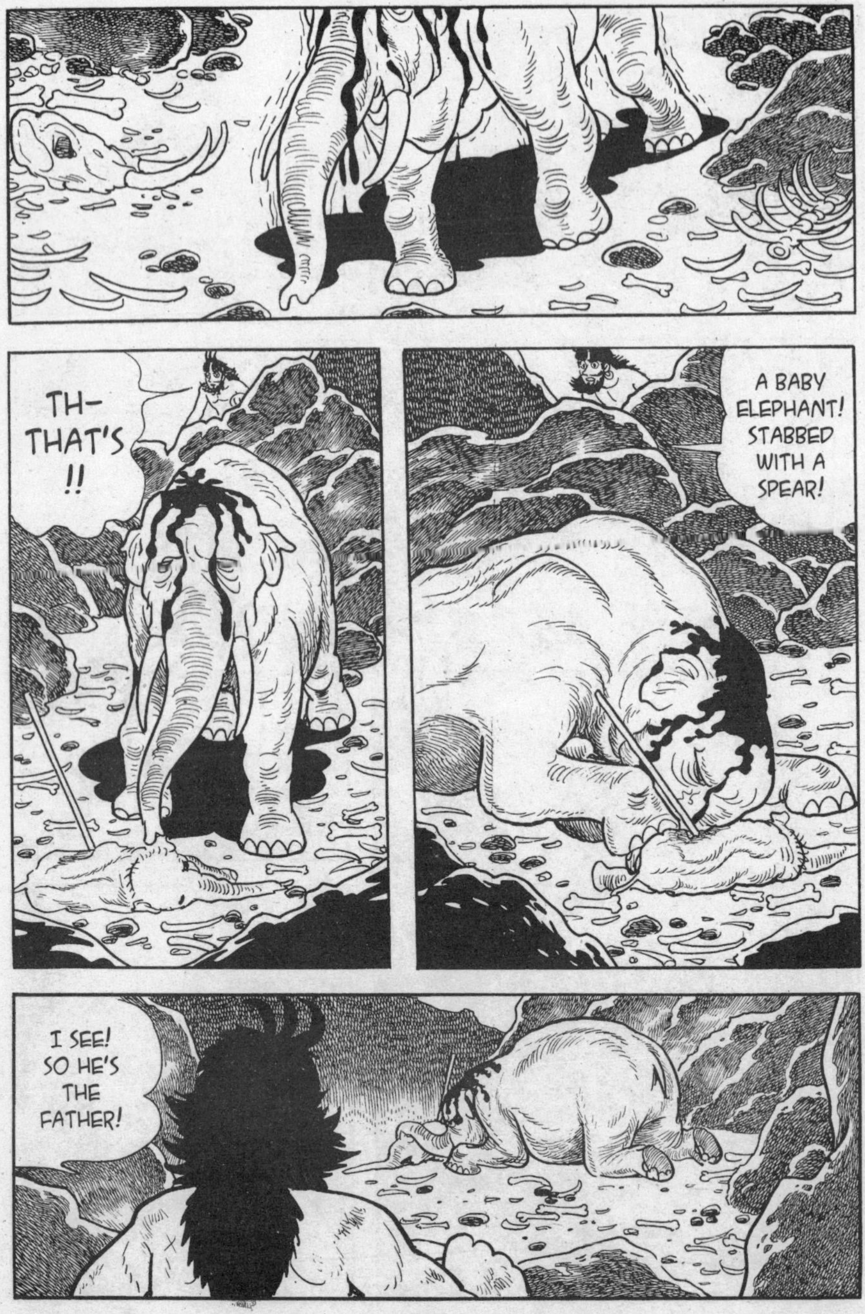

TH-THAT'S !!
A BABY ELEPHANT! STABBED WITH A SPEAR!
I SEE! SO HE'S THE FATHER!

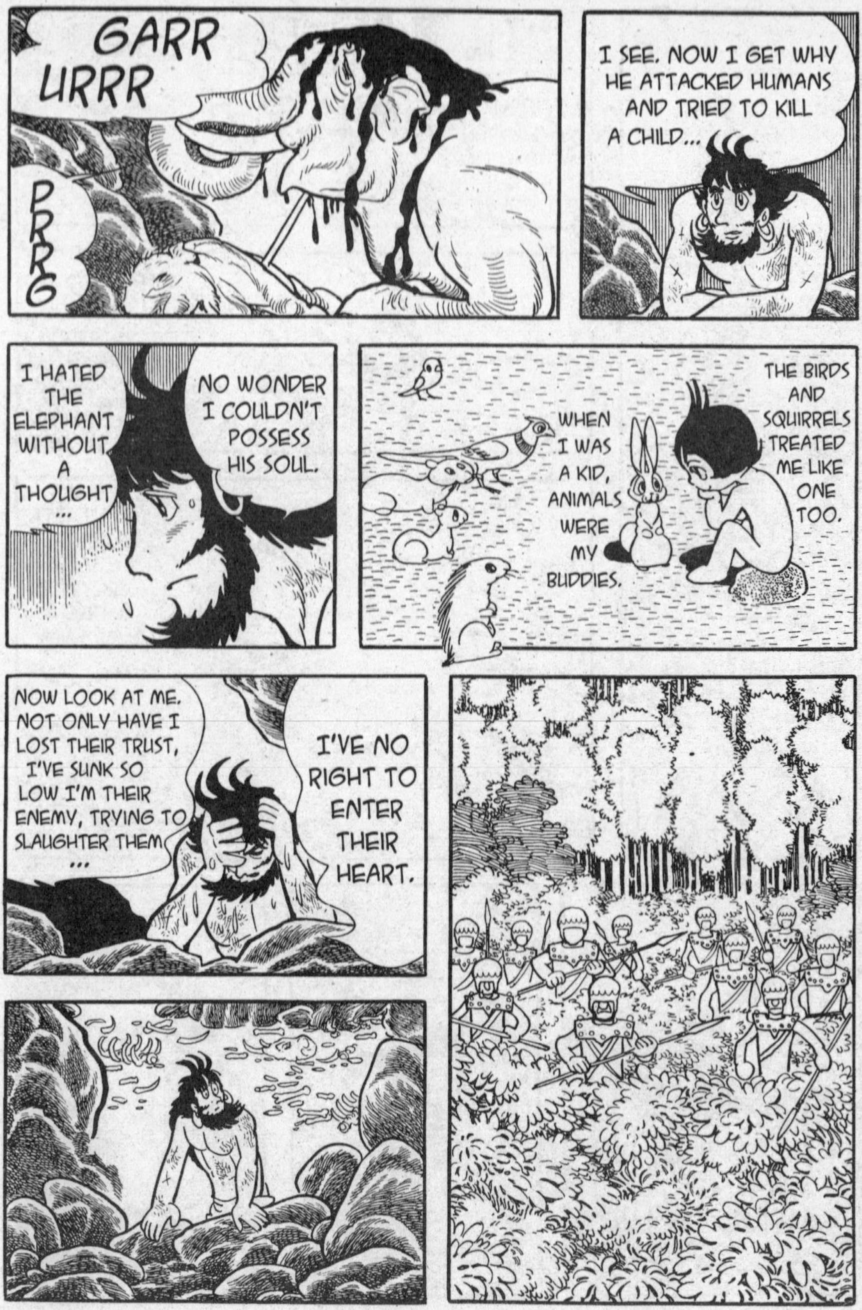
GARR URRR
DRRRG
I SEE. NOW I GET WHY HE ATTACKED HUMANS AND TRIED TO KILL A CHILD...
I HATED THE ELEPHANT WITHOUT A THOUGHT...
NO WONDER I COULDN'T POSSESS HIS SOUL.
THE BIRDS AND SQUIRRELS TREATED ME LIKE ONE TOO.
WHEN I WAS A KID, ANIMALS WERE MY BUDDIES.
NOW LOOK AT ME. NOT ONLY HAVE I LOST THEIR TRUST, I'VE SUNK SO LOW I'M THEIR ENEMY, TRYING TO SLAUGHTER THEM...
I'VE NO RIGHT TO ENTER THEIR HEART.

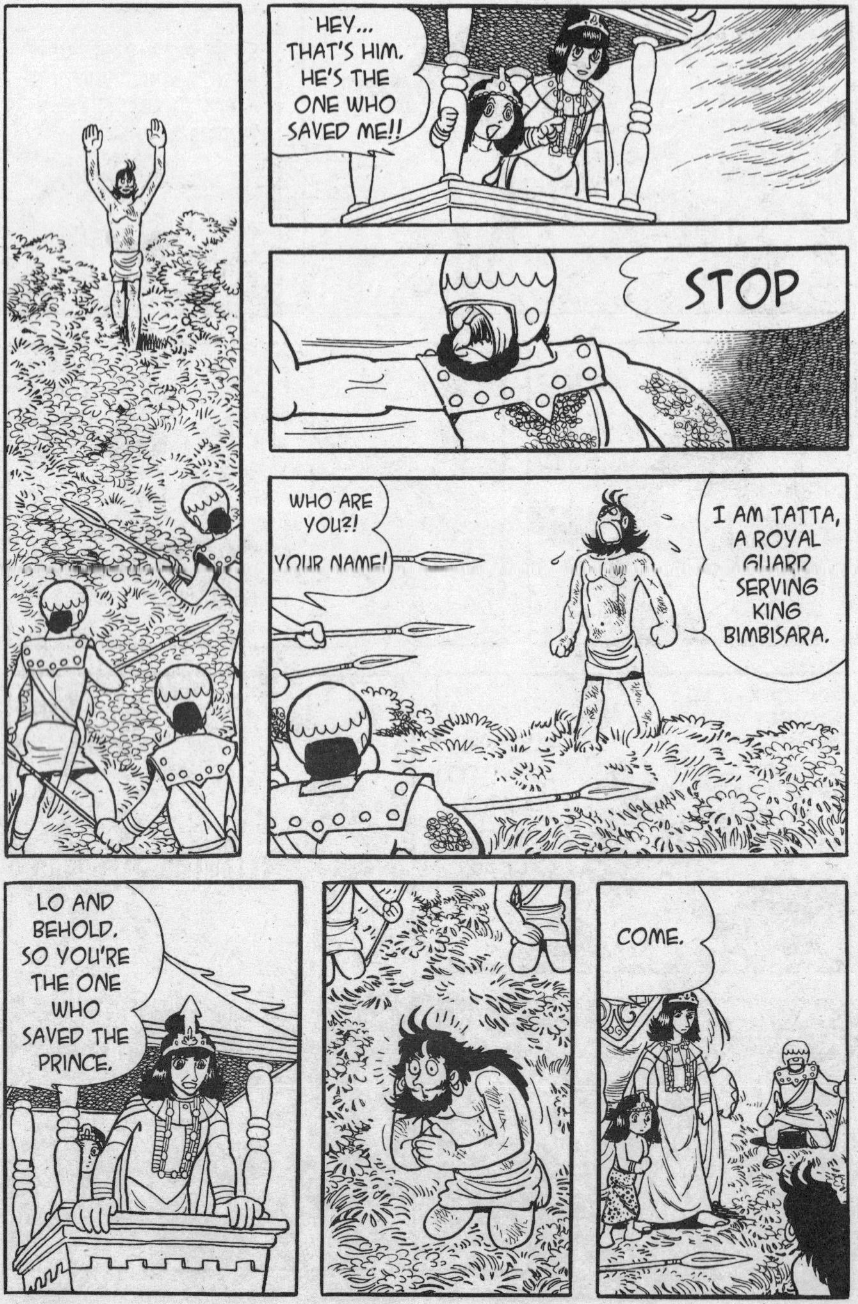
HEY... THAT'S HIM. HE'S THE ONE WHO SAVED ME!!
STOP
WHO ARE YOU?!
YOUR NAME!
I AM TATTA, A ROYAL GUARD SERVING KING BIMBISARA.
LO AND BEHOLD. SO YOU'RE THE ONE WHO SAVED THE PRINCE.
COME.

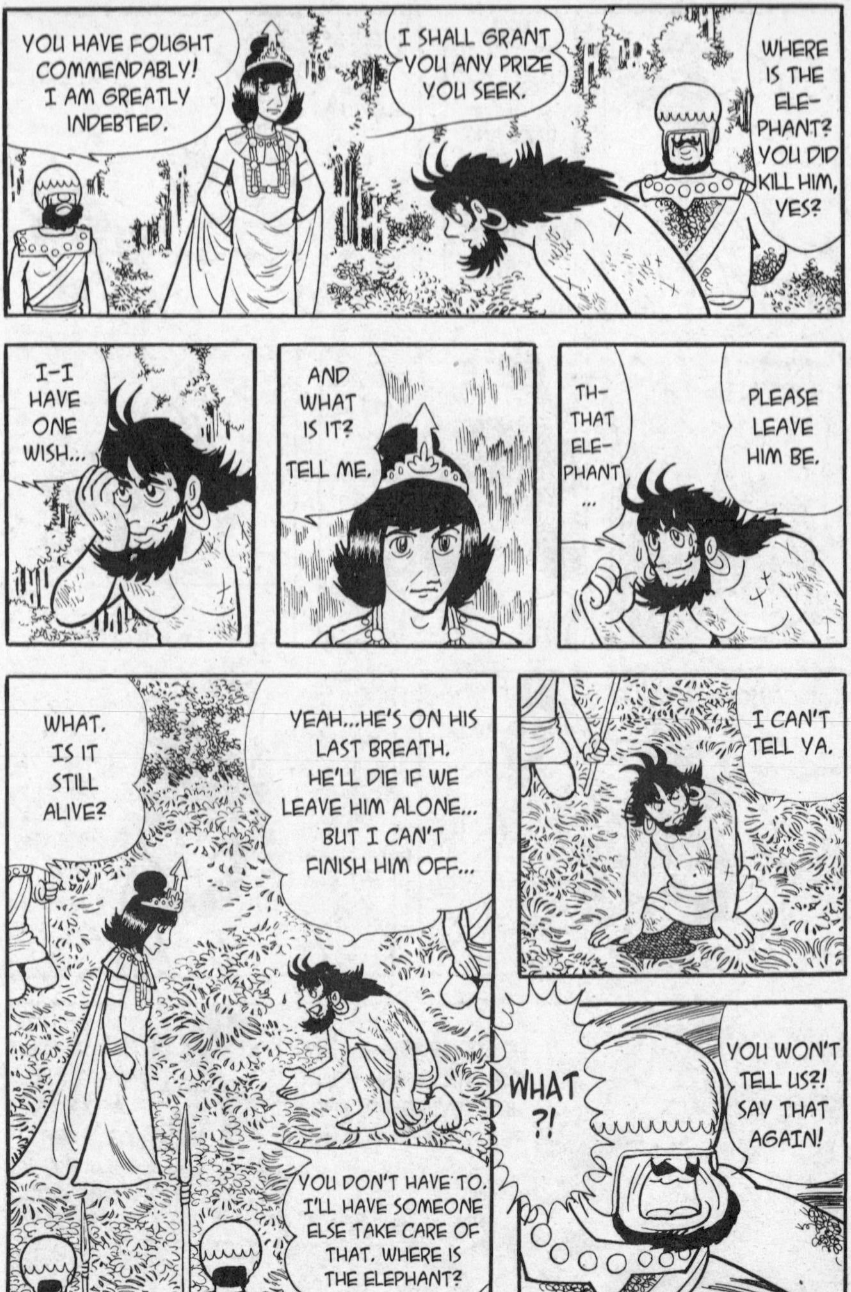

YOU HAVE FOUGHT COMMENDABLY! I AM GREATLY INDEBTED.
I SHALL GRANT YOU ANY PRIZE YOU SEEK.
WHERE IS THE ELE-PHANT? YOU DID KILL HIM, YES?
I-I HAVE ONE WISH...
AND WHAT IS IT? TELL ME.
TH-THAT ELE-PHANT...
PLEASE LEAVE HIM BE.
WHAT. IS IT STILL ALIVE?
YEAH...HE'S ON HIS LAST BREATH. HE'LL DIE IF WE LEAVE HIM ALONE... BUT I CAN'T FINISH HIM OFF...
YOU DON'T HAVE TO. I'LL HAVE SOMEONE ELSE TAKE CARE OF THAT. WHERE IS THE ELEPHANT?
I CAN'T TELL YA.
WHAT ?!
YOU WON'T TELL US?! SAY THAT AGAIN!

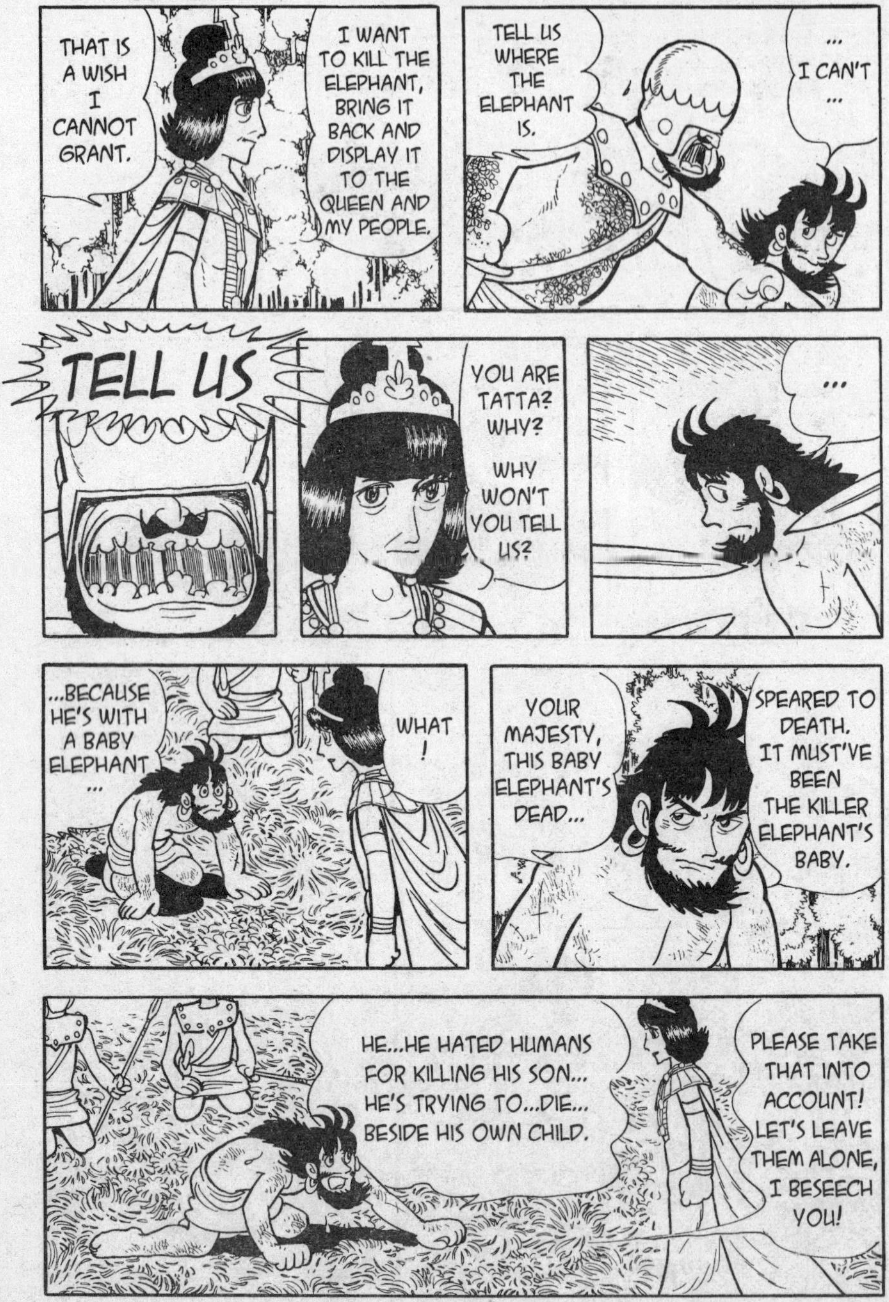
THAT IS A WISH I CANNOT GRANT.
I WANT TO KILL THE ELEPHANT, BRING IT BACK AND DISPLAY IT TO THE QUEEN AND MY PEOPLE.
TELL US WHERE THE ELEPHANT IS.
... I CAN'T ...
TELL US
YOU ARE TATTA? WHY?
WHY WON'T YOU TELL US?
...
...BECAUSE HE'S WITH A BABY ELEPHANT ...
WHAT !
YOUR MAJESTY, THIS BABY ELEPHANT'S DEAD...
SPEARED TO DEATH. IT MUST'VE BEEN THE KILLER ELEPHANT'S BABY.
HE...HE HATED HUMANS FOR KILLING HIS SON... HE'S TRYING TO...DIE... BESIDE HIS OWN CHILD.
PLEASE TAKE THAT INTO ACCOUNT! LET'S LEAVE THEM ALONE, I BESEECH YOU!

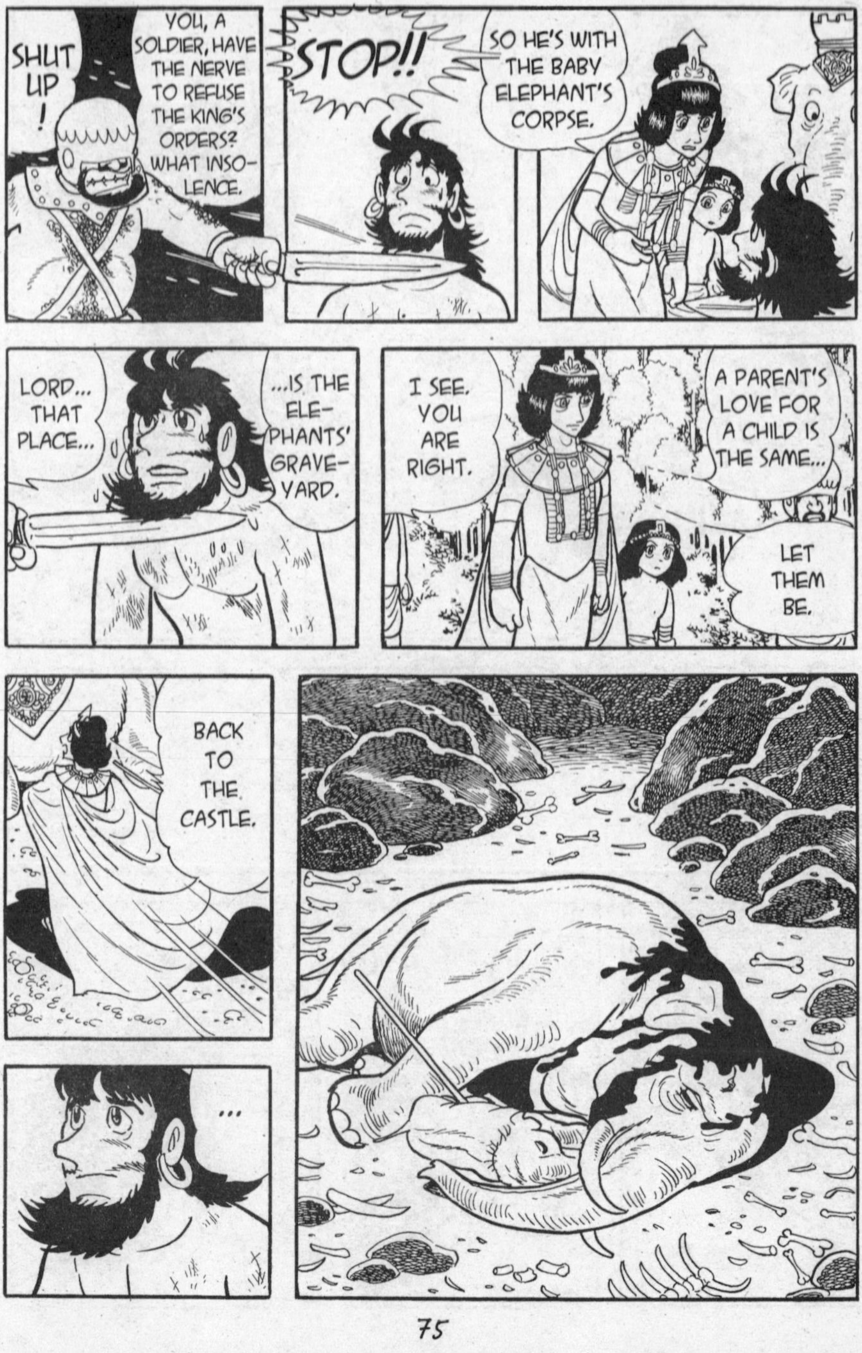
SHUT UP!
YOU, A SOLDIER, HAVE THE NERVE TO REFUSE THE KING'S ORDERS? WHAT INSOLENCE.
STOP!!
SO HE'S WITH THE BABY ELEPHANT'S CORPSE.
LORD... THAT PLACE...
...IS THE ELEPHANTS' GRAVEYARD.
I SEE. YOU ARE RIGHT.
A PARENT'S LOVE FOR A CHILD IS THE SAME...
LET THEM BE.
BACK TO THE CASTLE.
...

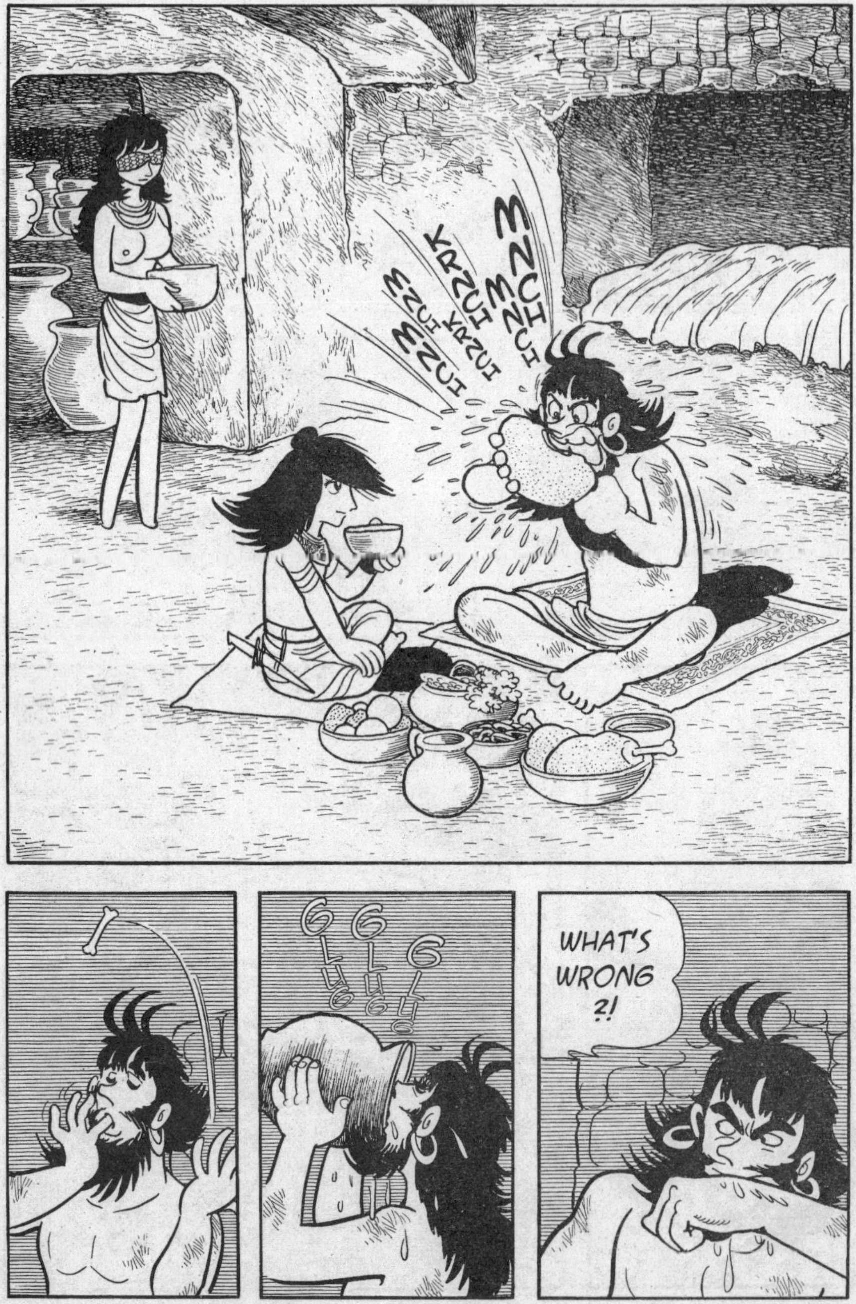
EZUI EZUI
KRZUI KRZUI
MNCH MNCH
GLUG GLUG GLUG
WHAT'S WRONG ?!

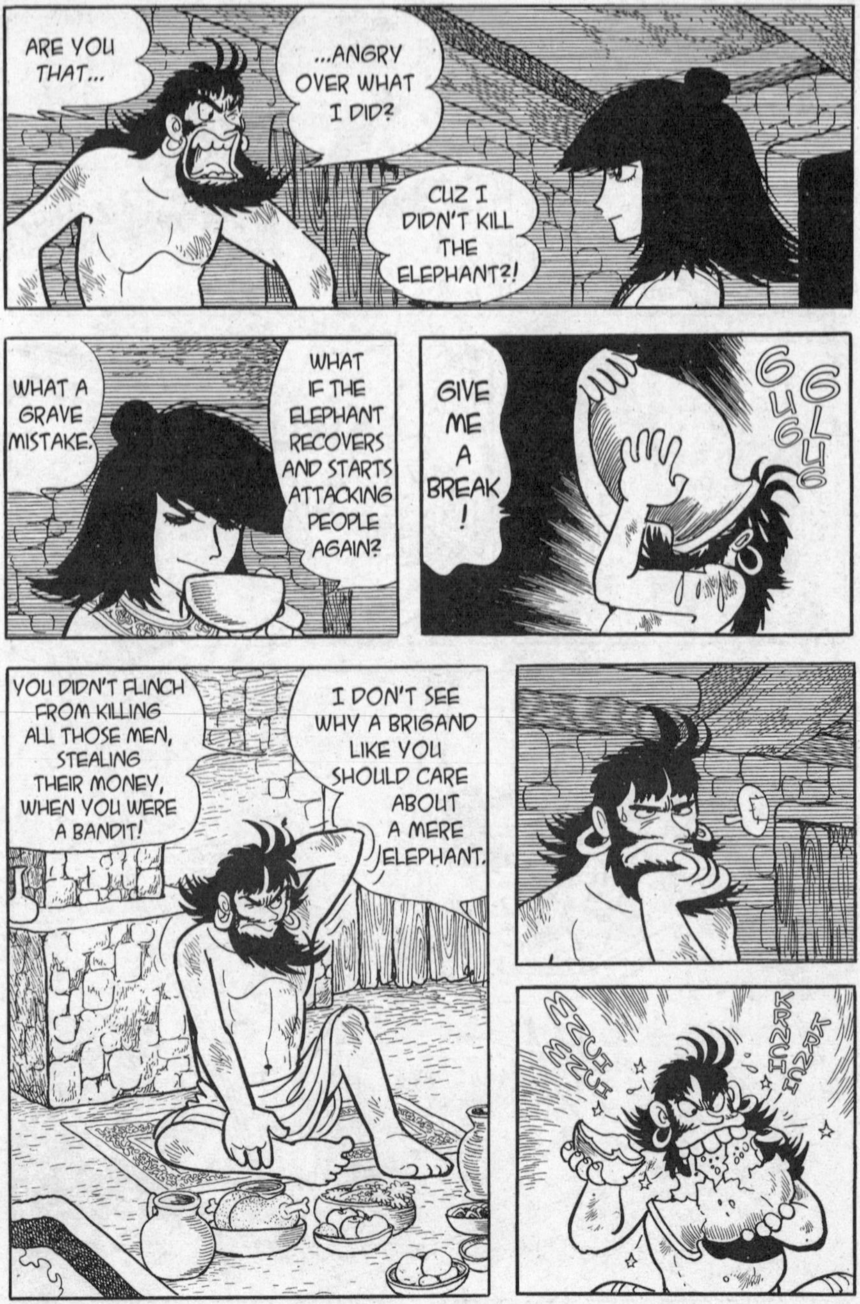
ARE YOU THAT...
...ANGRY OVER WHAT I DID?
CUZ I DIDN'T KILL THE ELEPHANT?!
WHAT A GRAVE MISTAKE.
WHAT IF THE ELEPHANT RECOVERS AND STARTS ATTACKING PEOPLE AGAIN?
GIVE ME A BREAK!
GUG GLUG
YOU DIDN'T FLINCH FROM KILLING ALL THOSE MEN, STEALING THEIR MONEY, WHEN YOU WERE A BANDIT!
I DON'T SEE WHY A BRIGAND LIKE YOU SHOULD CARE ABOUT A MERE ELEPHANT.
MUNCH MUNCH
KRNCH KRNCH

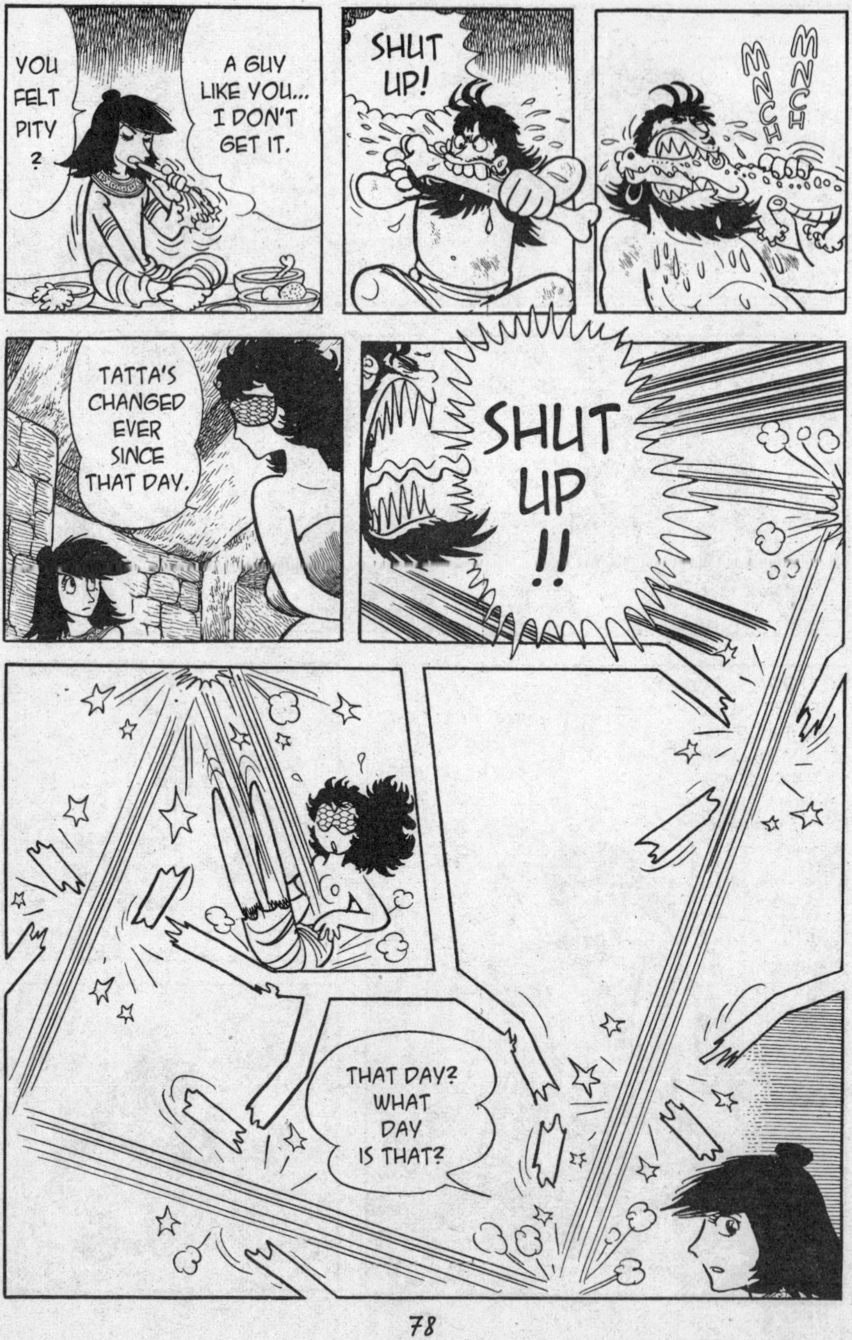
YOU FELT PITY ?
A GUY LIKE YOU... I DON'T GET IT.
SHUT UP!
MNCH MNCH
TATTA'S CHANGED EVER SINCE THAT DAY.
SHUT UP !!
THAT DAY? WHAT DAY IS THAT?

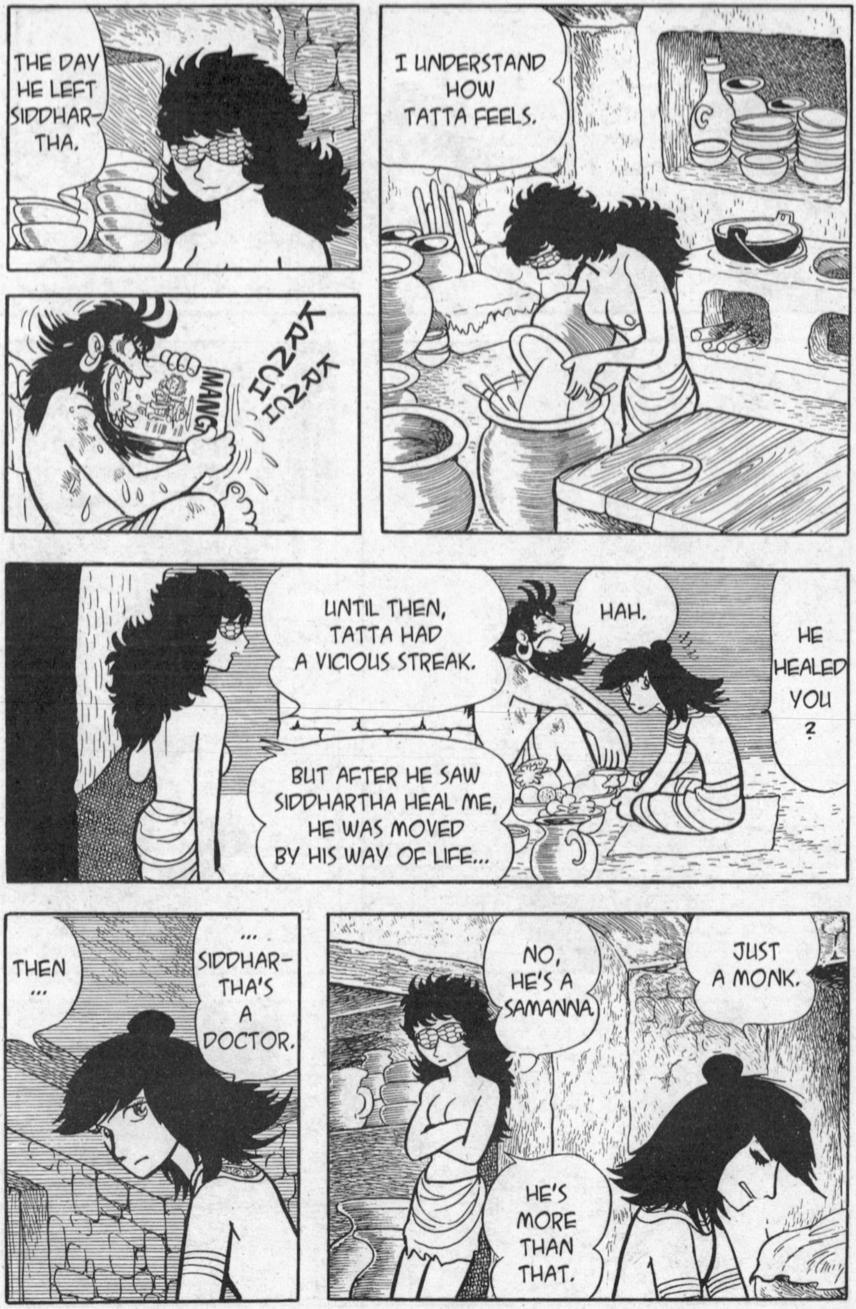
THE DAY HE LEFT SIDDHARTHA.
I UNDERSTAND HOW TATTA FEELS.
MANG
KRZUI KRZUI
UNTIL THEN, TATTA HAD A VICIOUS STREAK.
BUT AFTER HE SAW SIDDHARTHA HEAL ME, HE WAS MOVED BY HIS WAY OF LIFE...
HAH.
HE HEALED YOU?
THEN ...
... SIDDHARTHA'S A DOCTOR.
NO, HE'S A SAMANNA.
JUST A MONK.
HE'S MORE THAN THAT.

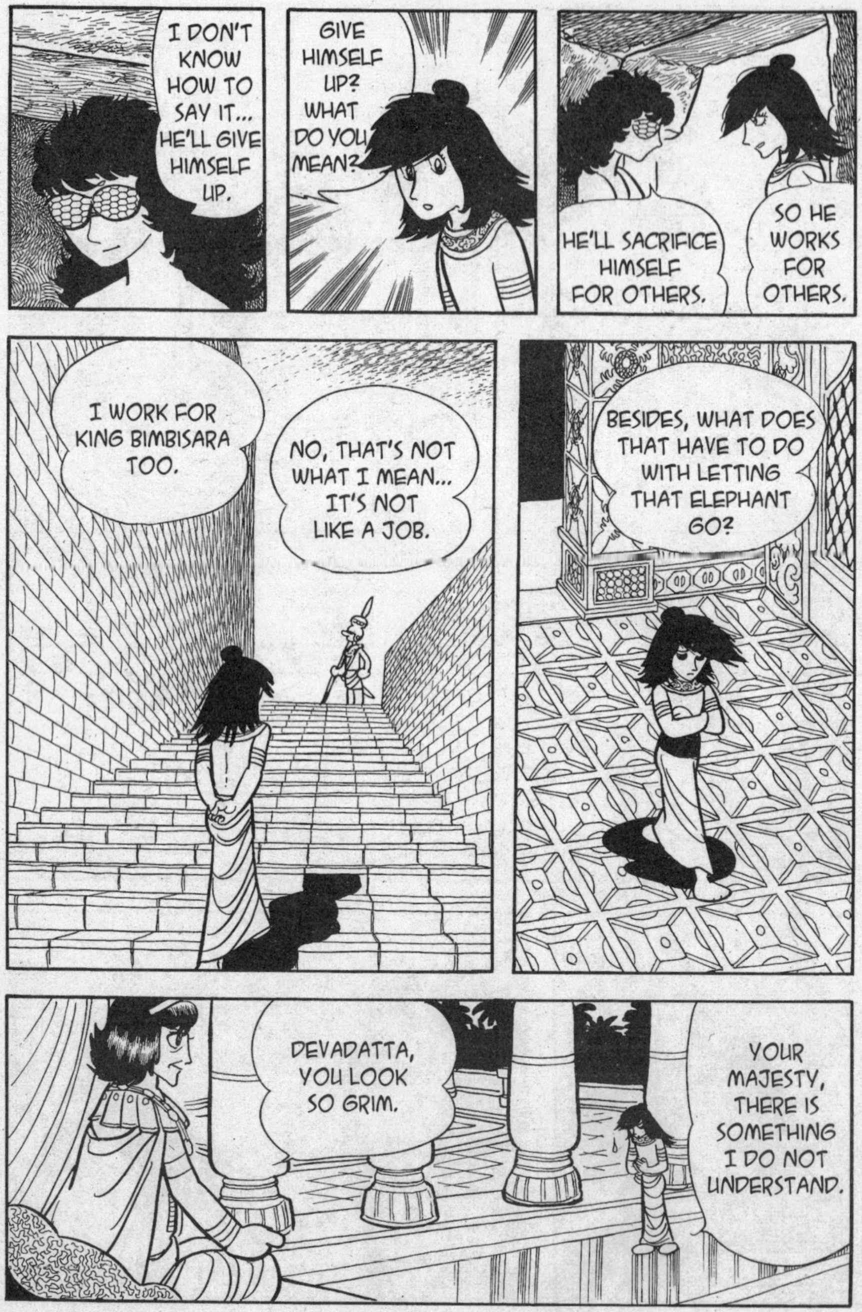
I DON'T KNOW HOW TO SAY IT... HE'LL GIVE HIMSELF UP.
GIVE HIMSELF UP? WHAT DO YOU MEAN?
HE'LL SACRIFICE HIMSELF FOR OTHERS.
SO HE WORKS FOR OTHERS.
I WORK FOR KING BIMBISARA TOO.
NO, THAT'S NOT WHAT I MEAN... IT'S NOT LIKE A JOB.
BESIDES, WHAT DOES THAT HAVE TO DO WITH LETTING THAT ELEPHANT GO?
DEVADATTA, YOU LOOK SO GRIM.
YOUR MAJESTY, THERE IS SOMETHING I DO NOT UNDERSTAND.

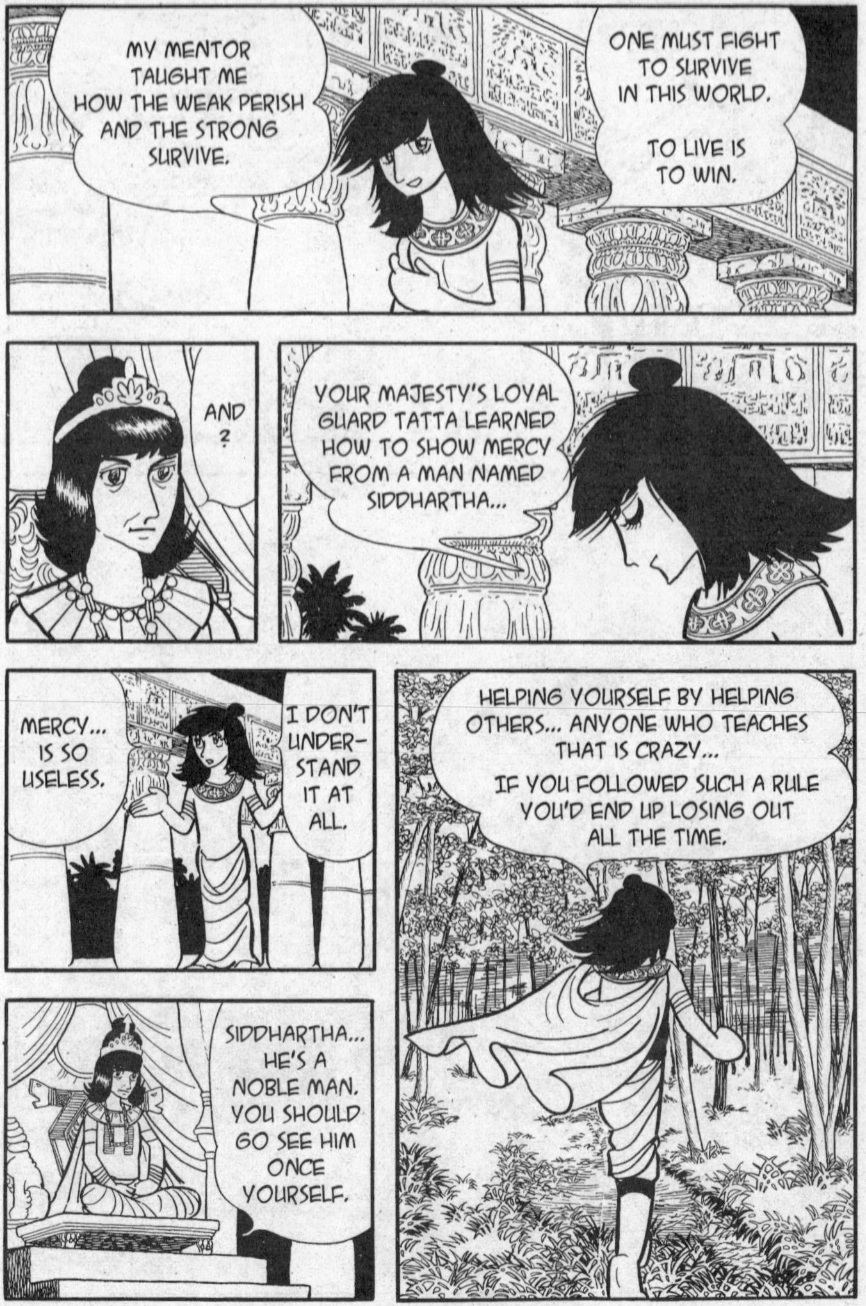
MY MENTOR TAUGHT ME HOW THE WEAK PERISH AND THE STRONG SURVIVE.
ONE MUST FIGHT TO SURVIVE IN THIS WORLD.
TO LIVE IS TO WIN.
AND ?
YOUR MAJESTY'S LOYAL GUARD TATTA LEARNED HOW TO SHOW MERCY FROM A MAN NAMED SIDDHARTHA...
MERCY... IS SO USELESS.
I DON'T UNDER-STAND IT AT ALL.
HELPING YOURSELF BY HELPING OTHERS... ANYONE WHO TEACHES THAT IS CRAZY...
IF YOU FOLLOWED SUCH A RULE YOU'D END UP LOSING OUT ALL THE TIME.
SIDDHARTHA... HE'S A NOBLE MAN. YOU SHOULD GO SEE HIM ONCE YOURSELF.

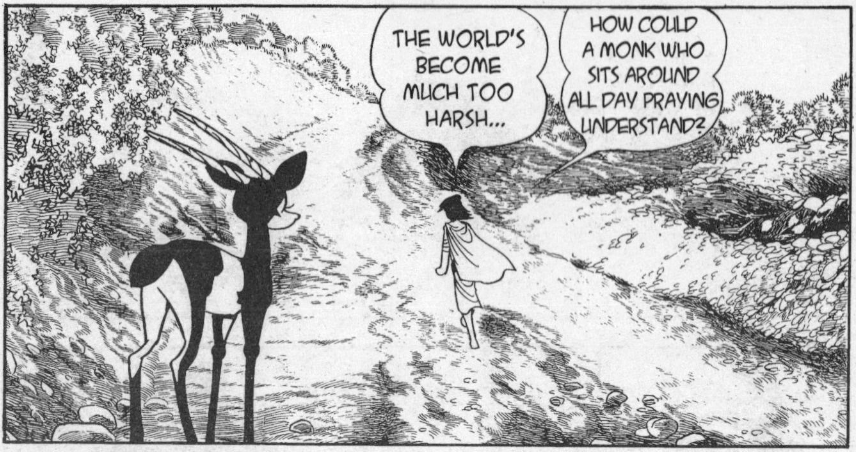
THE WORLD'S BECOME MUCH TOO HARSH...
HOW COULD A MONK WHO SITS AROUND ALL DAY PRAYING UNDERSTAND?

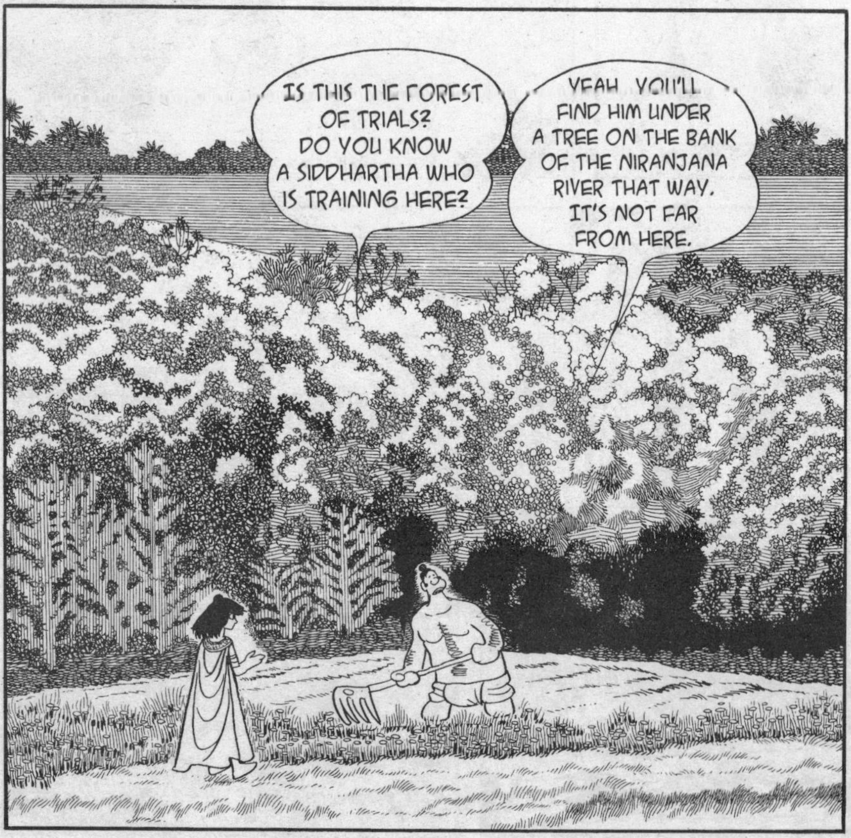
IS THIS THE FOREST OF TRIALS? DO YOU KNOW A SIDDHARTHA WHO IS TRAINING HERE?
YEAH. YOU'LL FIND HIM UNDER A TREE ON THE BANK OF THE NIRANJANA RIVER THAT WAY. IT'S NOT FAR FROM HERE.

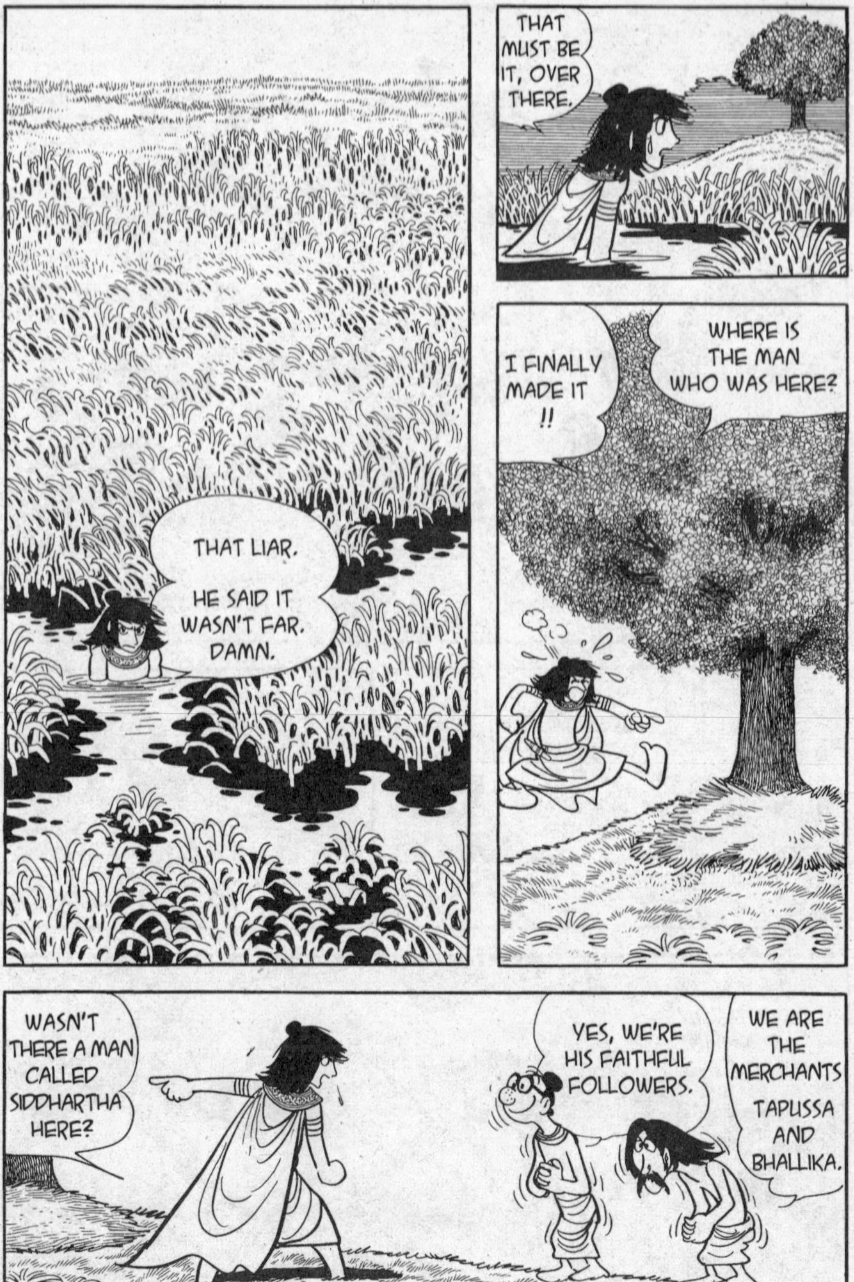
THAT MUST BE IT, OVER THERE.
THAT LIAR.
HE SAID IT WASN'T FAR. DAMN.
WHERE IS THE MAN WHO WAS HERE?
I FINALLY MADE IT !!
WASN'T THERE A MAN CALLED SIDDHARTHA HERE?
YES, WE'RE HIS FAITHFUL FOLLOWERS.
WE ARE THE MERCHANTS TAPUSSA AND BHALLIKA.

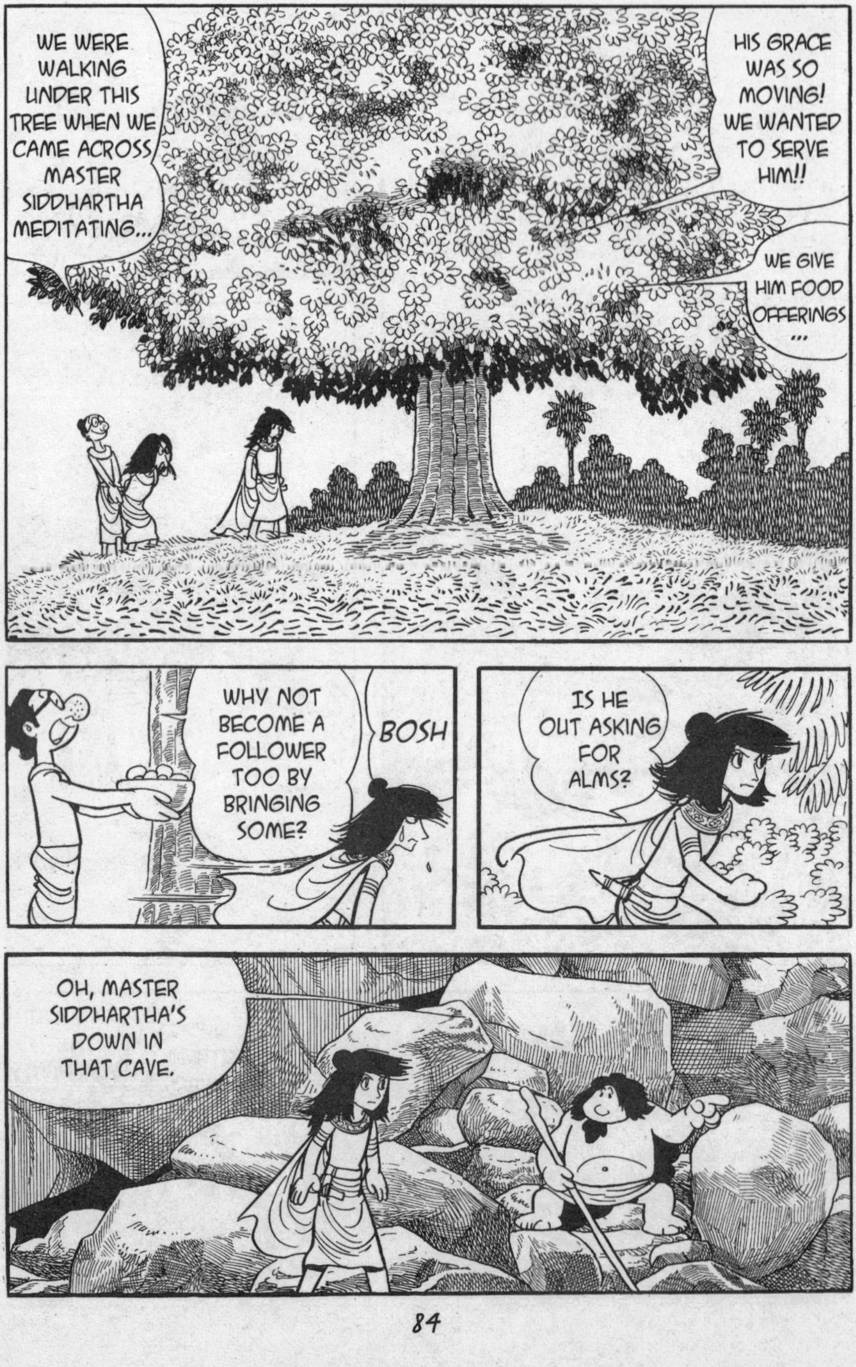
WE WERE WALKING UNDER THIS TREE WHEN WE CAME ACROSS MASTER SIDDHARTHA MEDITATING...
HIS GRACE WAS SO MOVING! WE WANTED TO SERVE HIM!!
WE GIVE HIM FOOD OFFERINGS ...
WHY NOT BECOME A FOLLOWER TOO BY BRINGING SOME?
BOSH
IS HE OUT ASKING FOR ALMS?
OH, MASTER SIDDHARTHA'S DOWN IN THAT CAVE.

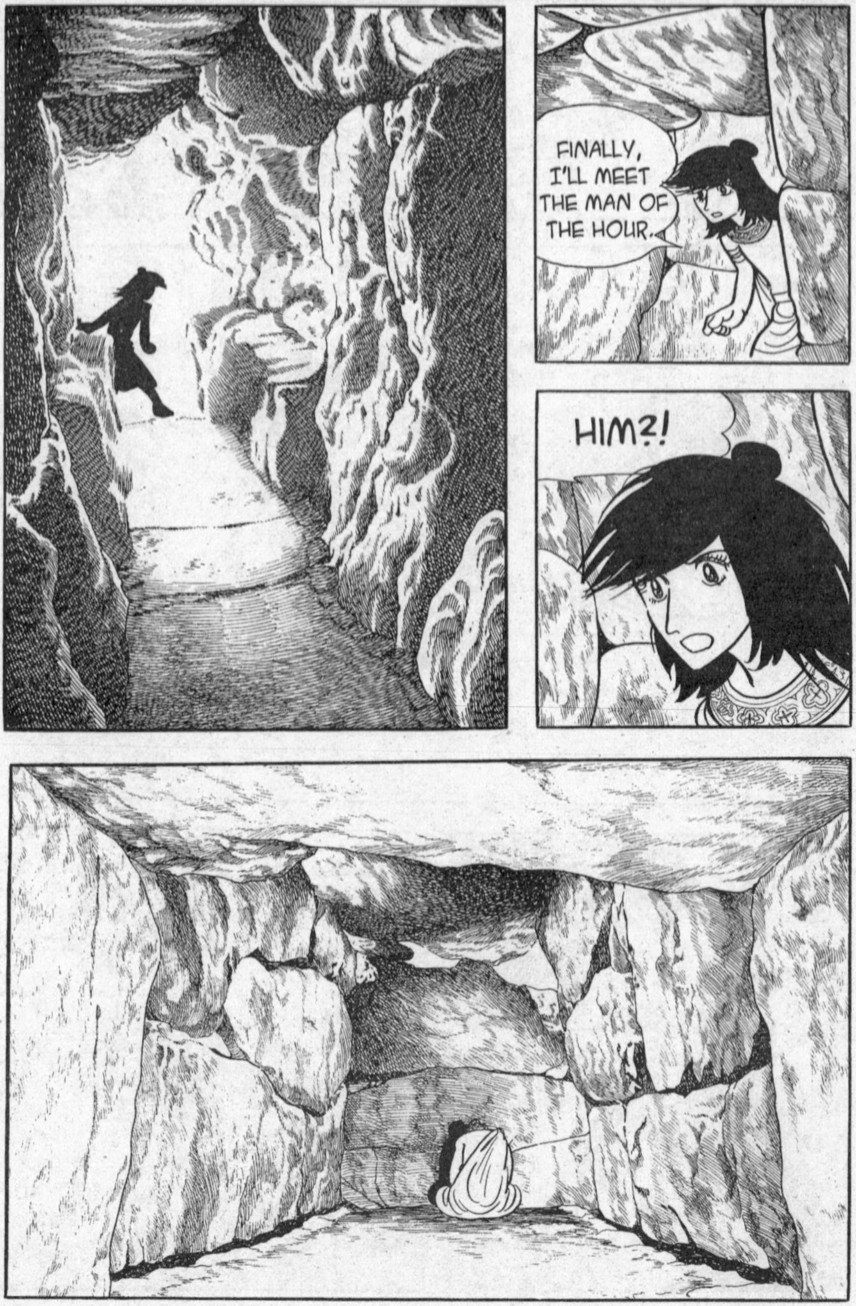
FINALLY, I'LL MEET THE MAN OF THE HOUR...
HIM?!

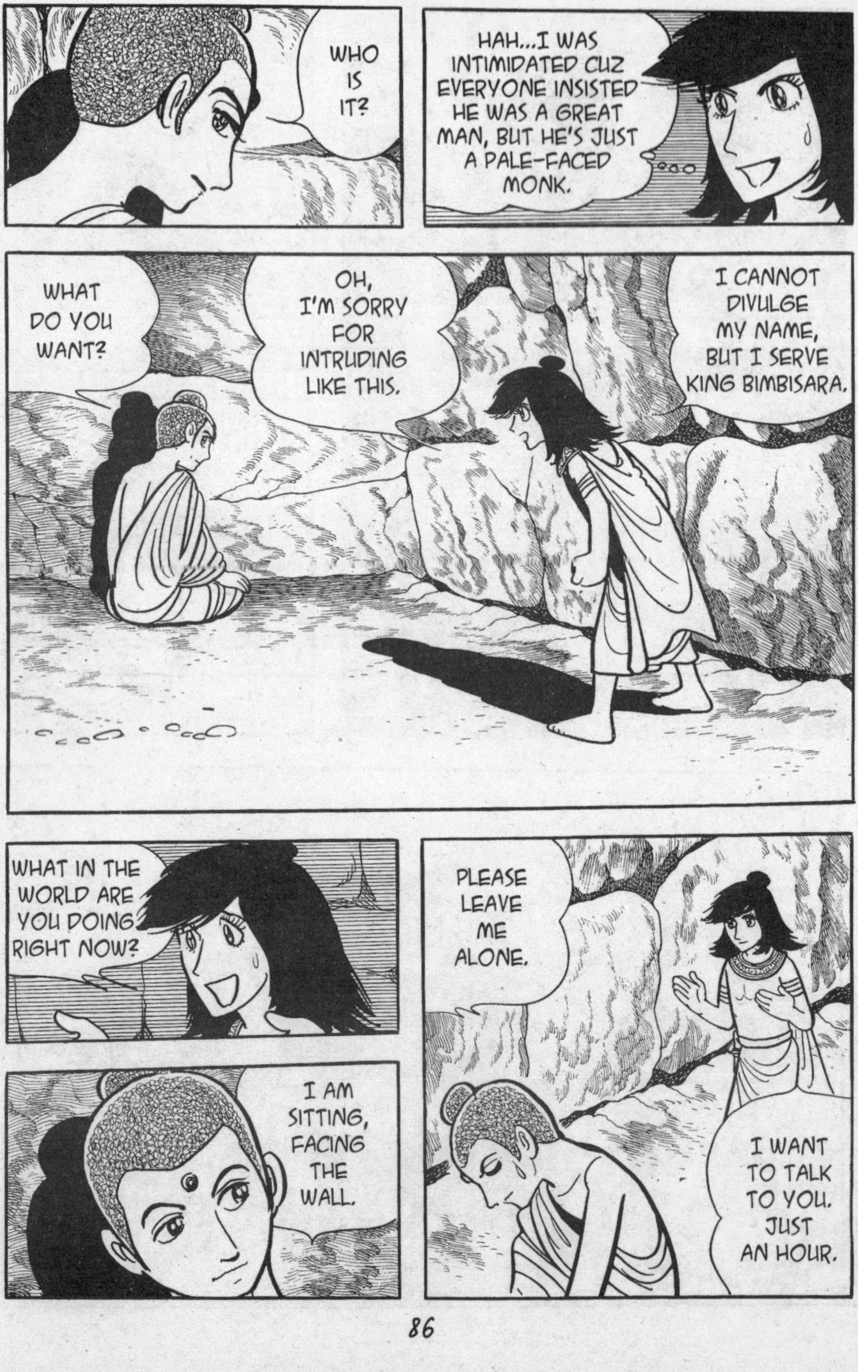
WHO IS IT?
HAH...I WAS INTIMIDATED CUZ EVERYONE INSISTED HE WAS A GREAT MAN, BUT HE'S JUST A PALE-FACED MONK.
WHAT DO YOU WANT?
OH, I'M SORRY FOR INTRUDING LIKE THIS.
I CANNOT DIVULGE MY NAME, BUT I SERVE KING BIMBISARA.
WHAT IN THE WORLD ARE YOU DOING RIGHT NOW?
I AM SITTING, FACING THE WALL.
PLEASE LEAVE ME ALONE.
I WANT TO TALK TO YOU. JUST AN HOUR.

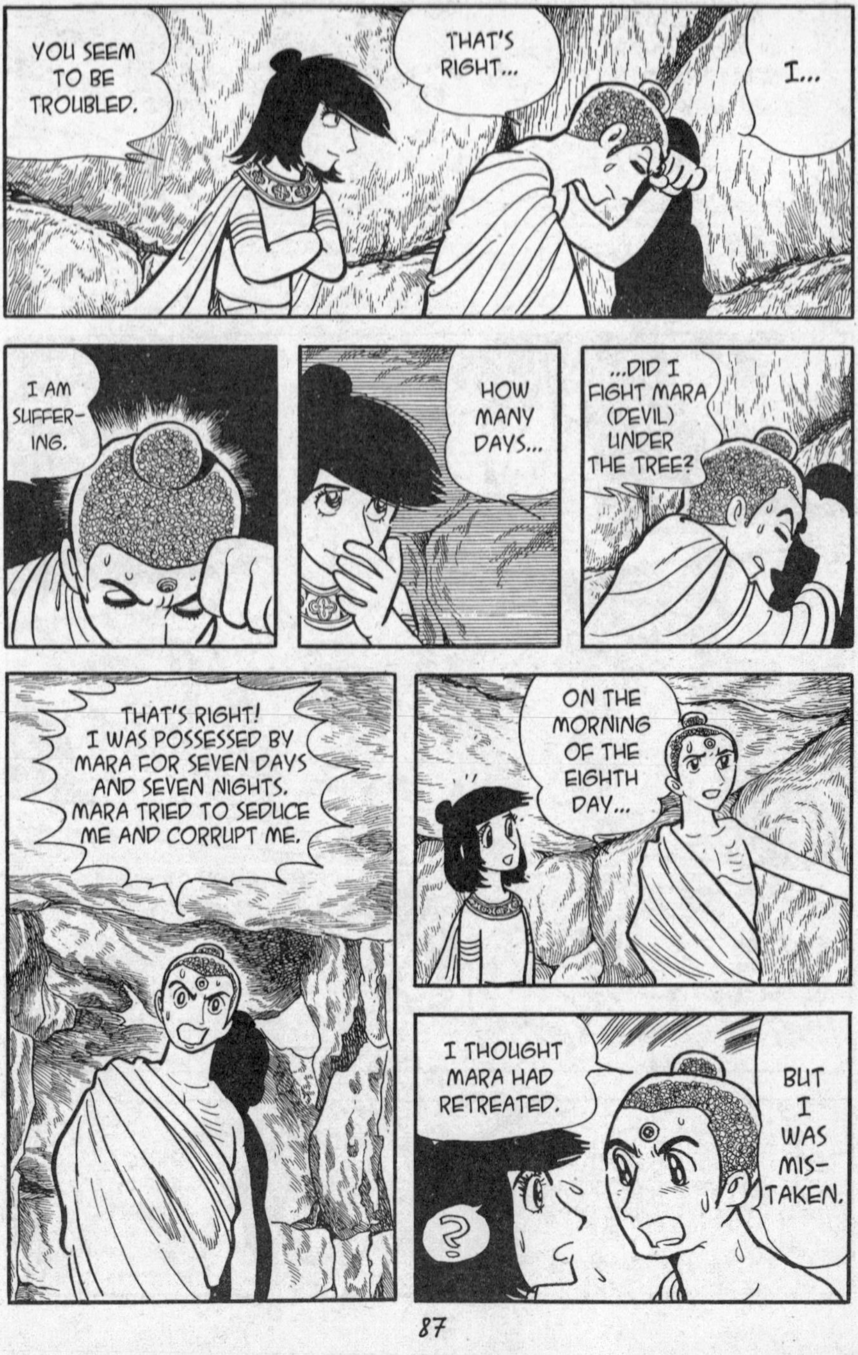
YOU SEEM TO BE TROUBLED.
THAT'S RIGHT...
I...
I AM SUFFER-ING.
HOW MANY DAYS...
...DID I FIGHT MARA (DEVIL) UNDER THE TREE?
THAT'S RIGHT! I WAS POSSESSED BY MARA FOR SEVEN DAYS AND SEVEN NIGHTS. MARA TRIED TO SEDUCE ME AND CORRUPT ME.
ON THE MORNING OF THE EIGHTH DAY...
I THOUGHT MARA HAD RETREATED.
BUT I WAS MIS-TAKEN.
?

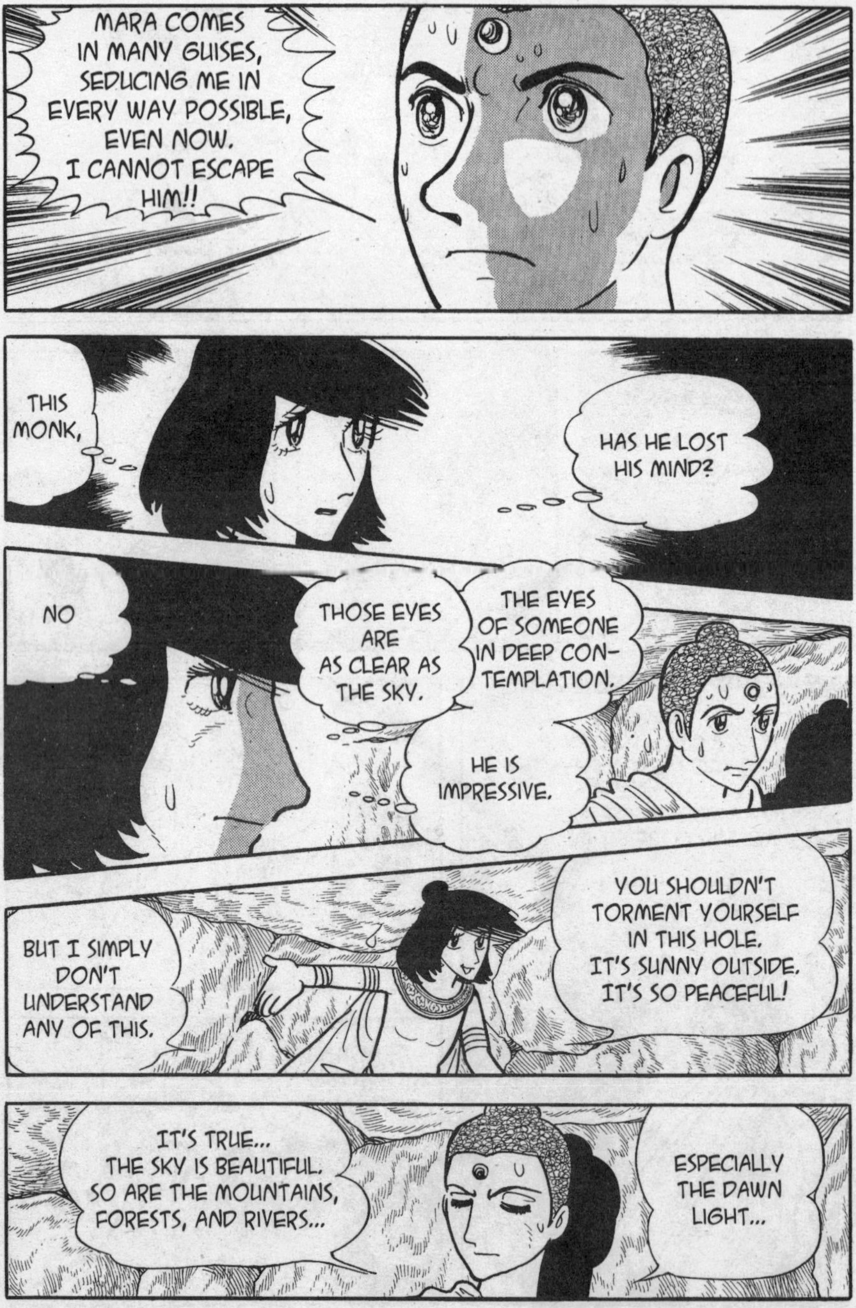
MARA COMES IN MANY GUISES, SEDUCING ME IN EVERY WAY POSSIBLE, EVEN NOW. I CANNOT ESCAPE HIM!!
THIS MONK,
HAS HE LOST HIS MIND?
NO
THOSE EYES ARE AS CLEAR AS THE SKY.
THE EYES OF SOMEONE IN DEEP CON-TEMPLATION.
HE IS IMPRESSIVE.
BUT I SIMPLY DON'T UNDERSTAND ANY OF THIS.
YOU SHOULDN'T TORMENT YOURSELF IN THIS HOLE. IT'S SUNNY OUTSIDE. IT'S SO PEACEFUL!
IT'S TRUE... THE SKY IS BEAUTIFUL. SO ARE THE MOUNTAINS, FORESTS, AND RIVERS...
ESPECIALLY THE DAWN LIGHT...

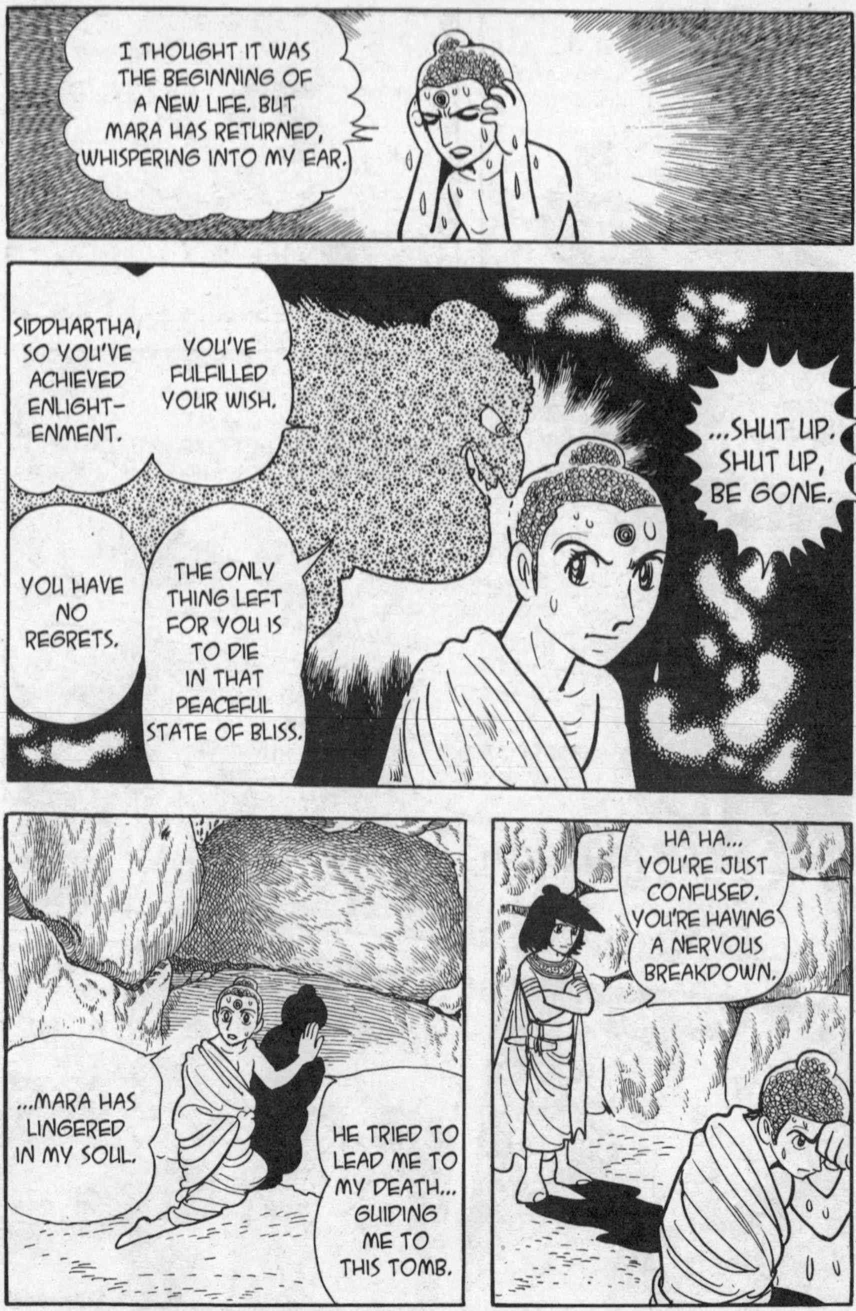
I THOUGHT IT WAS THE BEGINNING OF A NEW LIFE. BUT MARA HAS RETURNED, WHISPERING INTO MY EAR.
SIDDHARTHA, SO YOU'VE ACHIEVED ENLIGHT-ENMENT.
YOU'VE FULFILLED YOUR WISH.
YOU HAVE NO REGRETS.
THE ONLY THING LEFT FOR YOU IS TO DIE IN THAT PEACEFUL STATE OF BLISS.
...SHUT UP. SHUT UP, BE GONE.
...MARA HAS LINGERED IN MY SOUL.
HE TRIED TO LEAD ME TO MY DEATH... GUIDING ME TO THIS TOMB.
HA HA... YOU'RE JUST CONFUSED. YOU'RE HAVING A NERVOUS BREAKDOWN.

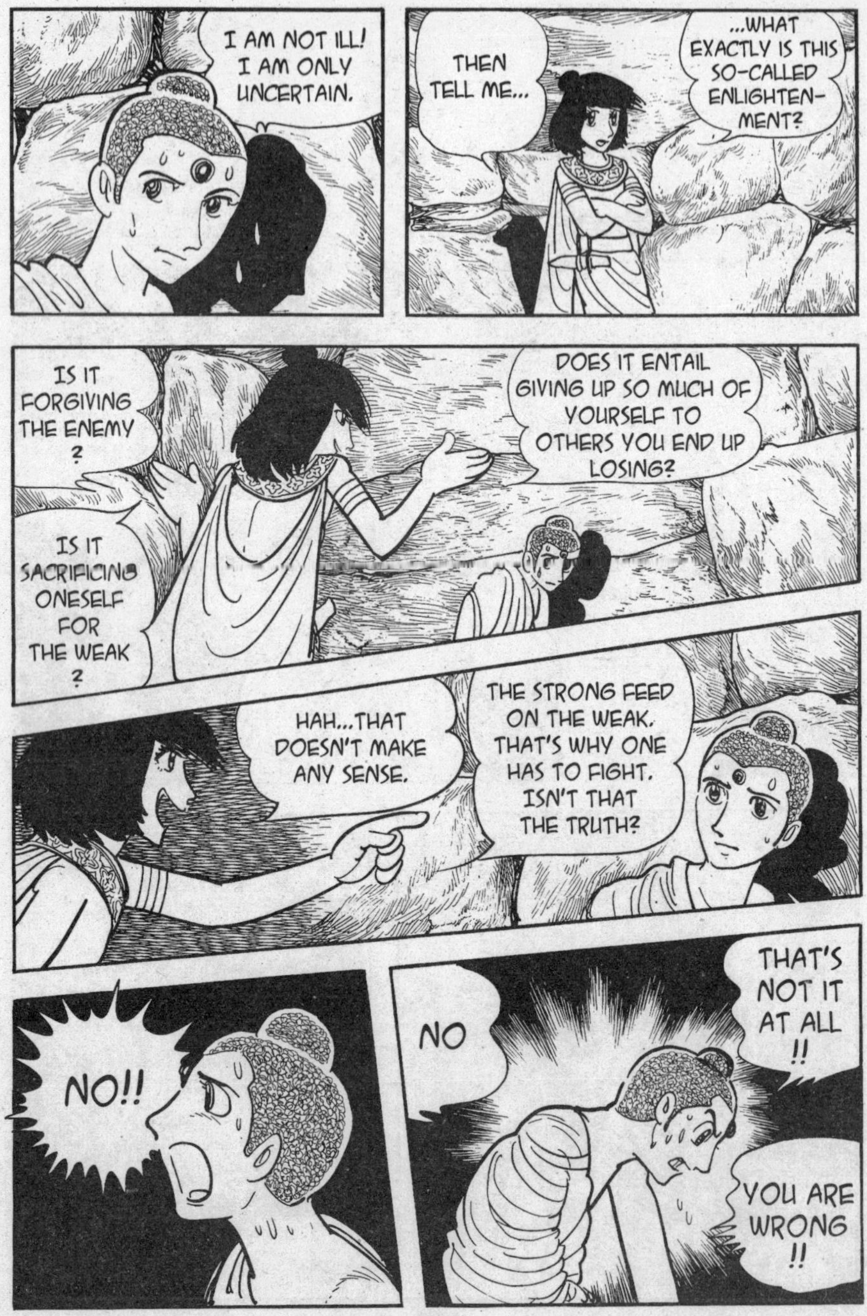
I AM NOT ILL! I AM ONLY UNCERTAIN.
THEN TELL ME...
...WHAT EXACTLY IS THIS SO-CALLED ENLIGHTENMENT?
IS IT FORGIVING THE ENEMY?
DOES IT ENTAIL GIVING UP SO MUCH OF YOURSELF TO OTHERS YOU END UP LOSING?
IS IT SACRIFICING ONESELF FOR THE WEAK?
THE STRONG FEED ON THE WEAK. THAT'S WHY ONE HAS TO FIGHT. ISN'T THAT THE TRUTH?
HAH...THAT DOESN'T MAKE ANY SENSE.
NO!!
NO
THAT'S NOT IT AT ALL!!
YOU ARE WRONG!!

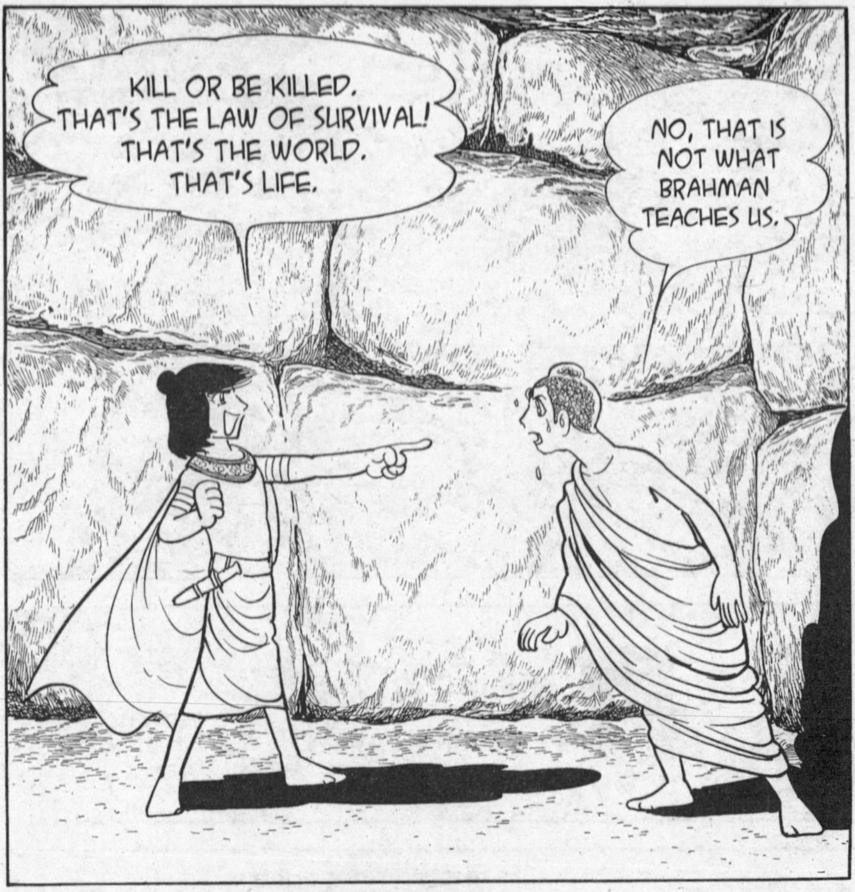
KILL OR BE KILLED. THAT'S THE LAW OF SURVIVAL! THAT'S THE WORLD. THAT'S LIFE.
NO, THAT IS NOT WHAT BRAHMAN TEACHES US.

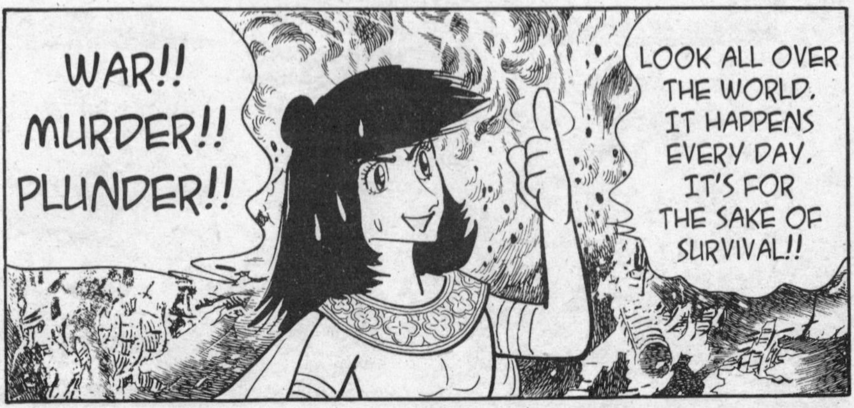
WAR!! MURDER!! PLUNDER!!
LOOK ALL OVER THE WORLD. IT HAPPENS EVERY DAY. IT'S FOR THE SAKE OF SURVIVAL!!

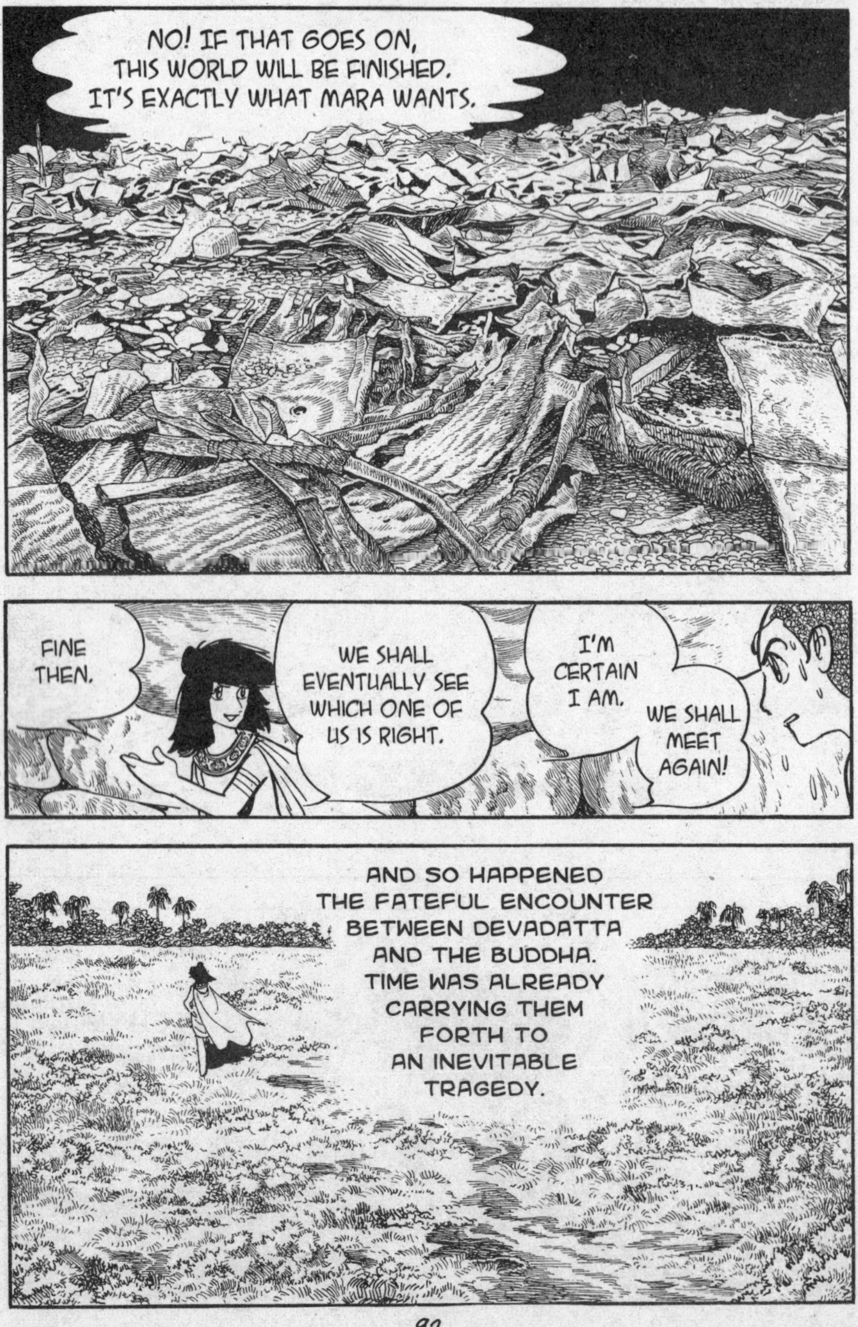
NO! IF THAT GOES ON, THIS WORLD WILL BE FINISHED. IT'S EXACTLY WHAT MARA WANTS.
FINE THEN.
WE SHALL EVENTUALLY SEE WHICH ONE OF US IS RIGHT.
I'M CERTAIN I AM.
WE SHALL MEET AGAIN!
AND SO HAPPENED THE FATEFUL ENCOUNTER BETWEEN DEVADATTA AND THE BUDDHA. TIME WAS ALREADY CARRYING THEM FORTH TO AN INEVITABLE TRAGEDY.

CHAPTER TWO

OPPONENTS

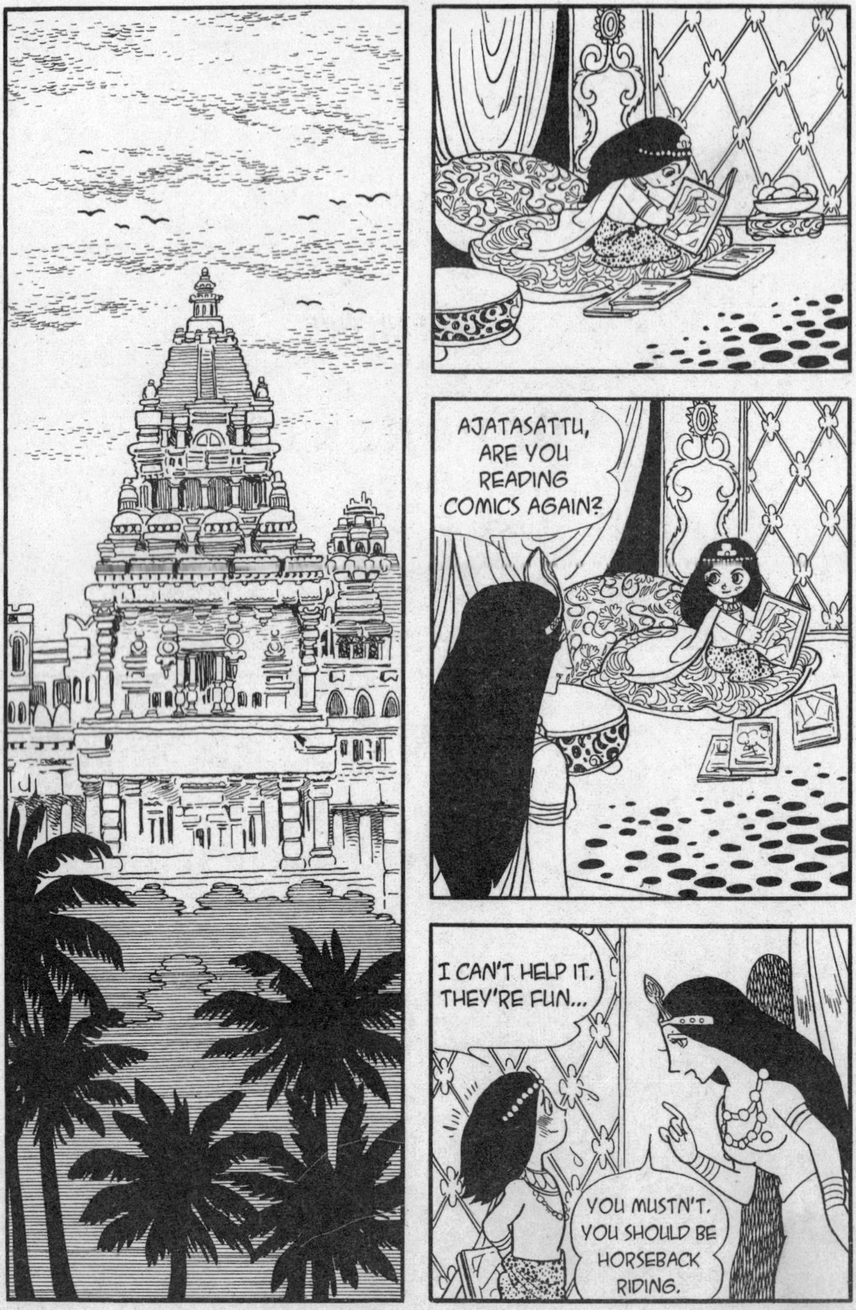
AJATASATTU, ARE YOU READING COMICS AGAIN?
I CAN'T HELP IT. THEY'RE FUN...
YOU MUSTN'T. YOU SHOULD BE HORSEBACK RIDING.

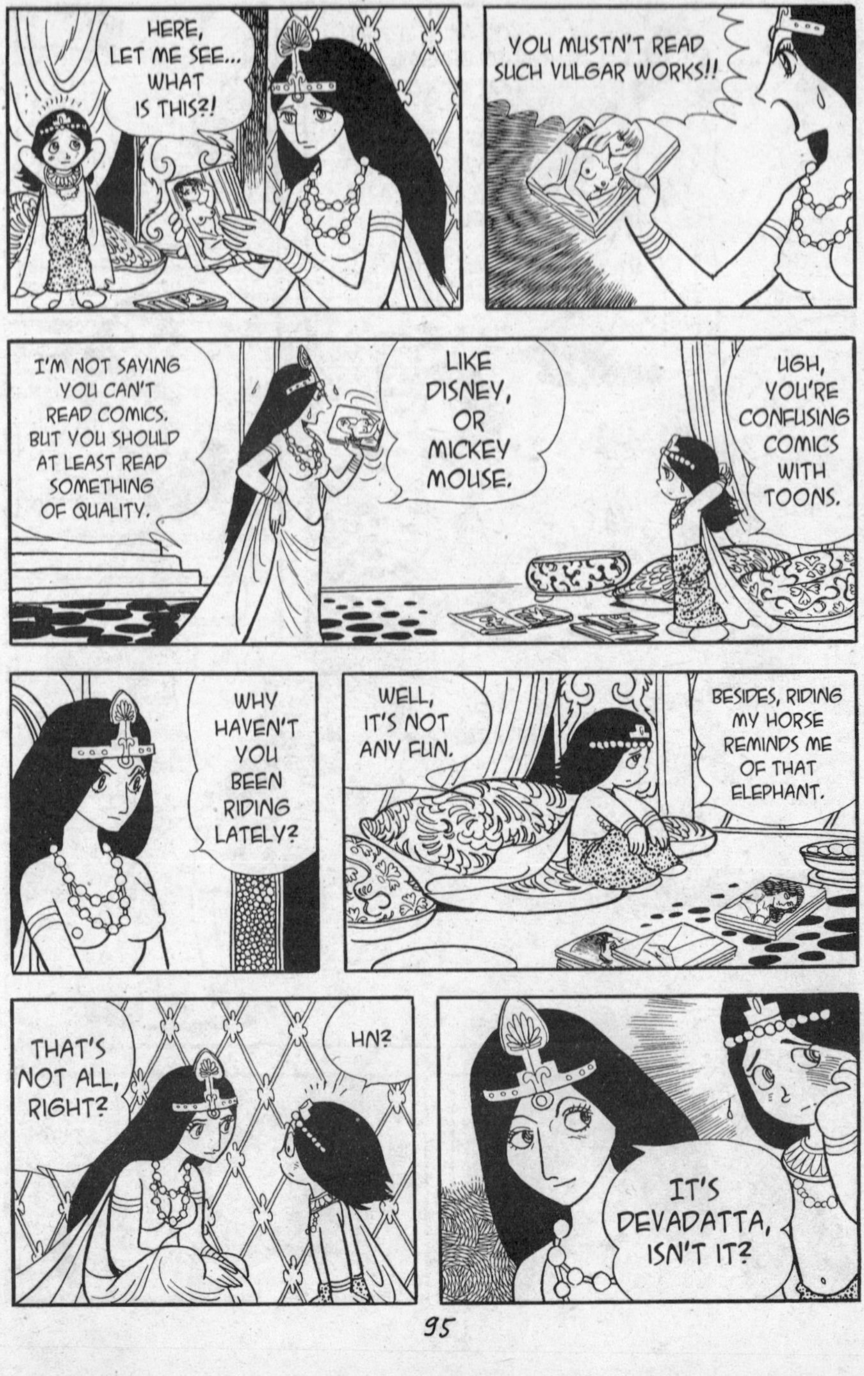

HERE, LET ME SEE... WHAT IS THIS?!
YOU MUSTN'T READ SUCH VULGAR WORKS!!
I'M NOT SAYING YOU CAN'T READ COMICS. BUT YOU SHOULD AT LEAST READ SOMETHING OF QUALITY.
LIKE DISNEY, OR MICKEY MOUSE.
UGH, YOU'RE CONFUSING COMICS WITH TOONS.
WHY HAVEN'T YOU BEEN RIDING LATELY?
WELL, IT'S NOT ANY FUN.
BESIDES, RIDING MY HORSE REMINDS ME OF THAT ELEPHANT.
THAT'S NOT ALL, RIGHT?
HN?
IT'S DEVADATTA, ISN'T IT?

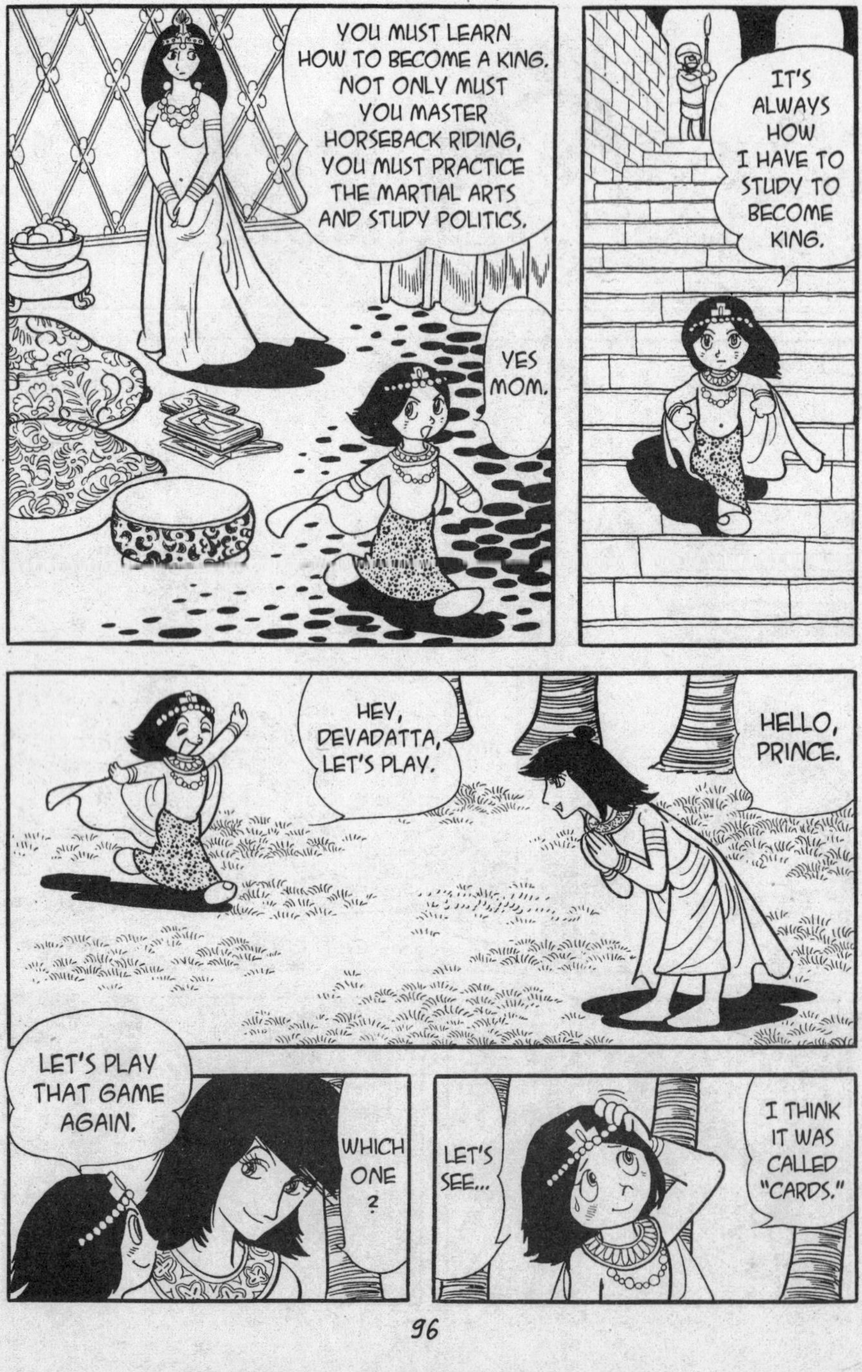
YOU MUST LEARN HOW TO BECOME A KING. NOT ONLY MUST YOU MASTER HORSEBACK RIDING, YOU MUST PRACTICE THE MARTIAL ARTS AND STUDY POLITICS.
YES MOM.
IT'S ALWAYS HOW I HAVE TO STUDY TO BECOME KING.
HEY, DEVADATTA, LET'S PLAY.
HELLO, PRINCE.
LET'S PLAY THAT GAME AGAIN.
WHICH ONE ?
LET'S SEE...
I THINK IT WAS CALLED "CARDS."

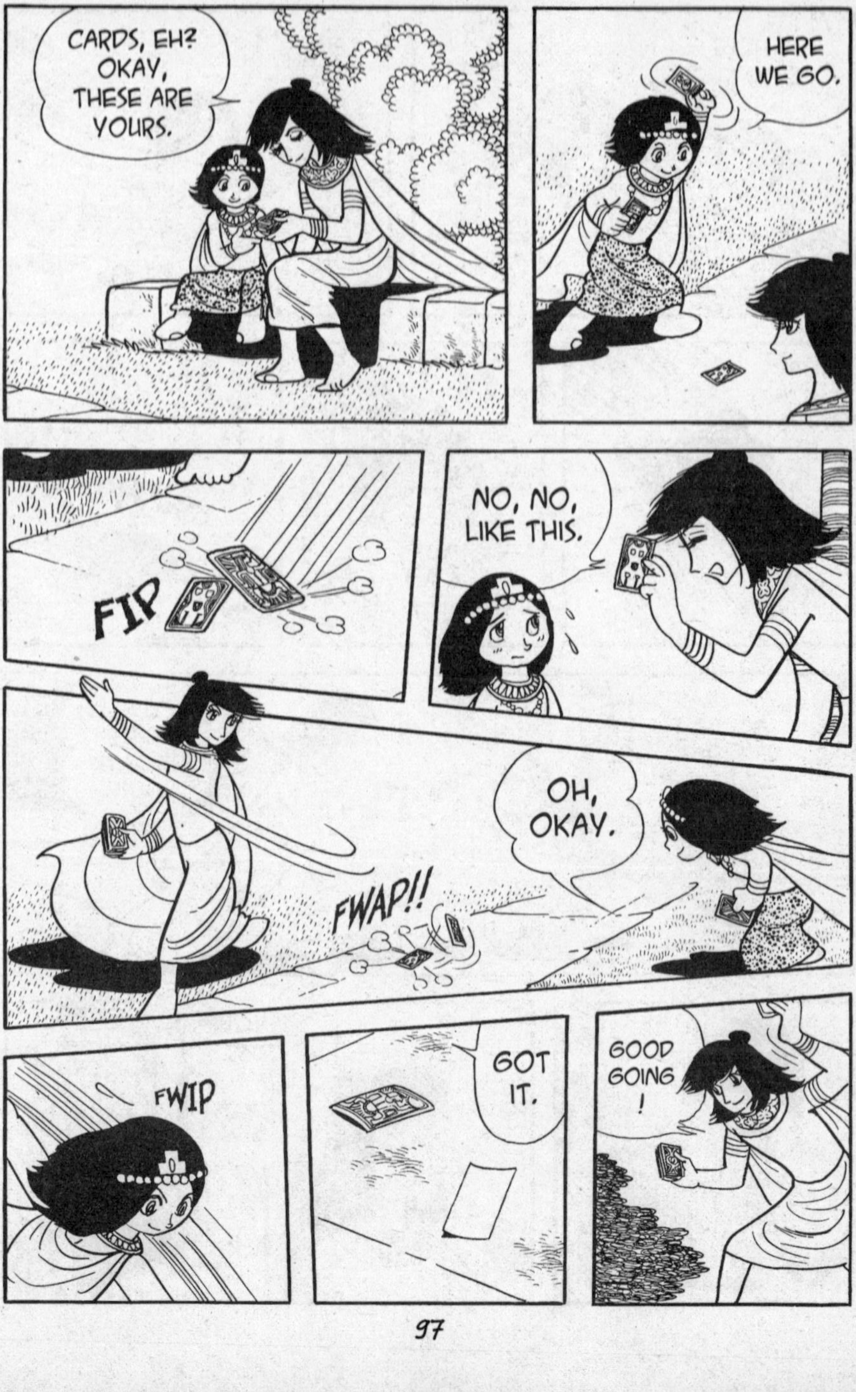
CARDS, EH? OKAY, THESE ARE YOURS.
HERE WE GO.
FIP
NO, NO, LIKE THIS.
OH, OKAY.
FWAP!!
FWIP
GOT IT.
GOOD GOING!

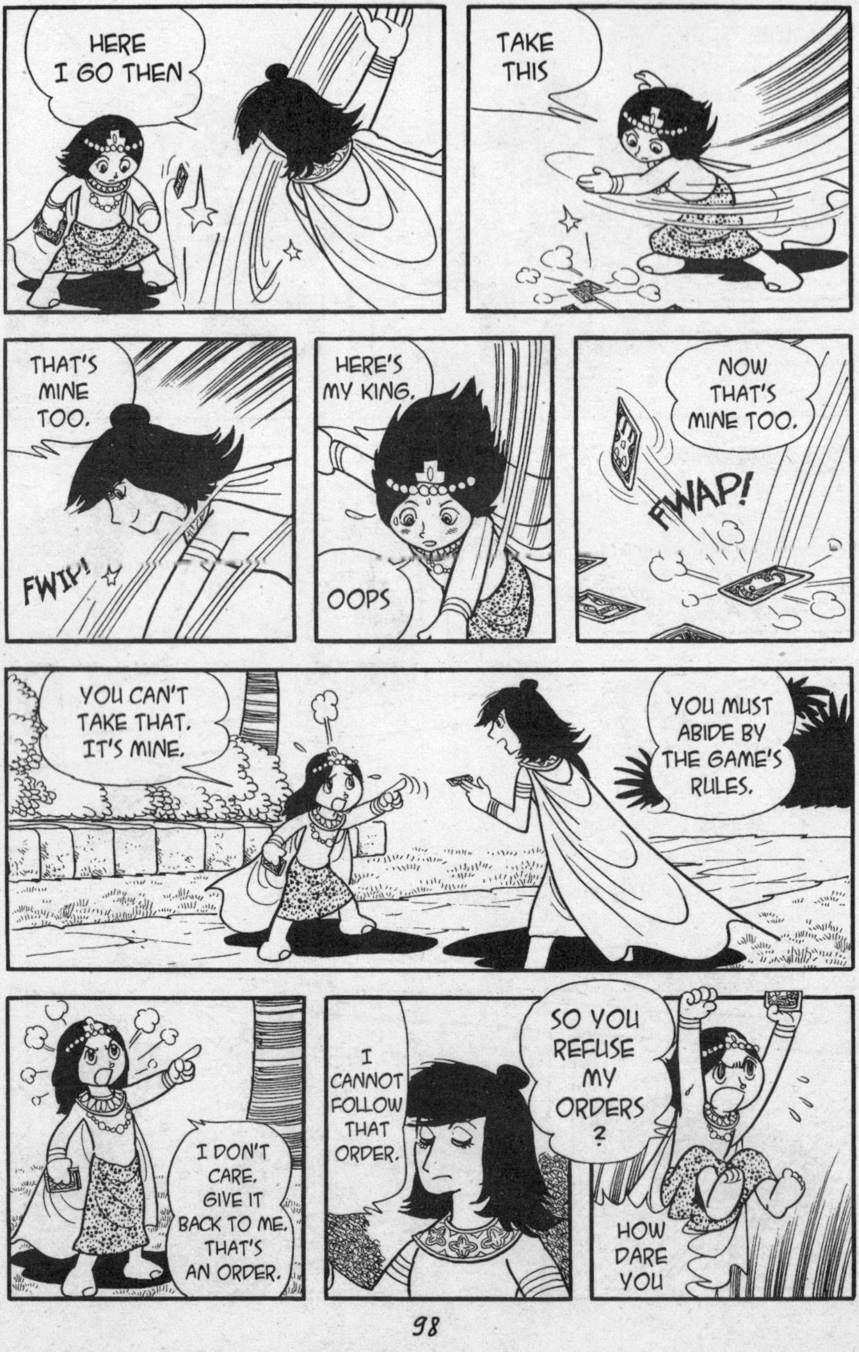
HERE I GO THEN
TAKE THIS
THAT'S MINE TOO.
FWIP!
HERE'S MY KING.
OOPS
NOW THAT'S MINE TOO.
FWAP!
YOU CAN'T TAKE THAT. IT'S MINE.
YOU MUST ABIDE BY THE GAME'S RULES.
I DON'T CARE. GIVE IT BACK TO ME. THAT'S AN ORDER.
I CANNOT FOLLOW THAT ORDER.
SO YOU REFUSE MY ORDERS ?
HOW DARE YOU

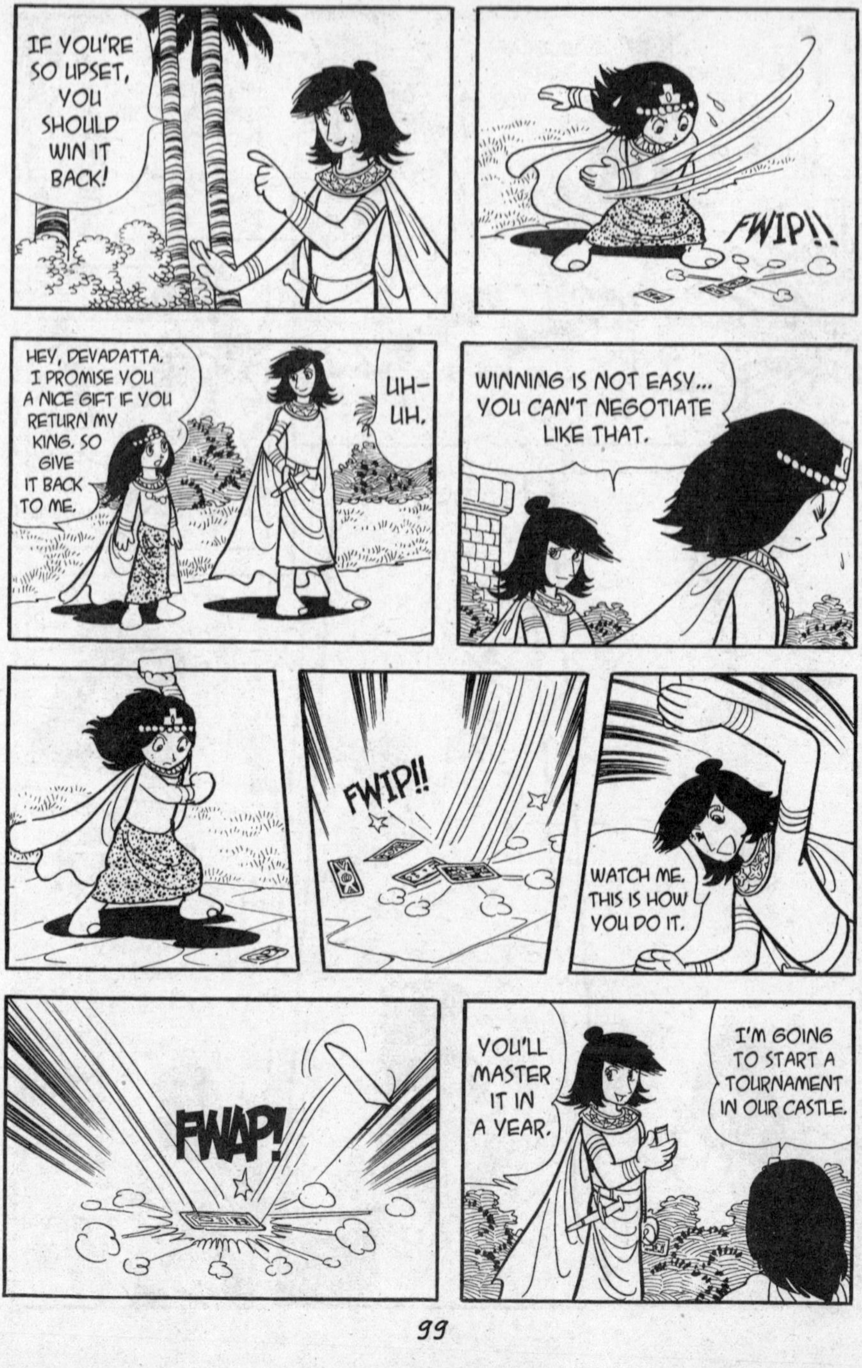
IF YOU'RE SO UPSET, YOU SHOULD WIN IT BACK!
FWIP!!
HEY, DEVADATTA. I PROMISE YOU A NICE GIFT IF YOU RETURN MY KING. SO GIVE IT BACK TO ME.
UH-UH.
WINNING IS NOT EASY... YOU CAN'T NEGOTIATE LIKE THAT.
FWIP!!
WATCH ME. THIS IS HOW YOU DO IT.
FWAP!
YOU'LL MASTER IT IN A YEAR.
I'M GOING TO START A TOURNAMENT IN OUR CASTLE.

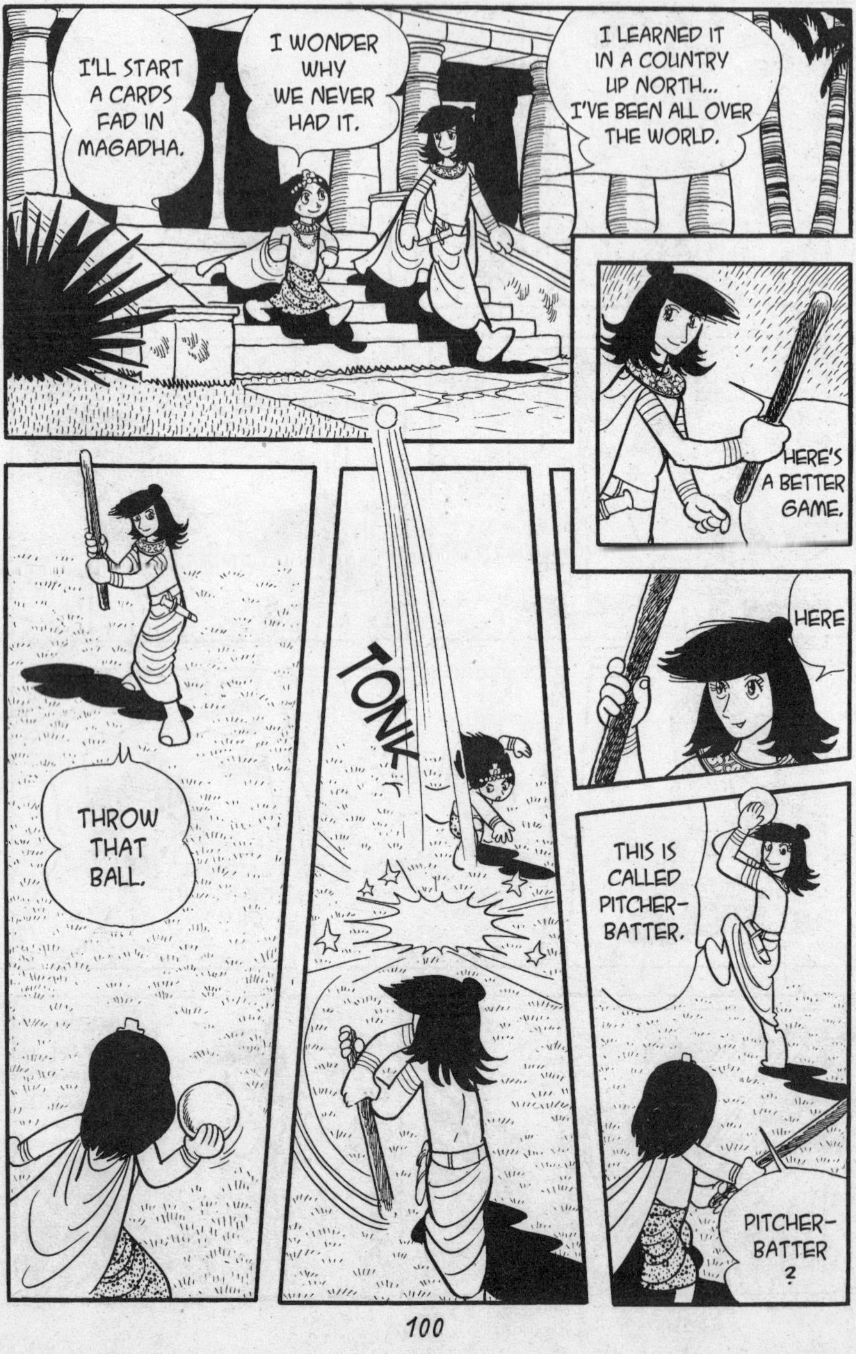
I'LL START A CARDS FAD IN MAGADHA.
I WONDER WHY WE NEVER HAD IT.
I LEARNED IT IN A COUNTRY UP NORTH... I'VE BEEN ALL OVER THE WORLD.
HERE'S A BETTER GAME.
HERE
THIS IS CALLED PITCHER-BATTER.
PITCHER-BATTER?
THROW THAT BALL.
TONK

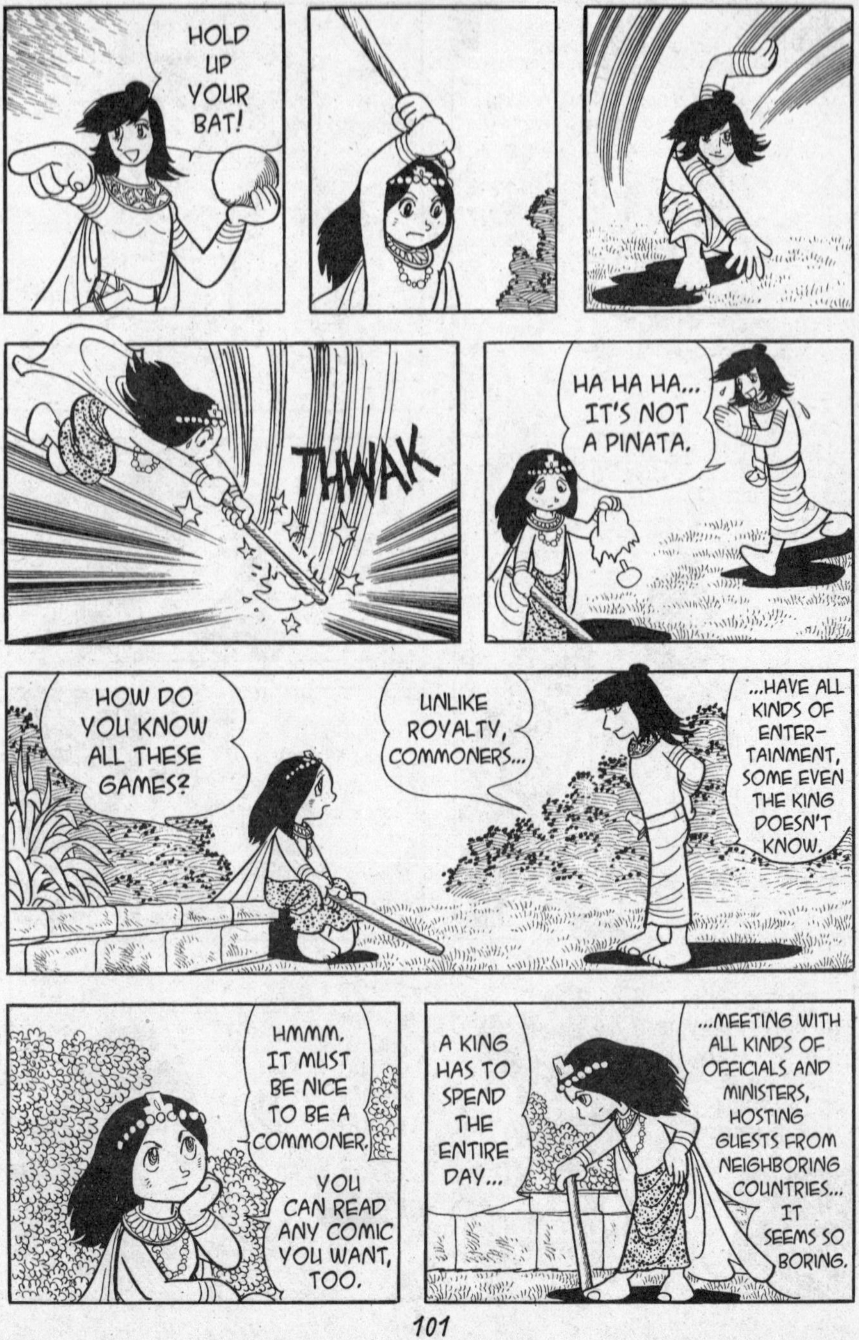
HOLD UP YOUR BAT!
THWAK
HA HA HA... IT'S NOT A PINATA.
HOW DO YOU KNOW ALL THESE GAMES?
UNLIKE ROYALTY, COMMONERS...
...HAVE ALL KINDS OF ENTER-TAINMENT, SOME EVEN THE KING DOESN'T KNOW.
HMMM. IT MUST BE NICE TO BE A COMMONER.
YOU CAN READ ANY COMIC YOU WANT, TOO.
A KING HAS TO SPEND THE ENTIRE DAY...
...MEETING WITH ALL KINDS OF OFFICIALS AND MINISTERS, HOSTING GUESTS FROM NEIGHBORING COUNTRIES... IT SEEMS SO BORING.

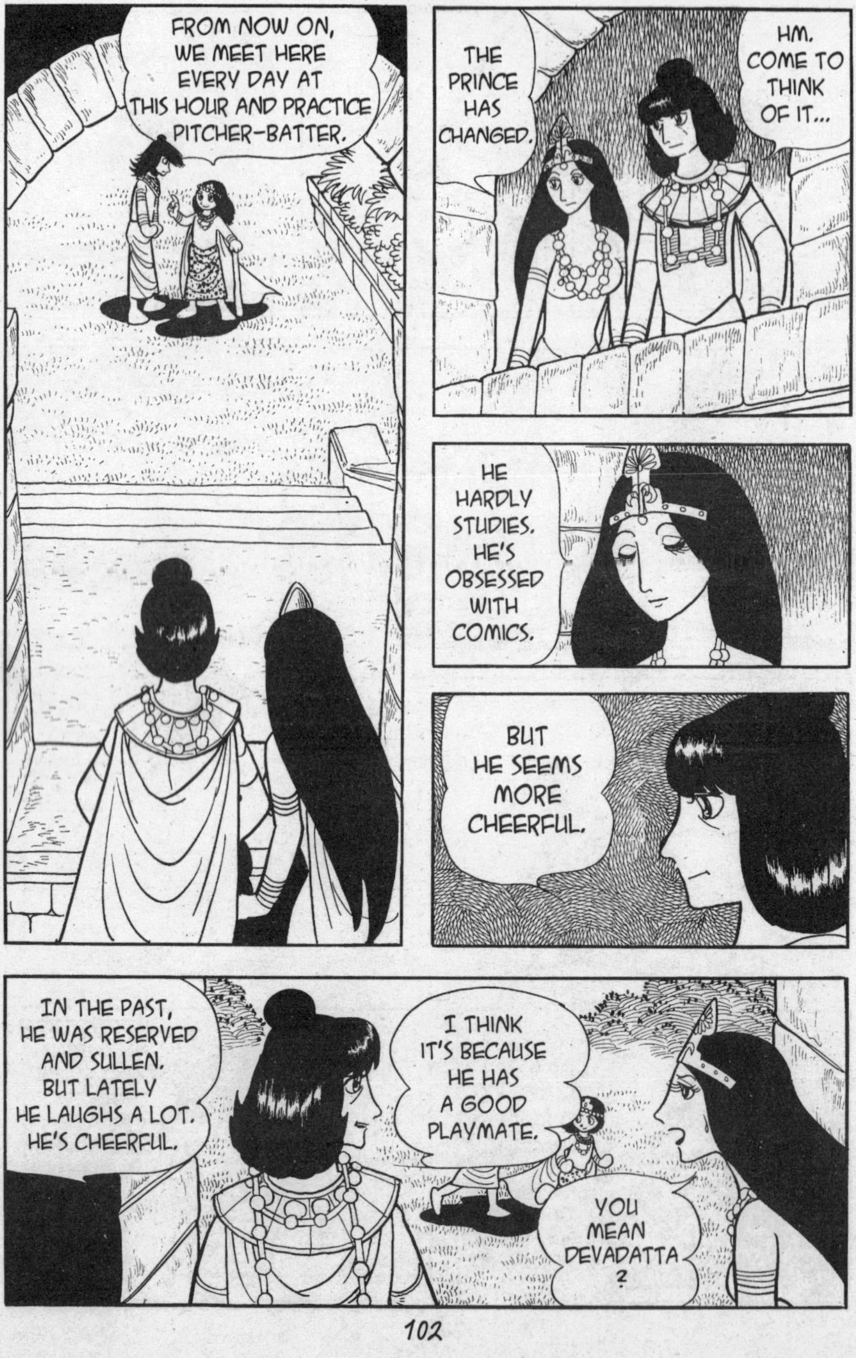
FROM NOW ON, WE MEET HERE EVERY DAY AT THIS HOUR AND PRACTICE PITCHER-BATTER.
HM. COME TO THINK OF IT...
THE PRINCE HAS CHANGED.
HE HARDLY STUDIES. HE'S OBSESSED WITH COMICS.
BUT HE SEEMS MORE CHEERFUL.
IN THE PAST, HE WAS RESERVED AND SULLEN. BUT LATELY HE LAUGHS A LOT. HE'S CHEERFUL.
I THINK IT'S BECAUSE HE HAS A GOOD PLAYMATE.
YOU MEAN DEVADATTA?

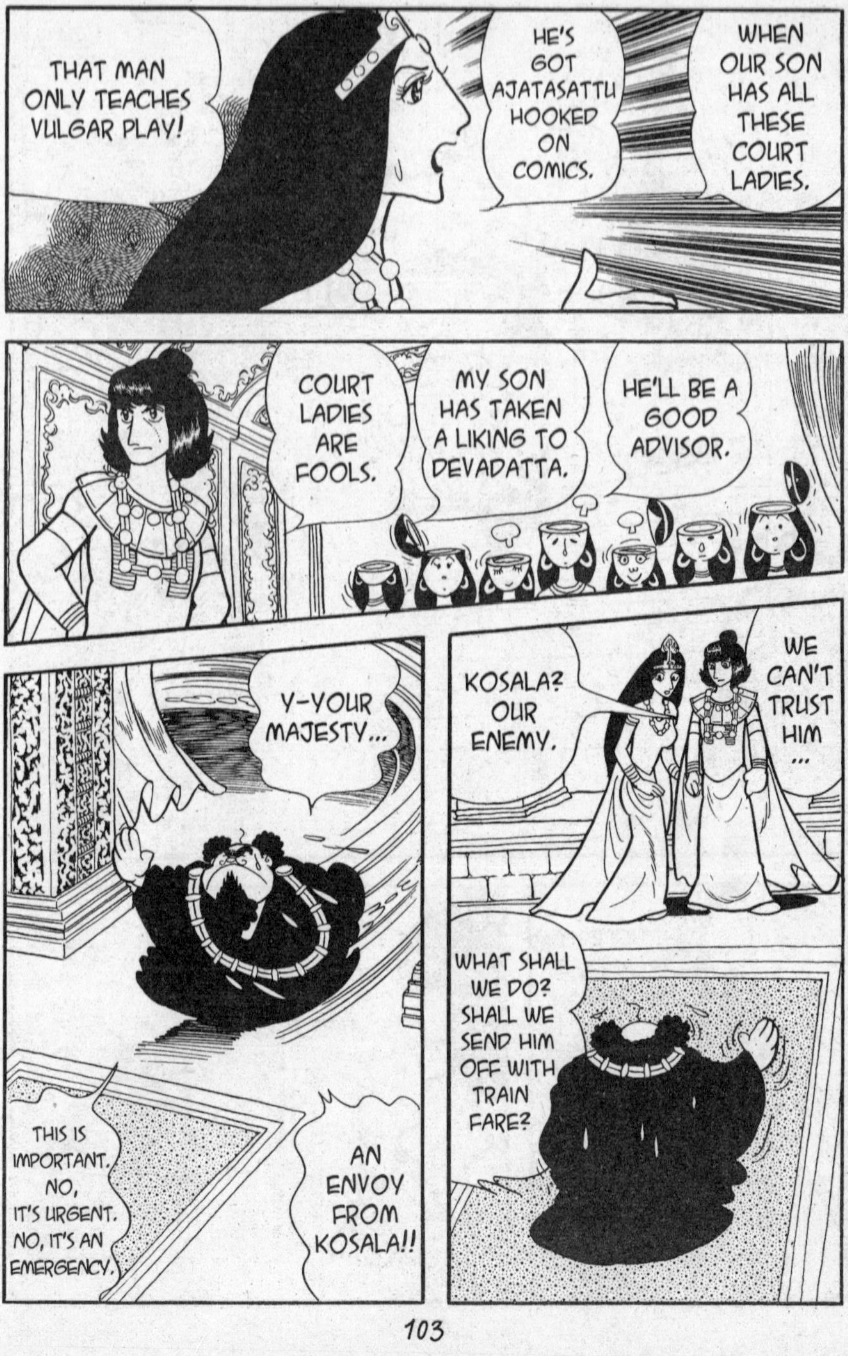
WHEN OUR SON HAS ALL THESE COURT LADIES.
HE'S GOT AJATASATTU HOOKED ON COMICS.
THAT MAN ONLY TEACHES VULGAR PLAY!
HE'LL BE A GOOD ADVISOR.
MY SON HAS TAKEN A LIKING TO DEVADATTA.
COURT LADIES ARE FOOLS.
WE CAN'T TRUST HIM ...
KOSALA? OUR ENEMY.
WHAT SHALL WE DO? SHALL WE SEND HIM OFF WITH TRAIN FARE?
Y-YOUR MAJESTY...
AN ENVOY FROM KOSALA!!
THIS IS IMPORTANT. NO, IT'S URGENT. NO, IT'S AN EMERGENCY.

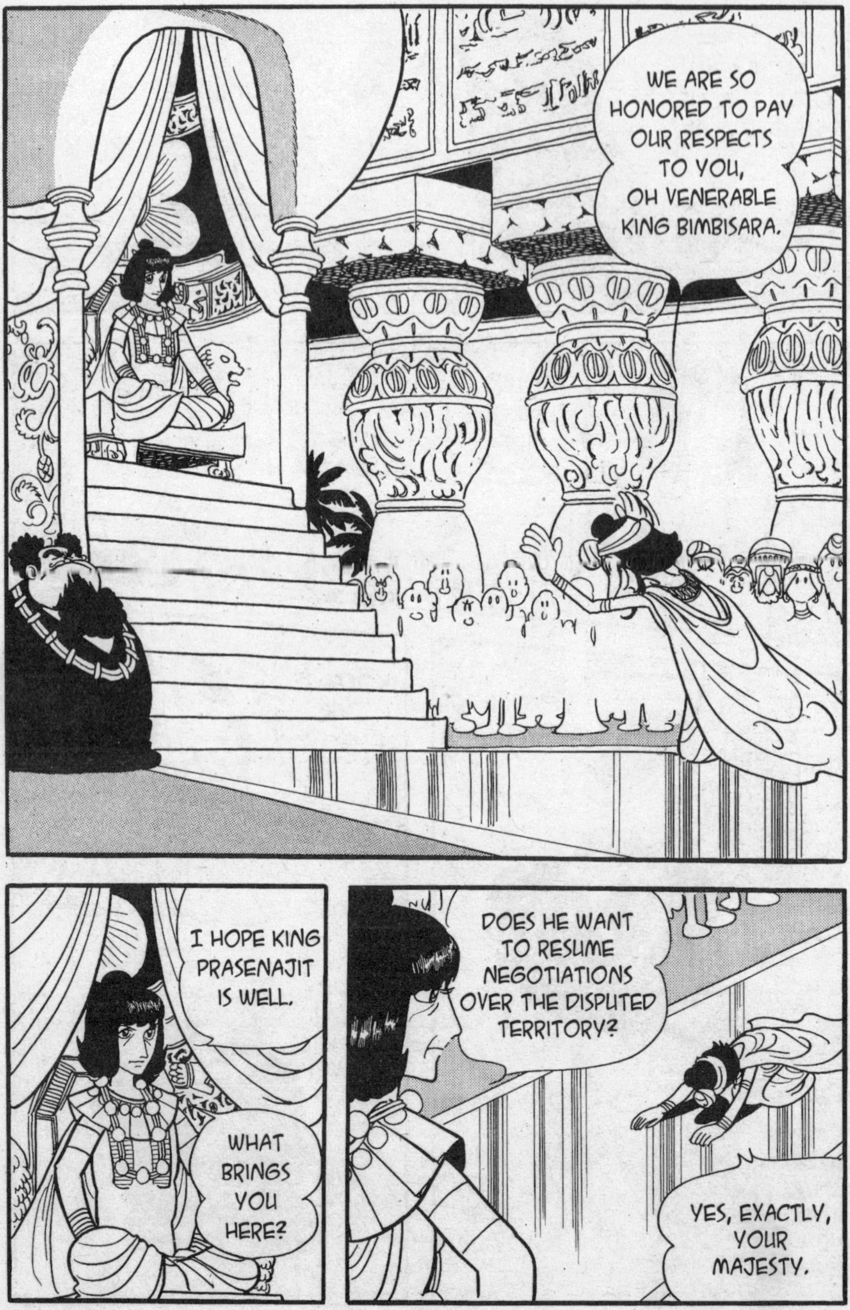
WE ARE SO HONORED TO PAY OUR RESPECTS TO YOU, OH VENERABLE KING BIMBISARA.
I HOPE KING PRASENAJIT IS WELL.
WHAT BRINGS YOU HERE?
DOES HE WANT TO RESUME NEGOTIATIONS OVER THE DISPUTED TERRITORY?
YES, EXACTLY, YOUR MAJESTY.

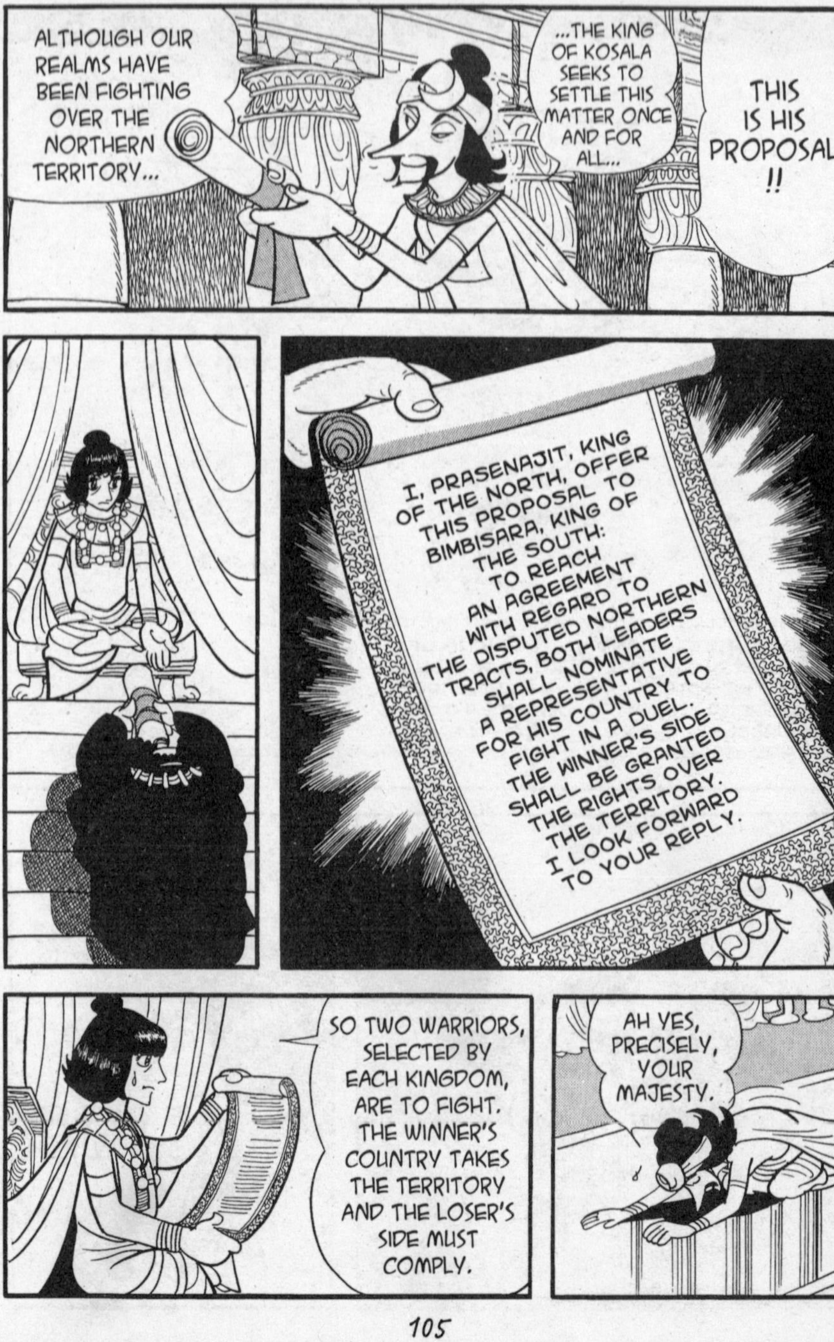
ALTHOUGH OUR REALMS HAVE BEEN FIGHTING OVER THE NORTHERN TERRITORY...
...THE KING OF KOSALA SEEKS TO SETTLE THIS MATTER ONCE AND FOR ALL...
THIS IS HIS PROPOSAL !!
I, PRASENAJIT, KING OF THE NORTH, OFFER THIS PROPOSAL TO BIMBISARA, KING OF THE SOUTH: TO REACH AN AGREEMENT WITH REGARD TO THE DISPUTED NORTHERN TRACTS, BOTH LEADERS SHALL NOMINATE A REPRESENTATIVE FOR HIS COUNTRY TO FIGHT IN A DUEL. THE WINNER'S SIDE SHALL BE GRANTED THE RIGHTS OVER THE TERRITORY. I LOOK FORWARD TO YOUR REPLY.
SO TWO WARRIORS, SELECTED BY EACH KINGDOM, ARE TO FIGHT. THE WINNER'S COUNTRY TAKES THE TERRITORY AND THE LOSER'S SIDE MUST COMPLY.
AH YES, PRECISELY, YOUR MAJESTY.

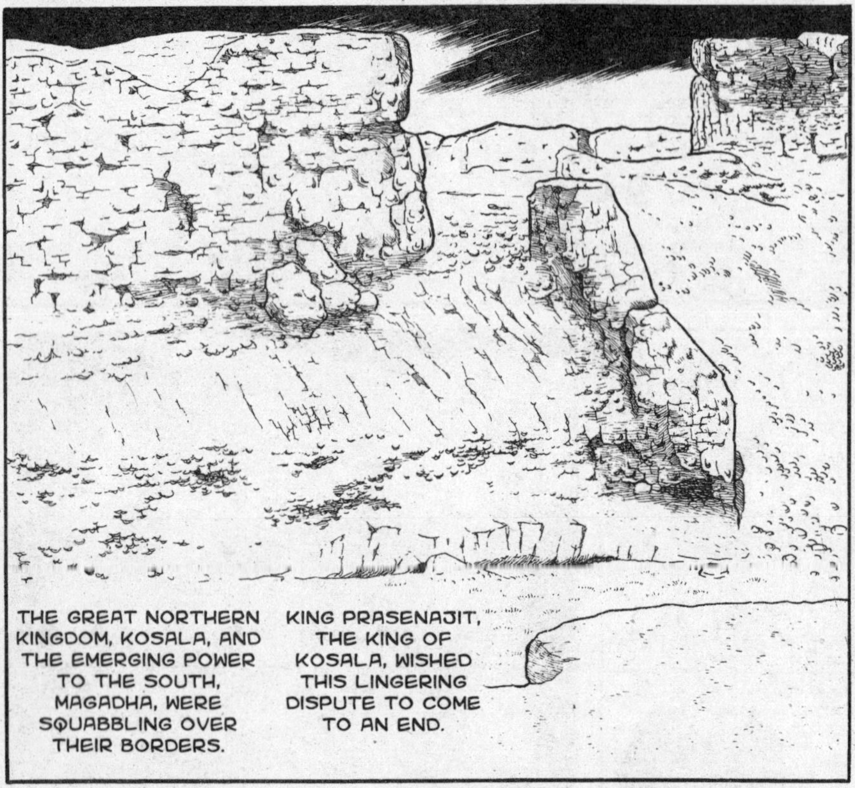
THE GREAT NORTHERN KINGDOM, KOSALA, AND THE EMERGING POWER TO THE SOUTH, MAGADHA, WERE SQUABBLING OVER THEIR BORDERS.
KING PRASENAJIT, THE KING OF KOSALA, WISHED THIS LINGERING DISPUTE TO COME TO AN END.

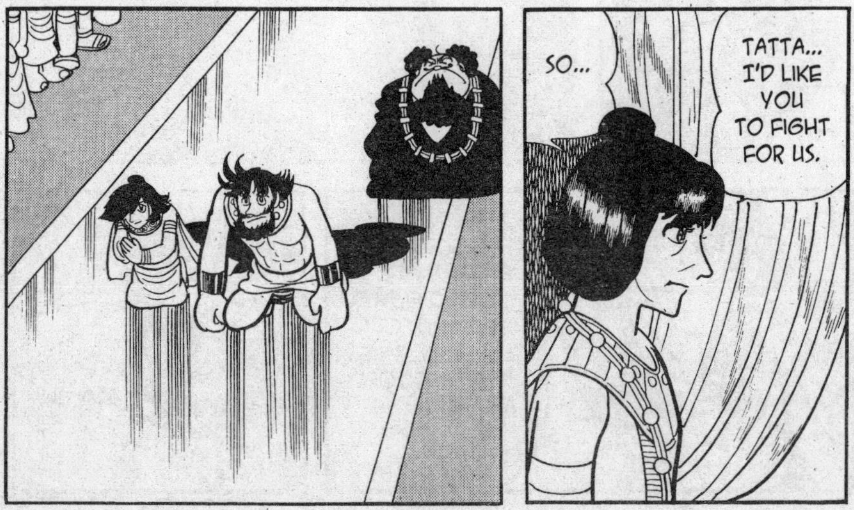
TATTA... I'D LIKE YOU TO FIGHT FOR US.
SO...

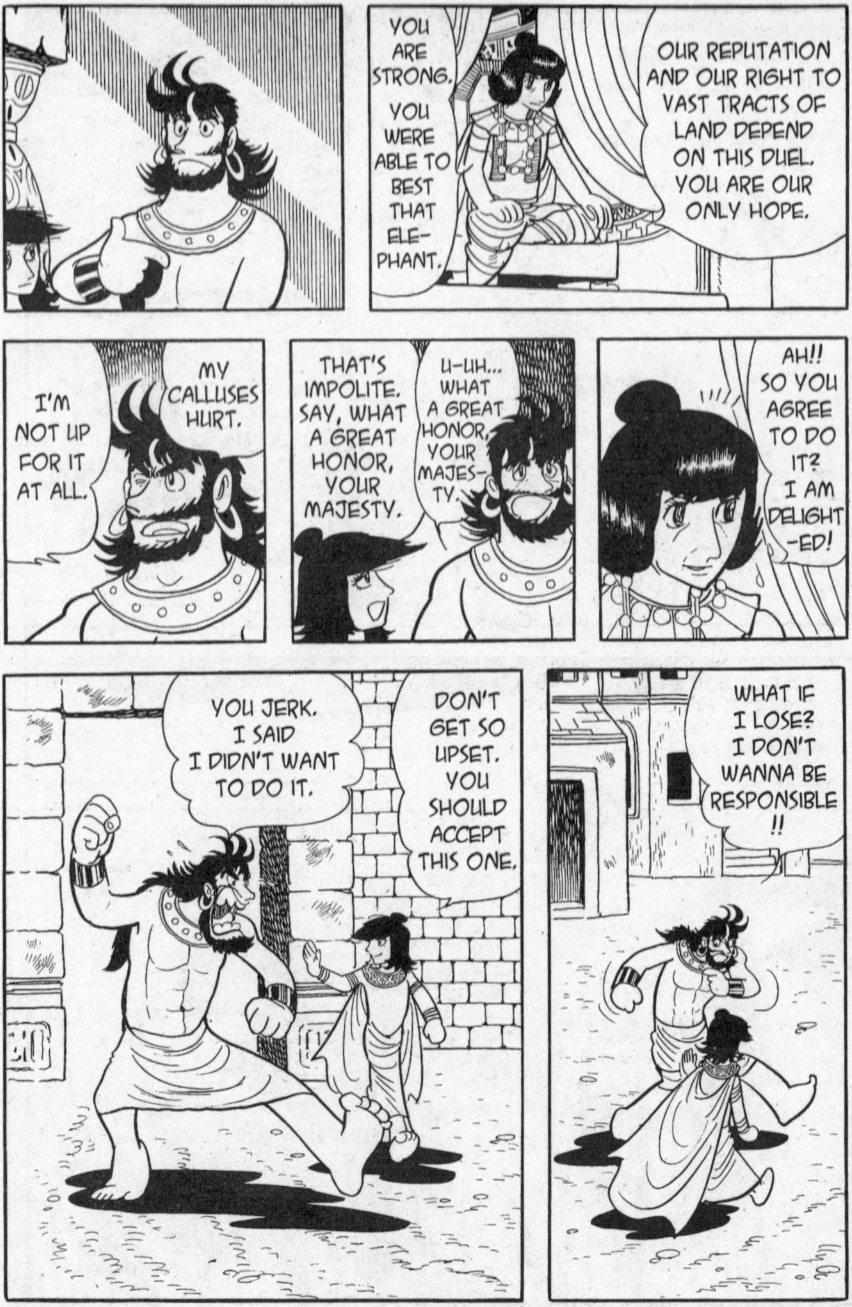
YOU ARE STRONG.
YOU WERE ABLE TO BEST THAT ELE-PHANT.
OUR REPUTATION AND OUR RIGHT TO VAST TRACTS OF LAND DEPEND ON THIS DUEL. YOU ARE OUR ONLY HOPE.
MY CALLUSES HURT.
I'M NOT UP FOR IT AT ALL.
THAT'S IMPOLITE. SAY, WHAT A GREAT HONOR, YOUR MAJESTY.
U-UH... WHAT A GREAT HONOR, YOUR MAJES-TY.
AH!! SO YOU AGREE TO DO IT? I AM DELIGHT-ED!
YOU JERK. I SAID I DIDN'T WANT TO DO IT.
DON'T GET SO UPSET. YOU SHOULD ACCEPT THIS ONE.
WHAT IF I LOSE? I DON'T WANNA BE RESPONSIBLE !!

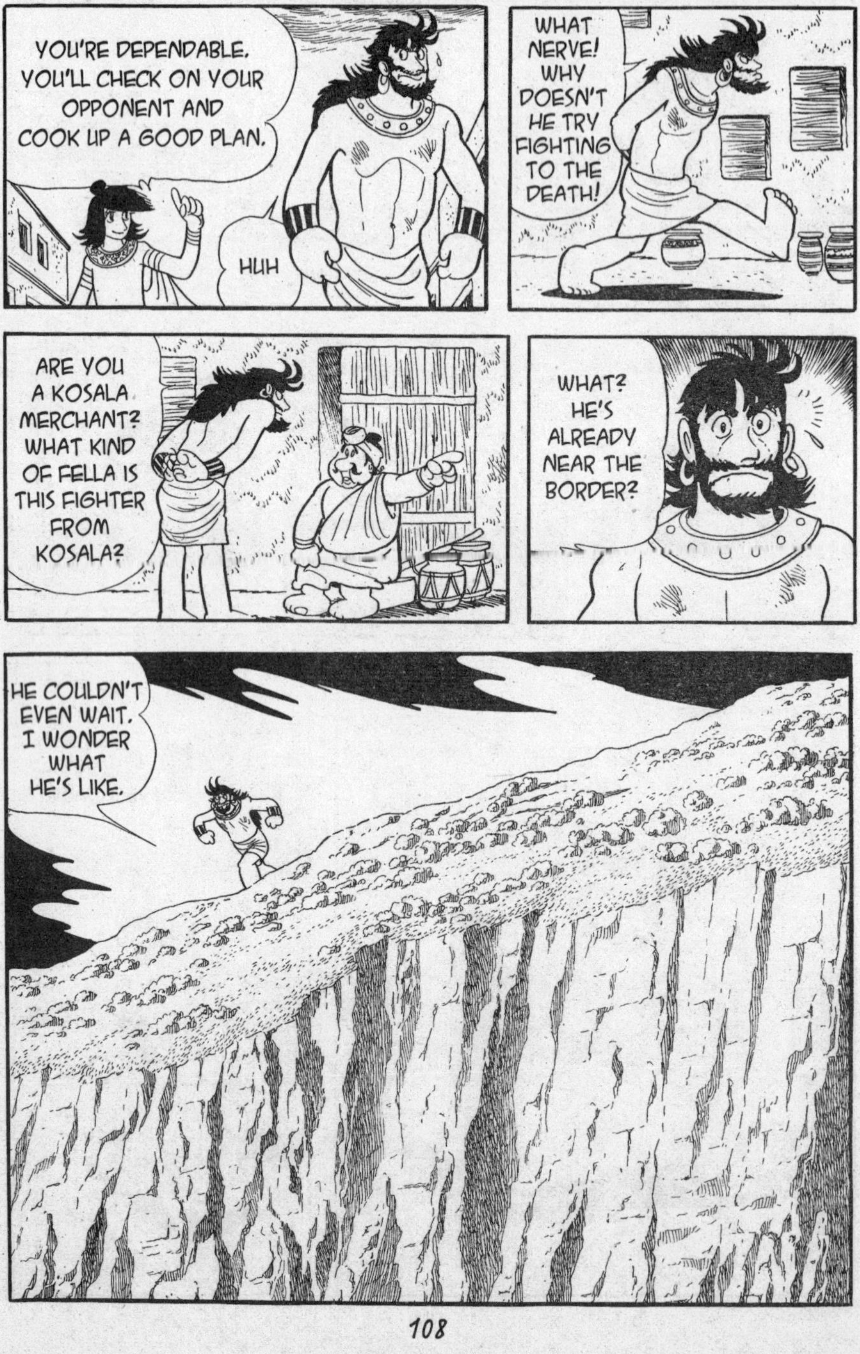
YOU'RE DEPENDABLE. YOU'LL CHECK ON YOUR OPPONENT AND COOK UP A GOOD PLAN.
HUH
WHAT NERVE! WHY DOESN'T HE TRY FIGHTING TO THE DEATH!
ARE YOU A KOSALA MERCHANT? WHAT KIND OF FELLA IS THIS FIGHTER FROM KOSALA?
WHAT? HE'S ALREADY NEAR THE BORDER?
HE COULDN'T EVEN WAIT. I WONDER WHAT HE'S LIKE.

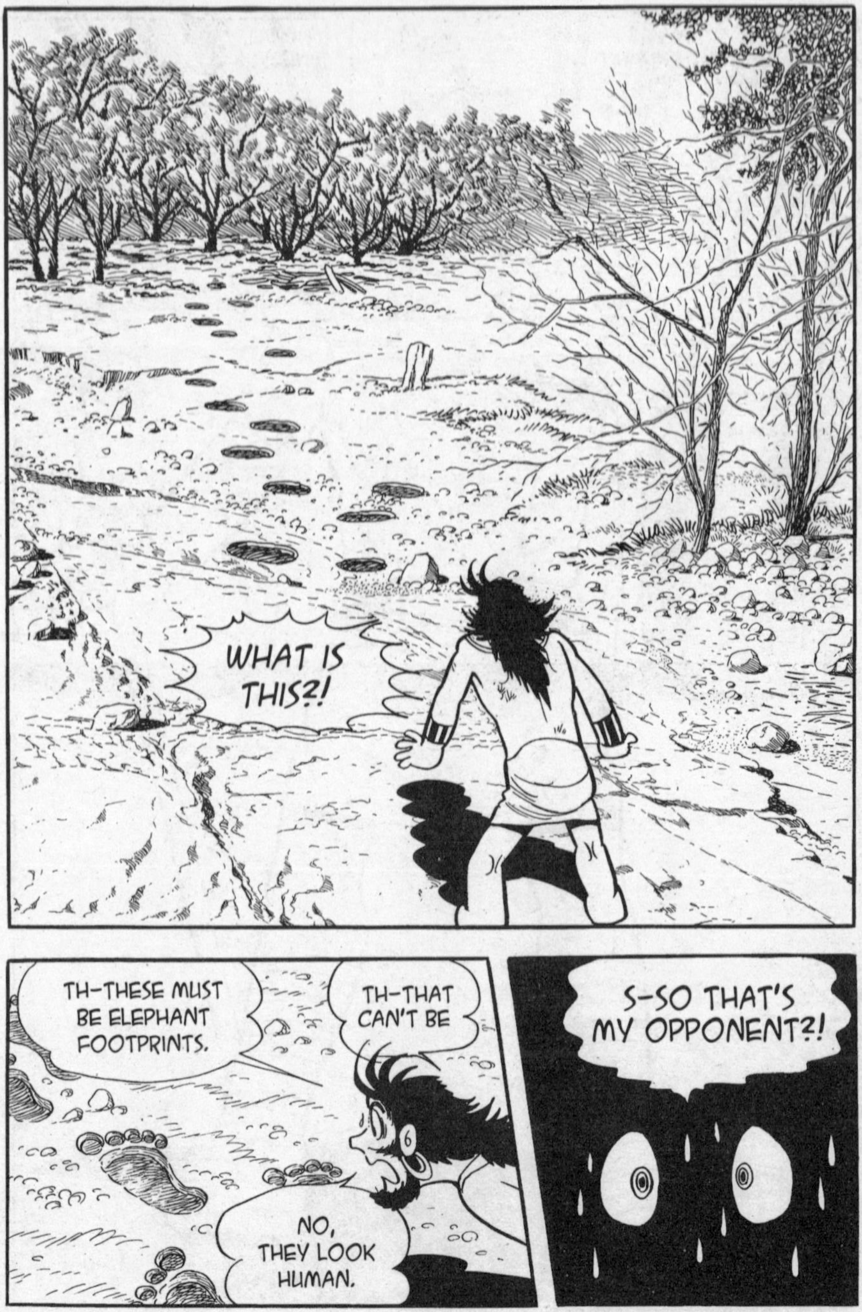
WHAT IS THIS?!
TH-THESE MUST BE ELEPHANT FOOTPRINTS.
TH-THAT CAN'T BE
NO, THEY LOOK HUMAN.
S-SO THAT'S MY OPPONENT?!

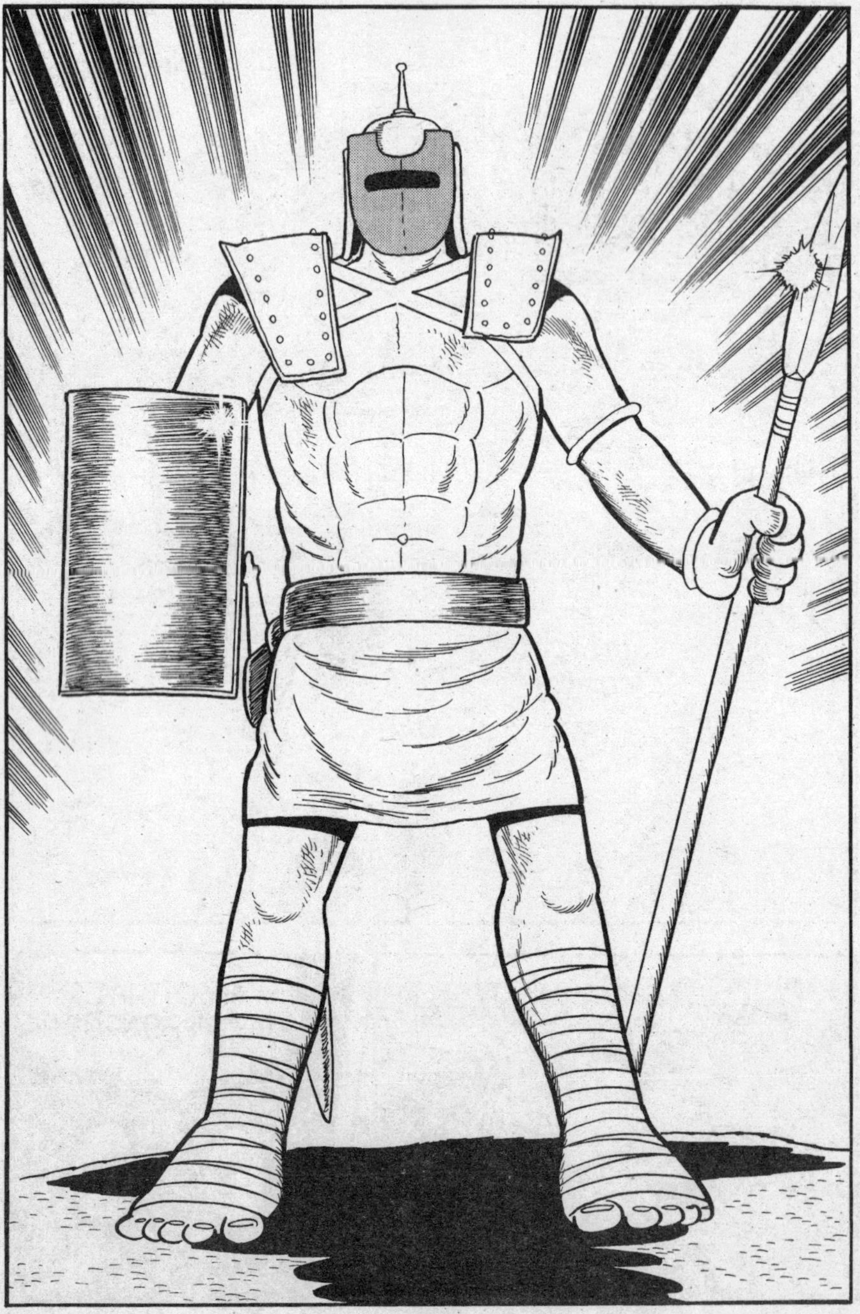

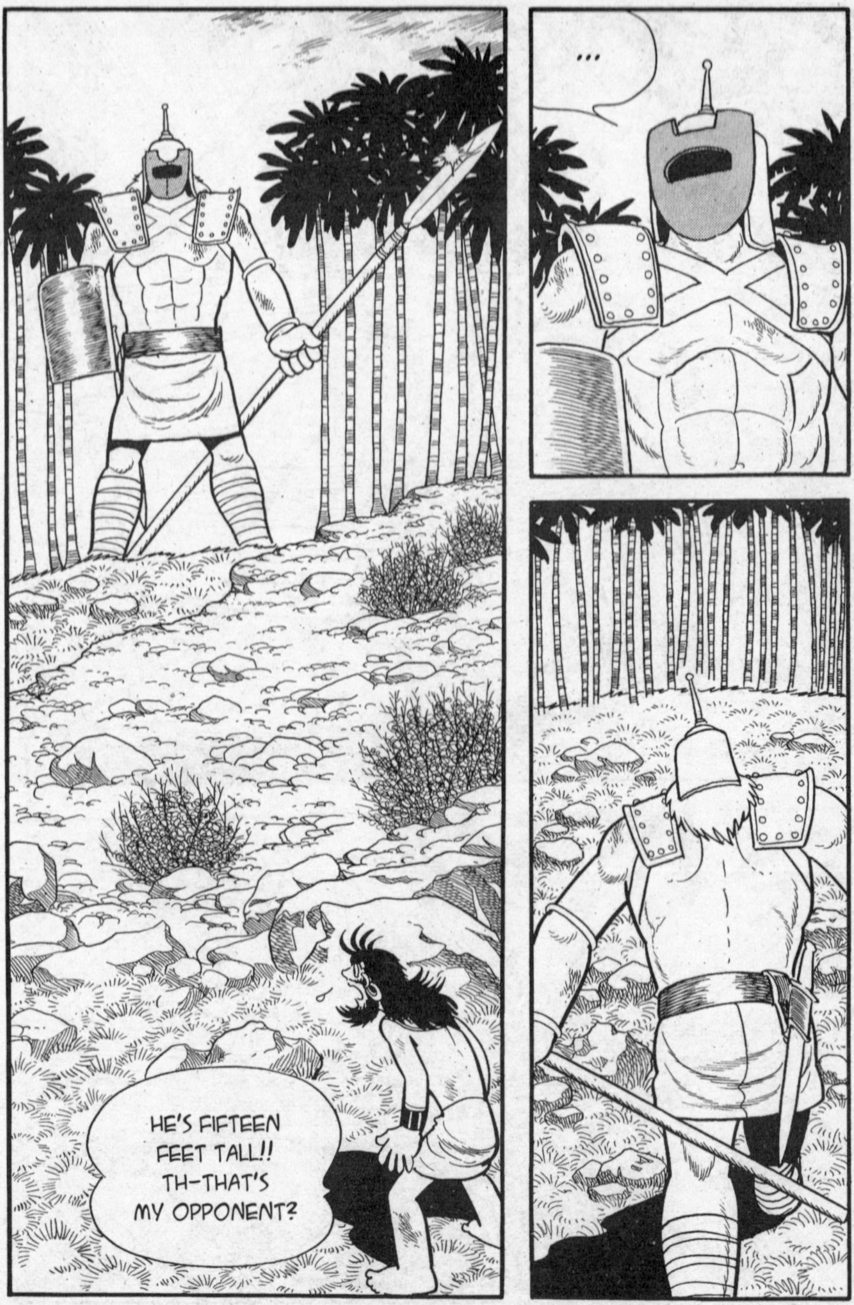
HE'S FIFTEEN FEET TALL!! TH-THAT'S MY OPPONENT?
...

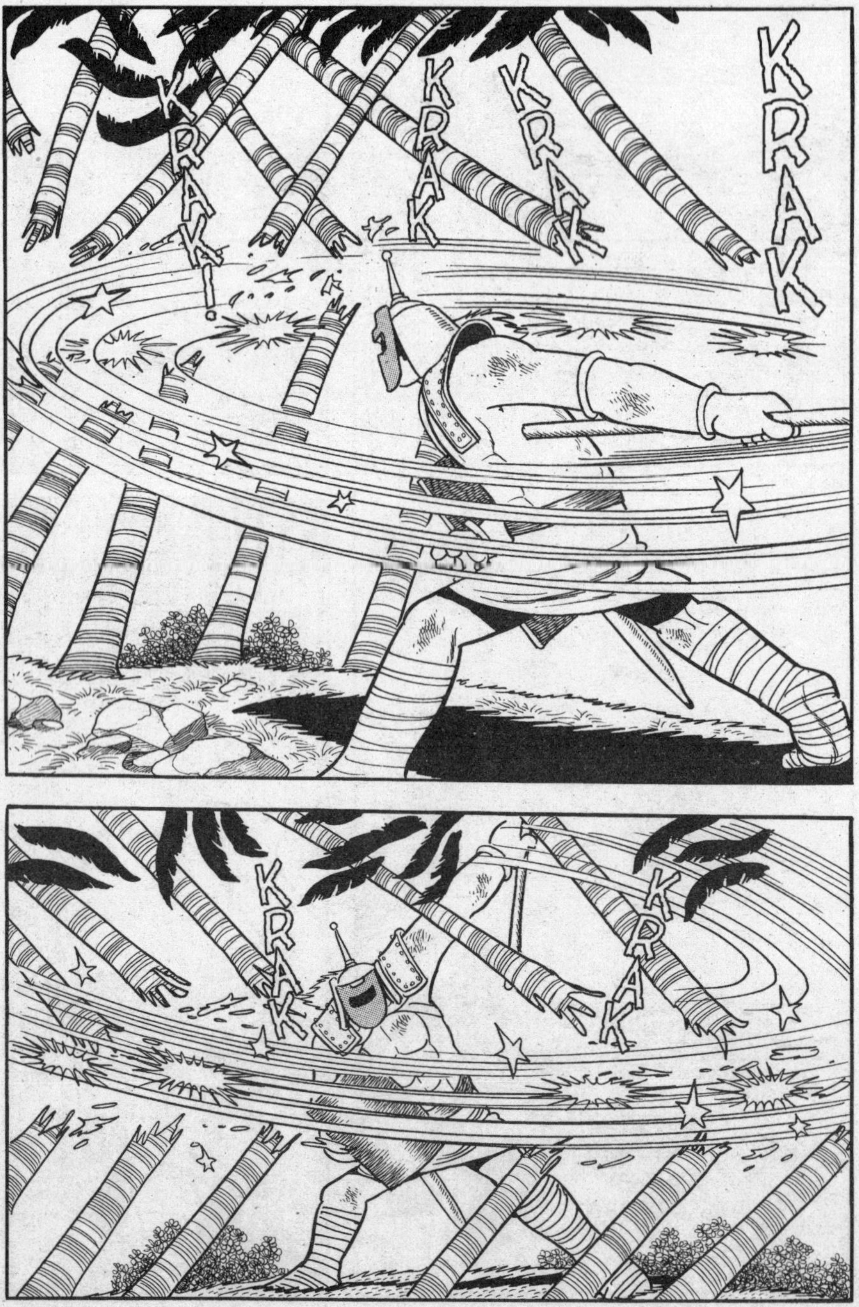
KRAK!
KRAK
KRAK
KRAK
KRAK
KRAK

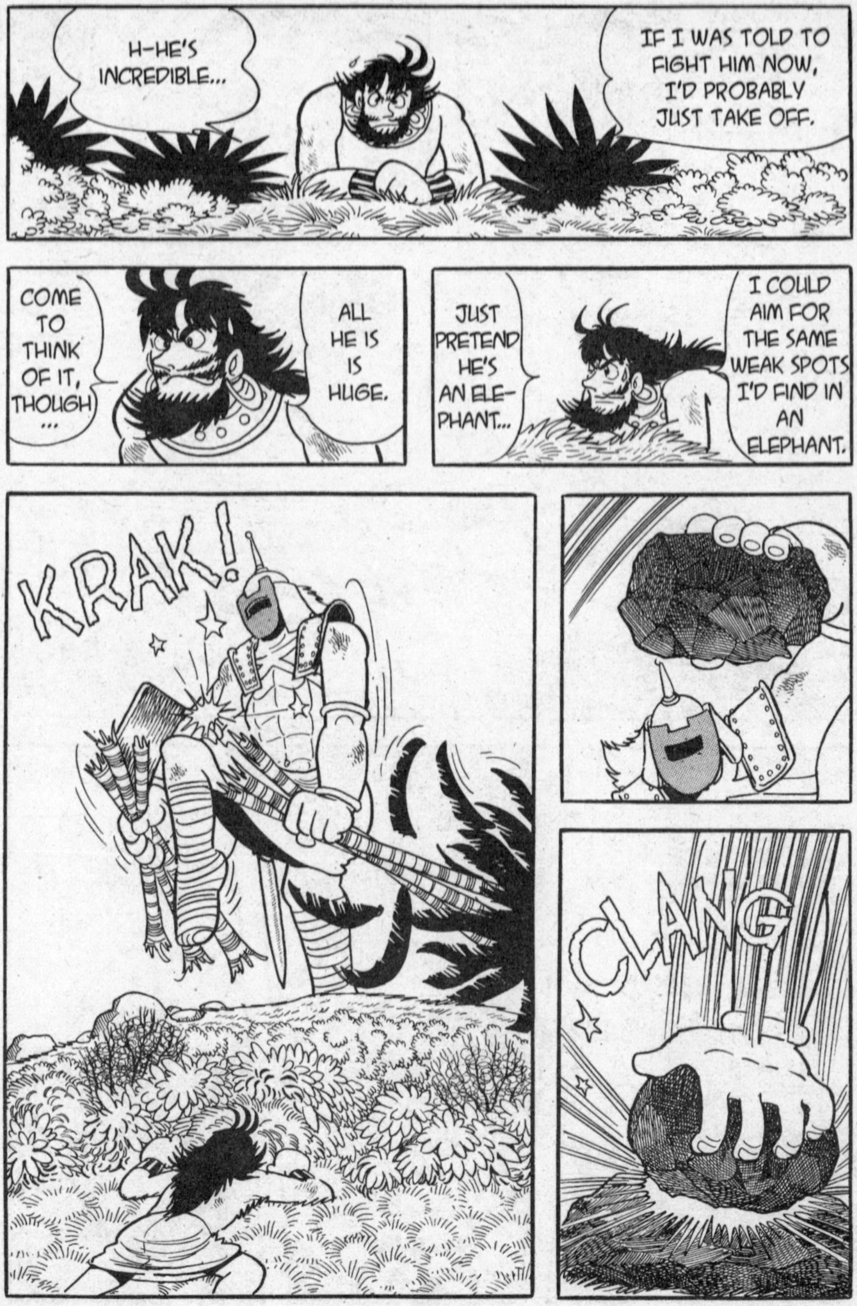
H-HE'S INCREDIBLE...
IF I WAS TOLD TO FIGHT HIM NOW, I'D PROBABLY JUST TAKE OFF.
COME TO THINK OF IT, THOUGH...
ALL HE IS IS HUGE.
JUST PRETEND HE'S AN ELEPHANT...
I COULD AIM FOR THE SAME WEAK SPOTS I'D FIND IN AN ELEPHANT.
KRAK!
CLANG

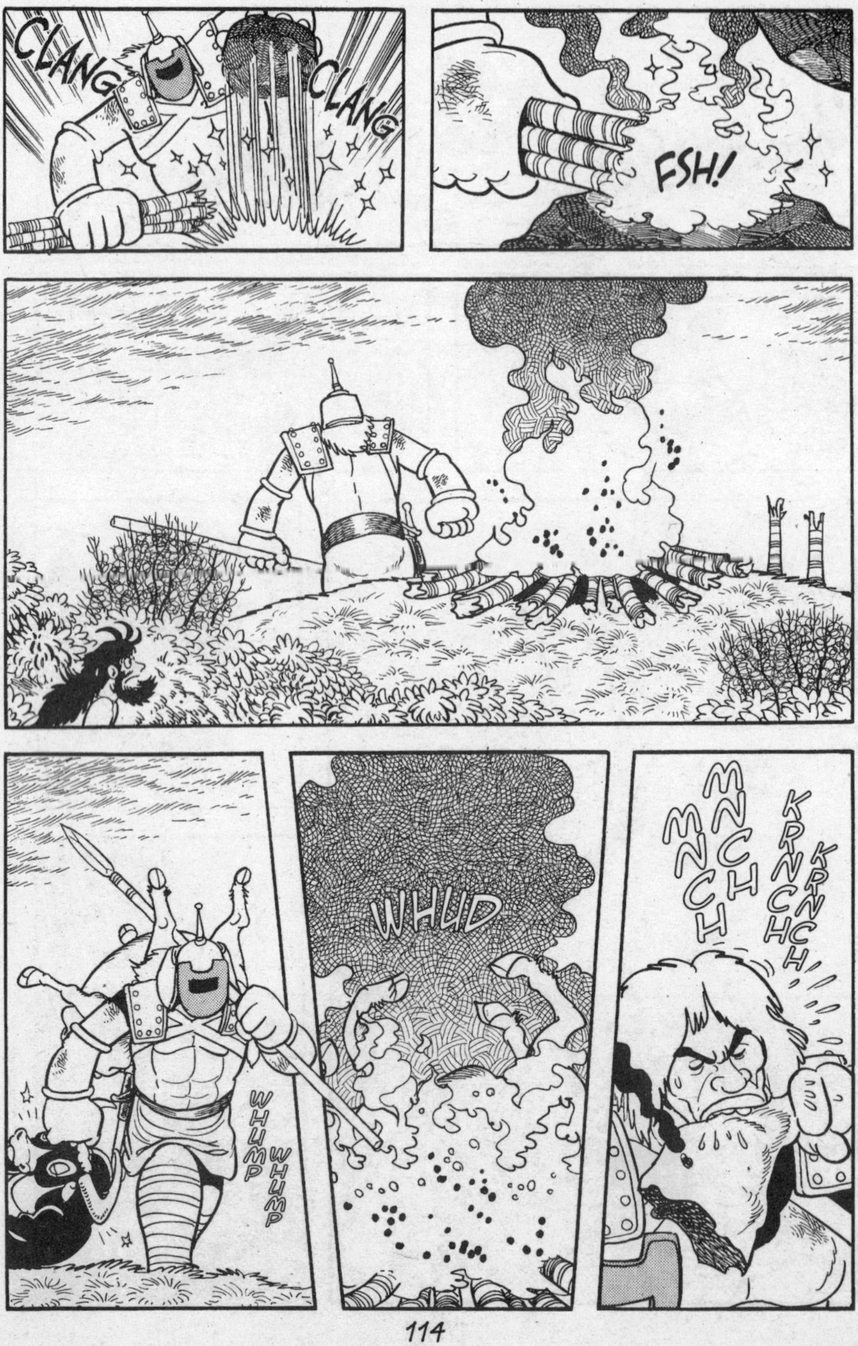
CLANG
CLANG
FSH!
WHUD
WHUMP
WHUMP
MNCH
MNCH
KRNCH
KRNCH

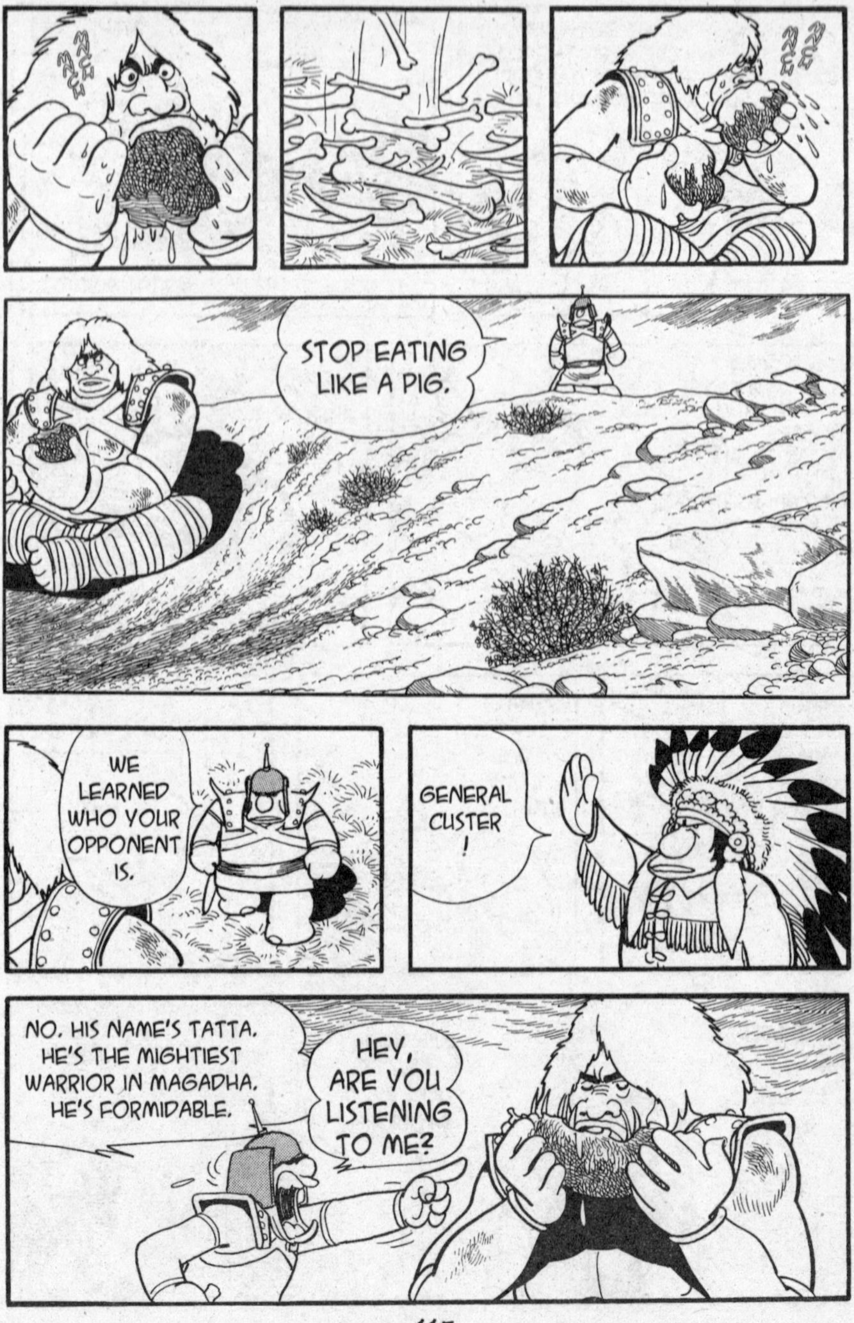
STOP EATING LIKE A PIG.
WE LEARNED WHO YOUR OPPONENT IS.
GENERAL CUSTER !
NO. HIS NAME'S TATTA. HE'S THE MIGHTIEST WARRIOR IN MAGADHA. HE'S FORMIDABLE.
HEY, ARE YOU LISTENING TO ME?

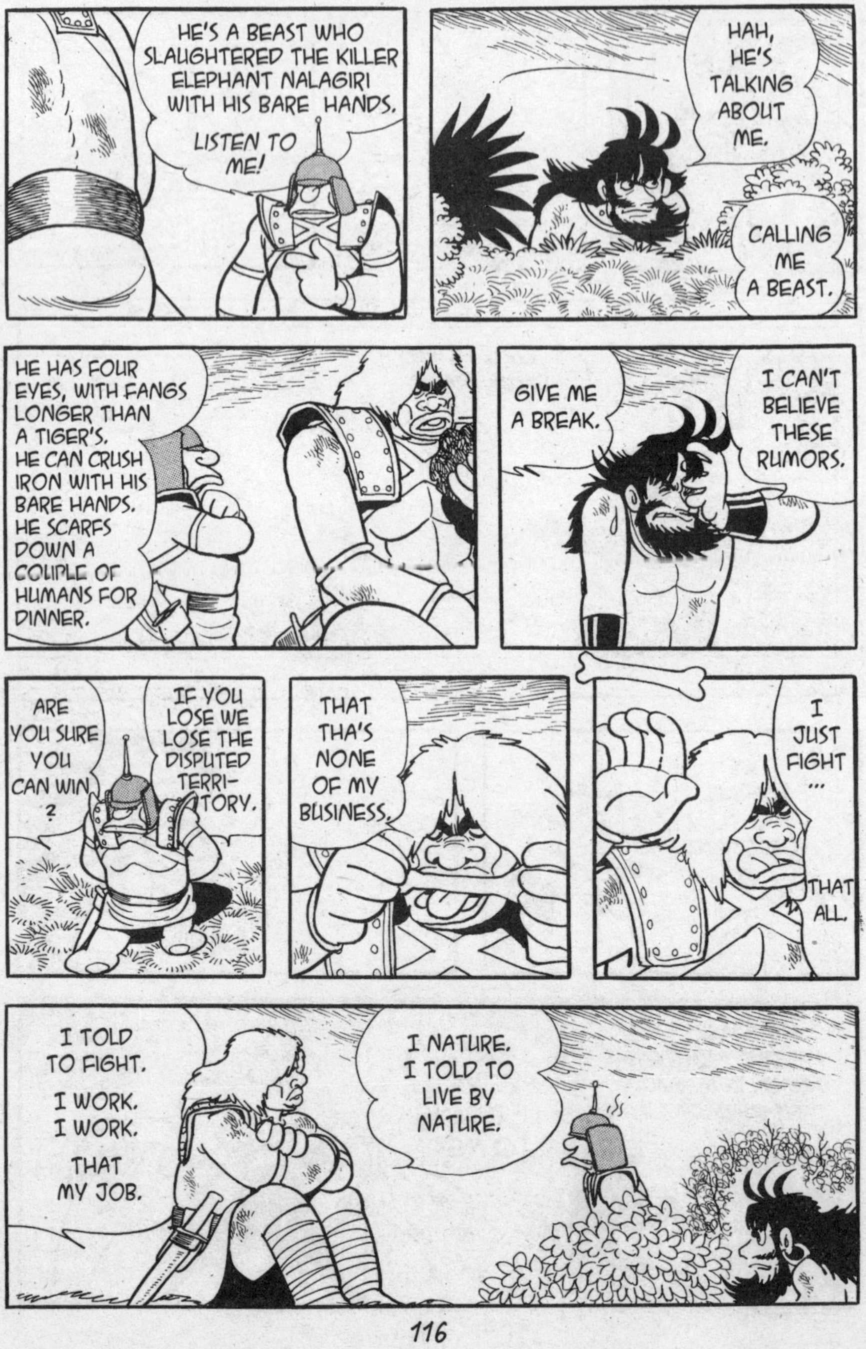

HE'S A BEAST WHO SLAUGHTERED THE KILLER ELEPHANT NALAGIRI WITH HIS BARE HANDS.
LISTEN TO ME!
HAH, HE'S TALKING ABOUT ME.
CALLING ME A BEAST.
HE HAS FOUR EYES, WITH FANGS LONGER THAN A TIGER'S. HE CAN CRUSH IRON WITH HIS BARE HANDS. HE SCARFS DOWN A COUPLE OF HUMANS FOR DINNER.
GIVE ME A BREAK.
I CAN'T BELIEVE THESE RUMORS.
ARE YOU SURE YOU CAN WIN ?
IF YOU LOSE WE LOSE THE DISPUTED TERRI-TORY.
THAT THA'S NONE OF MY BUSINESS.
I JUST FIGHT ...
THAT ALL.
I TOLD TO FIGHT.
I WORK. I WORK.
THAT MY JOB.
I NATURE. I TOLD TO LIVE BY NATURE.

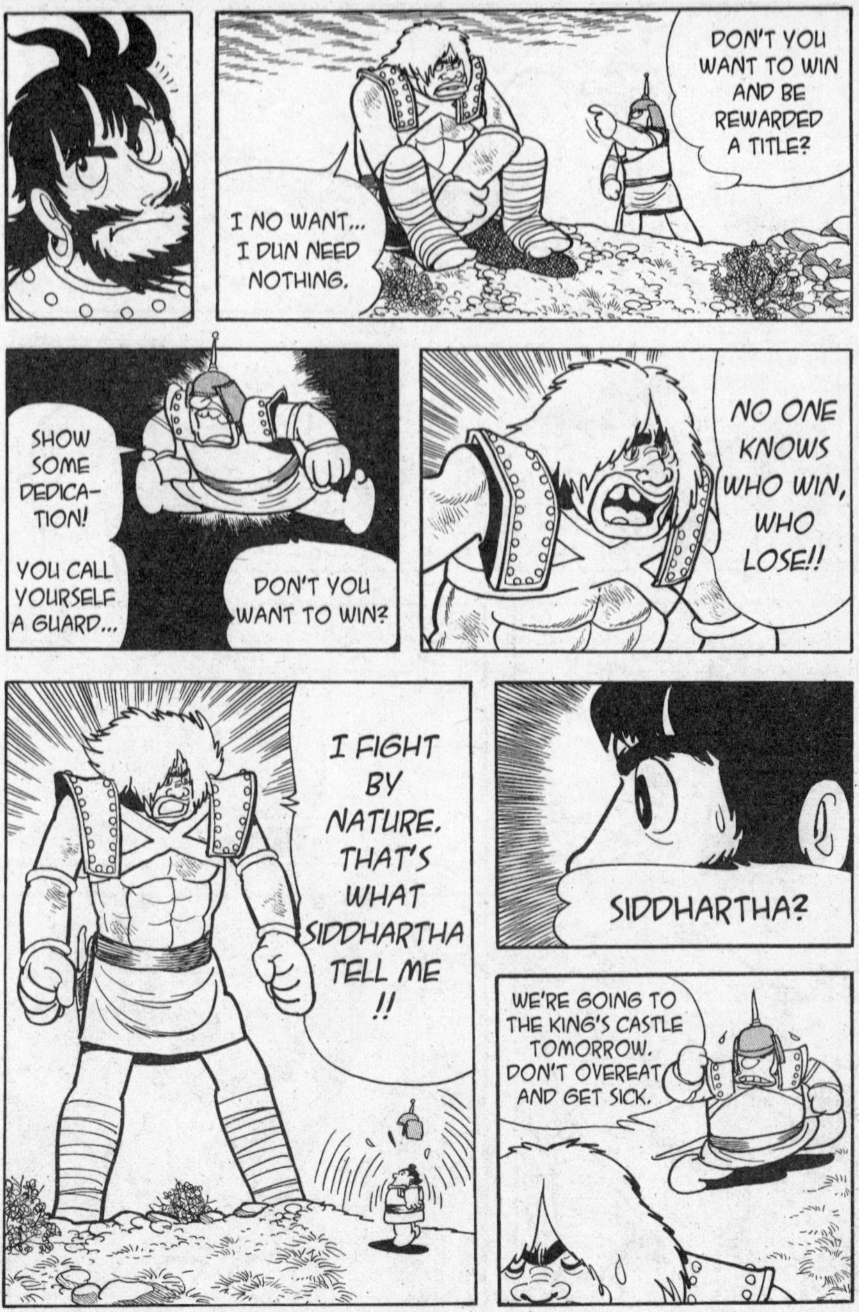
DON'T YOU WANT TO WIN AND BE REWARDED A TITLE?
I NO WANT... I DUN NEED NOTHING.
SHOW SOME DEDICA-TION!
YOU CALL YOURSELF A GUARD...
DON'T YOU WANT TO WIN?
NO ONE KNOWS WHO WIN, WHO LOSE!!
I FIGHT BY NATURE. THAT'S WHAT SIDDHARTHA TELL ME !!
SIDDHARTHA?
WE'RE GOING TO THE KING'S CASTLE TOMORROW. DON'T OVEREAT AND GET SICK.

HEY, GIANT!

YOU JUST MENTIONED SIDDHAR-THA.

I HEARD YOU FROM THE BUSHES.

YOU MEAN THE SAMANNA, SIDDHAR-THA?

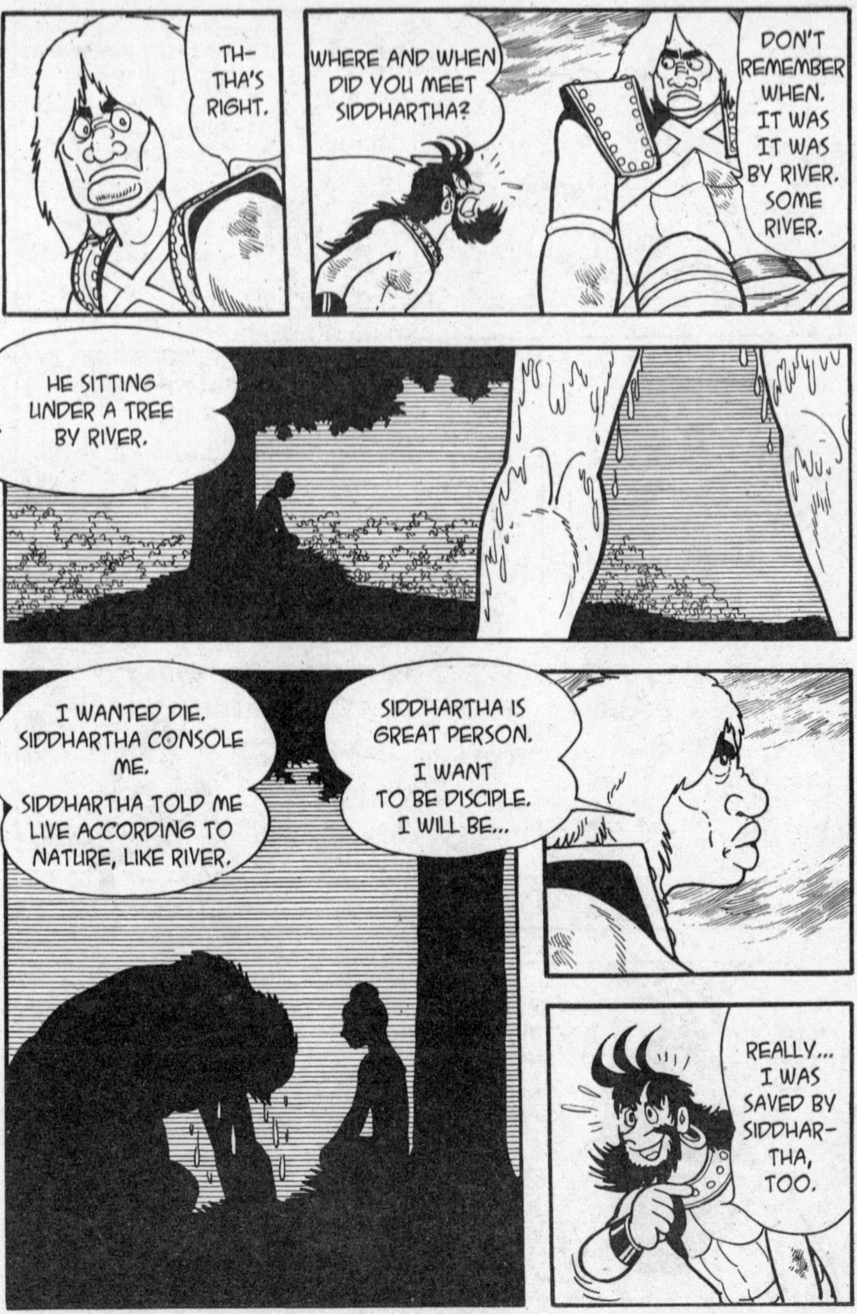
TH-
THA'S
RIGHT.
WHERE AND WHEN DID YOU MEET SIDDHARTHA?
DON'T REMEMBER WHEN. IT WAS IT WAS BY RIVER. SOME RIVER.
HE SITTING UNDER A TREE BY RIVER.
I WANTED DIE. SIDDHARTHA CONSOLE ME.
SIDDHARTHA TOLD ME LIVE ACCORDING TO NATURE, LIKE RIVER.
SIDDHARTHA IS GREAT PERSON.
I WANT TO BE DISCIPLE. I WILL BE...
REALLY... I WAS SAVED BY SIDDHAR-THA, TOO.

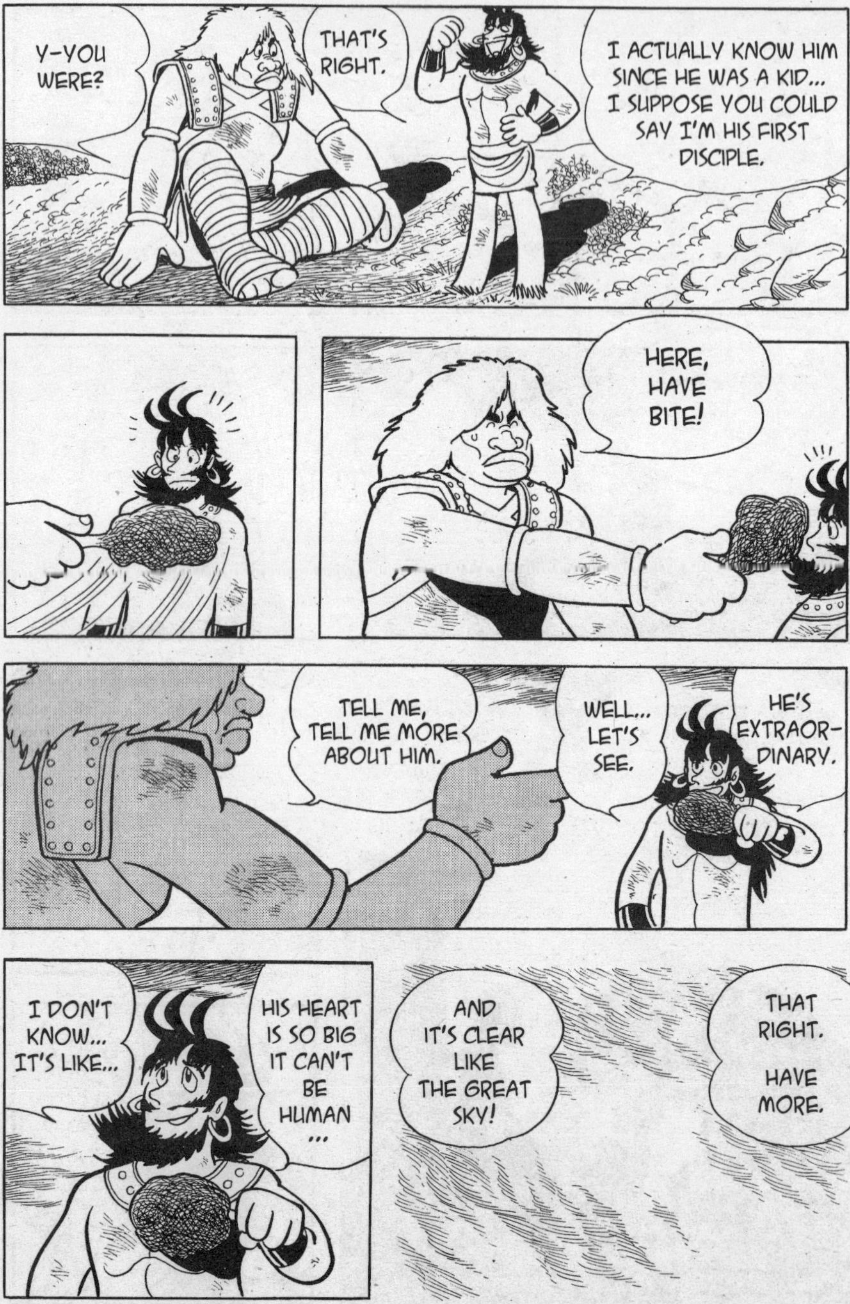
Y-YOU WERE?
THAT'S RIGHT.
I ACTUALLY KNOW HIM SINCE HE WAS A KID... I SUPPOSE YOU COULD SAY I'M HIS FIRST DISCIPLE.
HERE, HAVE BITE!
TELL ME, TELL ME MORE ABOUT HIM.
WELL... LET'S SEE.
HE'S EXTRAOR-DINARY.
I DON'T KNOW... IT'S LIKE...
HIS HEART IS SO BIG IT CAN'T BE HUMAN ...
AND IT'S CLEAR LIKE THE GREAT SKY!
THAT RIGHT. HAVE MORE.

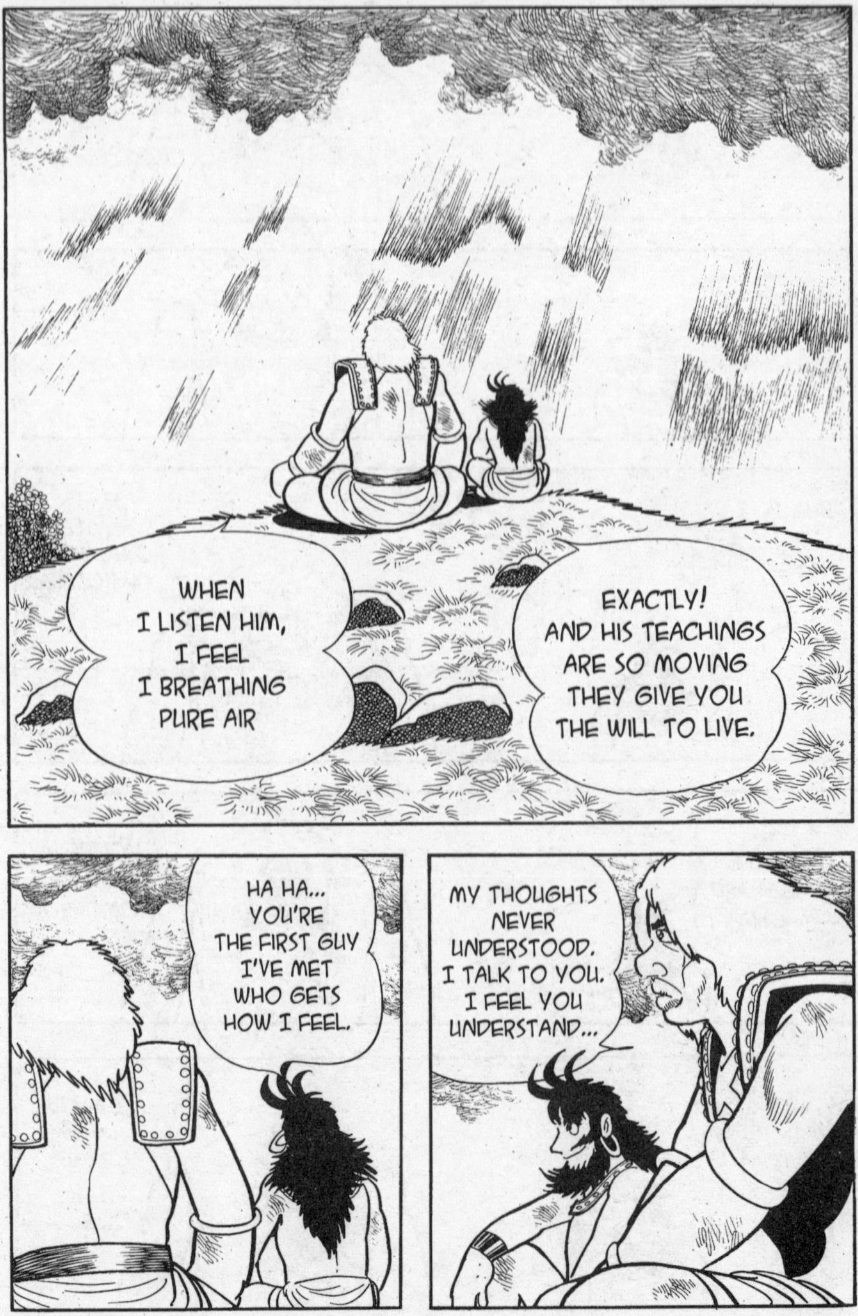
WHEN I LISTEN HIM, I FEEL I BREATHING PURE AIR
EXACTLY! AND HIS TEACHINGS ARE SO MOVING THEY GIVE YOU THE WILL TO LIVE.
HA HA... YOU'RE THE FIRST GUY I'VE MET WHO GETS HOW I FEEL.
MY THOUGHTS NEVER UNDERSTOOD. I TALK TO YOU. I FEEL YOU UNDERSTAND...

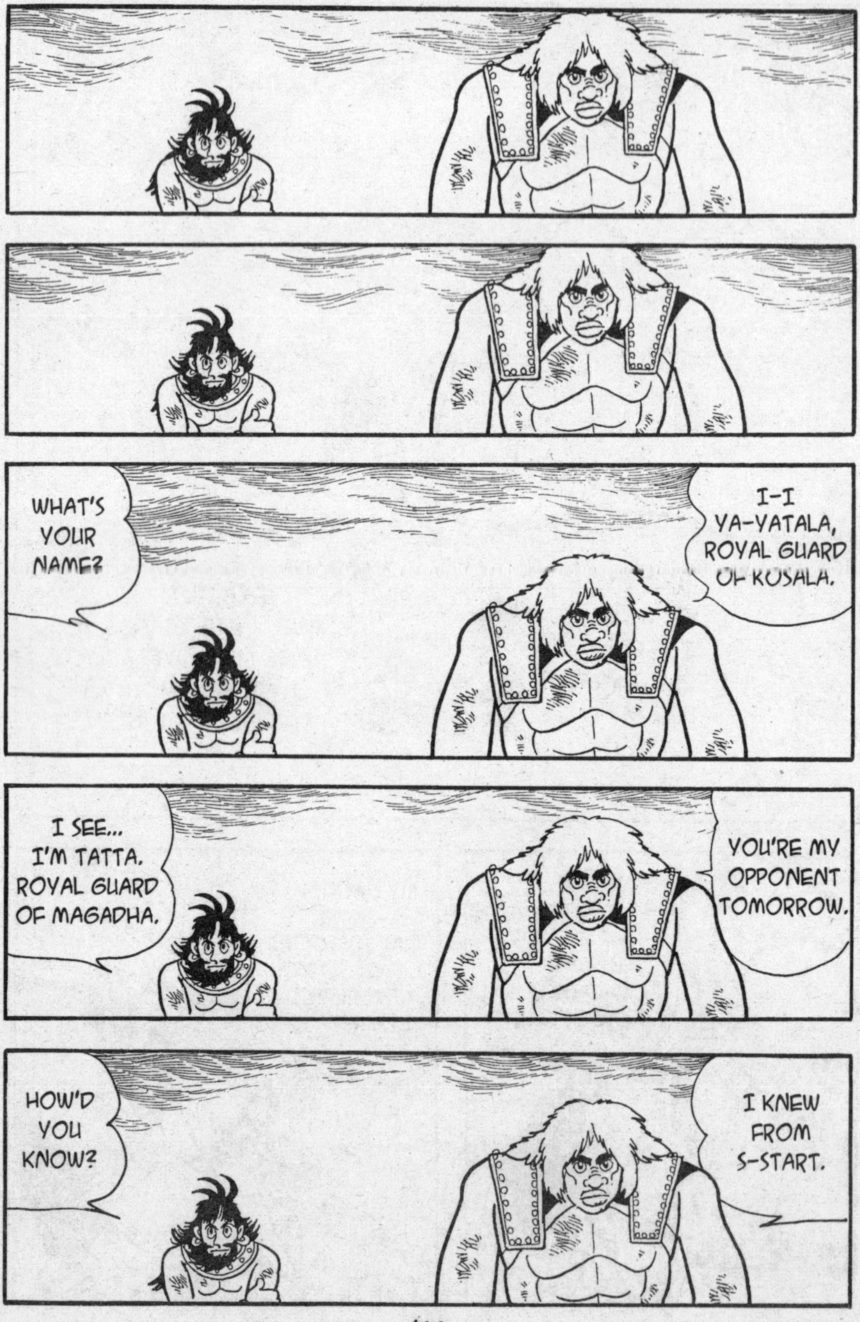
WHAT'S YOUR NAME?
I-I YA-YATALA, ROYAL GUARD OF KOSALA.
I SEE... I'M TATTA. ROYAL GUARD OF MAGADHA.
YOU'RE MY OPPONENT TOMORROW.
HOW'D YOU KNOW?
I KNEW FROM S-START.

COMMANDER SAY YOU HAVE FOUR EYES, TIGER FANGS...
HA HA... GIVE ME A BREAK.
I-I GLAD. I DON'T WANT TO FIGHT NO DEMON.
WHAT A TWIST OF FATE...WE'RE BOTH DISCIPLES OF SIDDHARTHA WHO CAN RELATE TO EACH OTHER...
...BUT ONE OF US HAS TO DIE TOMORROW ...
TH-THAT IS HOW IS... I FOLLOW WAY OF THINGS...
NO HARD FEELINGS ...
I'LL SEE YOU TOMORROW AT THE CASTLE.

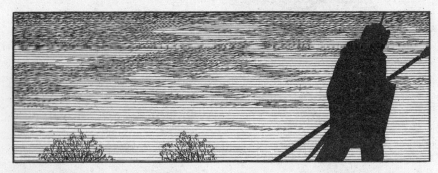

YOU'RE SO QUIET...

...

124

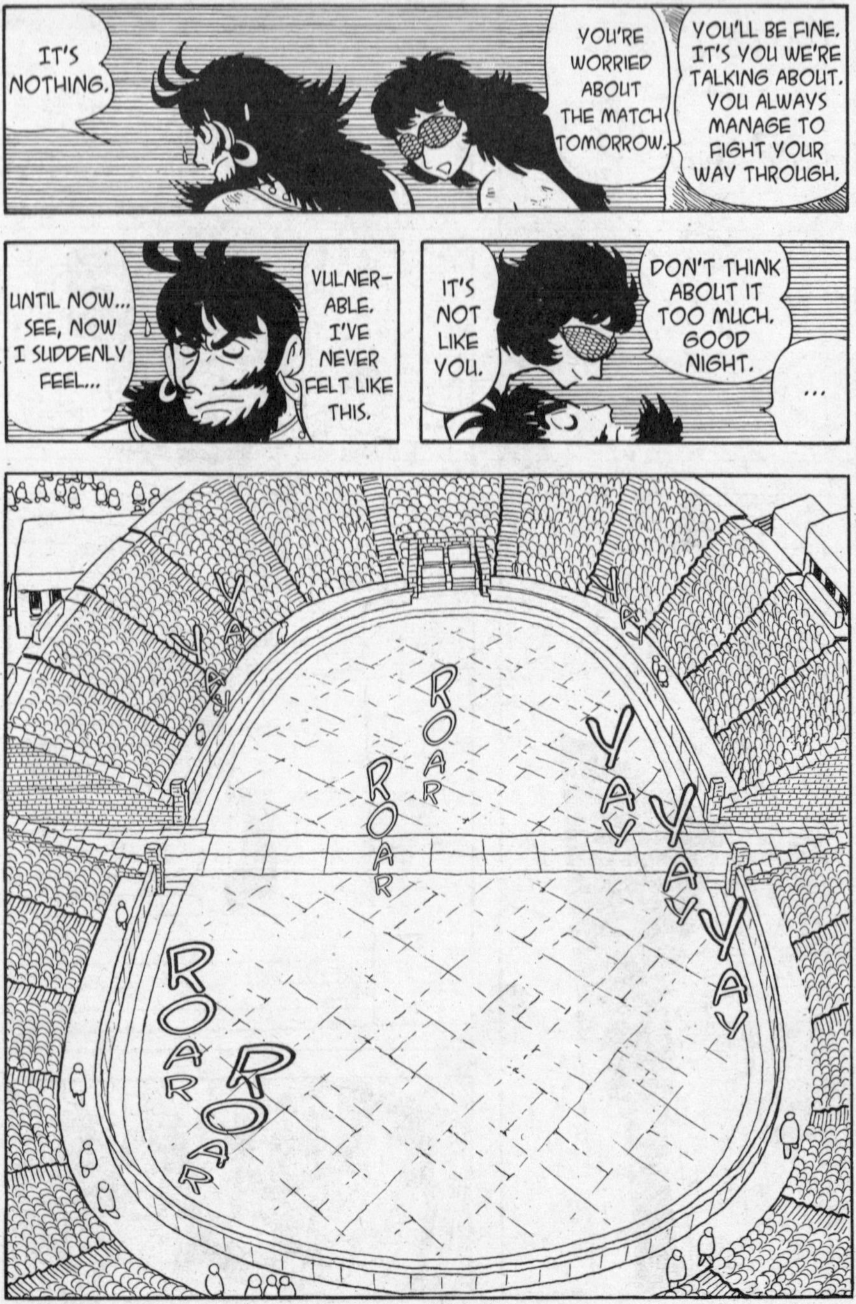
IT'S NOTHING.
YOU'RE WORRIED ABOUT THE MATCH TOMORROW.
YOU'LL BE FINE. IT'S YOU WE'RE TALKING ABOUT. YOU ALWAYS MANAGE TO FIGHT YOUR WAY THROUGH.
UNTIL NOW... SEE, NOW I SUDDENLY FEEL...
VULNERABLE. I'VE NEVER FELT LIKE THIS.
IT'S NOT LIKE YOU.
DON'T THINK ABOUT IT TOO MUCH. GOOD NIGHT.
...
YAY
ROAR
ROAR
YAY YAY YAY
ROAR ROAR ROAR
YAY YAY YAY

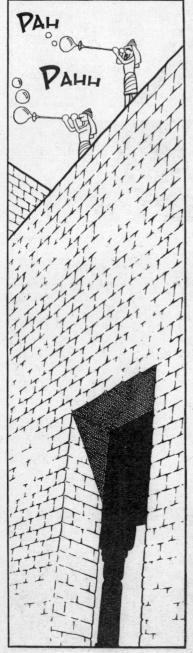

PAH

PAHH

LADIES AND GENTLEMEN, THE KING AND QUEEN.

126

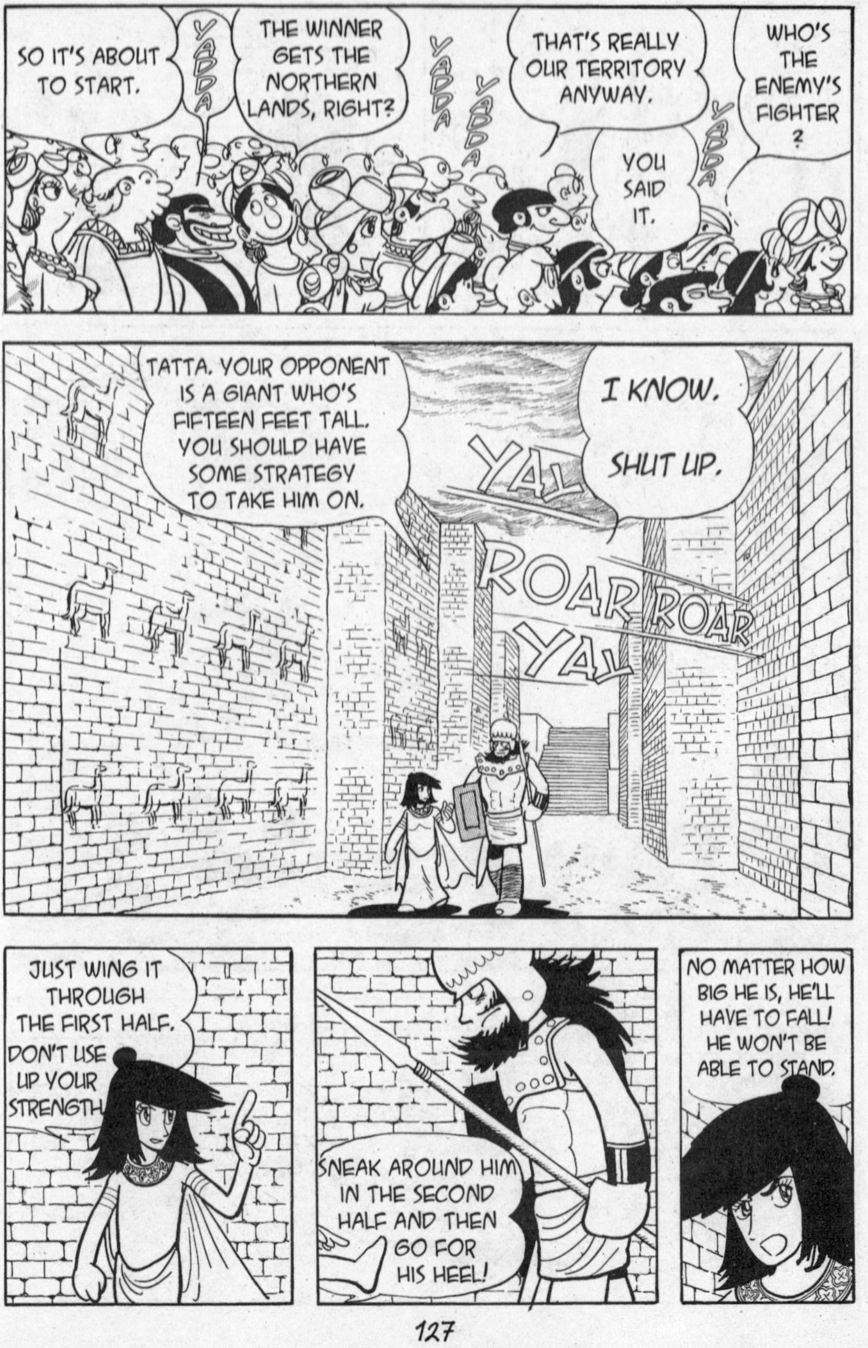

SO IT'S ABOUT TO START.
YADDA
THE WINNER GETS THE NORTHERN LANDS, RIGHT?
YADDA
YADDA
THAT'S REALLY OUR TERRITORY ANYWAY.
YOU SAID IT.
YADDA
WHO'S THE ENEMY'S FIGHTER ?
TATTA. YOUR OPPONENT IS A GIANT WHO'S FIFTEEN FEET TALL. YOU SHOULD HAVE SOME STRATEGY TO TAKE HIM ON.
I KNOW.
SHUT UP.
YAL
ROAR
ROAR
YAL
JUST WING IT THROUGH THE FIRST HALF.
DON'T USE UP YOUR STRENGTH.
SNEAK AROUND HIM IN THE SECOND HALF AND THEN GO FOR HIS HEEL!
NO MATTER HOW BIG HE IS, HE'LL HAVE TO FALL! HE WON'T BE ABLE TO STAND.

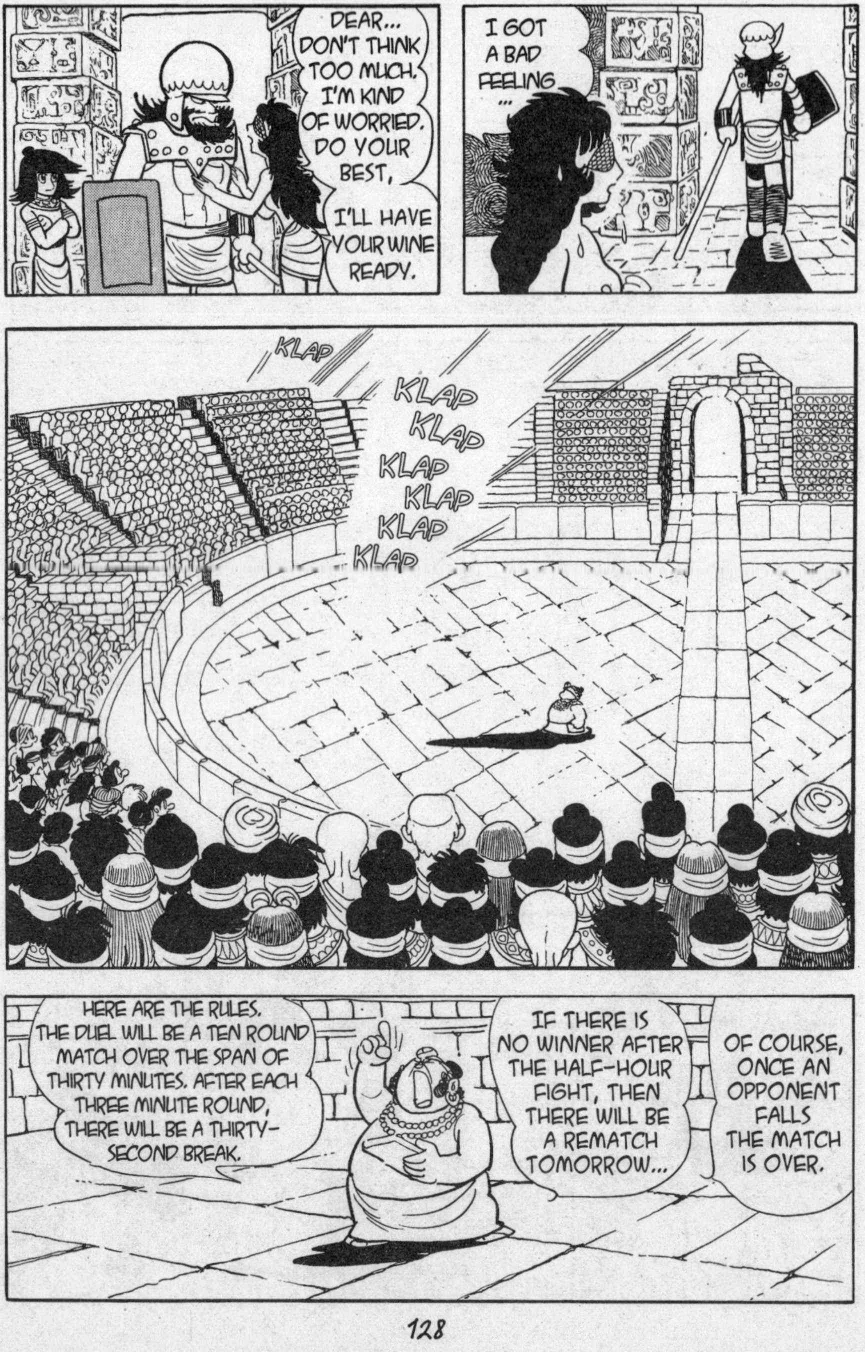
DEAR... DON'T THINK TOO MUCH. I'M KIND OF WORRIED. DO YOUR BEST,
I'LL HAVE YOUR WINE READY.
I GOT A BAD FEELING ...
KLAP
KLAP KLAP KLAP KLAP KLAP KLAP
HERE ARE THE RULES. THE DUEL WILL BE A TEN ROUND MATCH OVER THE SPAN OF THIRTY MINUTES. AFTER EACH THREE MINUTE ROUND, THERE WILL BE A THIRTY-SECOND BREAK.
IF THERE IS NO WINNER AFTER THE HALF-HOUR FIGHT, THEN THERE WILL BE A REMATCH TOMORROW...
OF COURSE, ONCE AN OPPONENT FALLS THE MATCH IS OVER.

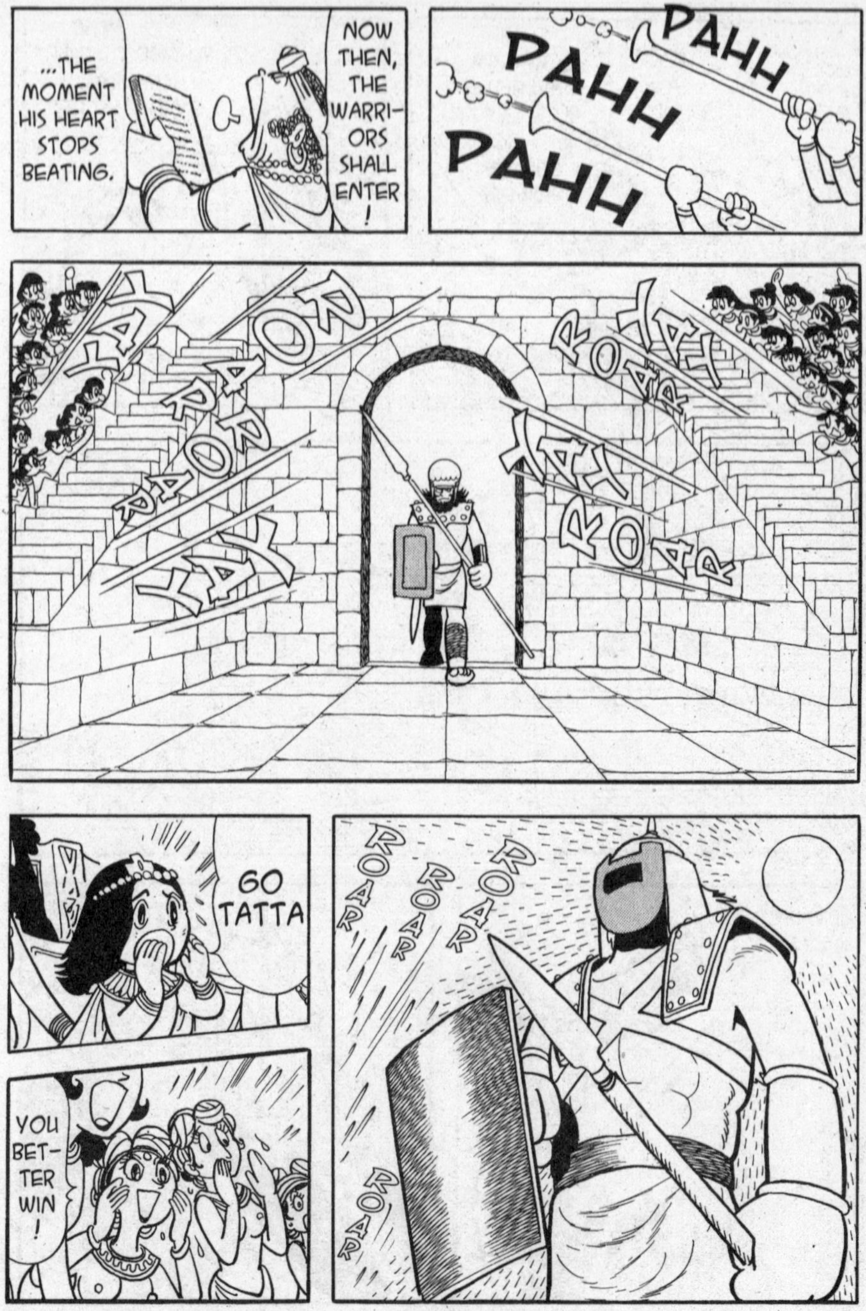
NOW THEN, THE WARRIORS SHALL ENTER!
...THE MOMENT HIS HEART STOPS BEATING.
PAHH
PAHH
PAHH
PAHH
YAY
ROAR
YAY
ROAR
ROAR
YAY
YAY
ROAR
GO TATTA
YOU BETTER WIN!
ROAR
ROAR
ROAR
ROAR
ROAR

THIS IS NO GOOD.

HE'S A GIANT.

IS HE STUFFED? MAYBE THEY BLEW HIM UP WITH SOME BAKING POWDER.

A SINGLE BLOW WILL FINISH TATTA.

YOU MUST PLEDGE TO FIGHT HONORABLY BY THE SACRED ALTAR!

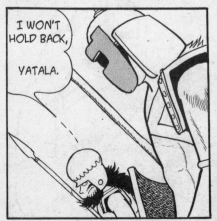

I WON'T HOLD BACK, YATALA.

VERY WELL THEN, COMMENCE.

CHAPTER THREE

SHOWDOWN

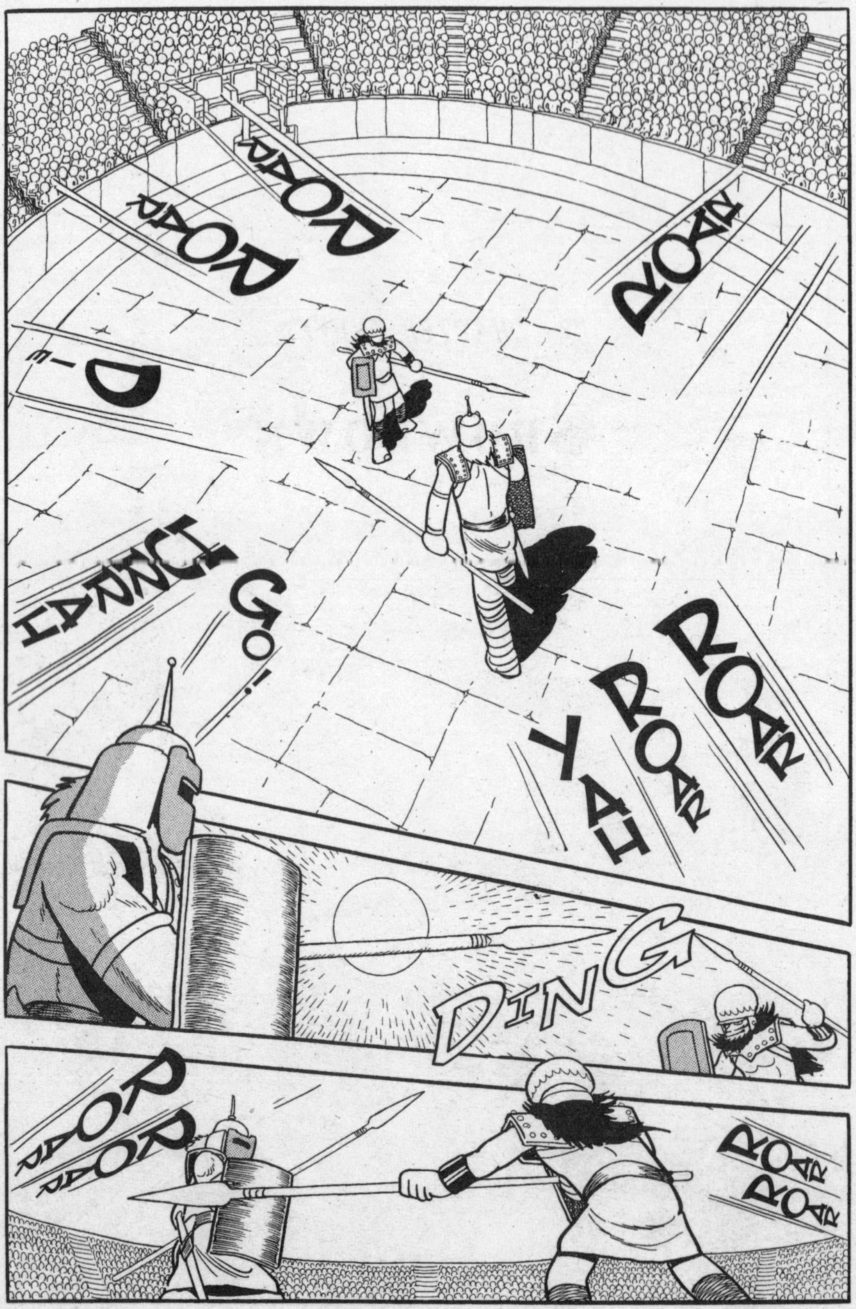
ROAR ROAR
ROAR
GO!
ROAR ROAR YAH
DING
ROAR ROAR
ROAR ROAR

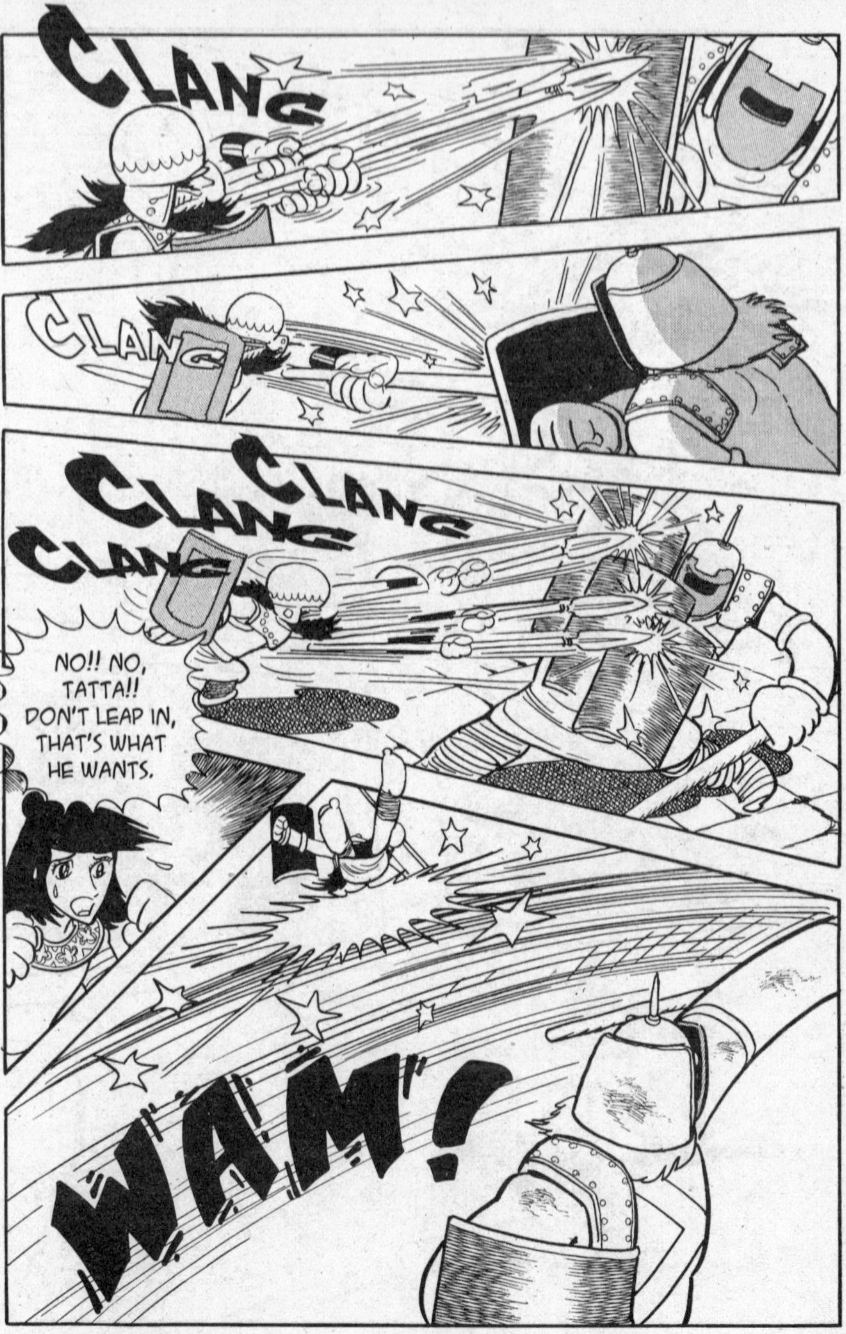
CLANG
CLANG
CLANG
CLANG
CLANG
NO!! NO, TATTA!! DON'T LEAP IN, THAT'S WHAT HE WANTS.
WAM!

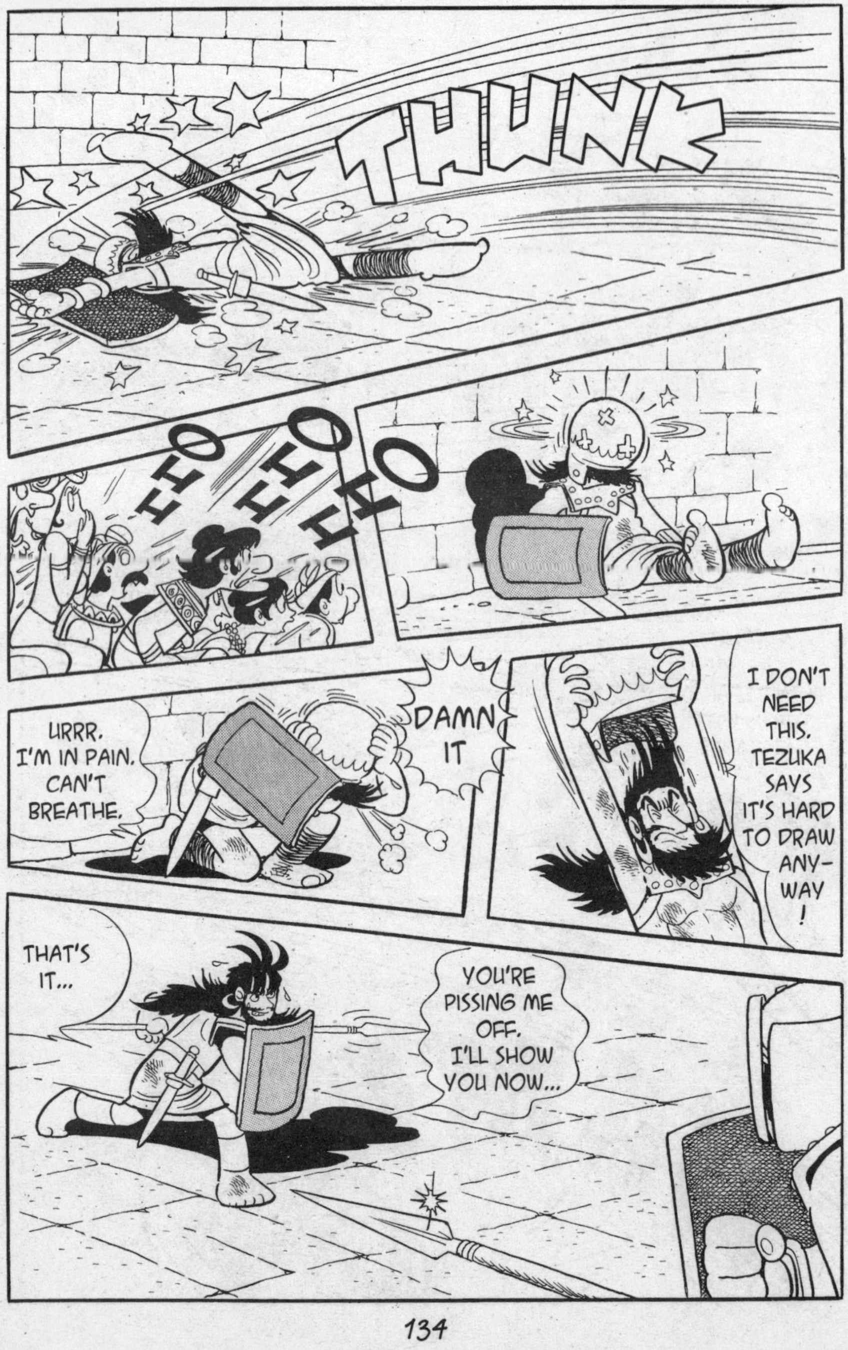
THUNK
URRR. I'M IN PAIN. CAN'T BREATHE.
DAMN IT
I DON'T NEED THIS. TEZUKA SAYS IT'S HARD TO DRAW ANYWAY!
THAT'S IT...
YOU'RE PISSING ME OFF. I'LL SHOW YOU NOW...

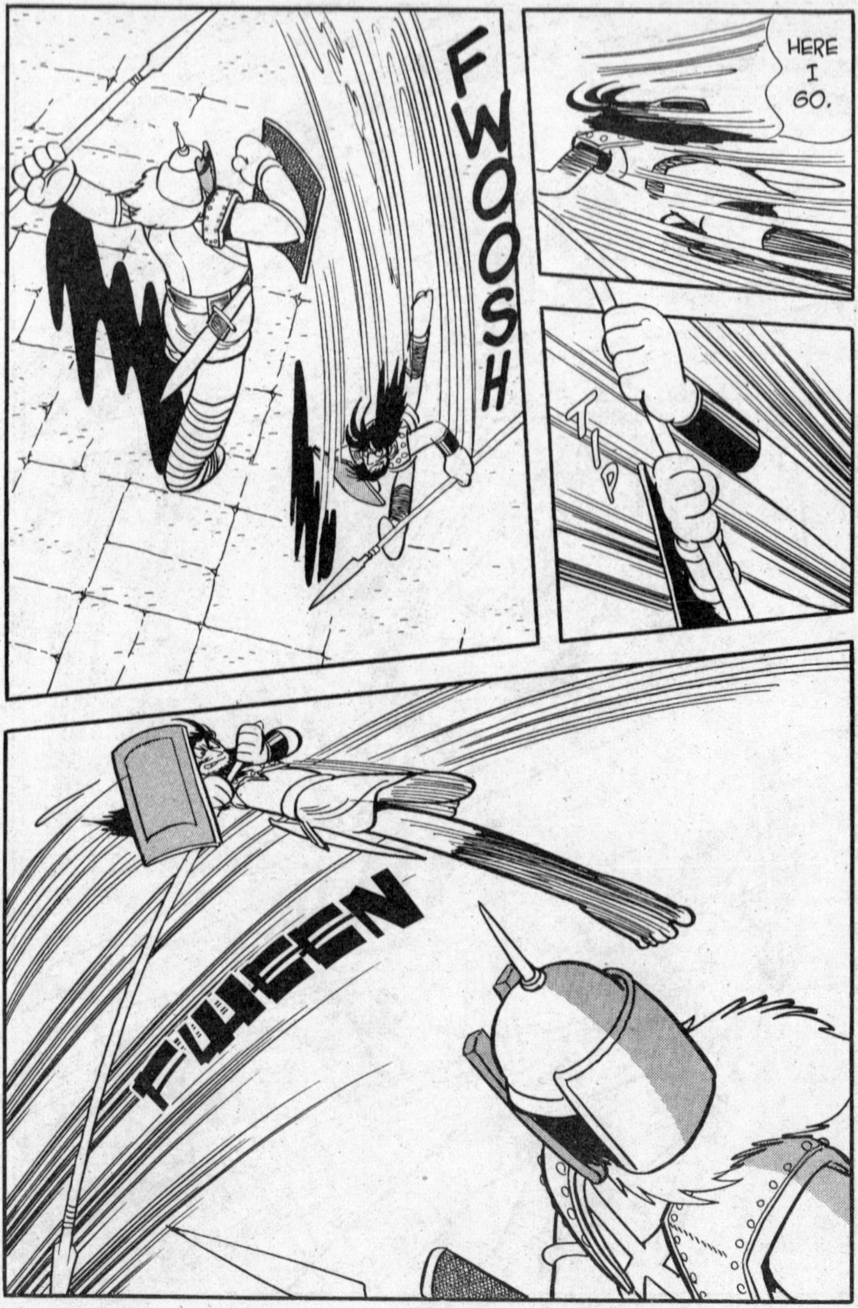
FWOOSH
HERE I GO.
TIP
FWEEN

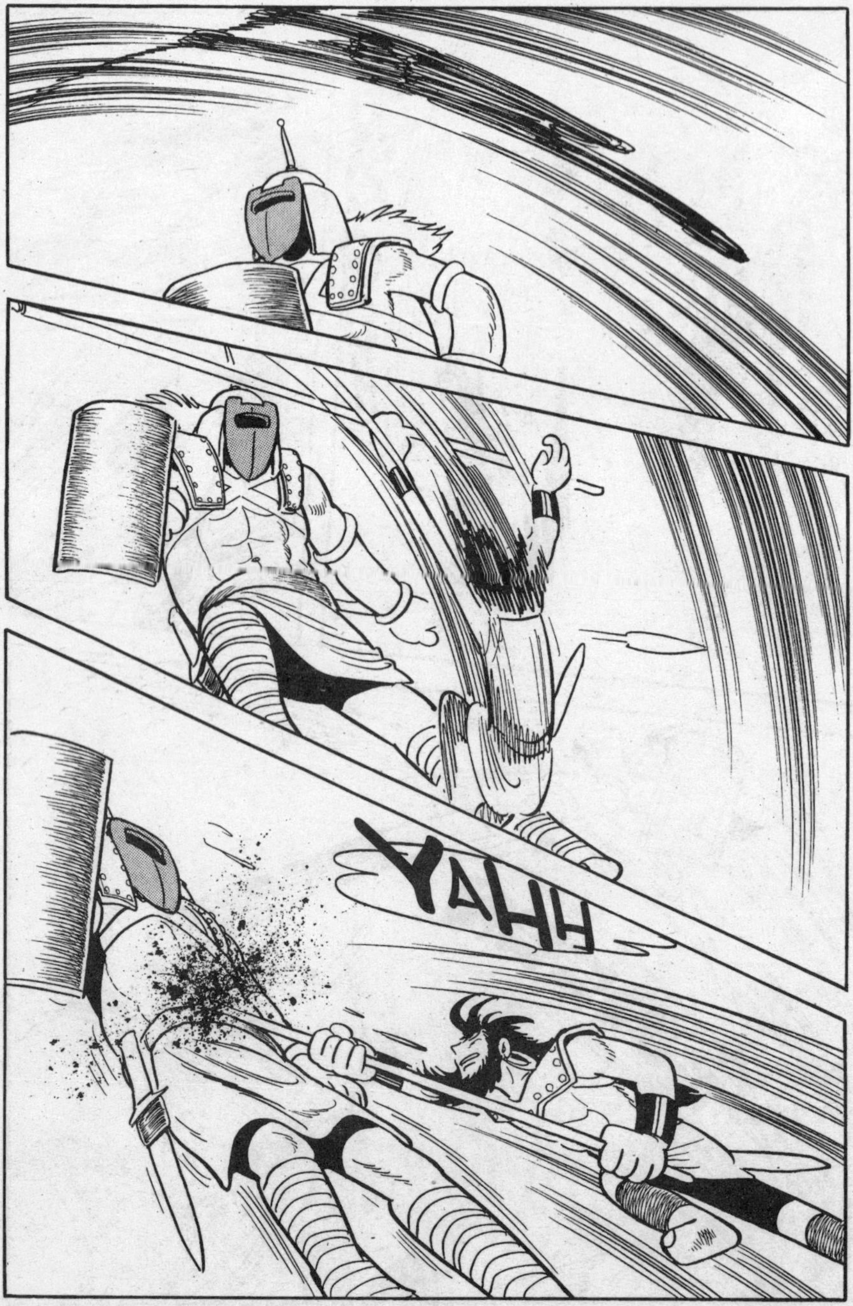
YAHH

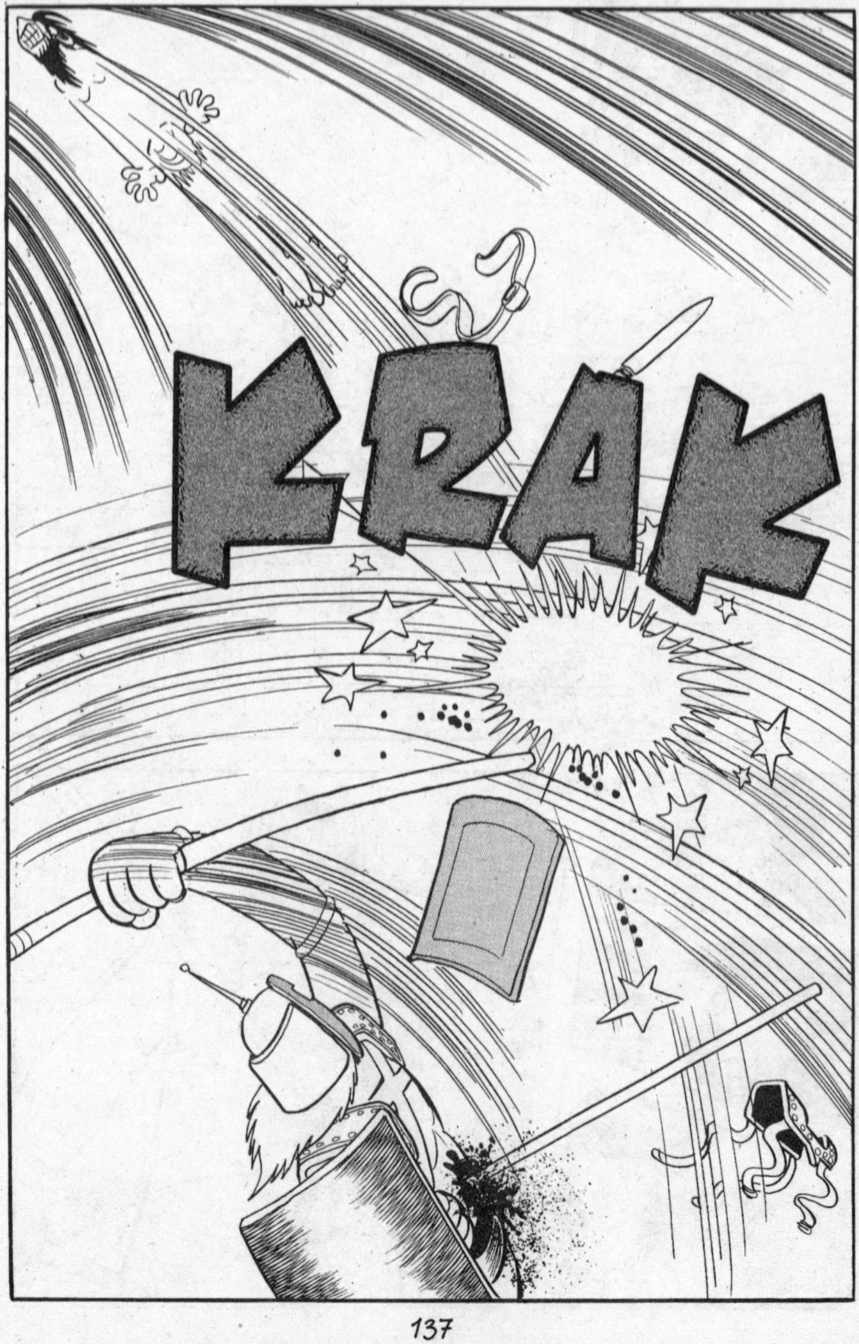
KRAK

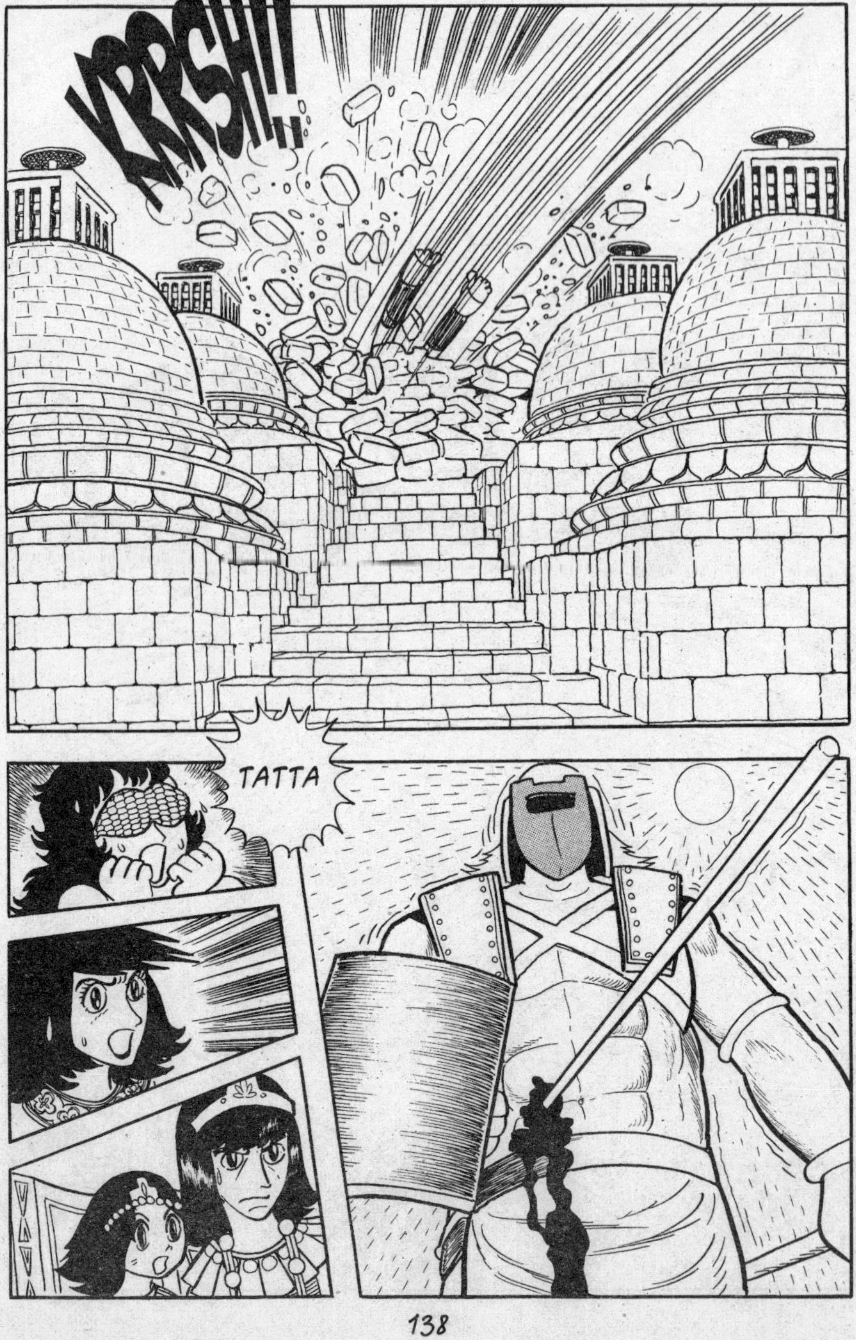
KRRSH!!!
TATTA

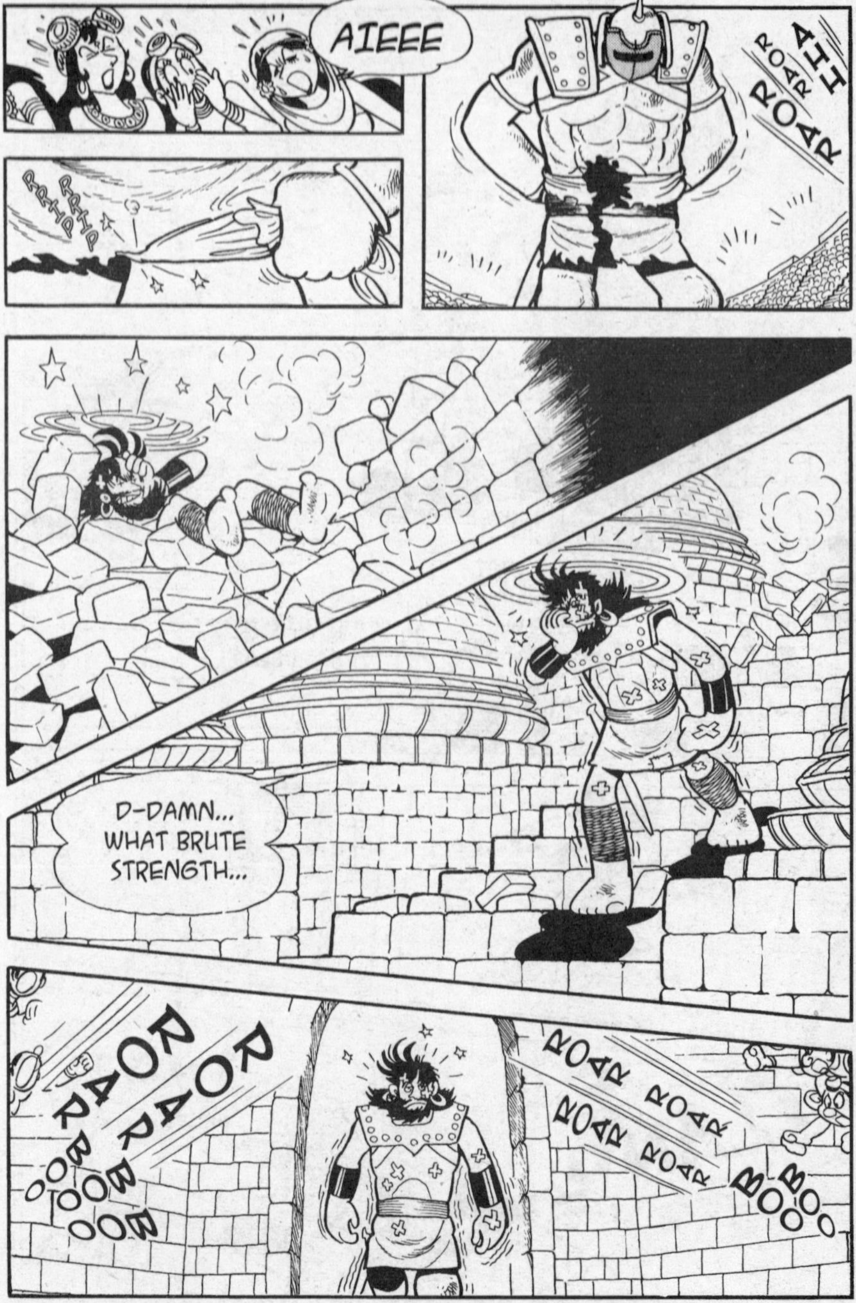
AIEEE
ROAR ROAR AHH
RRRIP RRRIP
D-DAMN... WHAT BRUTE STRENGTH...
ROAR ROAR BOOO
ROAR ROAR
ROAR ROAR ROAR
BOOO

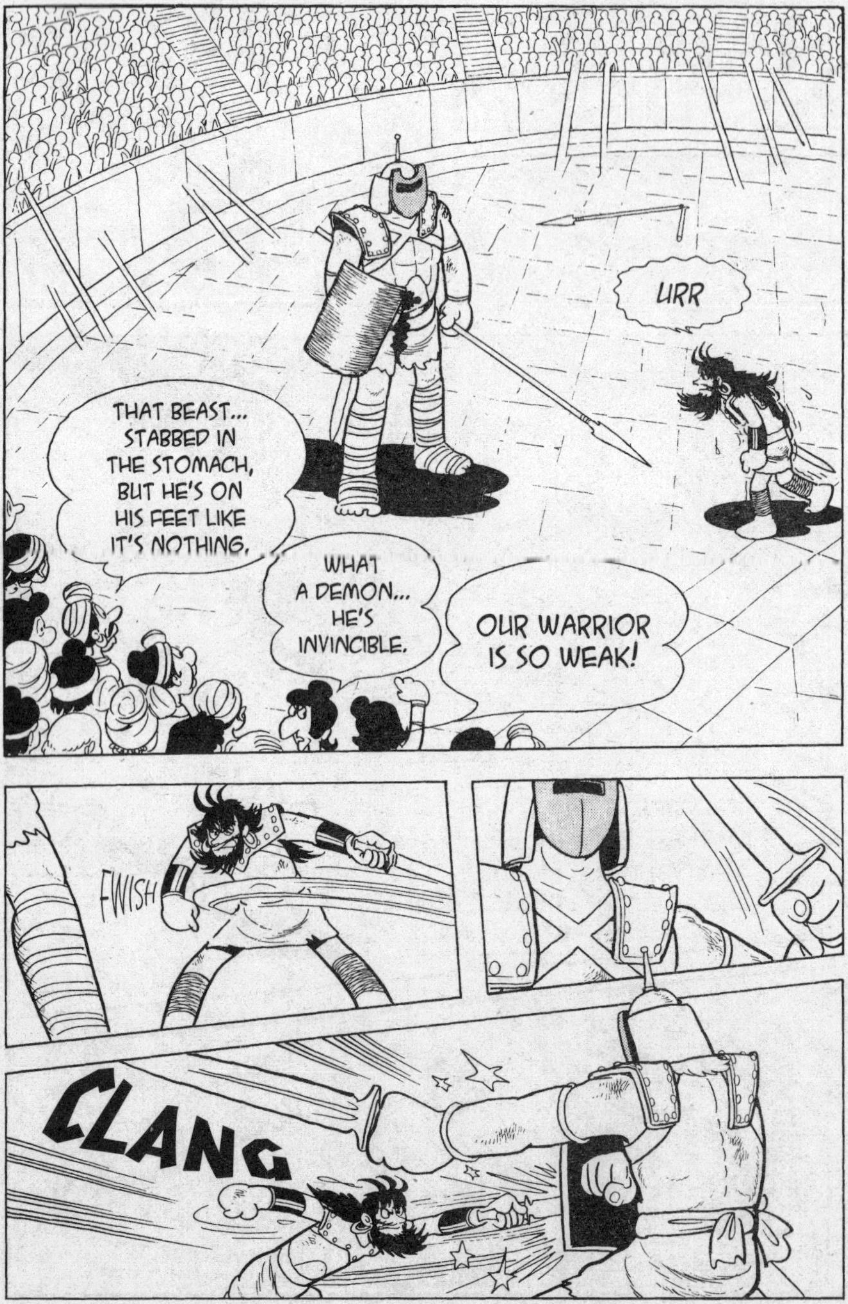
URR
THAT BEAST... STABBED IN THE STOMACH, BUT HE'S ON HIS FEET LIKE IT'S NOTHING.
WHAT A DEMON... HE'S INVINCIBLE.
OUR WARRIOR IS SO WEAK!
FWISH
CLANG

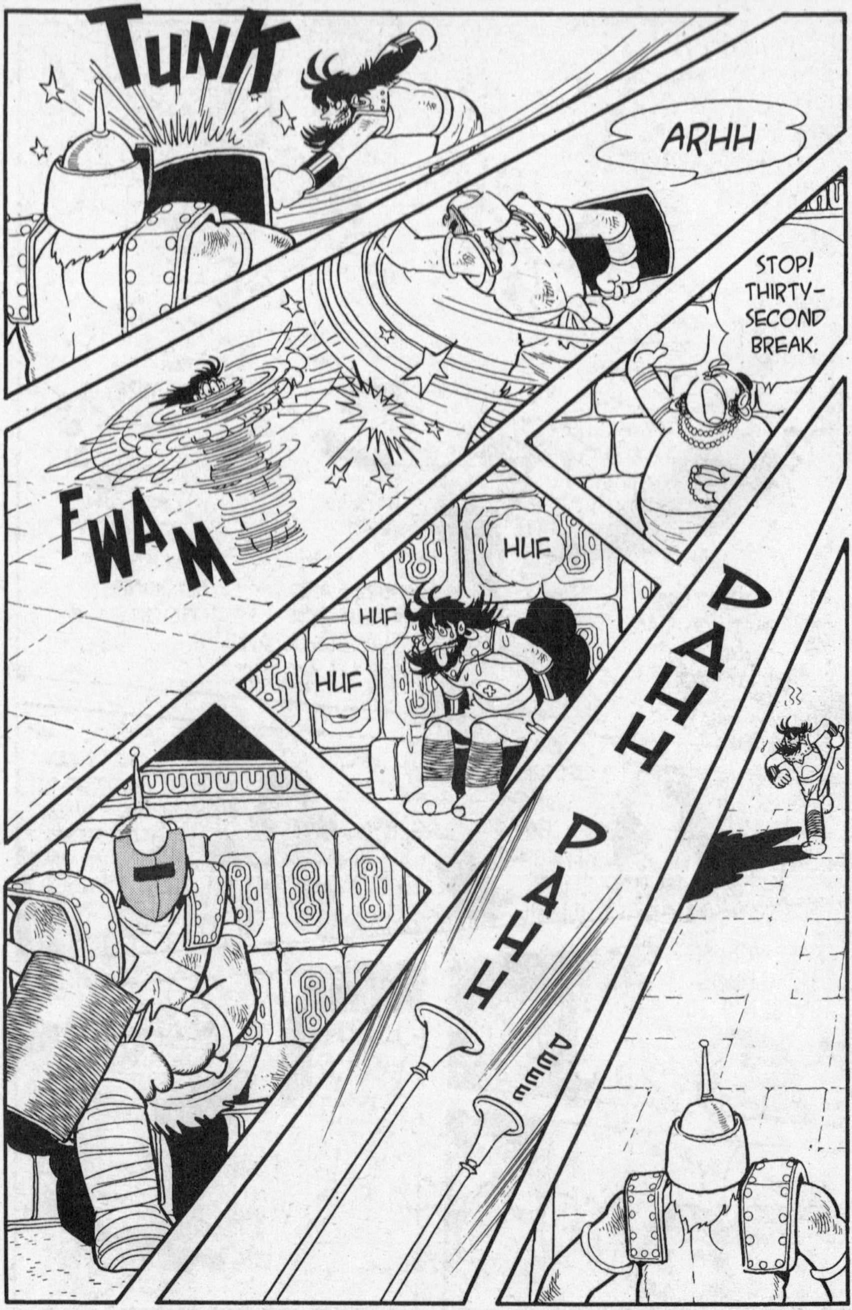
TUNK
ARHH
FWAM
STOP! THIRTY-SECOND BREAK.
HUF
HUF
HUF
PAHH
PAHH

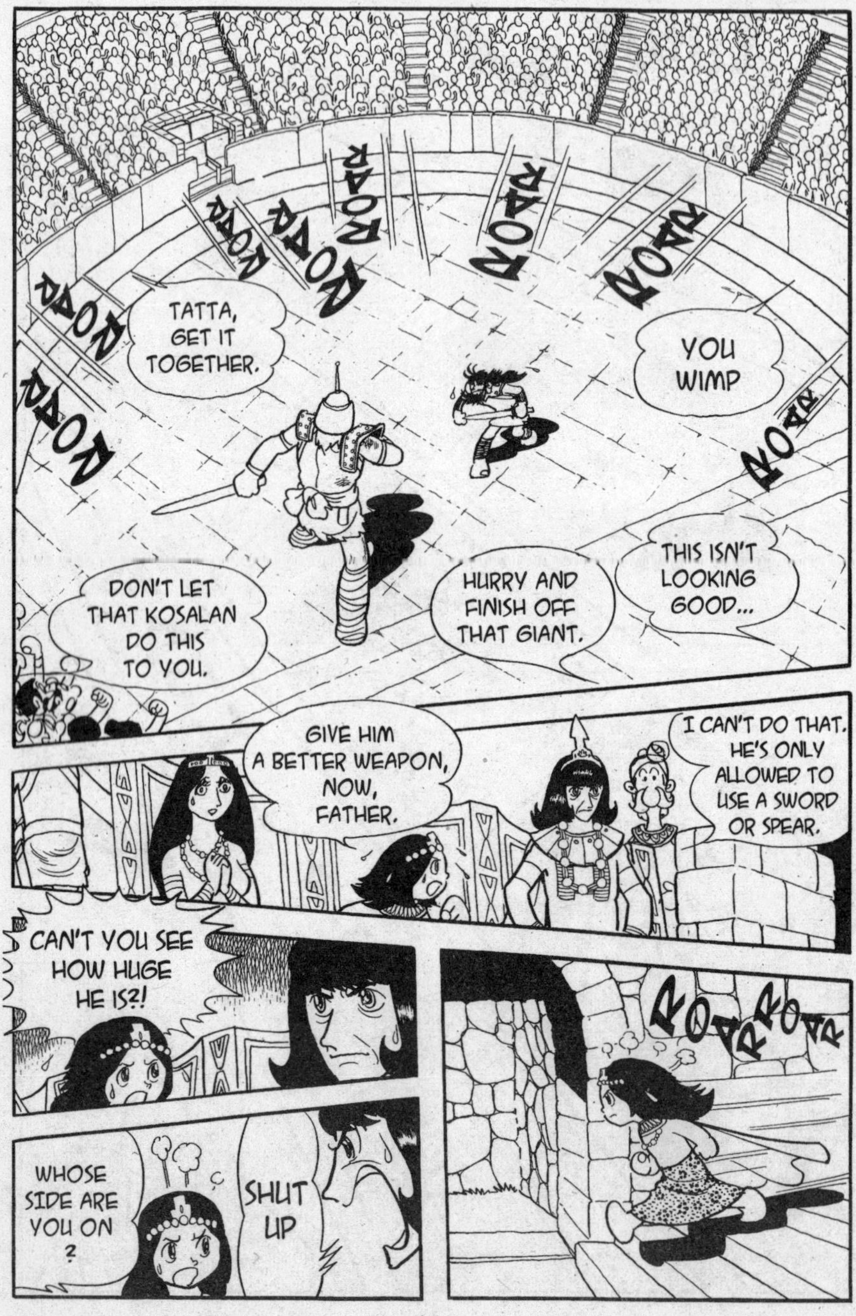
ROAR
ROAR
ROAR
ROAR
ROAR
ROAR
ROAR
ROAR
ROAR
TATTA, GET IT TOGETHER.
YOU WIMP
DON'T LET THAT KOSALAN DO THIS TO YOU.
HURRY AND FINISH OFF THAT GIANT.
THIS ISN'T LOOKING GOOD...
GIVE HIM A BETTER WEAPON, NOW, FATHER.
I CAN'T DO THAT. HE'S ONLY ALLOWED TO USE A SWORD OR SPEAR.
CAN'T YOU SEE HOW HUGE HE IS?!
WHOSE SIDE ARE YOU ON ?
SHUT UP
ROAR
ROAR

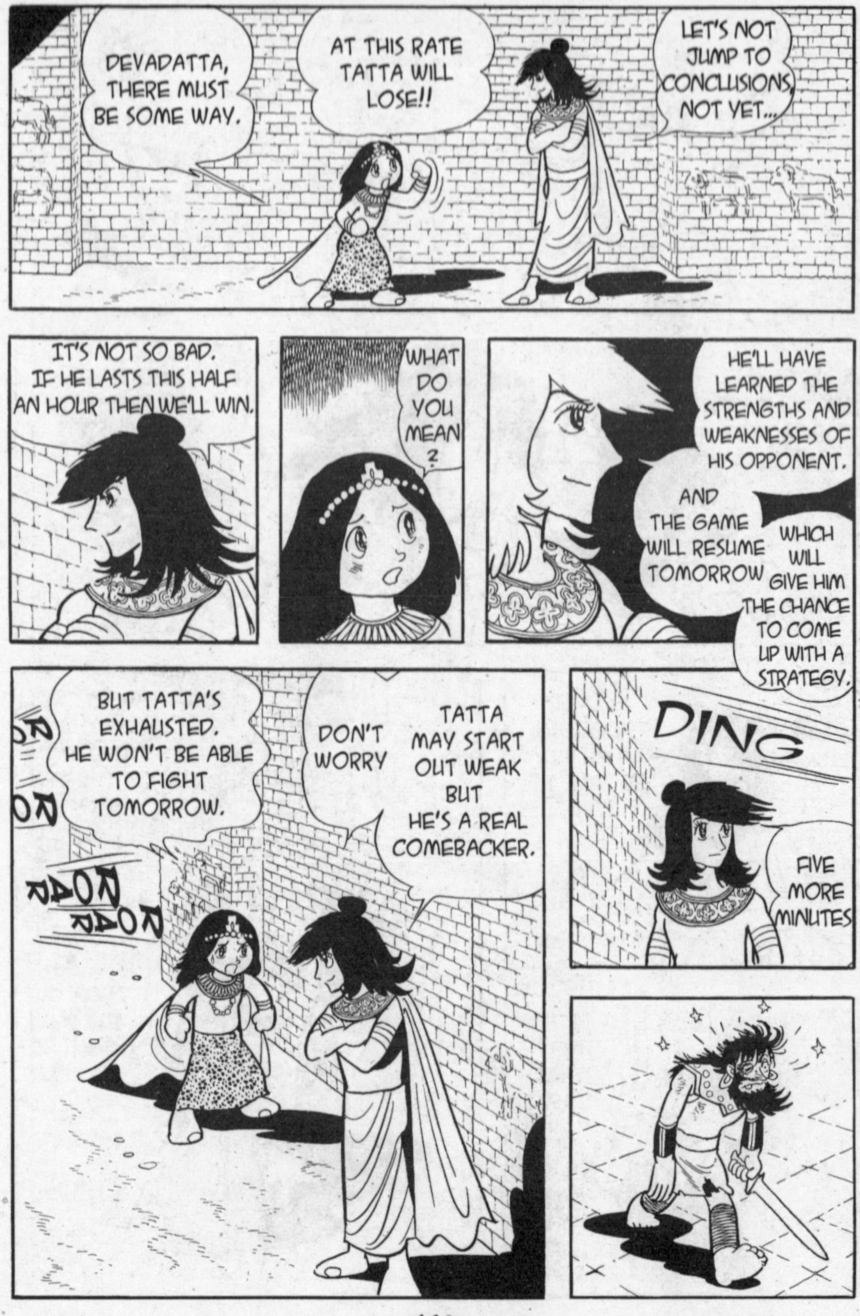
DEVADATTA, THERE MUST BE SOME WAY.
AT THIS RATE TATTA WILL LOSE!!
LET'S NOT JUMP TO CONCLUSIONS, NOT YET...
IT'S NOT SO BAD. IF HE LASTS THIS HALF AN HOUR THEN WE'LL WIN.
WHAT DO YOU MEAN?
HE'LL HAVE LEARNED THE STRENGTHS AND WEAKNESSES OF HIS OPPONENT.
AND THE GAME WILL RESUME TOMORROW
WHICH WILL GIVE HIM THE CHANCE TO COME UP WITH A STRATEGY.
BUT TATTA'S EXHAUSTED. HE WON'T BE ABLE TO FIGHT TOMORROW.
DON'T WORRY
TATTA MAY START OUT WEAK BUT HE'S A REAL COMEBACKER.
DING
FIVE MORE MINUTES

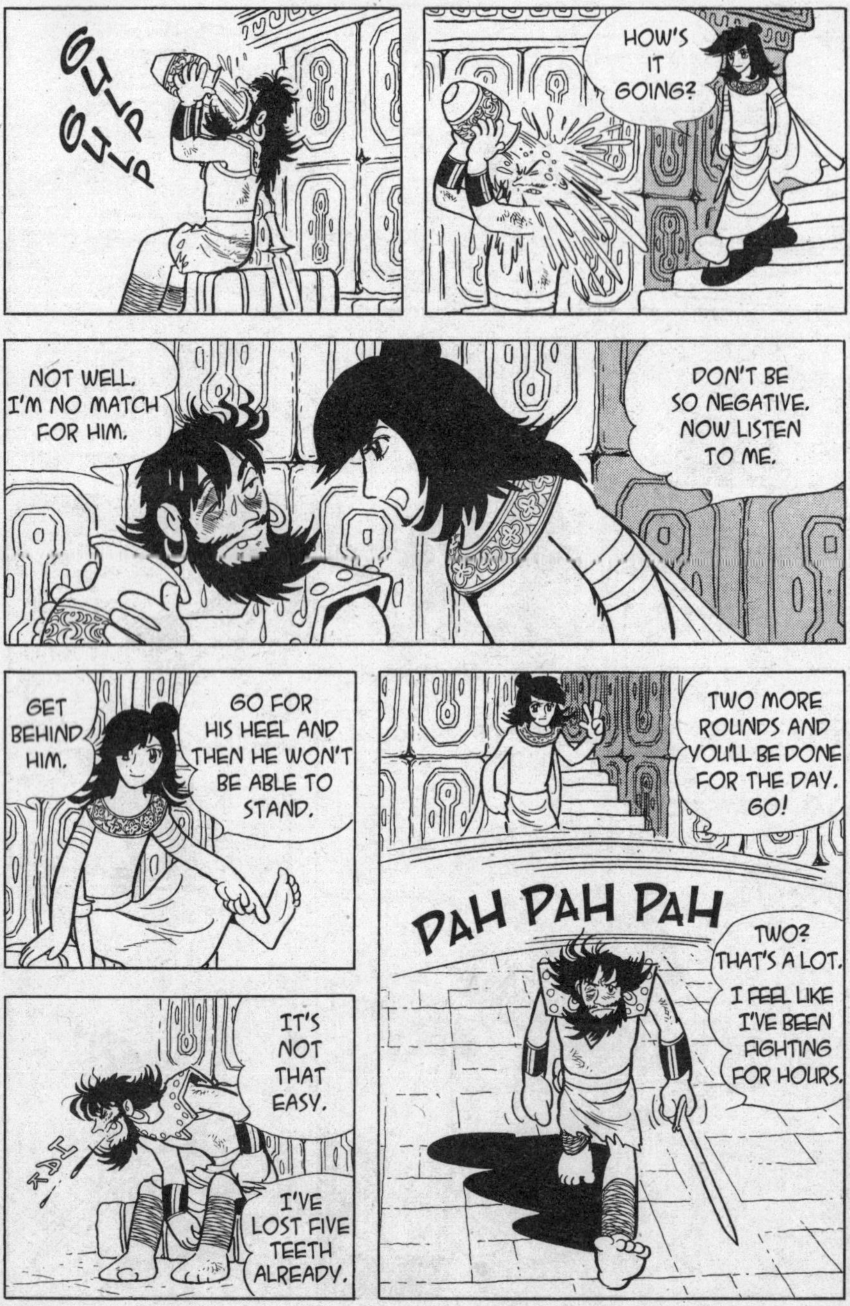
GULP GULP
HOW'S IT GOING?
NOT WELL. I'M NO MATCH FOR HIM.
DON'T BE SO NEGATIVE. NOW LISTEN TO ME.
GET BEHIND HIM.
GO FOR HIS HEEL AND THEN HE WON'T BE ABLE TO STAND.
IT'S NOT THAT EASY.
I'VE LOST FIVE TEETH ALREADY.
TWO MORE ROUNDS AND YOU'LL BE DONE FOR THE DAY. GO!
PAH PAH PAH
TWO? THAT'S A LOT.
I FEEL LIKE I'VE BEEN FIGHTING FOR HOURS.

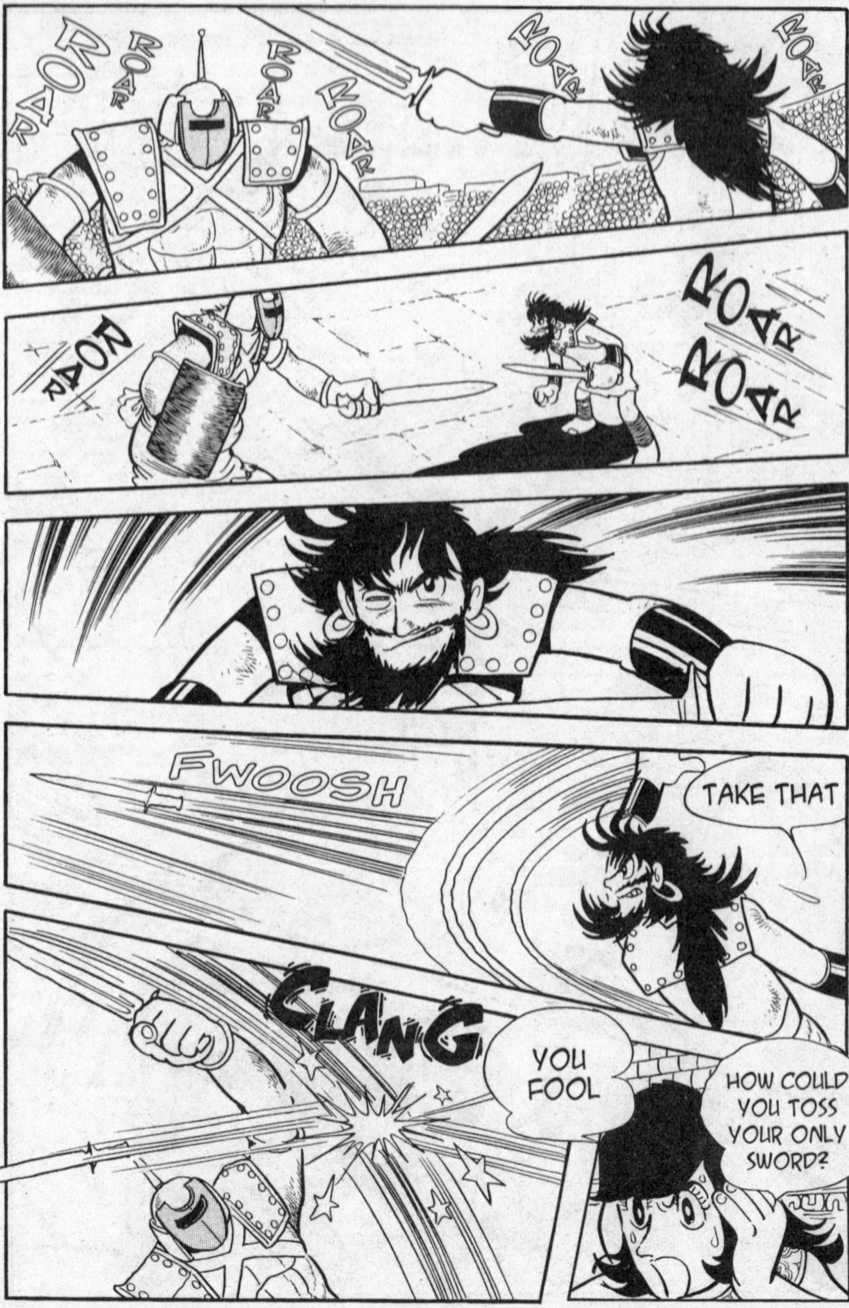
ROAR
ROAR
ROAR
ROAR
ROAR
ROAR
ROAR
ROAR
ROAR
FWOOSH
TAKE THAT
CLANG
YOU FOOL
HOW COULD YOU TOSS YOUR ONLY SWORD?

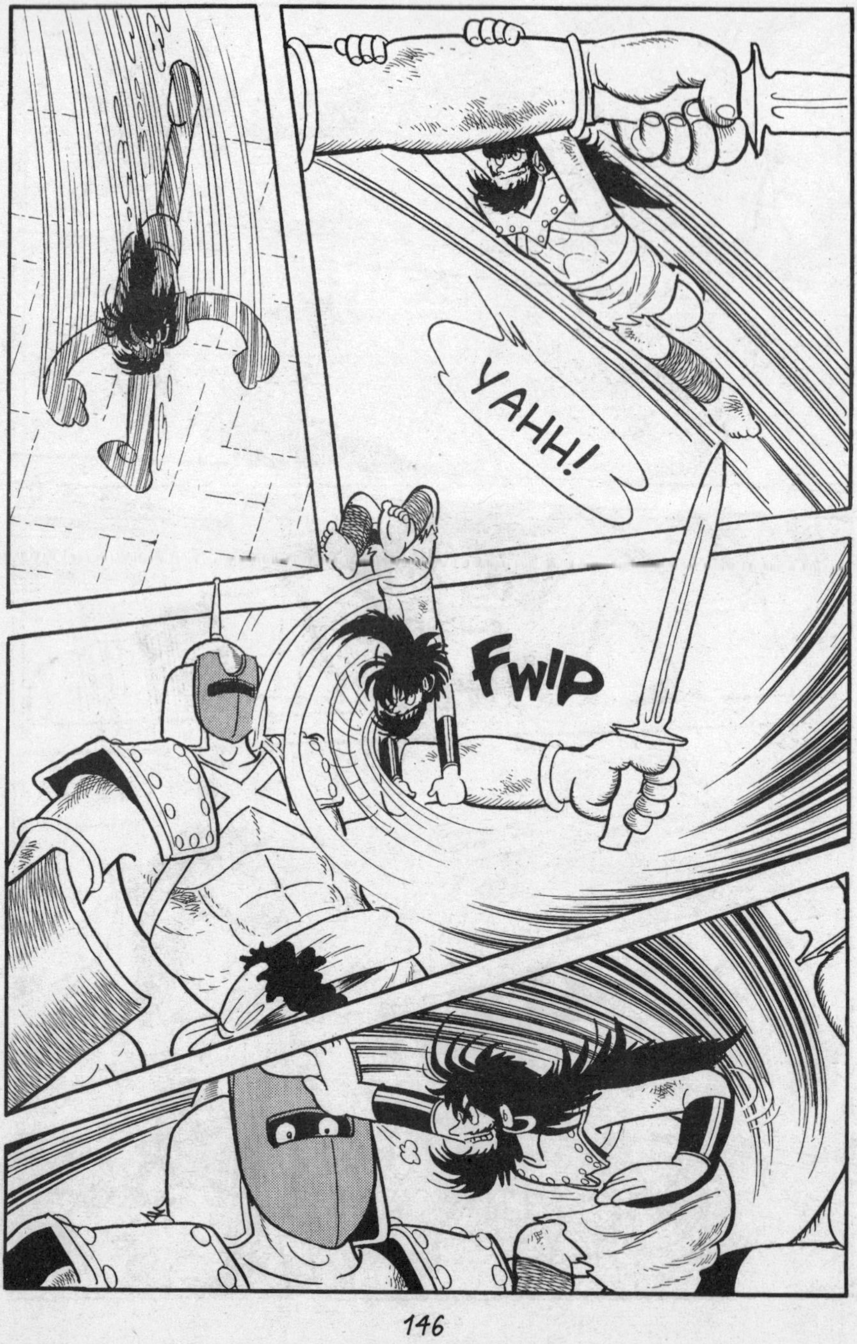
YAHH!
FWIP

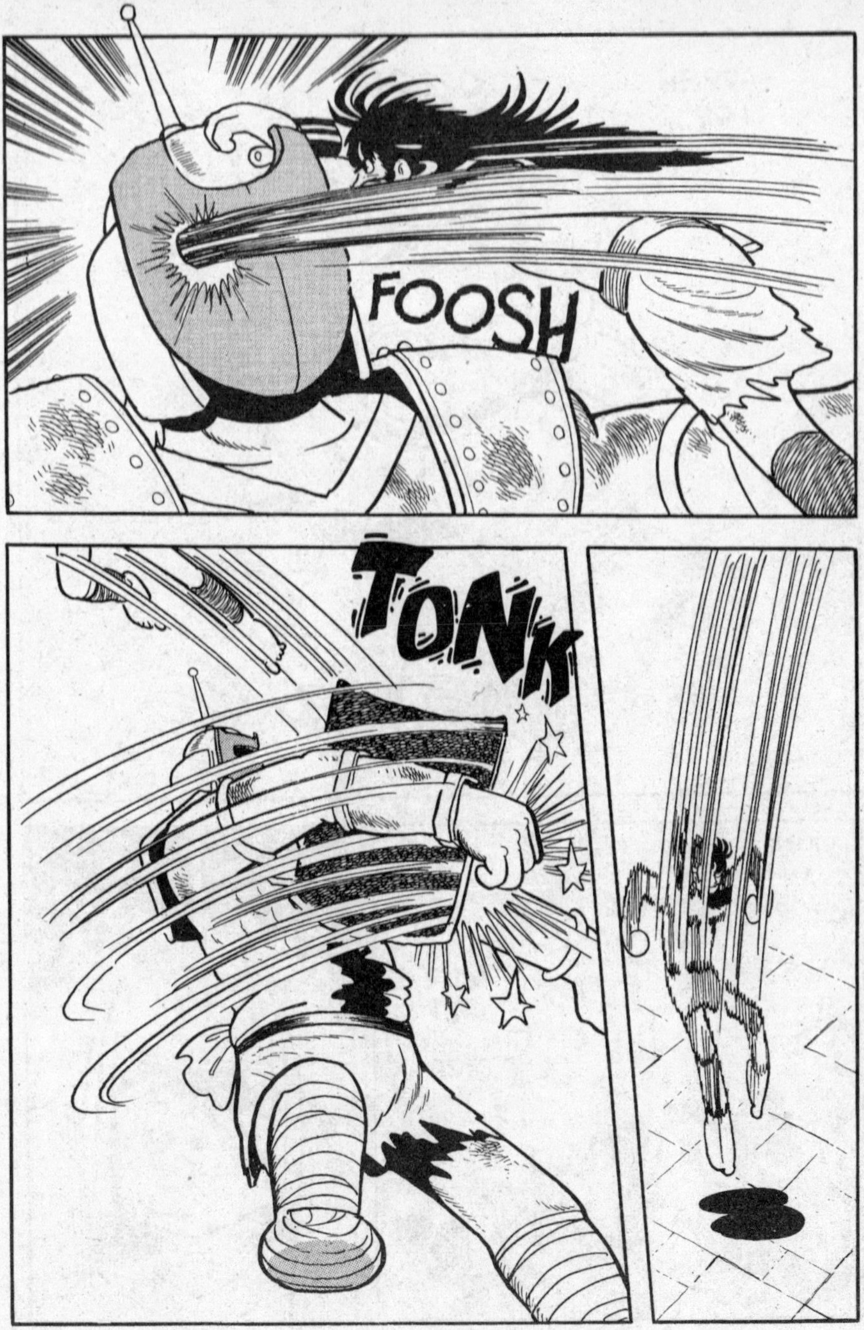
FOOSH
TONK

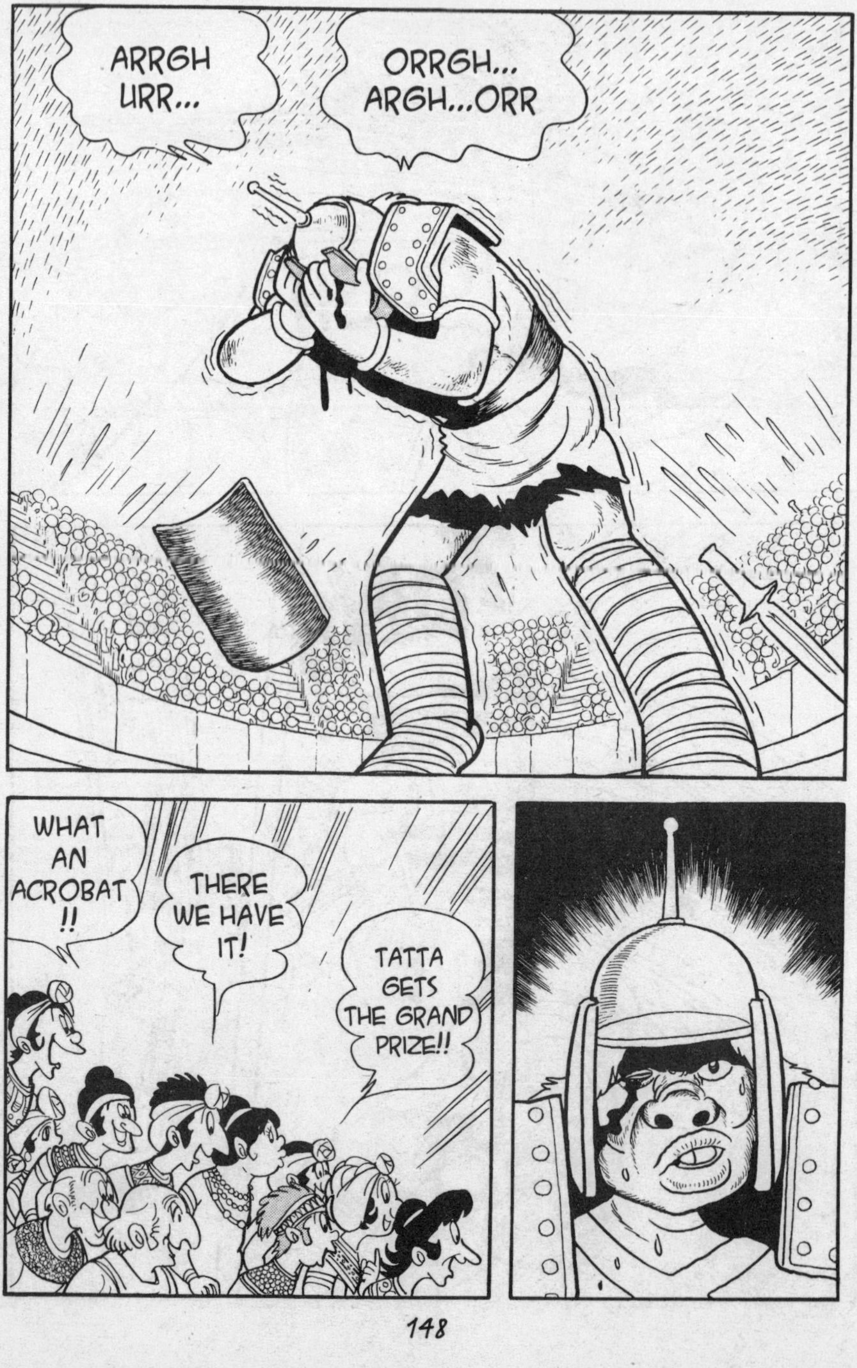
ARRGH URR...
ORRGH... ARGH...ORR
WHAT AN ACROBAT !!
THERE WE HAVE IT!
TATTA GETS THE GRAND PRIZE!!

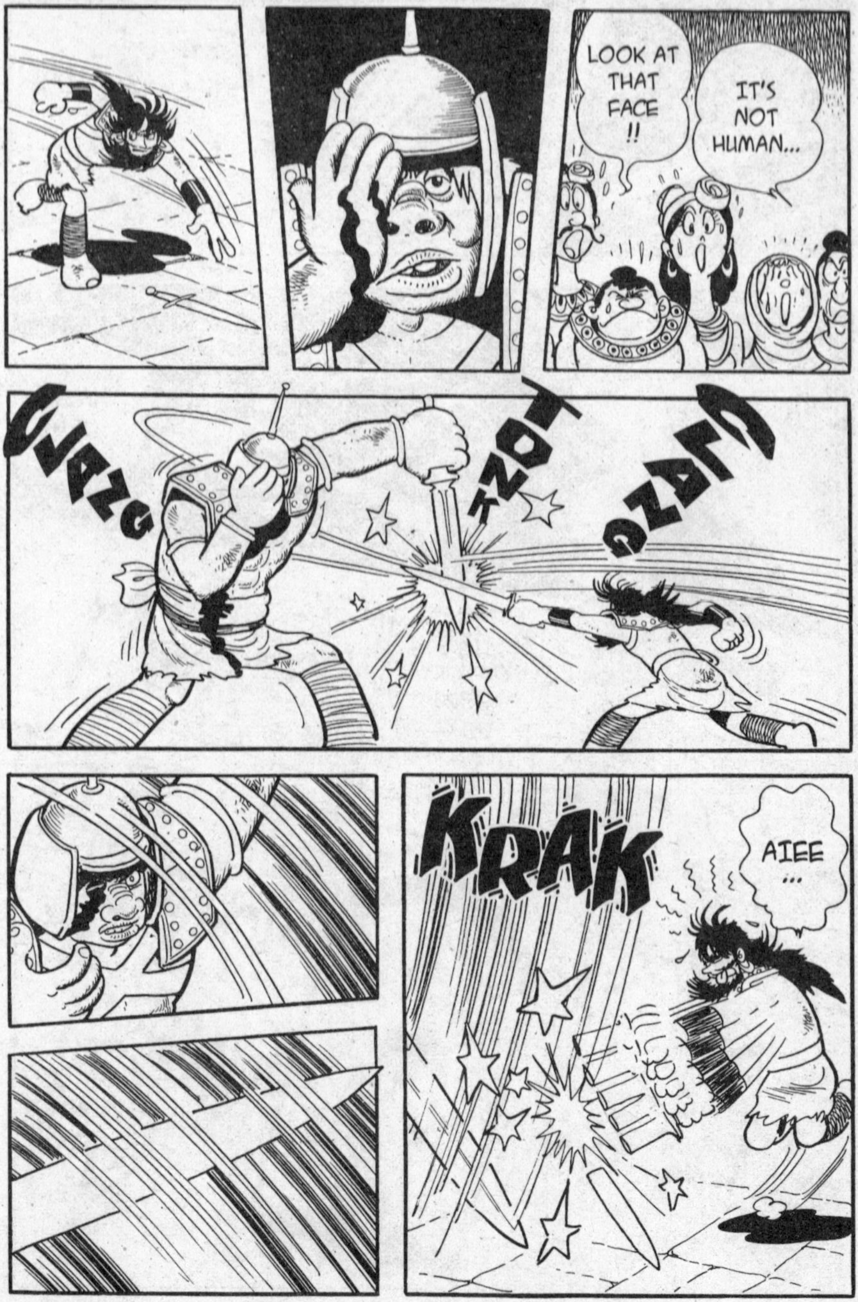

LOOK AT THAT FACE !!
IT'S NOT HUMAN...
KRAK
AIEE ...

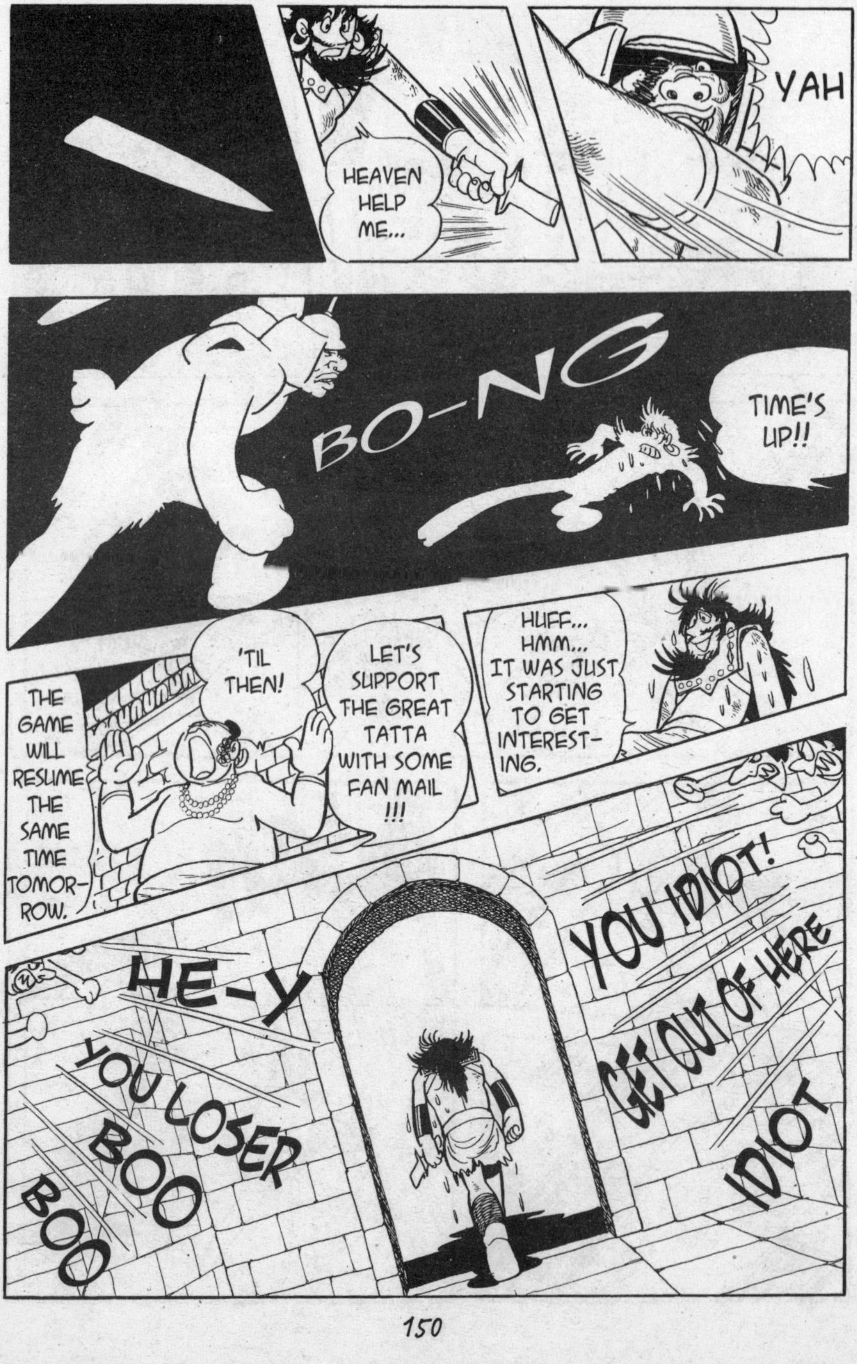
HEAVEN HELP ME...
YAH
BO-NG
TIME'S UP!!
THE GAME WILL RESUME THE SAME TIME TOMORROW.
'TIL THEN!
LET'S SUPPORT THE GREAT TATTA WITH SOME FAN MAIL !!!
HUFF... HMM... IT WAS JUST STARTING TO GET INTERESTING.
HE-Y
YOU LOSER
BOO
BOO
YOU IDIOT!
GET OUT OF HERE
IDIOT

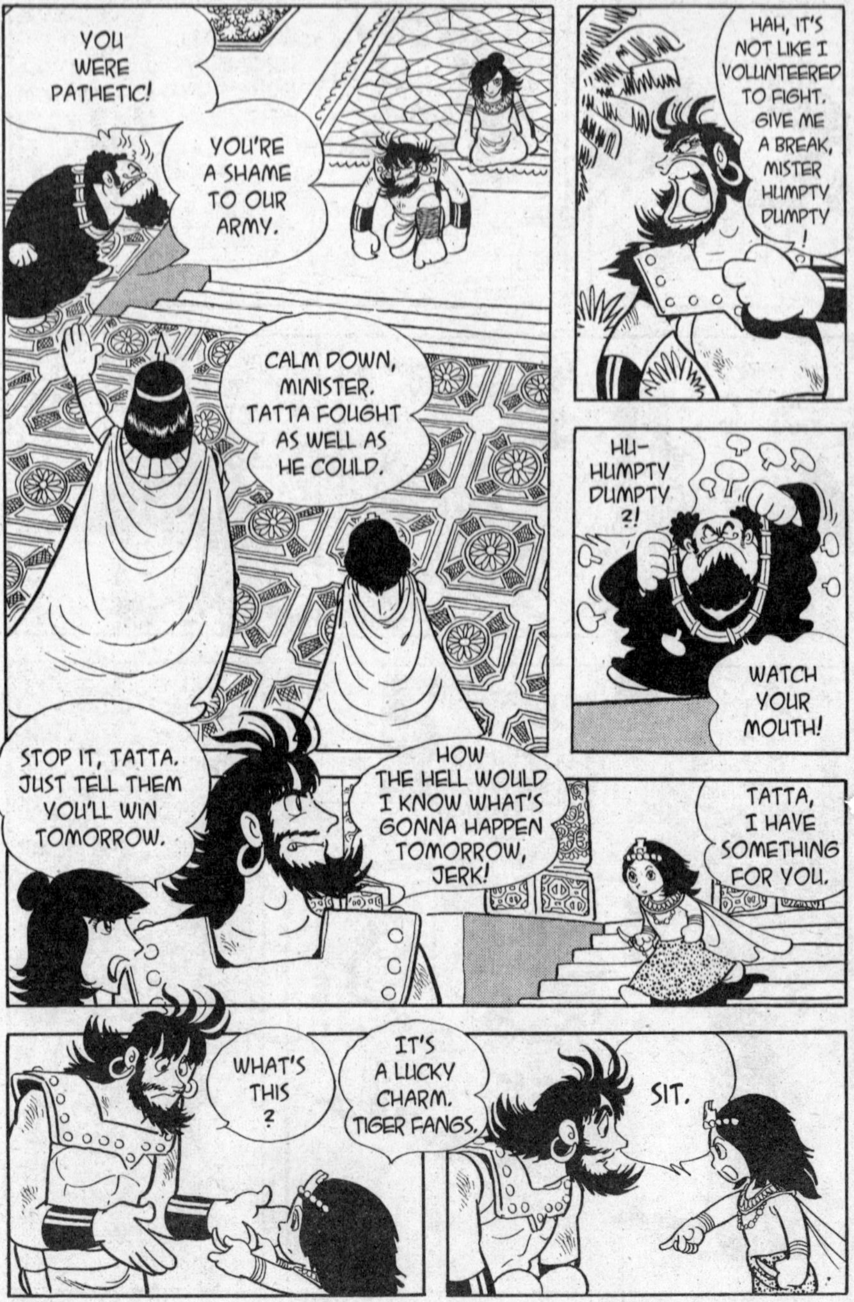
YOU WERE PATHETIC!
YOU'RE A SHAME TO OUR ARMY.
HAH, IT'S NOT LIKE I VOLUNTEERED TO FIGHT. GIVE ME A BREAK, MISTER HUMPTY DUMPTY!
CALM DOWN, MINISTER. TATTA FOUGHT AS WELL AS HE COULD.
HU-HUMPTY DUMPTY?!
WATCH YOUR MOUTH!
STOP IT, TATTA. JUST TELL THEM YOU'LL WIN TOMORROW.
HOW THE HELL WOULD I KNOW WHAT'S GONNA HAPPEN TOMORROW, JERK!
TATTA, I HAVE SOMETHING FOR YOU.
WHAT'S THIS?
IT'S A LUCKY CHARM. TIGER FANGS.
SIT.

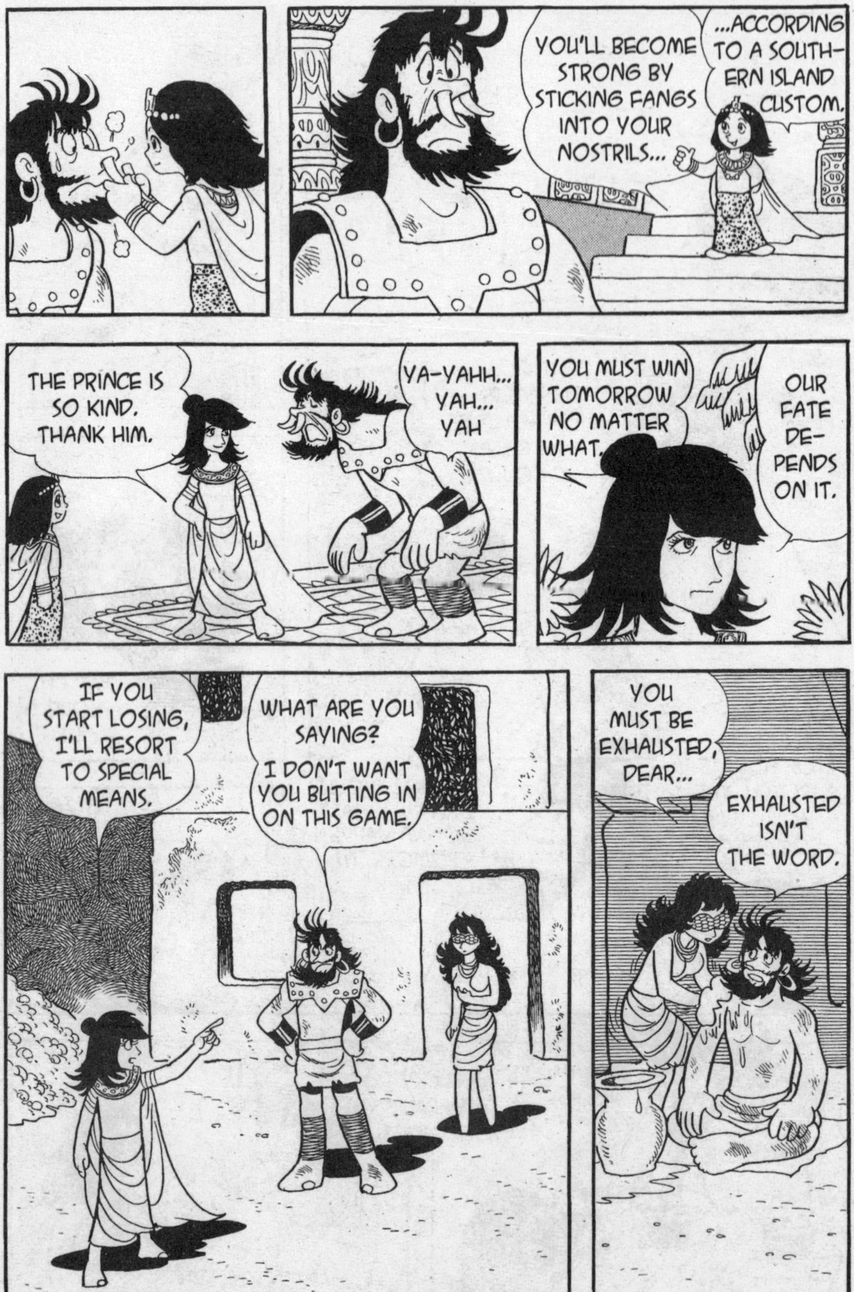

YOU'LL BECOME STRONG BY STICKING FANGS INTO YOUR NOSTRILS...
...ACCORDING TO A SOUTH-ERN ISLAND CUSTOM.
THE PRINCE IS SO KIND. THANK HIM.
YA-YAHH... YAH... YAH
YOU MUST WIN TOMORROW NO MATTER WHAT.
OUR FATE DE-PENDS ON IT.
IF YOU START LOSING, I'LL RESORT TO SPECIAL MEANS.
WHAT ARE YOU SAYING?
I DON'T WANT YOU BUTTING IN ON THIS GAME.
YOU MUST BE EXHAUSTED, DEAR...
EXHAUSTED ISN'T THE WORD.

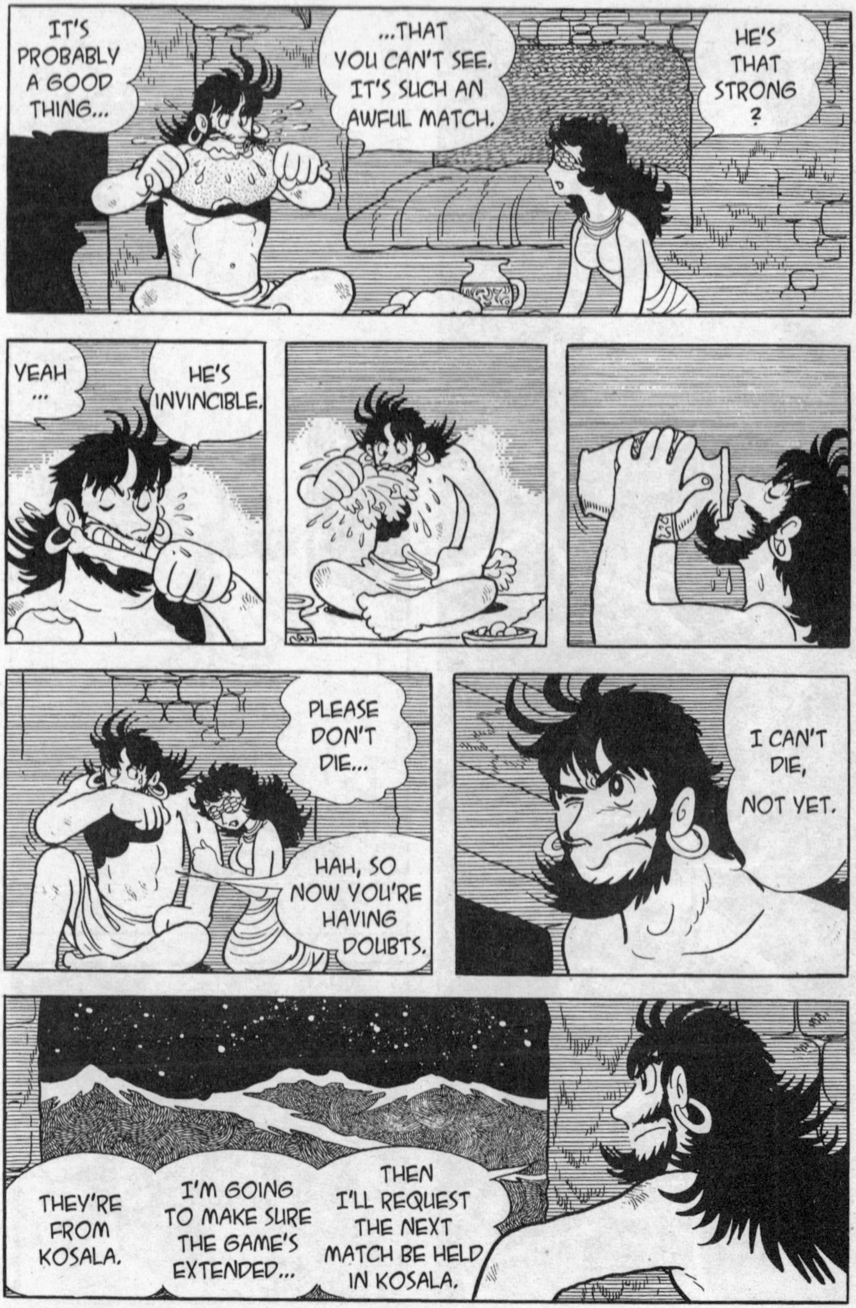
IT'S PROBABLY A GOOD THING...
...THAT YOU CAN'T SEE. IT'S SUCH AN AWFUL MATCH.
HE'S THAT STRONG ?
YEAH ...
HE'S INVINCIBLE.
PLEASE DON'T DIE...
HAH, SO NOW YOU'RE HAVING DOUBTS.
I CAN'T DIE, NOT YET.
THEY'RE FROM KOSALA.
I'M GOING TO MAKE SURE THE GAME'S EXTENDED...
THEN I'LL REQUEST THE NEXT MATCH BE HELD IN KOSALA.

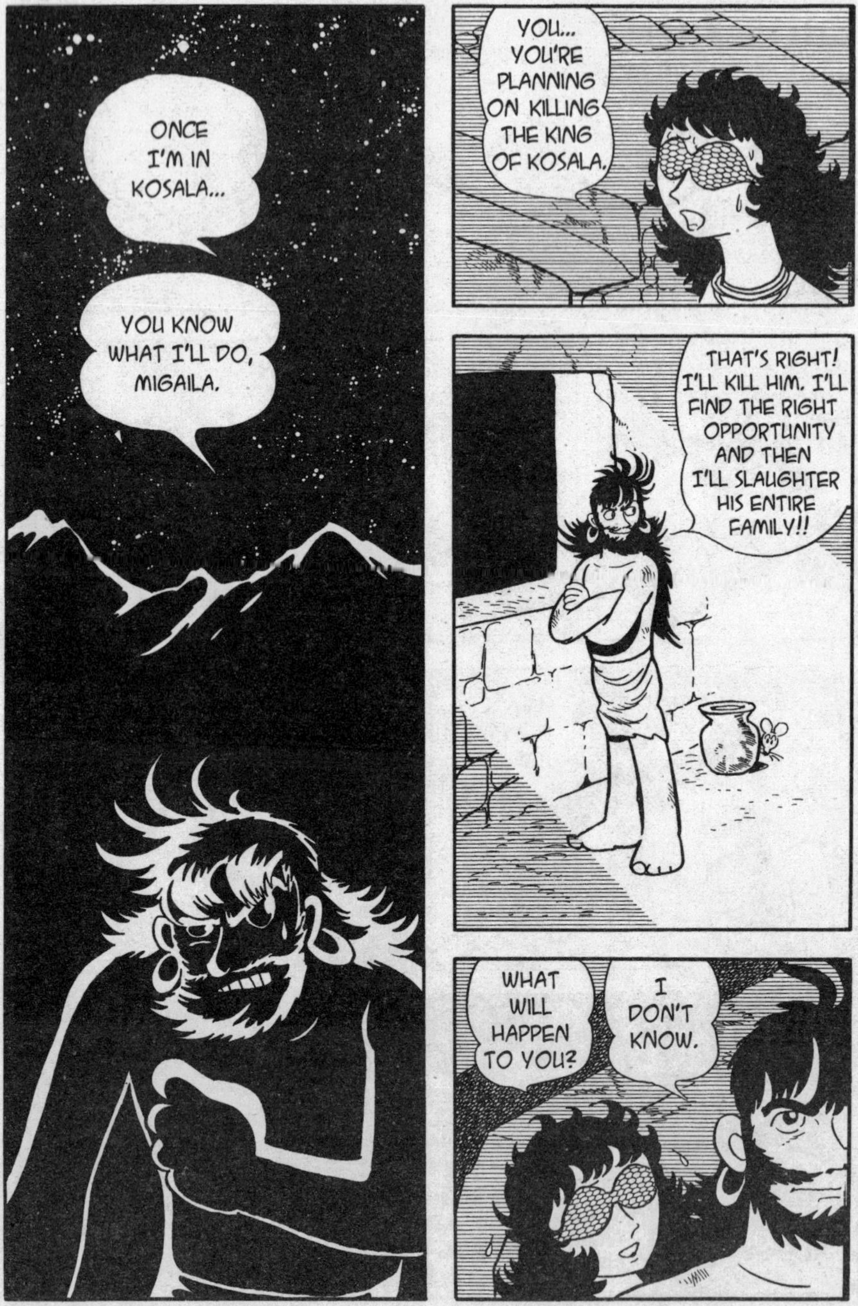

ONCE I'M IN KOSALA...
YOU KNOW WHAT I'LL DO, MIGAILA.
YOU... YOU'RE PLANNING ON KILLING THE KING OF KOSALA.
THAT'S RIGHT! I'LL KILL HIM. I'LL FIND THE RIGHT OPPORTUNITY AND THEN I'LL SLAUGHTER HIS ENTIRE FAMILY!!
WHAT WILL HAPPEN TO YOU?
I DON'T KNOW.

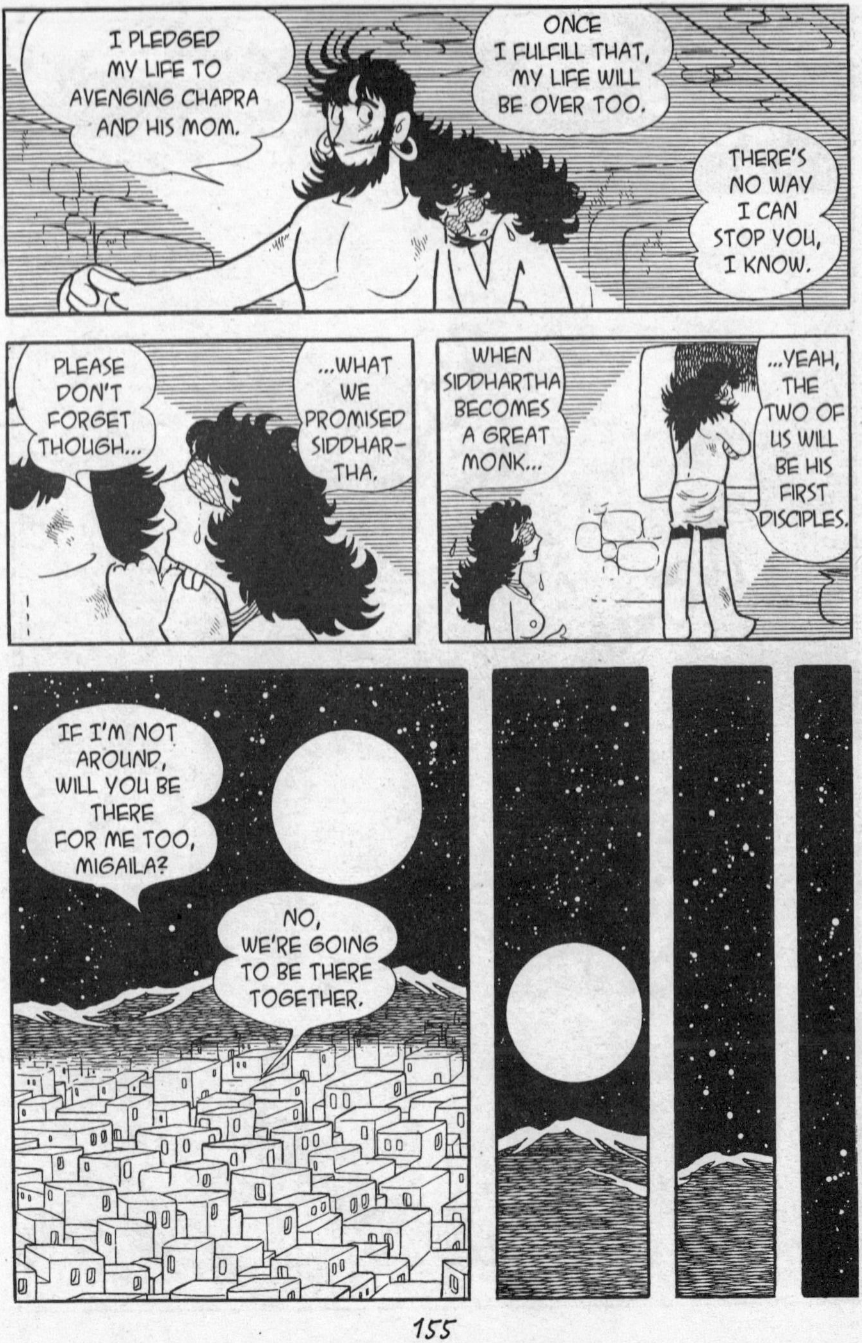
I PLEDGED MY LIFE TO AVENGING CHAPRA AND HIS MOM.
ONCE I FULFILL THAT, MY LIFE WILL BE OVER TOO.
THERE'S NO WAY I CAN STOP YOU, I KNOW.
PLEASE DON'T FORGET THOUGH...
...WHAT WE PROMISED SIDDHAR-THA.
WHEN SIDDHARTHA BECOMES A GREAT MONK...
...YEAH, THE TWO OF US WILL BE HIS FIRST DISCIPLES.
IF I'M NOT AROUND, WILL YOU BE THERE FOR ME TOO, MIGAILA?
NO, WE'RE GOING TO BE THERE TOGETHER.

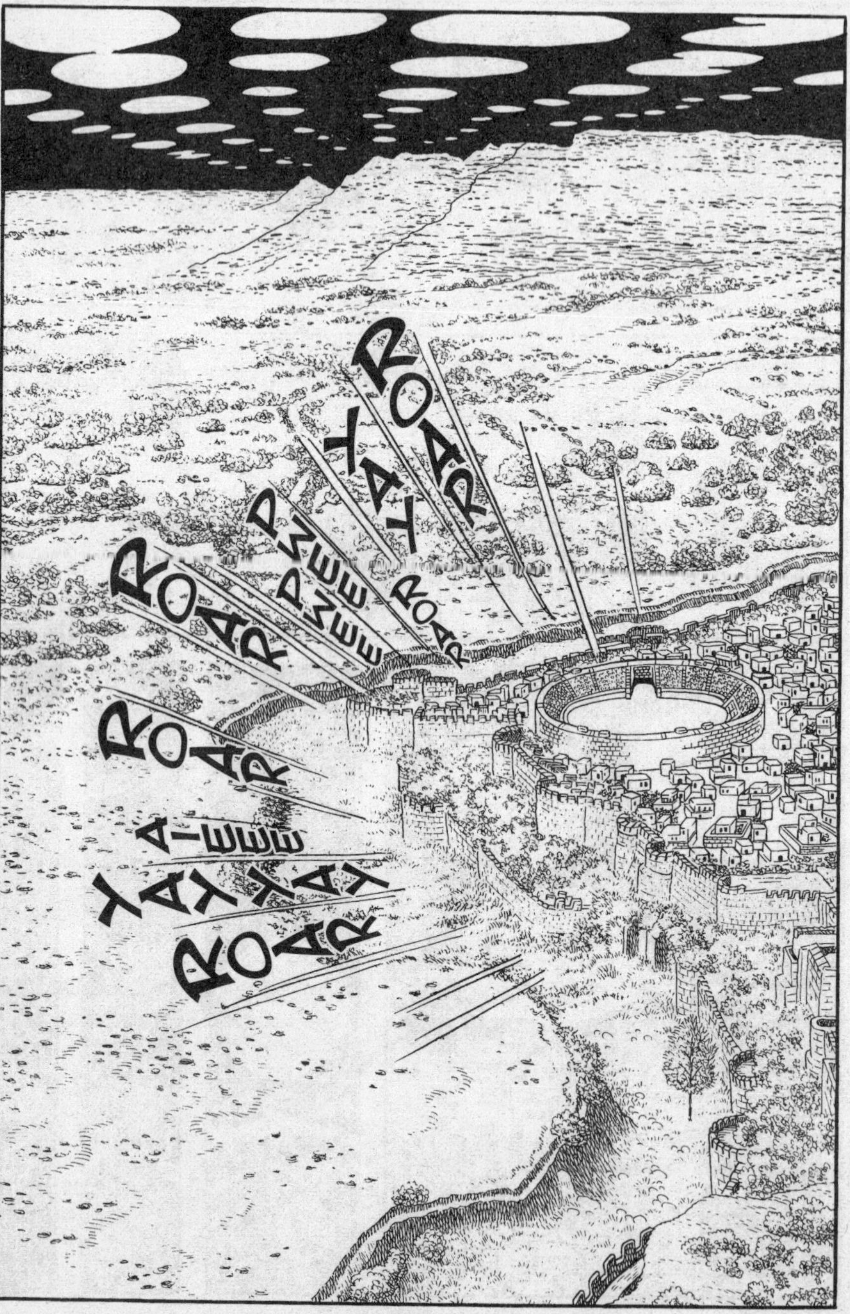
ROAR
YAY
ROAR
PWEE
WEE
WEE
ROAR
ROAR
YAY A-WWW
YAY
ROAR

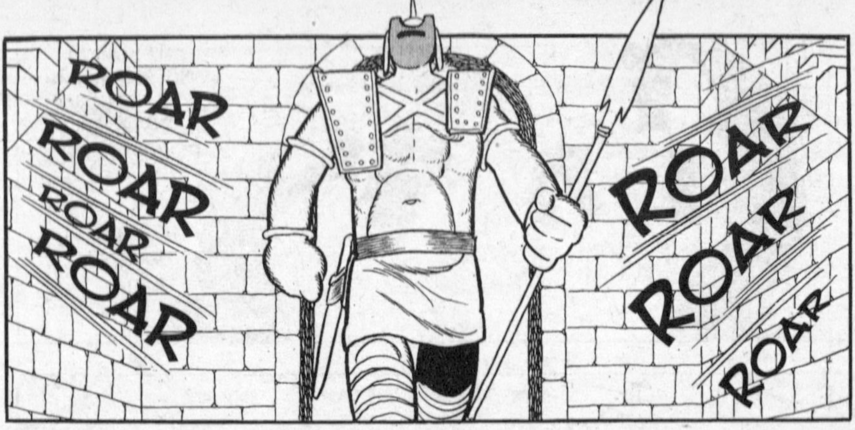
ROAR
ROAR
ROAR
ROAR
ROAR
ROAR
ROAR
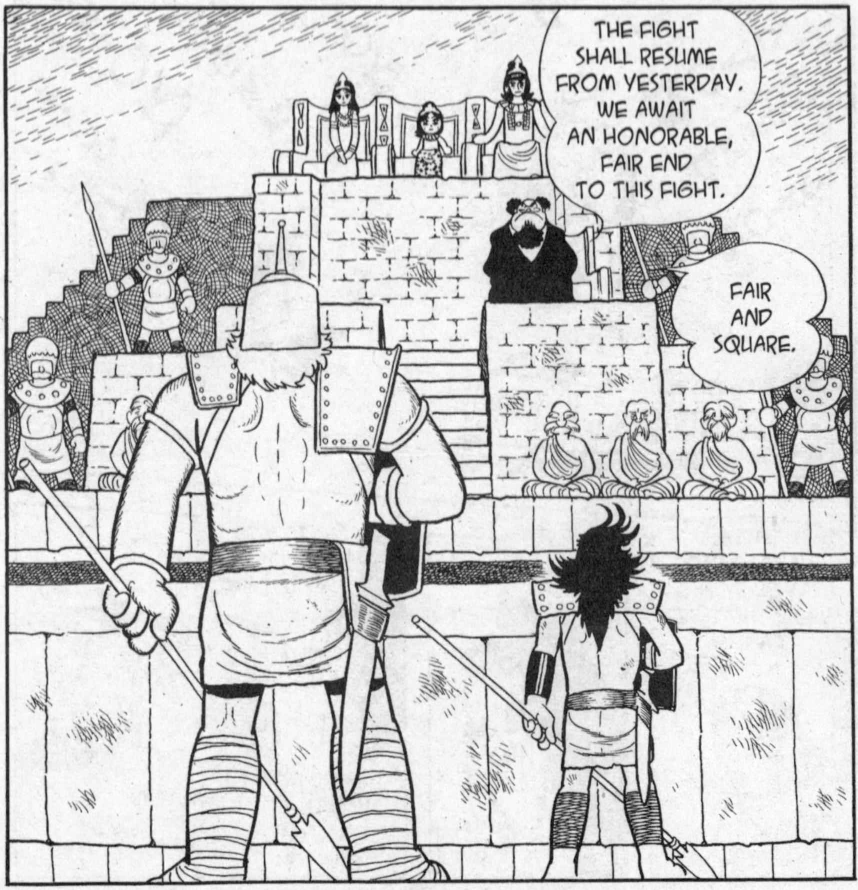
THE FIGHT SHALL RESUME FROM YESTERDAY. WE AWAIT AN HONORABLE, FAIR END TO THIS FIGHT.
FAIR AND SQUARE.

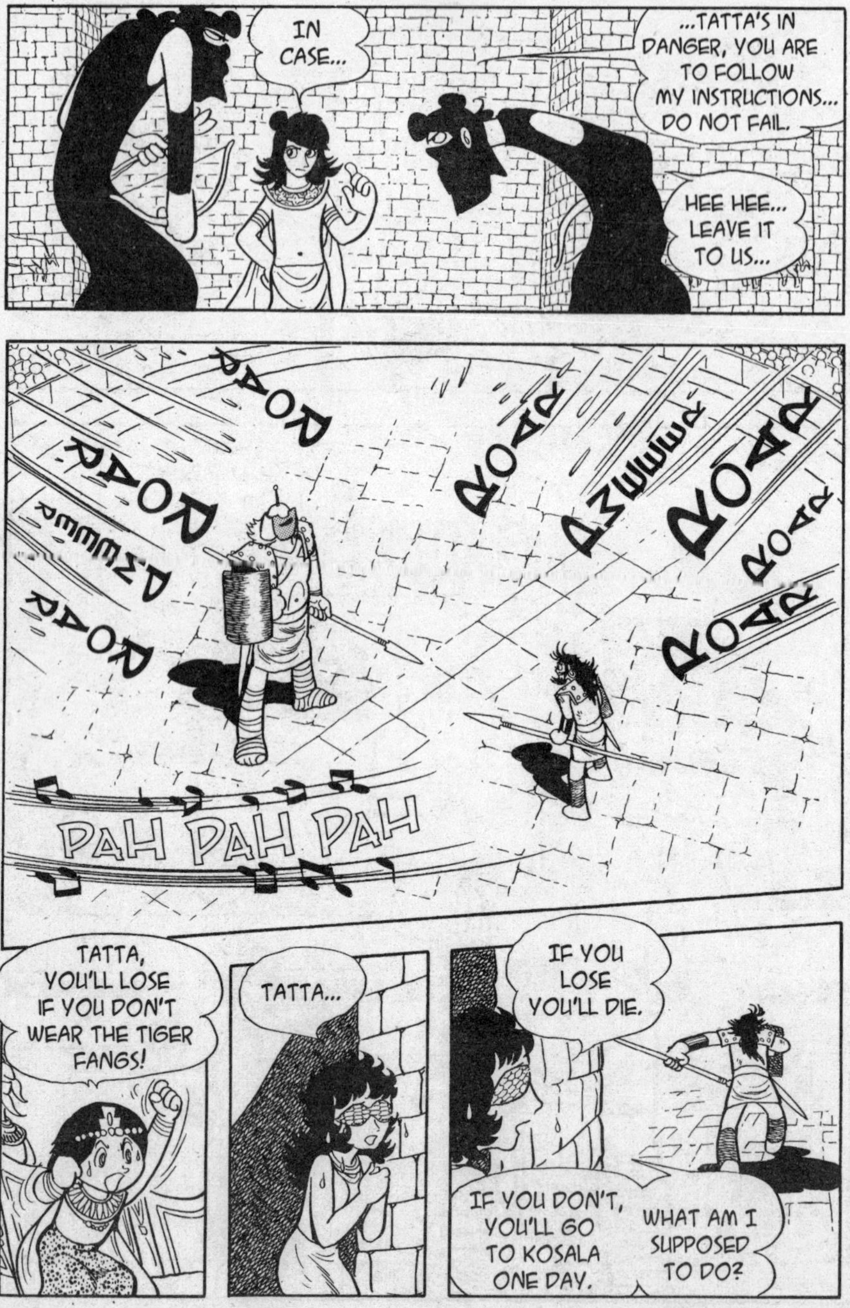
IN CASE...
...TATTA'S IN DANGER, YOU ARE TO FOLLOW MY INSTRUCTIONS... DO NOT FAIL.
HEE HEE... LEAVE IT TO US...
ROAR
ROAR
ROAR
PAH PAH PAH
TATTA, YOU'LL LOSE IF YOU DON'T WEAR THE TIGER FANGS!
TATTA...
IF YOU LOSE YOU'LL DIE.
IF YOU DON'T, YOU'LL GO TO KOSALA ONE DAY.
WHAT AM I SUPPOSED TO DO?

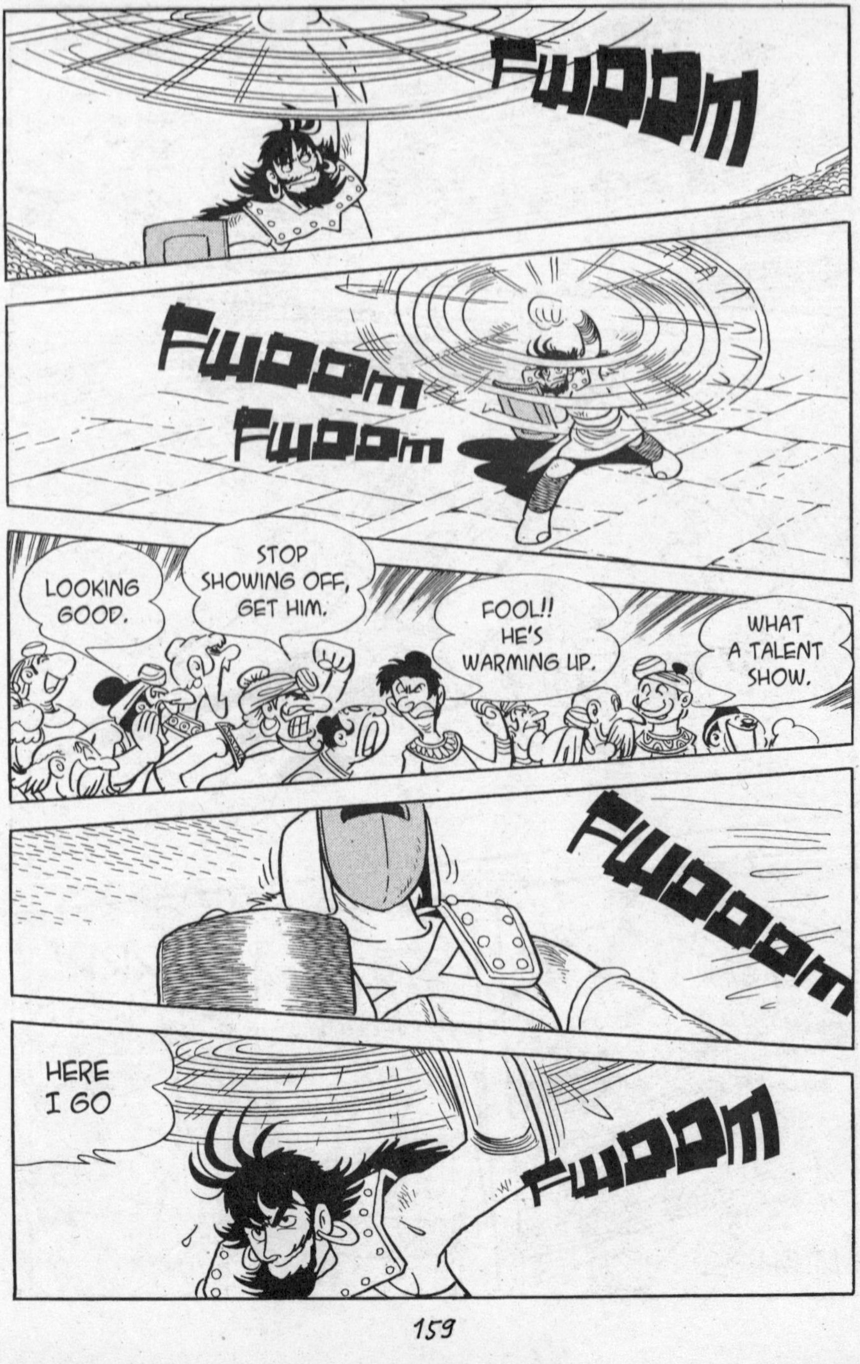
FWOOM
FWOOM
FWOOM
LOOKING GOOD.
STOP SHOWING OFF, GET HIM.
FOOL!! HE'S WARMING UP.
WHAT A TALENT SHOW.
FWOOOOM
HERE I GO
FWOOM

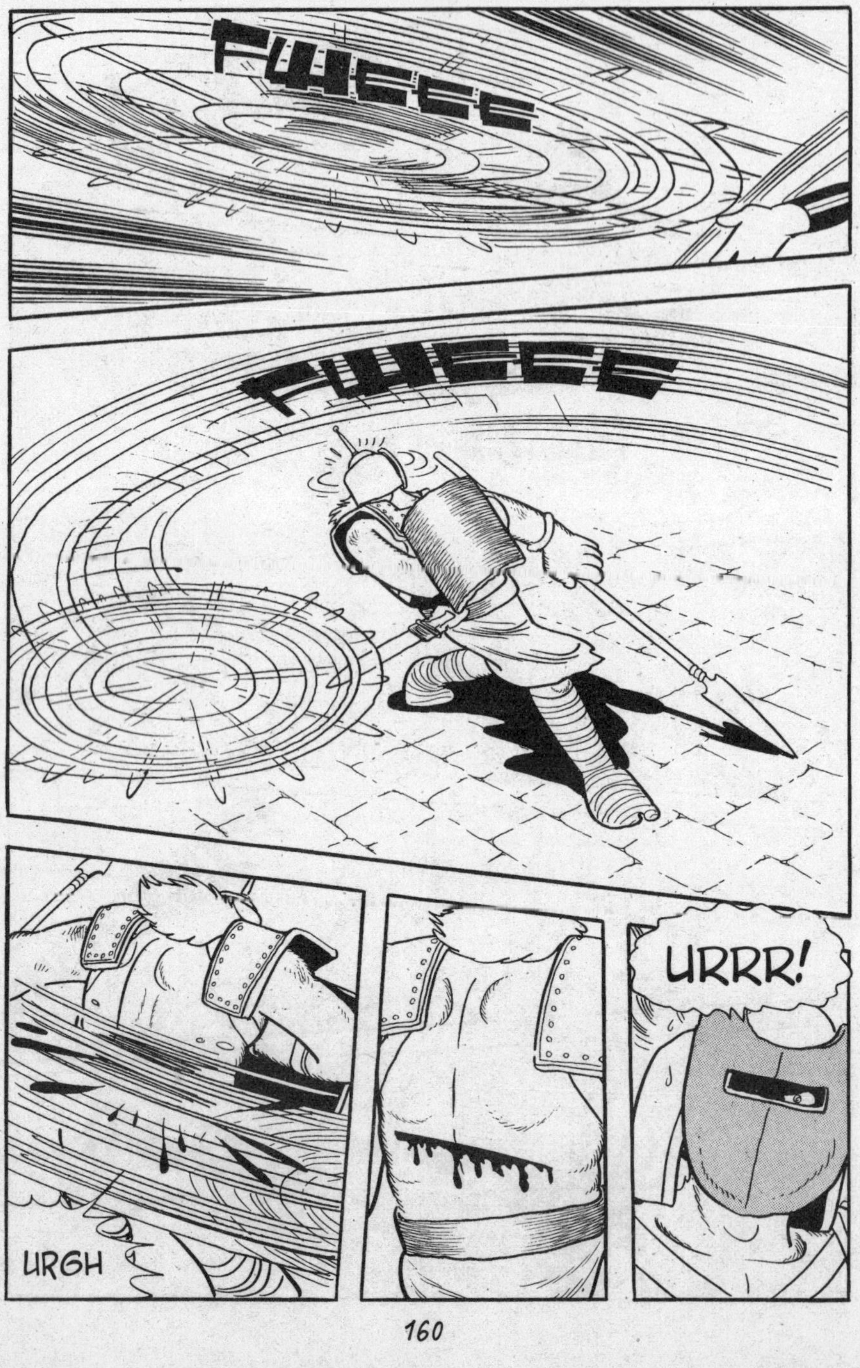
FWEEE
FWEEE
URGH
URRR!

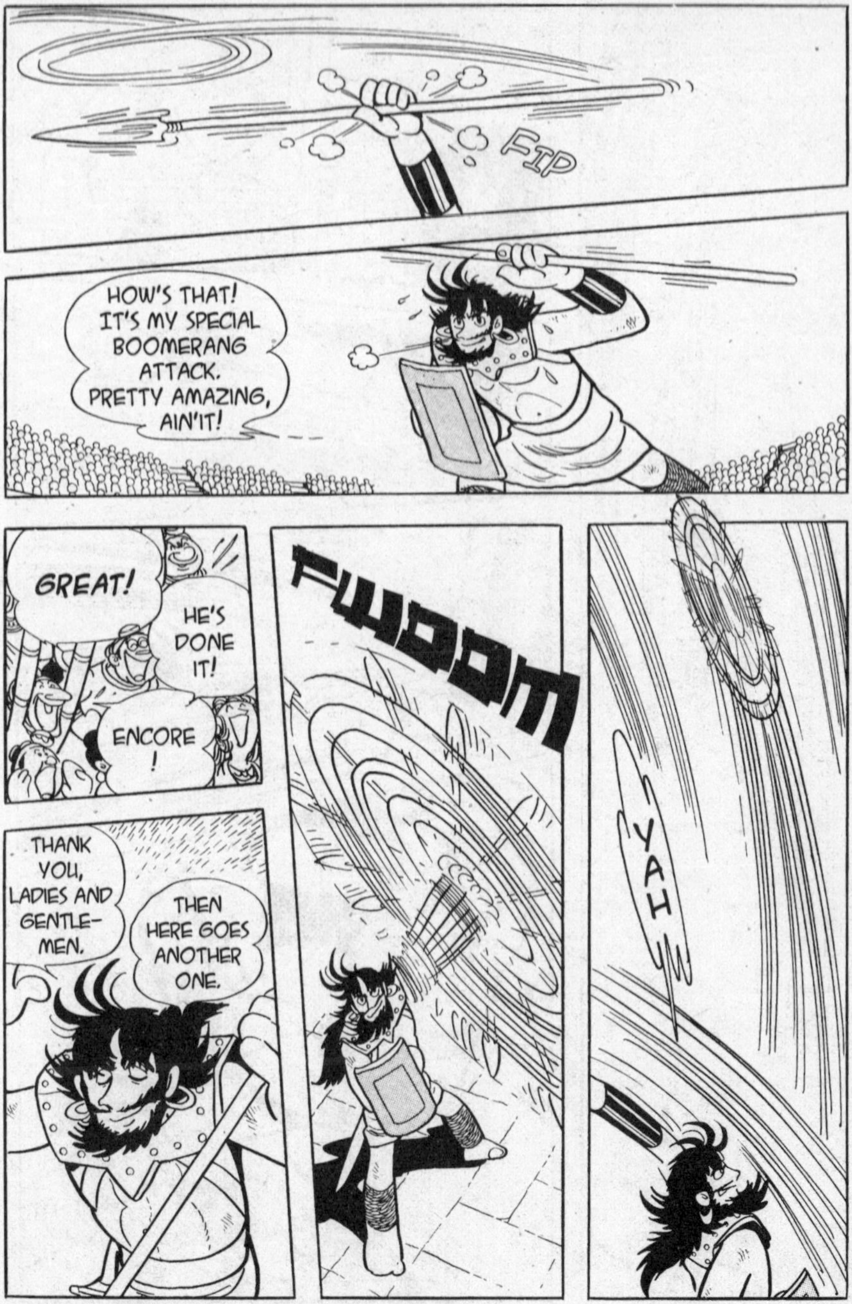
FIP
HOW'S THAT! IT'S MY SPECIAL BOOMERANG ATTACK. PRETTY AMAZING, AIN'T IT!
GREAT!
HE'S DONE IT!
ENCORE!
THANK YOU, LADIES AND GENTLE-MEN.
THEN HERE GOES ANOTHER ONE.
FWOOOM
YAH

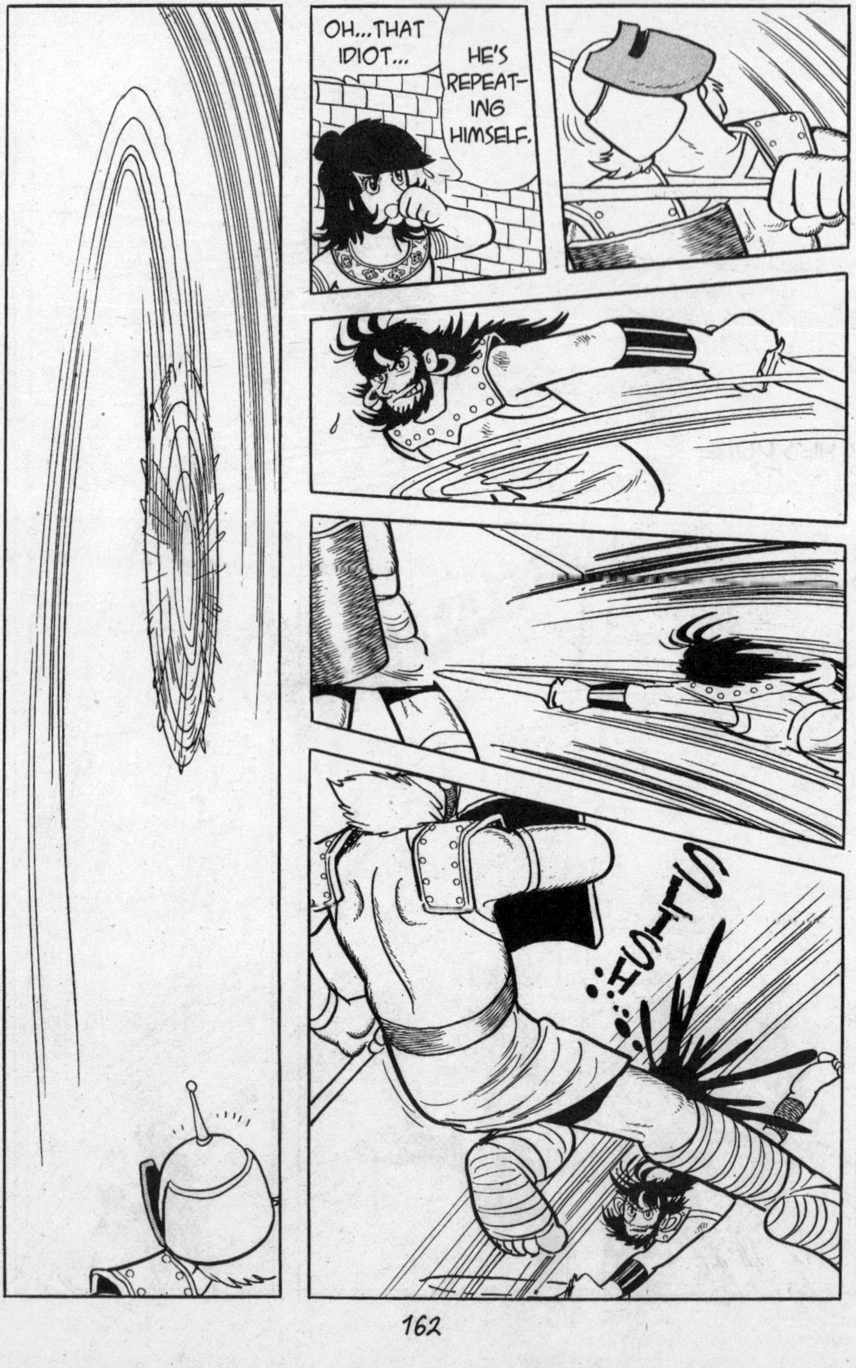
OH...THAT IDIOT...
HE'S REPEATING HIMSELF.

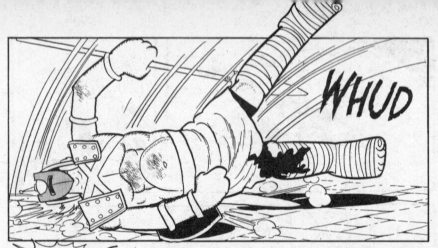

WHUD

HE'S DONE IT!

HURRY!

KILL HIM!

KILL!!

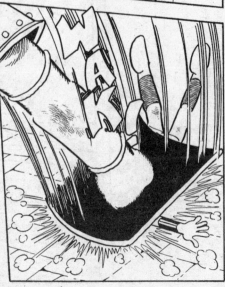

WAK

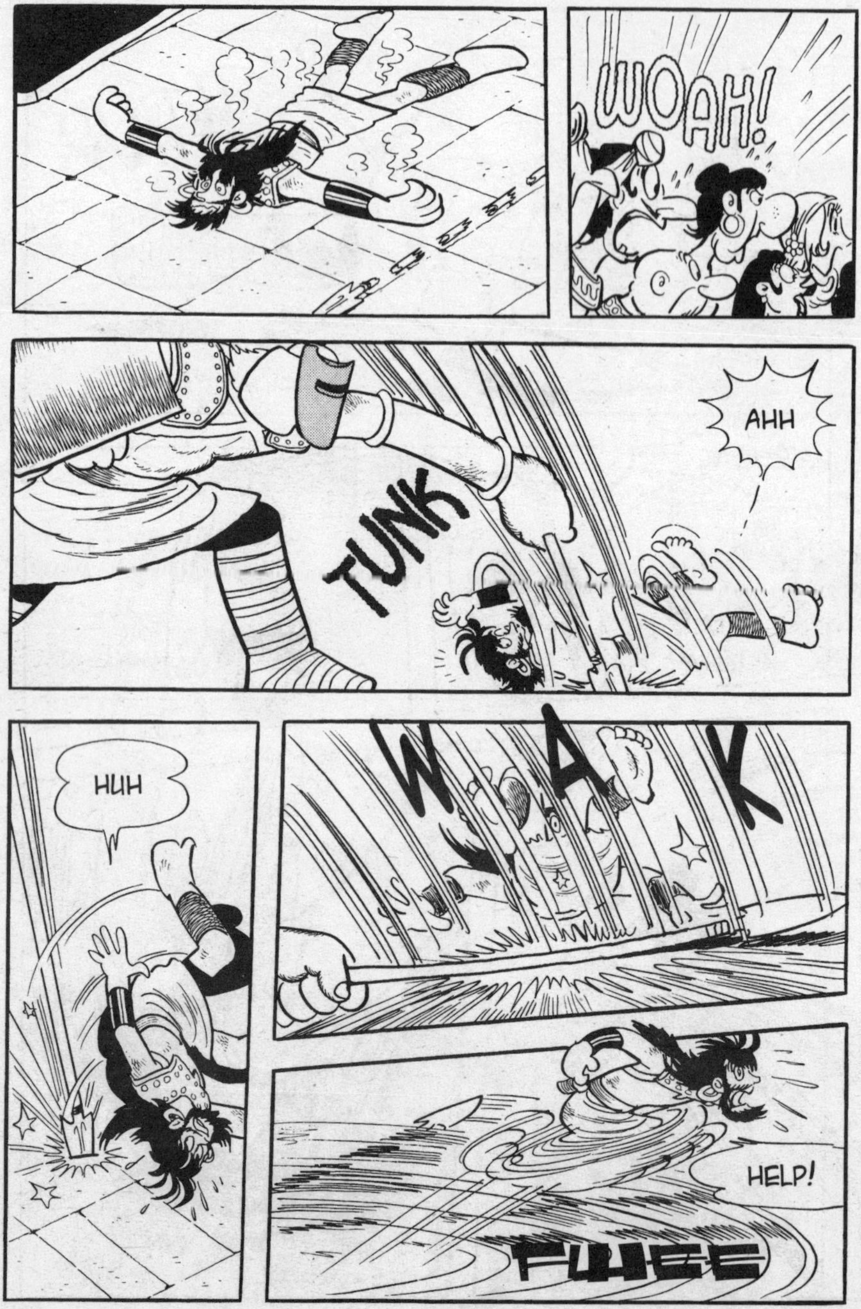
WOAH!
AHH
TUNK
HUH
WAK
HELP!
FWEE

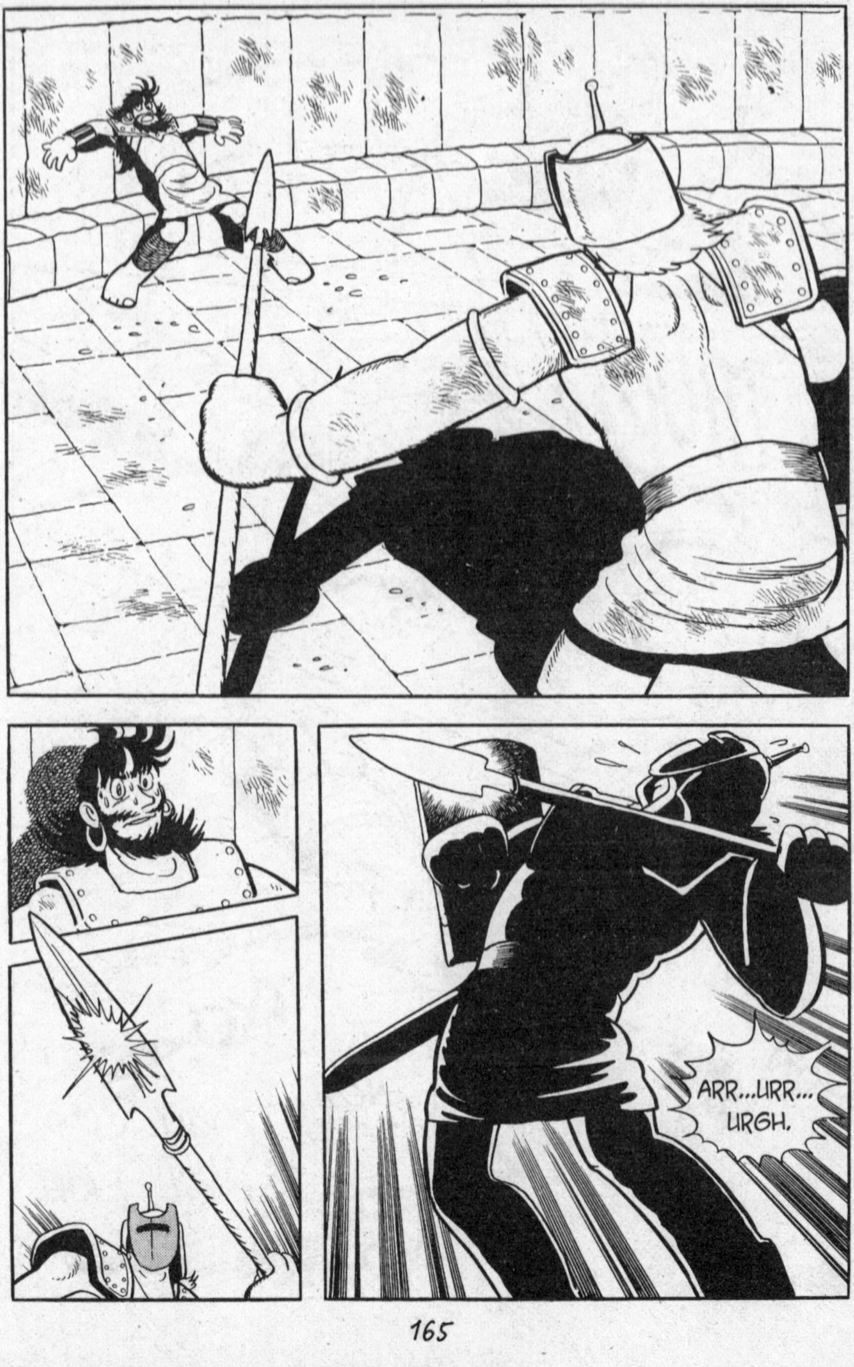
ARR...URR...
URGH.

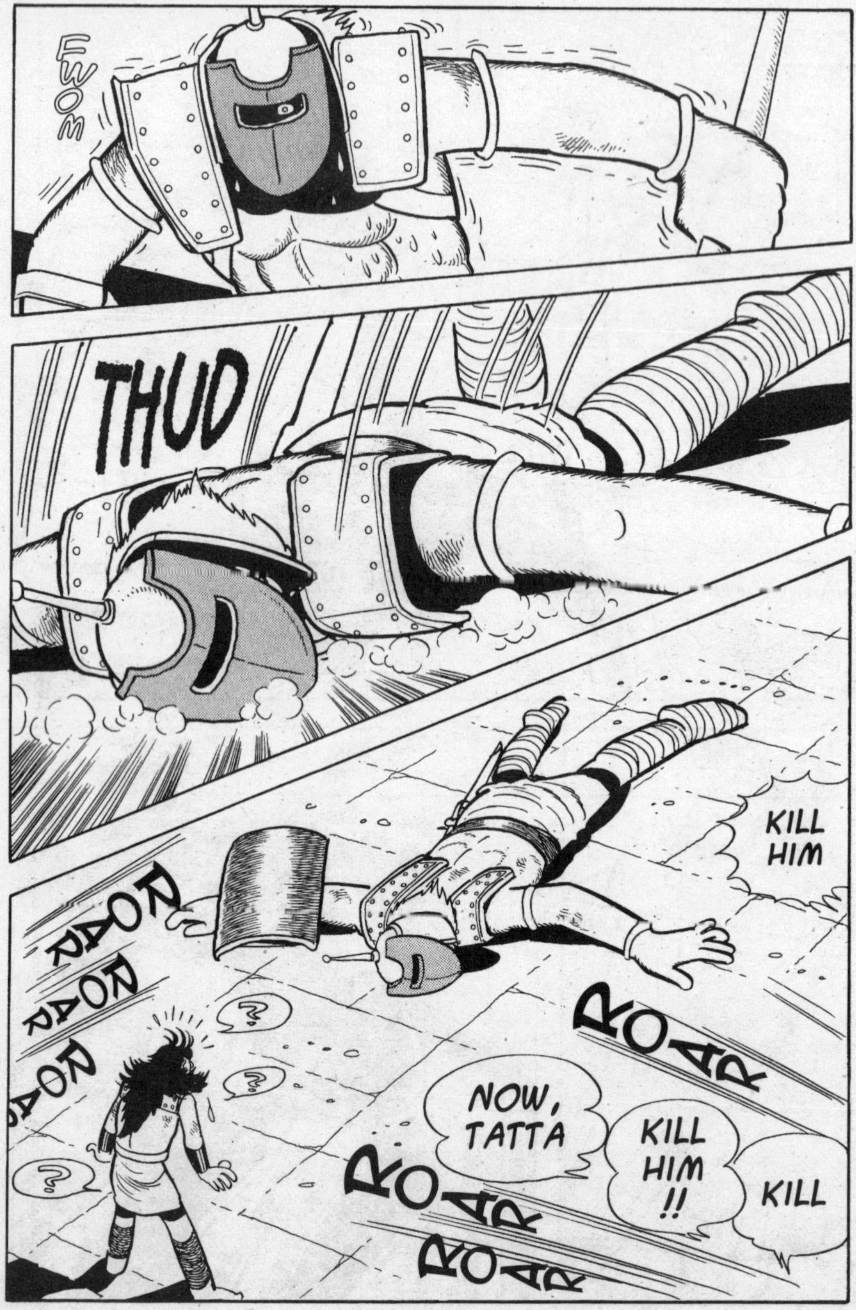
WOM
THUD
KILL HIM
ROAR ROAR ROAR
?
?
?
ROAR
NOW, TATTA
KILL HIM !!
KILL
ROAR
ROAR

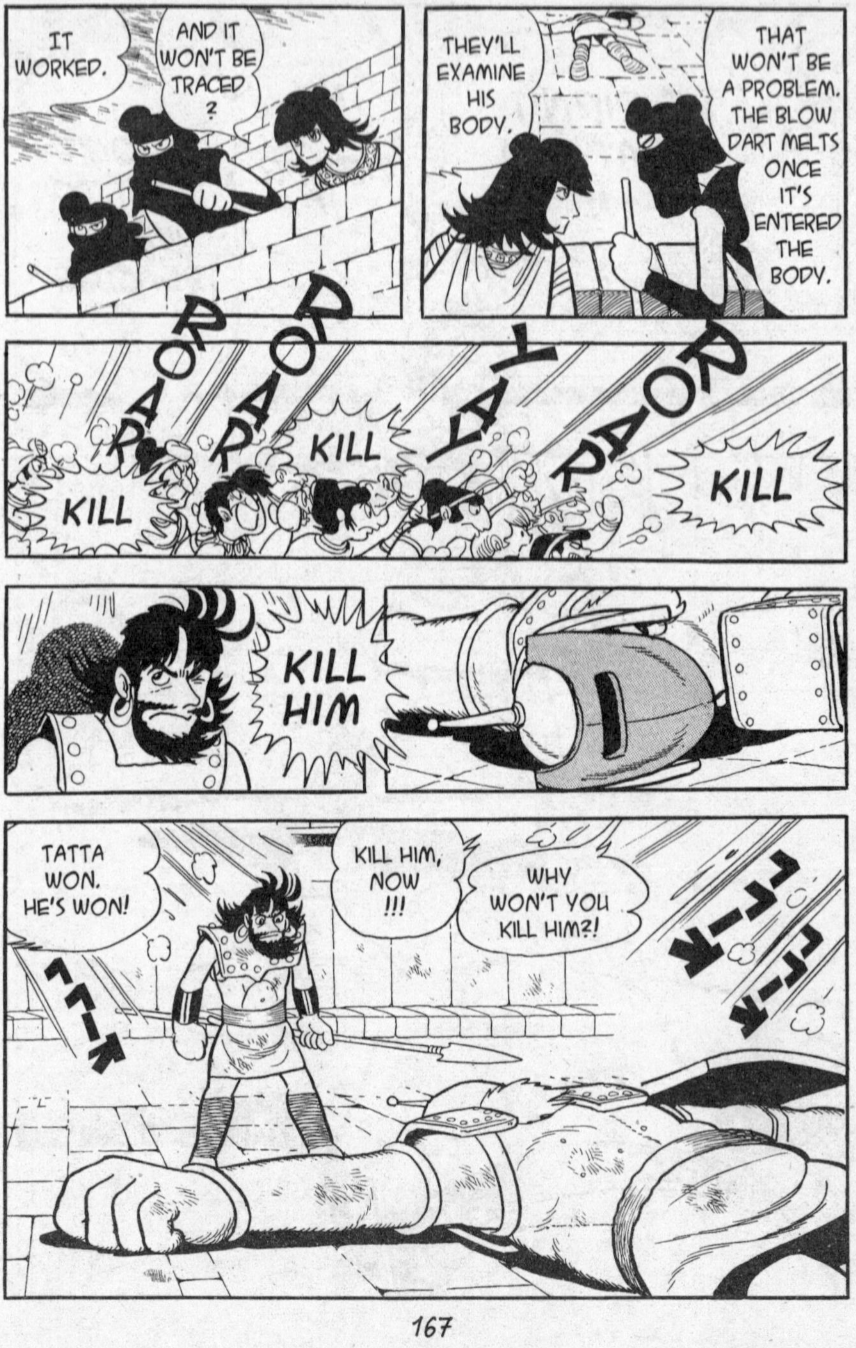
IT WORKED.
AND IT WON'T BE TRACED ?
THEY'LL EXAMINE HIS BODY.
THAT WON'T BE A PROBLEM. THE BLOW DART MELTS ONCE IT'S ENTERED THE BODY.
ROAR
ROAR
YAY
ROAR
KILL
KILL
KILL
KILL HIM
TATTA WON. HE'S WON!
KILL HIM, NOW !!!
WHY WON'T YOU KILL HIM?!

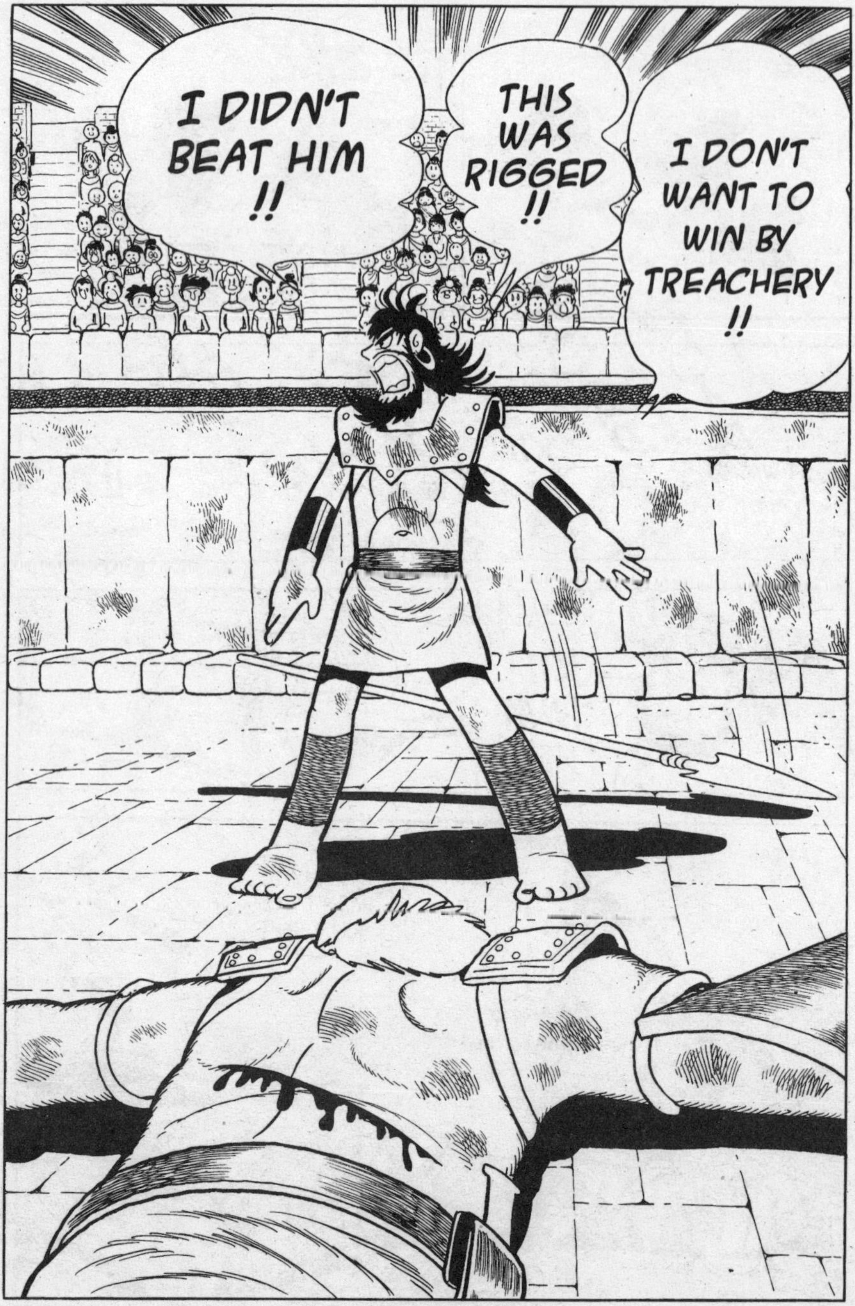
I DIDN'T BEAT HIM !!
THIS WAS RIGGED !!
I DON'T WANT TO WIN BY TREACHERY !!

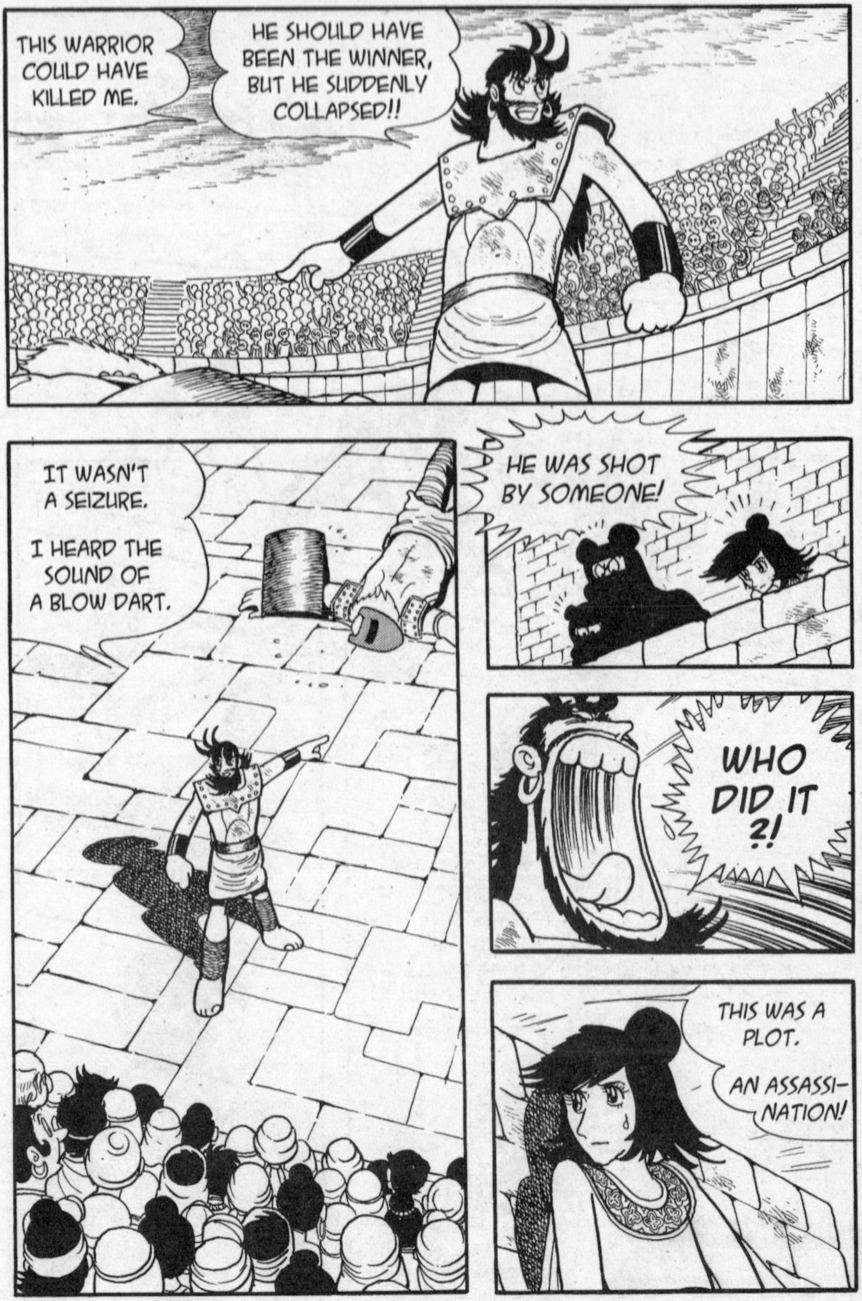

HE SHOULD HAVE BEEN THE WINNER, BUT HE SUDDENLY COLLAPSED!!
THIS WARRIOR COULD HAVE KILLED ME.
HE WAS SHOT BY SOMEONE!
IT WASN'T A SEIZURE.
I HEARD THE SOUND OF A BLOW DART.
WHO DID IT ?!
THIS WAS A PLOT.
AN ASSASSI-NATION!

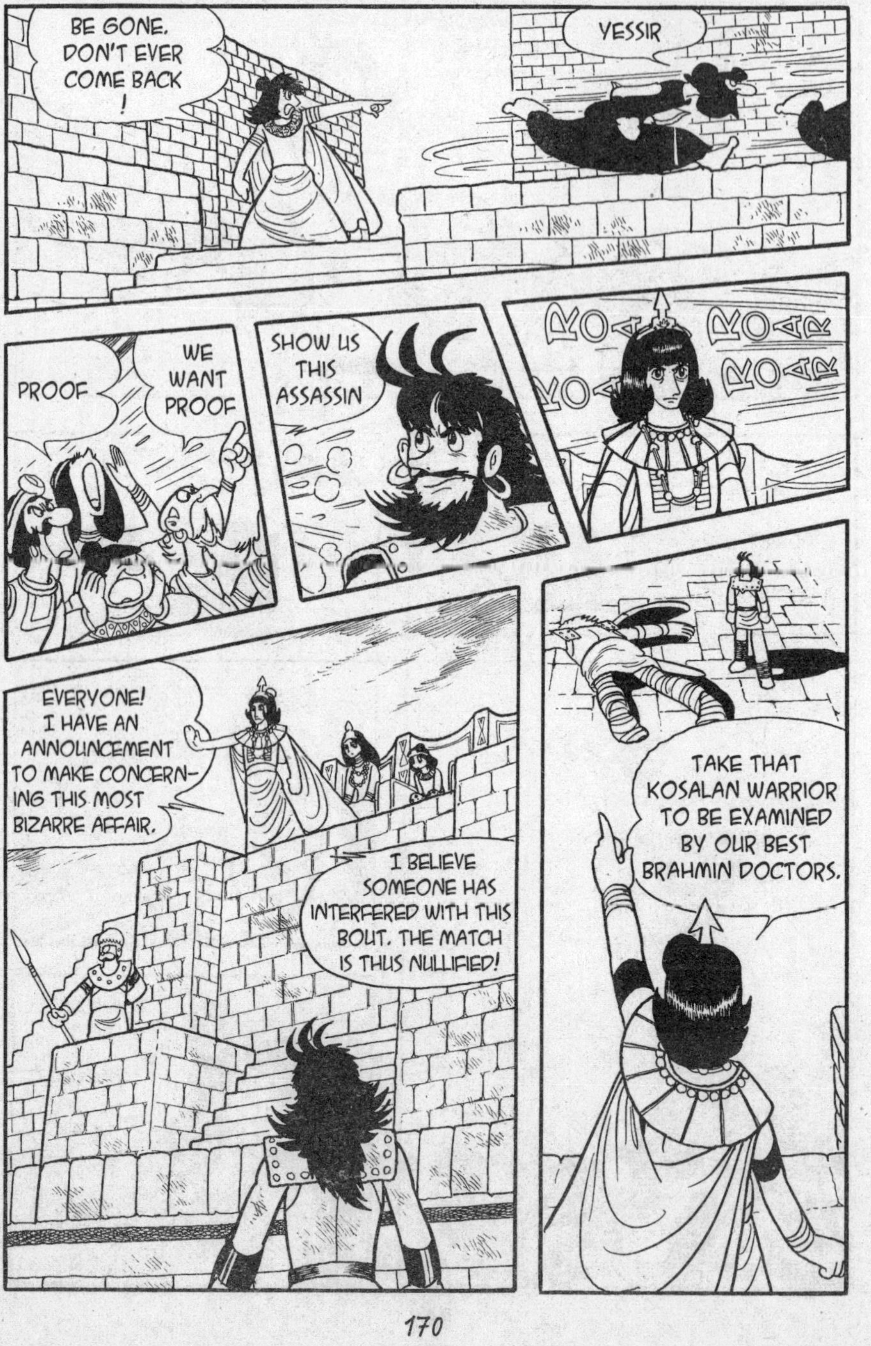

BE GONE. DON'T EVER COME BACK !
YESSIR
PROOF
WE WANT PROOF
SHOW US THIS ASSASSIN
ROAR ROAR ROAR ROAR
EVERYONE! I HAVE AN ANNOUNCEMENT TO MAKE CONCERNING THIS MOST BIZARRE AFFAIR.
I BELIEVE SOMEONE HAS INTERFERED WITH THIS BOUT. THE MATCH IS THUS NULLIFIED!
TAKE THAT KOSALAN WARRIOR TO BE EXAMINED BY OUR BEST BRAHMIN DOCTORS.

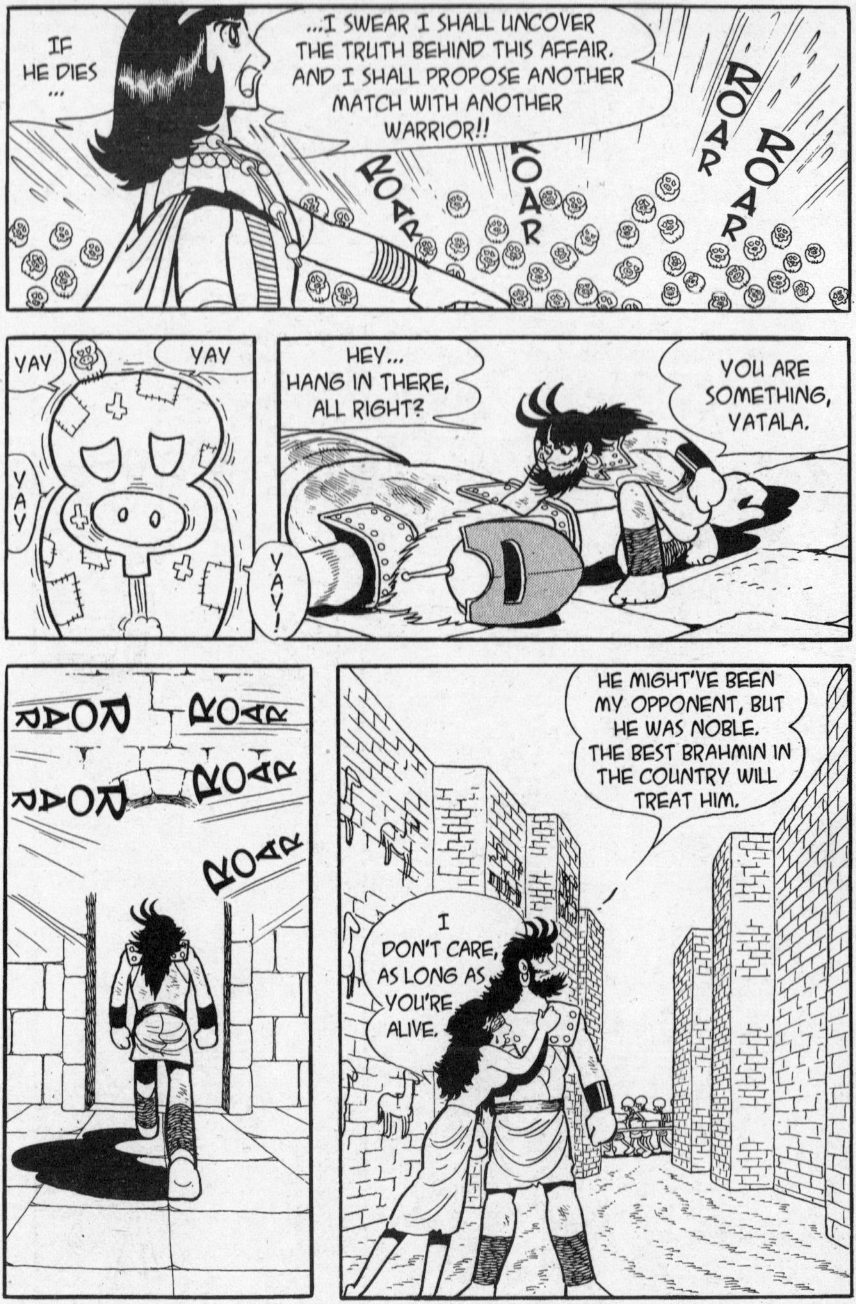
IF HE DIES ...
...I SWEAR I SHALL UNCOVER THE TRUTH BEHIND THIS AFFAIR. AND I SHALL PROPOSE ANOTHER MATCH WITH ANOTHER WARRIOR!!
ROAR
ROAR
ROAR
ROAR
ROAR
YAY
YAY
YAY
YAY!
HEY... HANG IN THERE, ALL RIGHT?
YOU ARE SOMETHING, YATALA.
ROAR
ROAR
ROAR
ROAR
ROAR
HE MIGHT'VE BEEN MY OPPONENT, BUT HE WAS NOBLE. THE BEST BRAHMIN IN THE COUNTRY WILL TREAT HIM.
I DON'T CARE, AS LONG AS YOU'RE ALIVE.

CHAPTER FOUR

CRISIS

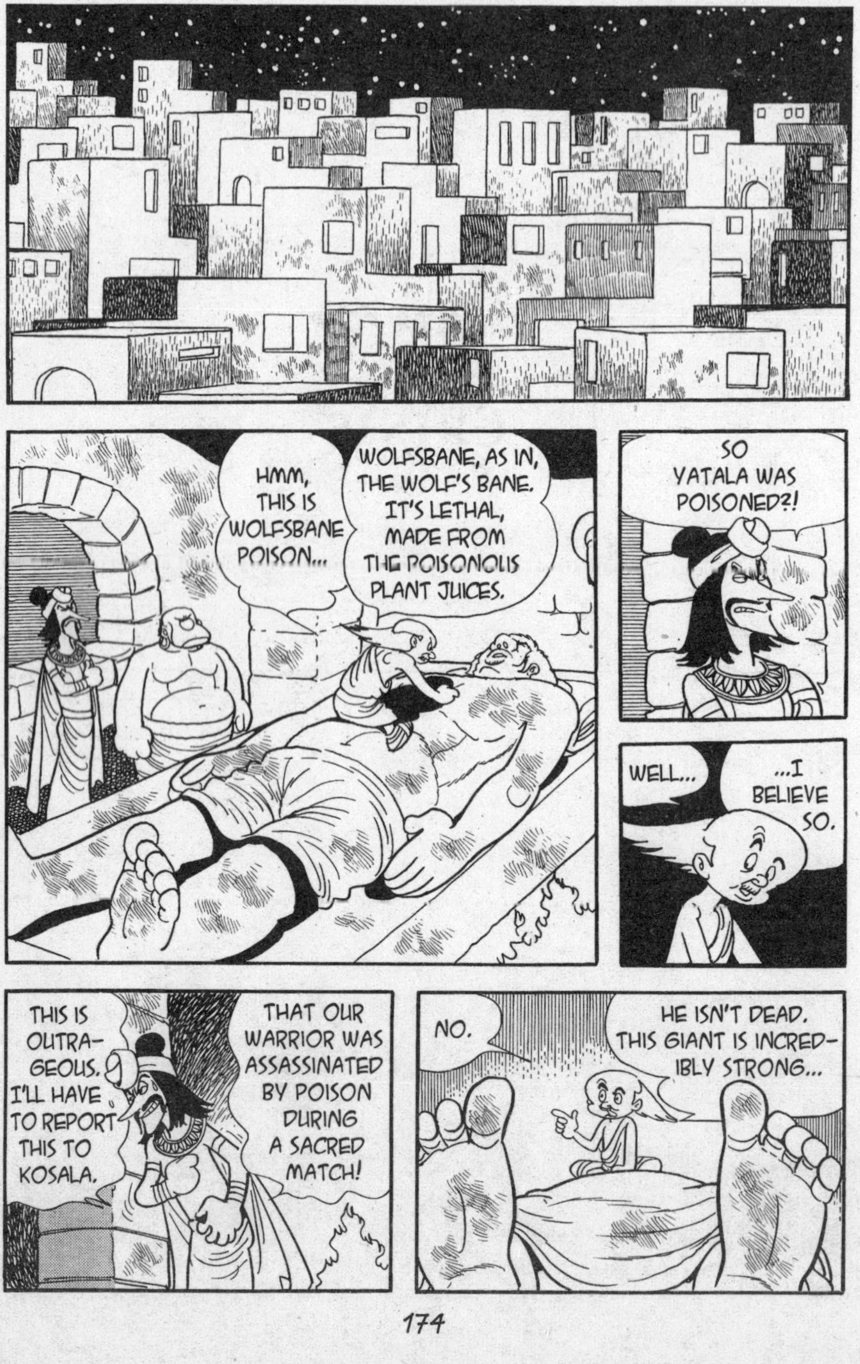

HMM, THIS IS WOLFSBANE POISON...
WOLFSBANE, AS IN, THE WOLF'S BANE. IT'S LETHAL, MADE FROM THE POISONOUS PLANT JUICES.
SO YATALA WAS POISONED?!
WELL...
...I BELIEVE SO.
THIS IS OUTRA-GEOUS. I'LL HAVE TO REPORT THIS TO KOSALA.
THAT OUR WARRIOR WAS ASSASSINATED BY POISON DURING A SACRED MATCH!
NO.
HE ISN'T DEAD. THIS GIANT IS INCRED-IBLY STRONG...

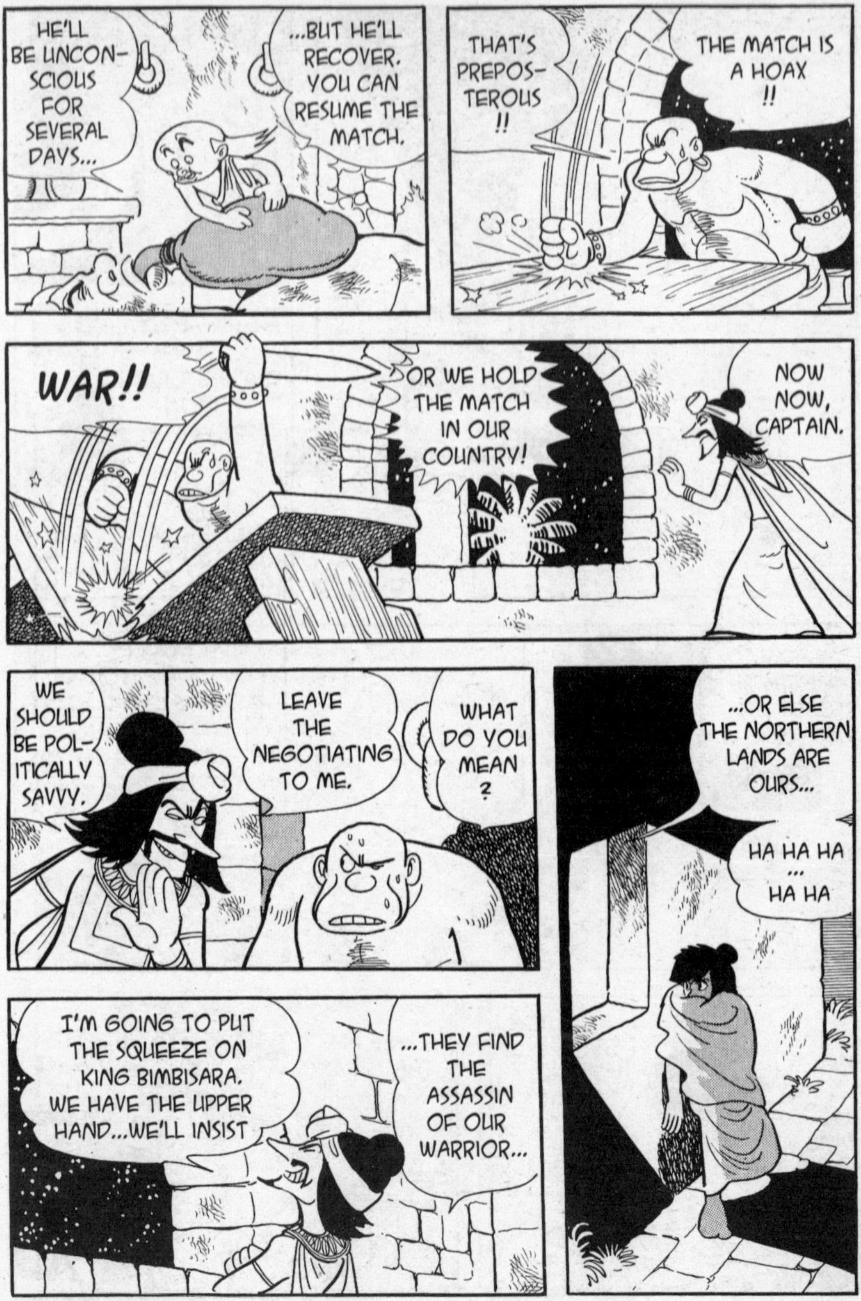
HE'LL BE UNCON-SCIOUS FOR SEVERAL DAYS...
...BUT HE'LL RECOVER. YOU CAN RESUME THE MATCH.
THAT'S PREPOS-TEROUS !!
THE MATCH IS A HOAX !!
WAR!!
OR WE HOLD THE MATCH IN OUR COUNTRY!
NOW NOW, CAPTAIN.
WE SHOULD BE POL-ITICALLY SAVVY.
LEAVE THE NEGOTIATING TO ME.
WHAT DO YOU MEAN ?
I'M GOING TO PUT THE SQUEEZE ON KING BIMBISARA. WE HAVE THE UPPER HAND...WE'LL INSIST
...THEY FIND THE ASSASSIN OF OUR WARRIOR...
...OR ELSE THE NORTHERN LANDS ARE OURS...
HA HA HA ... HA HA

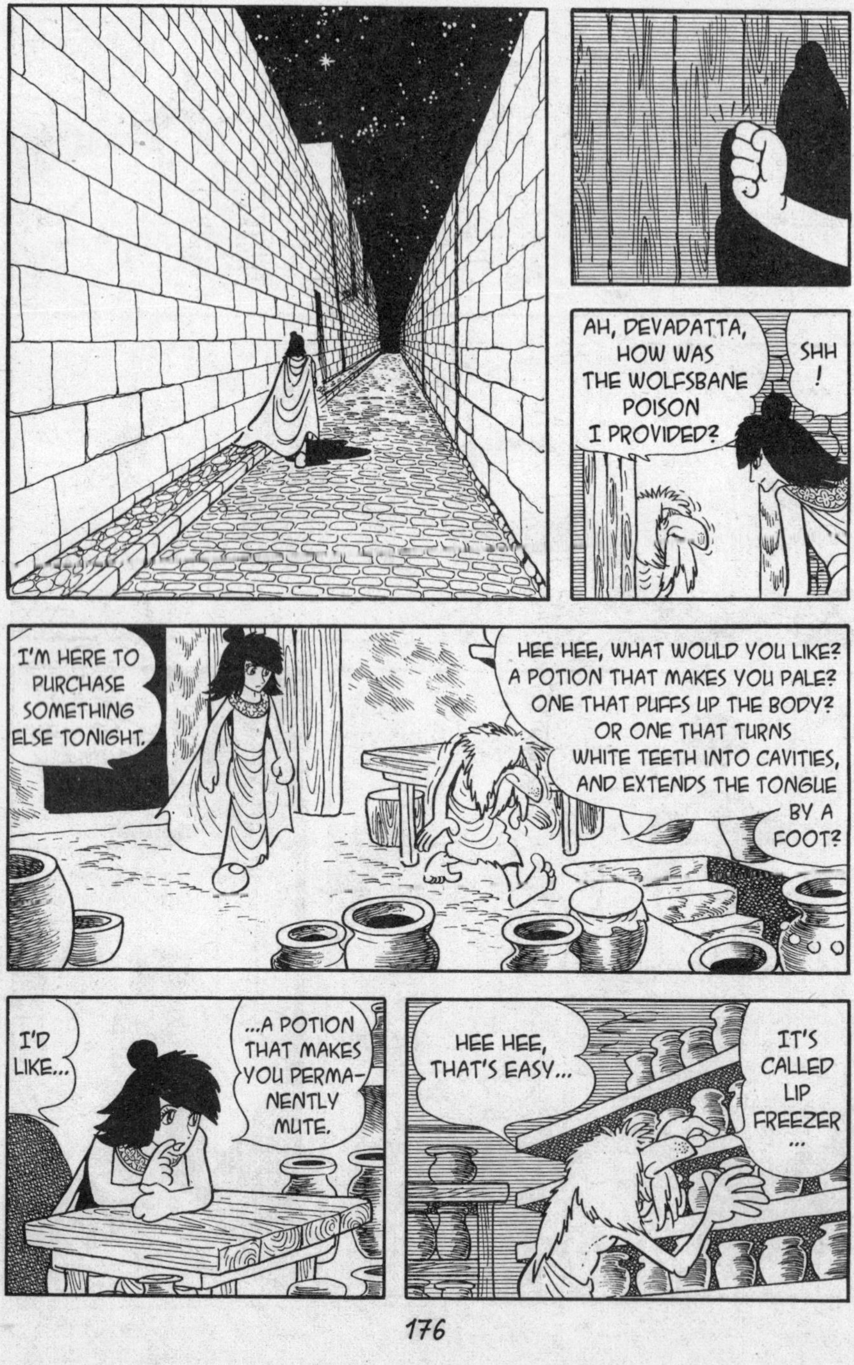
AH, DEVADATTA, HOW WAS THE WOLFSBANE POISON I PROVIDED?
SHH !
I'M HERE TO PURCHASE SOMETHING ELSE TONIGHT.
HEE HEE, WHAT WOULD YOU LIKE? A POTION THAT MAKES YOU PALE? ONE THAT PUFFS UP THE BODY? OR ONE THAT TURNS WHITE TEETH INTO CAVITIES, AND EXTENDS THE TONGUE BY A FOOT?
I'D LIKE...
...A POTION THAT MAKES YOU PERMA-NENTLY MUTE.
HEE HEE, THAT'S EASY...
IT'S CALLED LIP FREEZER ...

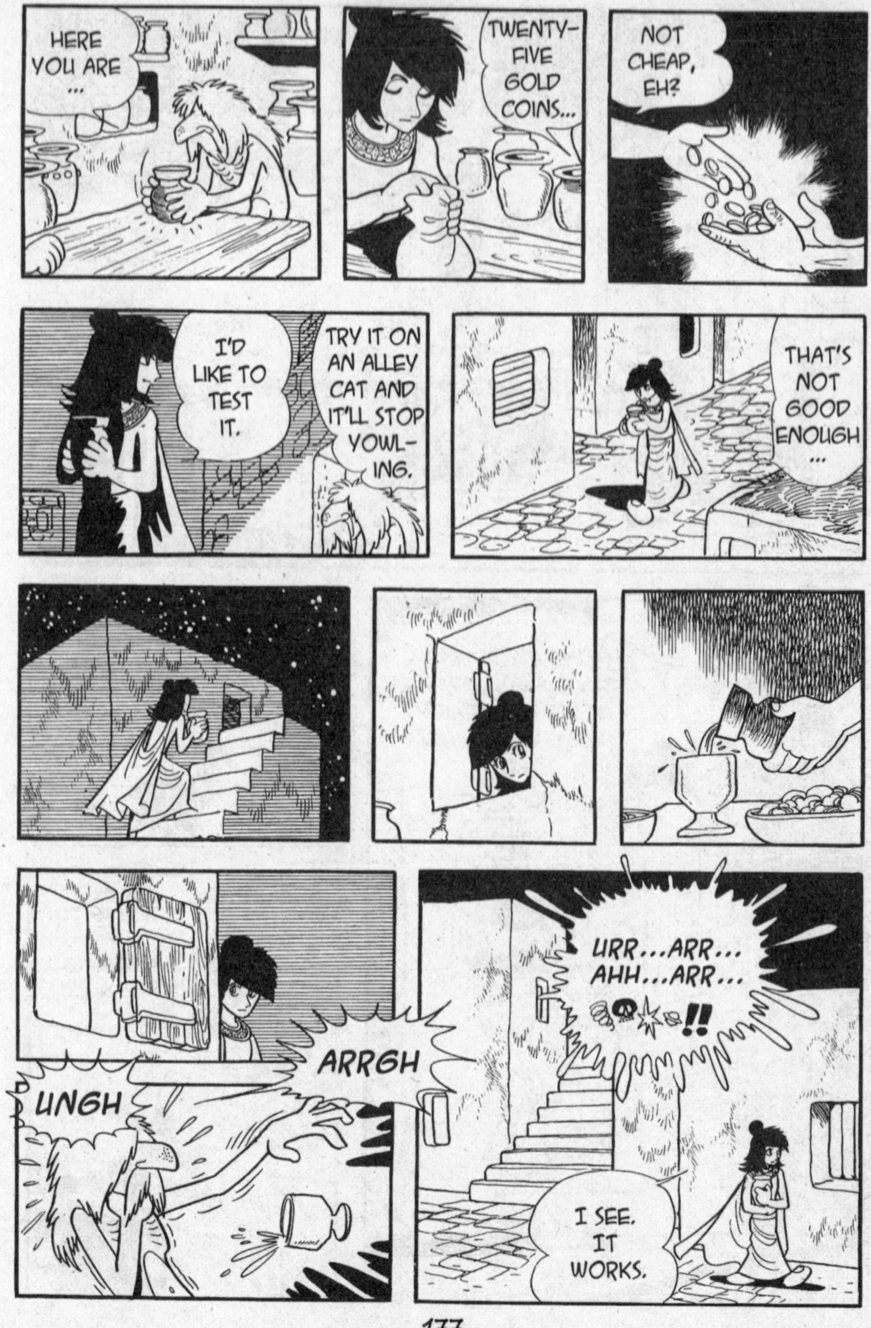
HERE YOU ARE ...
TWENTY-FIVE GOLD COINS...
NOT CHEAP, EH?
I'D LIKE TO TEST IT.
TRY IT ON AN ALLEY CAT AND IT'LL STOP YOWL-ING.
THAT'S NOT GOOD ENOUGH ...
ARRGH
UNGH
URR...ARR... AHH...ARR... !!
I SEE. IT WORKS.

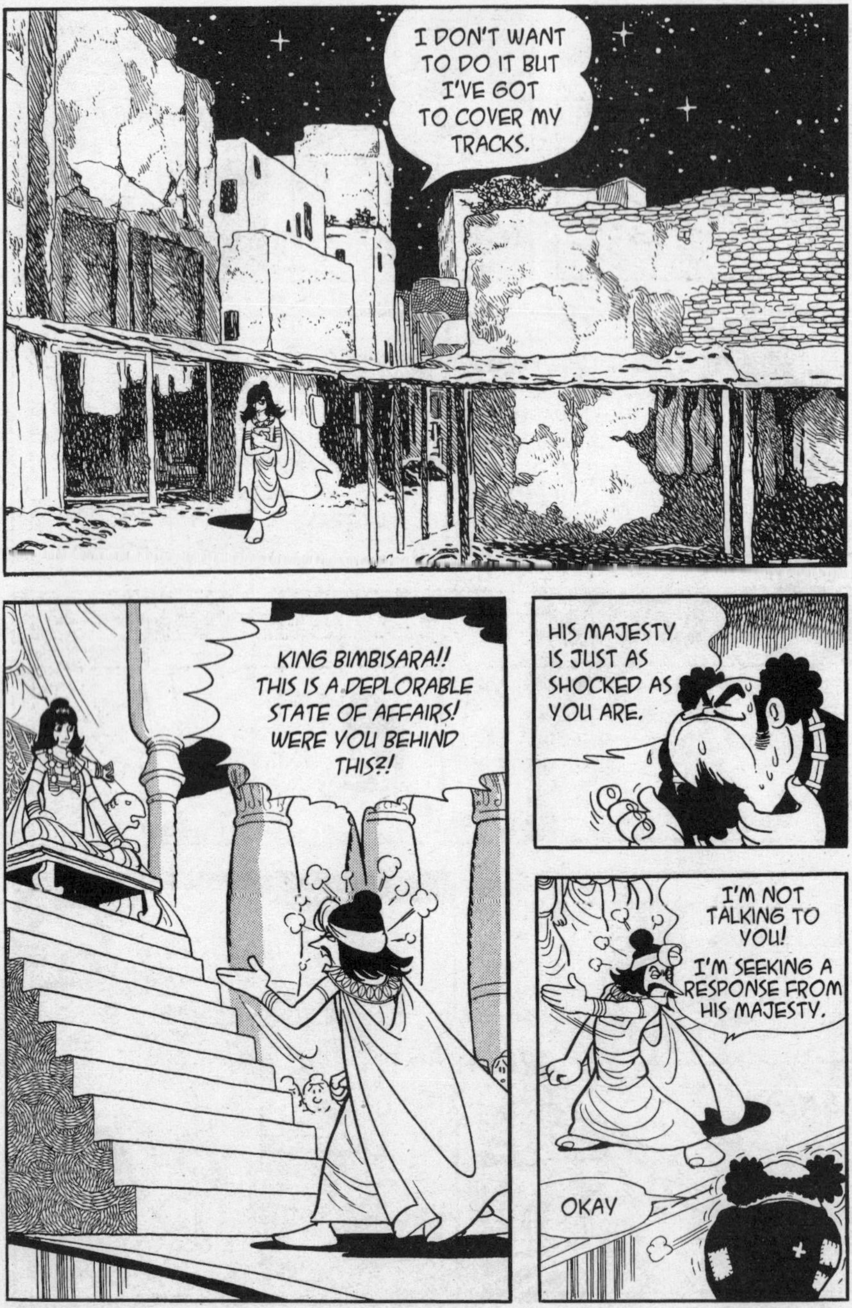
I DON'T WANT TO DO IT BUT I'VE GOT TO COVER MY TRACKS.
KING BIMBISARA!! THIS IS A DEPLORABLE STATE OF AFFAIRS! WERE YOU BEHIND THIS?!
HIS MAJESTY IS JUST AS SHOCKED AS YOU ARE.
I'M NOT TALKING TO YOU!
I'M SEEKING A RESPONSE FROM HIS MAJESTY.
OKAY

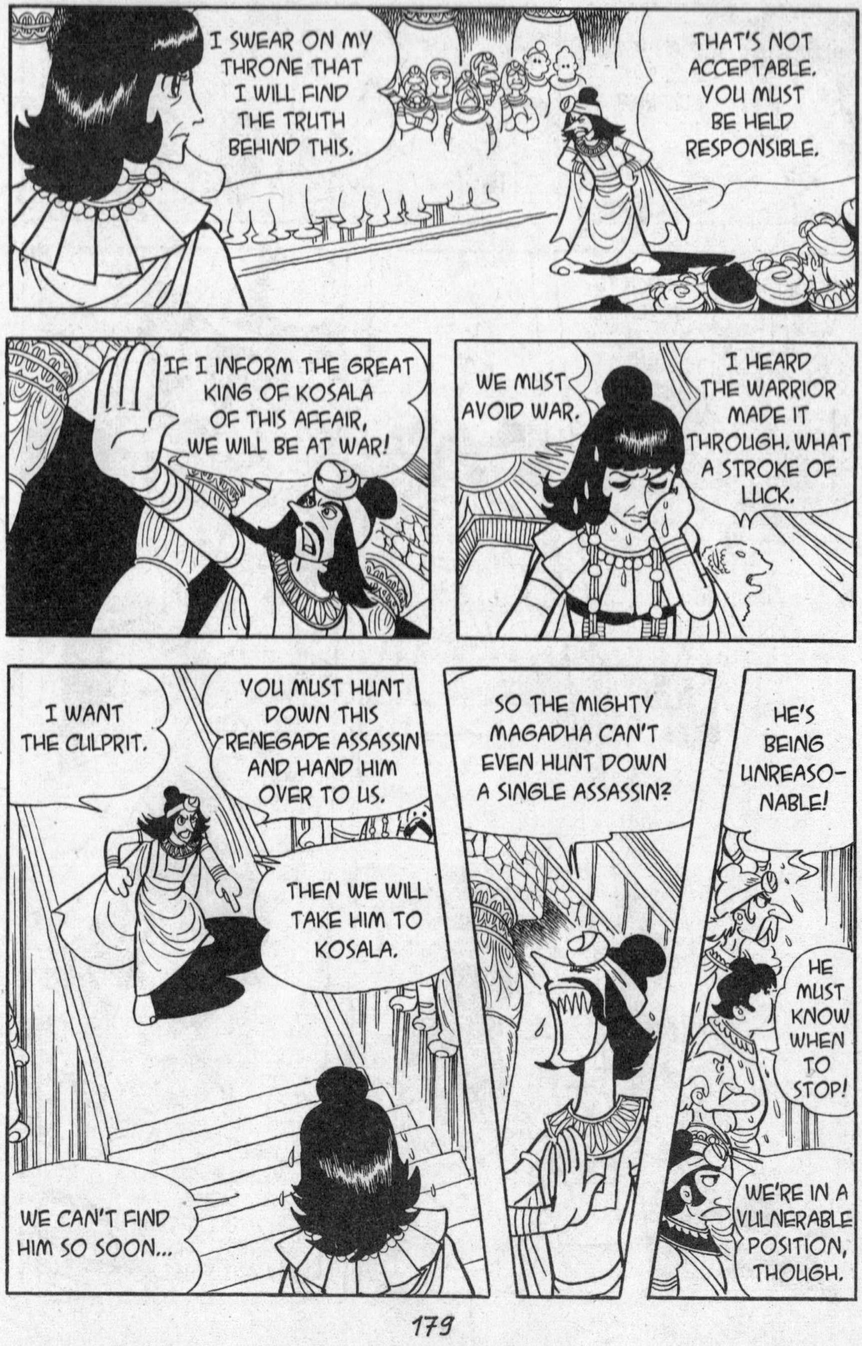
I SWEAR ON MY THRONE THAT I WILL FIND THE TRUTH BEHIND THIS.
THAT'S NOT ACCEPTABLE. YOU MUST BE HELD RESPONSIBLE.
IF I INFORM THE GREAT KING OF KOSALA OF THIS AFFAIR, WE WILL BE AT WAR!
WE MUST AVOID WAR.
I HEARD THE WARRIOR MADE IT THROUGH. WHAT A STROKE OF LUCK.
I WANT THE CULPRIT.
YOU MUST HUNT DOWN THIS RENEGADE ASSASSIN AND HAND HIM OVER TO US.
THEN WE WILL TAKE HIM TO KOSALA.
WE CAN'T FIND HIM SO SOON...
SO THE MIGHTY MAGADHA CAN'T EVEN HUNT DOWN A SINGLE ASSASSIN?
HE'S BEING UNREASO-NABLE!
HE MUST KNOW WHEN TO STOP!
WE'RE IN A VULNERABLE POSITION, THOUGH.

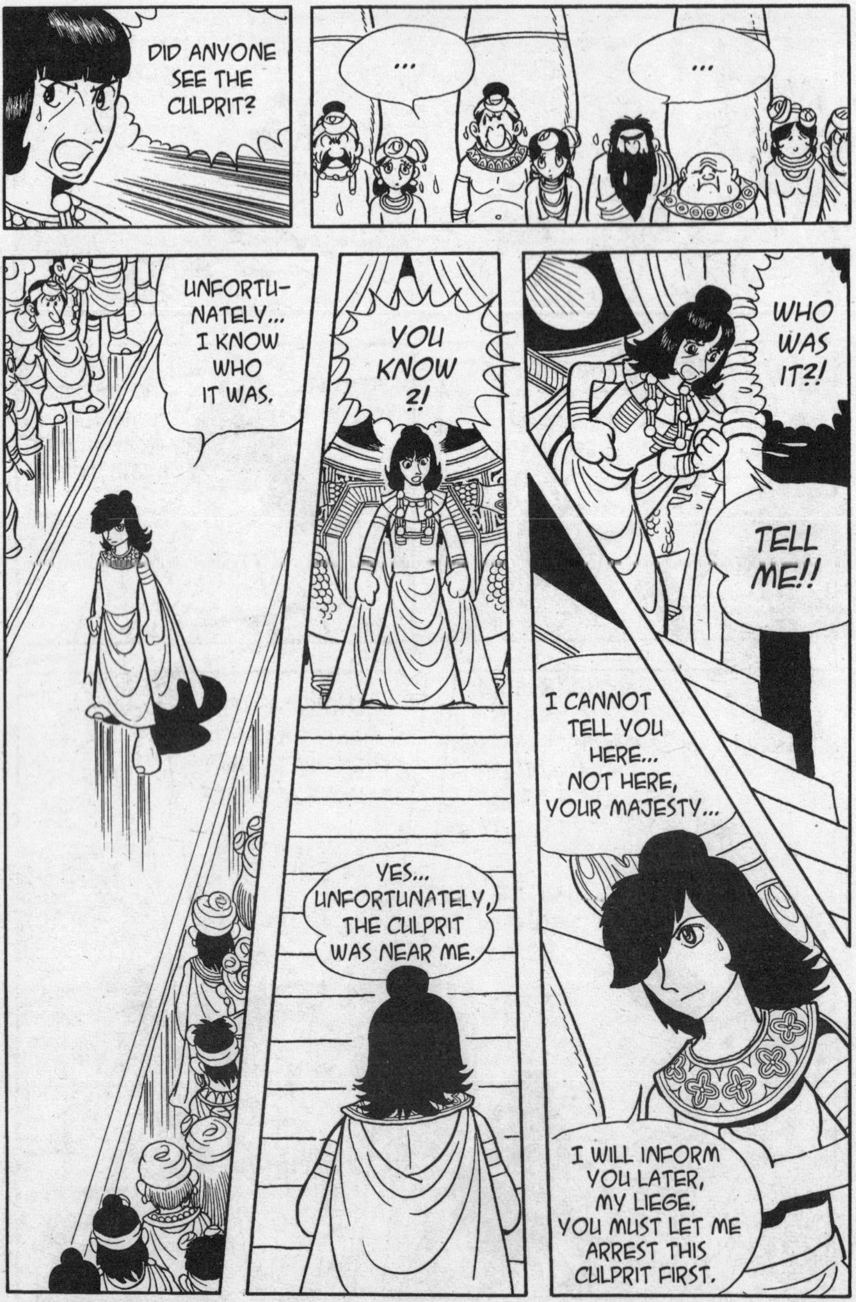
DID ANYONE SEE THE CULPRIT?
...
...
UNFORTU- NATELY... I KNOW WHO IT WAS.
YOU KNOW ?!
WHO WAS IT?!
TELL ME!!
YES... UNFORTUNATELY, THE CULPRIT WAS NEAR ME.
I CANNOT TELL YOU HERE... NOT HERE, YOUR MAJESTY...
I WILL INFORM YOU LATER, MY LIEGE. YOU MUST LET ME ARREST THIS CULPRIT FIRST.

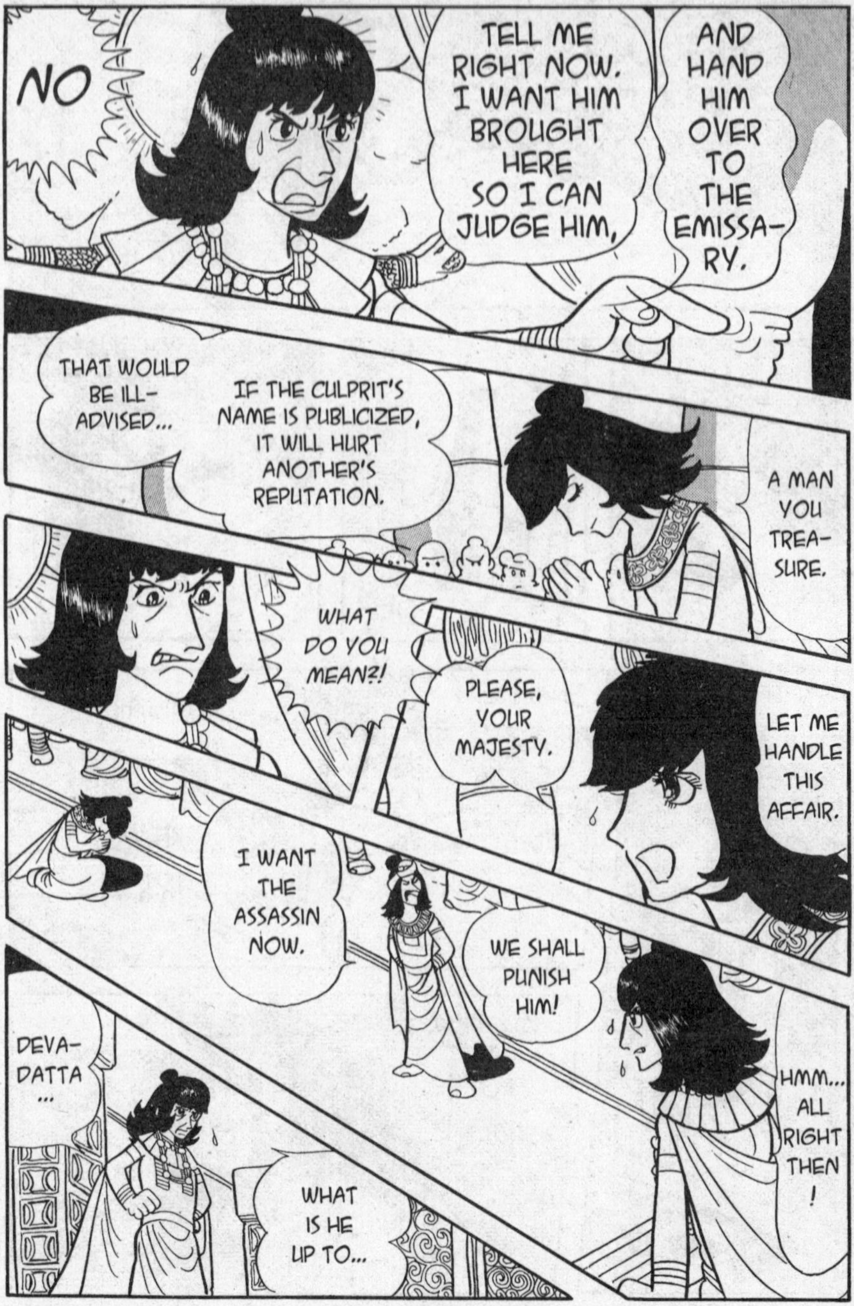
NO
TELL ME RIGHT NOW. I WANT HIM BROUGHT HERE SO I CAN JUDGE HIM,
AND HAND HIM OVER TO THE EMISSARY.
THAT WOULD BE ILL-ADVISED...
IF THE CULPRIT'S NAME IS PUBLICIZED, IT WILL HURT ANOTHER'S REPUTATION.
A MAN YOU TREASURE.
WHAT DO YOU MEAN?!
PLEASE, YOUR MAJESTY.
LET ME HANDLE THIS AFFAIR.
I WANT THE ASSASSIN NOW.
WE SHALL PUNISH HIM!
HMM... ALL RIGHT THEN!
DEVADATTA...
WHAT IS HE UP TO...

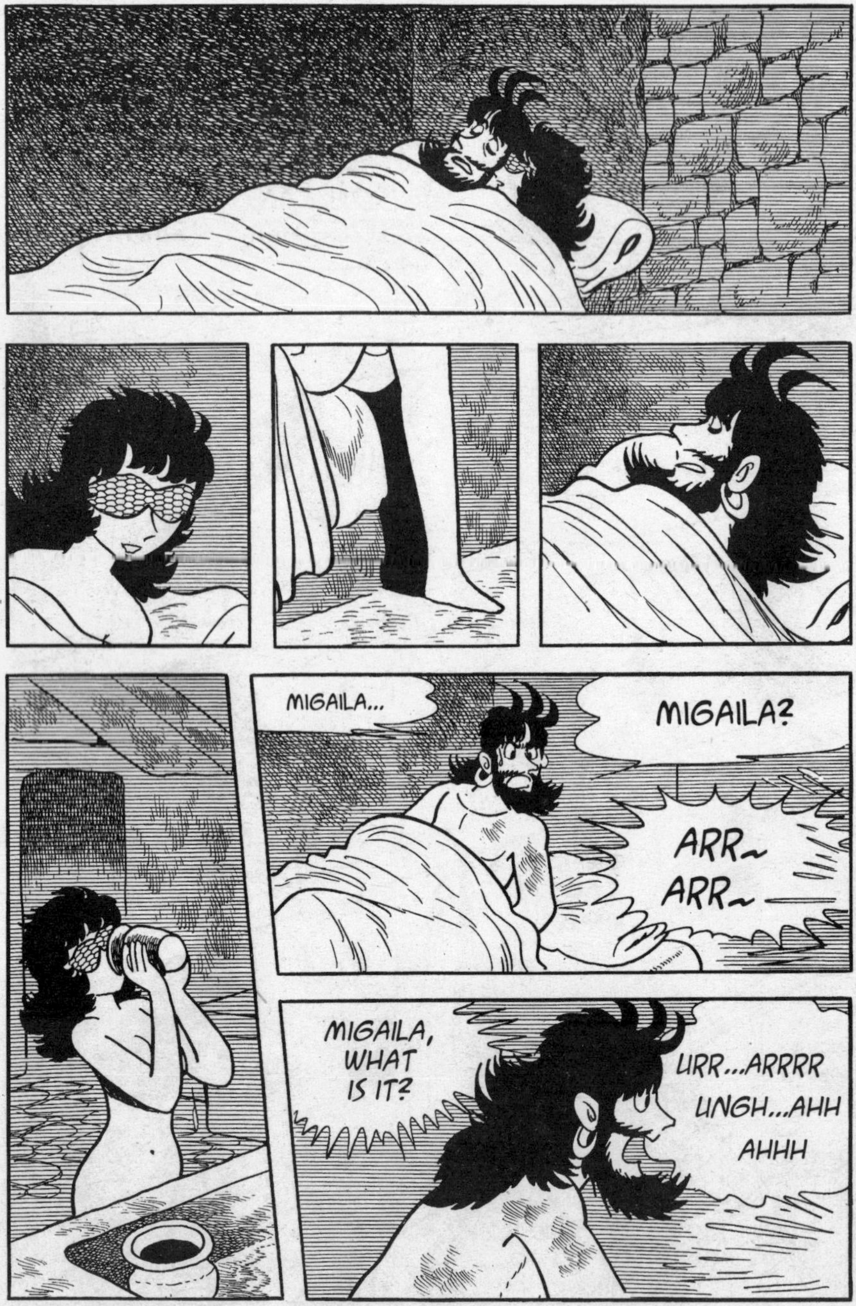
MIGAILA...
MIGAILA?
ARR~
ARR~
MIGAILA, WHAT IS IT?
URR...ARRRR
UNGH...AHH
AHHH

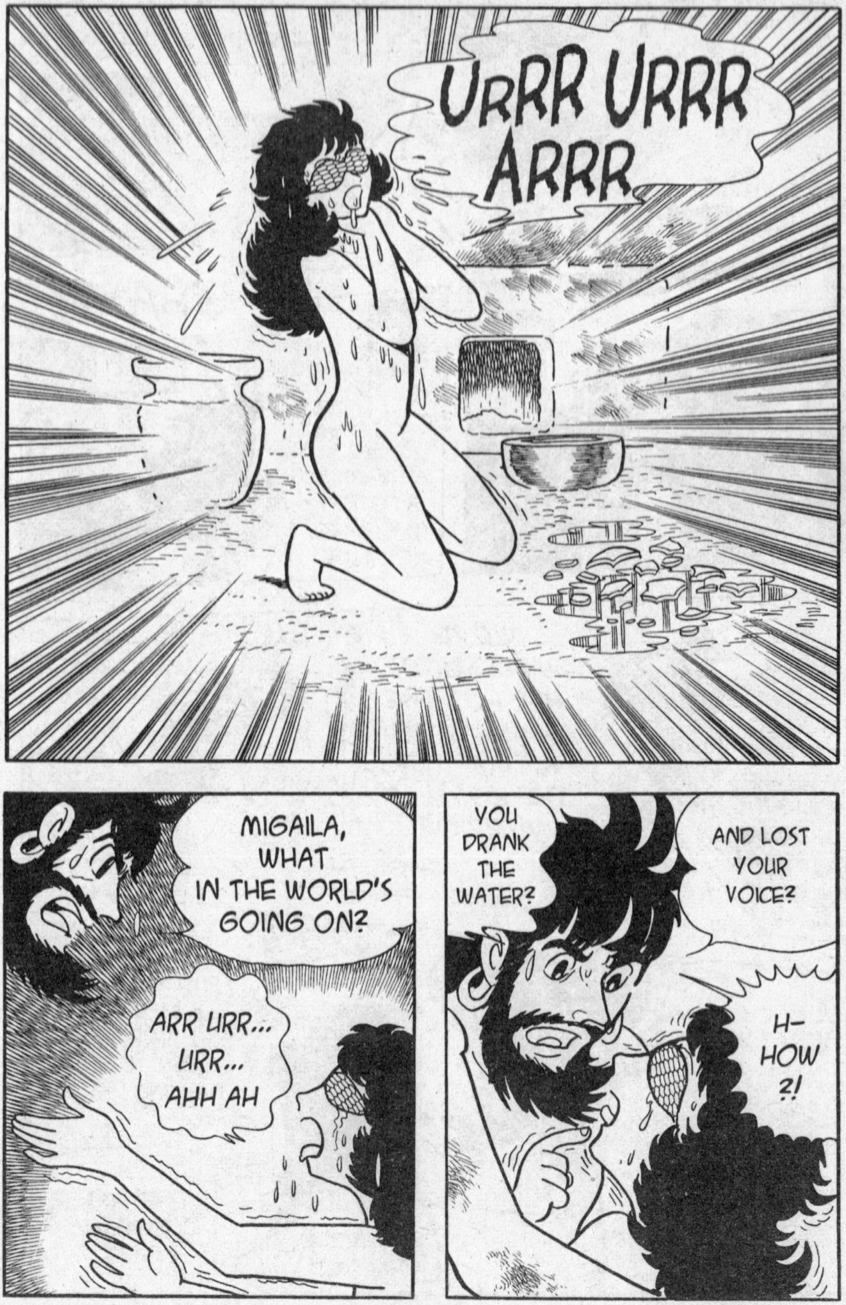
URRR URRR ARRR
MIGAILA, WHAT IN THE WORLD'S GOING ON?
ARR URR... URR... AHH AH
YOU DRANK THE WATER?
AND LOST YOUR VOICE?
H- HOW ?!

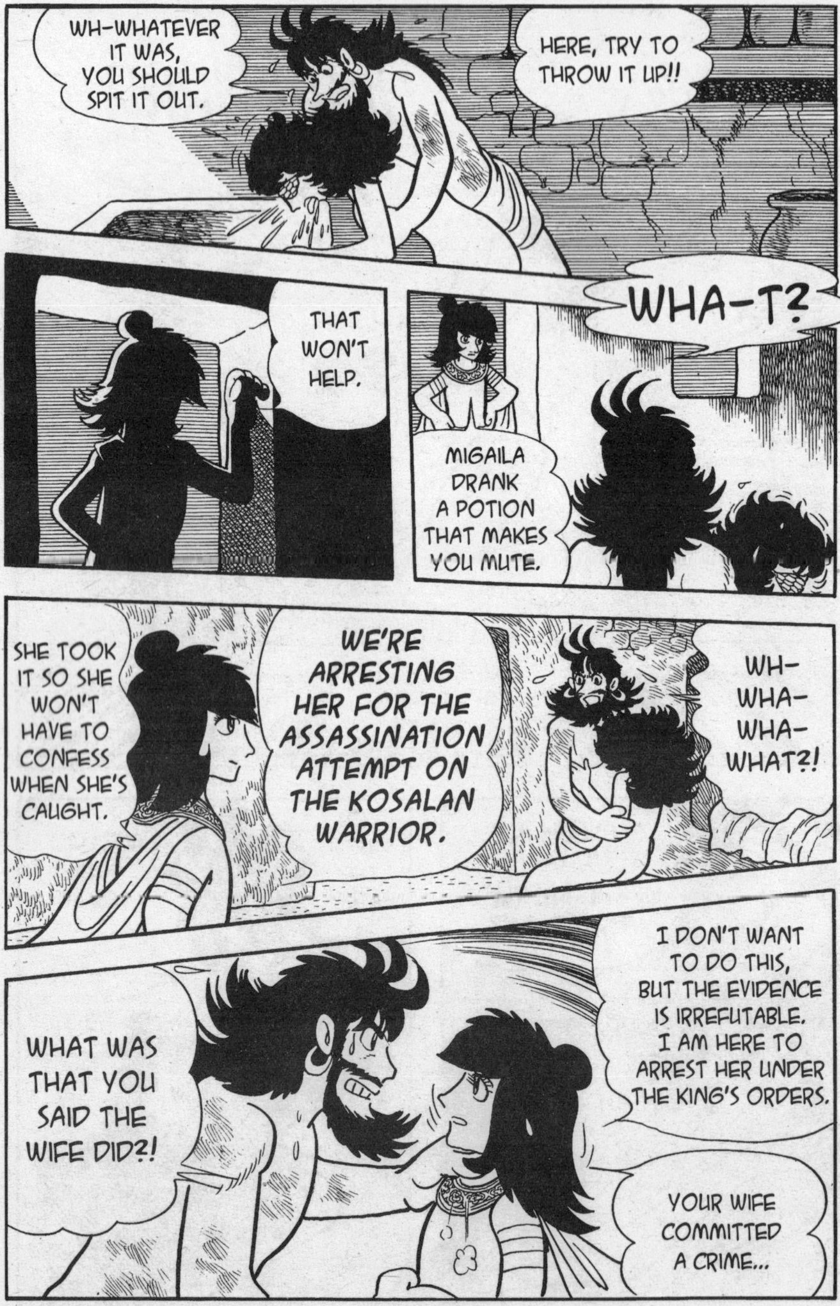
WH-WHATEVER IT WAS, YOU SHOULD SPIT IT OUT.
HERE, TRY TO THROW IT UP!!
WHA-T?
THAT WON'T HELP.
MIGAILA DRANK A POTION THAT MAKES YOU MUTE.
WH- WHA- WHA- WHAT?!
WE'RE ARRESTING HER FOR THE ASSASSINATION ATTEMPT ON THE KOSALAN WARRIOR.
SHE TOOK IT SO SHE WON'T HAVE TO CONFESS WHEN SHE'S CAUGHT.
I DON'T WANT TO DO THIS, BUT THE EVIDENCE IS IRREFUTABLE. I AM HERE TO ARREST HER UNDER THE KING'S ORDERS.
WHAT WAS THAT YOU SAID THE WIFE DID?!
YOUR WIFE COMMITTED A CRIME...

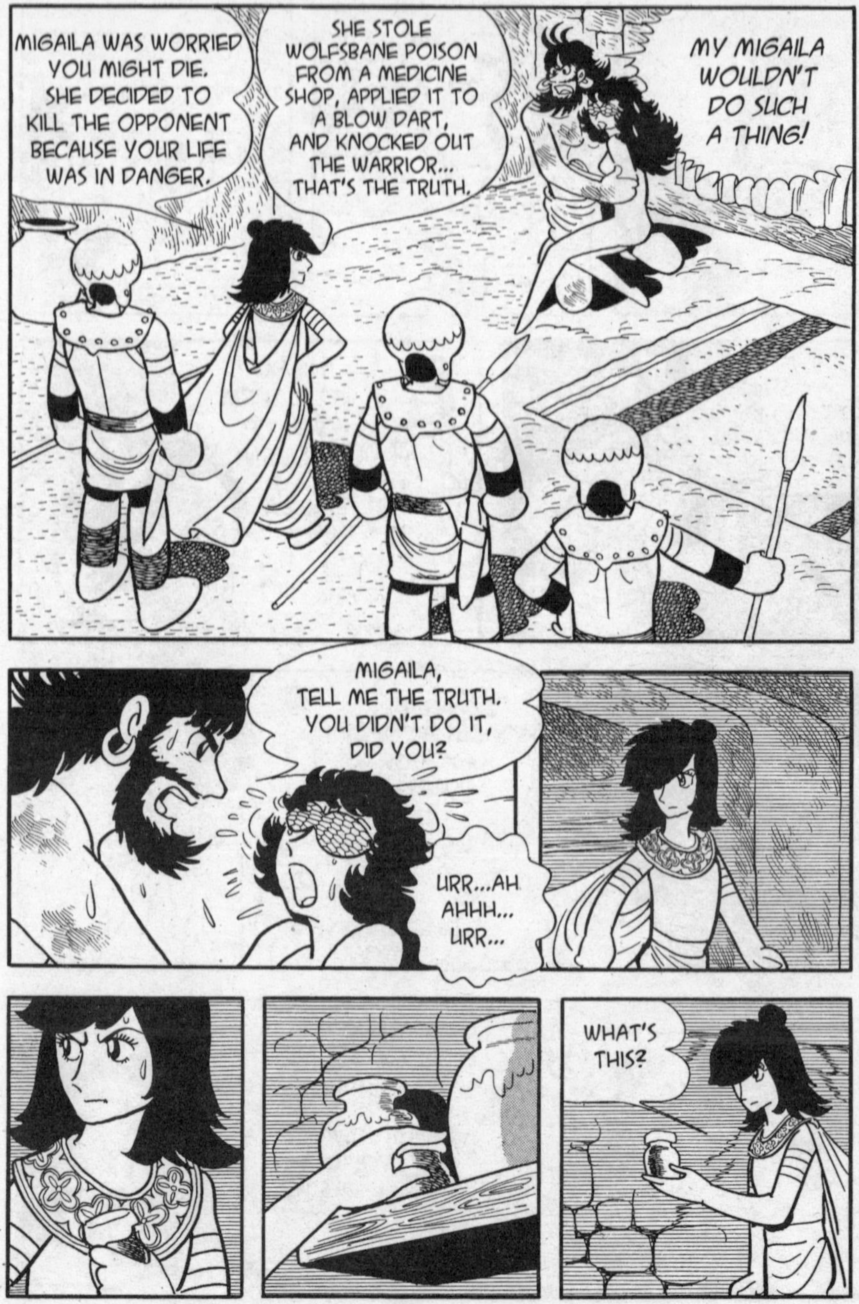
MIGAILA WAS WORRIED YOU MIGHT DIE. SHE DECIDED TO KILL THE OPPONENT BECAUSE YOUR LIFE WAS IN DANGER.
SHE STOLE WOLFSBANE POISON FROM A MEDICINE SHOP, APPLIED IT TO A BLOW DART, AND KNOCKED OUT THE WARRIOR... THAT'S THE TRUTH.
MY MIGAILA WOULDN'T DO SUCH A THING!
MIGAILA, TELL ME THE TRUTH. YOU DIDN'T DO IT, DID YOU?
URR...AH AHHH... URR...
WHAT'S THIS?

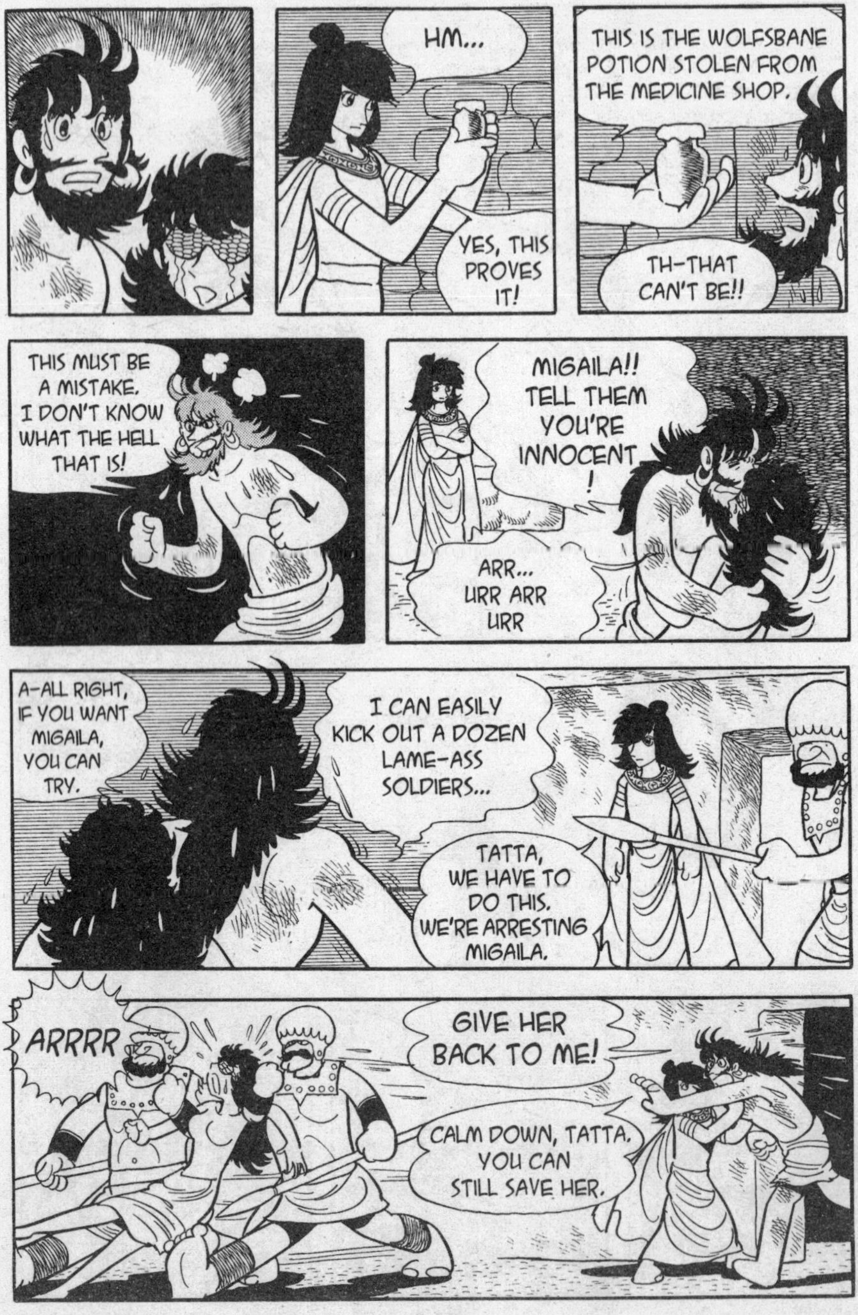
HM...
YES, THIS PROVES IT!
THIS IS THE WOLFSBANE POTION STOLEN FROM THE MEDICINE SHOP.
TH-THAT CAN'T BE!!
THIS MUST BE A MISTAKE. I DON'T KNOW WHAT THE HELL THAT IS!
MIGAILA!! TELL THEM YOU'RE INNOCENT!
ARR... URR ARR URR
A-ALL RIGHT, IF YOU WANT MIGAILA, YOU CAN TRY.
I CAN EASILY KICK OUT A DOZEN LAME-ASS SOLDIERS...
TATTA, WE HAVE TO DO THIS. WE'RE ARRESTING MIGAILA.
ARRRR
GIVE HER BACK TO ME!
CALM DOWN, TATTA. YOU CAN STILL SAVE HER.

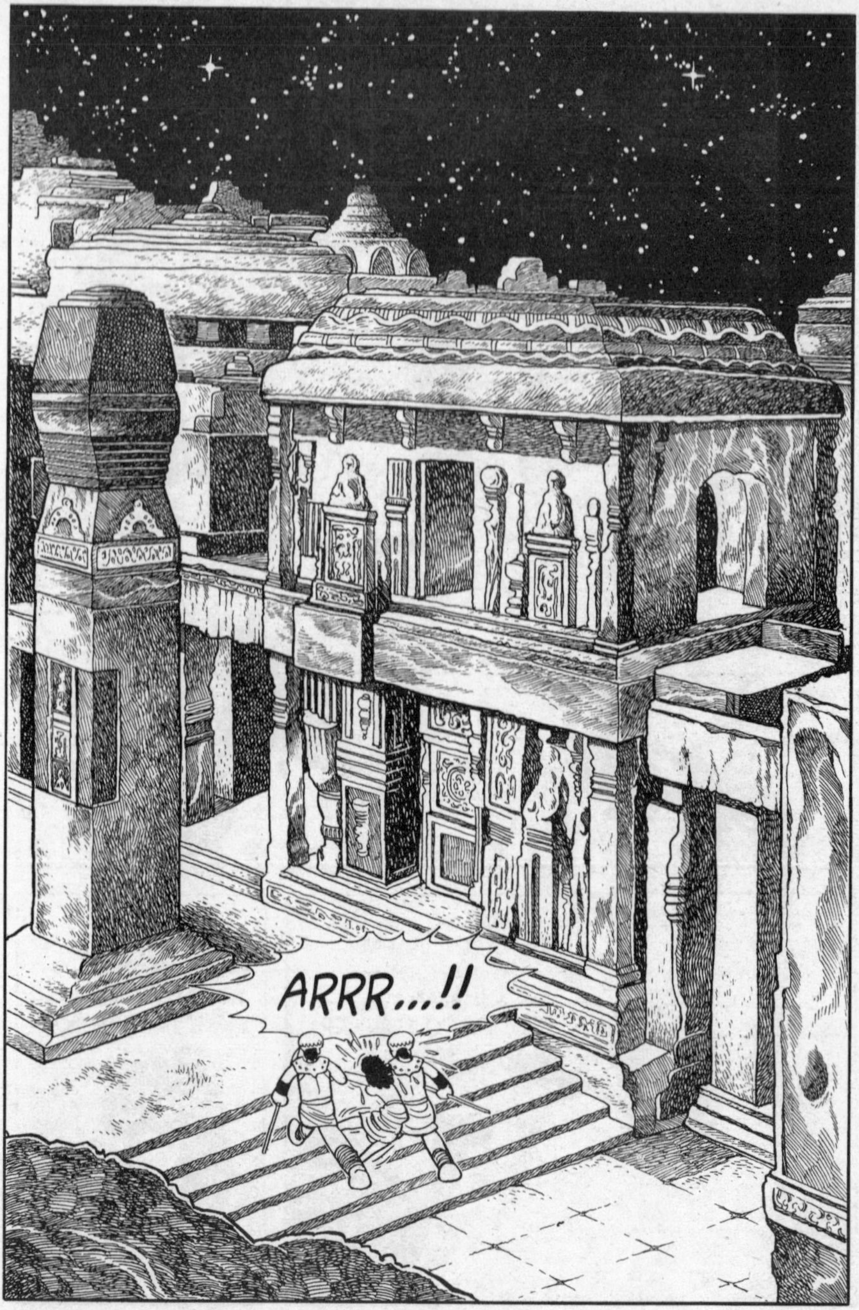
ARRR...!!

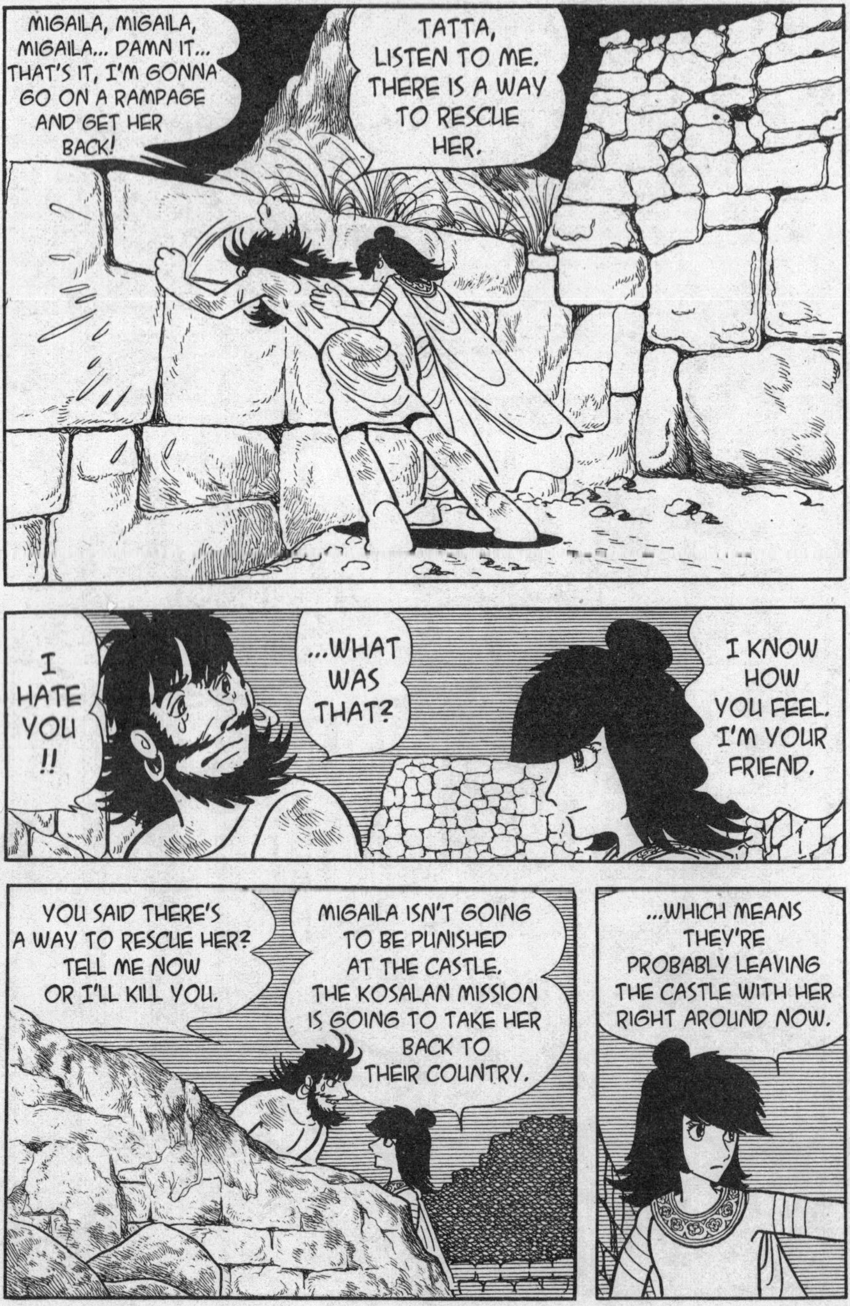

MIGAILA, MIGAILA, MIGAILA... DAMN IT... THAT'S IT, I'M GONNA GO ON A RAMPAGE AND GET HER BACK!
TATTA, LISTEN TO ME. THERE IS A WAY TO RESCUE HER.
I HATE YOU !!
...WHAT WAS THAT?
I KNOW HOW YOU FEEL. I'M YOUR FRIEND.
YOU SAID THERE'S A WAY TO RESCUE HER? TELL ME NOW OR I'LL KILL YOU.
MIGAILA ISN'T GOING TO BE PUNISHED AT THE CASTLE. THE KOSALAN MISSION IS GOING TO TAKE HER BACK TO THEIR COUNTRY.
...WHICH MEANS THEY'RE PROBABLY LEAVING THE CASTLE WITH HER RIGHT AROUND NOW.

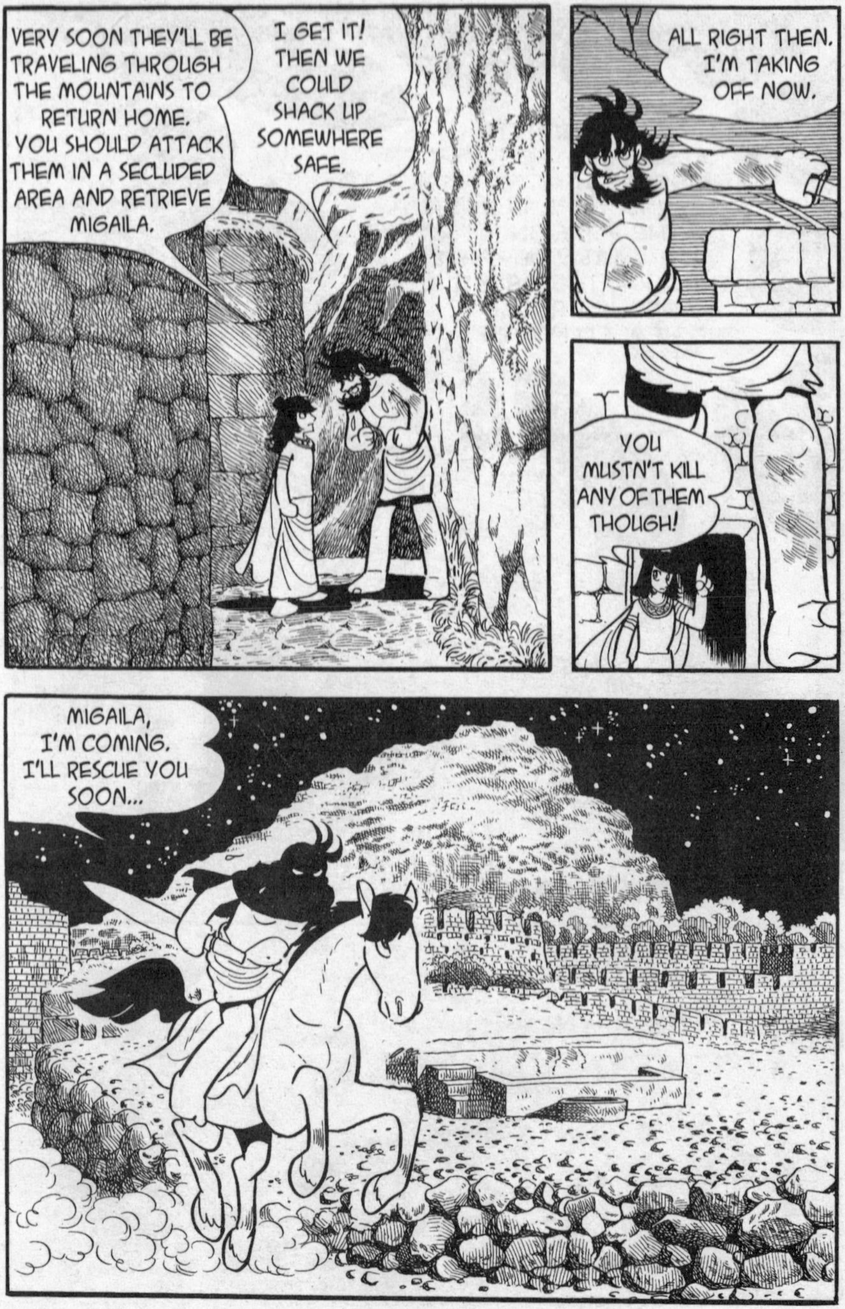
VERY SOON THEY'LL BE TRAVELING THROUGH THE MOUNTAINS TO RETURN HOME. YOU SHOULD ATTACK THEM IN A SECLUDED AREA AND RETRIEVE MIGAILA.
I GET IT! THEN WE COULD SHACK UP SOMEWHERE SAFE.
ALL RIGHT THEN. I'M TAKING OFF NOW.
YOU MUSTN'T KILL ANY OF THEM THOUGH!
MIGAILA, I'M COMING. I'LL RESCUE YOU SOON...

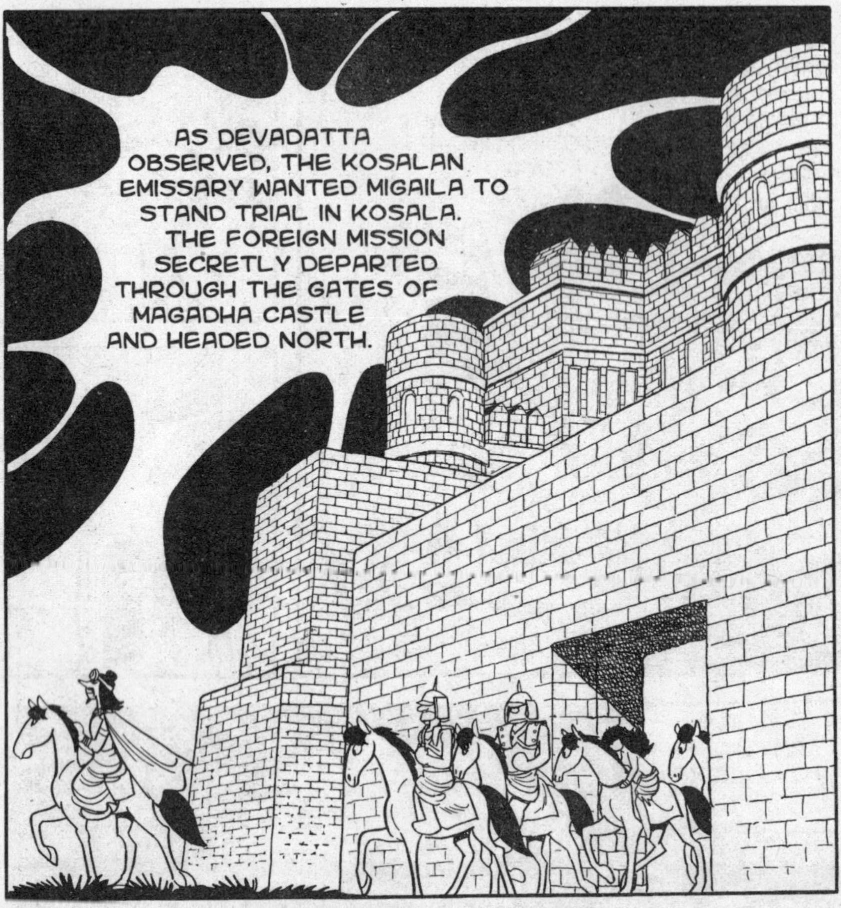
AS DEVADATTA OBSERVED, THE KOSALAN EMISSARY WANTED MIGAILA TO STAND TRIAL IN KOSALA. THE FOREIGN MISSION SECRETLY DEPARTED THROUGH THE GATES OF MAGADHA CASTLE AND HEADED NORTH.

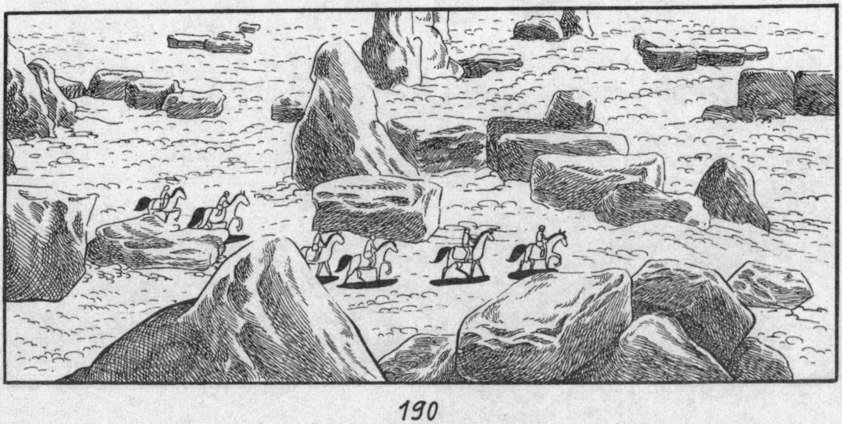

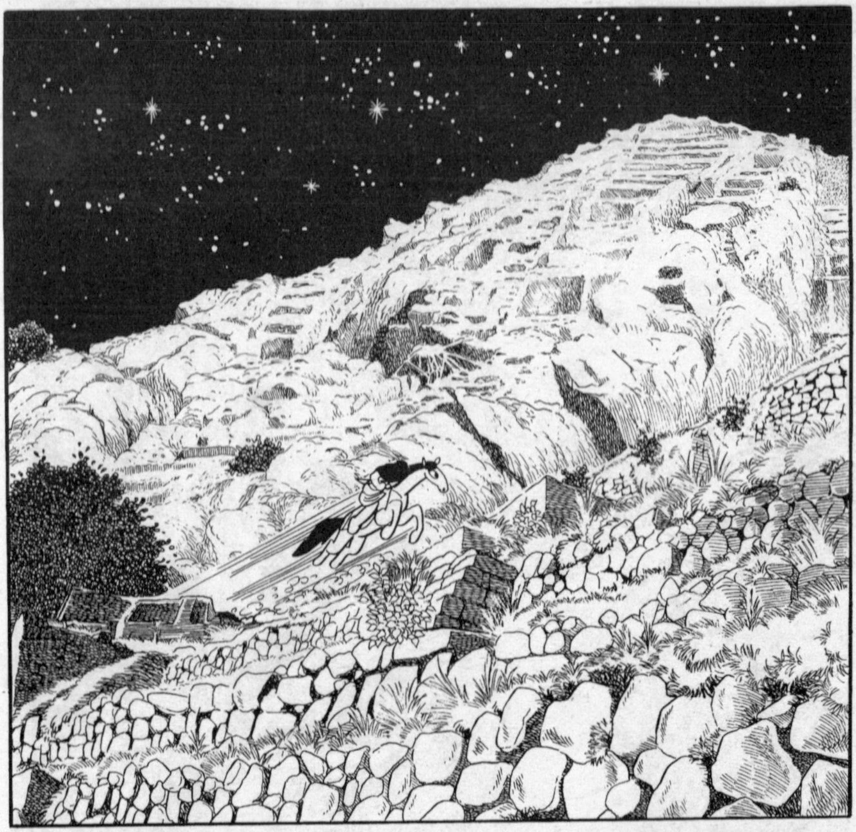

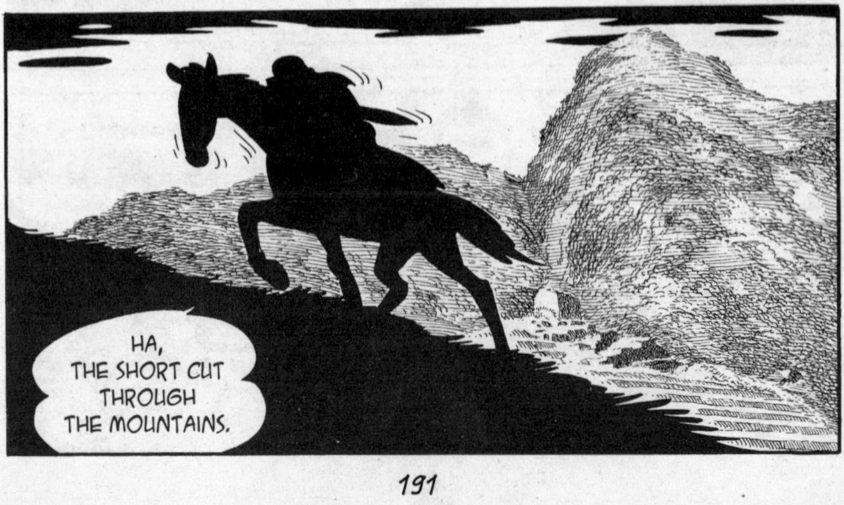

HA,
THE SHORT CUT
THROUGH
THE MOUNTAINS.

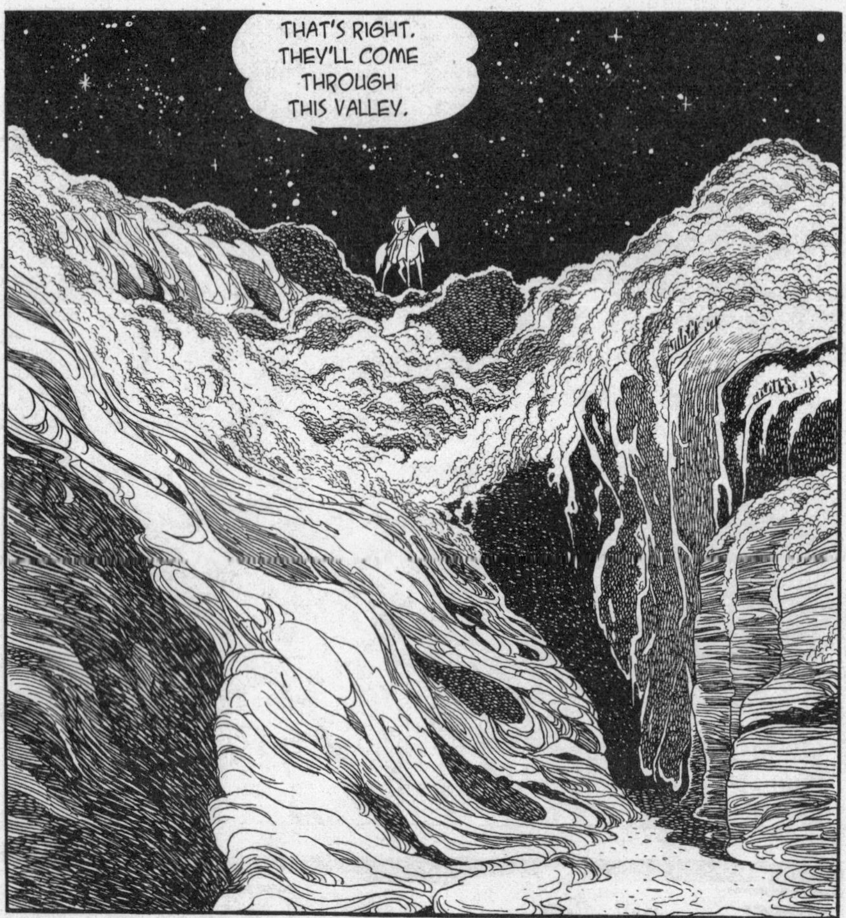
THAT'S RIGHT. THEY'LL COME THROUGH THIS VALLEY.

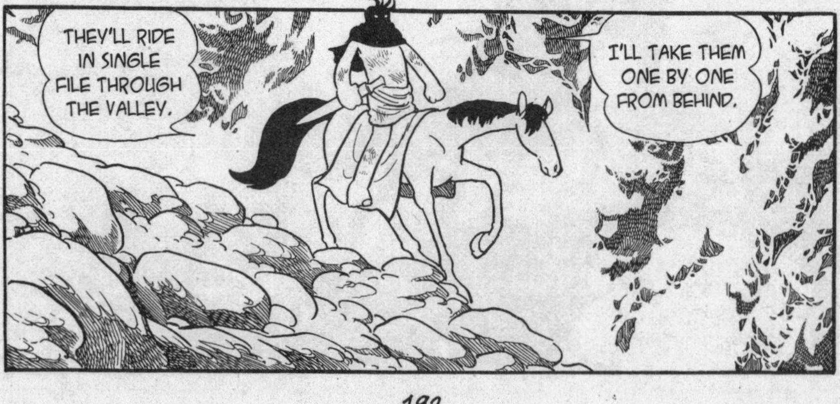
THEY'LL RIDE IN SINGLE FILE THROUGH THE VALLEY.
I'LL TAKE THEM ONE BY ONE FROM BEHIND.

REMINDS ME OF MY BANDIT DAYS.

HAD A GANG BACK THEN. NOW I'M ALONE.

GOOD...

...THEY'VE ENTERED THE VALLEY.

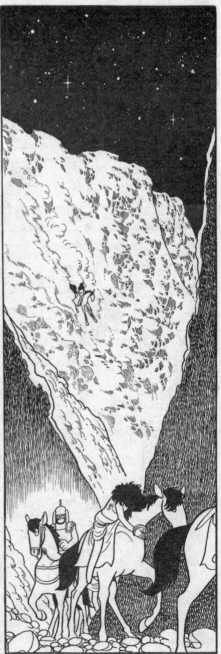

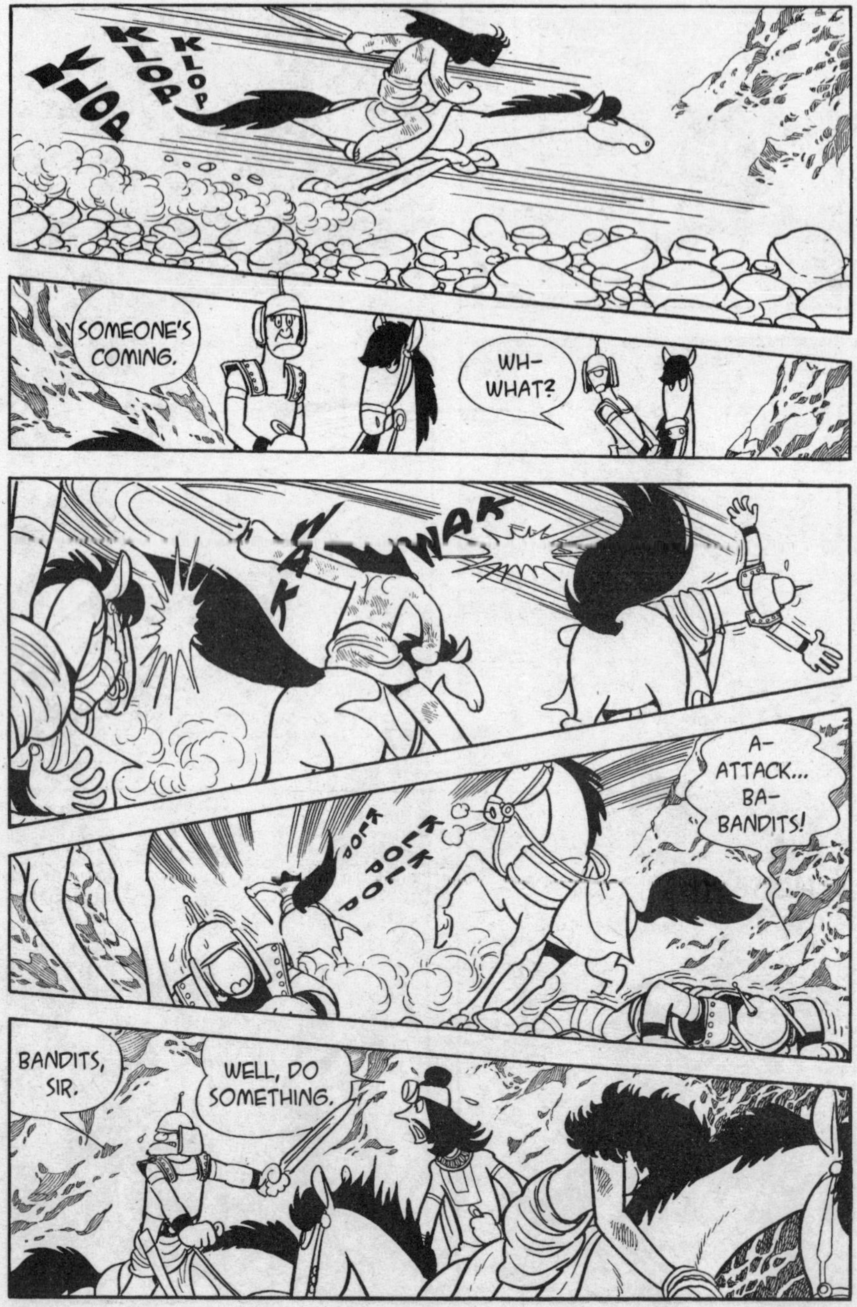
KLOP KLOP
KLOP KLOP
SOMEONE'S COMING.
WH- WHAT?
WAK
WAK
A- ATTACK... BA- BANDITS!
BANDITS, SIR.
WELL, DO SOMETHING.

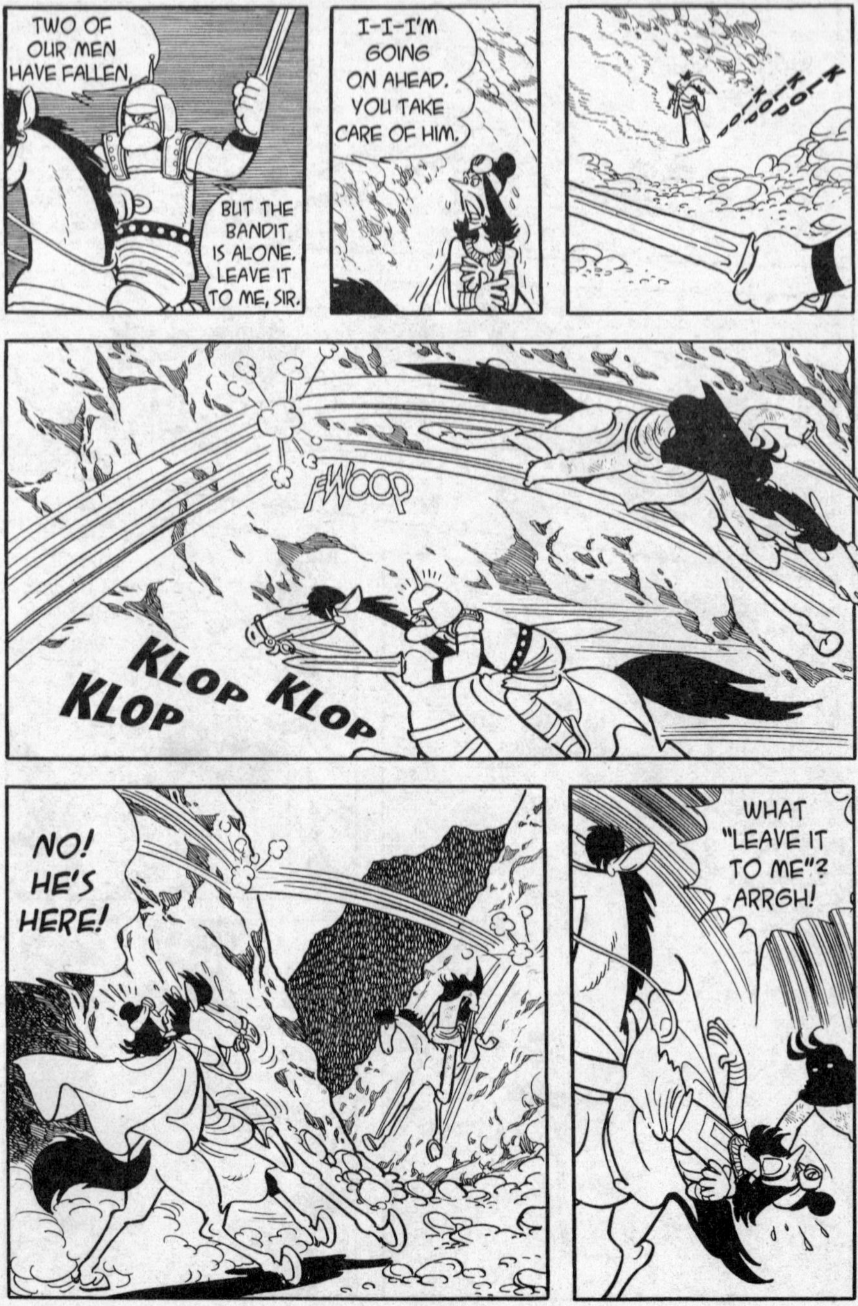
TWO OF OUR MEN HAVE FALLEN,
BUT THE BANDIT IS ALONE. LEAVE IT TO ME, SIR.
I-I-I'M GOING ON AHEAD. YOU TAKE CARE OF HIM.
KLOP KLOP KLOP
FWOOP
KLOP KLOP KLOP
NO! HE'S HERE!
WHAT "LEAVE IT TO ME"? ARRGH!

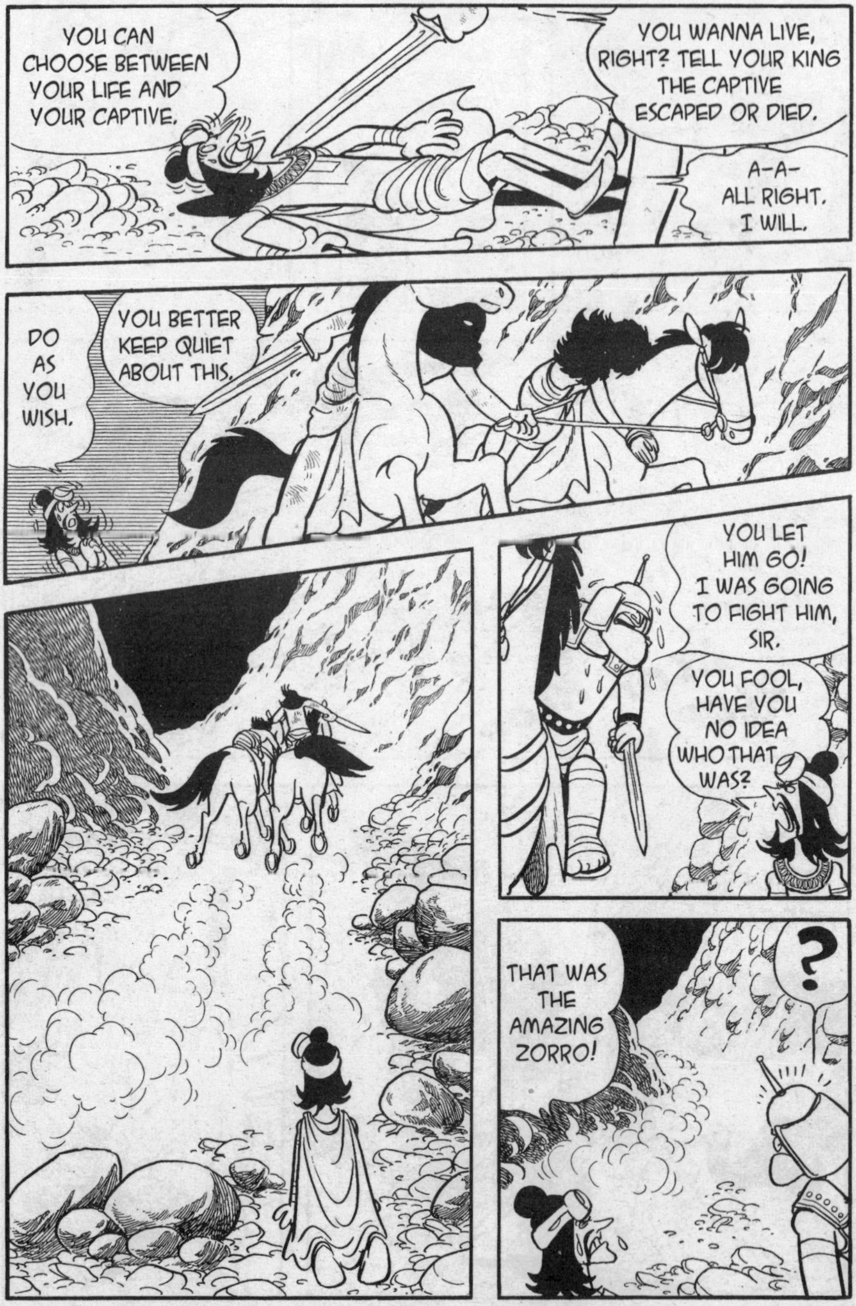
YOU CAN CHOOSE BETWEEN YOUR LIFE AND YOUR CAPTIVE.
YOU WANNA LIVE, RIGHT? TELL YOUR KING THE CAPTIVE ESCAPED OR DIED.
A-A- ALL RIGHT. I WILL.
YOU BETTER KEEP QUIET ABOUT THIS.
DO AS YOU WISH.
YOU LET HIM GO! I WAS GOING TO FIGHT HIM, SIR.
YOU FOOL, HAVE YOU NO IDEA WHO THAT WAS?
THAT WAS THE AMAZING ZORRO!
?

...

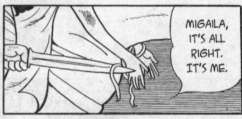

MIGAILA, IT'S ALL RIGHT. IT'S ME.

MIGAILA...

ARRR... URR... URR... URR...!!

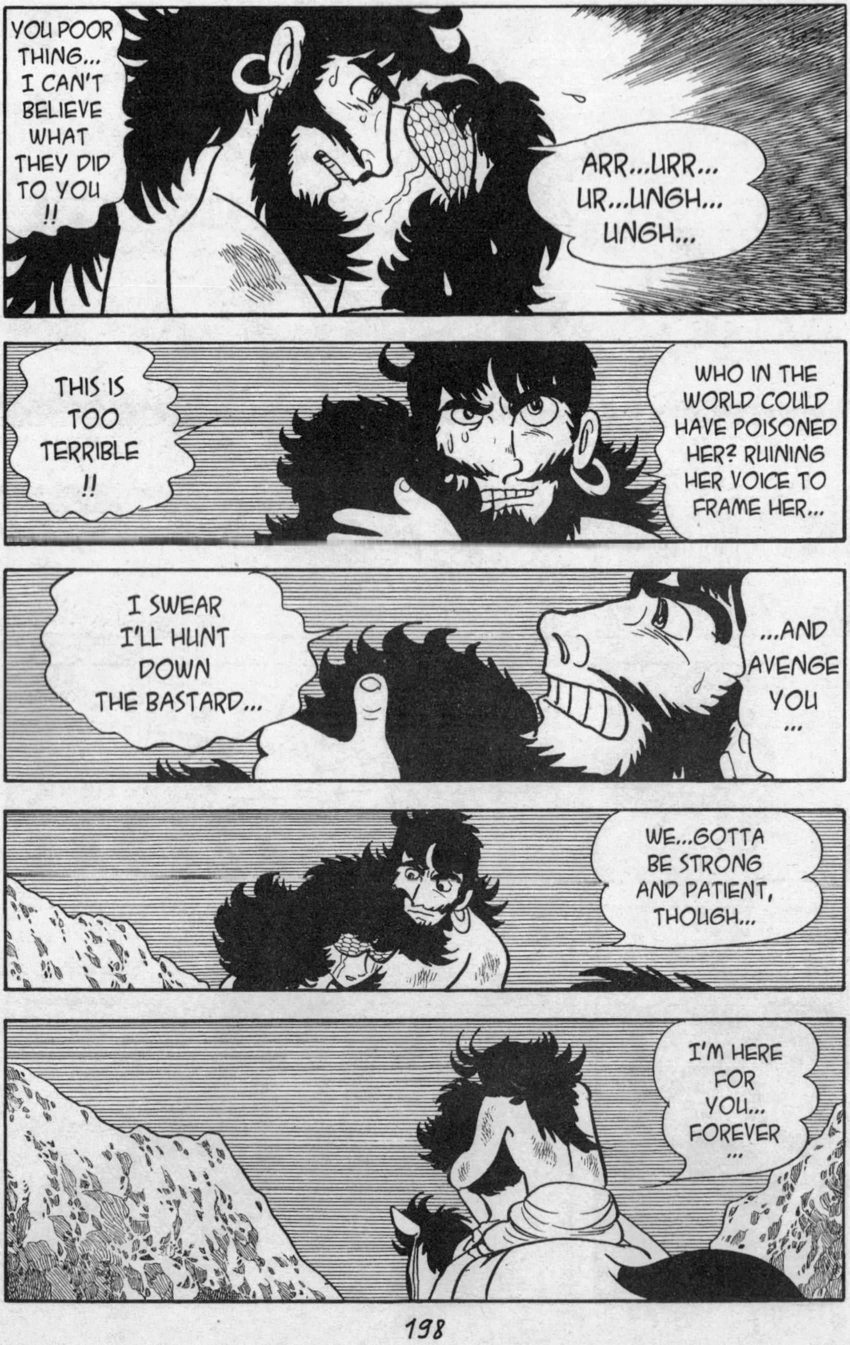
YOU POOR THING... I CAN'T BELIEVE WHAT THEY DID TO YOU !!
ARR...URR... UR...UNGH... UNGH...
WHO IN THE WORLD COULD HAVE POISONED HER? RUINING HER VOICE TO FRAME HER...
THIS IS TOO TERRIBLE !!
...AND AVENGE YOU ...
I SWEAR I'LL HUNT DOWN THE BASTARD...
WE...GOTTA BE STRONG AND PATIENT, THOUGH...
I'M HERE FOR YOU... FOREVER ...

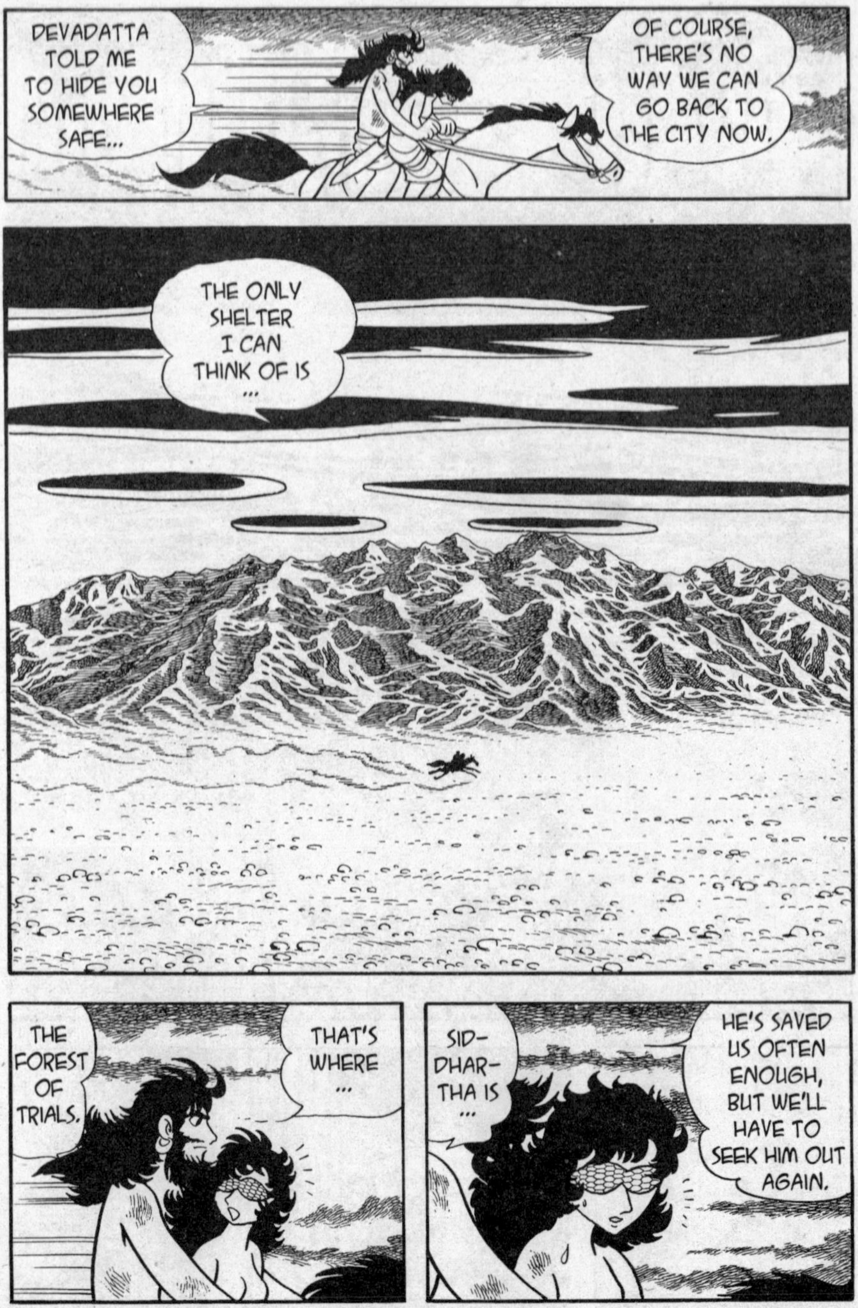
DEVADATTA TOLD ME TO HIDE YOU SOMEWHERE SAFE...
OF COURSE, THERE'S NO WAY WE CAN GO BACK TO THE CITY NOW.
THE ONLY SHELTER I CAN THINK OF IS ...
THE FOREST OF TRIALS.
THAT'S WHERE ...
SID-DHAR-THA IS ...
HE'S SAVED US OFTEN ENOUGH, BUT WE'LL HAVE TO SEEK HIM OUT AGAIN.

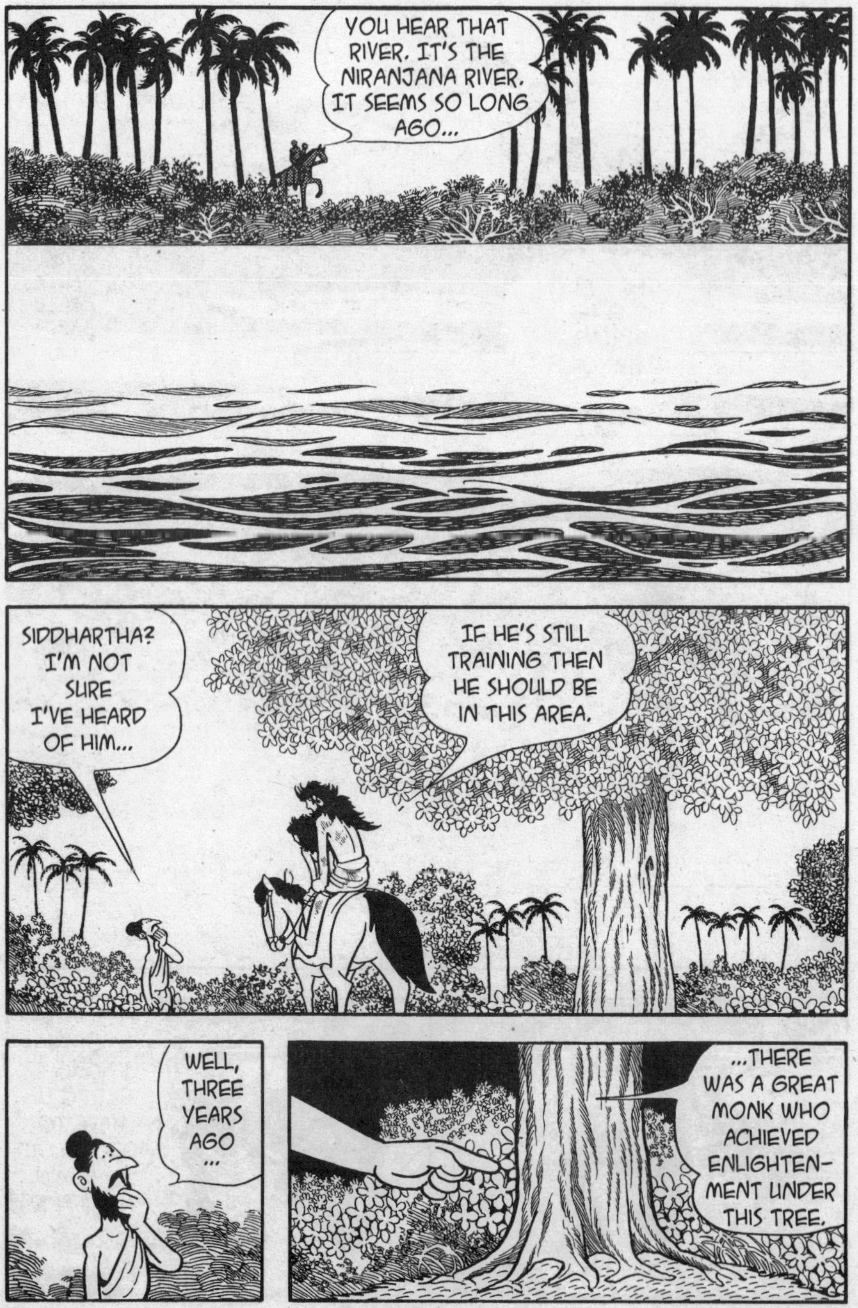
YOU HEAR THAT RIVER. IT'S THE NIRANJANA RIVER. IT SEEMS SO LONG AGO...
SIDDHARTHA? I'M NOT SURE I'VE HEARD OF HIM...
IF HE'S STILL TRAINING THEN HE SHOULD BE IN THIS AREA.
WELL, THREE YEARS AGO ...
...THERE WAS A GREAT MONK WHO ACHIEVED ENLIGHTEN-MENT UNDER THIS TREE.

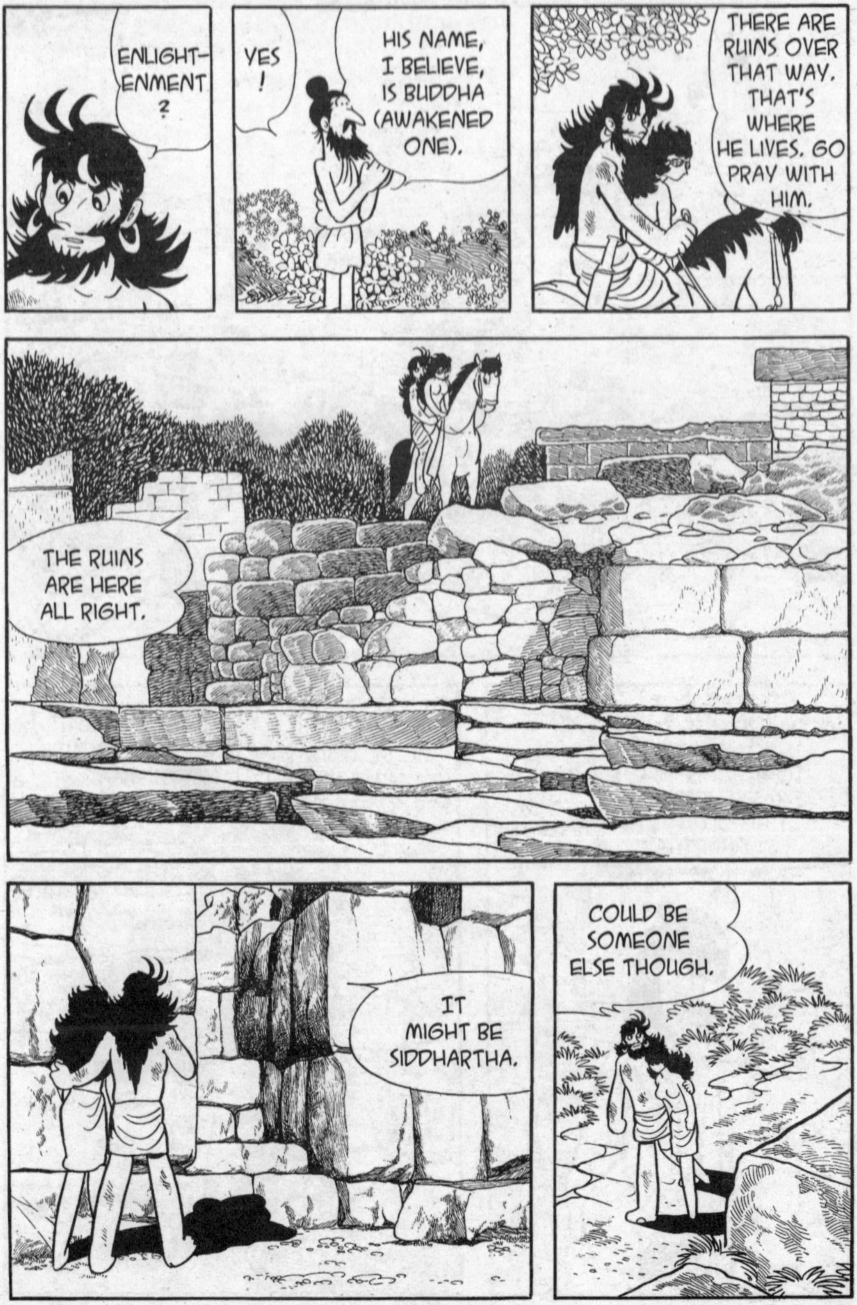
ENLIGHT-ENMENT?
YES!
HIS NAME, I BELIEVE, IS BUDDHA (AWAKENED ONE).
THERE ARE RUINS OVER THAT WAY. THAT'S WHERE HE LIVES. GO PRAY WITH HIM.
THE RUINS ARE HERE ALL RIGHT.
IT MIGHT BE SIDDHARTHA.
COULD BE SOMEONE ELSE THOUGH.

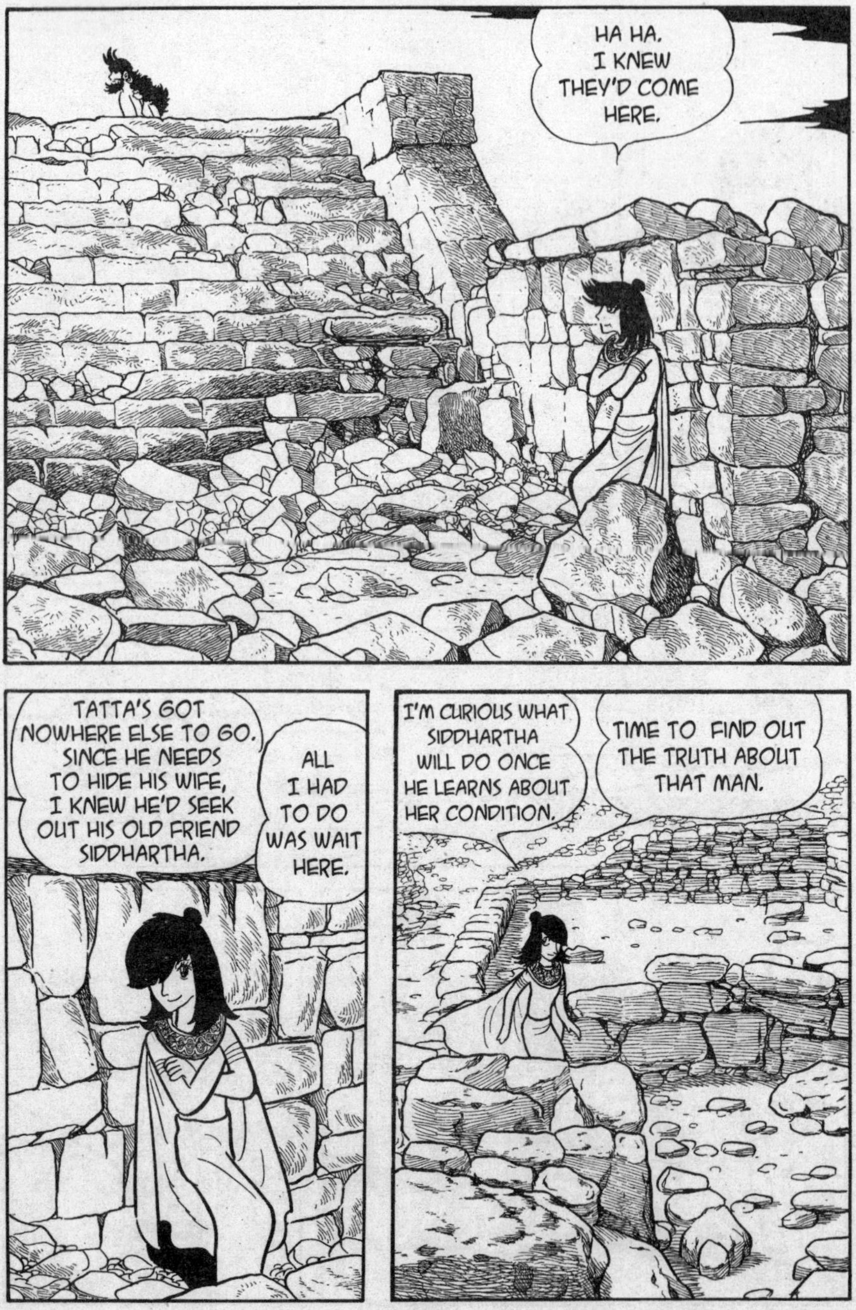
HA HA. I KNEW THEY'D COME HERE.
TATTA'S GOT NOWHERE ELSE TO GO. SINCE HE NEEDS TO HIDE HIS WIFE, I KNEW HE'D SEEK OUT HIS OLD FRIEND SIDDHARTHA.
ALL I HAD TO DO WAS WAIT HERE.
I'M CURIOUS WHAT SIDDHARTHA WILL DO ONCE HE LEARNS ABOUT HER CONDITION.
TIME TO FIND OUT THE TRUTH ABOUT THAT MAN.

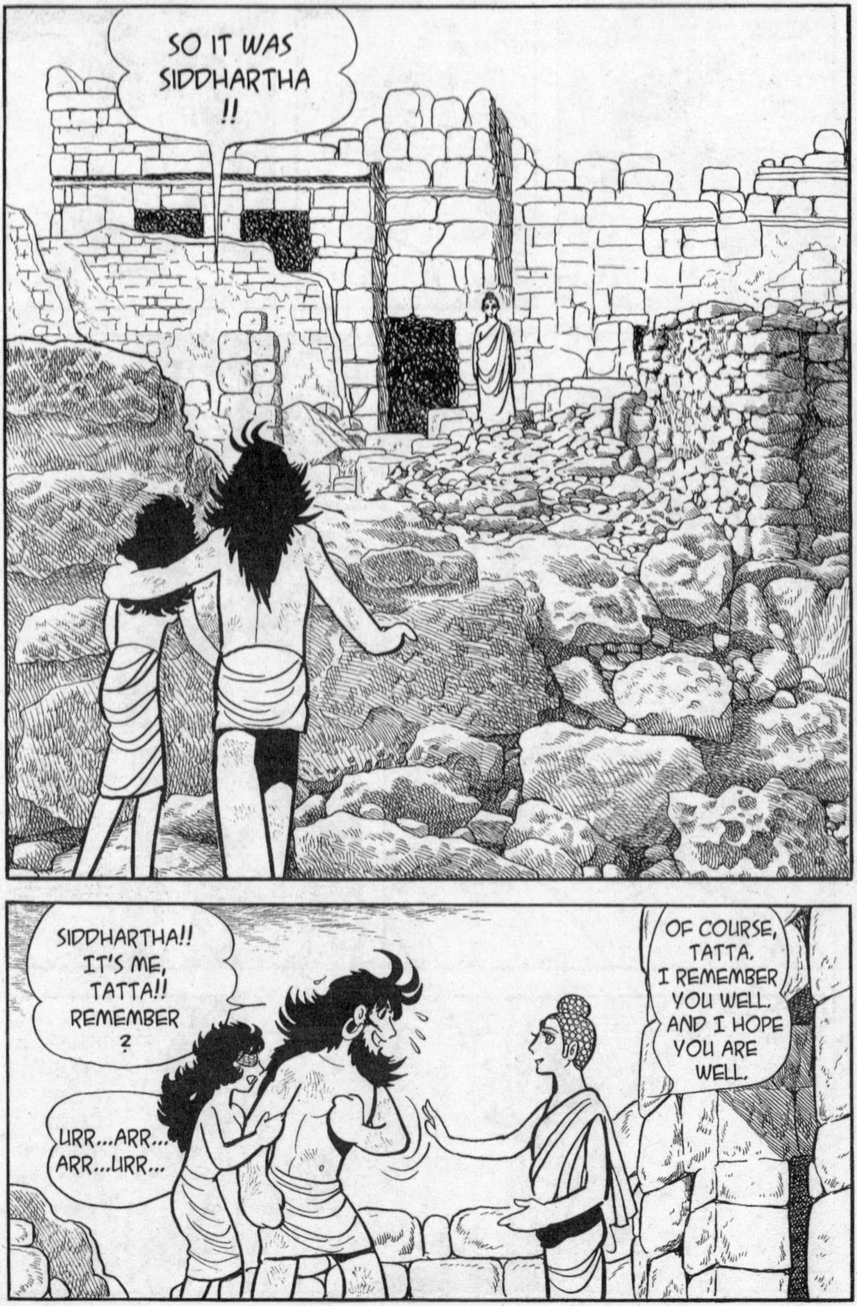
SO IT WAS SIDDHARTHA !!
SIDDHARTHA!! IT'S ME, TATTA!! REMEMBER ?
URR...ARR... ARR...URR...
OF COURSE, TATTA. I REMEMBER YOU WELL. AND I HOPE YOU ARE WELL.

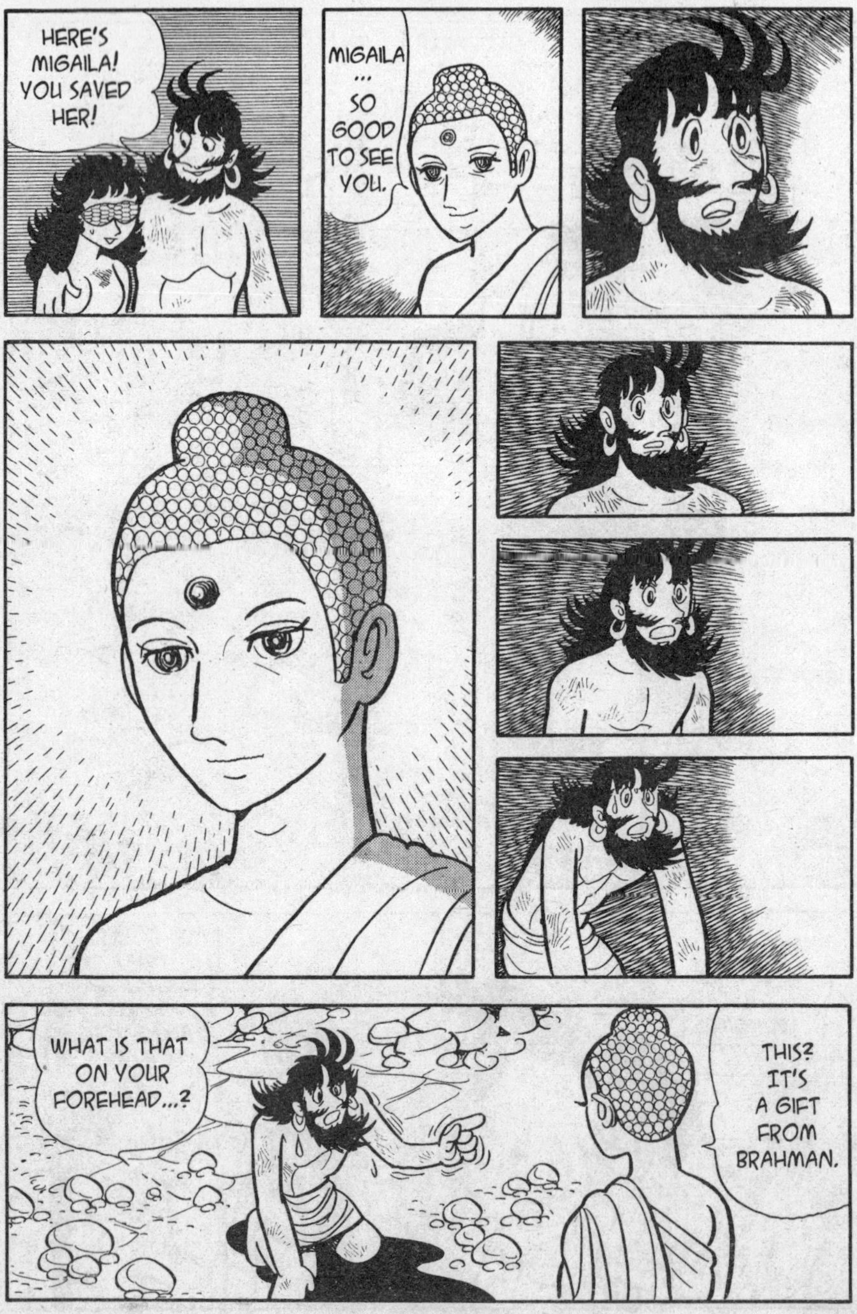
HERE'S MIGAILA! YOU SAVED HER!
MIGAILA ... SO GOOD TO SEE YOU.
WHAT IS THAT ON YOUR FOREHEAD...?
THIS? IT'S A GIFT FROM BRAHMAN.

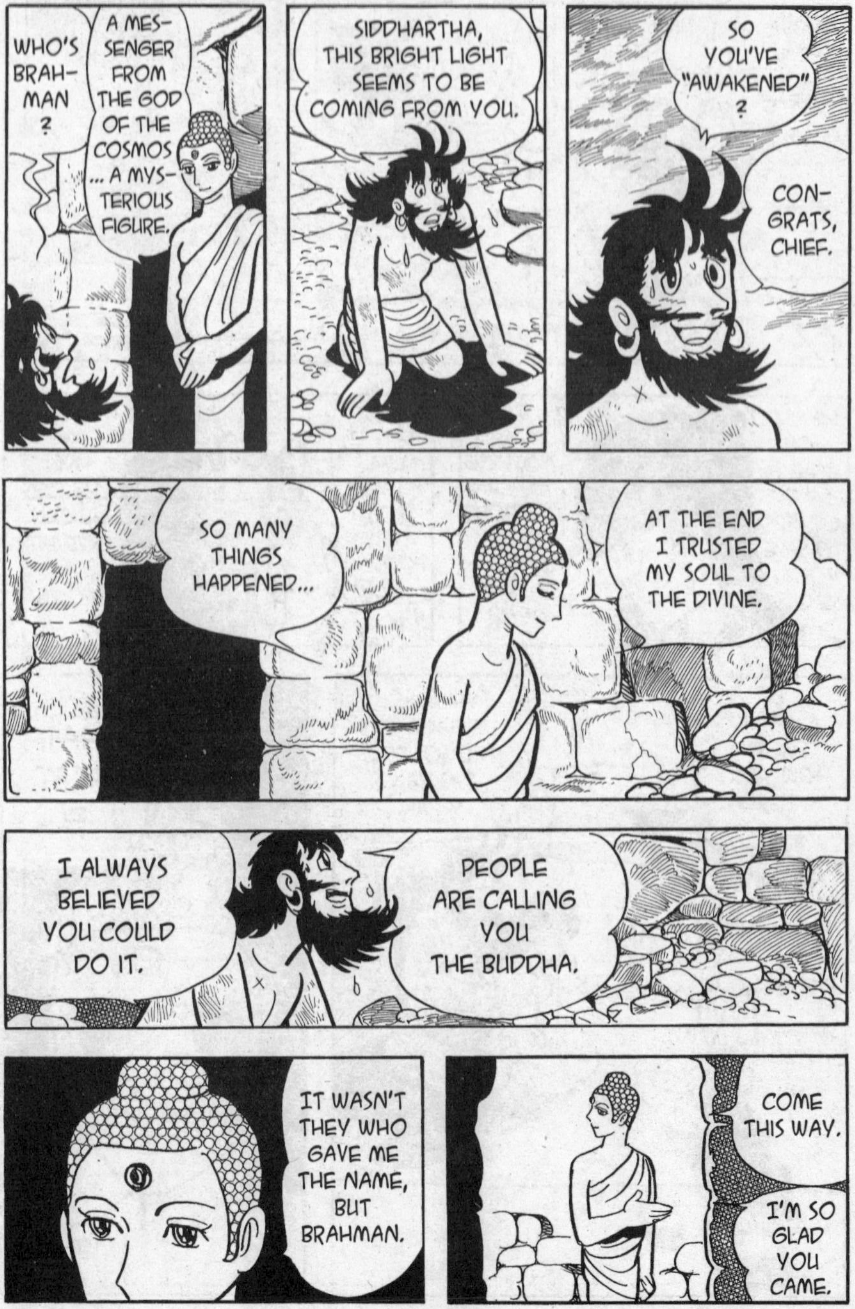
WHO'S BRAHMAN ?
A MESSENGER FROM THE GOD OF THE COSMOS ... A MYSTERIOUS FIGURE.
SIDDHARTHA, THIS BRIGHT LIGHT SEEMS TO BE COMING FROM YOU.
SO YOU'VE "AWAKENED" ?
CONGRATS, CHIEF.
SO MANY THINGS HAPPENED...
AT THE END I TRUSTED MY SOUL TO THE DIVINE.
I ALWAYS BELIEVED YOU COULD DO IT.
PEOPLE ARE CALLING YOU THE BUDDHA.
IT WASN'T THEY WHO GAVE ME THE NAME, BUT BRAHMAN.
COME THIS WAY.
I'M SO GLAD YOU CAME.

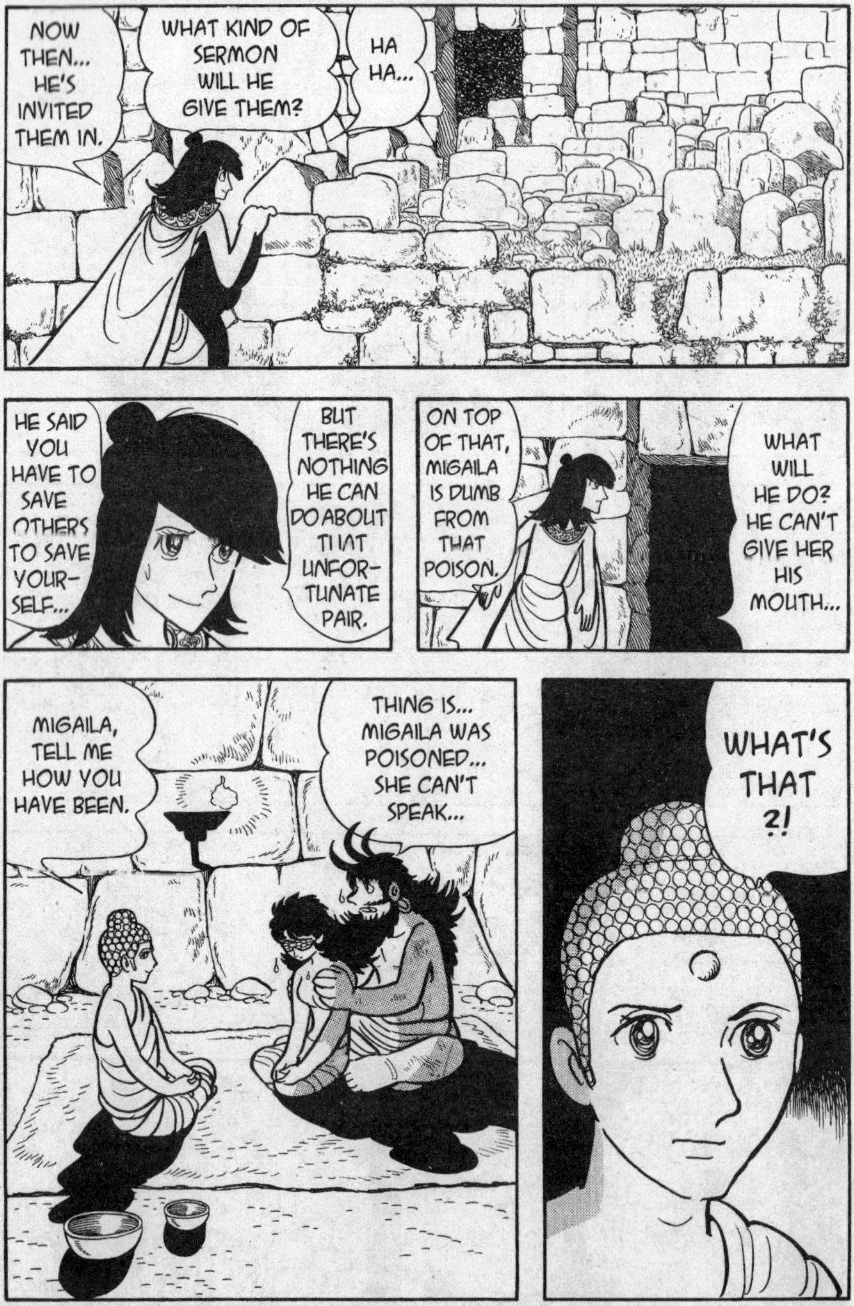
NOW THEN... HE'S INVITED THEM IN.
WHAT KIND OF SERMON WILL HE GIVE THEM?
HA HA...
HE SAID YOU HAVE TO SAVE OTHERS TO SAVE YOURSELF...
BUT THERE'S NOTHING HE CAN DO ABOUT THAT UNFORTUNATE PAIR.
ON TOP OF THAT, MIGAILA IS DUMB FROM THAT POISON.
WHAT WILL HE DO? HE CAN'T GIVE HER HIS MOUTH...
MIGAILA, TELL ME HOW YOU HAVE BEEN.
THING IS... MIGAILA WAS POISONED... SHE CAN'T SPEAK...
WHAT'S THAT ?!

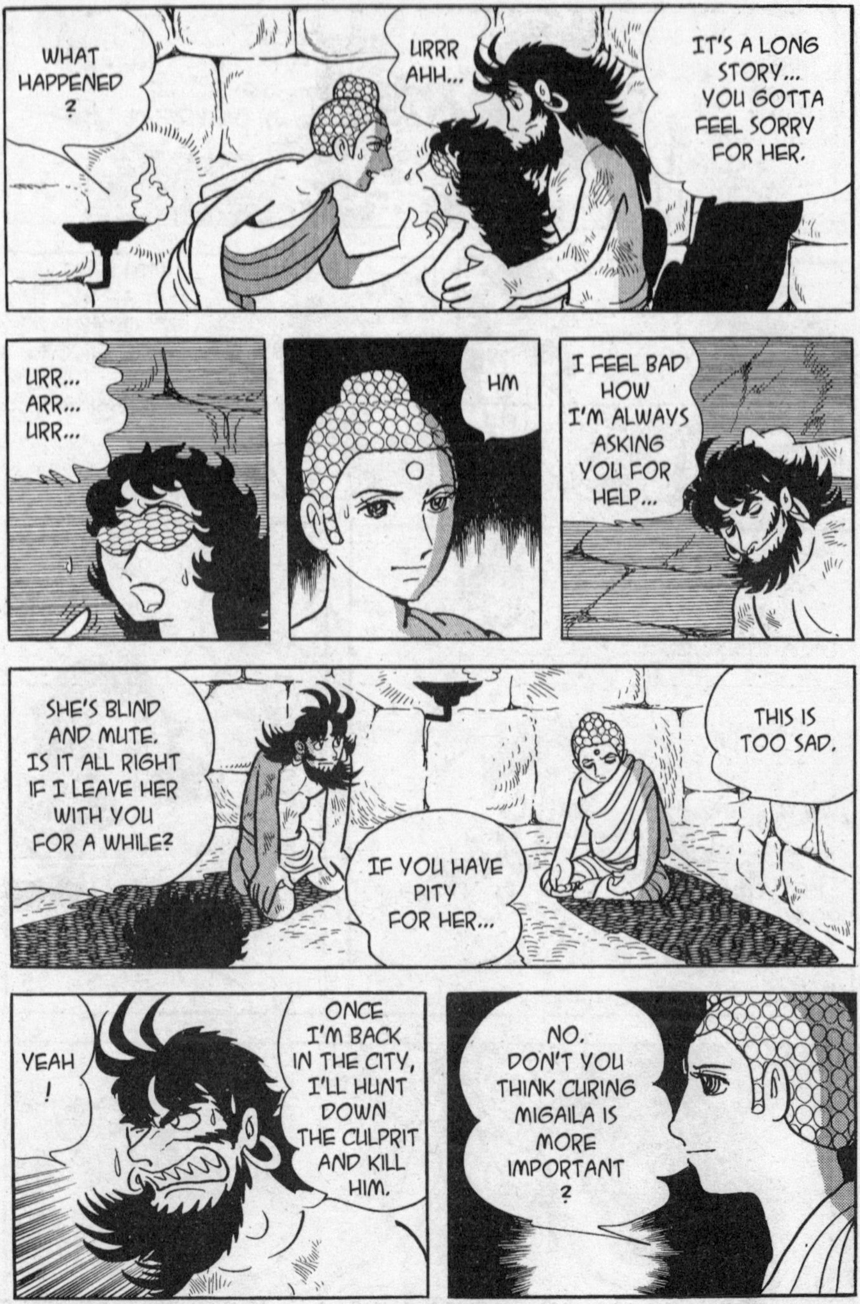
WHAT HAPPENED ?
URRR AHH...
IT'S A LONG STORY... YOU GOTTA FEEL SORRY FOR HER.
URR... ARR... URR...
HM
I FEEL BAD HOW I'M ALWAYS ASKING YOU FOR HELP...
SHE'S BLIND AND MUTE. IS IT ALL RIGHT IF I LEAVE HER WITH YOU FOR A WHILE?
IF YOU HAVE PITY FOR HER...
THIS IS TOO SAD.
YEAH !
ONCE I'M BACK IN THE CITY, I'LL HUNT DOWN THE CULPRIT AND KILL HIM.
NO. DON'T YOU THINK CURING MIGAILA IS MORE IMPORTANT ?

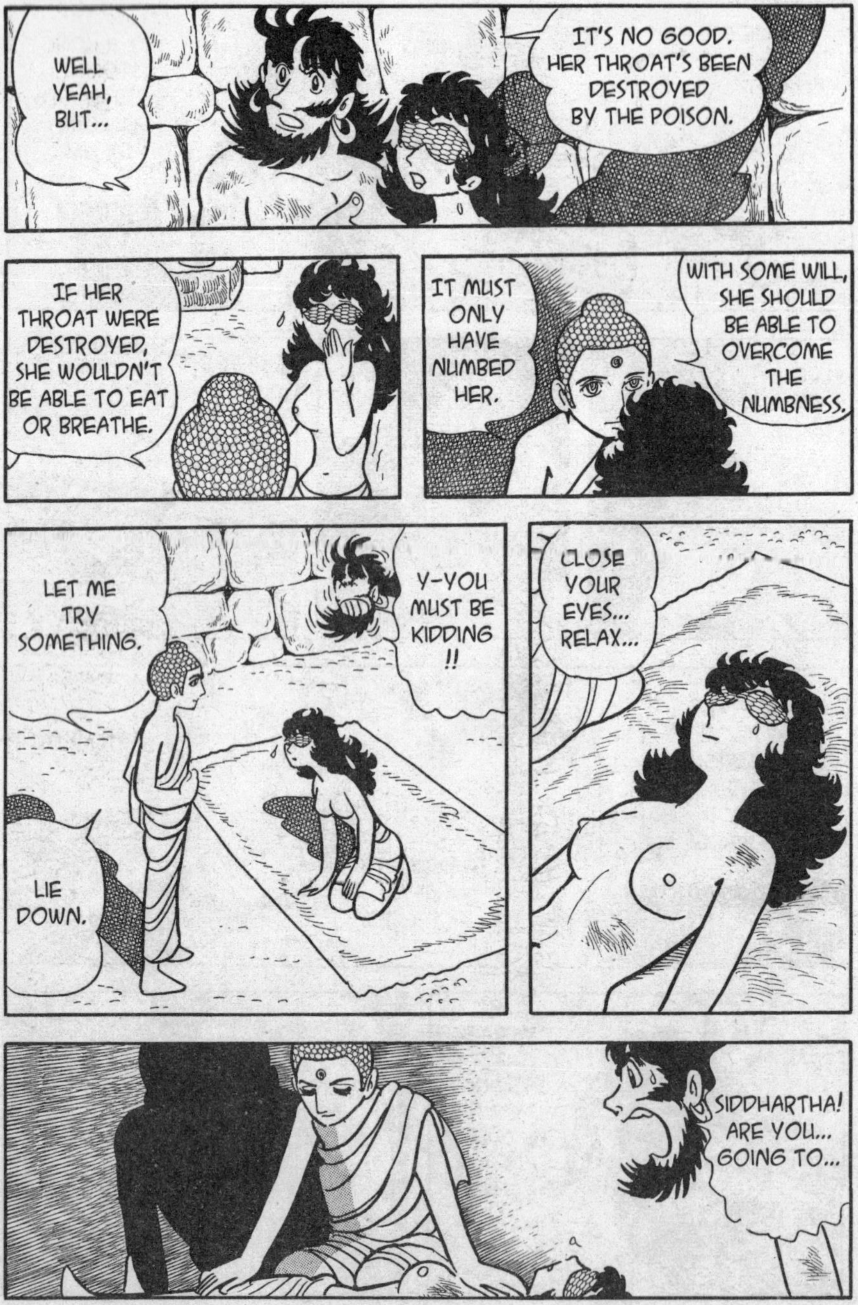
IT'S NO GOOD. HER THROAT'S BEEN DESTROYED BY THE POISON.
WELL YEAH, BUT...
IF HER THROAT WERE DESTROYED, SHE WOULDN'T BE ABLE TO EAT OR BREATHE.
IT MUST ONLY HAVE NUMBED HER.
WITH SOME WILL, SHE SHOULD BE ABLE TO OVERCOME THE NUMBNESS.
LET ME TRY SOMETHING.
Y-YOU MUST BE KIDDING !!
LIE DOWN.
CLOSE YOUR EYES... RELAX...
SIDDHARTHA! ARE YOU... GOING TO...

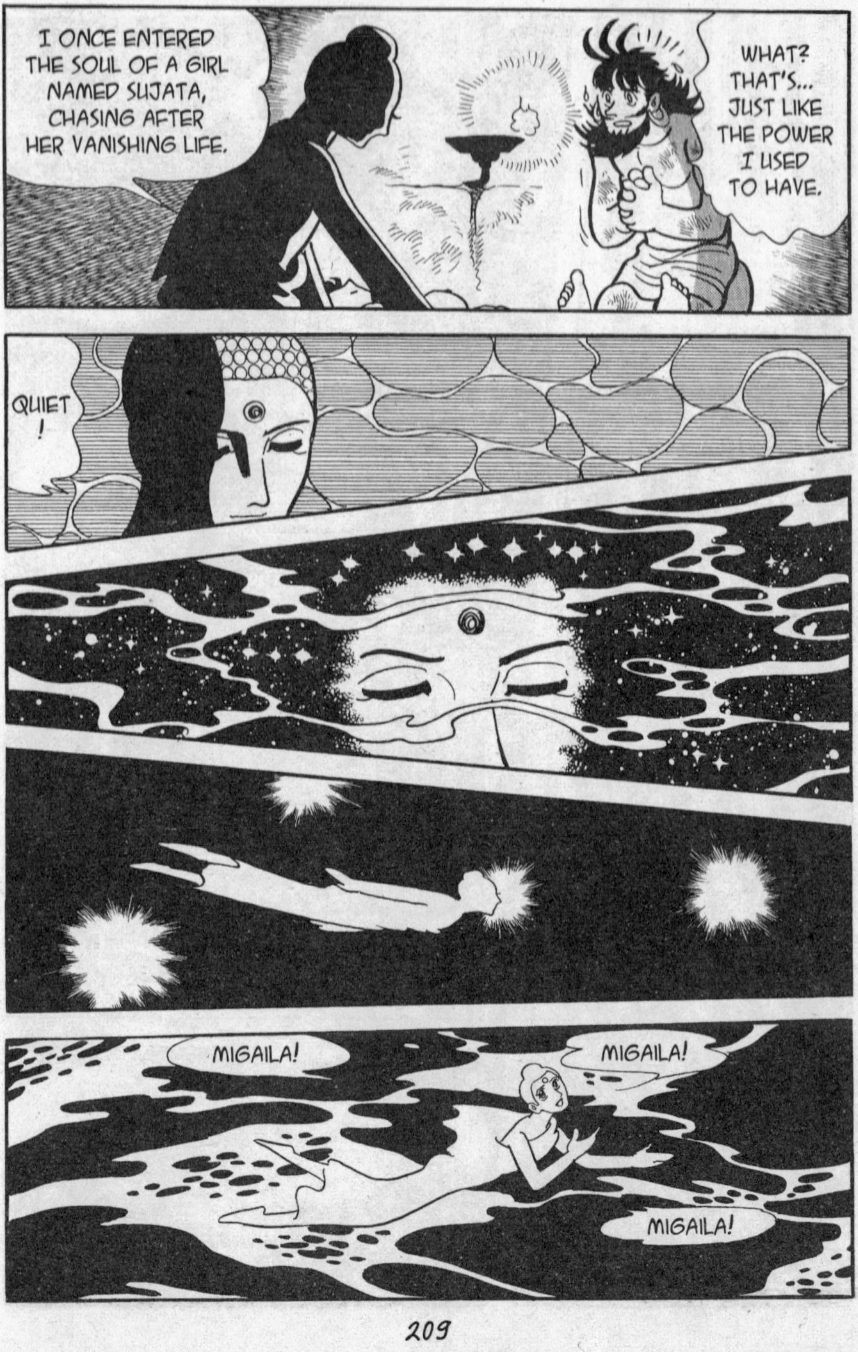

I ONCE ENTERED THE SOUL OF A GIRL NAMED SUJATA, CHASING AFTER HER VANISHING LIFE.
WHAT? THAT'S... JUST LIKE THE POWER I USED TO HAVE.
QUIET!
MIGAILA!
MIGAILA!
MIGAILA!

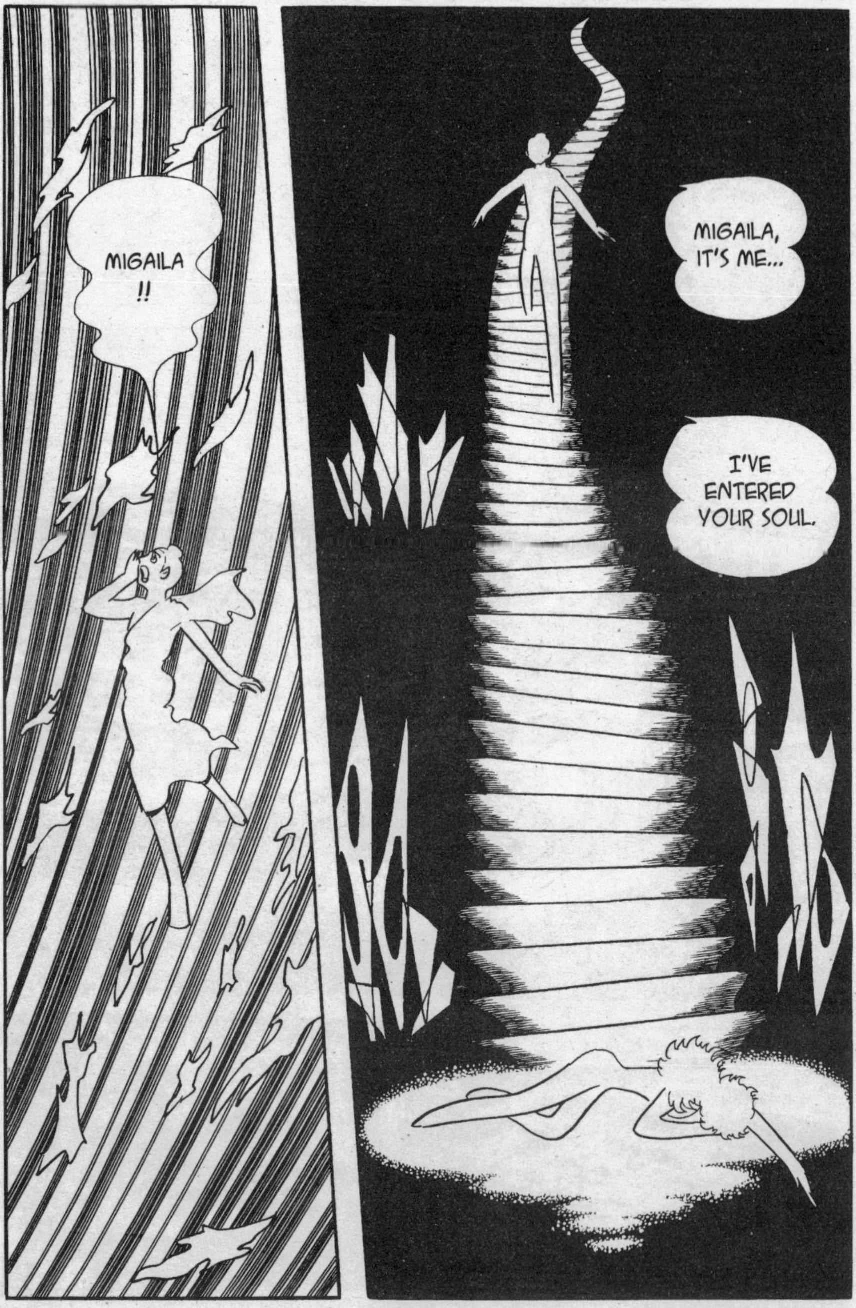
MIGAILA, IT'S ME...
I'VE ENTERED YOUR SOUL.
MIGAILA !!

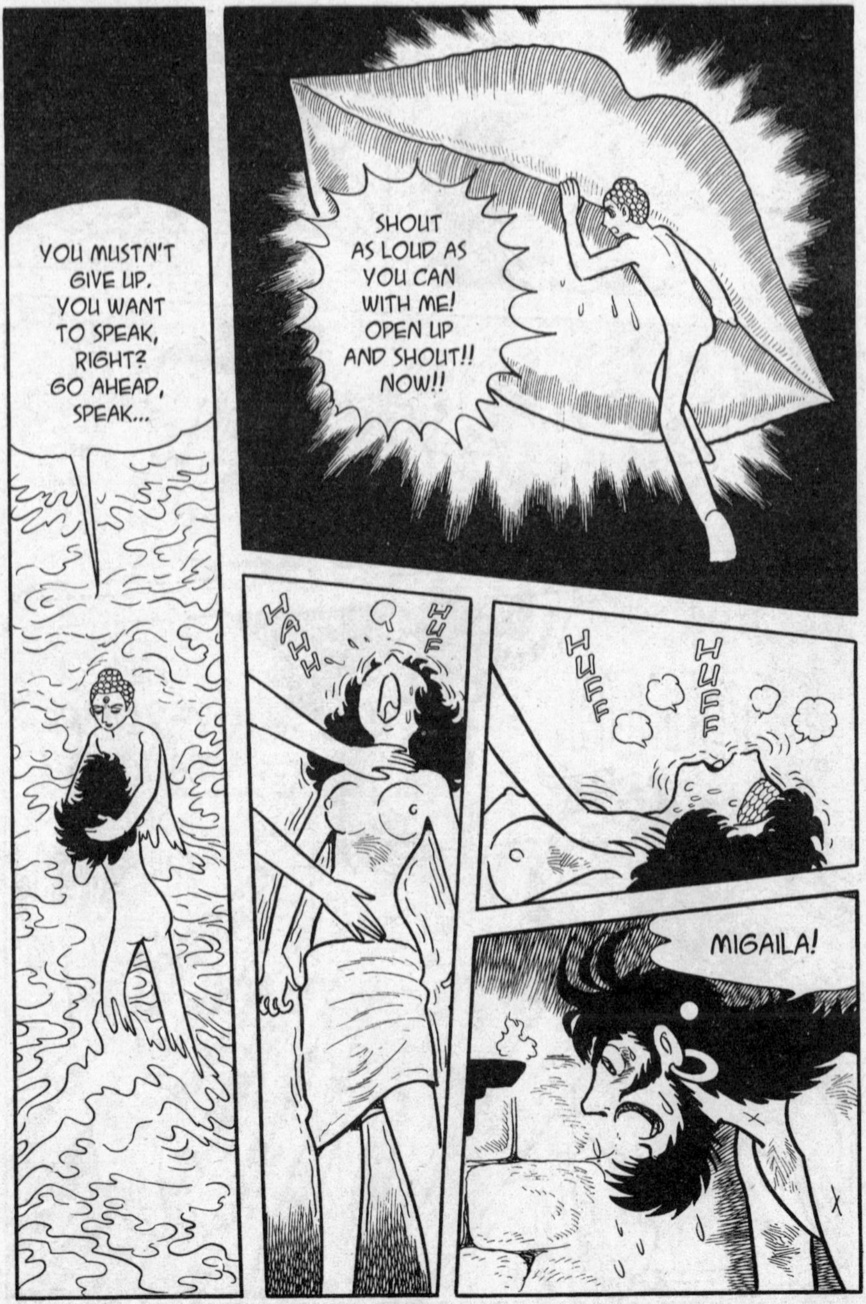
YOU MUSTN'T GIVE UP. YOU WANT TO SPEAK, RIGHT? GO AHEAD, SPEAK...
SHOUT AS LOUD AS YOU CAN WITH ME! OPEN UP AND SHOUT!! NOW!!
HAHH
HUF
HUFF
HUFF
MIGAILA!

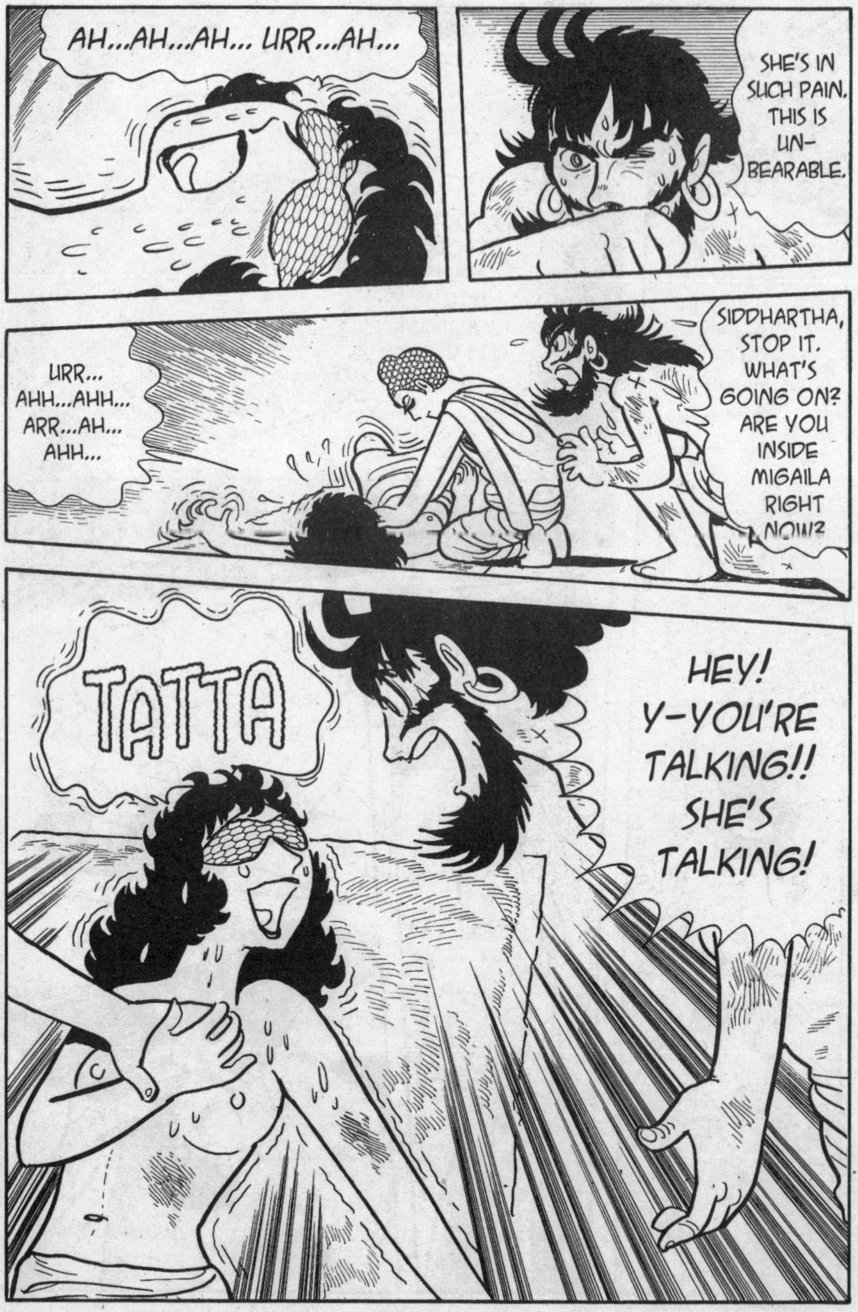
AH...AH...AH... URR...AH...
SHE'S IN SUCH PAIN. THIS IS UN-BEARABLE.
URR... AHH...AHH... ARR...AH... AHH...
SIDDHARTHA, STOP IT. WHAT'S GOING ON? ARE YOU INSIDE MIGAILA RIGHT NOW?
TATTA
HEY! Y-YOU'RE TALKING!! SHE'S TALKING!

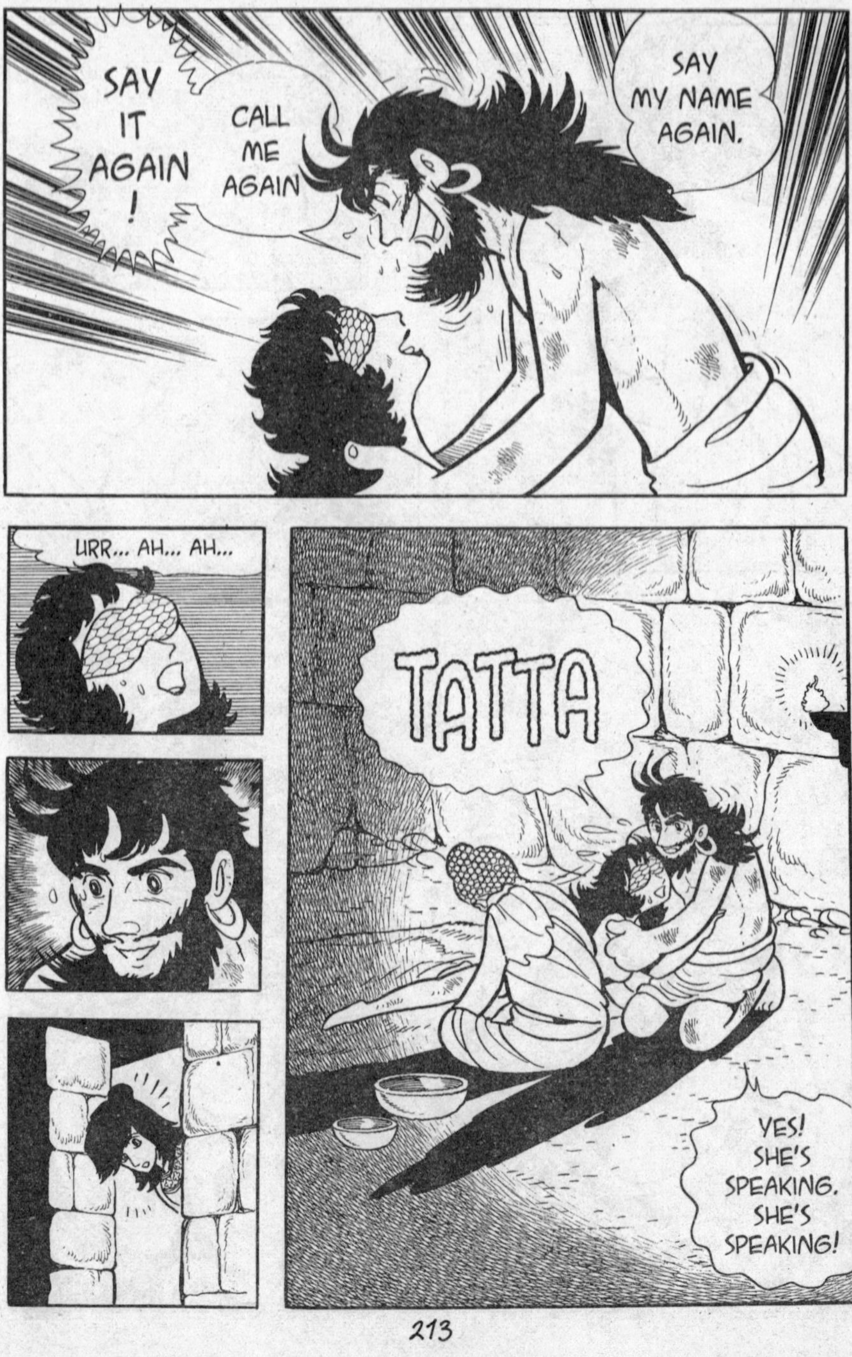
SAY MY NAME AGAIN.
CALL ME AGAIN
SAY IT AGAIN !
URR... AH... AH...
TATTA
YES! SHE'S SPEAKING. SHE'S SPEAKING!

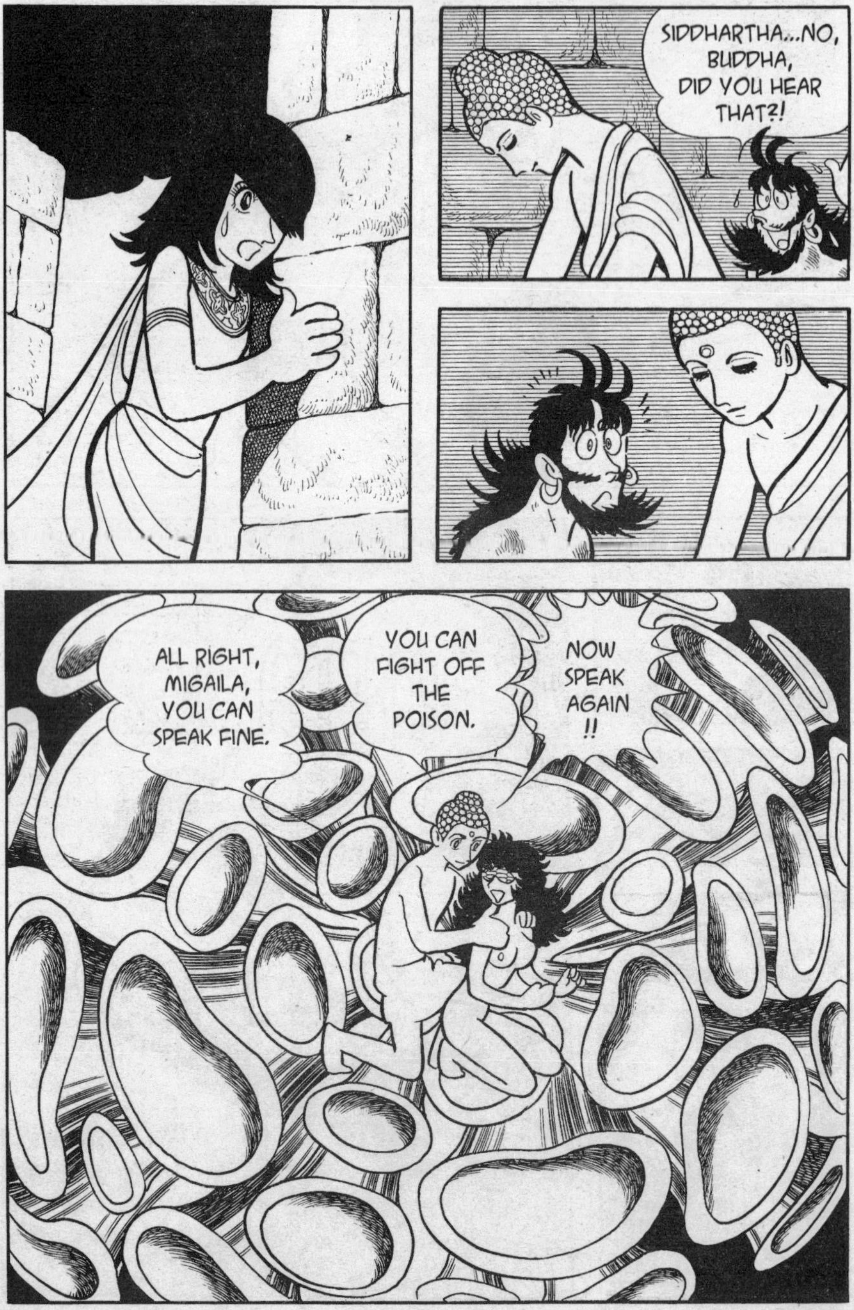
SIDDHARTHA...NO, BUDDHA, DID YOU HEAR THAT?!
ALL RIGHT, MIGAILA, YOU CAN SPEAK FINE.
YOU CAN FIGHT OFF THE POISON.
NOW SPEAK AGAIN !!

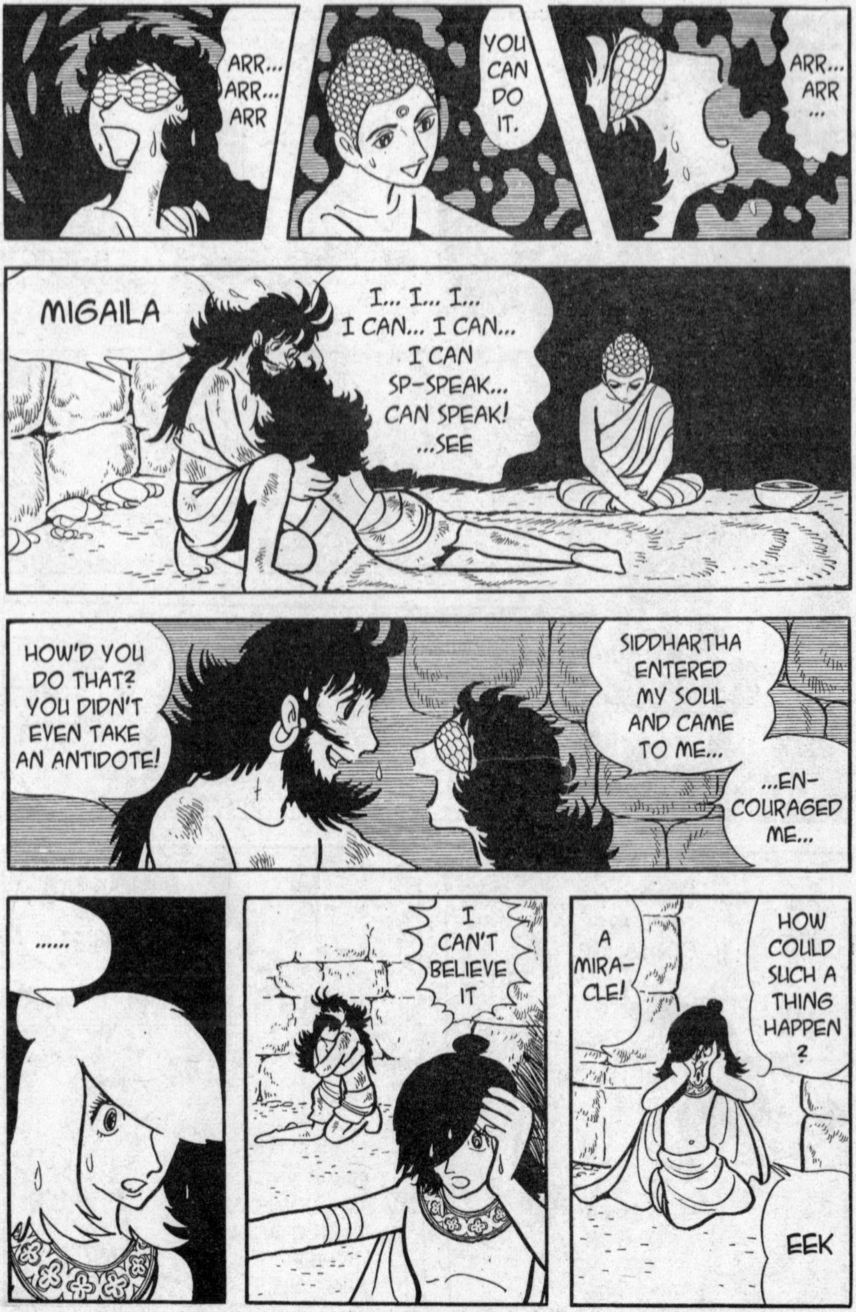
ARR... ARR... ARR
YOU CAN DO IT.
ARR... ARR ...
MIGAILA
I... I... I... I CAN... I CAN... I CAN SP-SPEAK... CAN SPEAK! ...SEE
HOW'D YOU DO THAT? YOU DIDN'T EVEN TAKE AN ANTIDOTE!
SIDDHARTHA ENTERED MY SOUL AND CAME TO ME...
...EN-COURAGED ME...
......
I CAN'T BELIEVE IT
A MIRA-CLE!
HOW COULD SUCH A THING HAPPEN ?
EEK

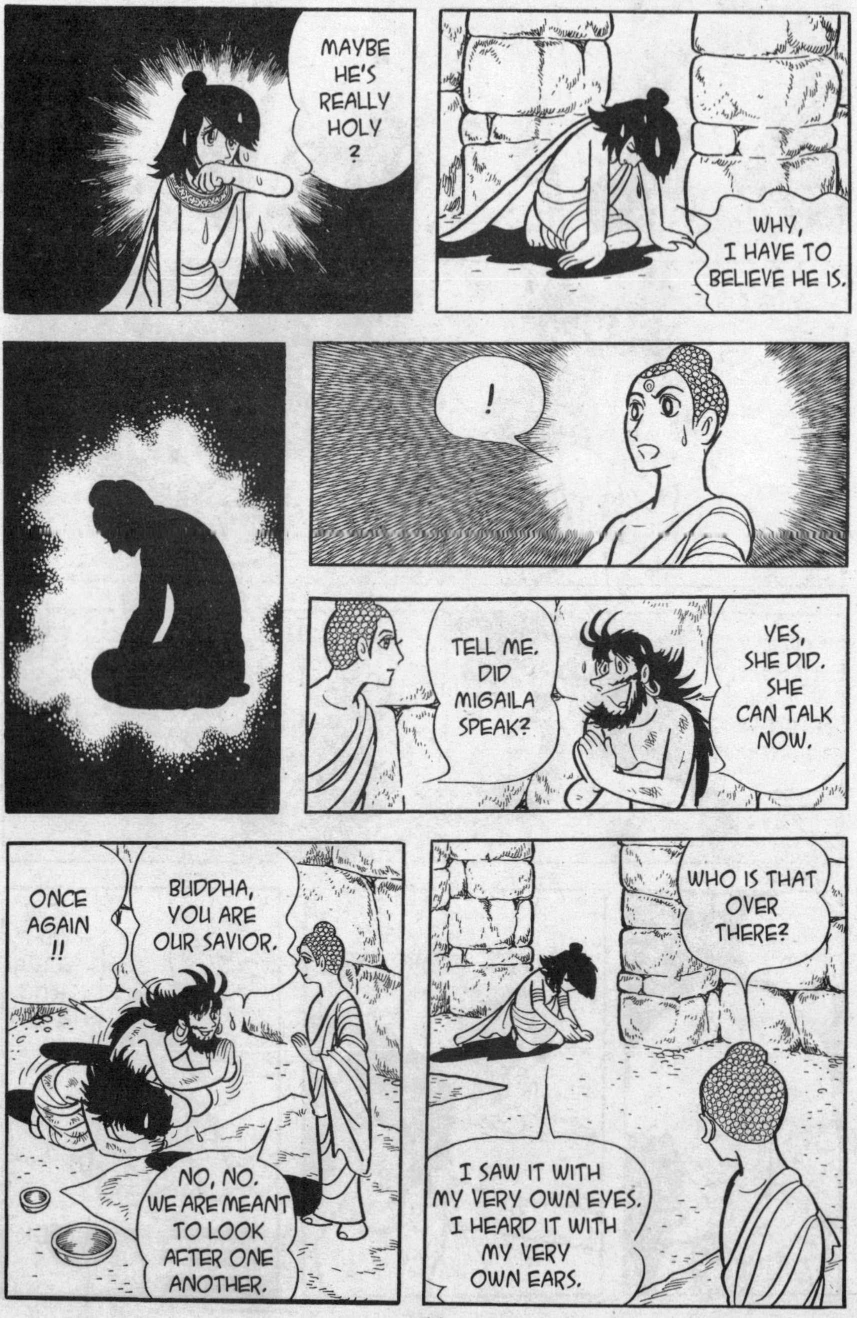
MAYBE HE'S REALLY HOLY ?
WHY, I HAVE TO BELIEVE HE IS.
!
TELL ME. DID MIGAILA SPEAK?
YES, SHE DID. SHE CAN TALK NOW.
ONCE AGAIN !!
BUDDHA, YOU ARE OUR SAVIOR.
NO, NO. WE ARE MEANT TO LOOK AFTER ONE ANOTHER.
WHO IS THAT OVER THERE?
I SAW IT WITH MY VERY OWN EYES. I HEARD IT WITH MY VERY OWN EARS.

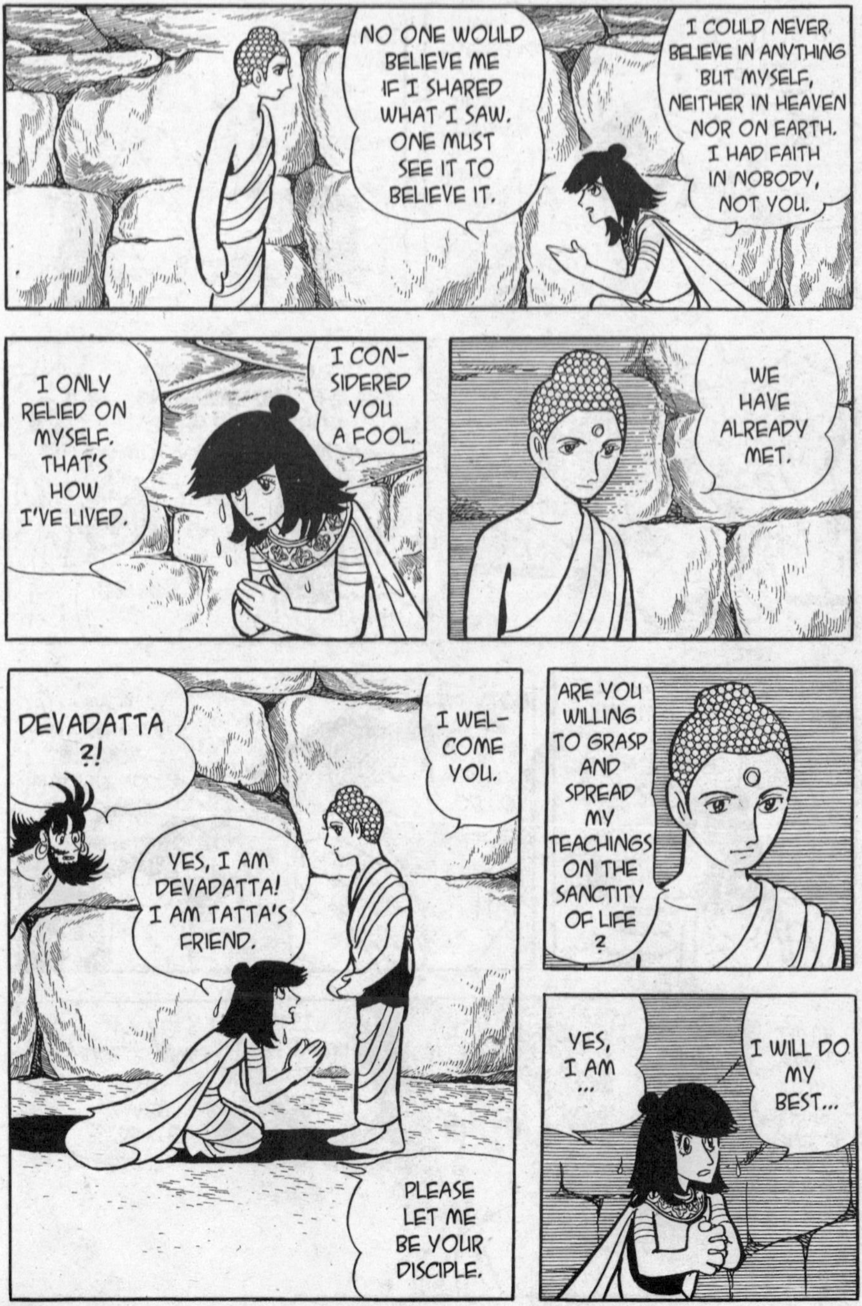
NO ONE WOULD BELIEVE ME IF I SHARED WHAT I SAW. ONE MUST SEE IT TO BELIEVE IT.
I COULD NEVER BELIEVE IN ANYTHING BUT MYSELF, NEITHER IN HEAVEN NOR ON EARTH. I HAD FAITH IN NOBODY, NOT YOU.
I CONSIDERED YOU A FOOL.
I ONLY RELIED ON MYSELF. THAT'S HOW I'VE LIVED.
WE HAVE ALREADY MET.
I WELCOME YOU.
DEVADATTA ?!
YES, I AM DEVADATTA! I AM TATTA'S FRIEND.
PLEASE LET ME BE YOUR DISCIPLE.
ARE YOU WILLING TO GRASP AND SPREAD MY TEACHINGS ON THE SANCTITY OF LIFE ?
I WILL DO MY BEST...
YES, I AM ...

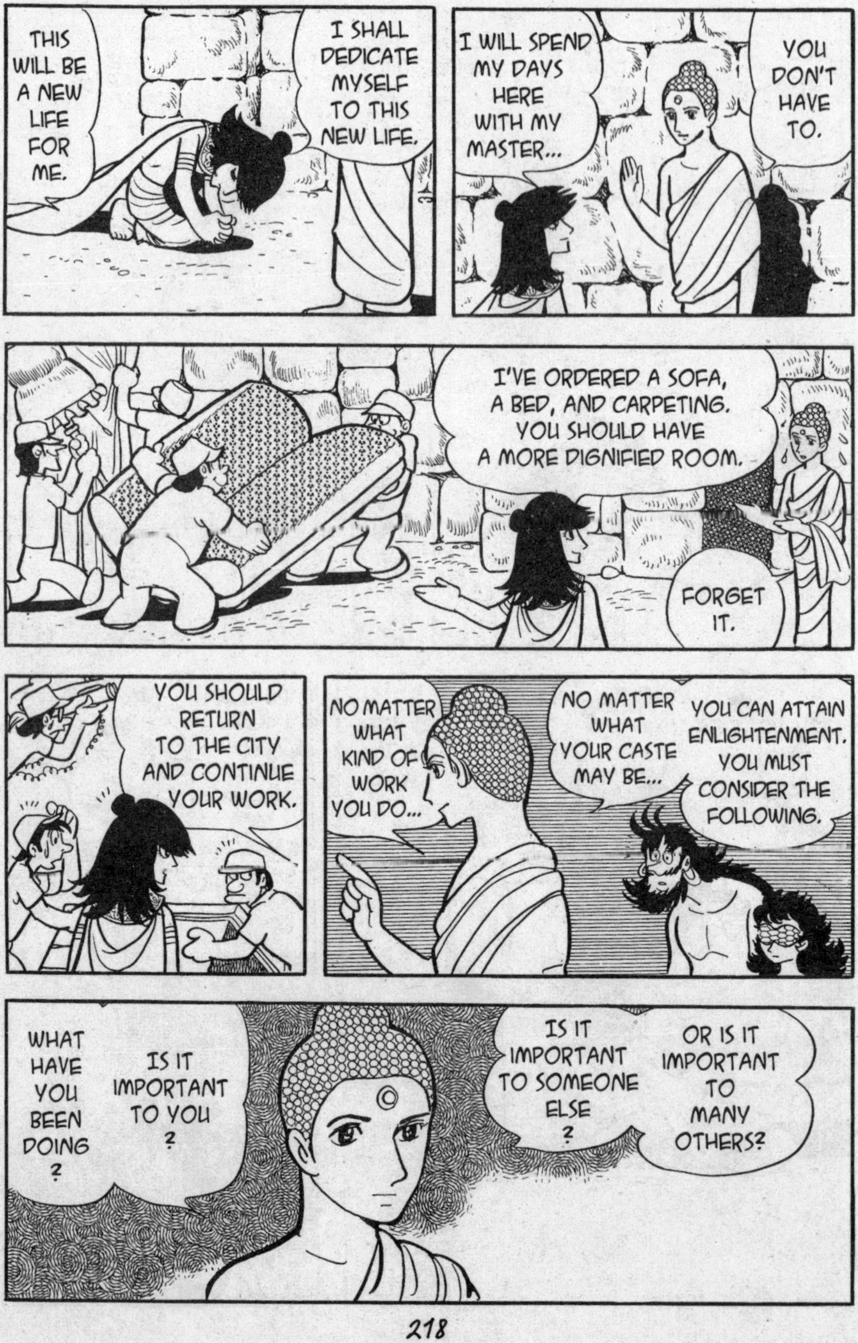
THIS WILL BE A NEW LIFE FOR ME.
I SHALL DEDICATE MYSELF TO THIS NEW LIFE.
I WILL SPEND MY DAYS HERE WITH MY MASTER...
YOU DON'T HAVE TO.
I'VE ORDERED A SOFA, A BED, AND CARPETING. YOU SHOULD HAVE A MORE DIGNIFIED ROOM.
FORGET IT.
YOU SHOULD RETURN TO THE CITY AND CONTINUE YOUR WORK.
NO MATTER WHAT KIND OF WORK YOU DO...
NO MATTER WHAT YOUR CASTE MAY BE...
YOU CAN ATTAIN ENLIGHTENMENT. YOU MUST CONSIDER THE FOLLOWING.
WHAT HAVE YOU BEEN DOING?
IS IT IMPORTANT TO YOU?
IS IT IMPORTANT TO SOMEONE ELSE?
OR IS IT IMPORTANT TO MANY OTHERS?

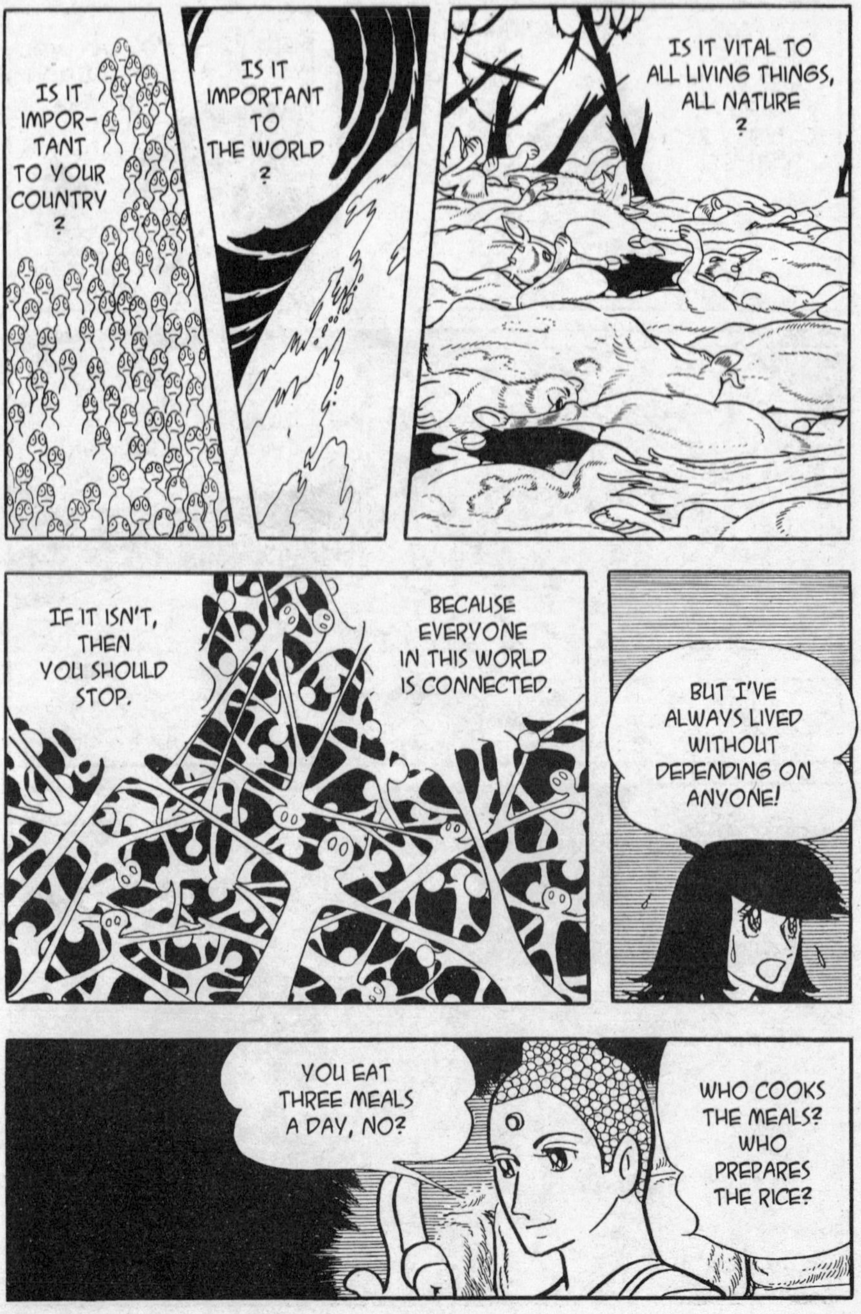
IS IT IMPORTANT TO YOUR COUNTRY ?
IS IT IMPORTANT TO THE WORLD ?
IS IT VITAL TO ALL LIVING THINGS, ALL NATURE ?
IF IT ISN'T, THEN YOU SHOULD STOP.
BECAUSE EVERYONE IN THIS WORLD IS CONNECTED.
BUT I'VE ALWAYS LIVED WITHOUT DEPENDING ON ANYONE!
YOU EAT THREE MEALS A DAY, NO?
WHO COOKS THE MEALS? WHO PREPARES THE RICE?

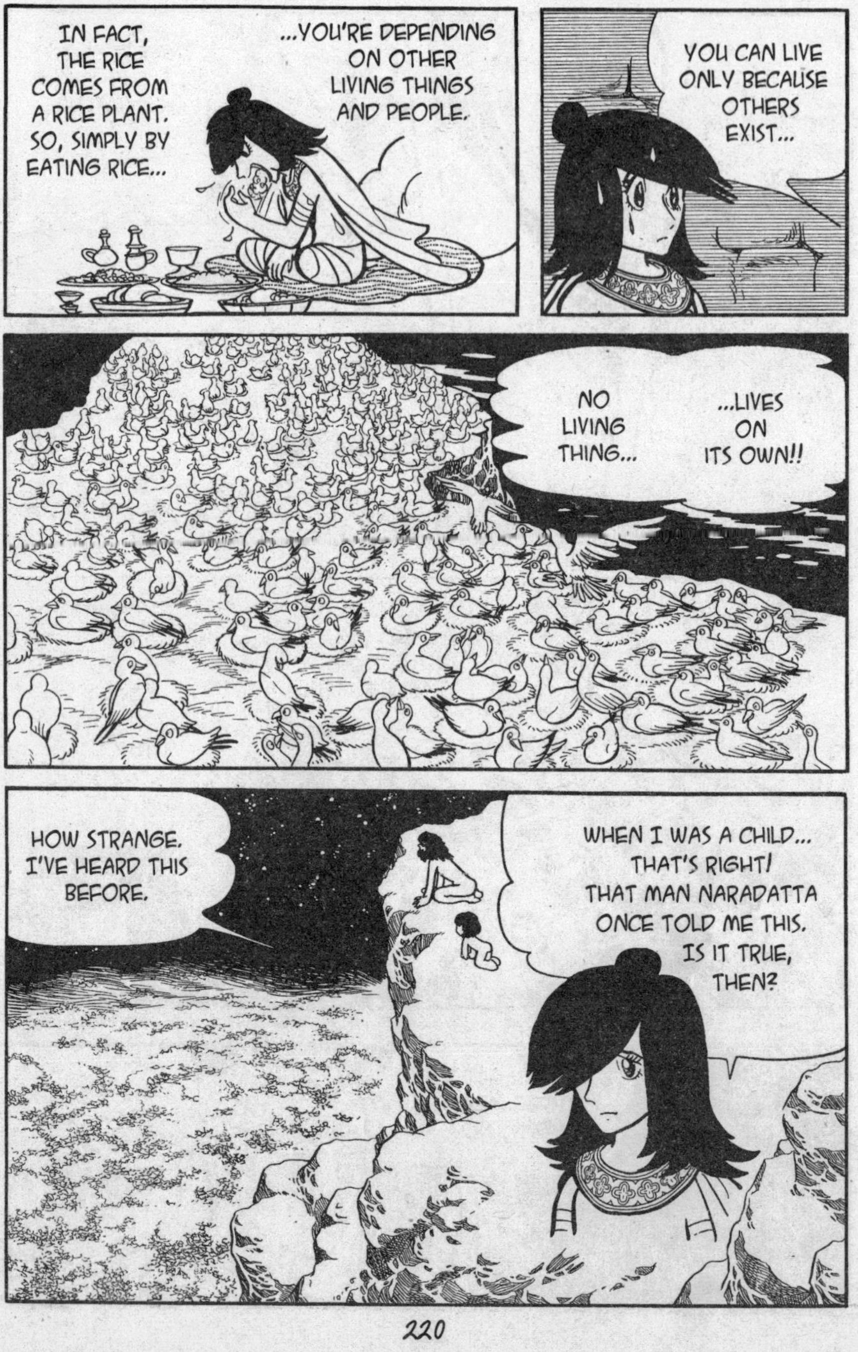
IN FACT, THE RICE COMES FROM A RICE PLANT. SO, SIMPLY BY EATING RICE...
...YOU'RE DEPENDING ON OTHER LIVING THINGS AND PEOPLE.
YOU CAN LIVE ONLY BECAUSE OTHERS EXIST...
NO LIVING THING...
...LIVES ON ITS OWN!!
HOW STRANGE. I'VE HEARD THIS BEFORE.
WHEN I WAS A CHILD... THAT'S RIGHT! THAT MAN NARADATTA ONCE TOLD ME THIS. IS IT TRUE, THEN?

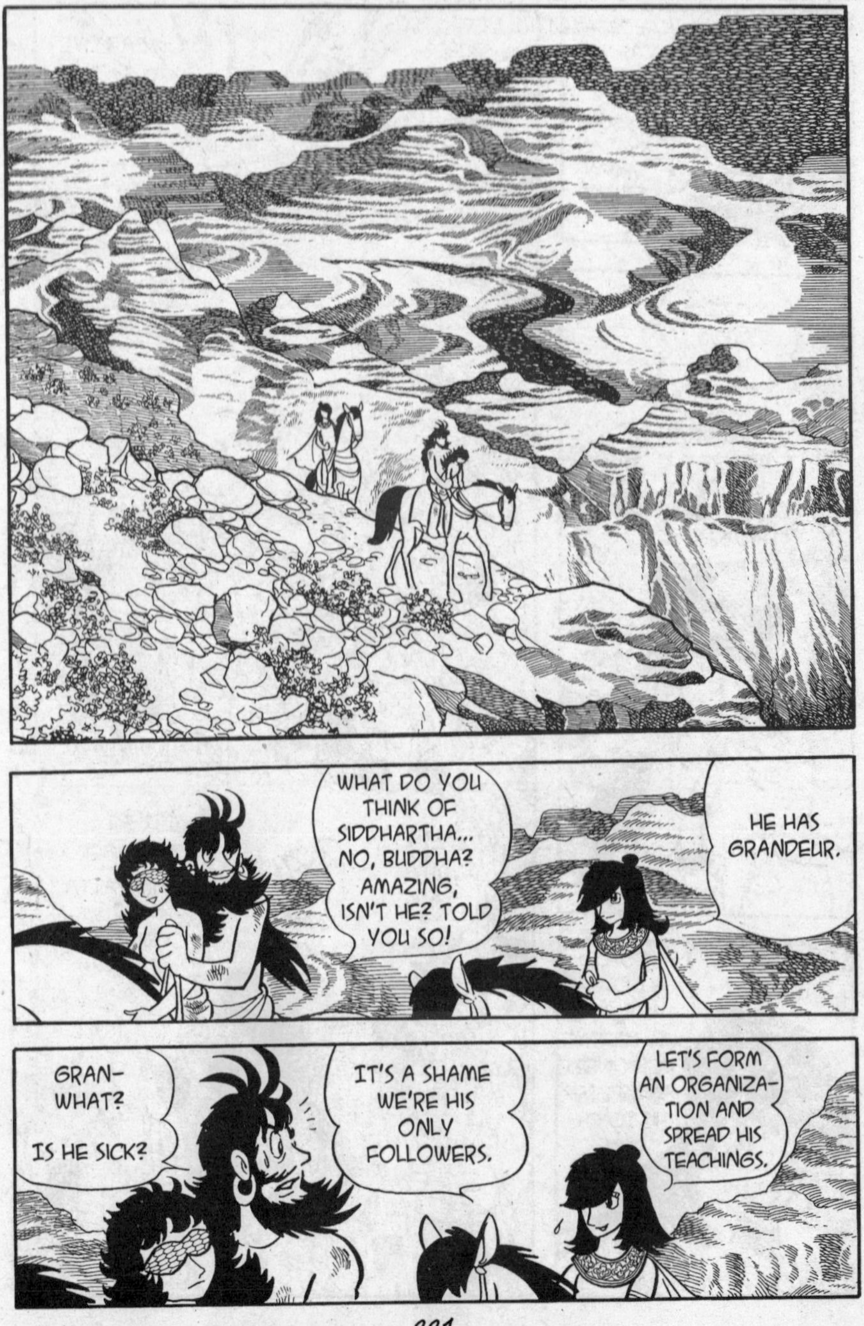
WHAT DO YOU THINK OF SIDDHARTHA... NO, BUDDHA? AMAZING, ISN'T HE? TOLD YOU SO!
HE HAS GRANDEUR.
LET'S FORM AN ORGANIZATION AND SPREAD HIS TEACHINGS.
IT'S A SHAME WE'RE HIS ONLY FOLLOWERS.
GRAN-WHAT?
IS HE SICK?

OR-ORGAN-IZASHUN? WHAT'S THAT? I KNOW WHAT AN ORGAN GRINDER IS...

AN ORGANIZATION IS A COMMUNITY.

BUDDHA WILL BE THE LEADER OF HUNDREDS, THOUSANDS...

NO, TENS OF THOUSANDS.

PEOPLE ALL OVER THE WORLD WILL BECOME FOLLOWERS AND SPREAD HIS TEACHINGS.

IT'S MY TASK...

...TO FORM THIS ORGANIZATION.

I'LL BE HIS MANAGER. THERE, AS OF TODAY, IS MY TASK!

222

CHAPTER FIVE

DEER PARK

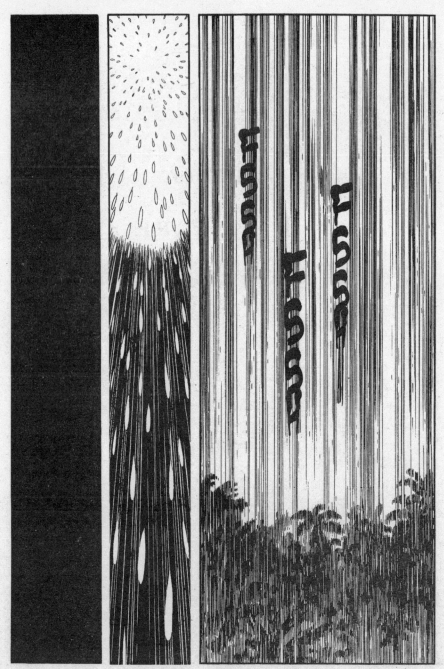

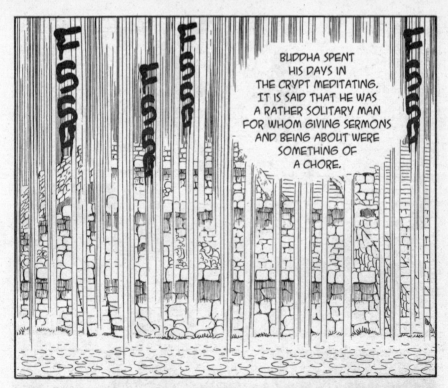

BUDDHA SPENT HIS DAYS IN THE CRYPT MEDITATING. IT IS SAID THAT HE WAS A RATHER SOLITARY MAN FOR WHOM GIVING SERMONS AND BEING ABOUT WERE SOMETHING OF A CHORE.

225

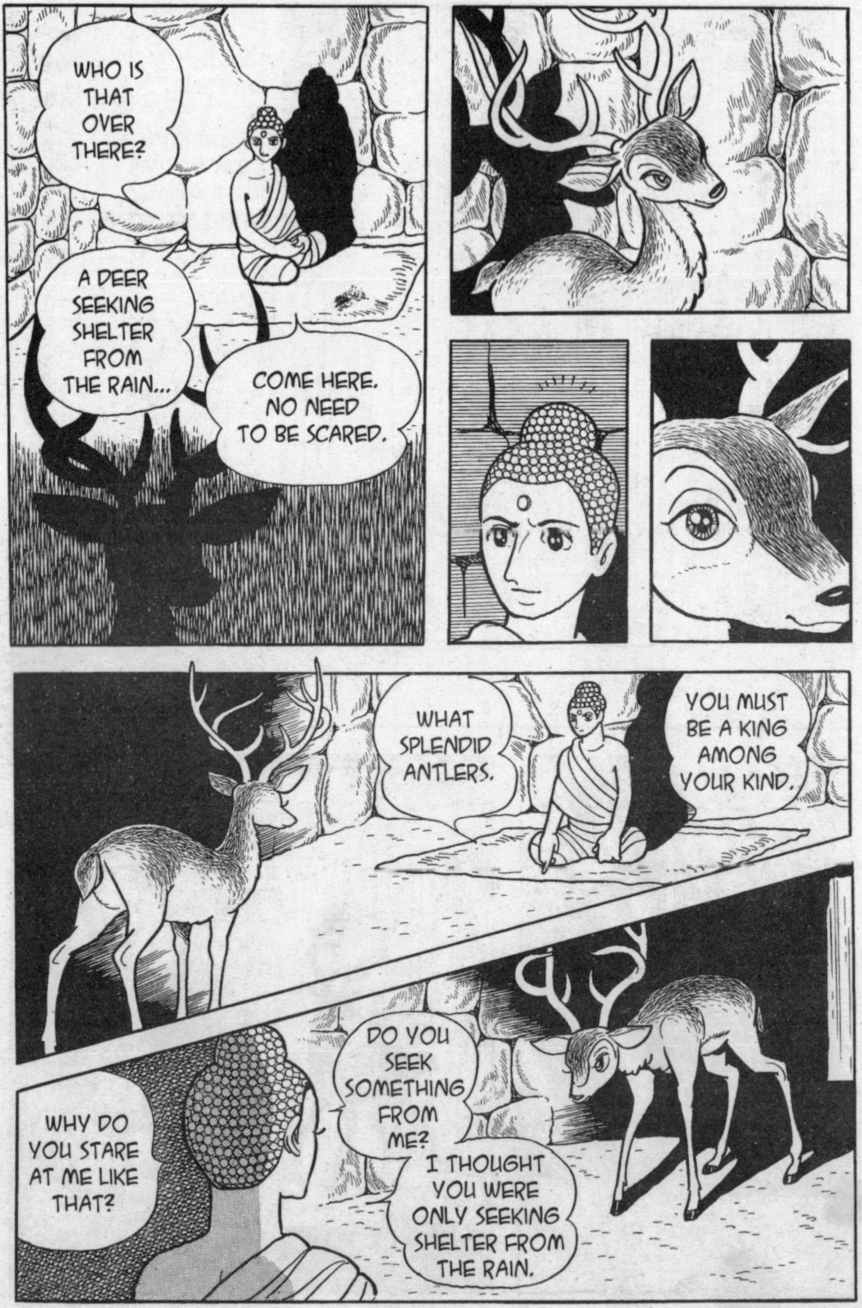
WHO IS THAT OVER THERE?
A DEER SEEKING SHELTER FROM THE RAIN...
COME HERE. NO NEED TO BE SCARED.
WHAT SPLENDID ANTLERS.
YOU MUST BE A KING AMONG YOUR KIND.
WHY DO YOU STARE AT ME LIKE THAT?
DO YOU SEEK SOMETHING FROM ME?
I THOUGHT YOU WERE ONLY SEEKING SHELTER FROM THE RAIN.

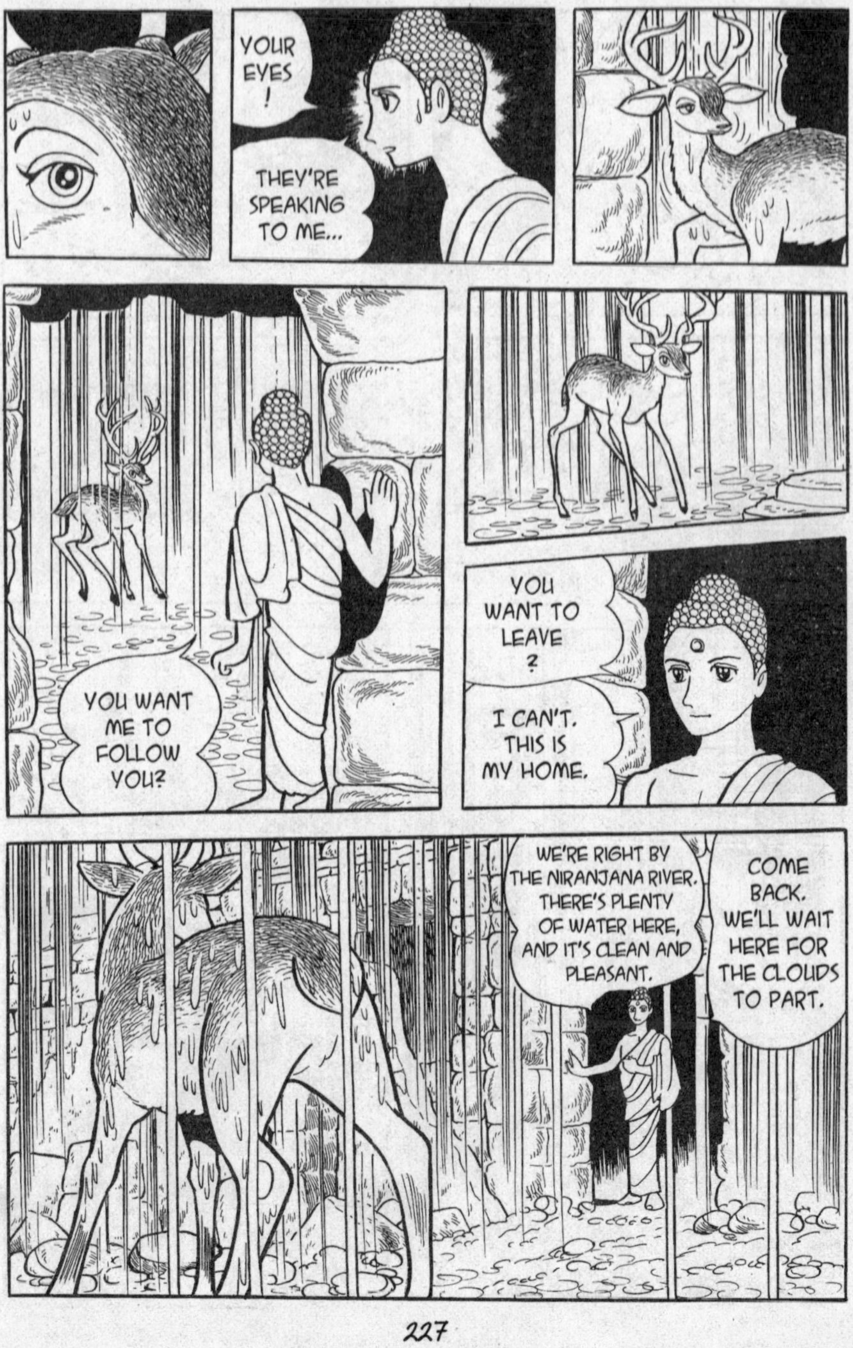
YOUR EYES !
THEY'RE SPEAKING TO ME...
YOU WANT ME TO FOLLOW YOU?
YOU WANT TO LEAVE ?
I CAN'T. THIS IS MY HOME.
WE'RE RIGHT BY THE NIRANJANA RIVER. THERE'S PLENTY OF WATER HERE, AND IT'S CLEAN AND PLEASANT.
COME BACK. WE'LL WAIT HERE FOR THE CLOUDS TO PART.

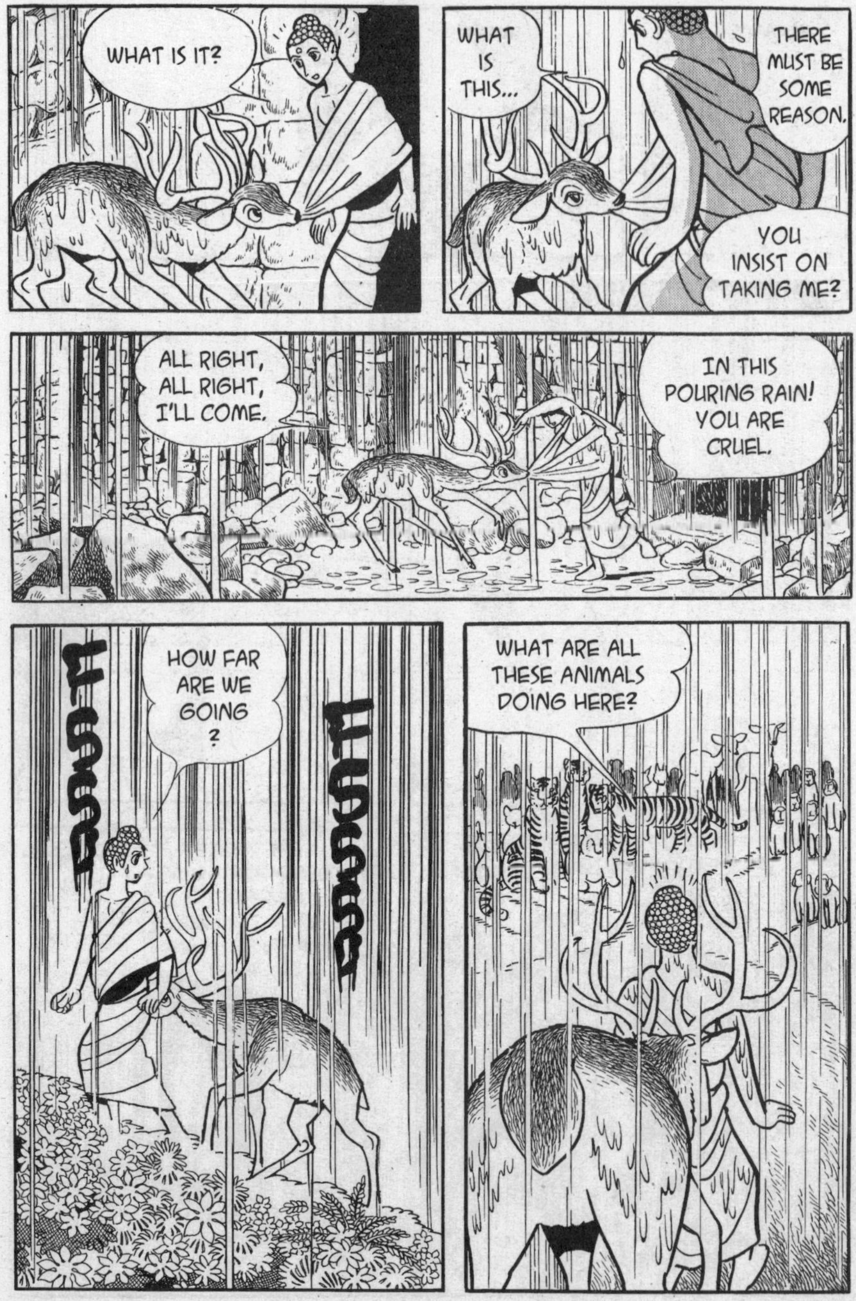
WHAT IS IT?
WHAT IS THIS...
THERE MUST BE SOME REASON.
YOU INSIST ON TAKING ME?
ALL RIGHT, ALL RIGHT, I'LL COME.
IN THIS POURING RAIN! YOU ARE CRUEL.
HOW FAR ARE WE GOING ?
WHAT ARE ALL THESE ANIMALS DOING HERE?

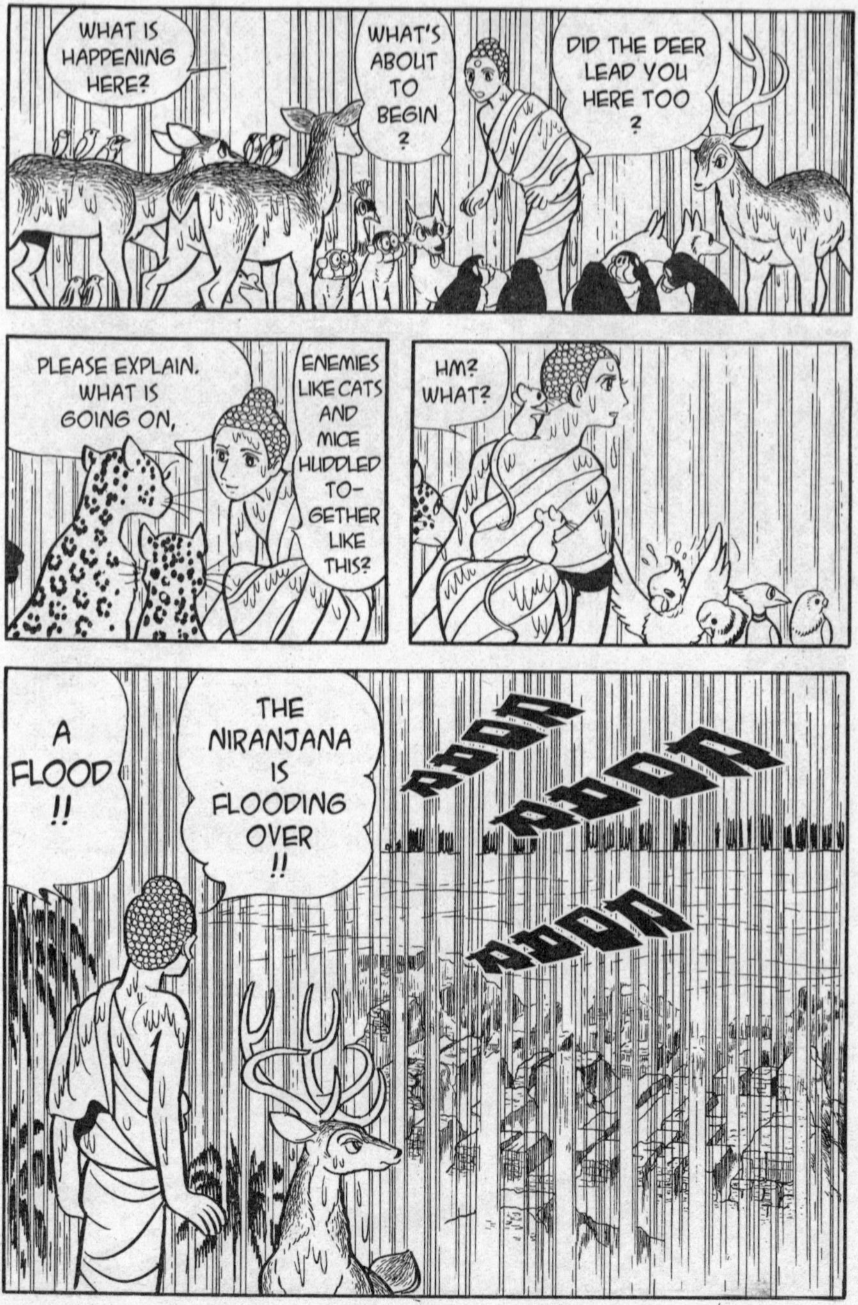
WHAT IS HAPPENING HERE?
WHAT'S ABOUT TO BEGIN?
DID THE DEER LEAD YOU HERE TOO?
PLEASE EXPLAIN. WHAT IS GOING ON,
ENEMIES LIKE CATS AND MICE HUDDLED TO-GETHER LIKE THIS?
HM? WHAT?
A FLOOD!!
THE NIRANJANA IS FLOODING OVER!!

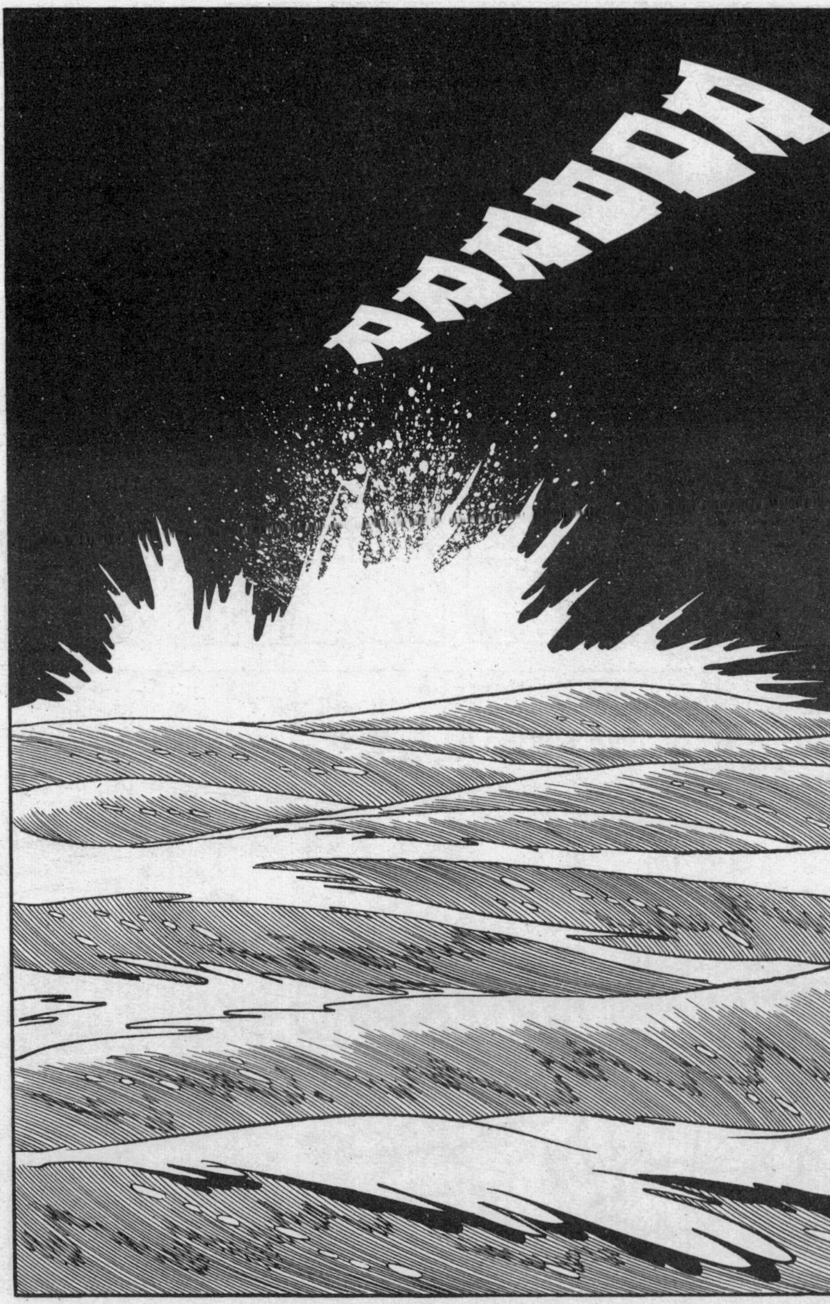

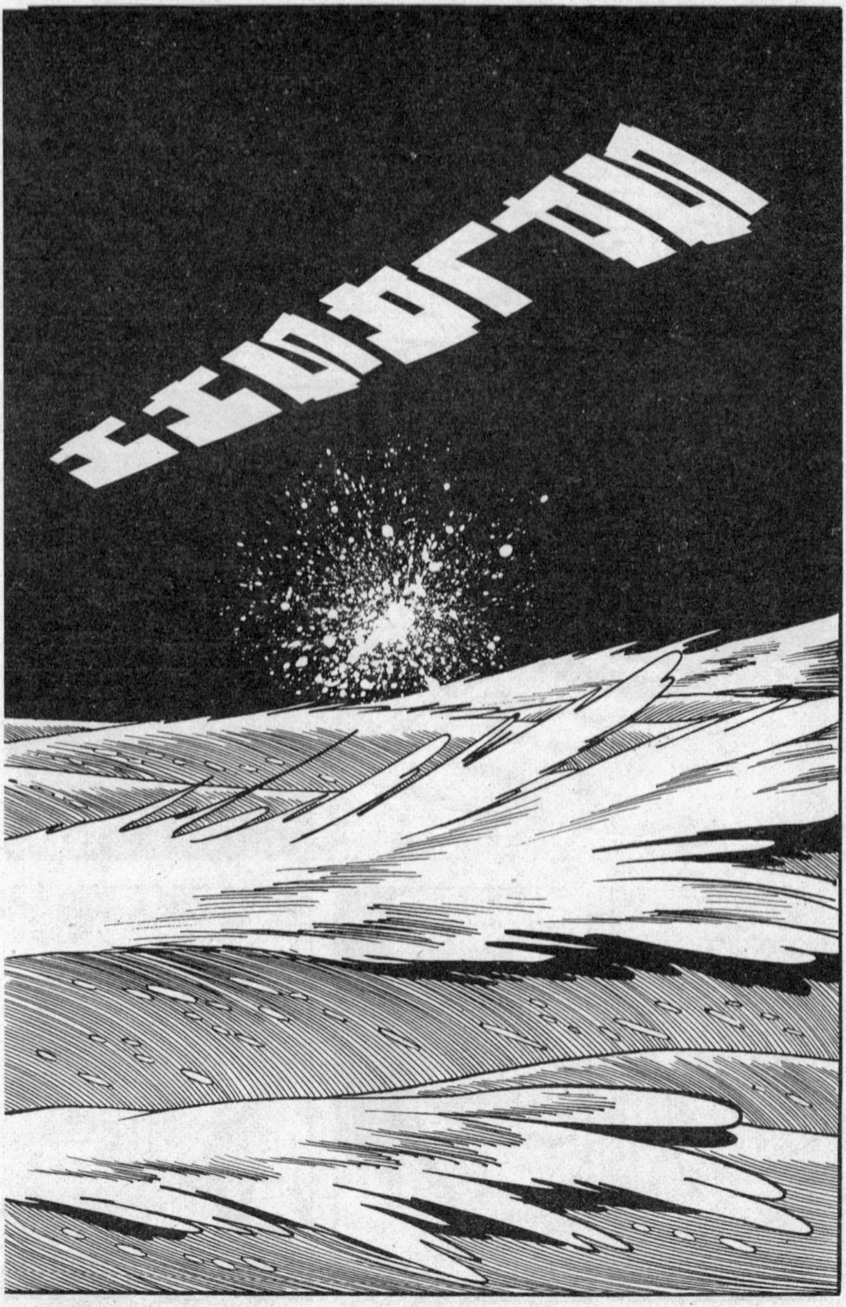

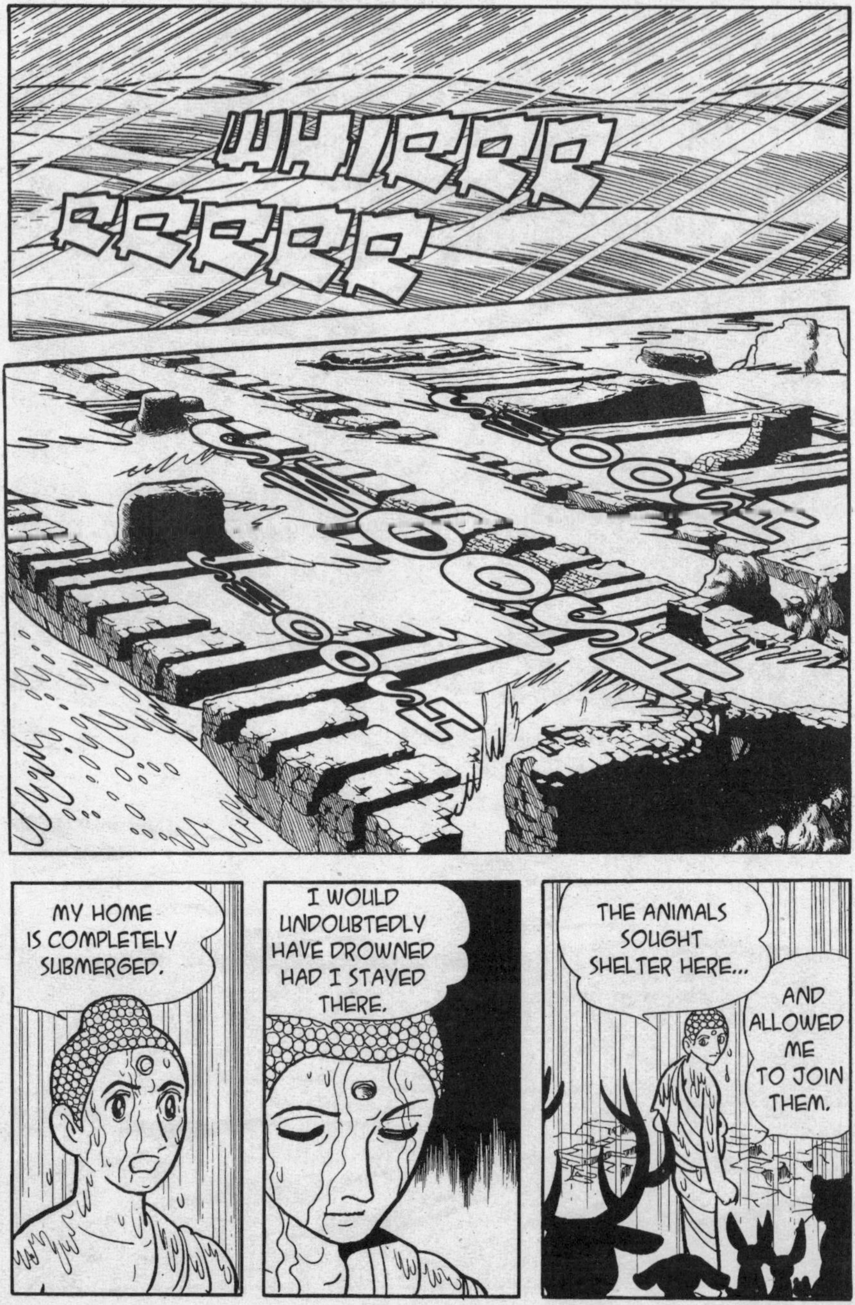
WHIRRR
CRRRR
SHOOSH
SWOOSH
SHOOSH
MY HOME IS COMPLETELY SUBMERGED.
I WOULD UNDOUBTEDLY HAVE DROWNED HAD I STAYED THERE.
THE ANIMALS SOUGHT SHELTER HERE...
AND ALLOWED ME TO JOIN THEM.

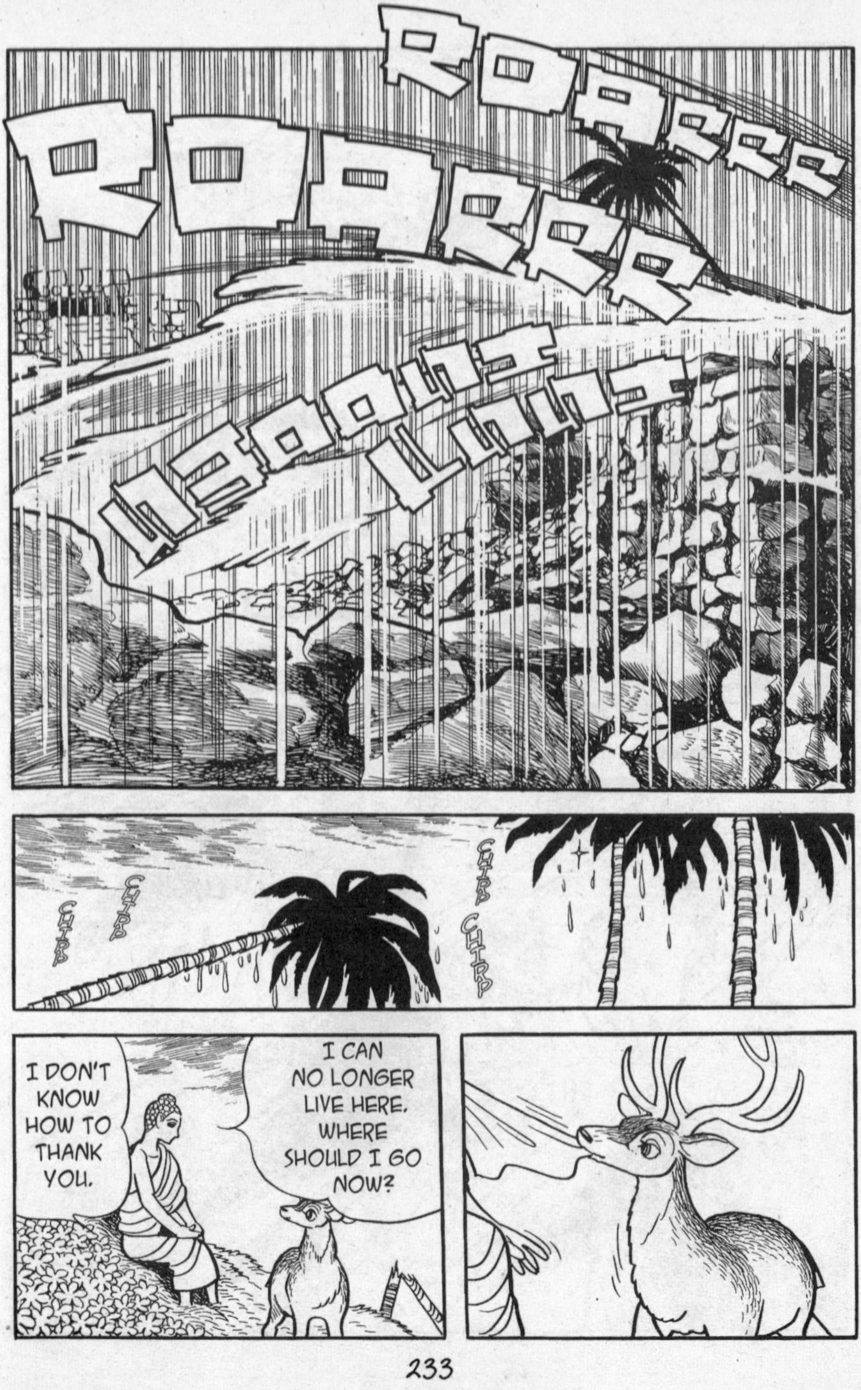
ROARRR
ROARRRR
CHIRP
CHIRP
CHIRP CHIRP
CHIRP
I DON'T KNOW HOW TO THANK YOU.
I CAN NO LONGER LIVE HERE. WHERE SHOULD I GO NOW?

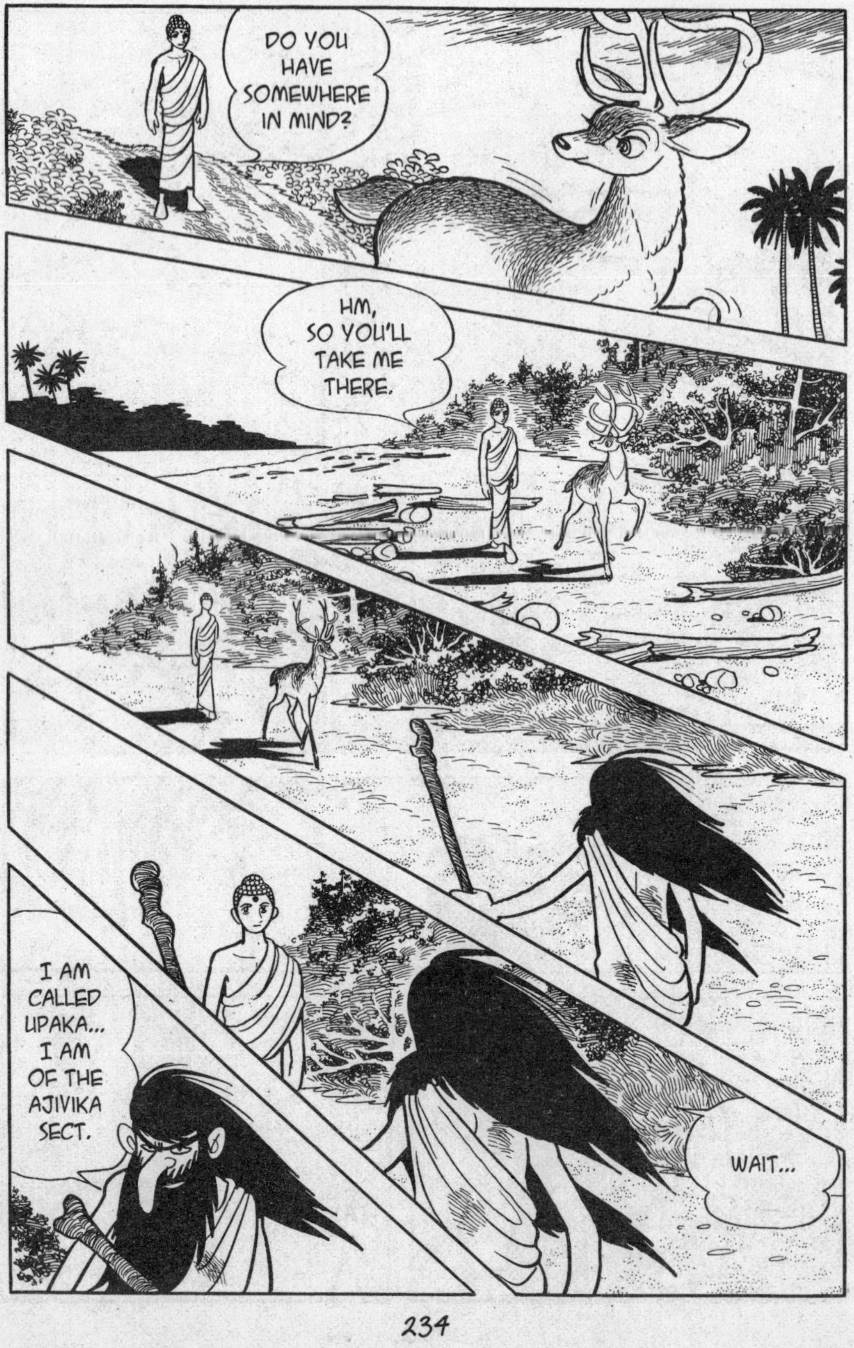
DO YOU HAVE SOMEWHERE IN MIND?
HM, SO YOU'LL TAKE ME THERE.
WAIT...
I AM CALLED UPAKA... I AM OF THE AJIVIKA SECT.

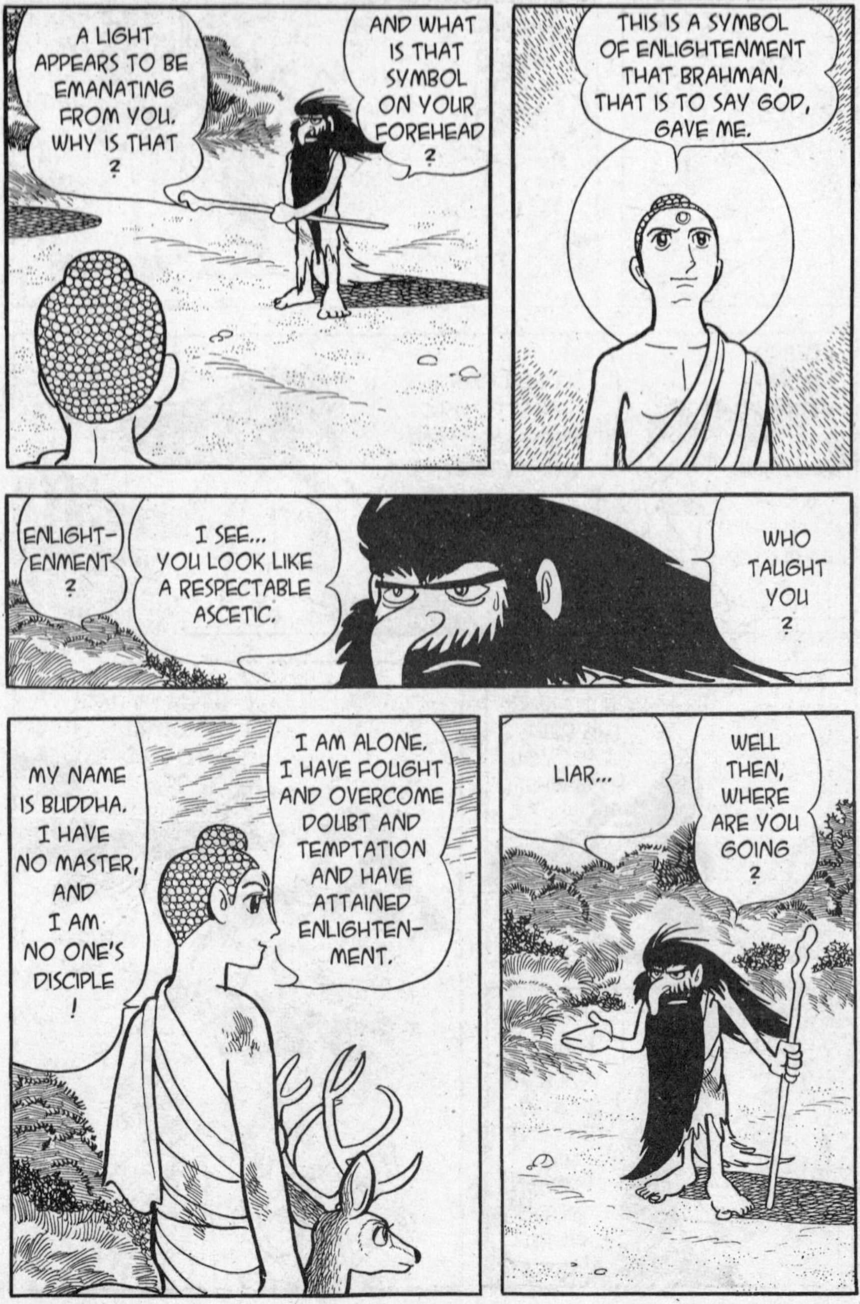
A LIGHT APPEARS TO BE EMANATING FROM YOU. WHY IS THAT ?
AND WHAT IS THAT SYMBOL ON YOUR FOREHEAD ?
THIS IS A SYMBOL OF ENLIGHTENMENT THAT BRAHMAN, THAT IS TO SAY GOD, GAVE ME.
ENLIGHT-ENMENT ?
I SEE... YOU LOOK LIKE A RESPECTABLE ASCETIC.
WHO TAUGHT YOU ?
MY NAME IS BUDDHA. I HAVE NO MASTER, AND I AM NO ONE'S DISCIPLE !
I AM ALONE. I HAVE FOUGHT AND OVERCOME DOUBT AND TEMPTATION AND HAVE ATTAINED ENLIGHTEN-MENT.
LIAR...
WELL THEN, WHERE ARE YOU GOING ?

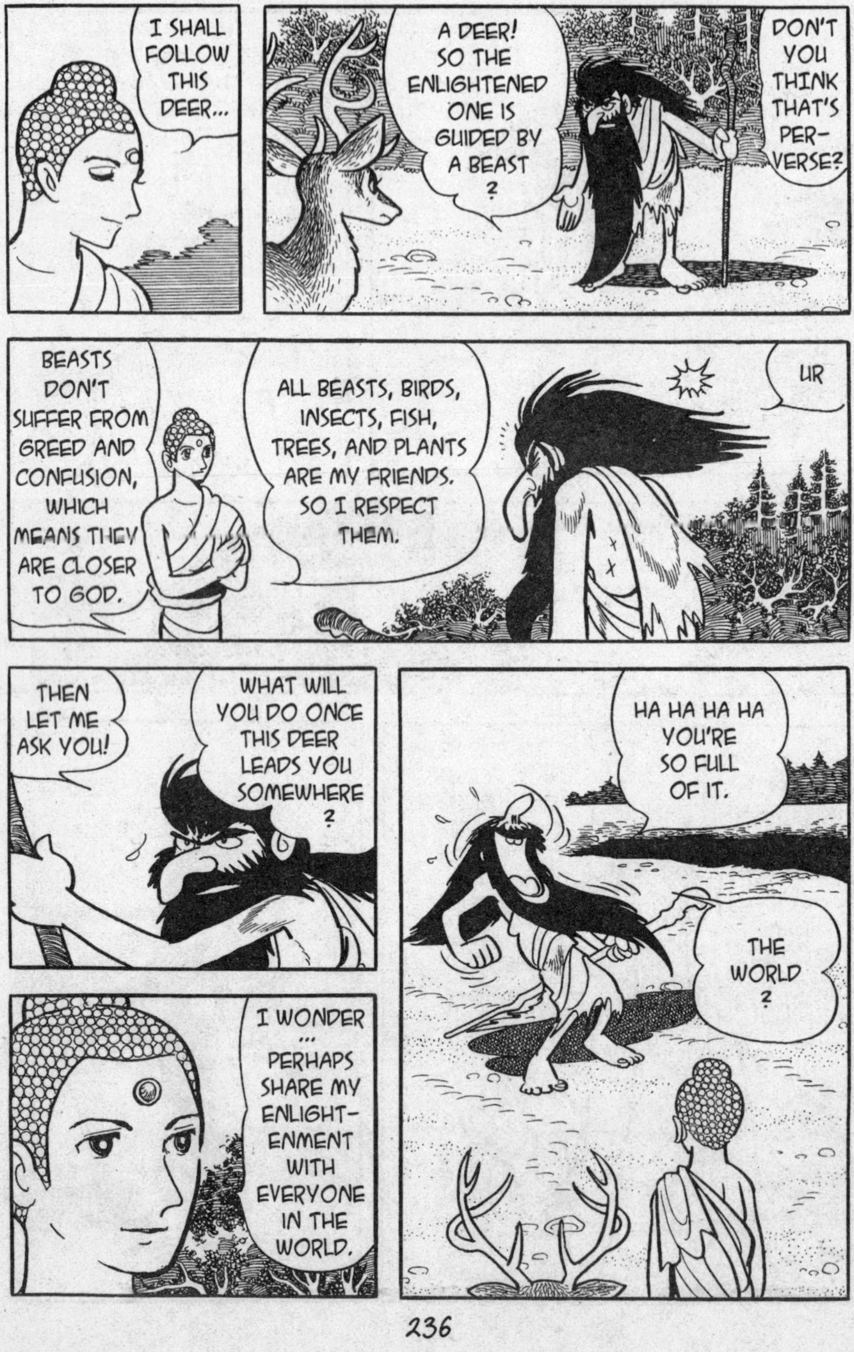
I SHALL FOLLOW THIS DEER...
A DEER! SO THE ENLIGHTENED ONE IS GUIDED BY A BEAST?
DON'T YOU THINK THAT'S PER-VERSE?
BEASTS DON'T SUFFER FROM GREED AND CONFUSION, WHICH MEANS THEY ARE CLOSER TO GOD.
ALL BEASTS, BIRDS, INSECTS, FISH, TREES, AND PLANTS ARE MY FRIENDS. SO I RESPECT THEM.
UR
THEN LET ME ASK YOU!
WHAT WILL YOU DO ONCE THIS DEER LEADS YOU SOMEWHERE?
I WONDER ... PERHAPS SHARE MY ENLIGHT-ENMENT WITH EVERYONE IN THE WORLD.
HA HA HA HA YOU'RE SO FULL OF IT.
THE WORLD?

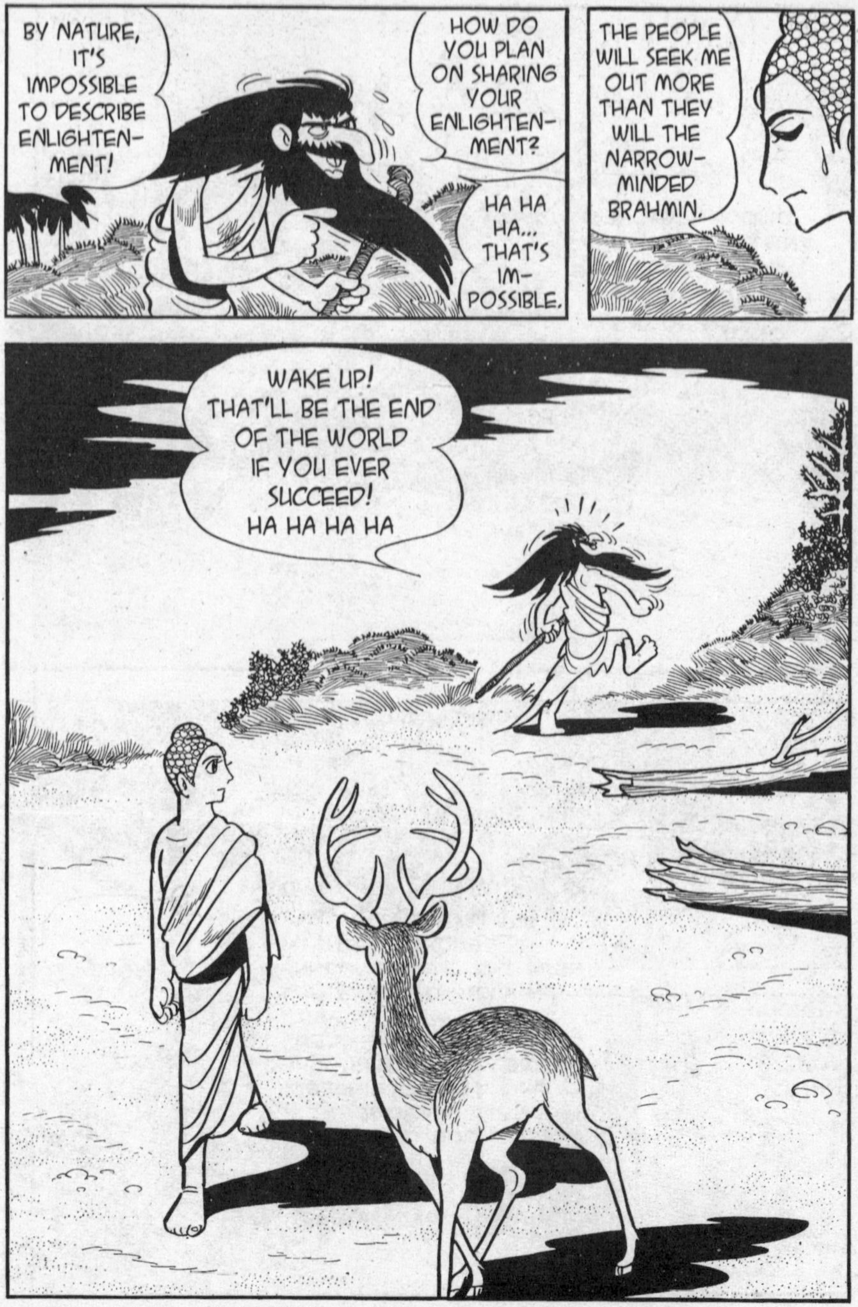
BY NATURE, IT'S IMPOSSIBLE TO DESCRIBE ENLIGHTENMENT!
HOW DO YOU PLAN ON SHARING YOUR ENLIGHTENMENT?
HA HA HA... THAT'S IMPOSSIBLE.
THE PEOPLE WILL SEEK ME OUT MORE THAN THEY WILL THE NARROW-MINDED BRAHMIN.
WAKE UP! THAT'LL BE THE END OF THE WORLD IF YOU EVER SUCCEED! HA HA HA HA

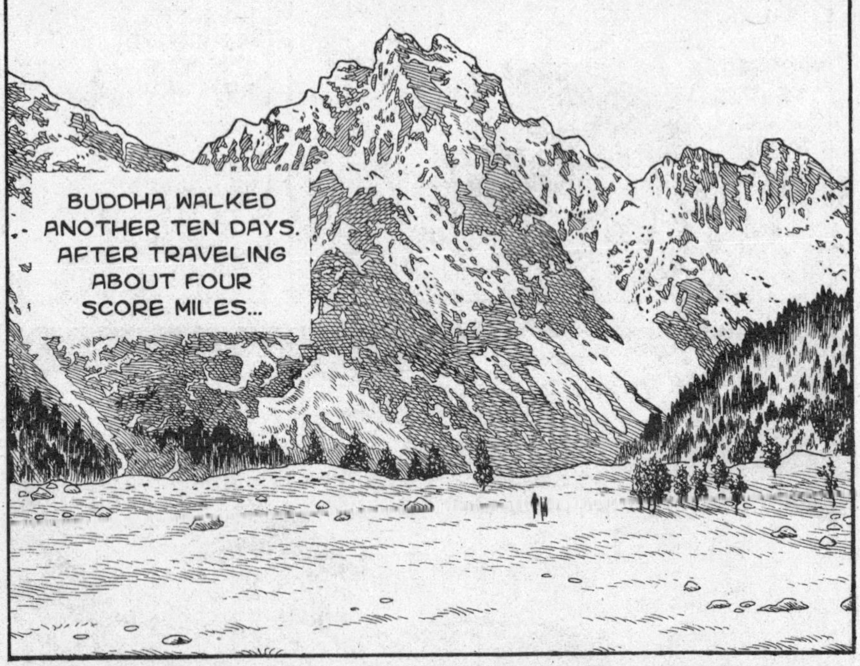
BUDDHA WALKED ANOTHER TEN DAYS. AFTER TRAVELING ABOUT FOUR SCORE MILES...
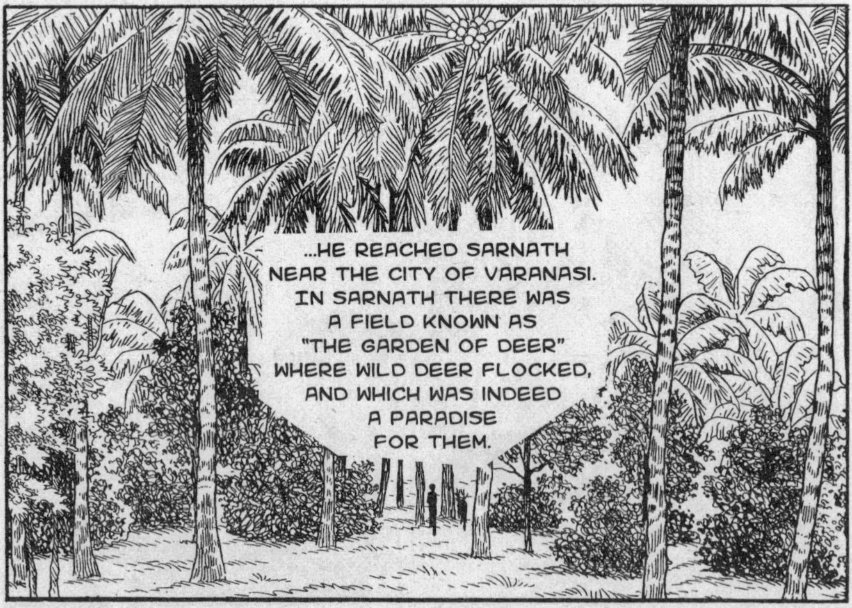
...HE REACHED SARNATH NEAR THE CITY OF VARANASI. IN SARNATH THERE WAS A FIELD KNOWN AS "THE GARDEN OF DEER" WHERE WILD DEER FLOCKED, AND WHICH WAS INDEED A PARADISE FOR THEM.

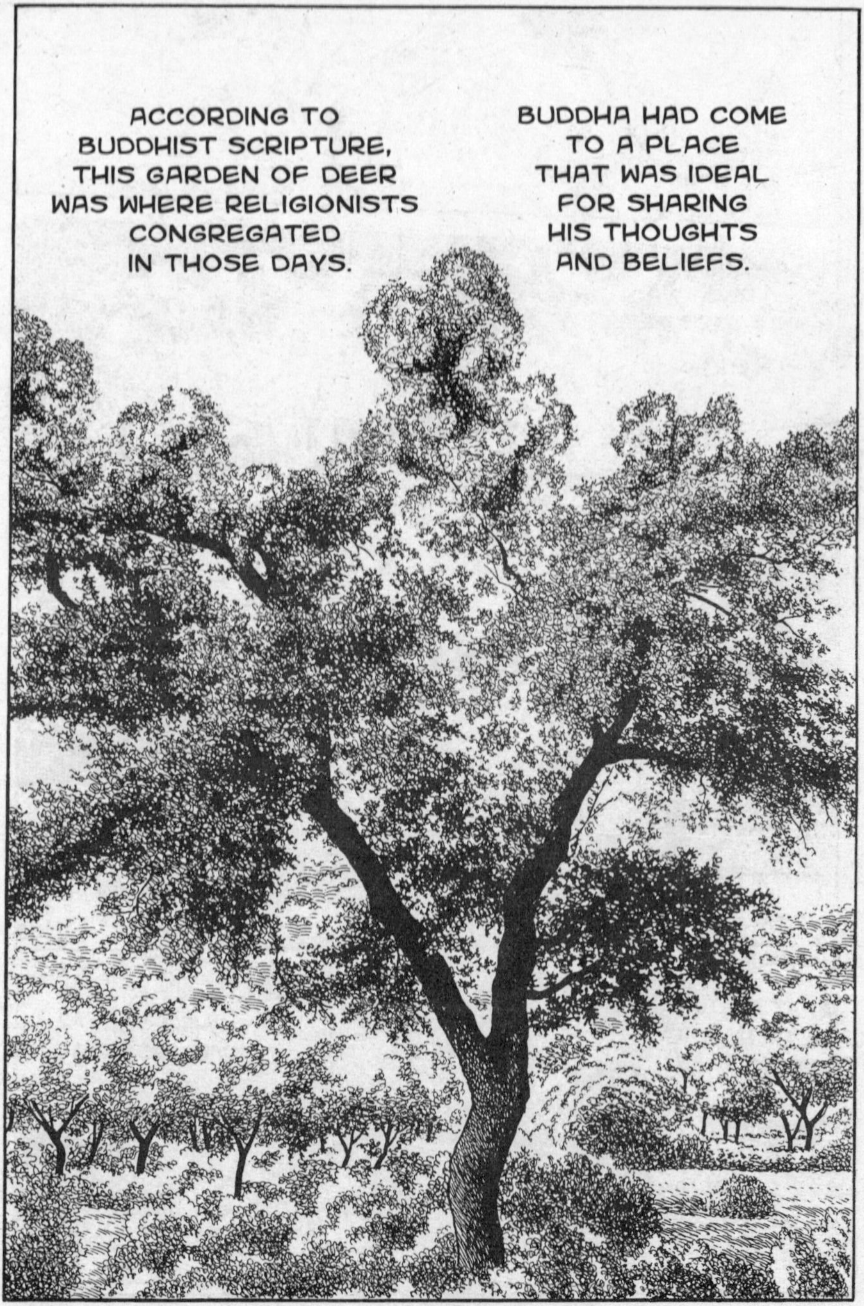
ACCORDING TO BUDDHIST SCRIPTURE, THIS GARDEN OF DEER WAS WHERE RELIGIONISTS CONGREGATED IN THOSE DAYS.
BUDDHA HAD COME TO A PLACE THAT WAS IDEAL FOR SHARING HIS THOUGHTS AND BELIEFS.

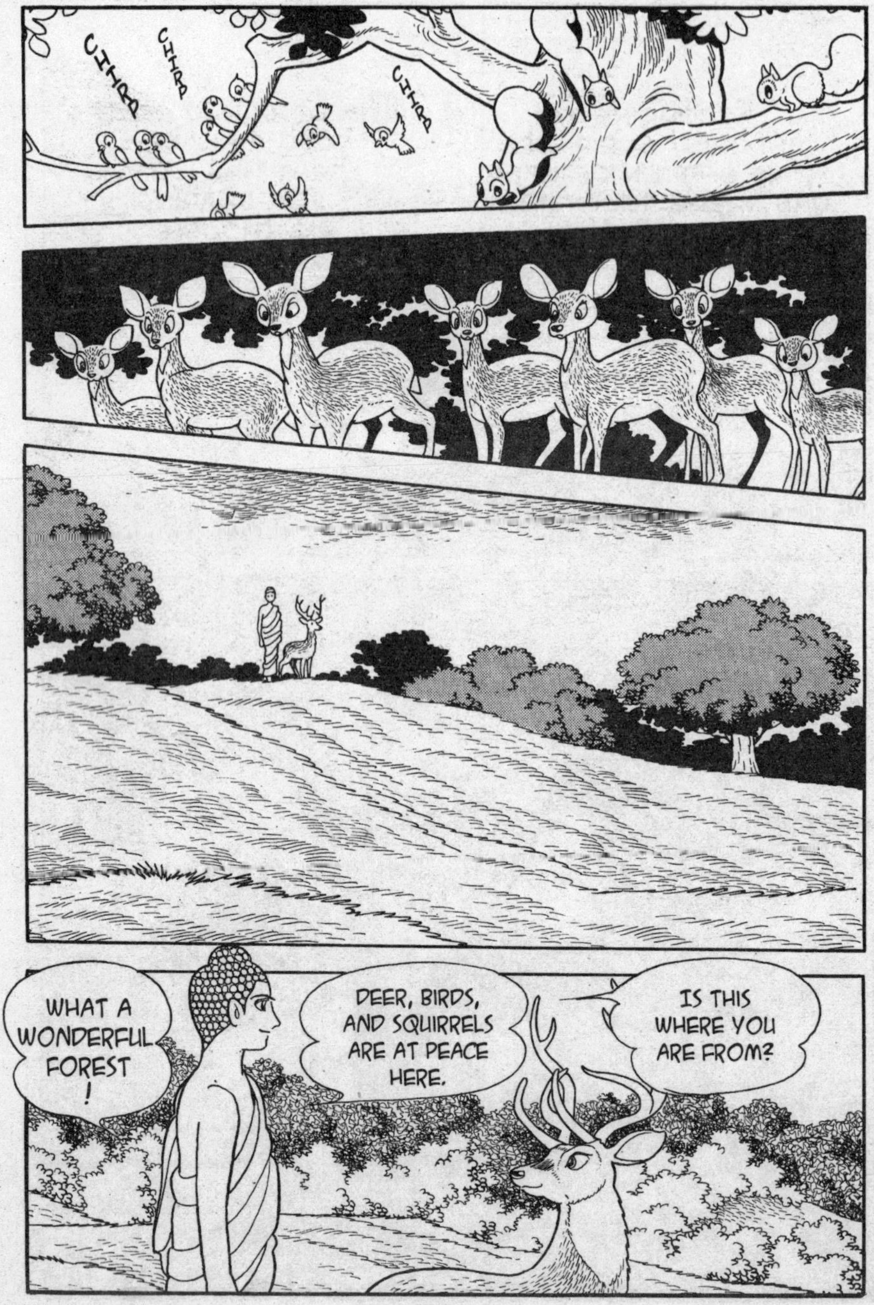
CHIRP
CHIRP
CHIRP
WHAT A WONDERFUL FOREST!
DEER, BIRDS, AND SQUIRRELS ARE AT PEACE HERE.
IS THIS WHERE YOU ARE FROM?

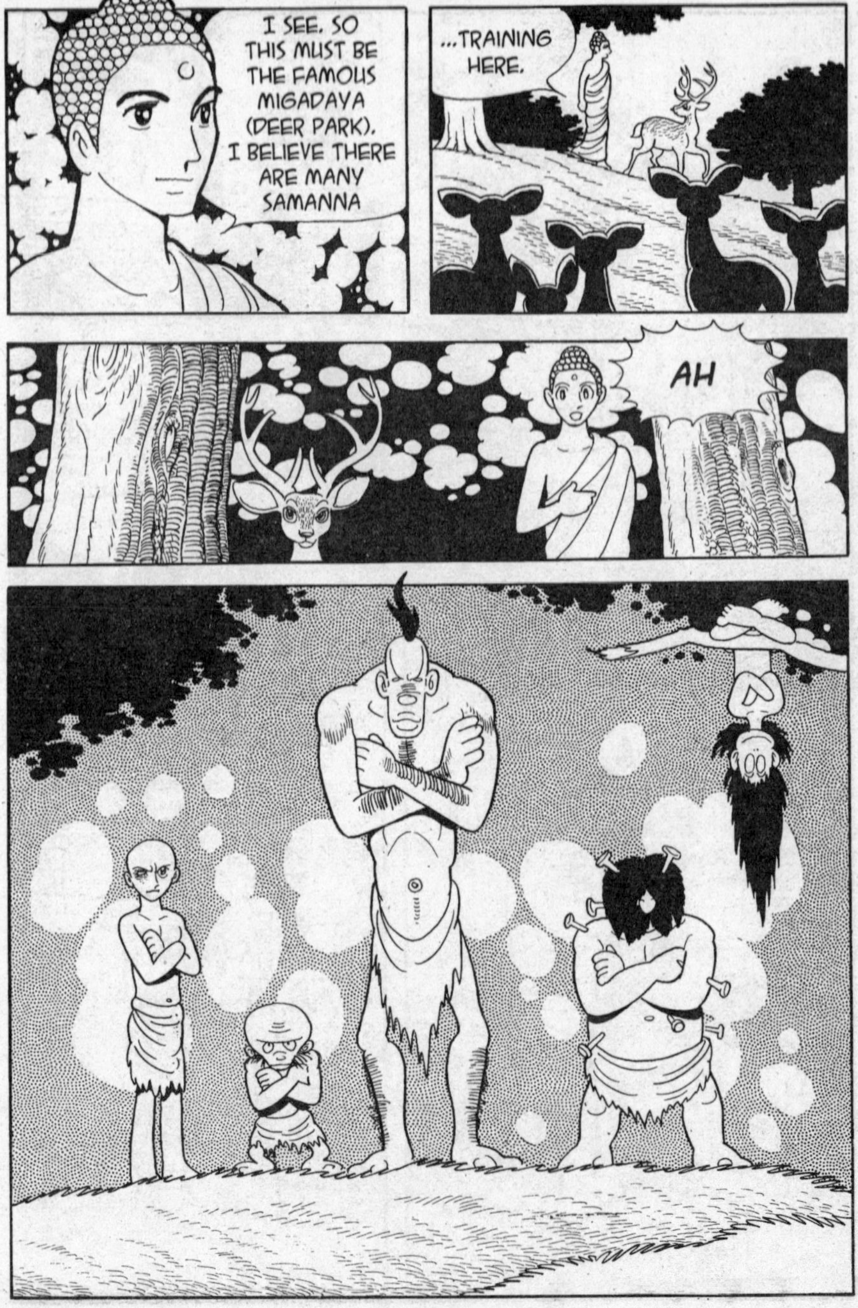
I SEE. SO THIS MUST BE THE FAMOUS MIGADAYA (DEER PARK). I BELIEVE THERE ARE MANY SAMANNA
...TRAINING HERE.
AH

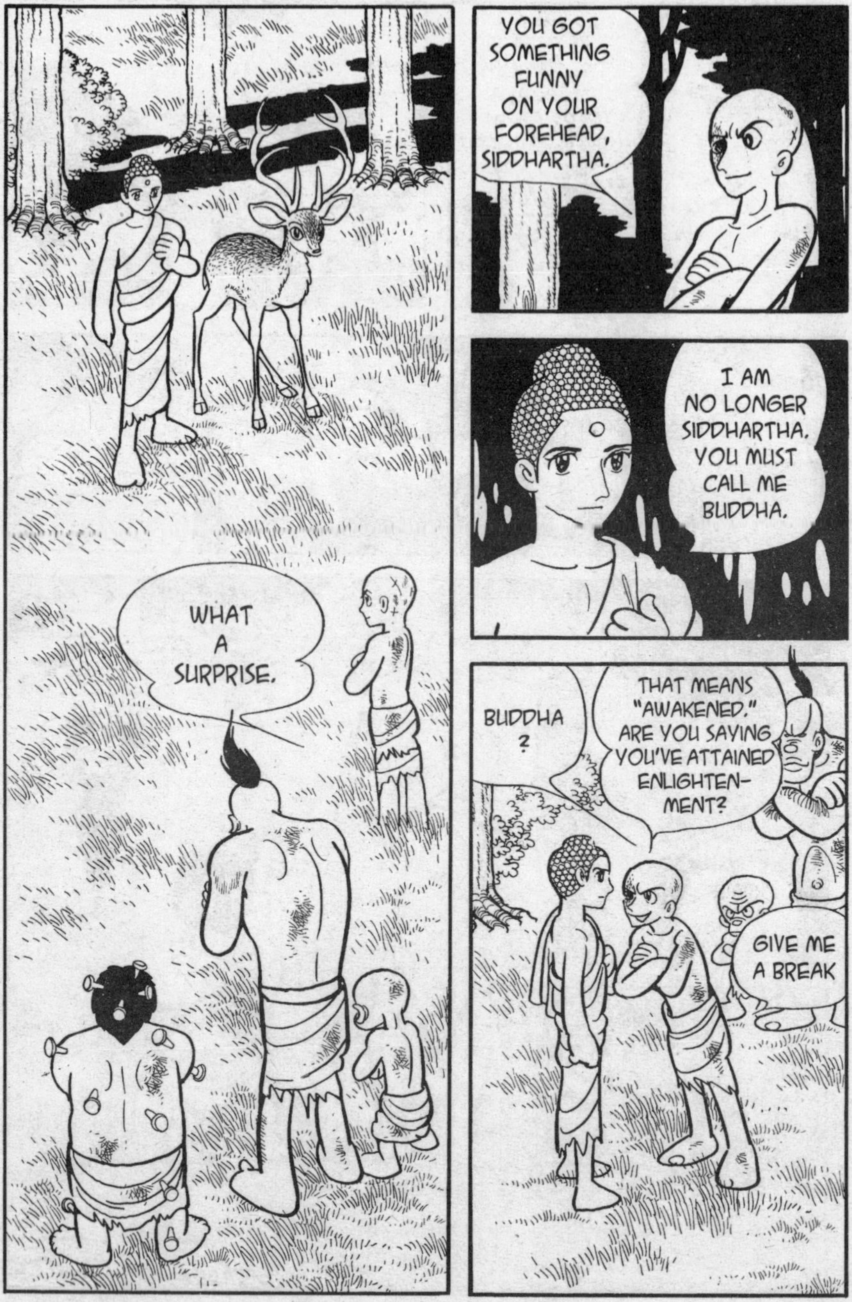
YOU GOT SOMETHING FUNNY ON YOUR FOREHEAD, SIDDHARTHA.
I AM NO LONGER SIDDHARTHA. YOU MUST CALL ME BUDDHA.
WHAT A SURPRISE.
BUDDHA ?
THAT MEANS "AWAKENED." ARE YOU SAYING YOU'VE ATTAINED ENLIGHTEN-MENT?
GIVE ME A BREAK

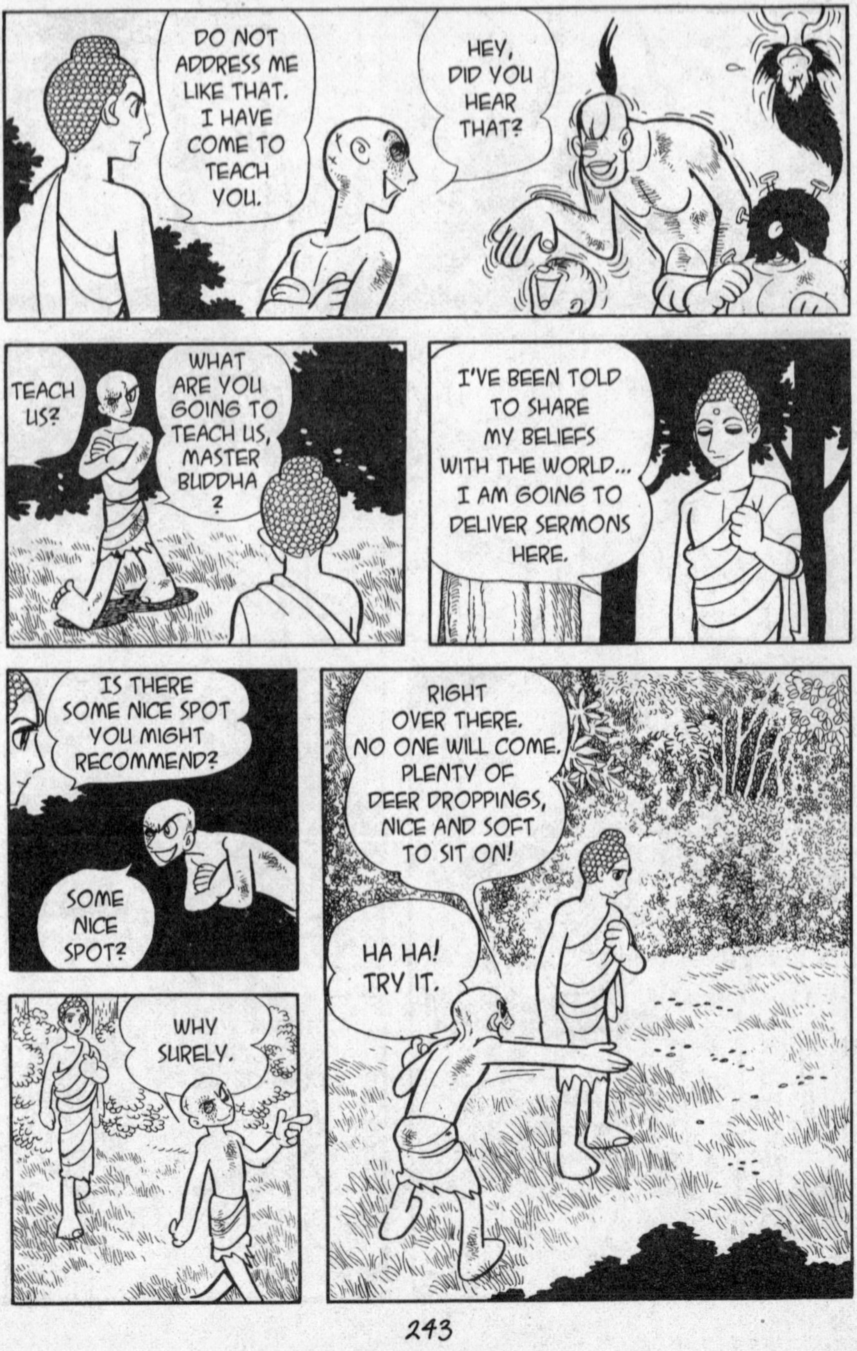
DO NOT ADDRESS ME LIKE THAT. I HAVE COME TO TEACH YOU.
HEY, DID YOU HEAR THAT?
TEACH US?
WHAT ARE YOU GOING TO TEACH US, MASTER BUDDHA?
I'VE BEEN TOLD TO SHARE MY BELIEFS WITH THE WORLD... I AM GOING TO DELIVER SERMONS HERE.
IS THERE SOME NICE SPOT YOU MIGHT RECOMMEND?
SOME NICE SPOT?
WHY SURELY.
RIGHT OVER THERE. NO ONE WILL COME. PLENTY OF DEER DROPPINGS, NICE AND SOFT TO SIT ON!
HA HA! TRY IT.

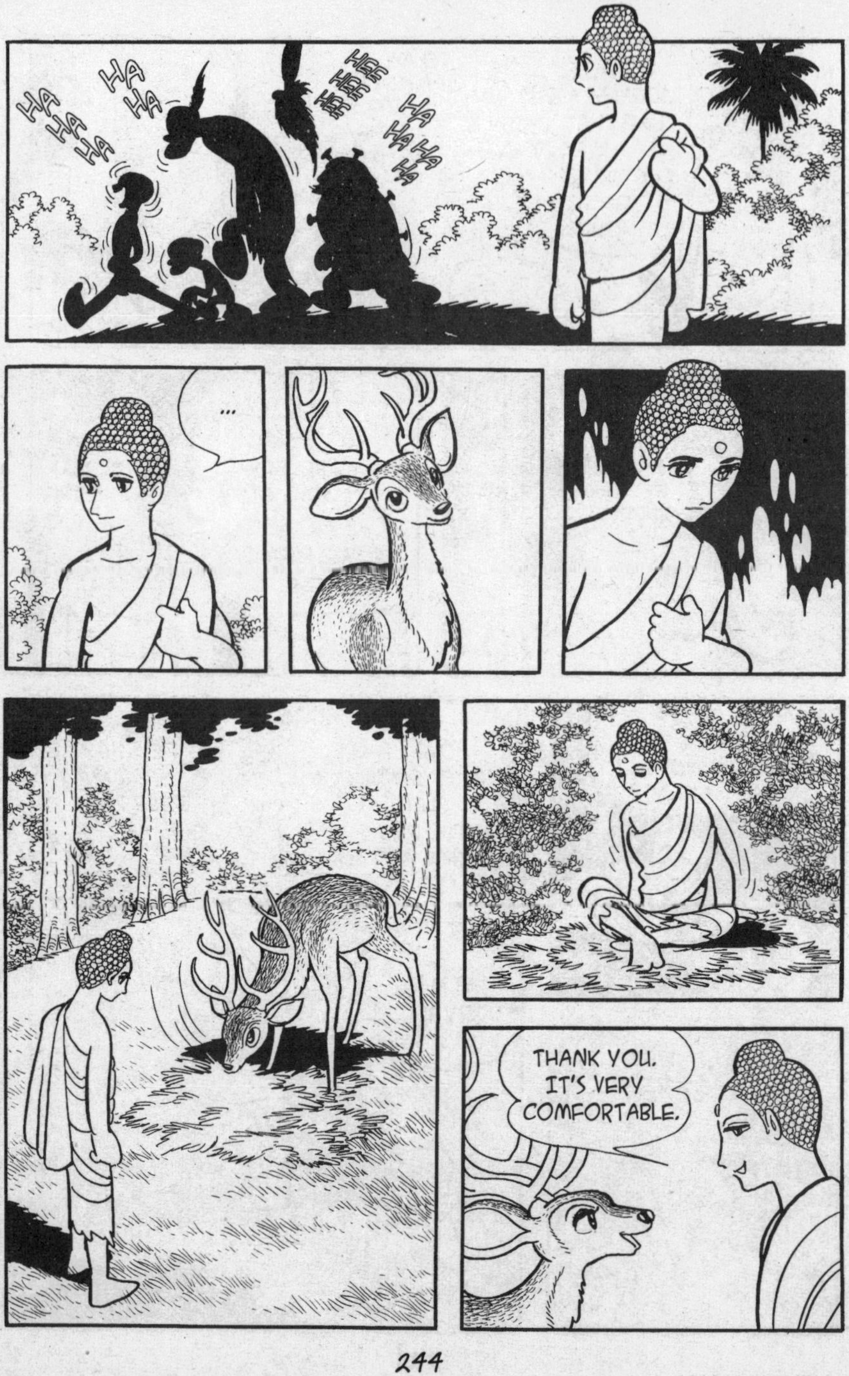
HA HA HA HA
HA HA
HEE HEE HEE
HA HA HA HA
...
THANK YOU. IT'S VERY COMFORTABLE.

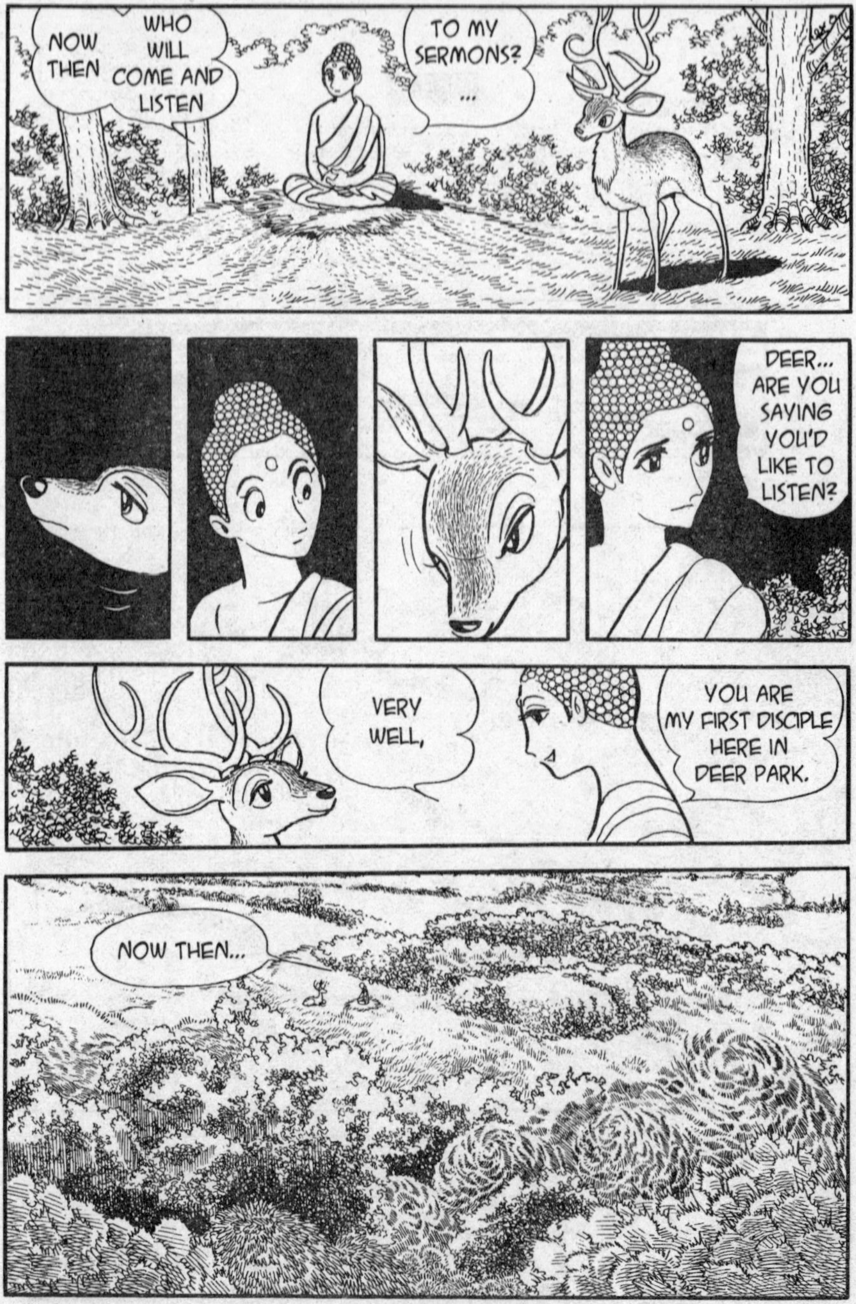
NOW THEN
WHO WILL COME AND LISTEN
TO MY SERMONS?
...
DEER... ARE YOU SAYING YOU'D LIKE TO LISTEN?
VERY WELL,
YOU ARE MY FIRST DISCIPLE HERE IN DEER PARK.
NOW THEN...

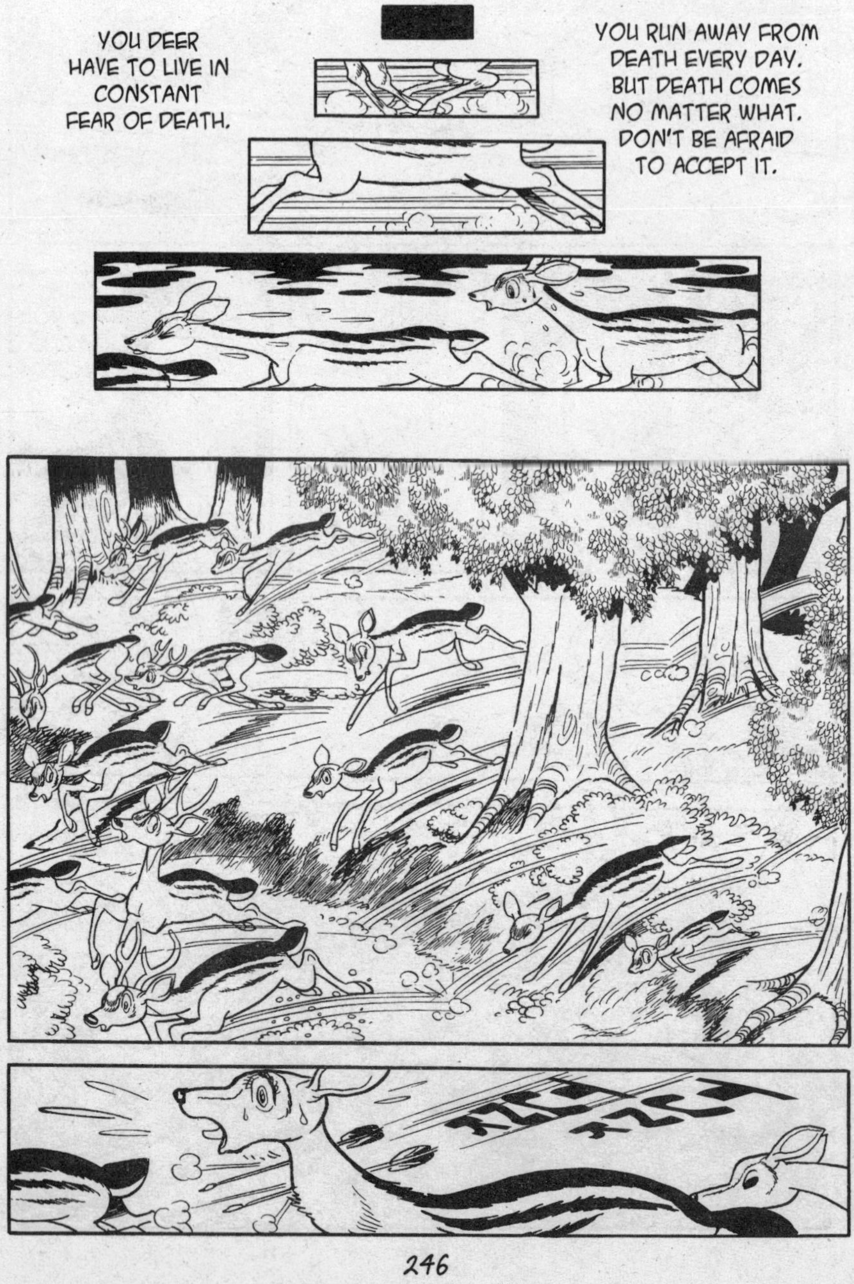
YOU DEER HAVE TO LIVE IN CONSTANT FEAR OF DEATH.
YOU RUN AWAY FROM DEATH EVERY DAY. BUT DEATH COMES NO MATTER WHAT. DON'T BE AFRAID TO ACCEPT IT.

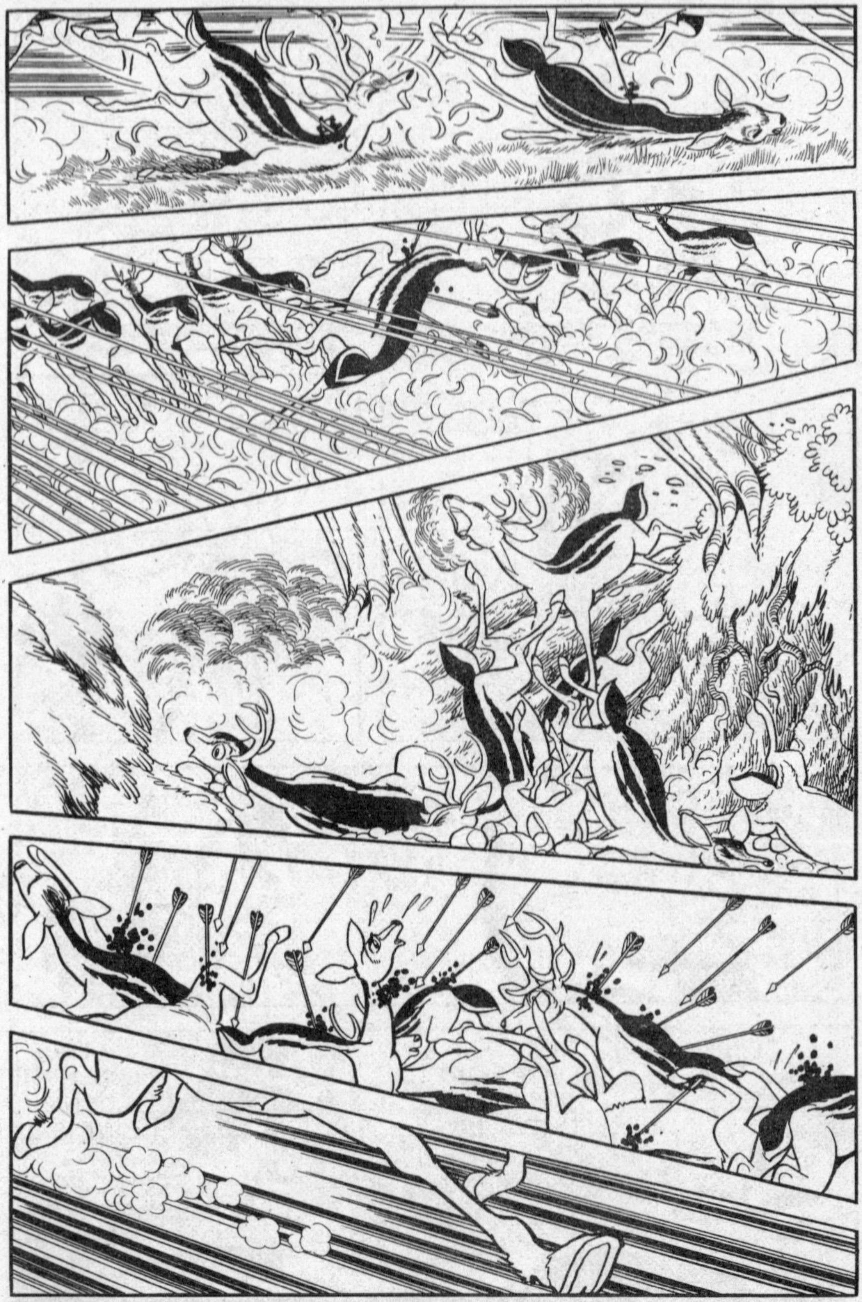

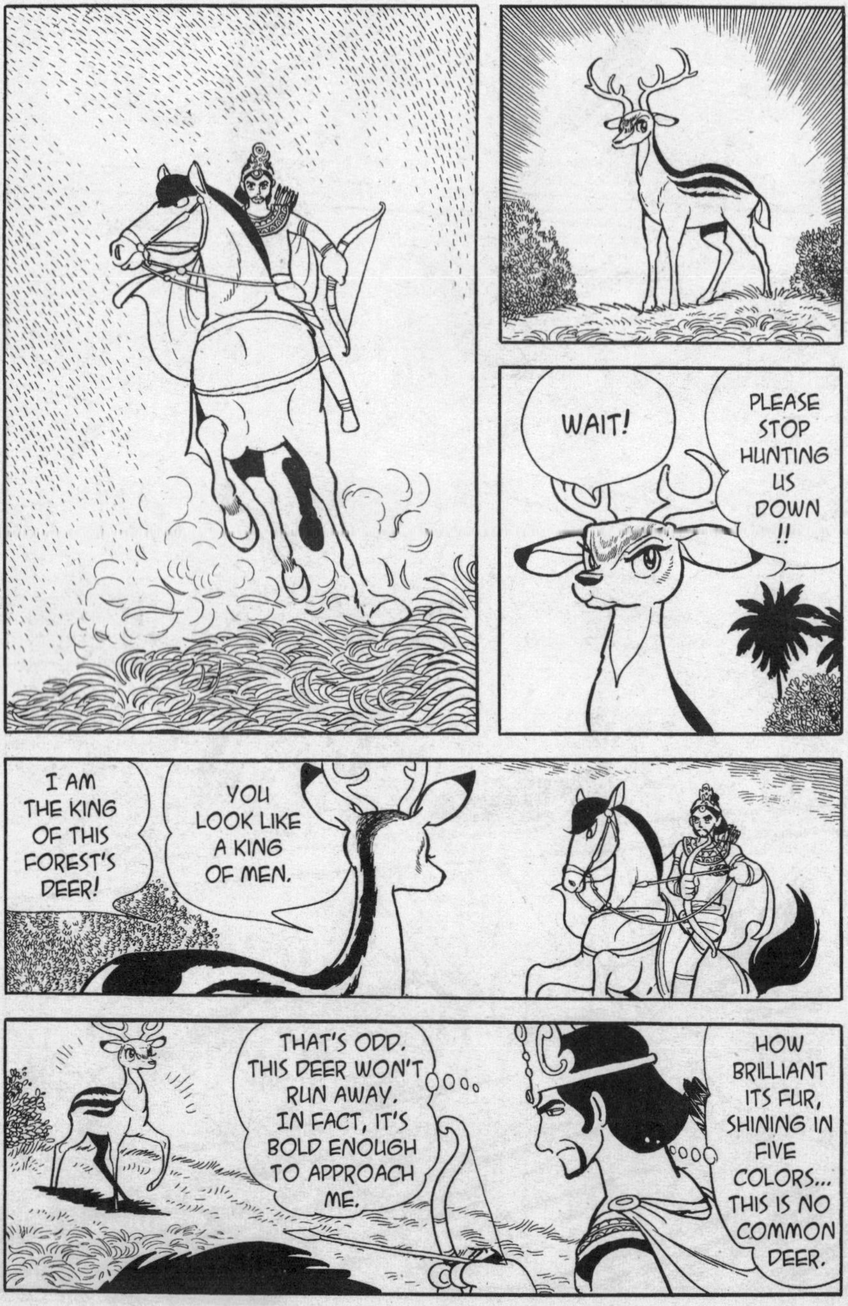

WAIT!
PLEASE STOP HUNTING US DOWN !!
I AM THE KING OF THIS FOREST'S DEER!
YOU LOOK LIKE A KING OF MEN.
THAT'S ODD. THIS DEER WON'T RUN AWAY. IN FACT, IT'S BOLD ENOUGH TO APPROACH ME.
HOW BRILLIANT ITS FUR, SHINING IN FIVE COLORS... THIS IS NO COMMON DEER.

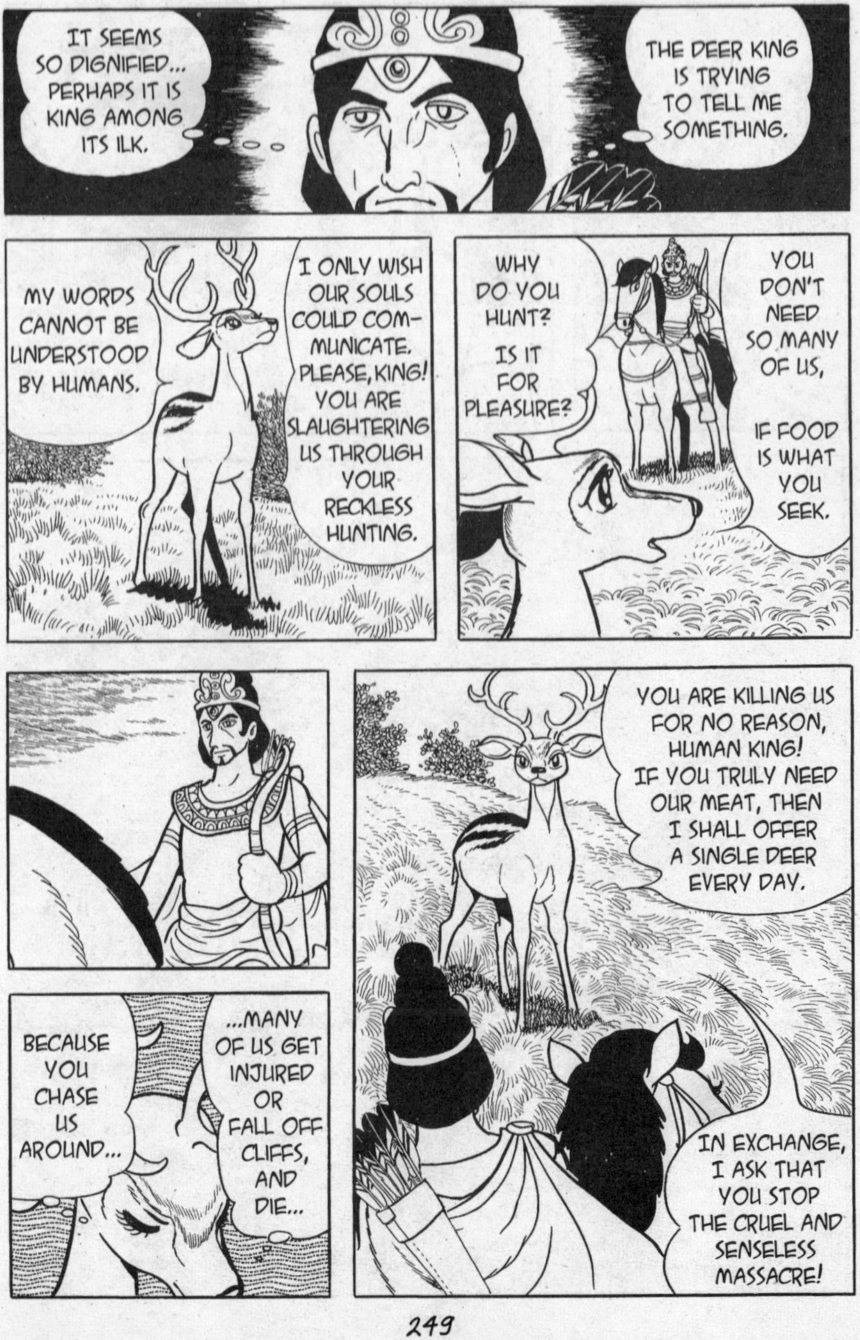
IT SEEMS SO DIGNIFIED... PERHAPS IT IS KING AMONG ITS ILK.
THE DEER KING IS TRYING TO TELL ME SOMETHING.
MY WORDS CANNOT BE UNDERSTOOD BY HUMANS.
I ONLY WISH OUR SOULS COULD COM-MUNICATE. PLEASE, KING! YOU ARE SLAUGHTERING US THROUGH YOUR RECKLESS HUNTING.
WHY DO YOU HUNT? IS IT FOR PLEASURE?
YOU DON'T NEED SO MANY OF US, IF FOOD IS WHAT YOU SEEK.
YOU ARE KILLING US FOR NO REASON, HUMAN KING! IF YOU TRULY NEED OUR MEAT, THEN I SHALL OFFER A SINGLE DEER EVERY DAY.
BECAUSE YOU CHASE US AROUND...
...MANY OF US GET INJURED OR FALL OFF CLIFFS, AND DIE...
IN EXCHANGE, I ASK THAT YOU STOP THE CRUEL AND SENSELESS MASSACRE!

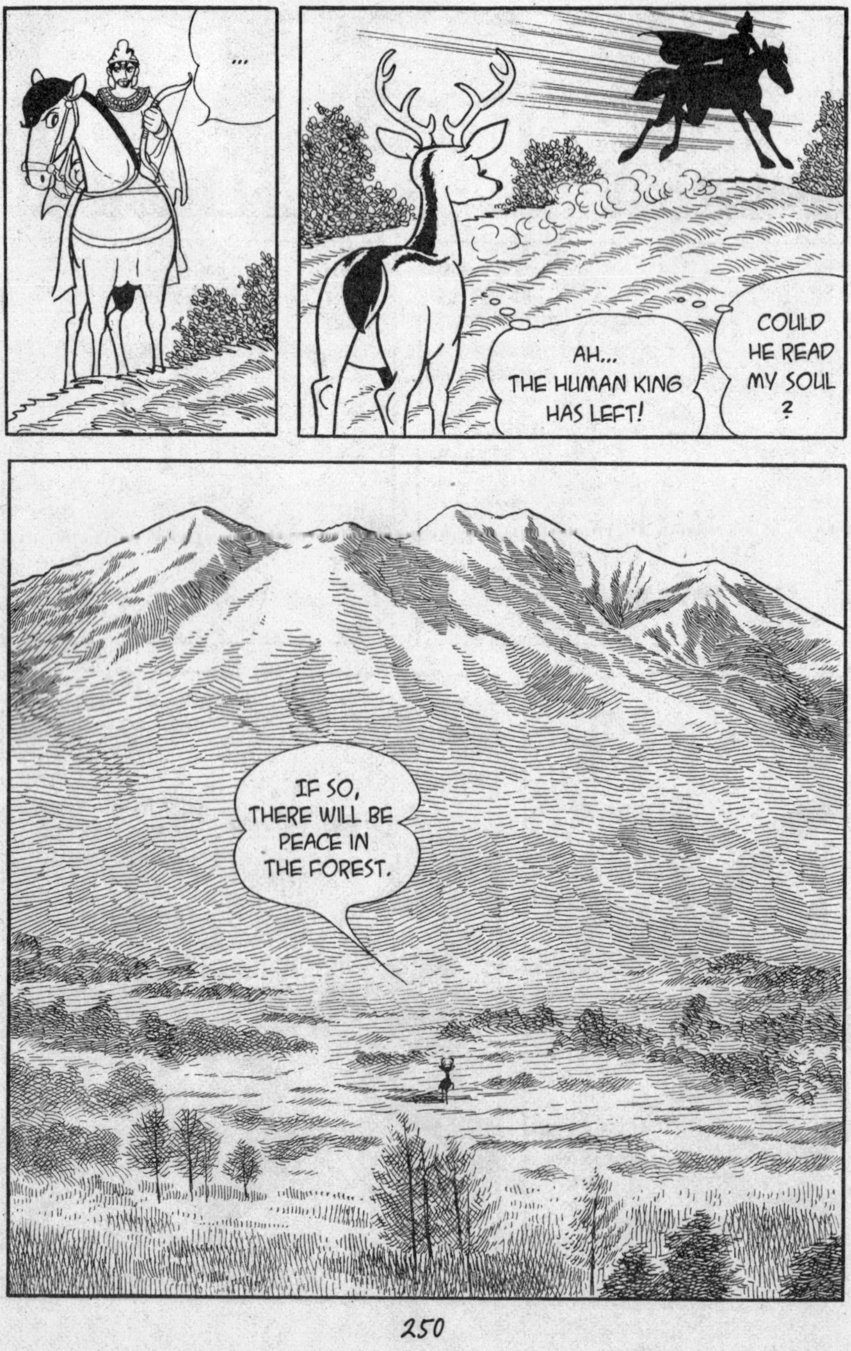
...
AH... THE HUMAN KING HAS LEFT!
COULD HE READ MY SOUL ?
IF SO, THERE WILL BE PEACE IN THE FOREST.

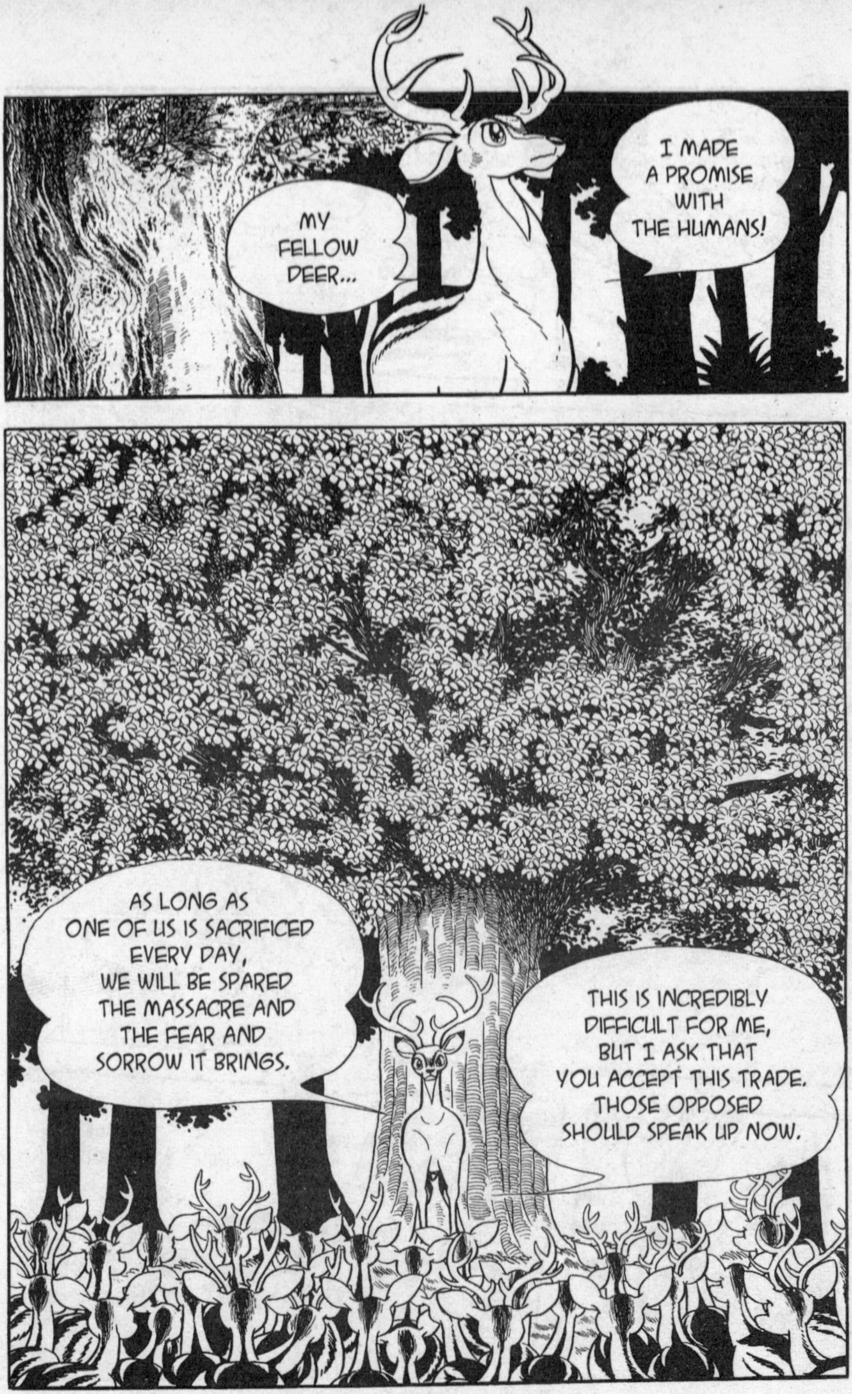
MY FELLOW DEER...
I MADE A PROMISE WITH THE HUMANS!
AS LONG AS ONE OF US IS SACRIFICED EVERY DAY, WE WILL BE SPARED THE MASSACRE AND THE FEAR AND SORROW IT BRINGS.
THIS IS INCREDIBLY DIFFICULT FOR ME, BUT I ASK THAT YOU ACCEPT THIS TRADE. THOSE OPPOSED SHOULD SPEAK UP NOW.

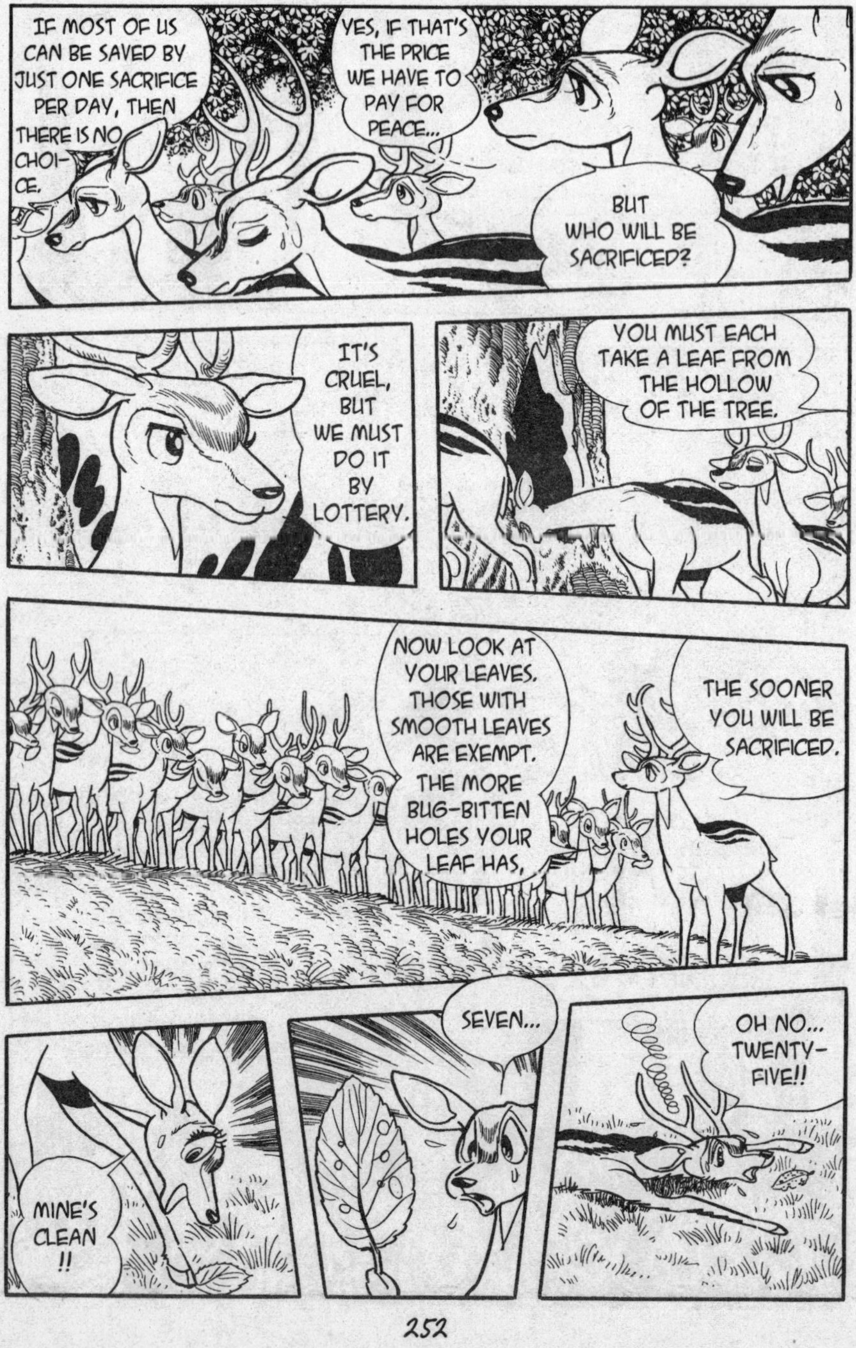
IF MOST OF US CAN BE SAVED BY JUST ONE SACRIFICE PER DAY, THEN THERE IS NO CHOI- CE.
YES, IF THAT'S THE PRICE WE HAVE TO PAY FOR PEACE...
BUT WHO WILL BE SACRIFICED?
IT'S CRUEL, BUT WE MUST DO IT BY LOTTERY.
YOU MUST EACH TAKE A LEAF FROM THE HOLLOW OF THE TREE.
NOW LOOK AT YOUR LEAVES. THOSE WITH SMOOTH LEAVES ARE EXEMPT. THE MORE BUG-BITTEN HOLES YOUR LEAF HAS,
THE SOONER YOU WILL BE SACRIFICED.
MINE'S CLEAN !!
SEVEN...
OH NO... TWENTY-FIVE!!

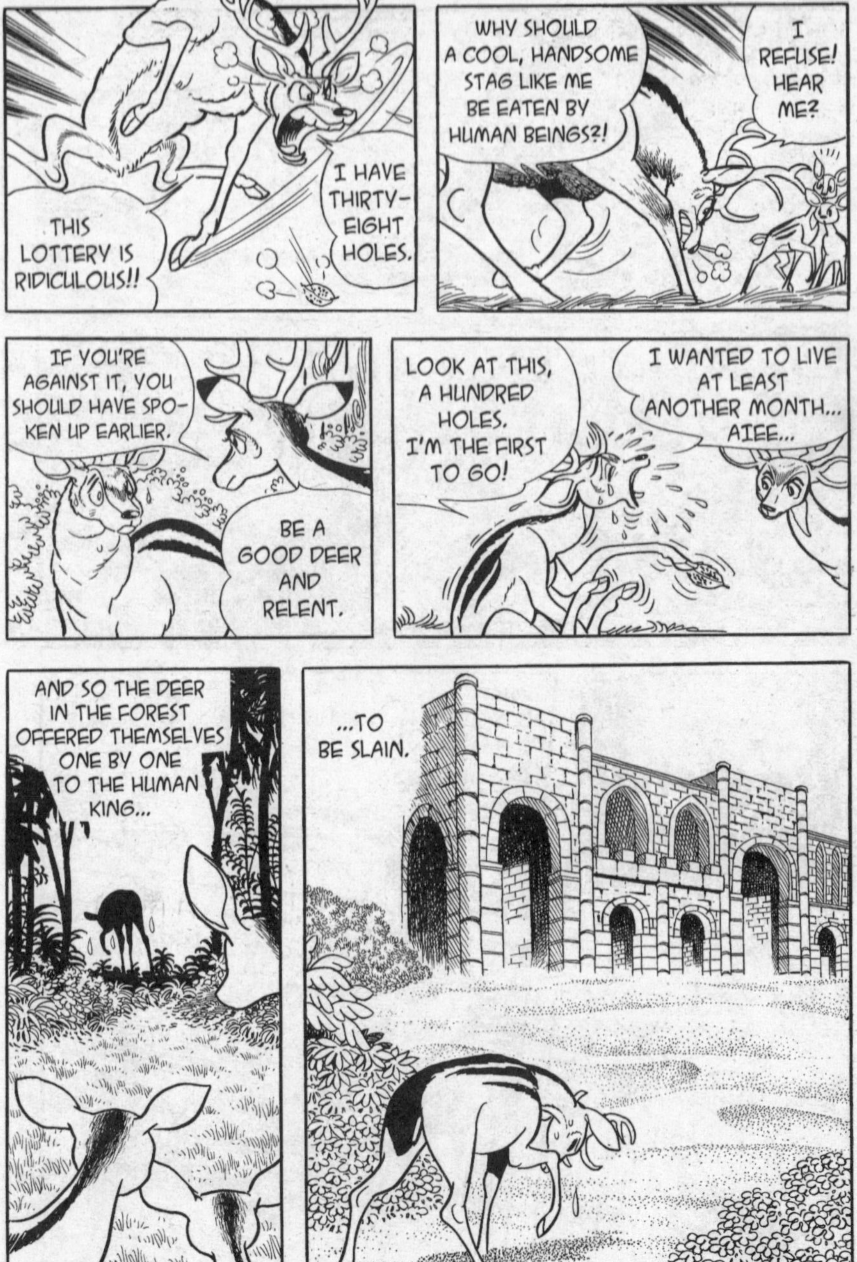
THIS LOTTERY IS RIDICULOUS!!
I HAVE THIRTY-EIGHT HOLES.
WHY SHOULD A COOL, HANDSOME STAG LIKE ME BE EATEN BY HUMAN BEINGS?!
I REFUSE! HEAR ME?
IF YOU'RE AGAINST IT, YOU SHOULD HAVE SPO-KEN UP EARLIER.
BE A GOOD DEER AND RELENT.
LOOK AT THIS, A HUNDRED HOLES. I'M THE FIRST TO GO!
I WANTED TO LIVE AT LEAST ANOTHER MONTH... AIEE...
AND SO THE DEER IN THE FOREST OFFERED THEMSELVES ONE BY ONE TO THE HUMAN KING...
...TO BE SLAIN.

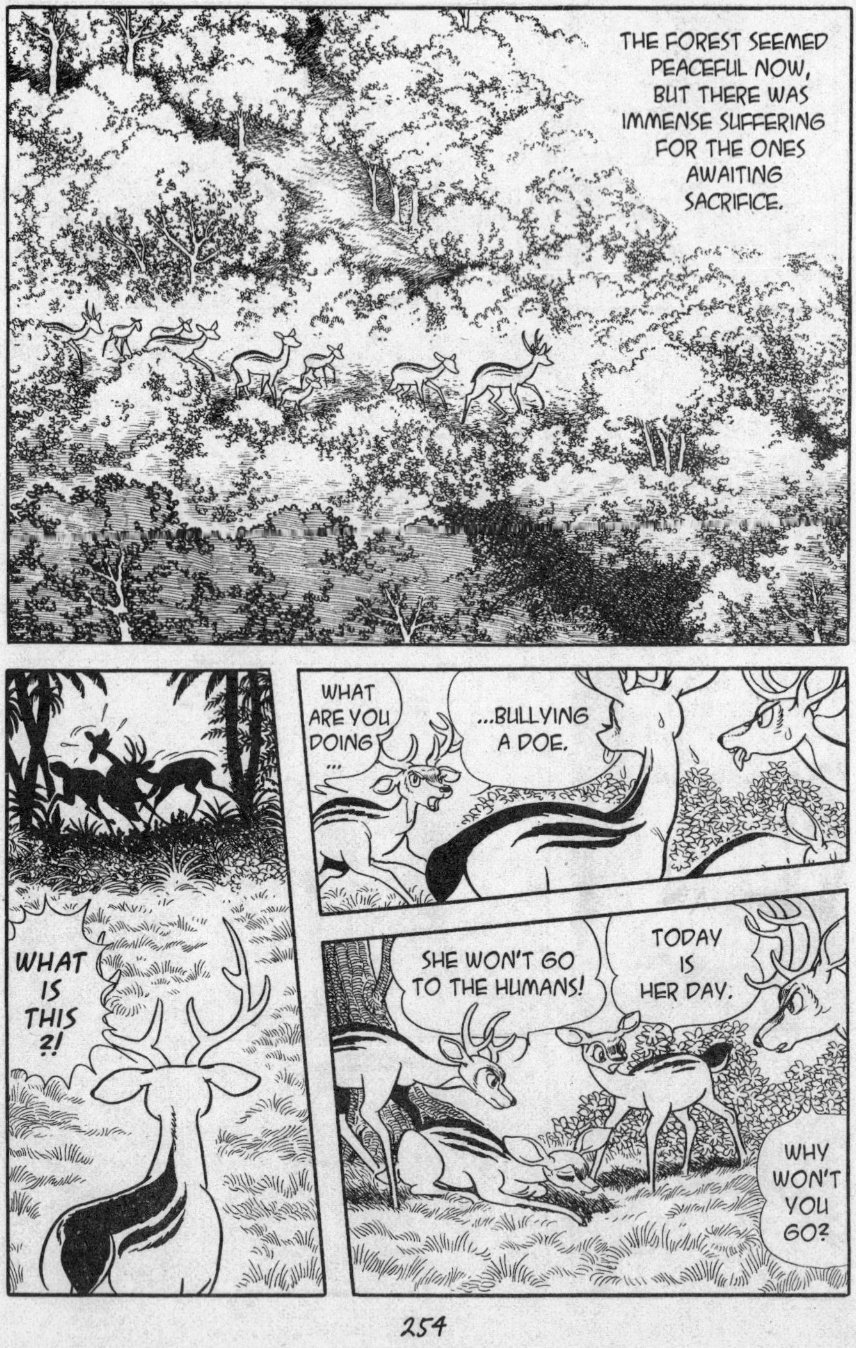
THE FOREST SEEMED PEACEFUL NOW, BUT THERE WAS IMMENSE SUFFERING FOR THE ONES AWAITING SACRIFICE.
WHAT IS THIS ?!
WHAT ARE YOU DOING ...
...BULLYING A DOE.
SHE WON'T GO TO THE HUMANS!
TODAY IS HER DAY.
WHY WON'T YOU GO?

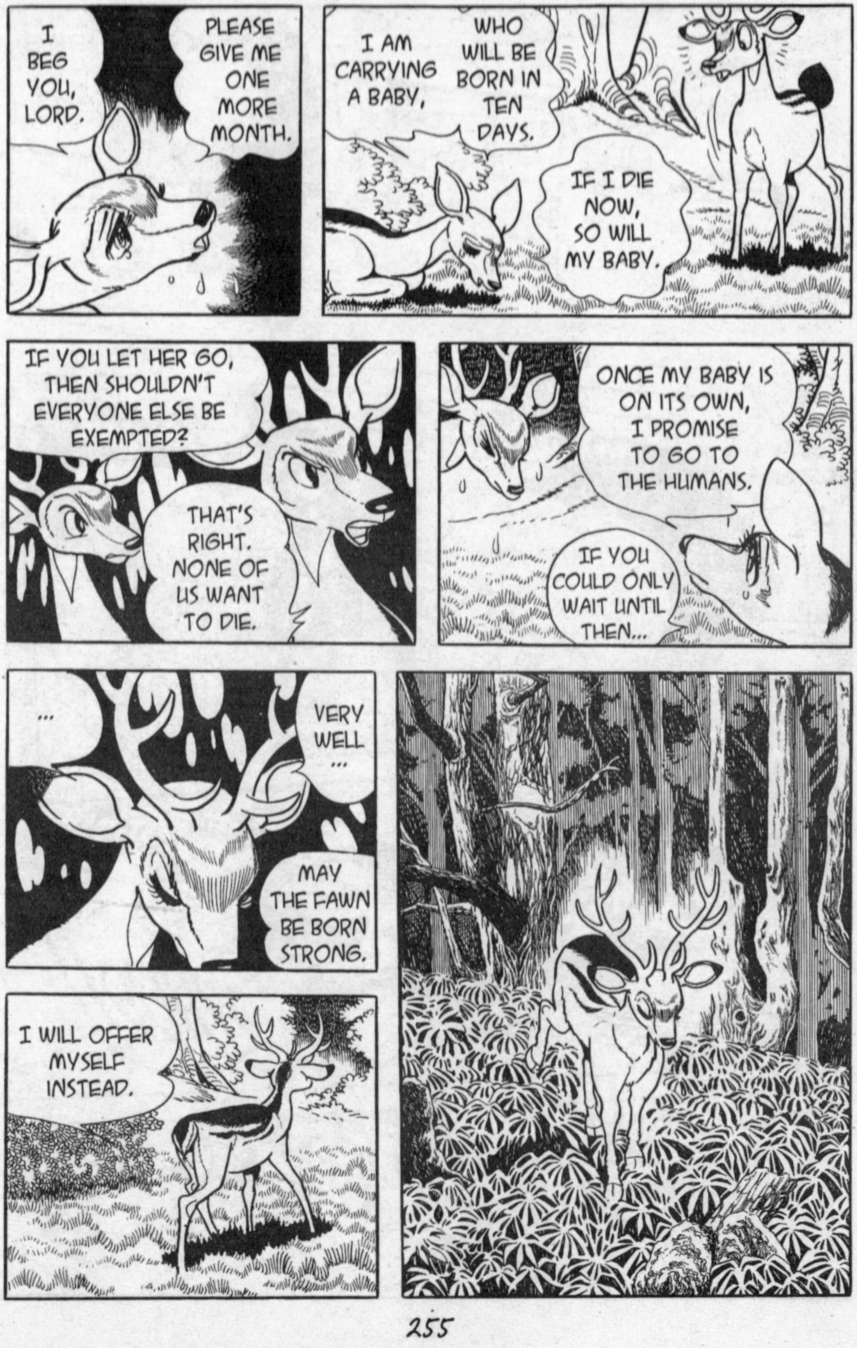
I BEG YOU, LORD.
PLEASE GIVE ME ONE MORE MONTH.
I AM CARRYING A BABY,
WHO WILL BE BORN IN TEN DAYS.
IF I DIE NOW, SO WILL MY BABY.
IF YOU LET HER GO, THEN SHOULDN'T EVERYONE ELSE BE EXEMPTED?
THAT'S RIGHT. NONE OF US WANT TO DIE.
ONCE MY BABY IS ON ITS OWN, I PROMISE TO GO TO THE HUMANS.
IF YOU COULD ONLY WAIT UNTIL THEN...
...
VERY WELL ...
MAY THE FAWN BE BORN STRONG.
I WILL OFFER MYSELF INSTEAD.

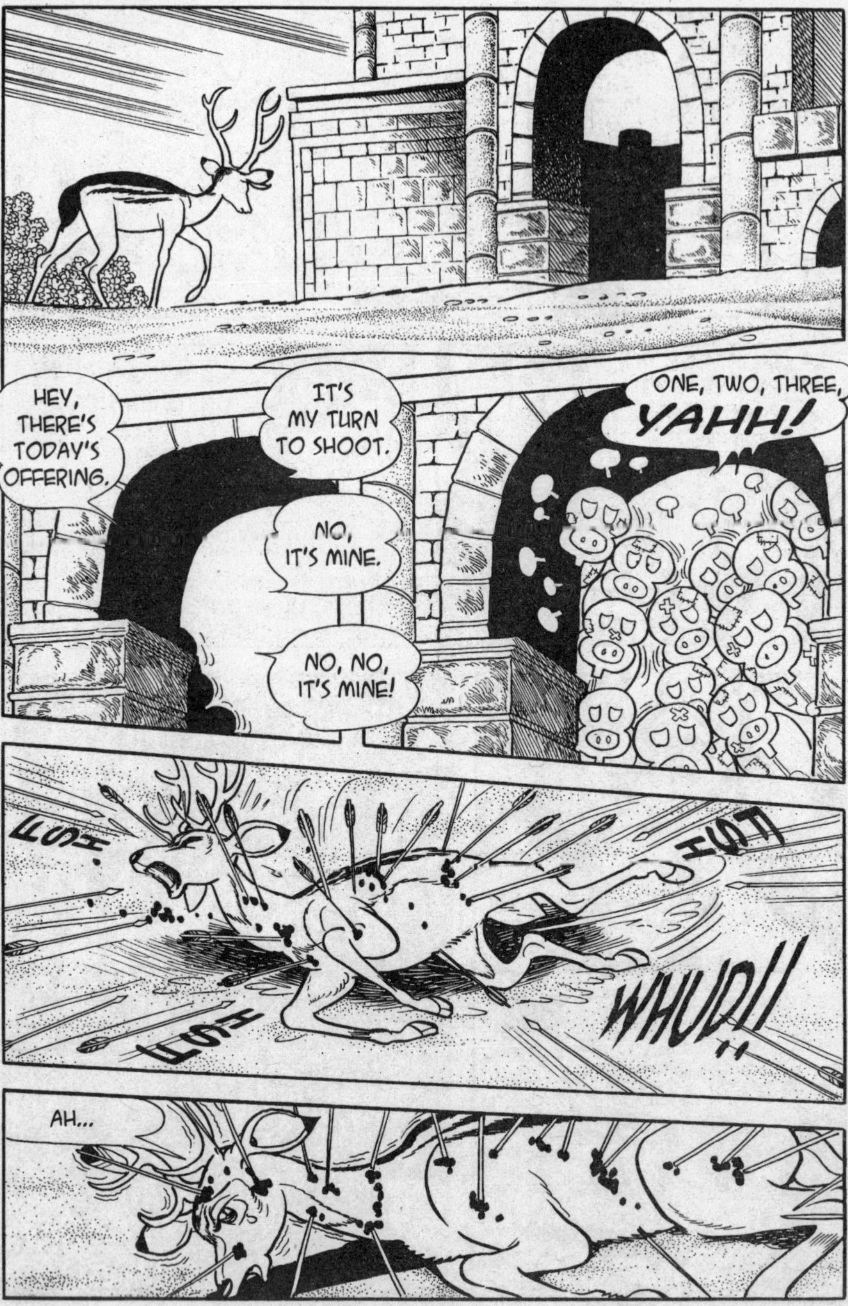
HEY, THERE'S TODAY'S OFFERING.
IT'S MY TURN TO SHOOT.
NO, IT'S MINE.
NO, NO, IT'S MINE!
ONE, TWO, THREE, YAHH!
WHUD!!
AH...

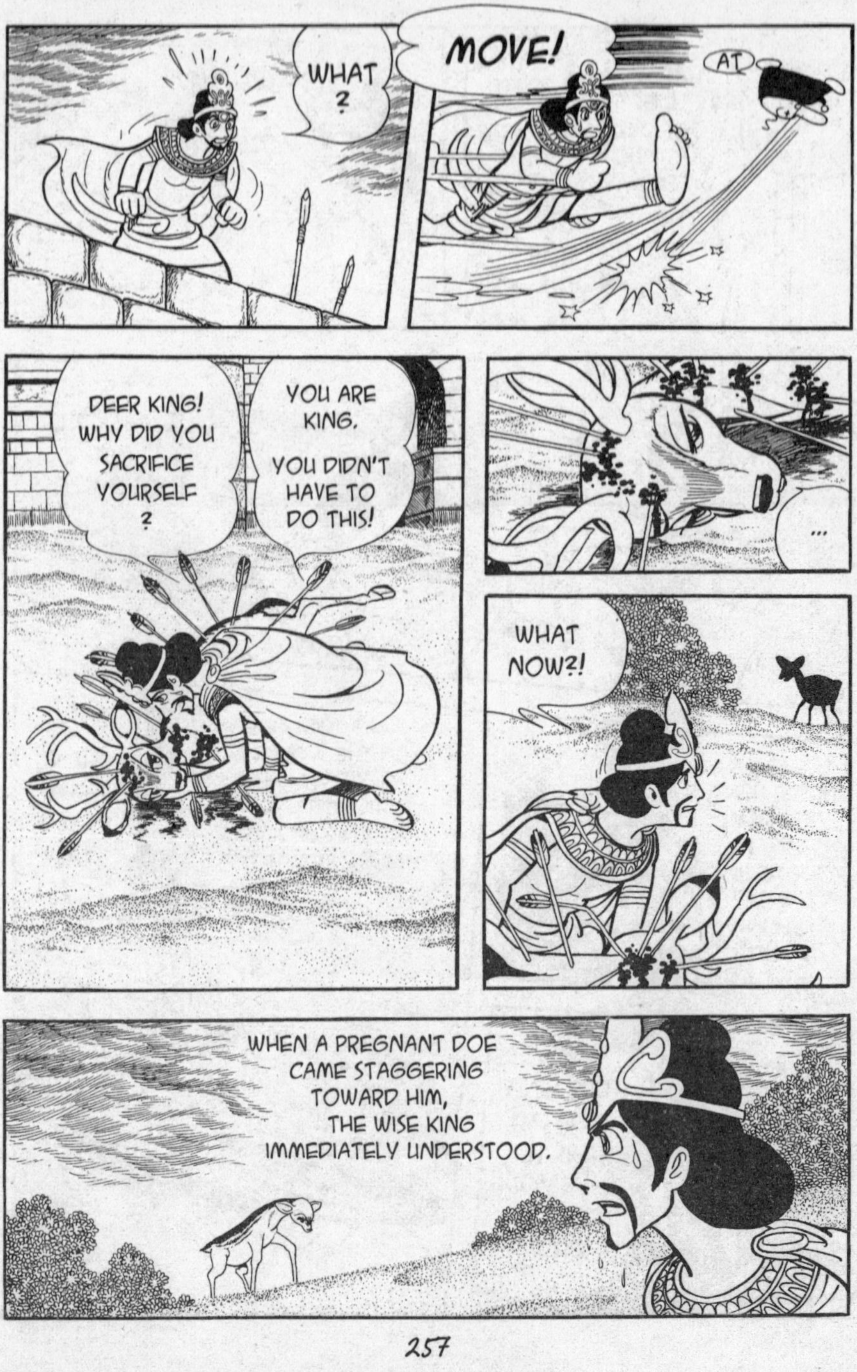
WHAT ?
MOVE!
AT
DEER KING! WHY DID YOU SACRIFICE YOURSELF ?
YOU ARE KING. YOU DIDN'T HAVE TO DO THIS!
...
WHAT NOW?!
WHEN A PREGNANT DOE CAME STAGGERING TOWARD HIM, THE WISE KING IMMEDIATELY UNDERSTOOD.

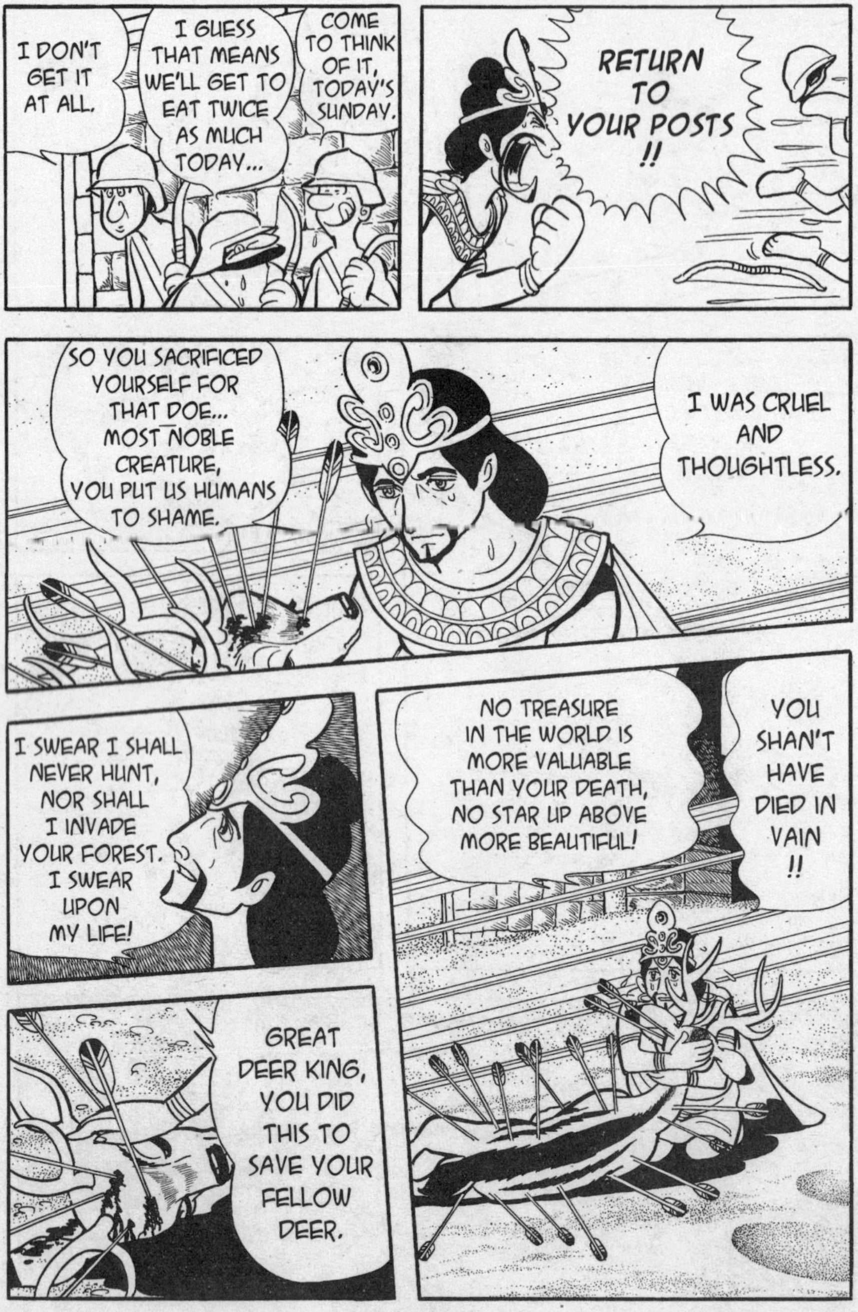
I DON'T GET IT AT ALL.
I GUESS THAT MEANS WE'LL GET TO EAT TWICE AS MUCH TODAY...
COME TO THINK OF IT, TODAY'S SUNDAY.
RETURN TO YOUR POSTS !!
SO YOU SACRIFICED YOURSELF FOR THAT DOE... MOST NOBLE CREATURE, YOU PUT US HUMANS TO SHAME.
I WAS CRUEL AND THOUGHTLESS.
I SWEAR I SHALL NEVER HUNT, NOR SHALL I INVADE YOUR FOREST. I SWEAR UPON MY LIFE!
GREAT DEER KING, YOU DID THIS TO SAVE YOUR FELLOW DEER.
NO TREASURE IN THE WORLD IS MORE VALUABLE THAN YOUR DEATH, NO STAR UP ABOVE MORE BEAUTIFUL!
YOU SHAN'T HAVE DIED IN VAIN !!

CHAPTER SIX

THE LEGEND OF SEBU THE OX

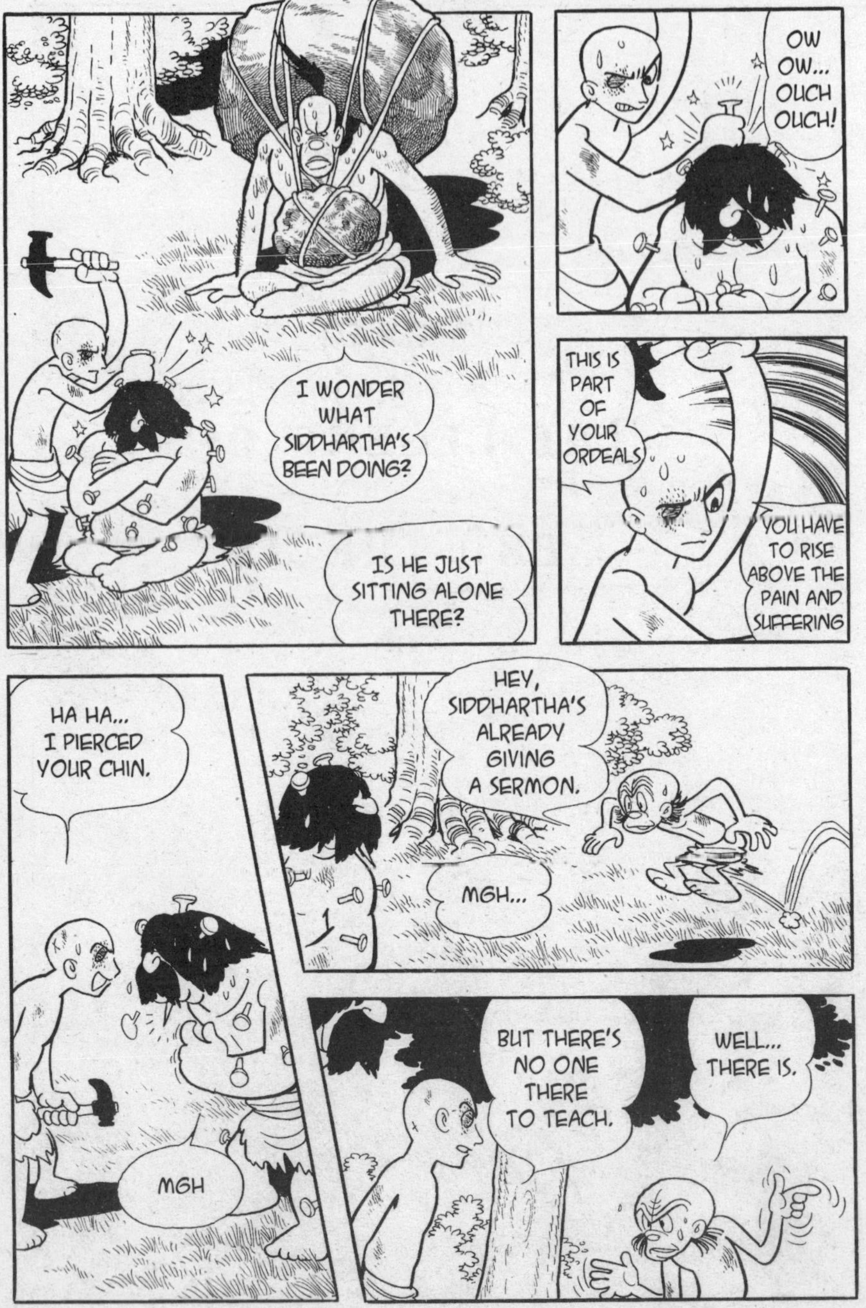
I WONDER WHAT SIDDHARTHA'S BEEN DOING?
IS HE JUST SITTING ALONE THERE?
OW OW... OUCH OUCH!
THIS IS PART OF YOUR ORDEALS.
YOU HAVE TO RISE ABOVE THE PAIN AND SUFFERING
HA HA... I PIERCED YOUR CHIN.
MGH
HEY, SIDDHARTHA'S ALREADY GIVING A SERMON.
MGH...
BUT THERE'S NO ONE THERE TO TEACH.
WELL... THERE IS.

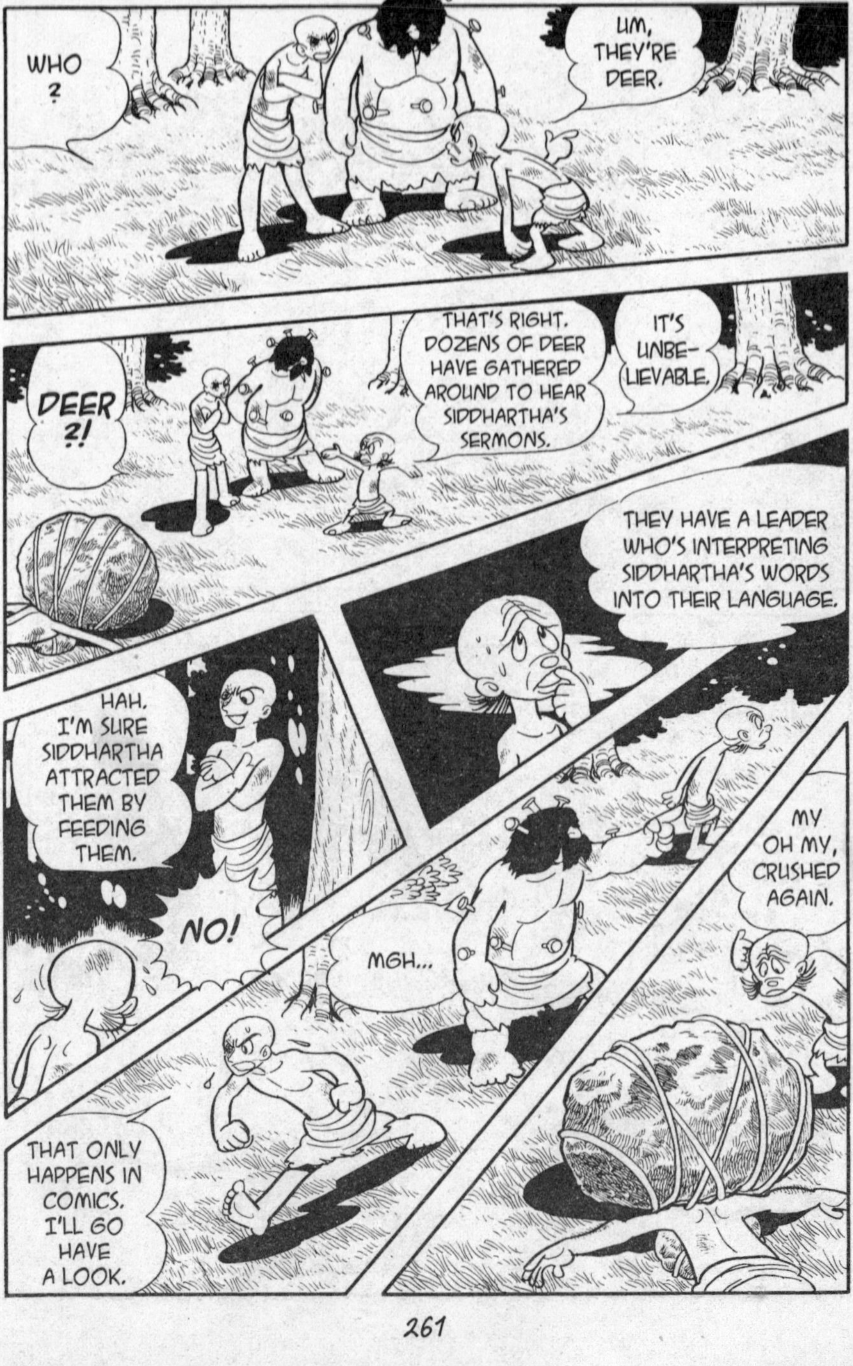
WHO ?
UM, THEY'RE DEER.
DEER ?!
THAT'S RIGHT. DOZENS OF DEER HAVE GATHERED AROUND TO HEAR SIDDHARTHA'S SERMONS.
IT'S UNBE-LIEVABLE.
THEY HAVE A LEADER WHO'S INTERPRETING SIDDHARTHA'S WORDS INTO THEIR LANGUAGE.
HAH, I'M SURE SIDDHARTHA ATTRACTED THEM BY FEEDING THEM.
NO!
MGH...
MY OH MY, CRUSHED AGAIN.
THAT ONLY HAPPENS IN COMICS. I'LL GO HAVE A LOOK.

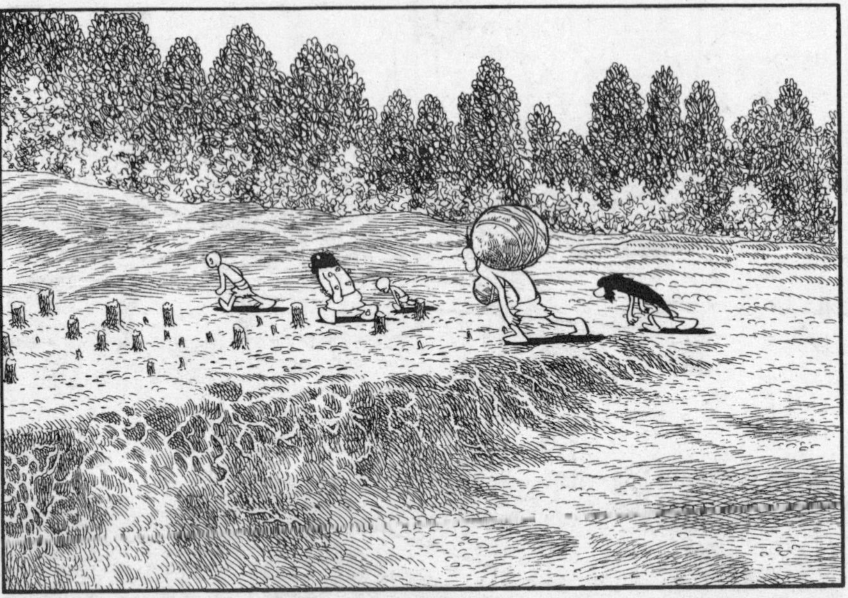

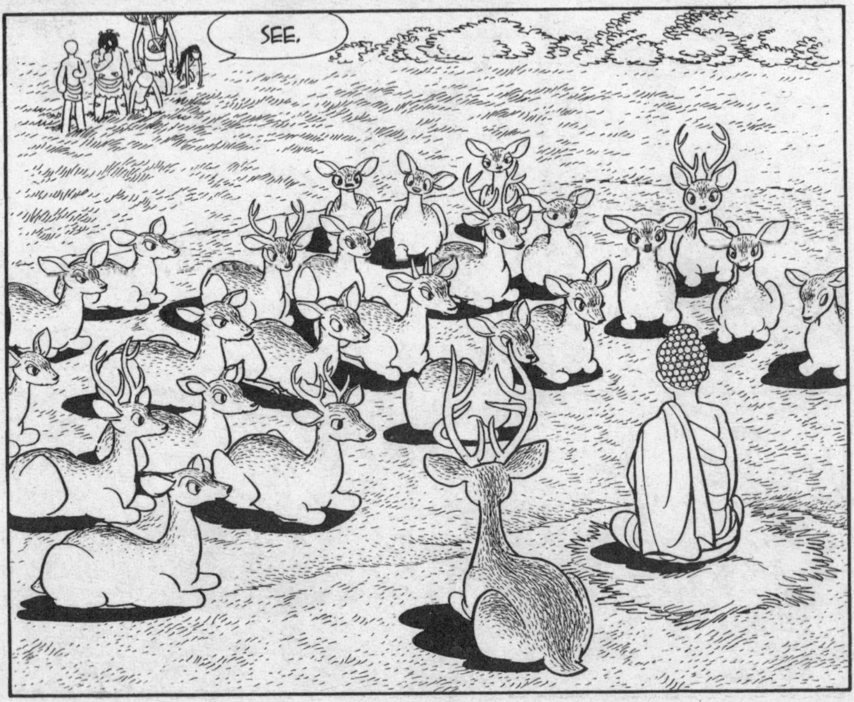
SEE.

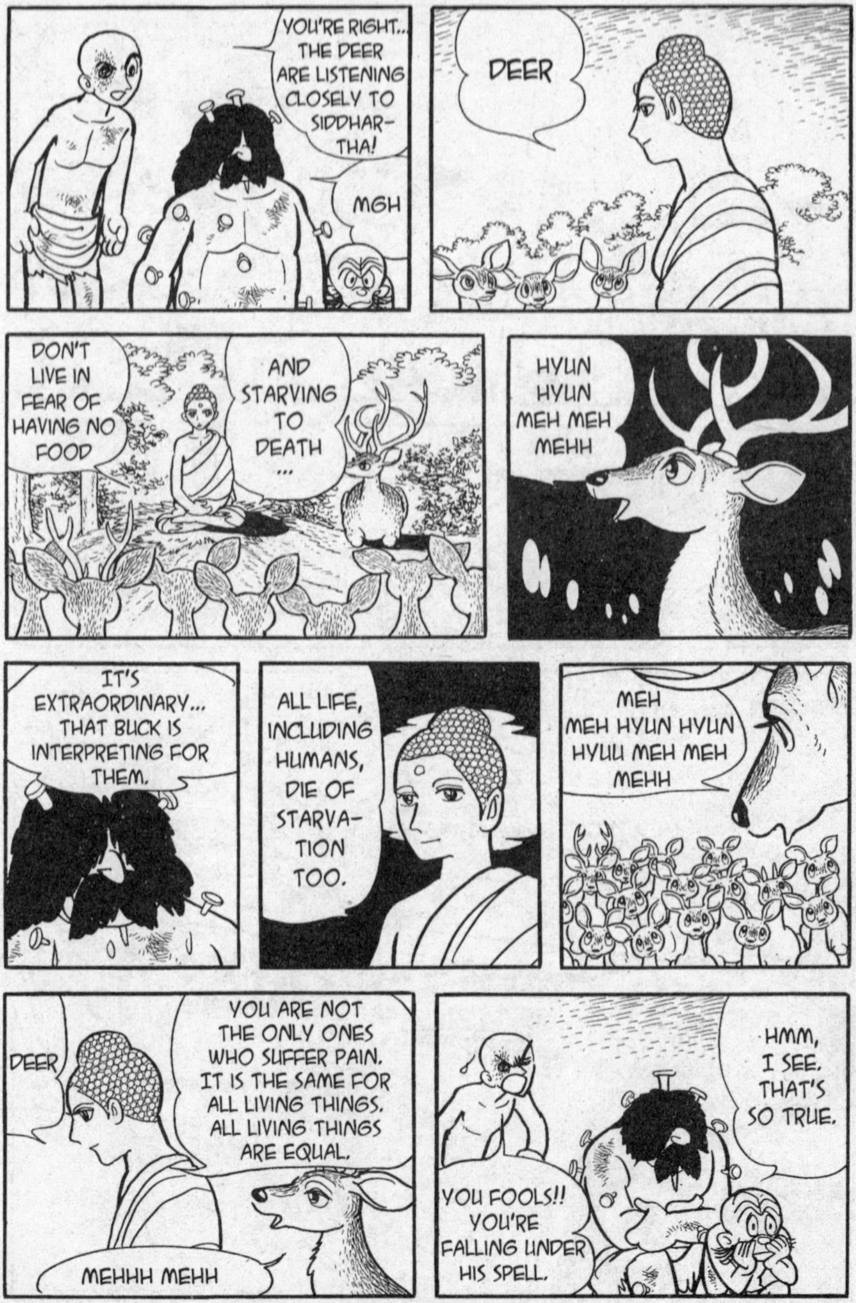
YOU'RE RIGHT... THE DEER ARE LISTENING CLOSELY TO SIDDHARTHA!
MGH
DEER
DON'T LIVE IN FEAR OF HAVING NO FOOD
AND STARVING TO DEATH ...
HYUN HYUN MEH MEH MEHH
IT'S EXTRAORDINARY... THAT BUCK IS INTERPRETING FOR THEM.
ALL LIFE, INCLUDING HUMANS, DIE OF STARVATION TOO.
MEH MEH HYUN HYUN HYUU MEH MEH MEHH
DEER
YOU ARE NOT THE ONLY ONES WHO SUFFER PAIN. IT IS THE SAME FOR ALL LIVING THINGS. ALL LIVING THINGS ARE EQUAL.
MEHHH MEHH
HMM, I SEE. THAT'S SO TRUE.
YOU FOOLS!! YOU'RE FALLING UNDER HIS SPELL.

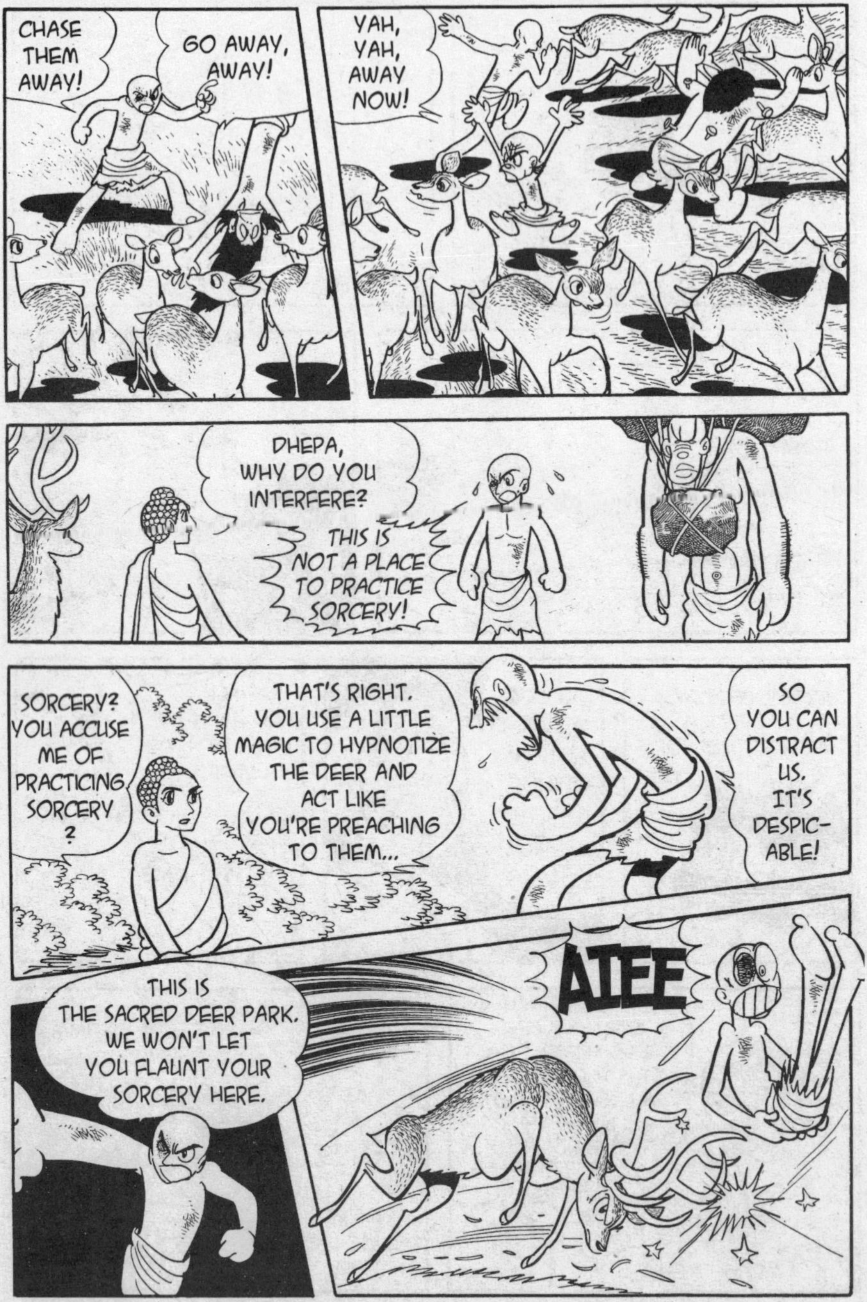
CHASE THEM AWAY!
GO AWAY, AWAY!
YAH, YAH, AWAY NOW!
DHEPA, WHY DO YOU INTERFERE?
THIS IS NOT A PLACE TO PRACTICE SORCERY!
SORCERY? YOU ACCUSE ME OF PRACTICING SORCERY?
THAT'S RIGHT. YOU USE A LITTLE MAGIC TO HYPNOTIZE THE DEER AND ACT LIKE YOU'RE PREACHING TO THEM...
SO YOU CAN DISTRACT US. IT'S DESPIC-ABLE!
THIS IS THE SACRED DEER PARK. WE WON'T LET YOU FLAUNT YOUR SORCERY HERE.
AIEE

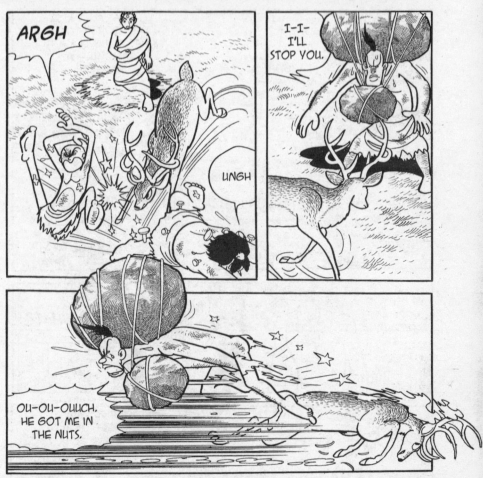

ARGH

I-I-I'LL STOP YOU.

UNGH

OU-OU-OUUCH. HE GOT ME IN THE NUTS.

OH NO, NOT AGAIN...

SEE WHAT IT DID TO ME? RUB SOME OINTMENT THERE.

CONSIDER IT AN ORDEAL AND COPE WITH IT.

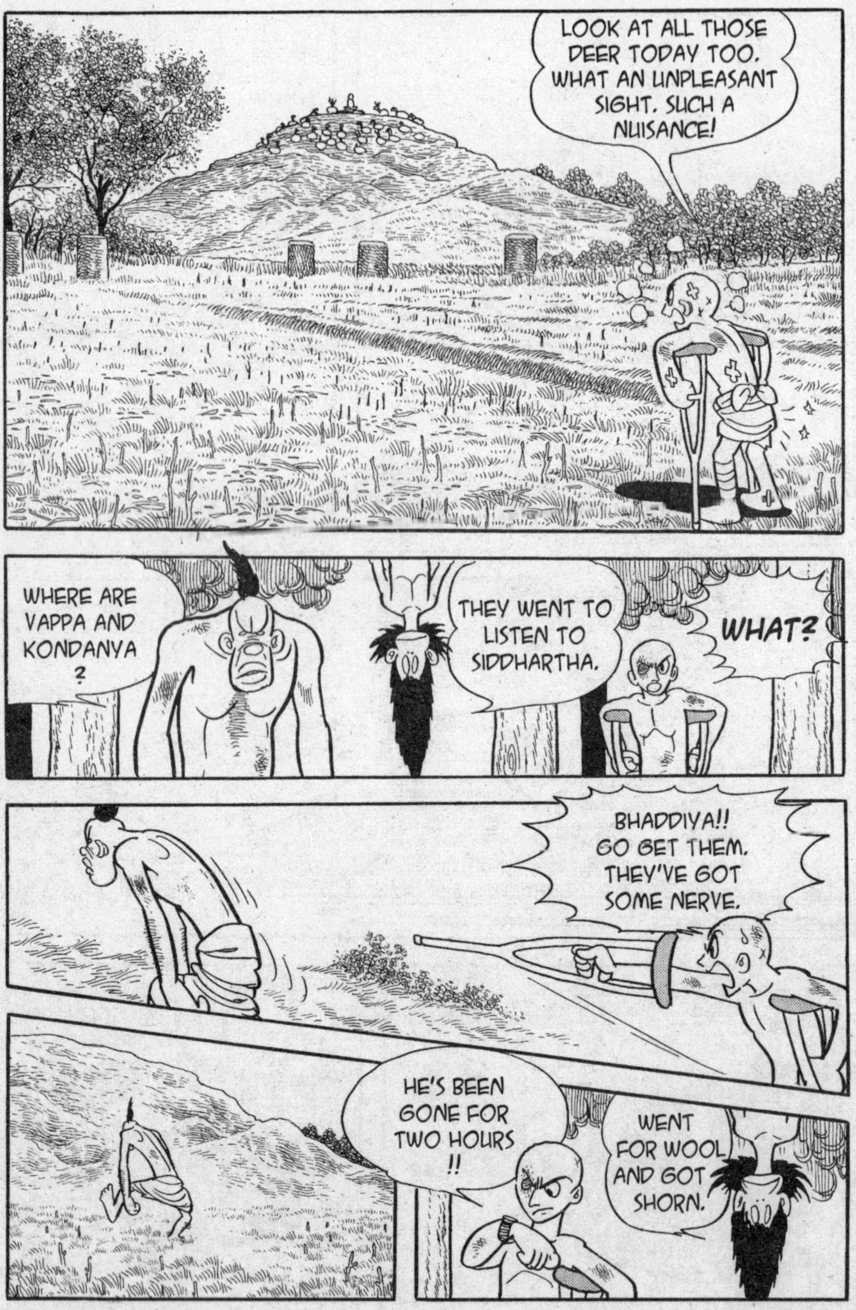
LOOK AT ALL THOSE DEER TODAY TOO. WHAT AN UNPLEASANT SIGHT. SUCH A NUISANCE!
WHERE ARE VAPPA AND KONDANYA ?
THEY WENT TO LISTEN TO SIDDHARTHA.
WHAT?
BHADDIYA!! GO GET THEM. THEY'VE GOT SOME NERVE.
HE'S BEEN GONE FOR TWO HOURS !!
WENT FOR WOOL AND GOT SHORN.

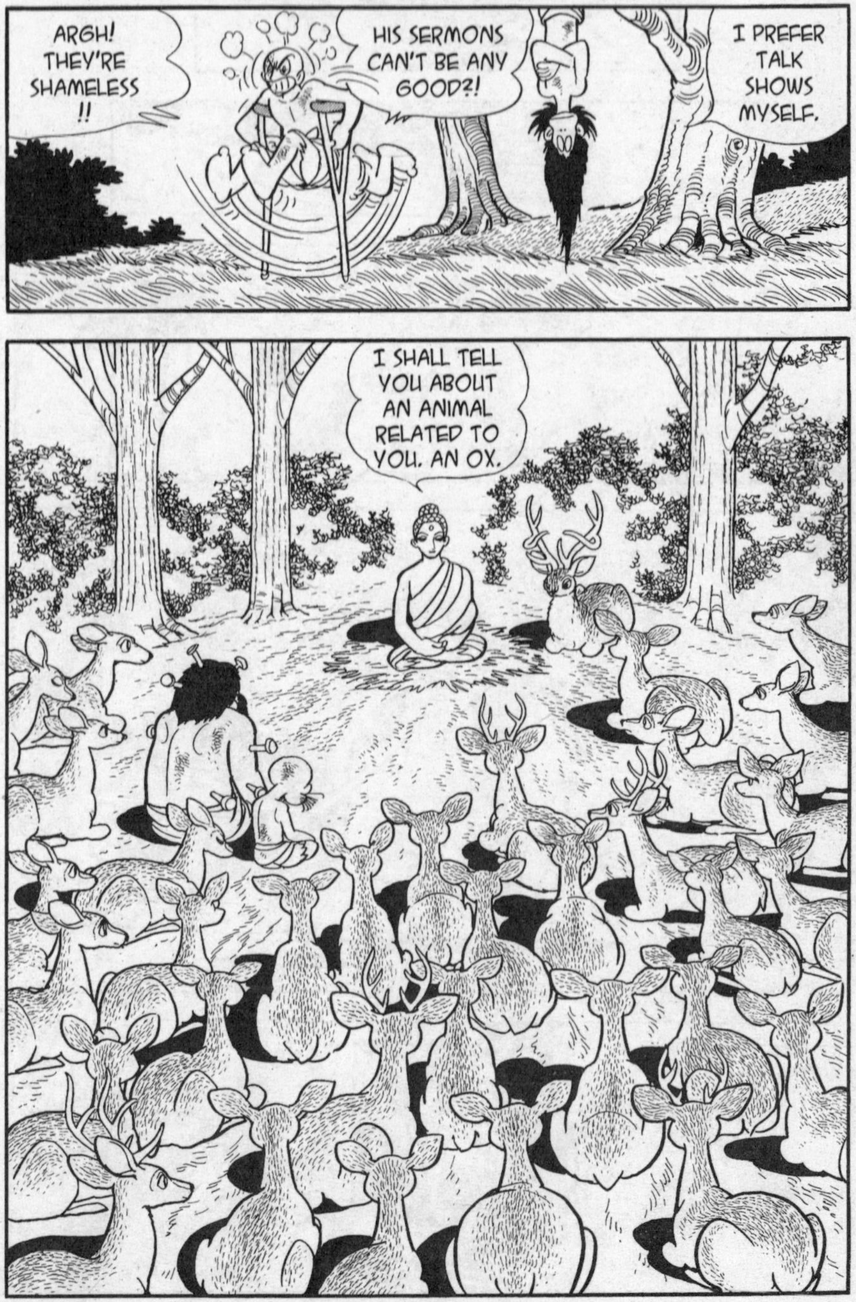
ARGH! THEY'RE SHAMELESS !!
HIS SERMONS CAN'T BE ANY GOOD?!
I PREFER TALK SHOWS MYSELF.
I SHALL TELL YOU ABOUT AN ANIMAL RELATED TO YOU. AN OX.

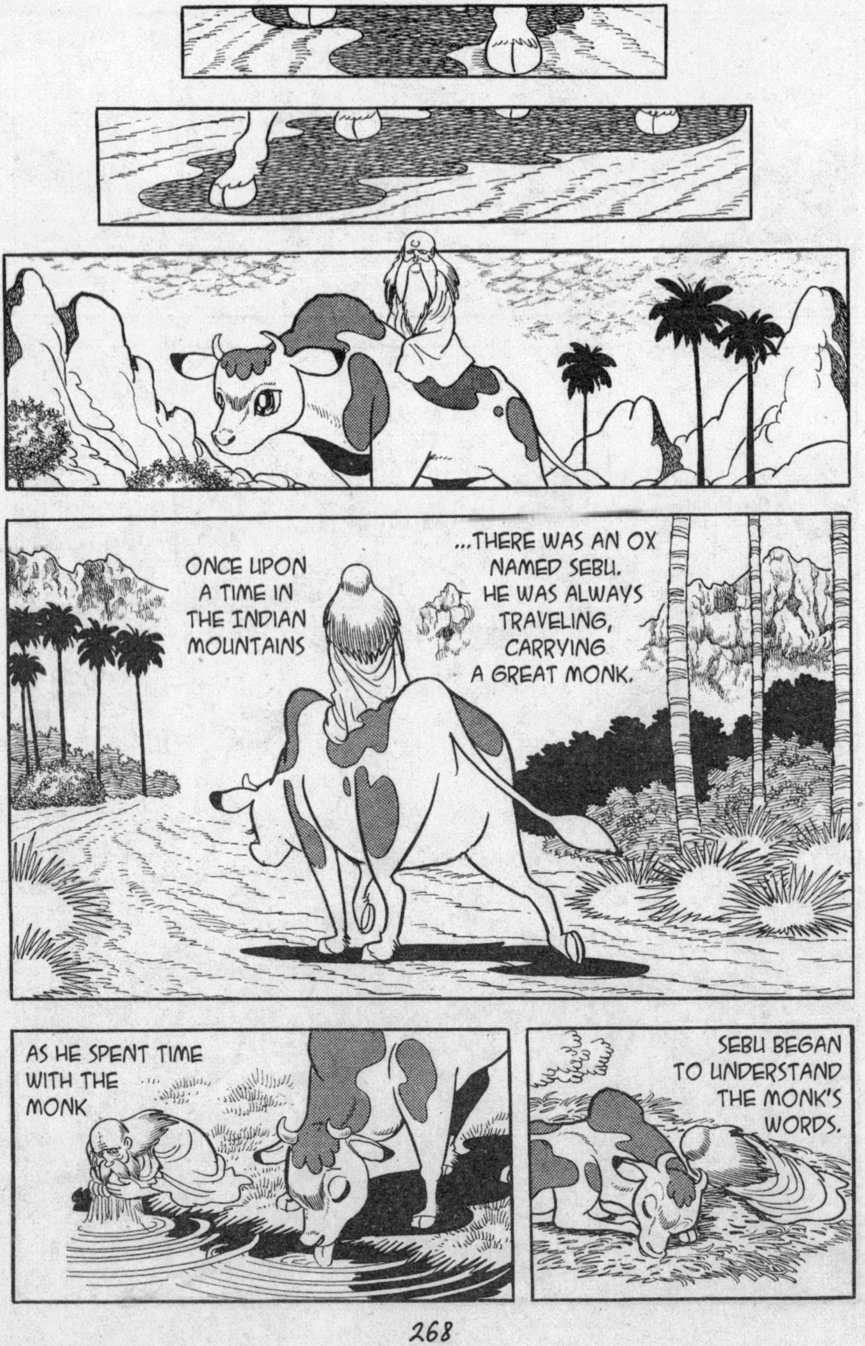
ONCE UPON A TIME IN THE INDIAN MOUNTAINS
...THERE WAS AN OX NAMED SEBU. HE WAS ALWAYS TRAVELING, CARRYING A GREAT MONK.
AS HE SPENT TIME WITH THE MONK
SEBU BEGAN TO UNDERSTAND THE MONK'S WORDS.

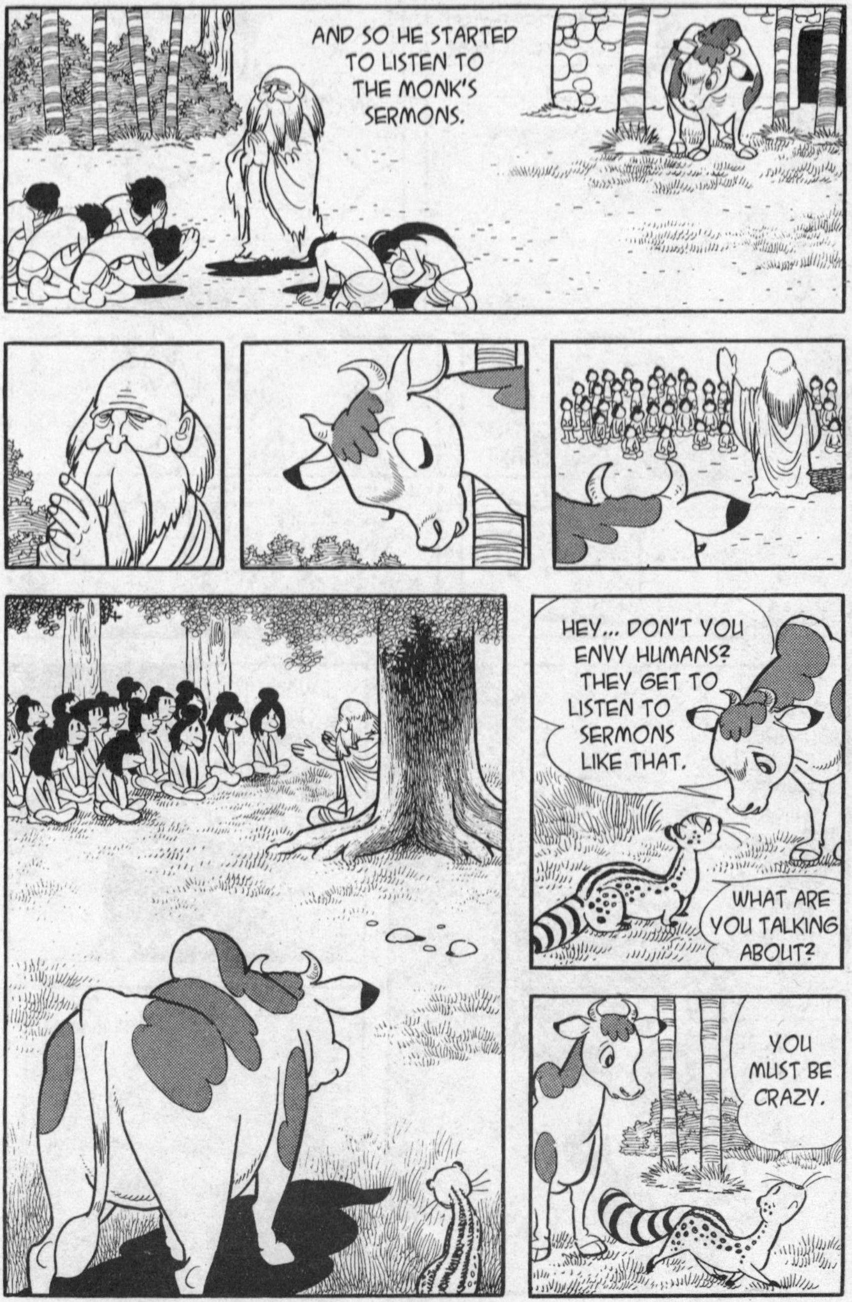
AND SO HE STARTED TO LISTEN TO THE MONK'S SERMONS.
HEY... DON'T YOU ENVY HUMANS? THEY GET TO LISTEN TO SERMONS LIKE THAT.
WHAT ARE YOU TALKING ABOUT?
YOU MUST BE CRAZY.

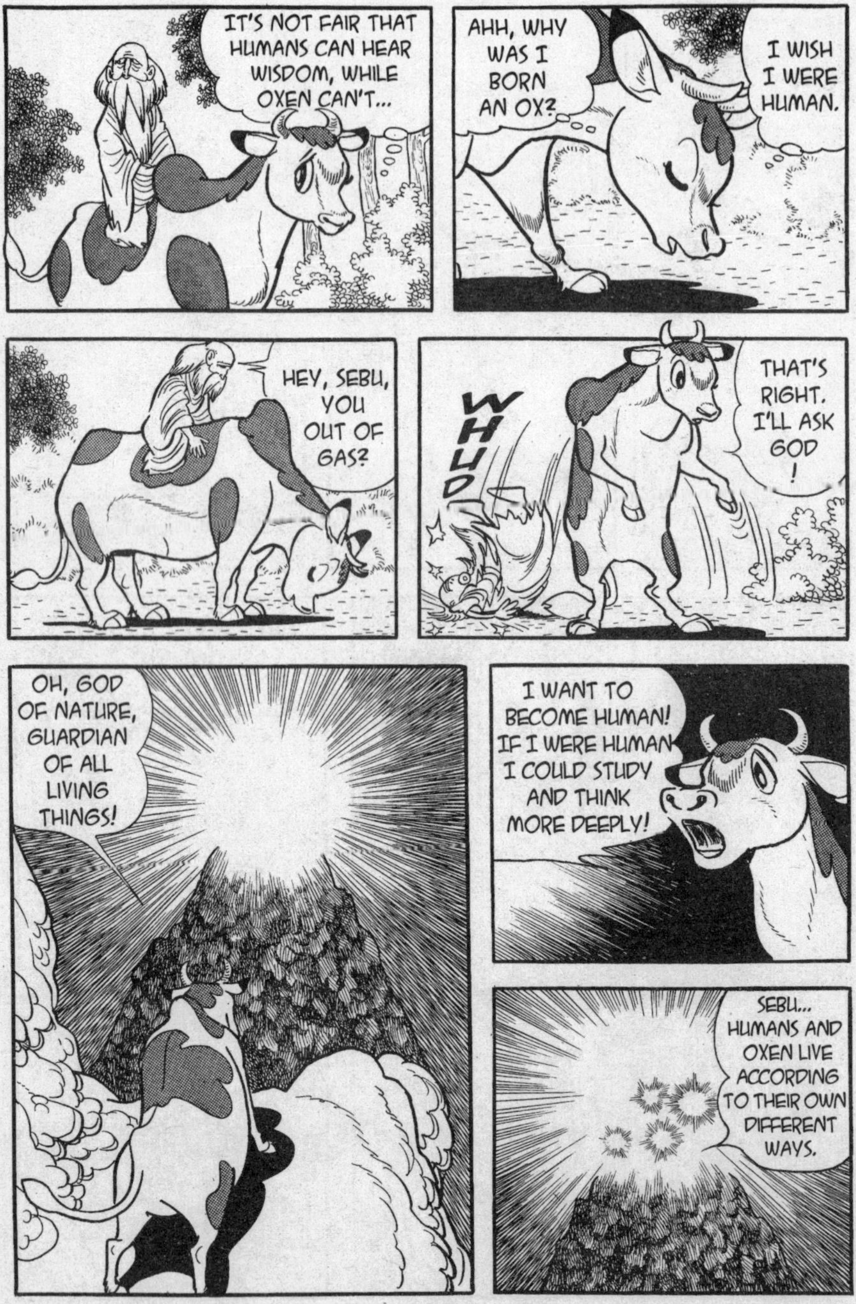
IT'S NOT FAIR THAT HUMANS CAN HEAR WISDOM, WHILE OXEN CAN'T...
AHH, WHY WAS I BORN AN OX?
I WISH I WERE HUMAN.
HEY, SEBU, YOU OUT OF GAS?
WHUD
THAT'S RIGHT. I'LL ASK GOD!
OH, GOD OF NATURE, GUARDIAN OF ALL LIVING THINGS!
I WANT TO BECOME HUMAN! IF I WERE HUMAN I COULD STUDY AND THINK MORE DEEPLY!
SEBU... HUMANS AND OXEN LIVE ACCORDING TO THEIR OWN DIFFERENT WAYS.

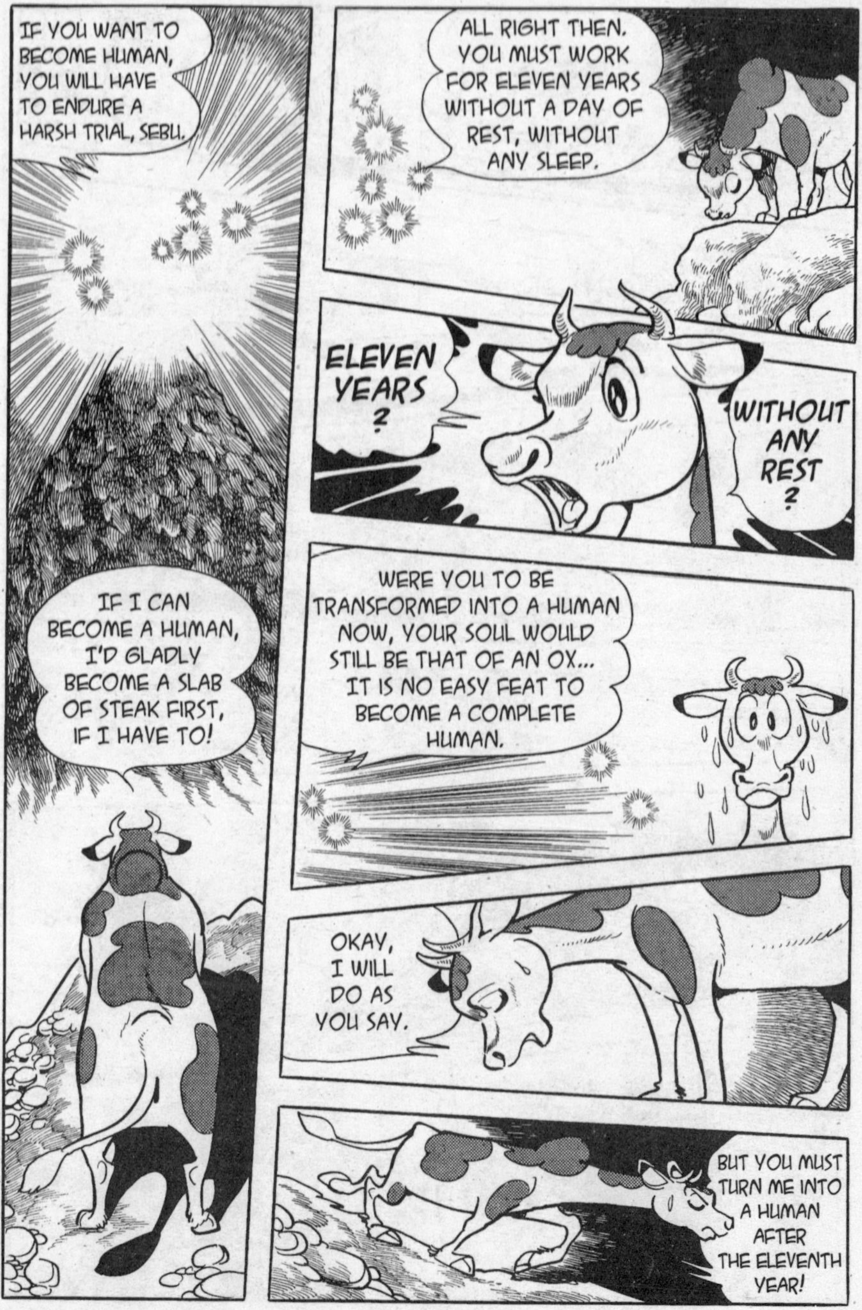

IF YOU WANT TO BECOME HUMAN, YOU WILL HAVE TO ENDURE A HARSH TRIAL, SEBU.
ALL RIGHT THEN. YOU MUST WORK FOR ELEVEN YEARS WITHOUT A DAY OF REST, WITHOUT ANY SLEEP.
ELEVEN YEARS?
WITHOUT ANY REST?
IF I CAN BECOME A HUMAN, I'D GLADLY BECOME A SLAB OF STEAK FIRST, IF I HAVE TO!
WERE YOU TO BE TRANSFORMED INTO A HUMAN NOW, YOUR SOUL WOULD STILL BE THAT OF AN OX... IT IS NO EASY FEAT TO BECOME A COMPLETE HUMAN.
OKAY, I WILL DO AS YOU SAY.
BUT YOU MUST TURN ME INTO A HUMAN AFTER THE ELEVENTH YEAR!

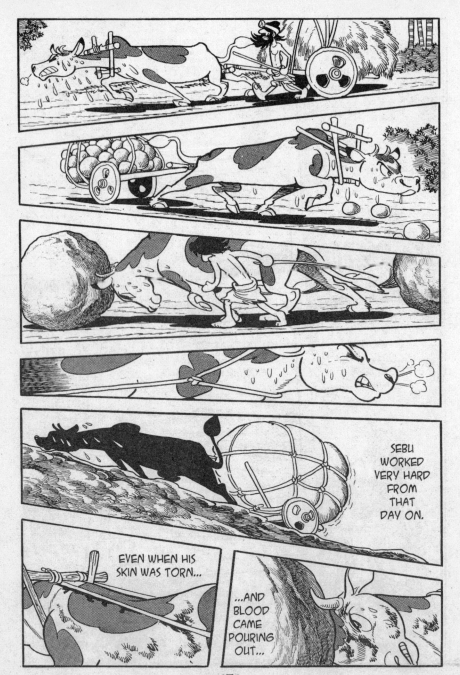

SEBU WORKED VERY HARD FROM THAT DAY ON.

EVEN WHEN HIS SKIN WAS TORN...

...AND BLOOD CAME POURING OUT...

272

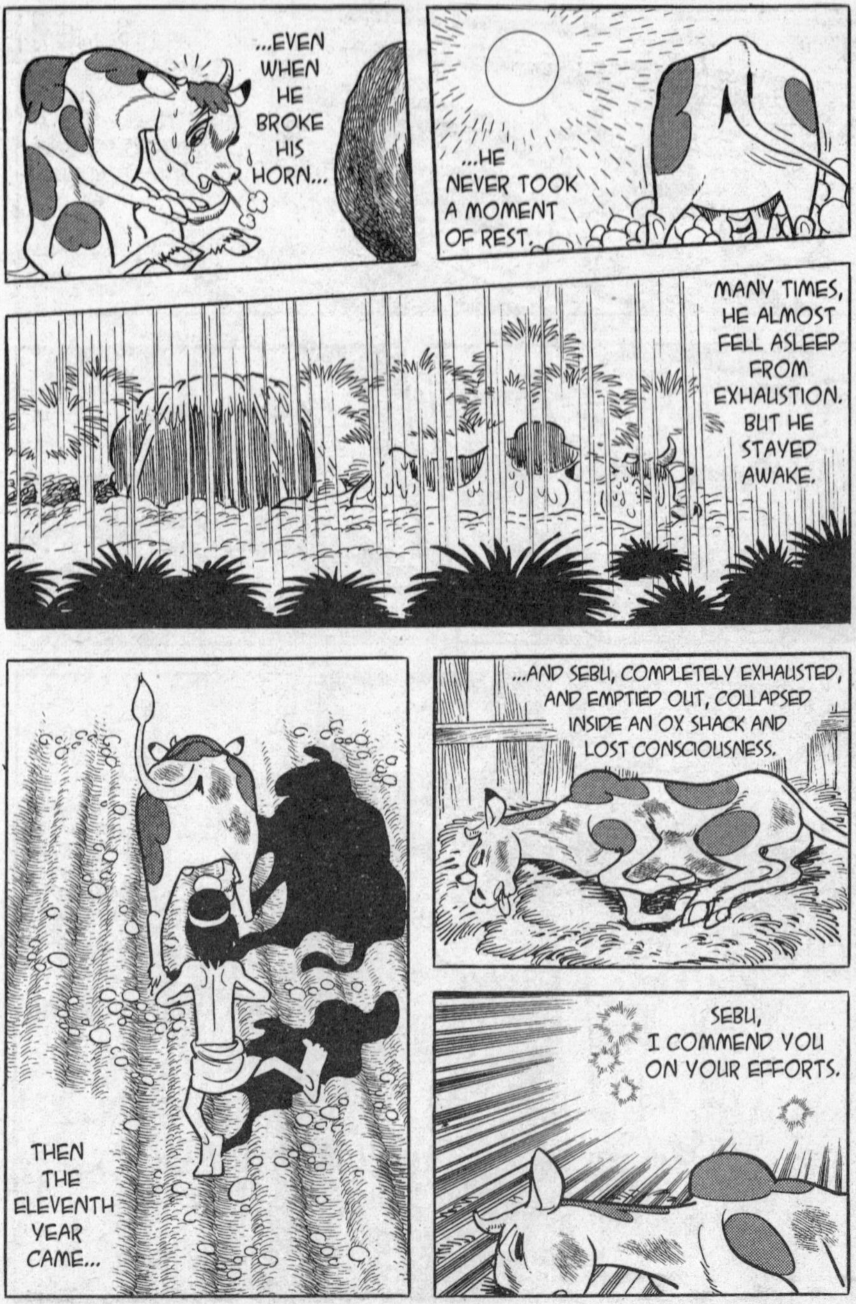
...EVEN WHEN HE BROKE HIS HORN...
...HE NEVER TOOK A MOMENT OF REST.
MANY TIMES, HE ALMOST FELL ASLEEP FROM EXHAUSTION. BUT HE STAYED AWAKE.
THEN THE ELEVENTH YEAR CAME...
...AND SEBU, COMPLETELY EXHAUSTED, AND EMPTIED OUT, COLLAPSED INSIDE AN OX SHACK AND LOST CONSCIOUSNESS.
SEBU, I COMMEND YOU ON YOUR EFFORTS.

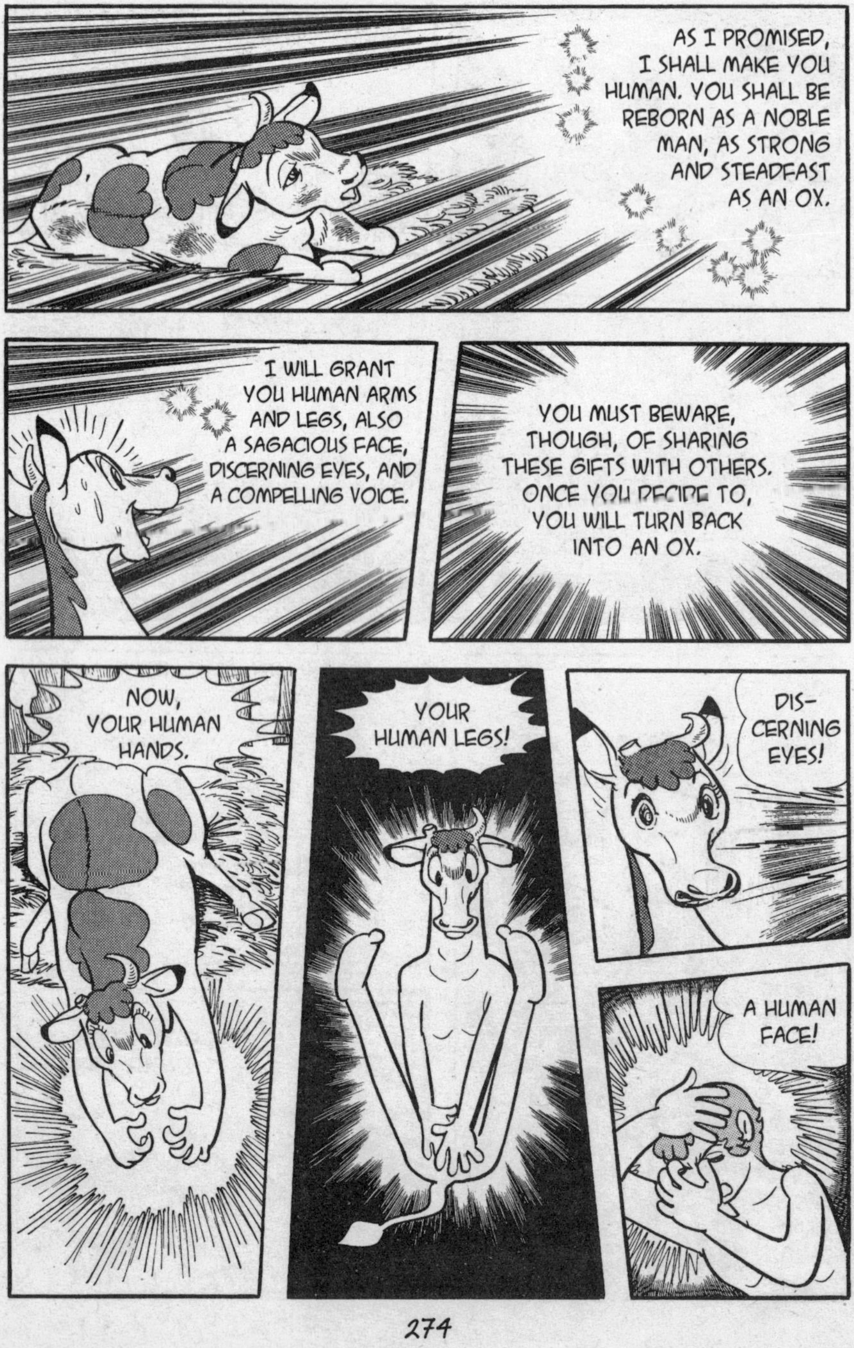
AS I PROMISED, I SHALL MAKE YOU HUMAN. YOU SHALL BE REBORN AS A NOBLE MAN, AS STRONG AND STEADFAST AS AN OX.
I WILL GRANT YOU HUMAN ARMS AND LEGS, ALSO A SAGACIOUS FACE, DISCERNING EYES, AND A COMPELLING VOICE.
YOU MUST BEWARE, THOUGH, OF SHARING THESE GIFTS WITH OTHERS. ONCE YOU DECIDE TO, YOU WILL TURN BACK INTO AN OX.
NOW, YOUR HUMAN HANDS.
YOUR HUMAN LEGS!
DIS-CERNING EYES!
A HUMAN FACE!

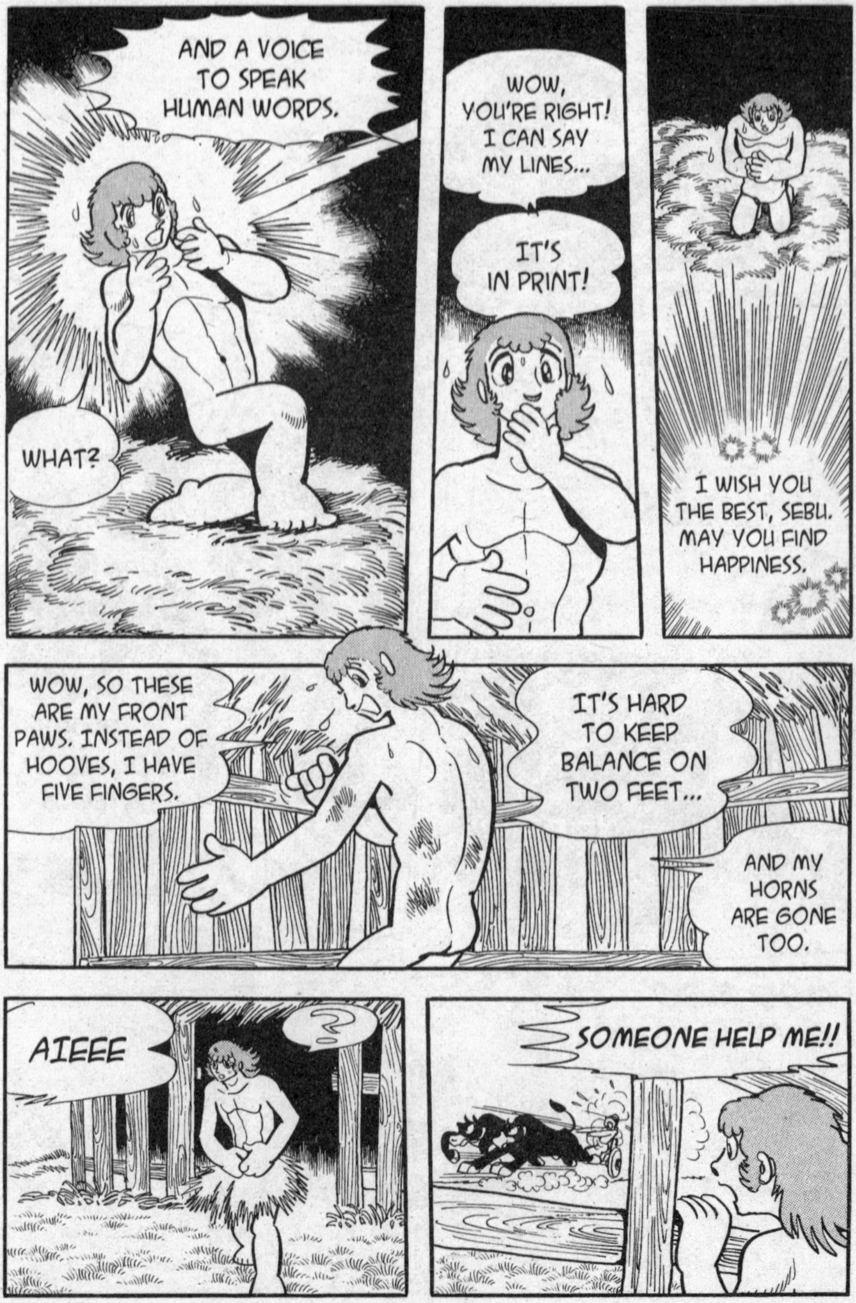
AND A VOICE TO SPEAK HUMAN WORDS.
WHAT?
WOW, YOU'RE RIGHT! I CAN SAY MY LINES...
IT'S IN PRINT!
I WISH YOU THE BEST, SEBU. MAY YOU FIND HAPPINESS.
WOW, SO THESE ARE MY FRONT PAWS. INSTEAD OF HOOVES, I HAVE FIVE FINGERS.
IT'S HARD TO KEEP BALANCE ON TWO FEET...
AND MY HORNS ARE GONE TOO.
AIEEE
?
SOMEONE HELP ME!!

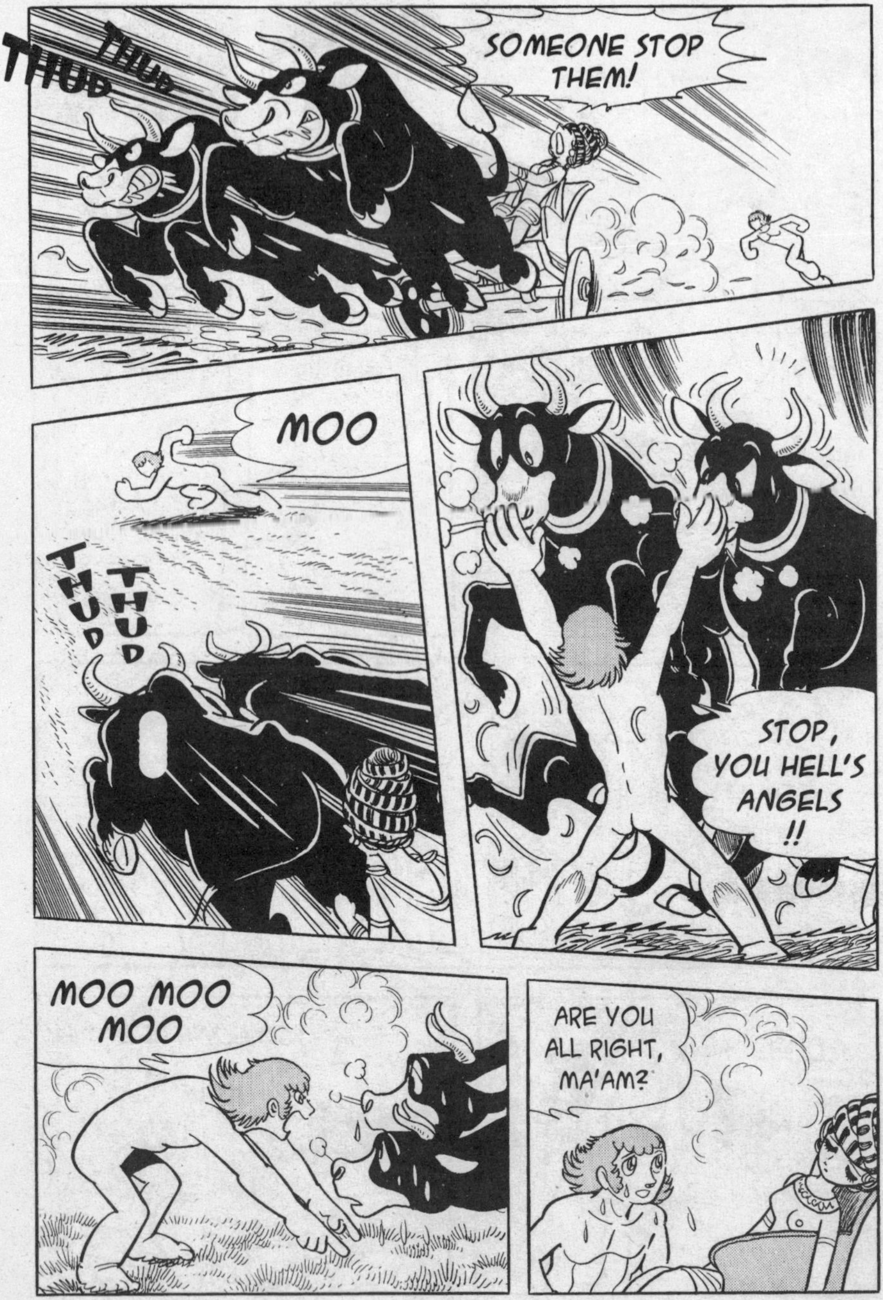
THUD
THUD
SOMEONE STOP THEM!
MOO
THUD THUD
THUD THUD
STOP, YOU HELL'S ANGELS !!
MOO MOO MOO
ARE YOU ALL RIGHT, MA'AM?

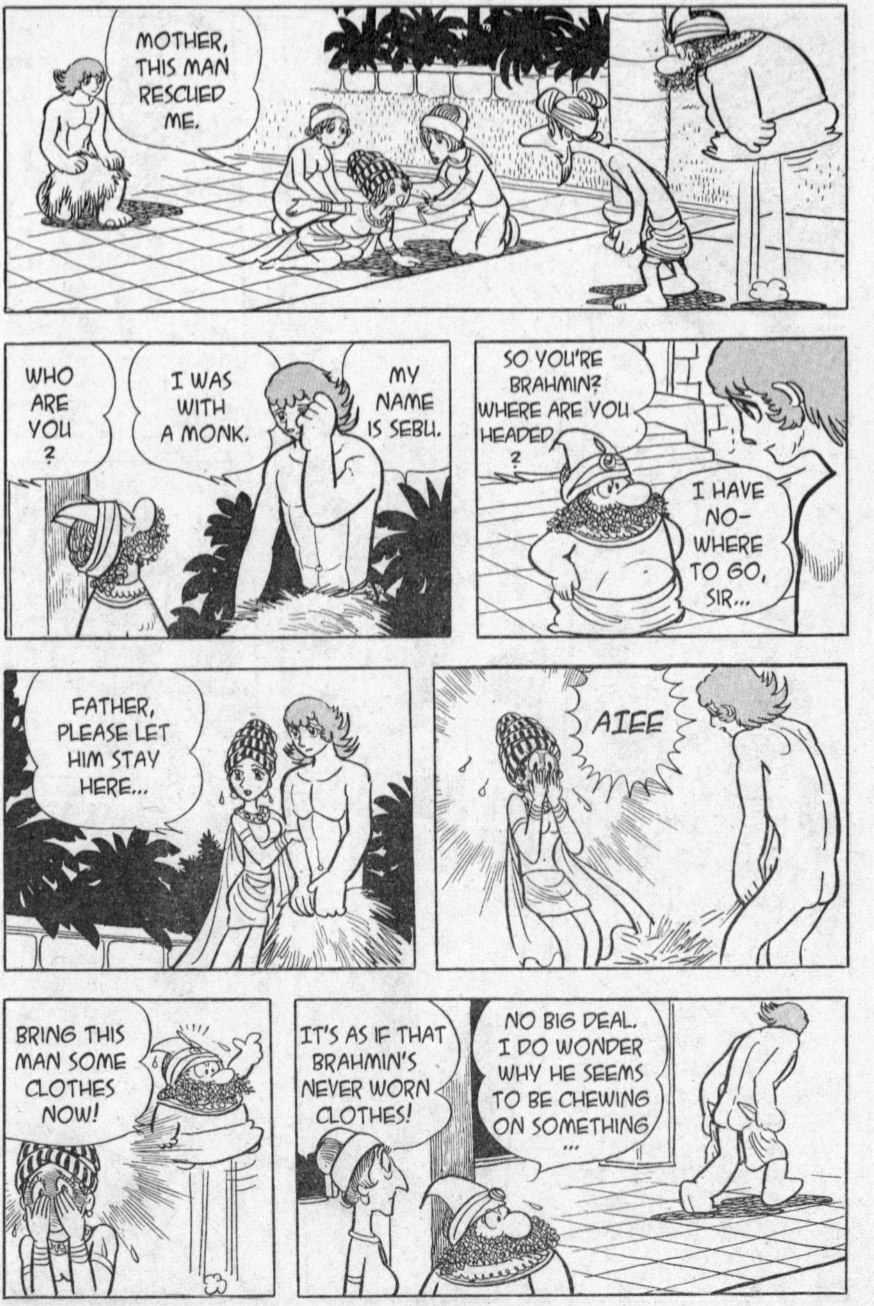
MOTHER, THIS MAN RESCUED ME.
WHO ARE YOU ?
I WAS WITH A MONK.
MY NAME IS SEBU.
SO YOU'RE BRAHMIN? WHERE ARE YOU HEADED ?
I HAVE NO-WHERE TO GO, SIR...
FATHER, PLEASE LET HIM STAY HERE...
AIEE
BRING THIS MAN SOME CLOTHES NOW!
IT'S AS IF THAT BRAHMIN'S NEVER WORN CLOTHES!
NO BIG DEAL. I DO WONDER WHY HE SEEMS TO BE CHEWING ON SOMETHING ...

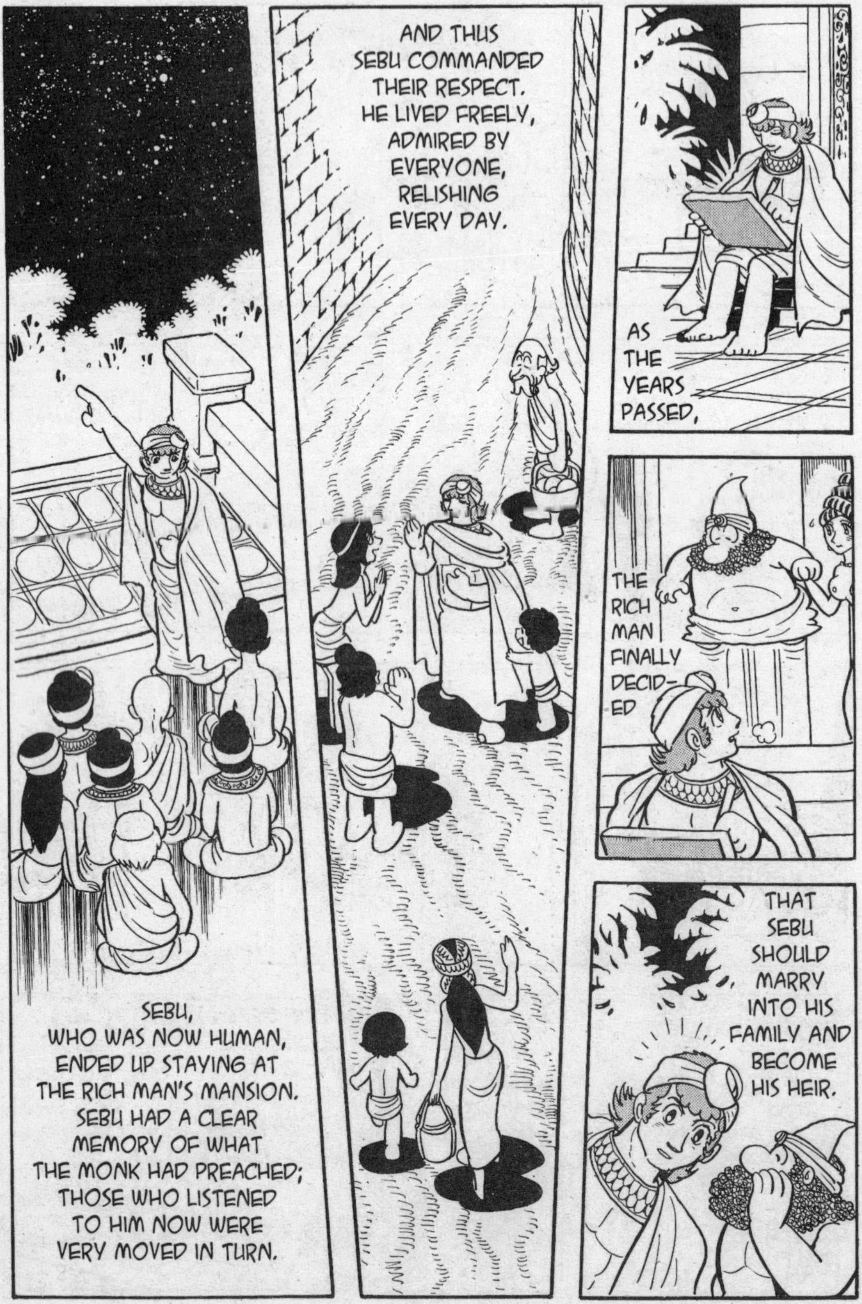
SEBU, WHO WAS NOW HUMAN, ENDED UP STAYING AT THE RICH MAN'S MANSION. SEBU HAD A CLEAR MEMORY OF WHAT THE MONK HAD PREACHED; THOSE WHO LISTENED TO HIM NOW WERE VERY MOVED IN TURN.
AND THUS SEBU COMMANDED THEIR RESPECT. HE LIVED FREELY, ADMIRED BY EVERYONE, RELISHING EVERY DAY.
AS THE YEARS PASSED,
THE RICH MAN FINALLY DECIDED
THAT SEBU SHOULD MARRY INTO HIS FAMILY AND BECOME HIS HEIR.

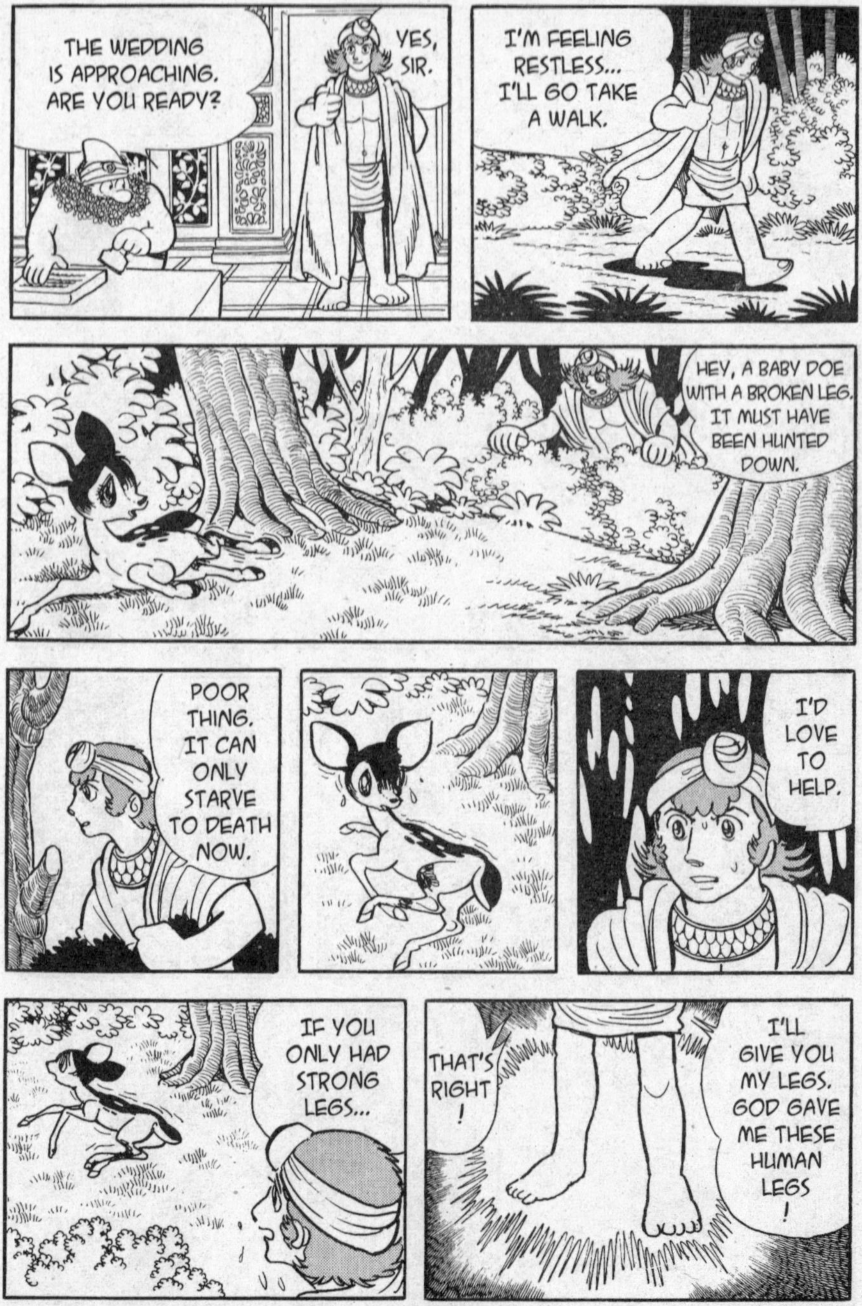

THE WEDDING IS APPROACHING. ARE YOU READY?
YES, SIR.
I'M FEELING RESTLESS... I'LL GO TAKE A WALK.
HEY, A BABY DOE WITH A BROKEN LEG. IT MUST HAVE BEEN HUNTED DOWN.
POOR THING. IT CAN ONLY STARVE TO DEATH NOW.
I'D LOVE TO HELP.
IF YOU ONLY HAD STRONG LEGS...
THAT'S RIGHT!
I'LL GIVE YOU MY LEGS. GOD GAVE ME THESE HUMAN LEGS!

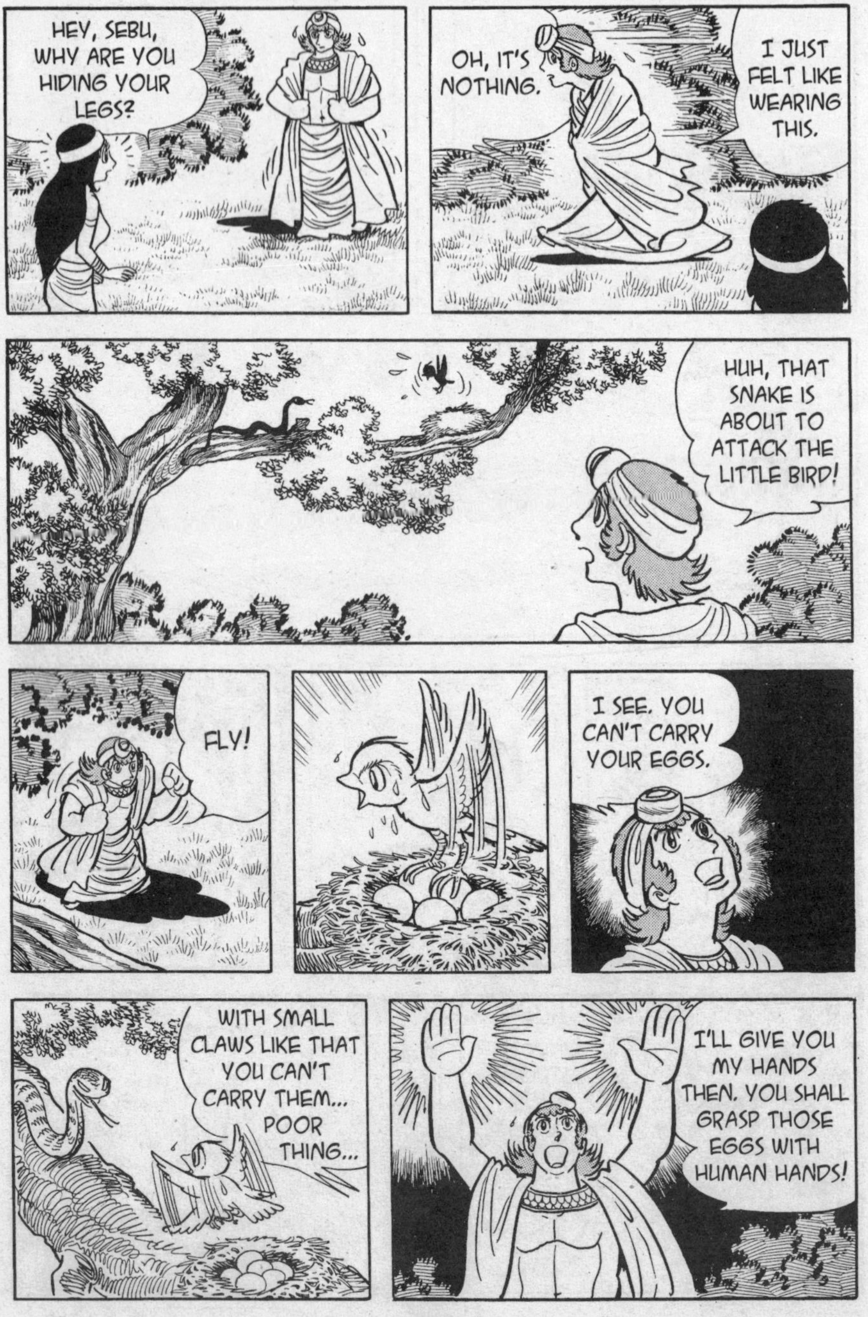
HEY, SEBU, WHY ARE YOU HIDING YOUR LEGS?
OH, IT'S NOTHING.
I JUST FELT LIKE WEARING THIS.
HUH, THAT SNAKE IS ABOUT TO ATTACK THE LITTLE BIRD!
FLY!
I SEE. YOU CAN'T CARRY YOUR EGGS.
WITH SMALL CLAWS LIKE THAT YOU CAN'T CARRY THEM... POOR THING...
I'LL GIVE YOU MY HANDS THEN. YOU SHALL GRASP THOSE EGGS WITH HUMAN HANDS!

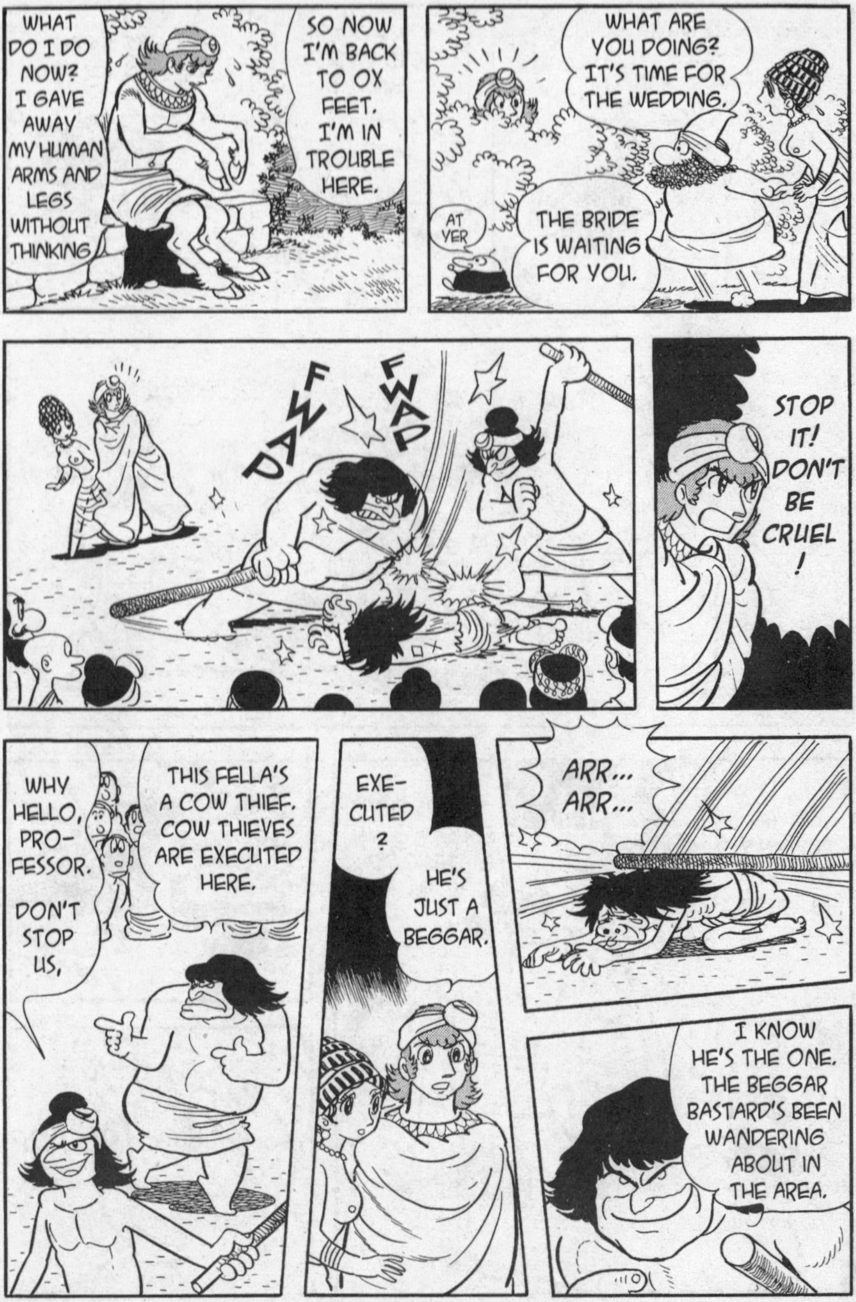

WHAT DO I DO NOW? I GAVE AWAY MY HUMAN ARMS AND LEGS WITHOUT THINKING
SO NOW I'M BACK TO OX FEET. I'M IN TROUBLE HERE.
WHAT ARE YOU DOING? IT'S TIME FOR THE WEDDING.
THE BRIDE IS WAITING FOR YOU.
AT YER
FWAP
FWAP
STOP IT! DON'T BE CRUEL!
WHY HELLO, PROFESSOR. DON'T STOP US,
THIS FELLA'S A COW THIEF. COW THIEVES ARE EXECUTED HERE.
EXECUTED?
HE'S JUST A BEGGAR.
ARR... ARR...
I KNOW HE'S THE ONE. THE BEGGAR BASTARD'S BEEN WANDERING ABOUT IN THE AREA.

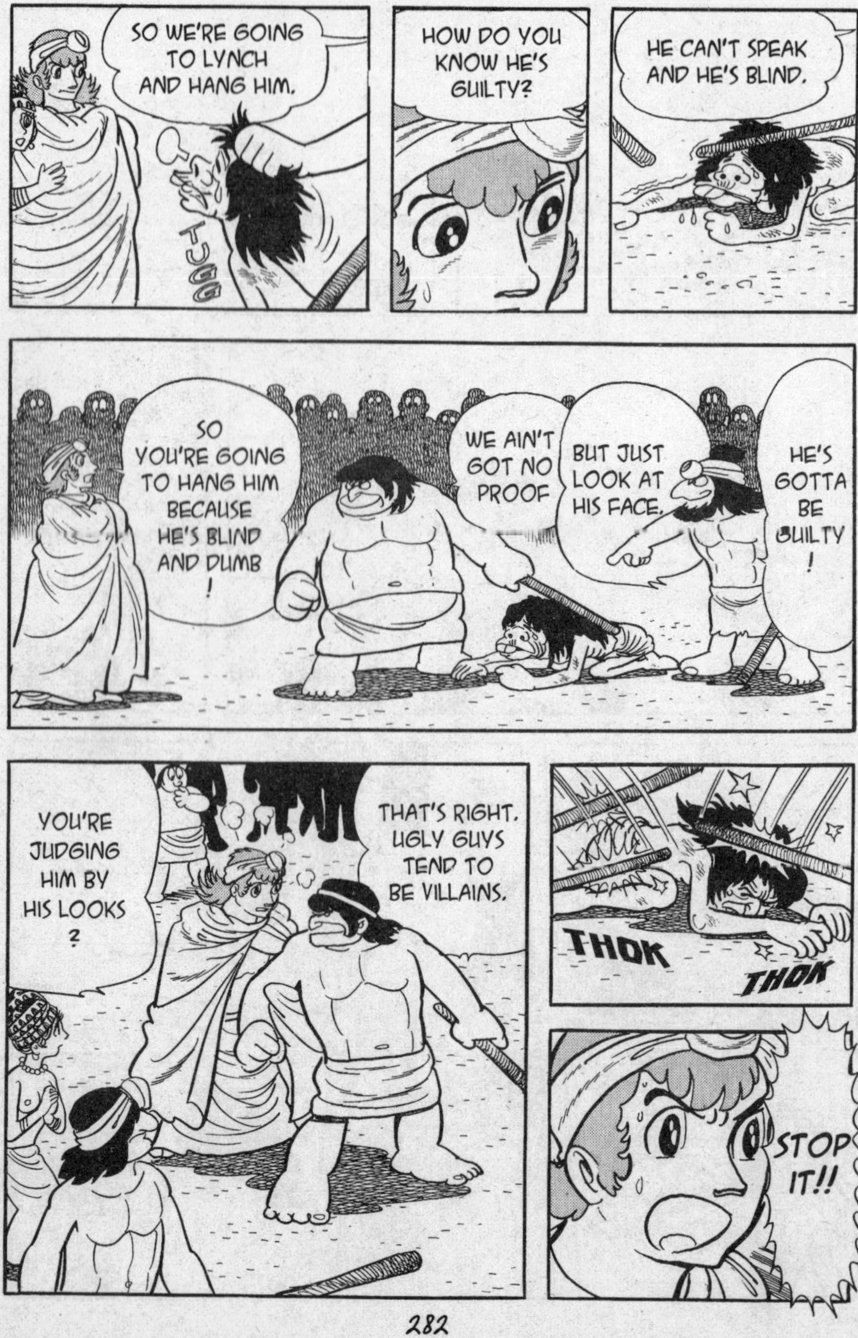
SO WE'RE GOING TO LYNCH AND HANG HIM.
TUGG
HOW DO YOU KNOW HE'S GUILTY?
HE CAN'T SPEAK AND HE'S BLIND.
SO YOU'RE GOING TO HANG HIM BECAUSE HE'S BLIND AND DUMB!
WE AIN'T GOT NO PROOF
BUT JUST LOOK AT HIS FACE.
HE'S GOTTA BE GUILTY!
YOU'RE JUDGING HIM BY HIS LOOKS?
THAT'S RIGHT. UGLY GUYS TEND TO BE VILLAINS.
THOK
THOK
STOP IT!!

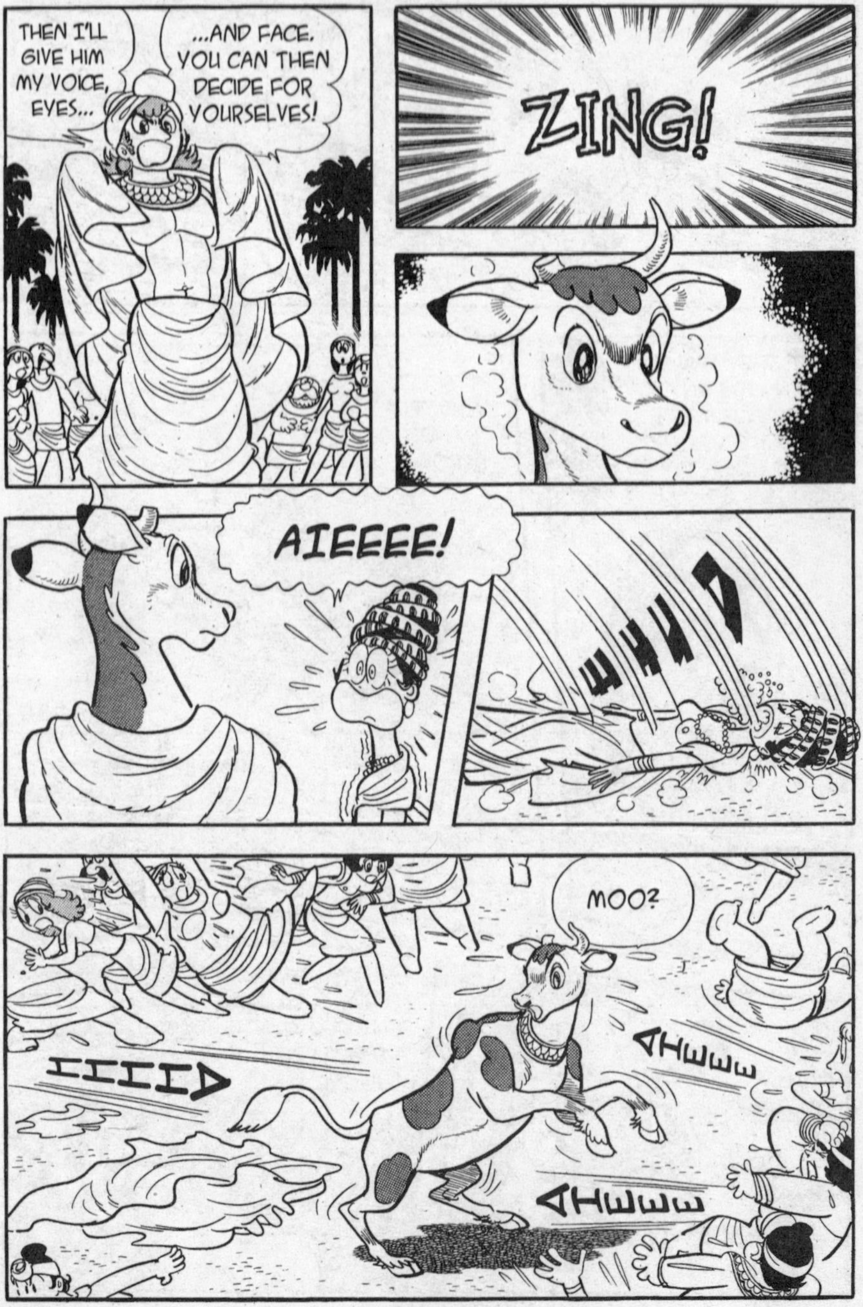
THEN I'LL GIVE HIM MY VOICE, EYES...
...AND FACE. YOU CAN THEN DECIDE FOR YOURSELVES!
ZING!
AIEEEE!
MOO?

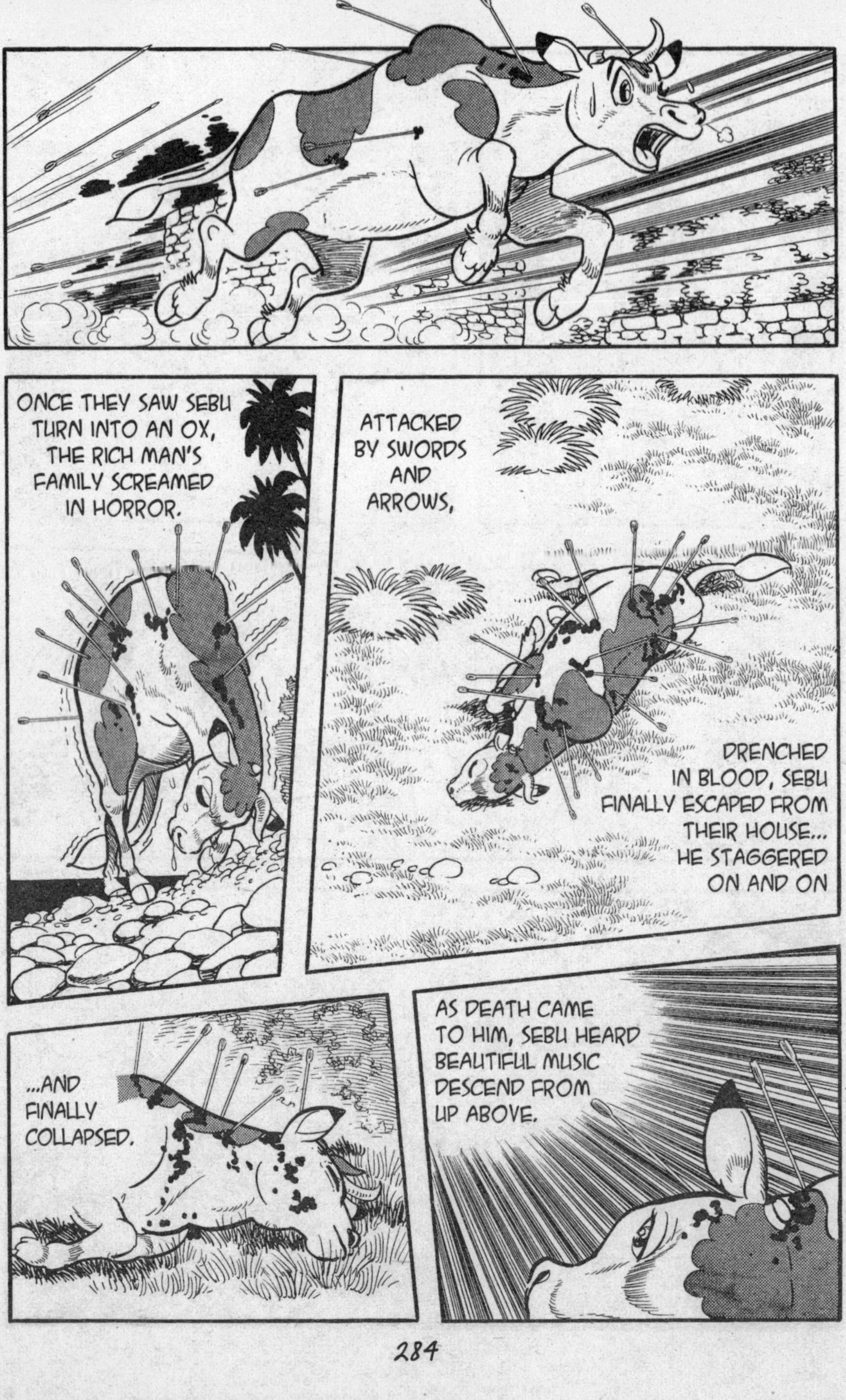
ONCE THEY SAW SEBU TURN INTO AN OX, THE RICH MAN'S FAMILY SCREAMED IN HORROR.
ATTACKED BY SWORDS AND ARROWS,
DRENCHED IN BLOOD, SEBU FINALLY ESCAPED FROM THEIR HOUSE... HE STAGGERED ON AND ON
...AND FINALLY COLLAPSED.
AS DEATH CAME TO HIM, SEBU HEARD BEAUTIFUL MUSIC DESCEND FROM UP ABOVE.

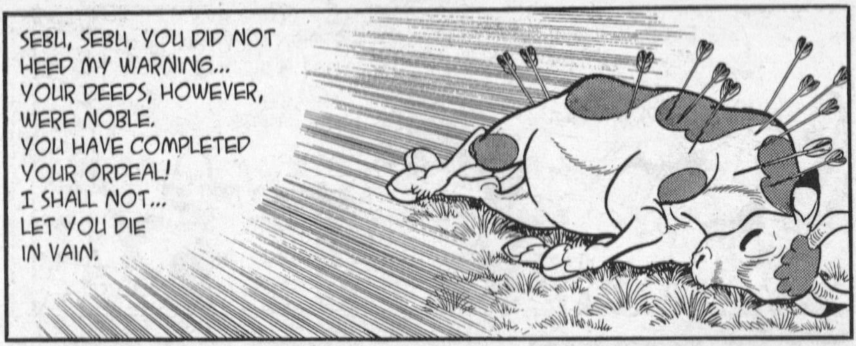
SEBU, SEBU, YOU DID NOT HEED MY WARNING... YOUR DEEDS, HOWEVER, WERE NOBLE. YOU HAVE COMPLETED YOUR ORDEAL! I SHALL NOT... LET YOU DIE IN VAIN.

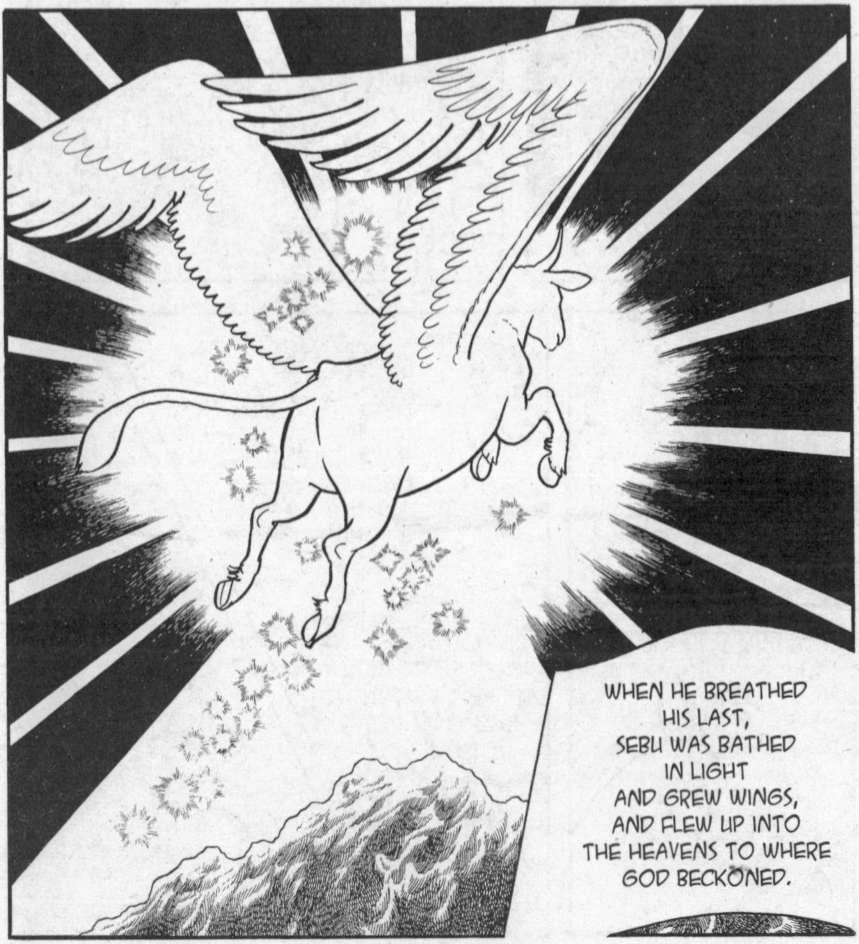
WHEN HE BREATHED HIS LAST, SEBU WAS BATHED IN LIGHT AND GREW WINGS, AND FLEW UP INTO THE HEAVENS TO WHERE GOD BECKONED.

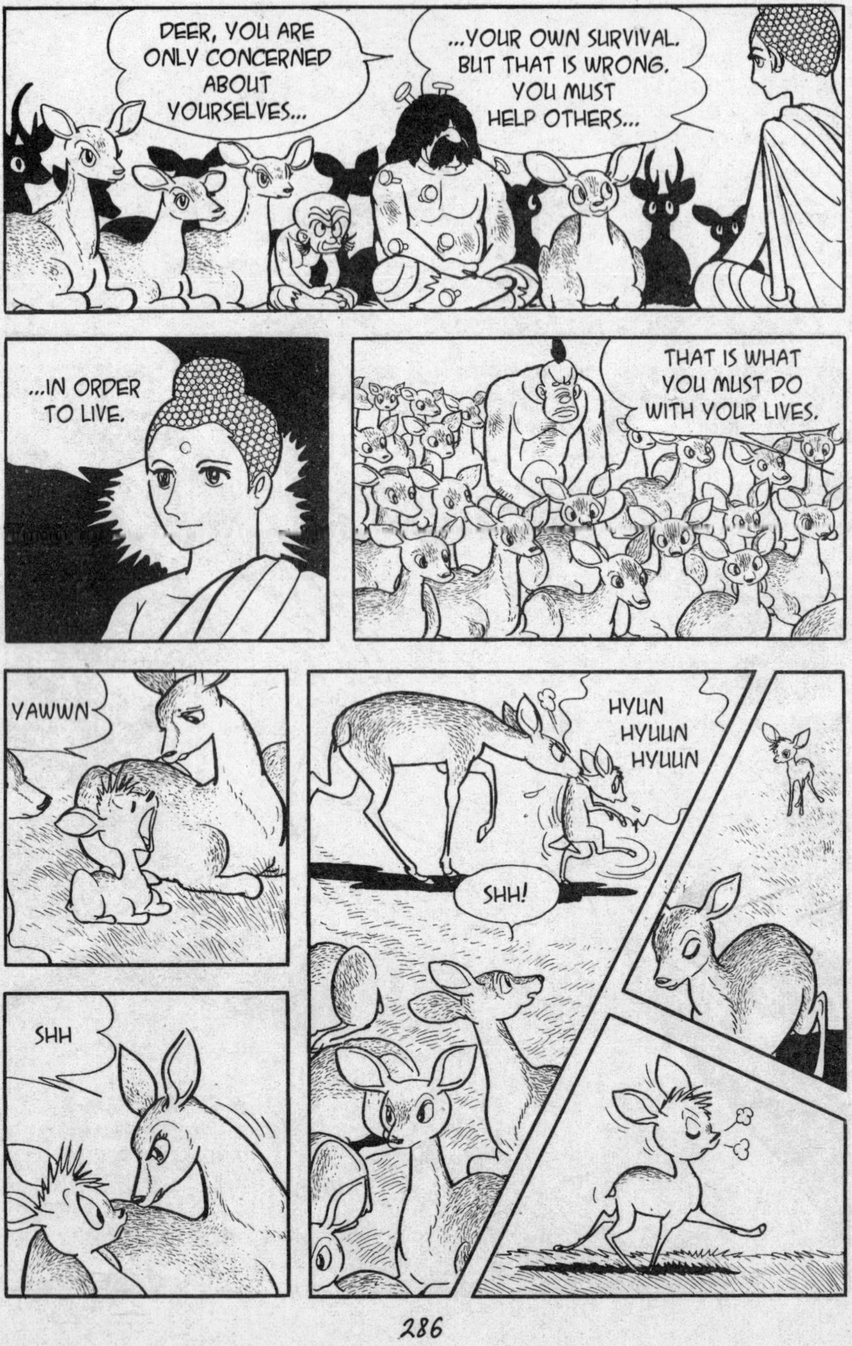

DEER, YOU ARE ONLY CONCERNED ABOUT YOURSELVES...
...YOUR OWN SURVIVAL. BUT THAT IS WRONG. YOU MUST HELP OTHERS...
...IN ORDER TO LIVE.
THAT IS WHAT YOU MUST DO WITH YOUR LIVES.
YAWWN
HYUN HYUUN HYUUN
SHH!
SHH

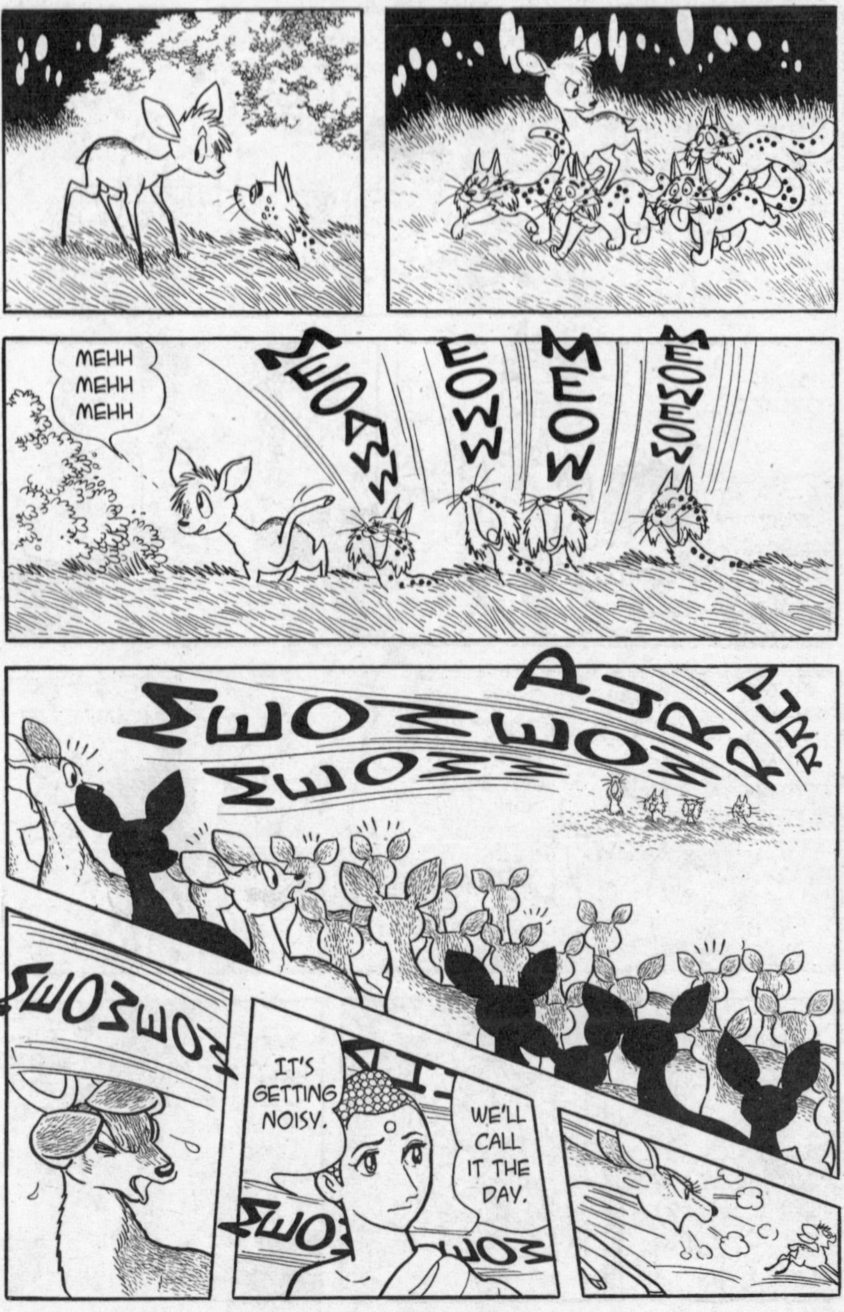
MEHH
MEHH
MEHH
MEOWW
MEOWW
MEOW
MEOWEOW
IT'S GETTING NOISY.
WE'LL CALL IT THE DAY.

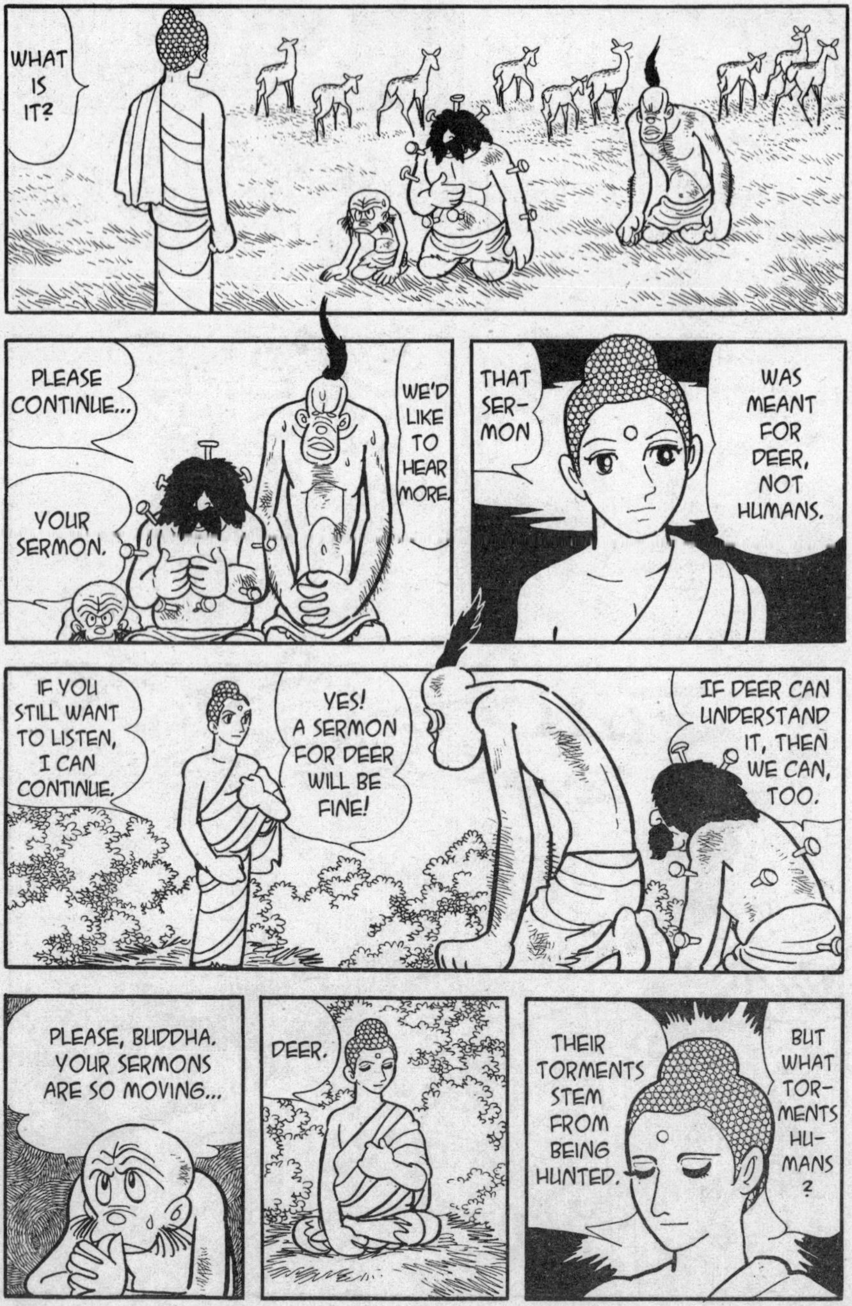
WHAT IS IT?
PLEASE CONTINUE...
YOUR SERMON.
WE'D LIKE TO HEAR MORE.
THAT SER-MON
WAS MEANT FOR DEER, NOT HUMANS.
IF YOU STILL WANT TO LISTEN, I CAN CONTINUE.
YES! A SERMON FOR DEER WILL BE FINE!
IF DEER CAN UNDERSTAND IT, THEN WE CAN, TOO.
PLEASE, BUDDHA. YOUR SERMONS ARE SO MOVING...
DEER.
THEIR TORMENTS STEM FROM BEING HUNTED.
BUT WHAT TOR-MENTS HU-MANS ?

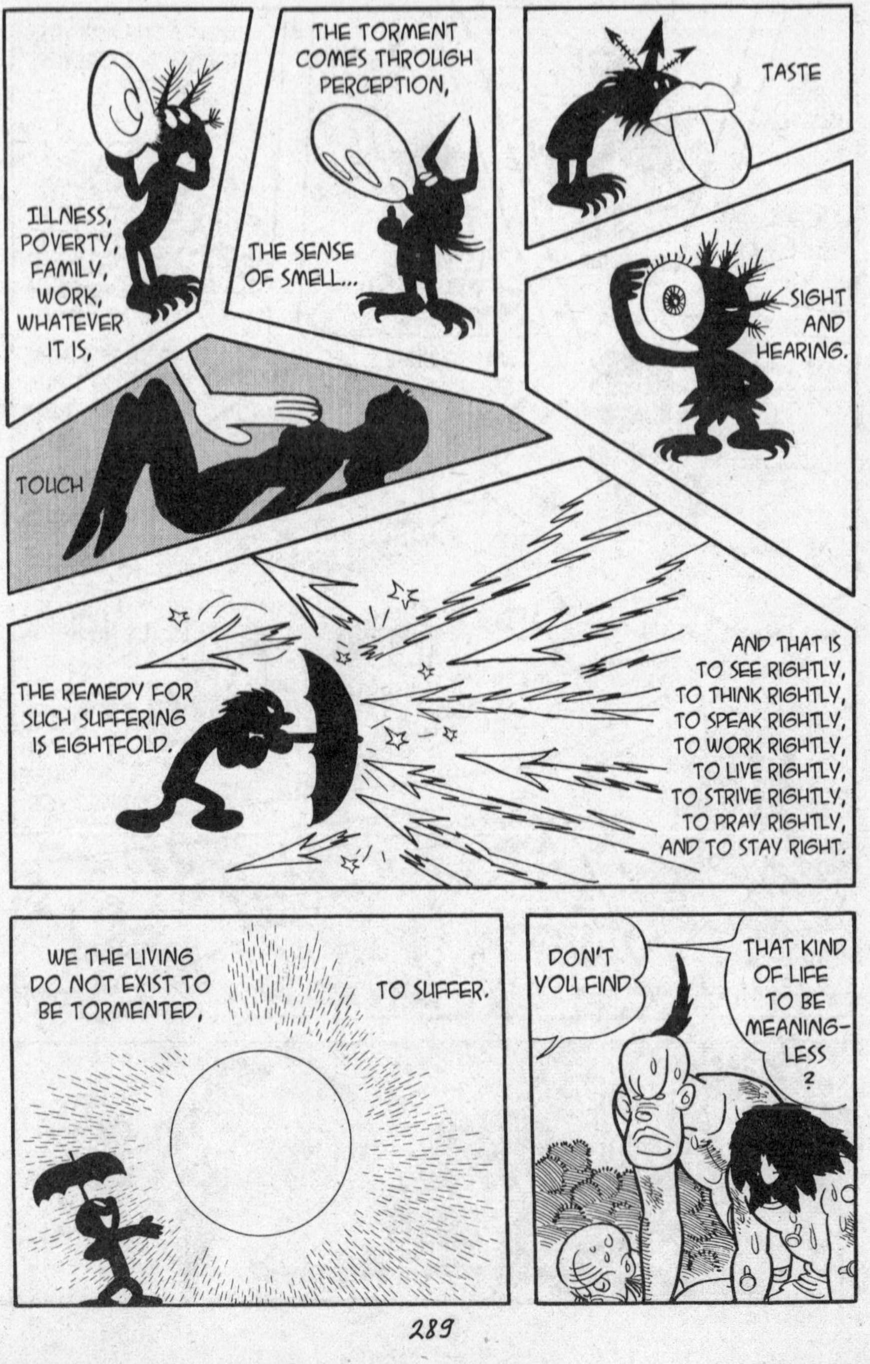
THE TORMENT COMES THROUGH PERCEPTION,
ILLNESS, POVERTY, FAMILY, WORK, WHATEVER IT IS,
THE SENSE OF SMELL...
TASTE
SIGHT AND HEARING.
TOUCH
THE REMEDY FOR SUCH SUFFERING IS EIGHTFOLD.
AND THAT IS TO SEE RIGHTLY, TO THINK RIGHTLY, TO SPEAK RIGHTLY, TO WORK RIGHTLY, TO LIVE RIGHTLY, TO STRIVE RIGHTLY, TO PRAY RIGHTLY, AND TO STAY RIGHT.
WE THE LIVING DO NOT EXIST TO BE TORMENTED,
TO SUFFER.
DON'T YOU FIND
THAT KIND OF LIFE TO BE MEANING-LESS ?

BUT ASCETICS
GO OUT OF THEIR WAY
WITH THEIR ORDEALS...
HURTING THEMSELVES, MAKING THEMSELVES SUFFER...
AND THAT'S HOW SOME OF THEM END THEIR LIVES.
IT'S NO DIFFERENT
FROM A DISSOLUTE LIFE OF PLEASURE
WHERE YOU DO WHAT PLEASES YOU.
BOTH ARE WASTED LIVES!
HEY, KONDANYA! HEY, BHADDIYA! WHAT'S WRONG?

I KNEW IT.

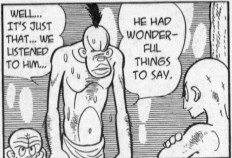

WELL... IT'S JUST THAT... WE LISTENED TO HIM...

HE HAD WONDERFUL THINGS TO SAY.

WONDERFUL? THAT DEPRAVED FRAUD HAS NOTHING TO SAY!

YOU DON'T UNDERSTAND. HIS WORDS ARE TRUTHFUL.

STOP IT! I'VE HAD ENOUGH.

HE'S SEDUCED YOU.

YOU SHOULD LISTEN TO HIM ONCE!

I'D RATHER WATCH A TALK SHOW.

291

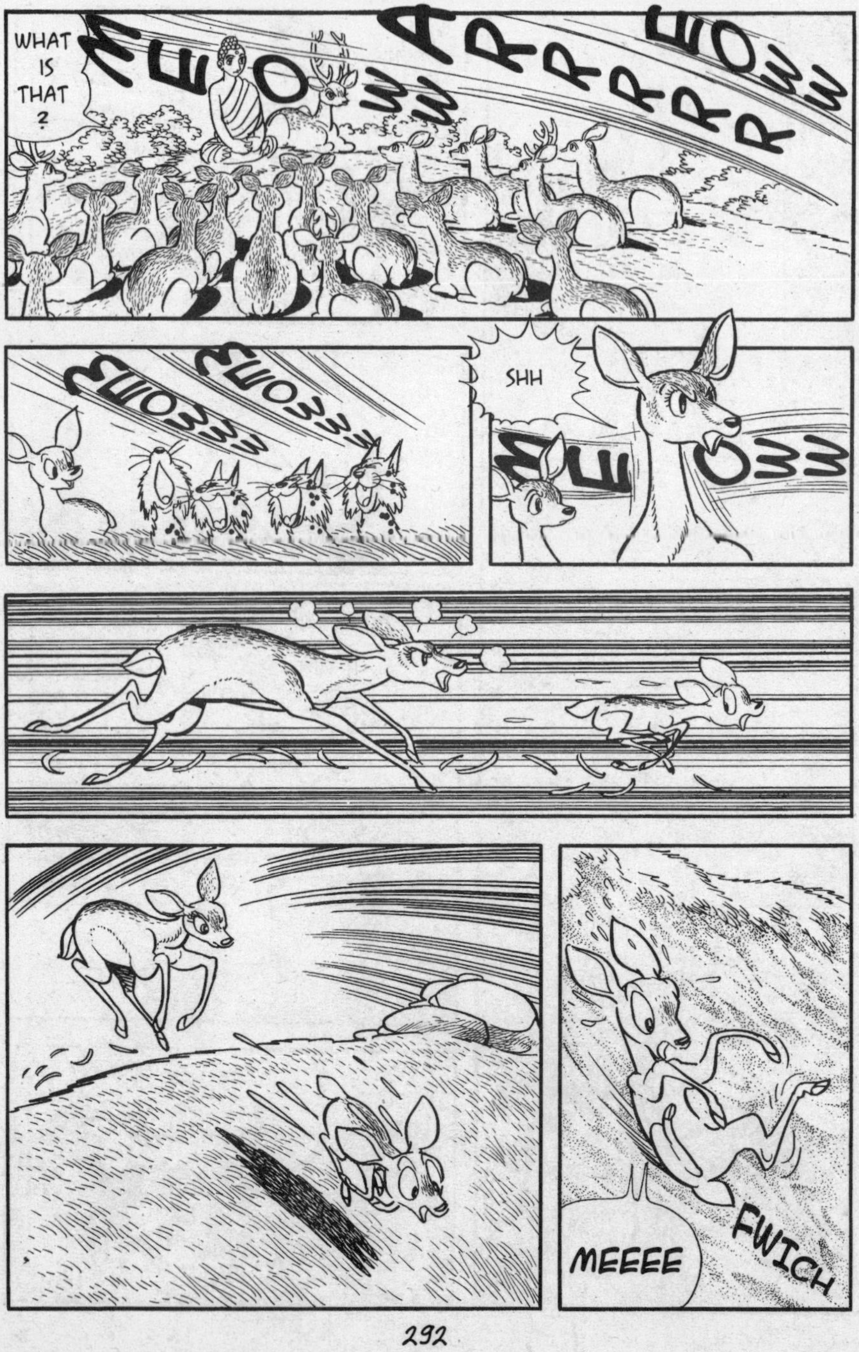
WHAT IS THAT ?
MEOW
ARRRRRW
AREOWW
MEOWW
MEOWW
SHH
MEOWW
MEEEE
FWICH

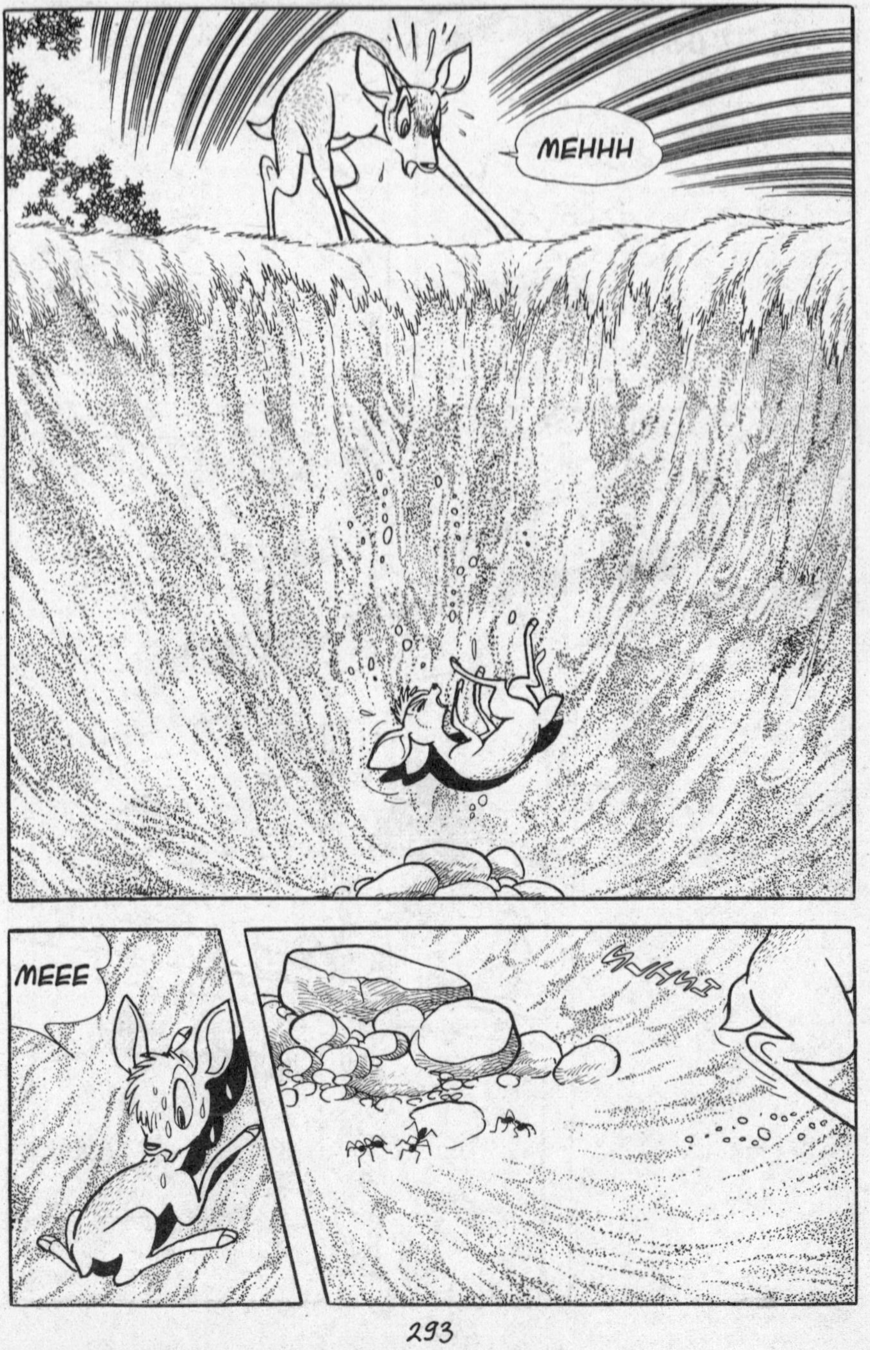
MEHHH
MEEE

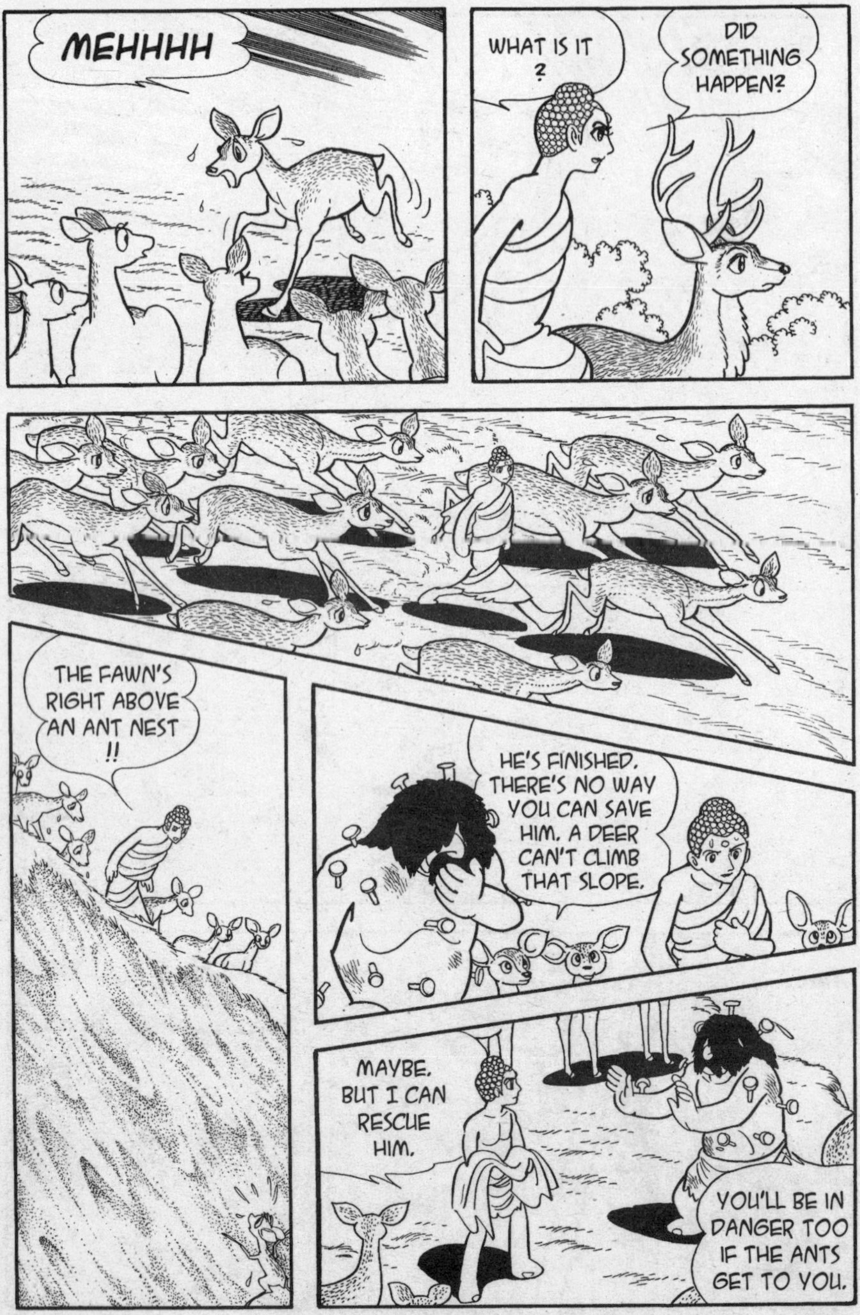
MEHHHH
WHAT IS IT ?
DID SOMETHING HAPPEN?
THE FAWN'S RIGHT ABOVE AN ANT NEST !!
HE'S FINISHED. THERE'S NO WAY YOU CAN SAVE HIM. A DEER CAN'T CLIMB THAT SLOPE.
MAYBE. BUT I CAN RESCUE HIM.
YOU'LL BE IN DANGER TOO IF THE ANTS GET TO YOU.

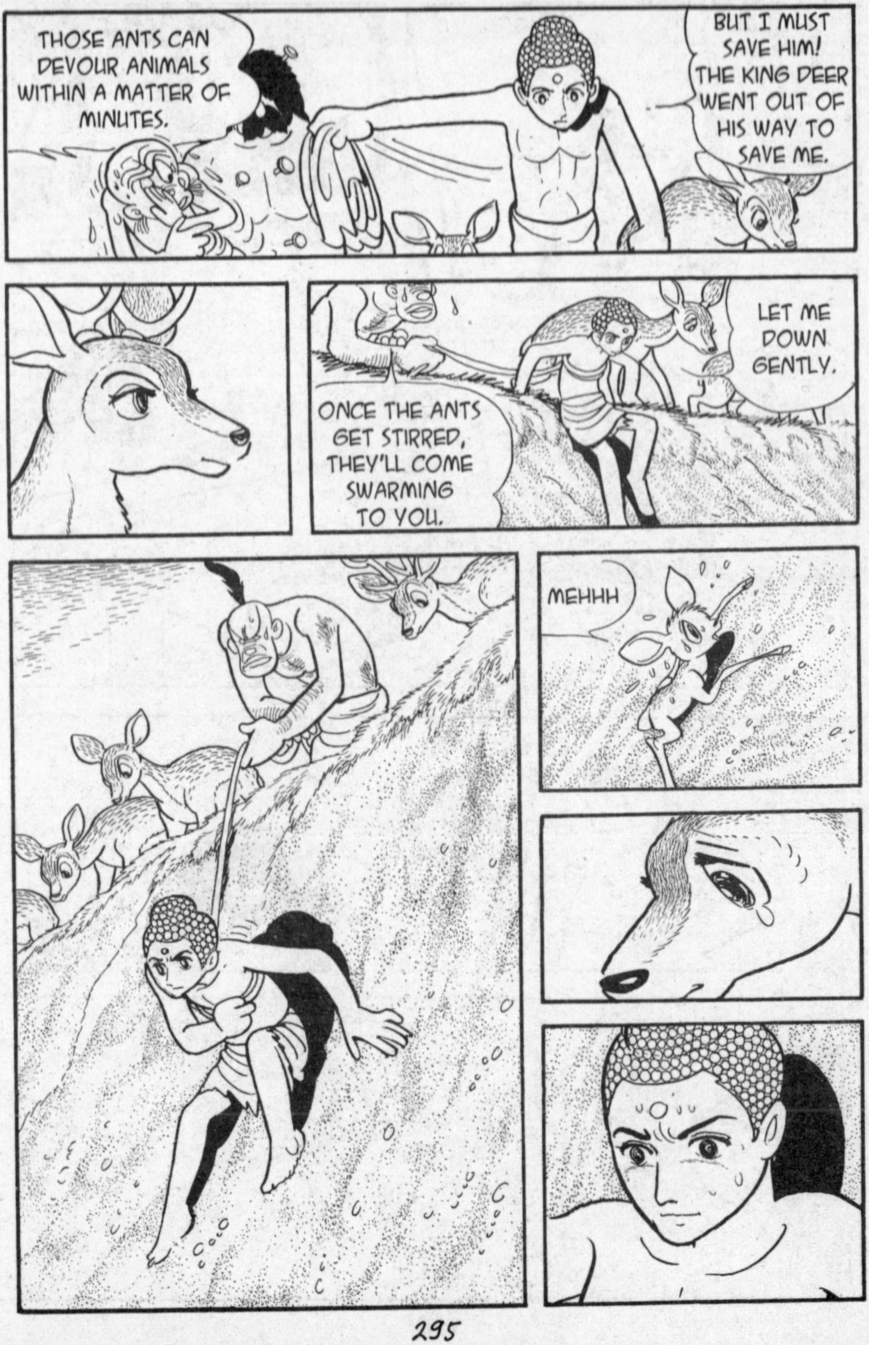
THOSE ANTS CAN DEVOUR ANIMALS WITHIN A MATTER OF MINUTES.
BUT I MUST SAVE HIM! THE KING DEER WENT OUT OF HIS WAY TO SAVE ME.
LET ME DOWN GENTLY.
ONCE THE ANTS GET STIRRED, THEY'LL COME SWARMING TO YOU.
MEHHH

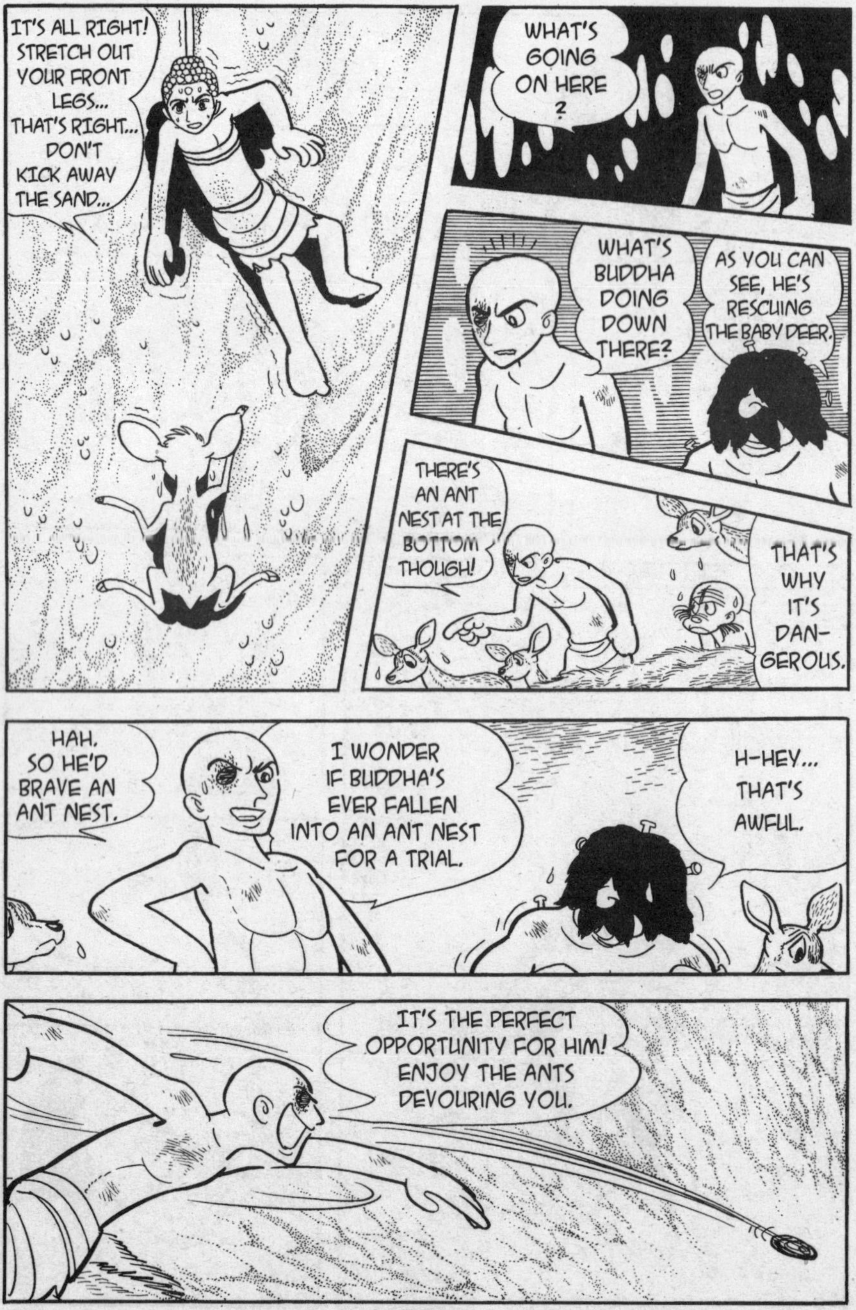

IT'S ALL RIGHT! STRETCH OUT YOUR FRONT LEGS... THAT'S RIGHT... DON'T KICK AWAY THE SAND...
WHAT'S GOING ON HERE ?
WHAT'S BUDDHA DOING DOWN THERE?
AS YOU CAN SEE, HE'S RESCUING THE BABY DEER.
THERE'S AN ANT NEST AT THE BOTTOM THOUGH!
THAT'S WHY IT'S DAN-GEROUS.
HAH. SO HE'D BRAVE AN ANT NEST.
I WONDER IF BUDDHA'S EVER FALLEN INTO AN ANT NEST FOR A TRIAL.
H-HEY... THAT'S AWFUL.
IT'S THE PERFECT OPPORTUNITY FOR HIM! ENJOY THE ANTS DEVOURING YOU.

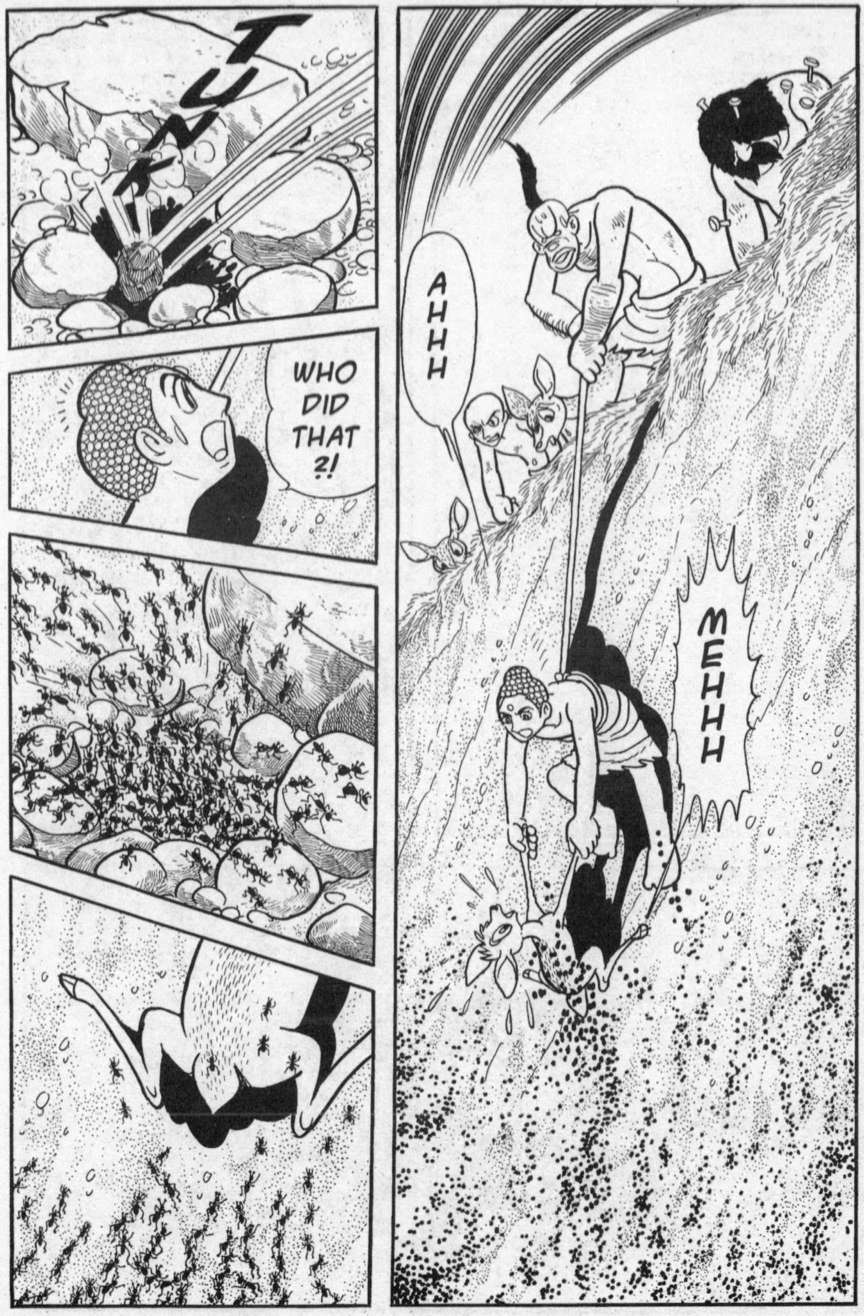
TUNK
WHO DID THAT ?!
AHHH
MEHHH

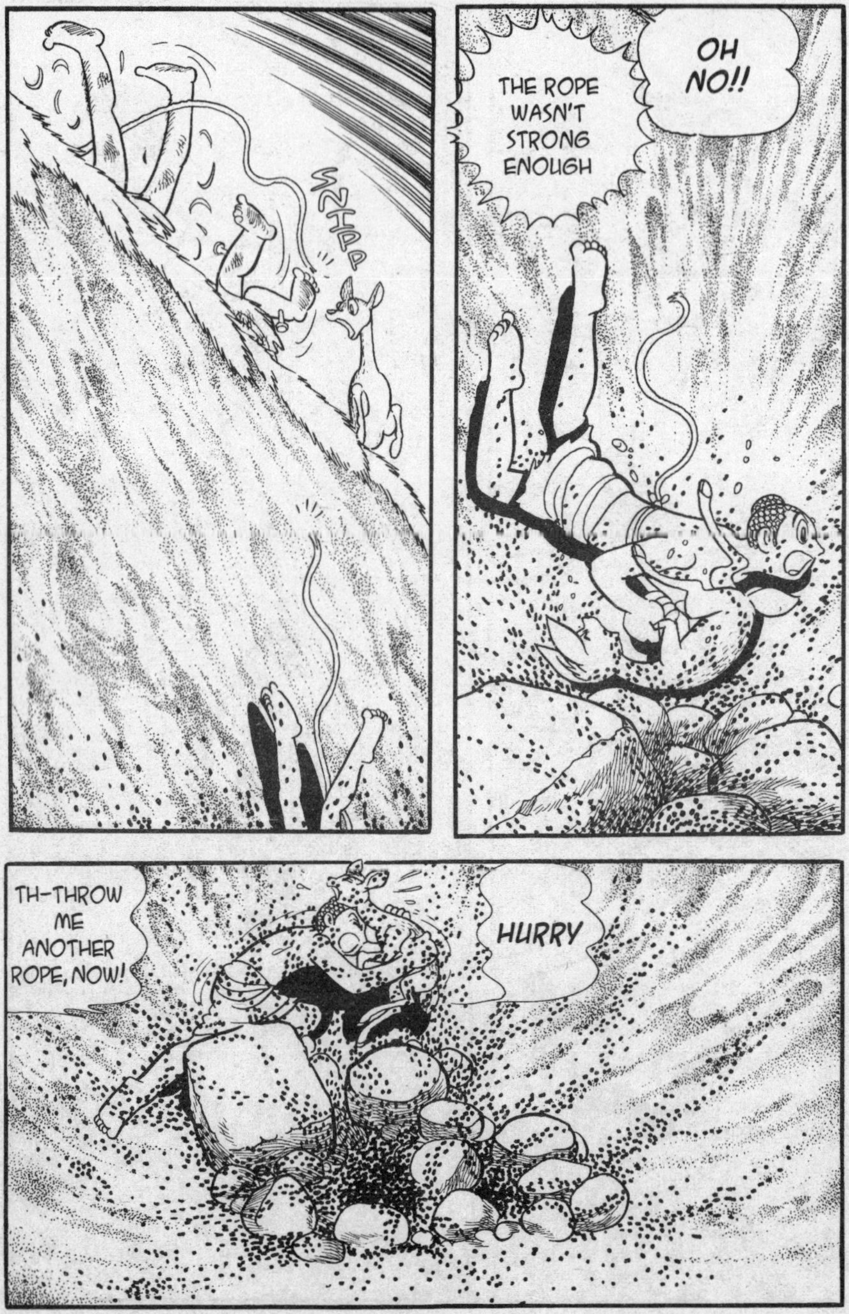
SNIPP
OH NO!!
THE ROPE WASN'T STRONG ENOUGH
HURRY
TH-THROW ME ANOTHER ROPE, NOW!

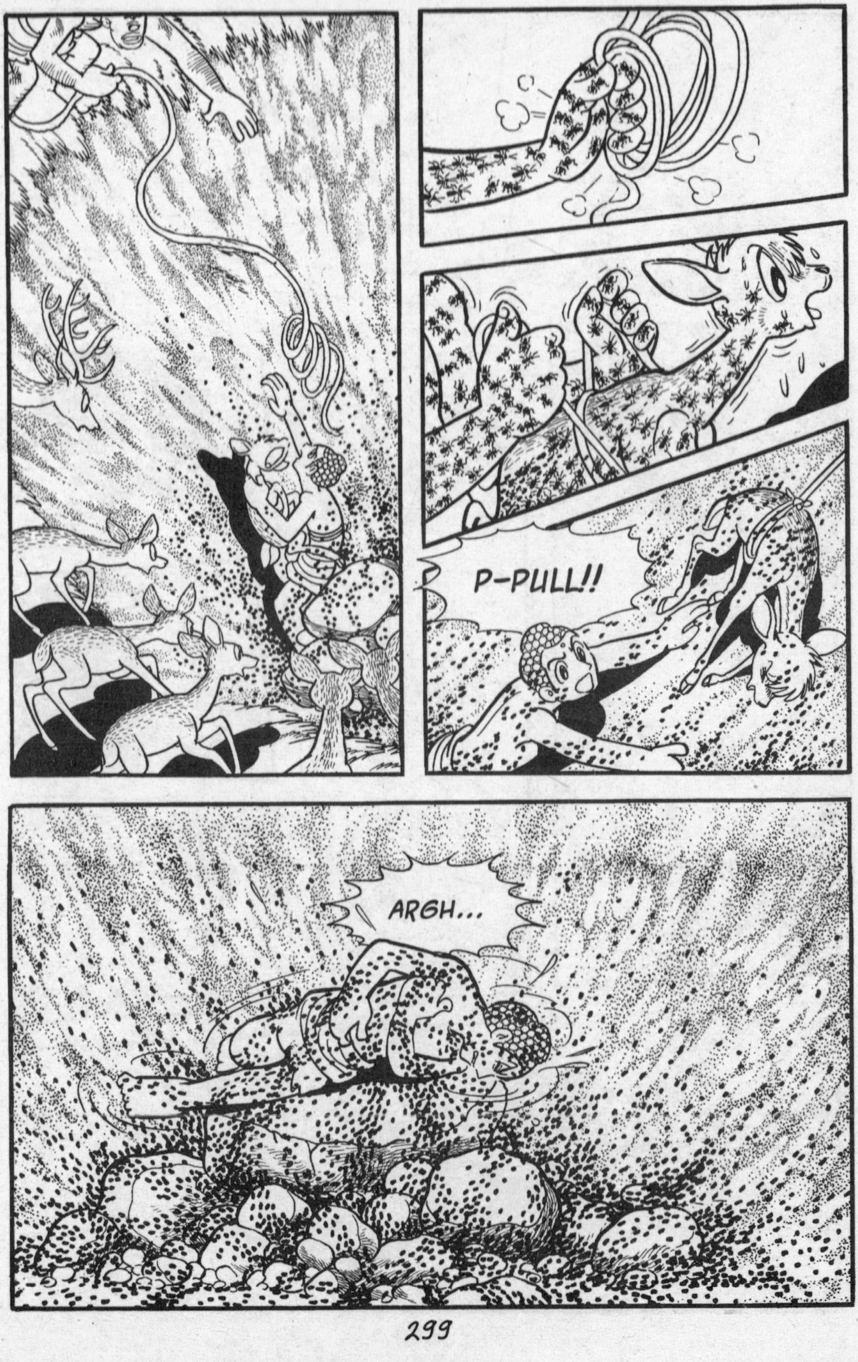
P-PULL!!
ARGH...

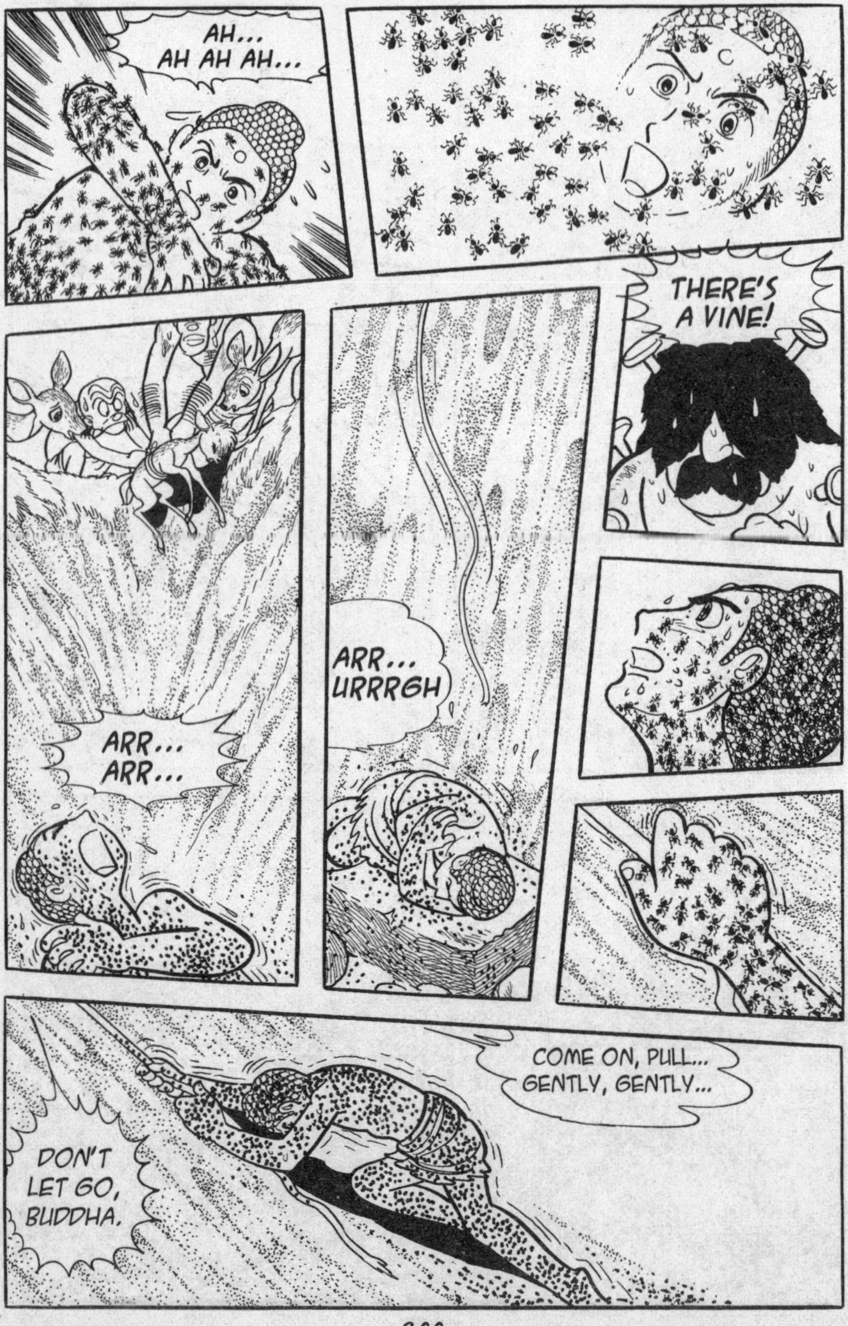
AH... AH AH AH...
THERE'S A VINE!
ARR... ARR...
ARR... URRRGH
COME ON, PULL... GENTLY, GENTLY...
DON'T LET GO, BUDDHA.

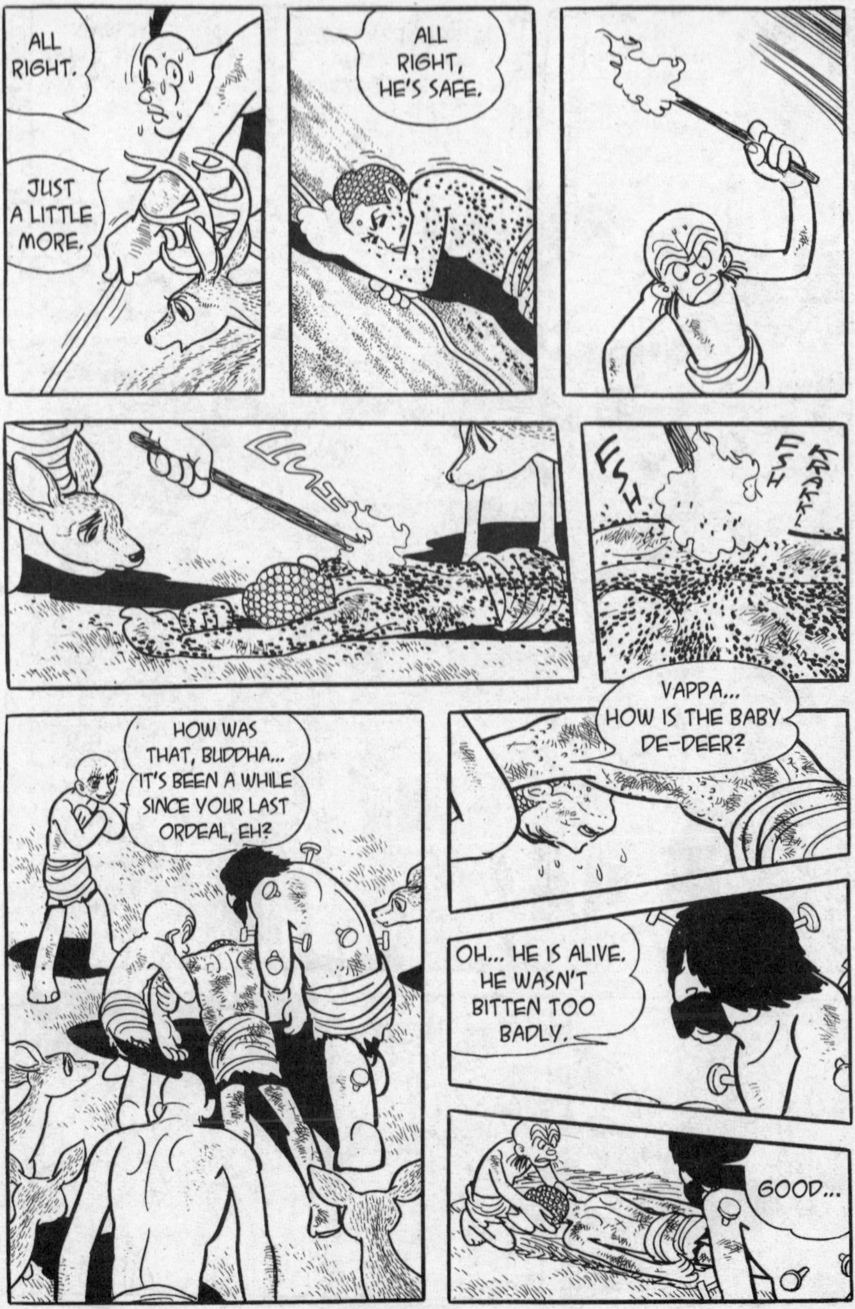
ALL RIGHT.
JUST A LITTLE MORE.
ALL RIGHT, HE'S SAFE.
FSH
FSH
KRAKKL
HOW WAS THAT, BUDDHA... IT'S BEEN A WHILE SINCE YOUR LAST ORDEAL, EH?
VAPPA... HOW IS THE BABY DE-DEER?
OH... HE IS ALIVE. HE WASN'T BITTEN TOO BADLY.
GOOD...

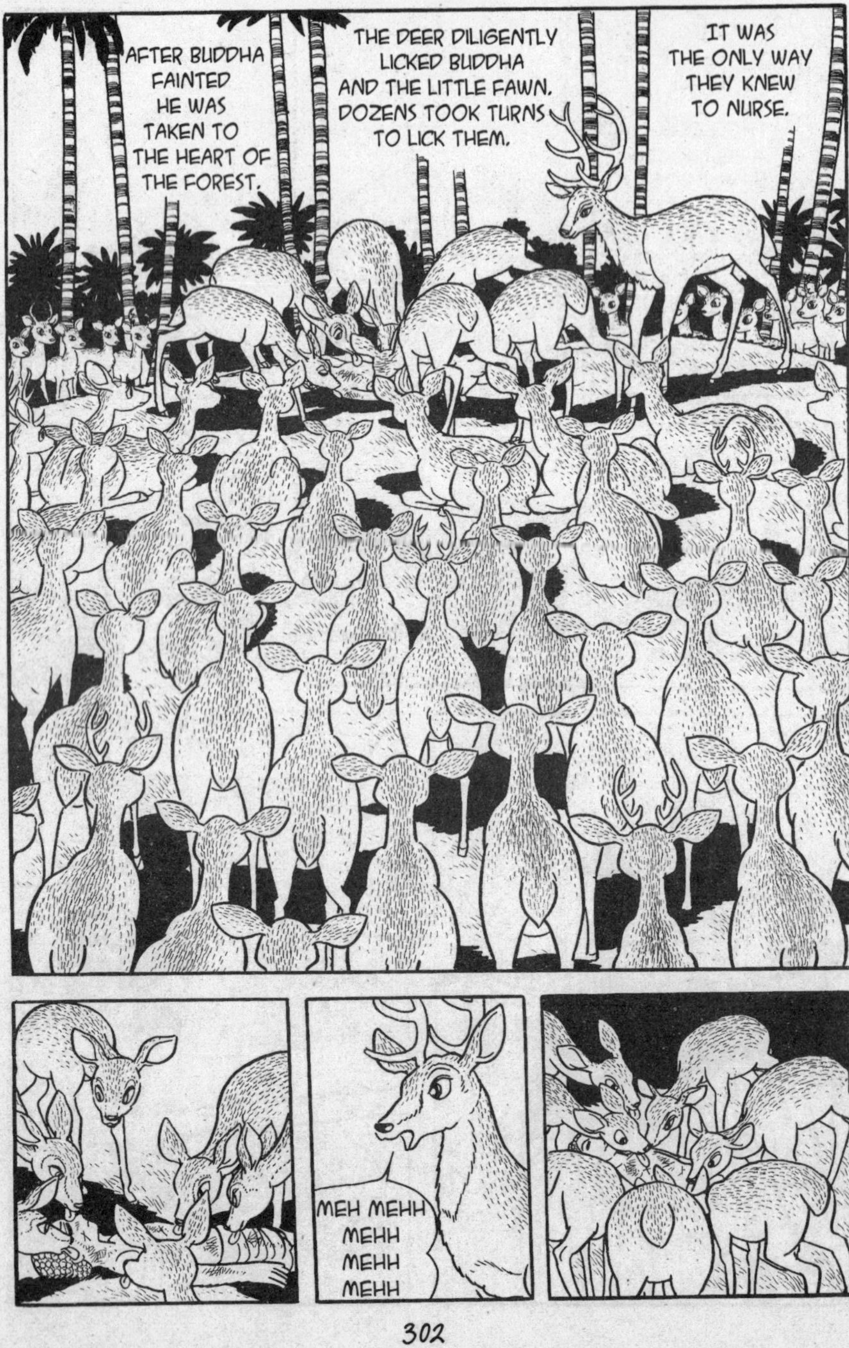
AFTER BUDDHA FAINTED HE WAS TAKEN TO THE HEART OF THE FOREST.
THE DEER DILIGENTLY LICKED BUDDHA AND THE LITTLE FAWN. DOZENS TOOK TURNS TO LICK THEM.
IT WAS THE ONLY WAY THEY KNEW TO NURSE.
MEH MEHH MEHH MEHH MEHH

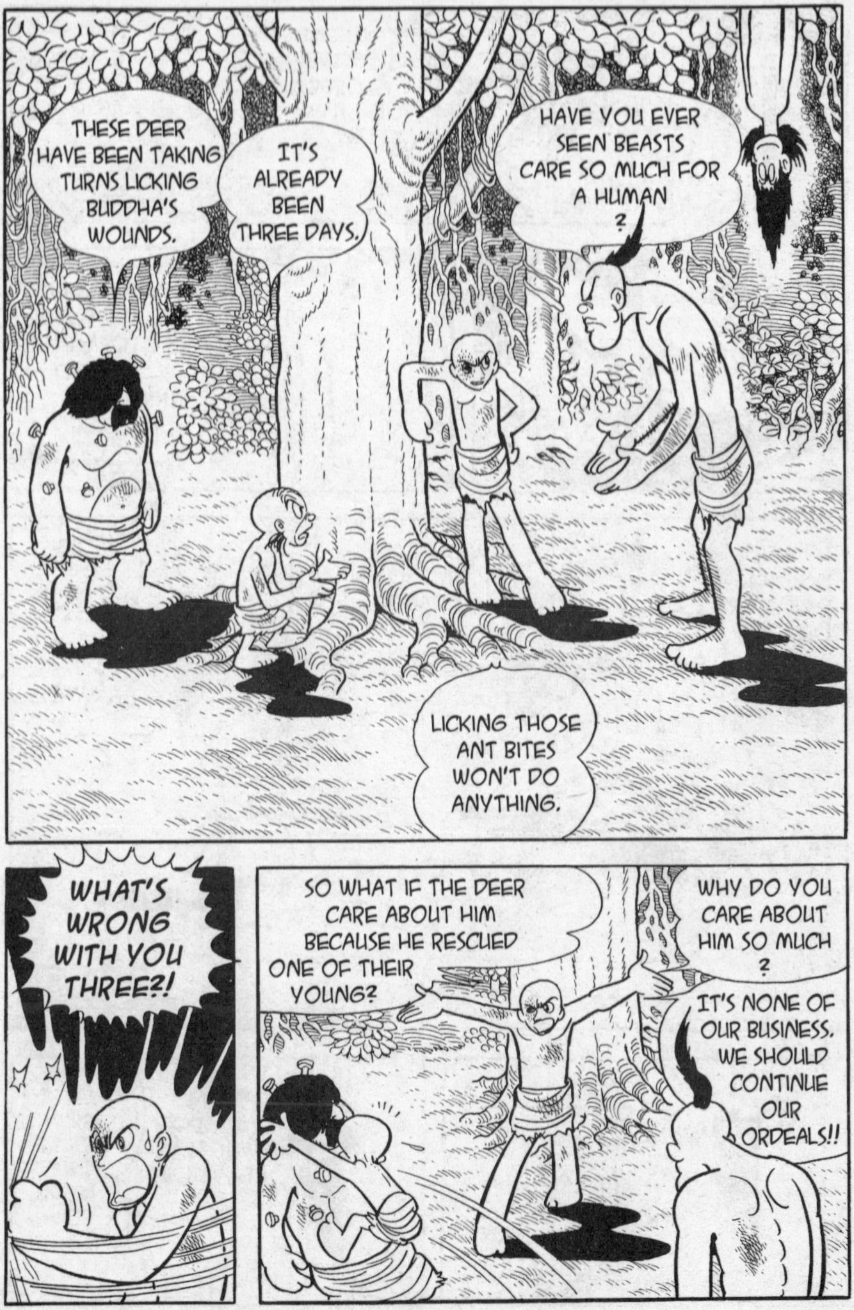
THESE DEER HAVE BEEN TAKING TURNS LICKING BUDDHA'S WOUNDS.
IT'S ALREADY BEEN THREE DAYS.
HAVE YOU EVER SEEN BEASTS CARE SO MUCH FOR A HUMAN?
LICKING THOSE ANT BITES WON'T DO ANYTHING.
WHAT'S WRONG WITH YOU THREE?!
SO WHAT IF THE DEER CARE ABOUT HIM BECAUSE HE RESCUED ONE OF THEIR YOUNG?
WHY DO YOU CARE ABOUT HIM SO MUCH?
IT'S NONE OF OUR BUSINESS. WE SHOULD CONTINUE OUR ORDEALS!!

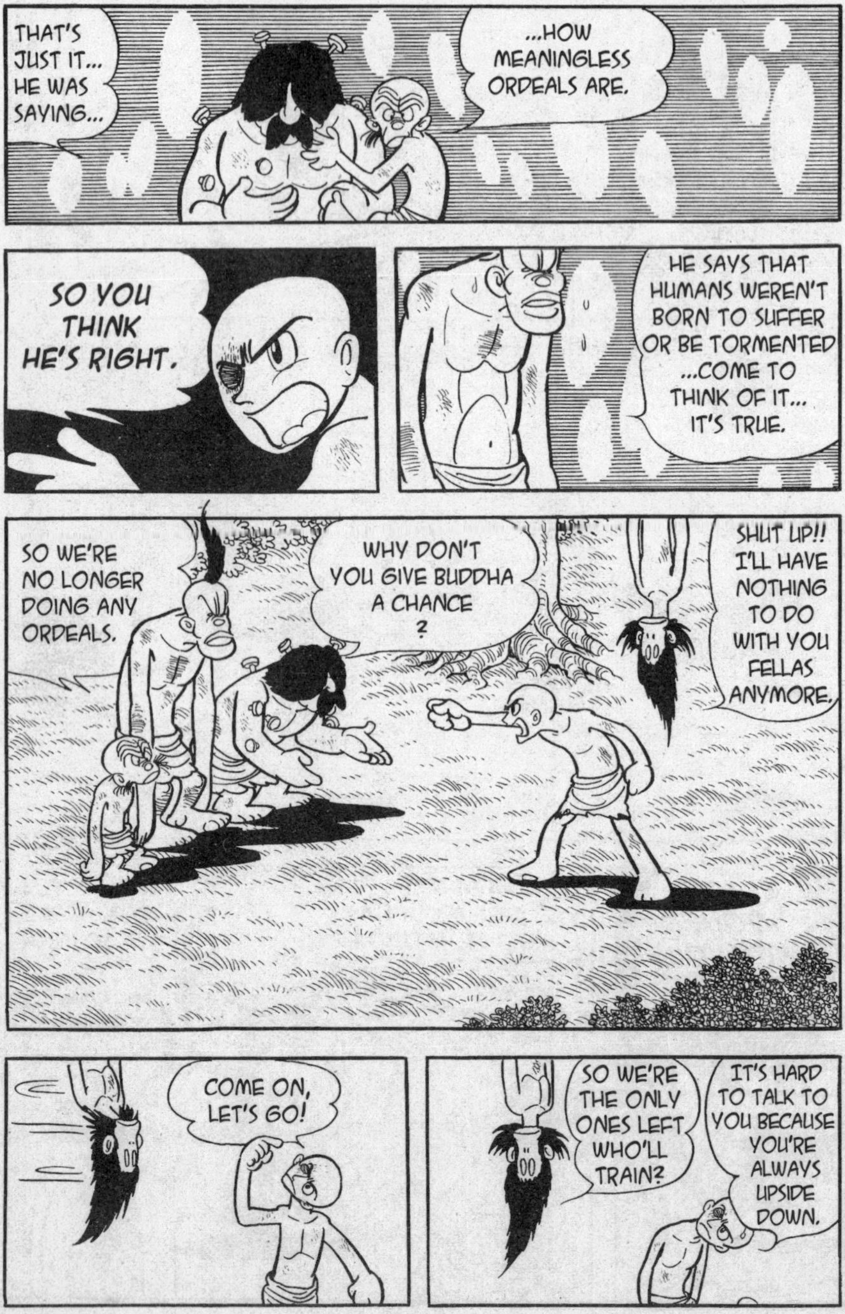
THAT'S JUST IT... HE WAS SAYING...
...HOW MEANINGLESS ORDEALS ARE.
SO YOU THINK HE'S RIGHT.
HE SAYS THAT HUMANS WEREN'T BORN TO SUFFER OR BE TORMENTED ...COME TO THINK OF IT... IT'S TRUE.
SO WE'RE NO LONGER DOING ANY ORDEALS.
WHY DON'T YOU GIVE BUDDHA A CHANCE ?
SHUT UP!! I'LL HAVE NOTHING TO DO WITH YOU FELLAS ANYMORE.
COME ON, LET'S GO!
SO WE'RE THE ONLY ONES LEFT WHO'LL TRAIN?
IT'S HARD TO TALK TO YOU BECAUSE YOU'RE ALWAYS UPSIDE DOWN.

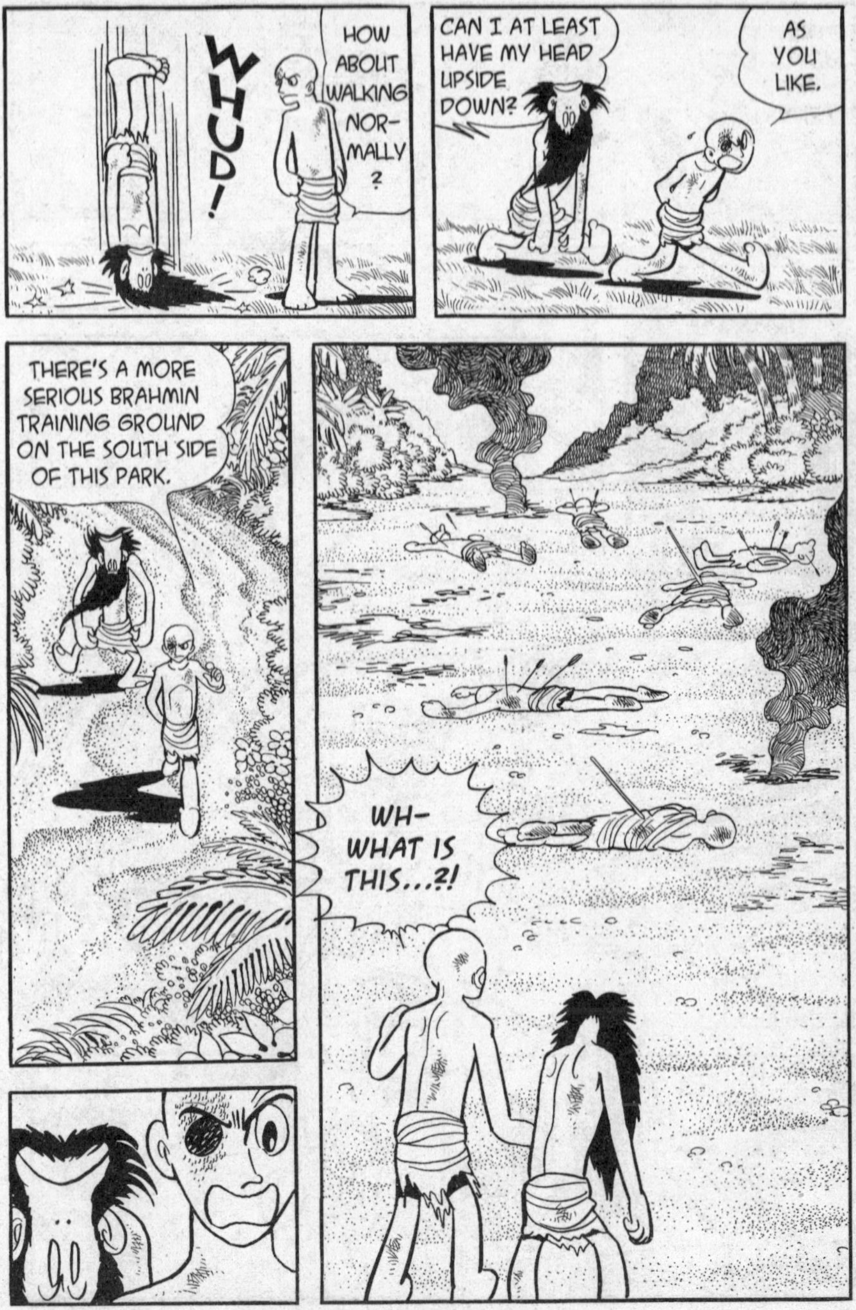
WHUD!
HOW ABOUT WALKING NOR-MALLY?
CAN I AT LEAST HAVE MY HEAD UPSIDE DOWN?
AS YOU LIKE.
THERE'S A MORE SERIOUS BRAHMIN TRAINING GROUND ON THE SOUTH SIDE OF THIS PARK.
WH-WHAT IS THIS...?!

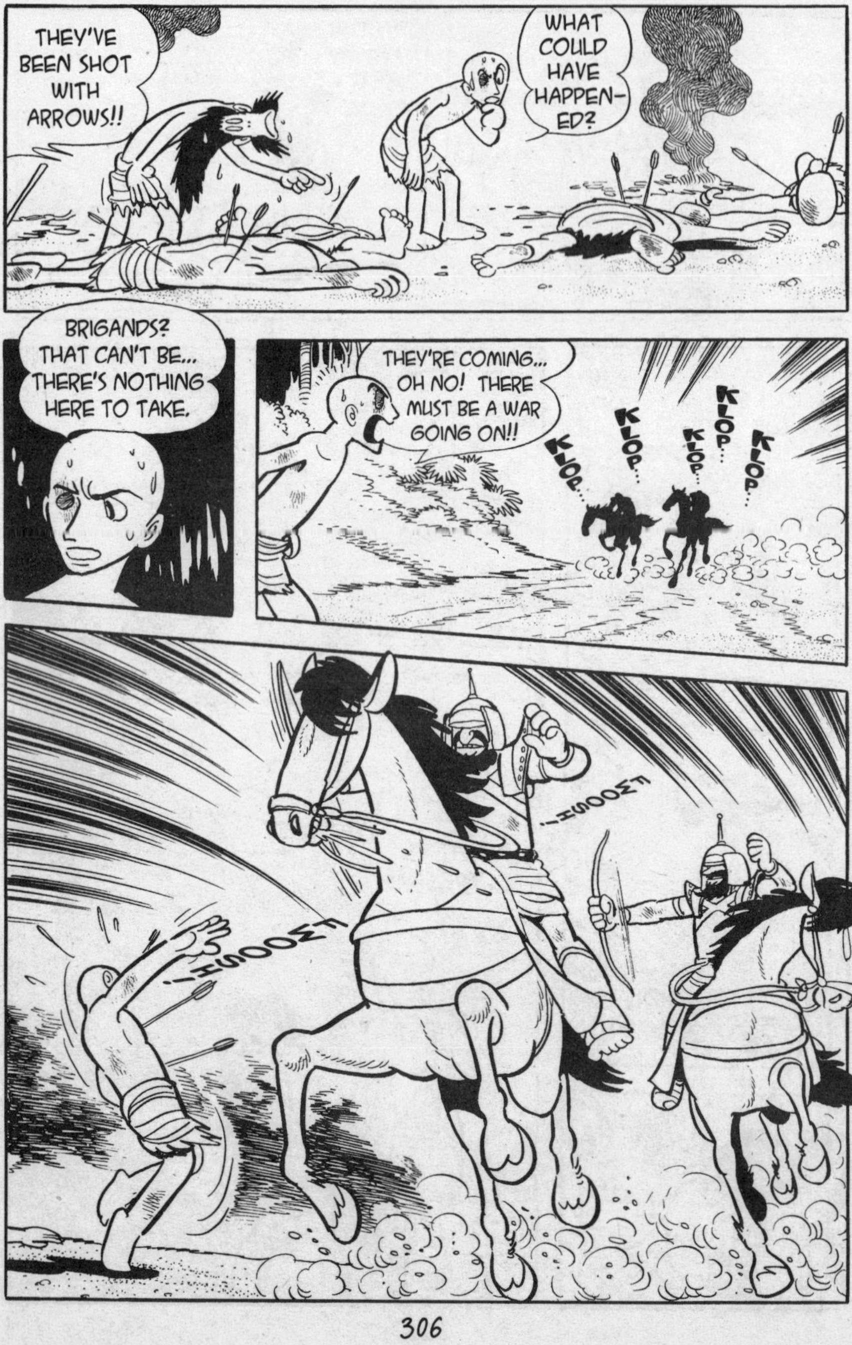

THEY'VE BEEN SHOT WITH ARROWS!!
WHAT COULD HAVE HAPPEN-ED?
BRIGANDS? THAT CAN'T BE... THERE'S NOTHING HERE TO TAKE.
THEY'RE COMING... OH NO! THERE MUST BE A WAR GOING ON!!
KLOP...
KLOP...
KLOP...
KLOP...
FWOOSH!
FWOOSH!

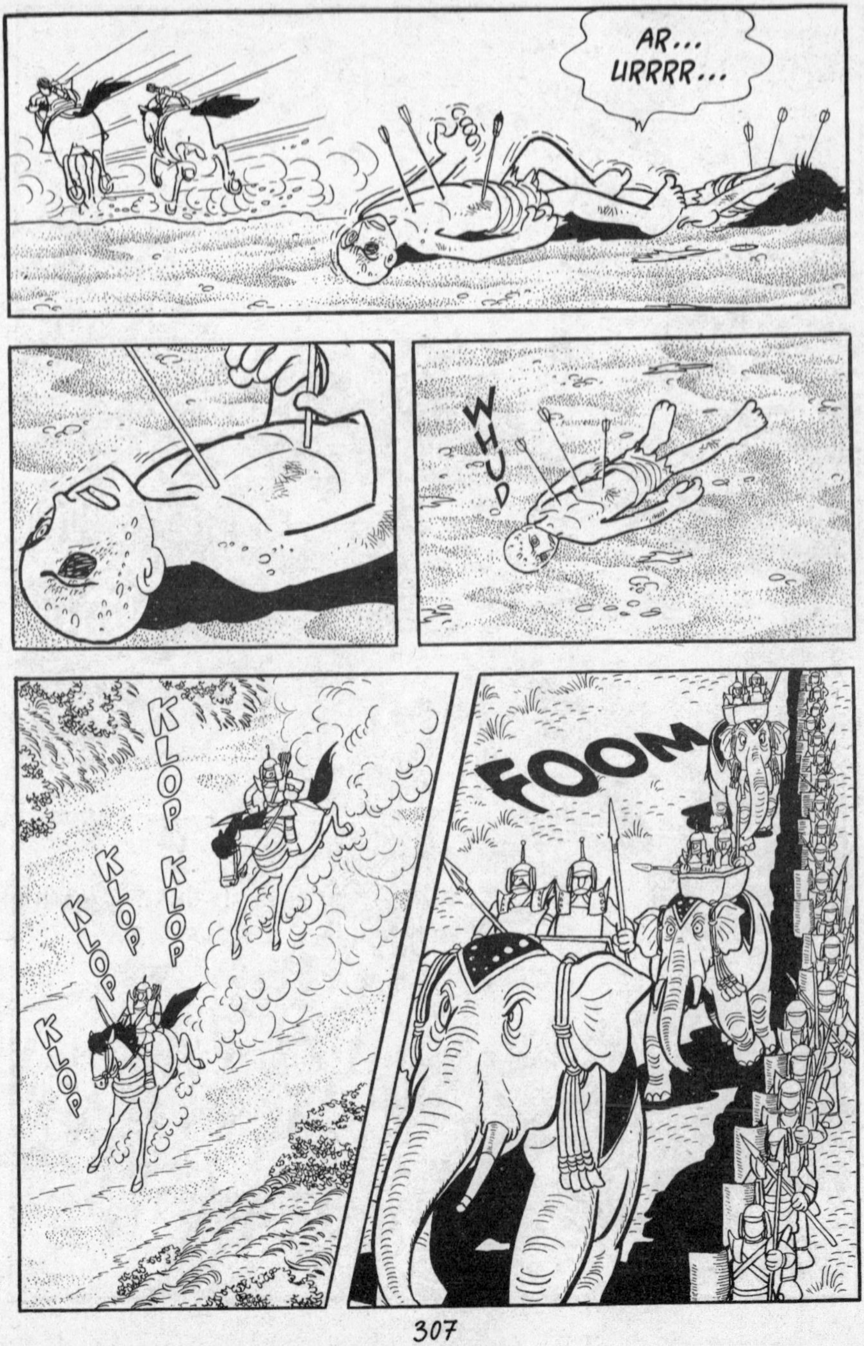
AR...
URRRR...
WHUD
KLOP KLOP
KLOP
KLOP KLOP
KLOP
KLOP
FOOM

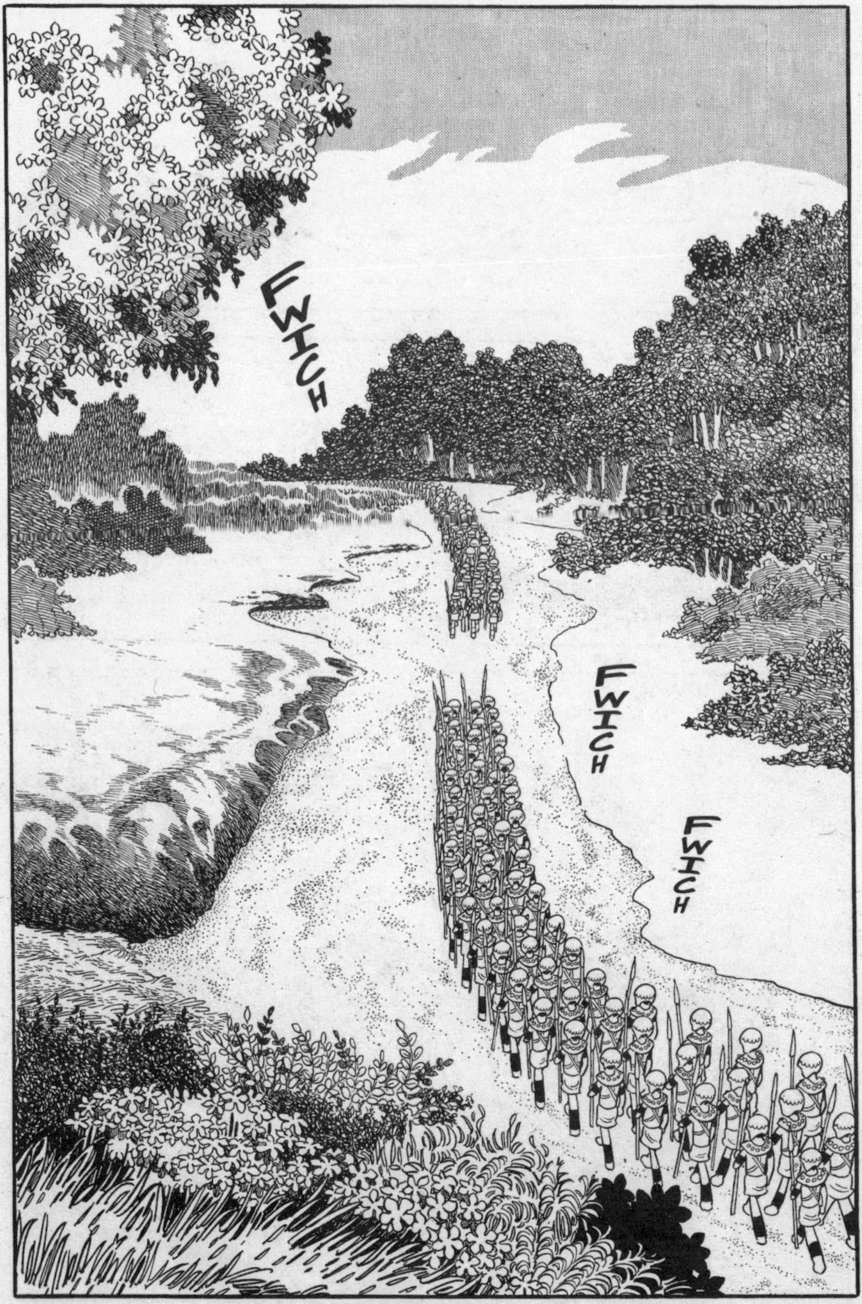
FWICH
FWICH
FWICH

CHAPTER SEVEN

FOOL'S WAY

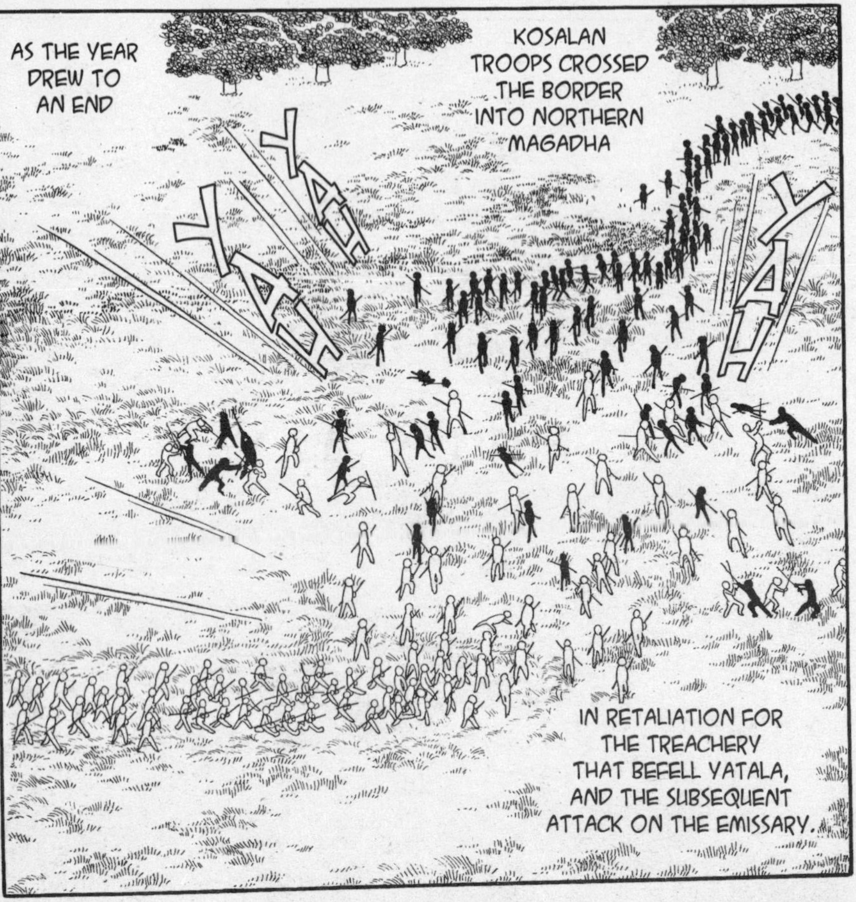
AS THE YEAR DREW TO AN END
KOSALAN TROOPS CROSSED THE BORDER INTO NORTHERN MAGADHA
YAAH
YAAH
YAAH
IN RETALIATION FOR THE TREACHERY THAT BEFELL YATALA, AND THE SUBSEQUENT ATTACK ON THE EMISSARY.

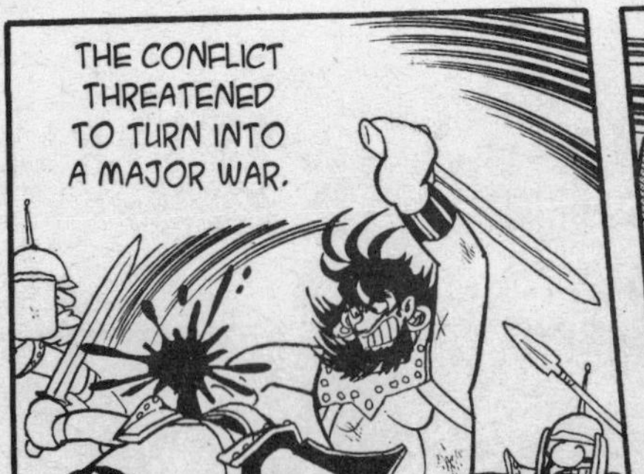
THE CONFLICT THREATENED TO TURN INTO A MAJOR WAR.

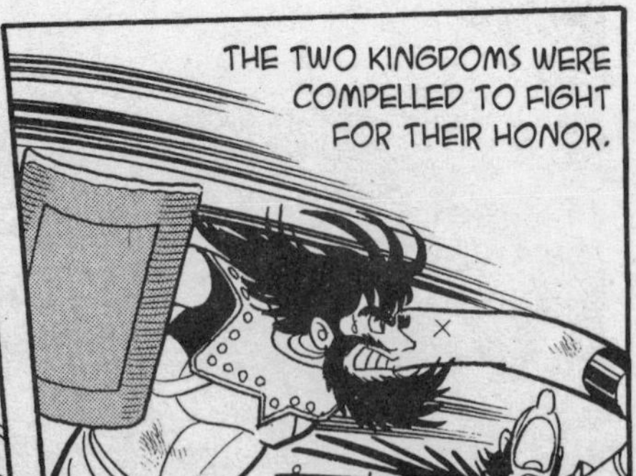
THE TWO KINGDOMS WERE COMPELLED TO FIGHT FOR THEIR HONOR.

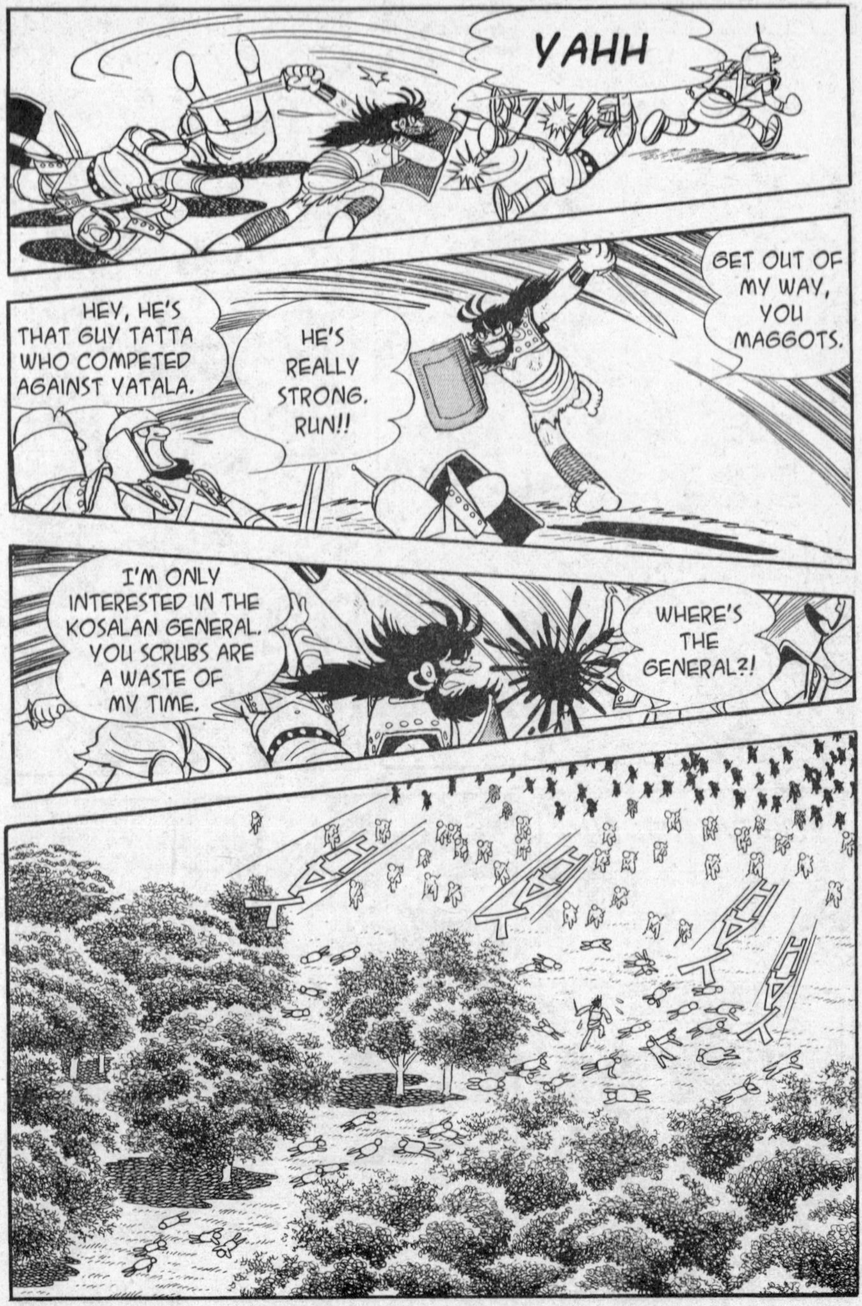
YAHH
GET OUT OF MY WAY, YOU MAGGOTS.
HEY, HE'S THAT GUY TATTA WHO COMPETED AGAINST YATALA.
HE'S REALLY STRONG. RUN!!
I'M ONLY INTERESTED IN THE KOSALAN GENERAL. YOU SCRUBS ARE A WASTE OF MY TIME.
WHERE'S THE GENERAL?!

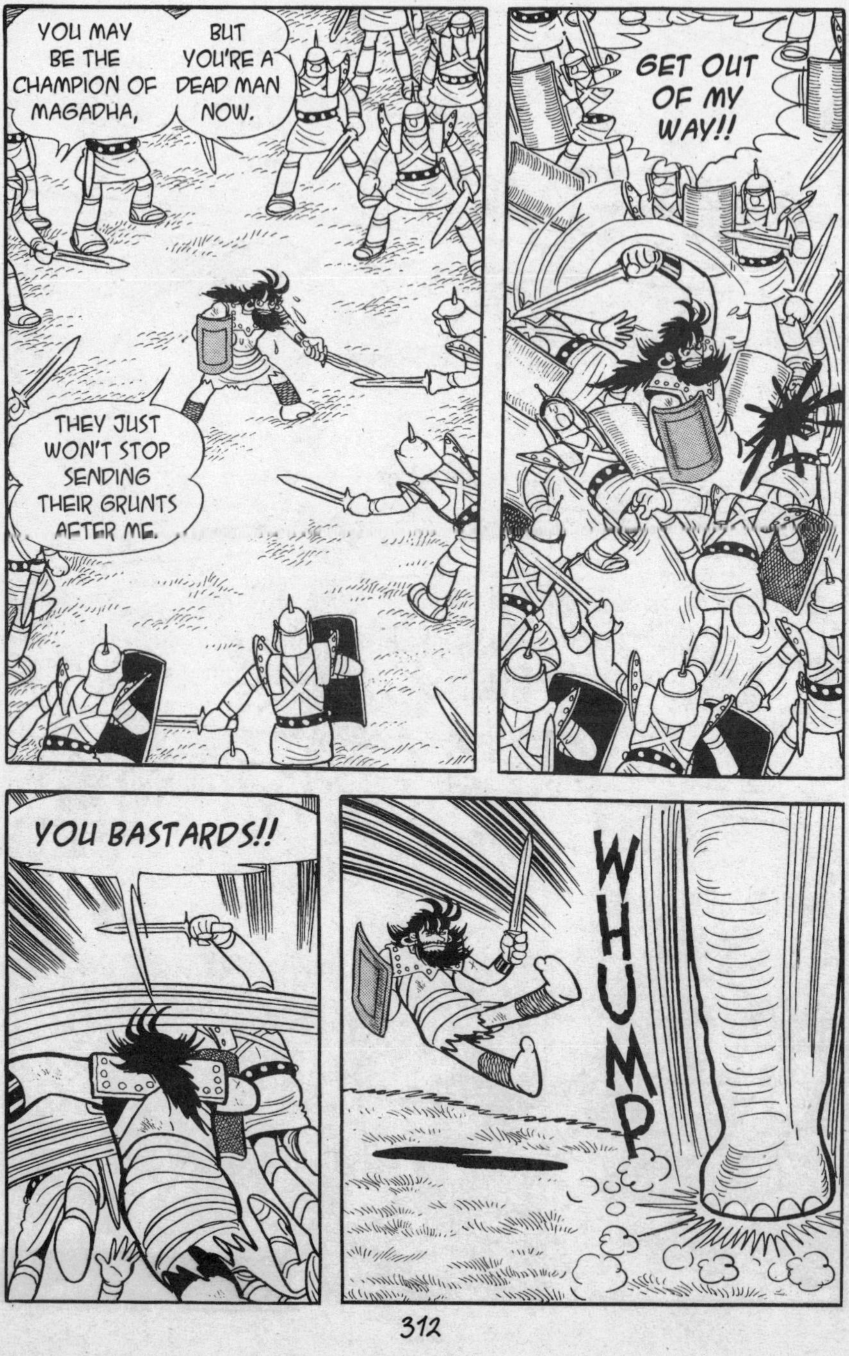
YOU MAY BE THE CHAMPION OF MAGADHA,
BUT YOU'RE A DEAD MAN NOW.
THEY JUST WON'T STOP SENDING THEIR GRUNTS AFTER ME.
GET OUT OF MY WAY!!
YOU BASTARDS!!
WHUMP

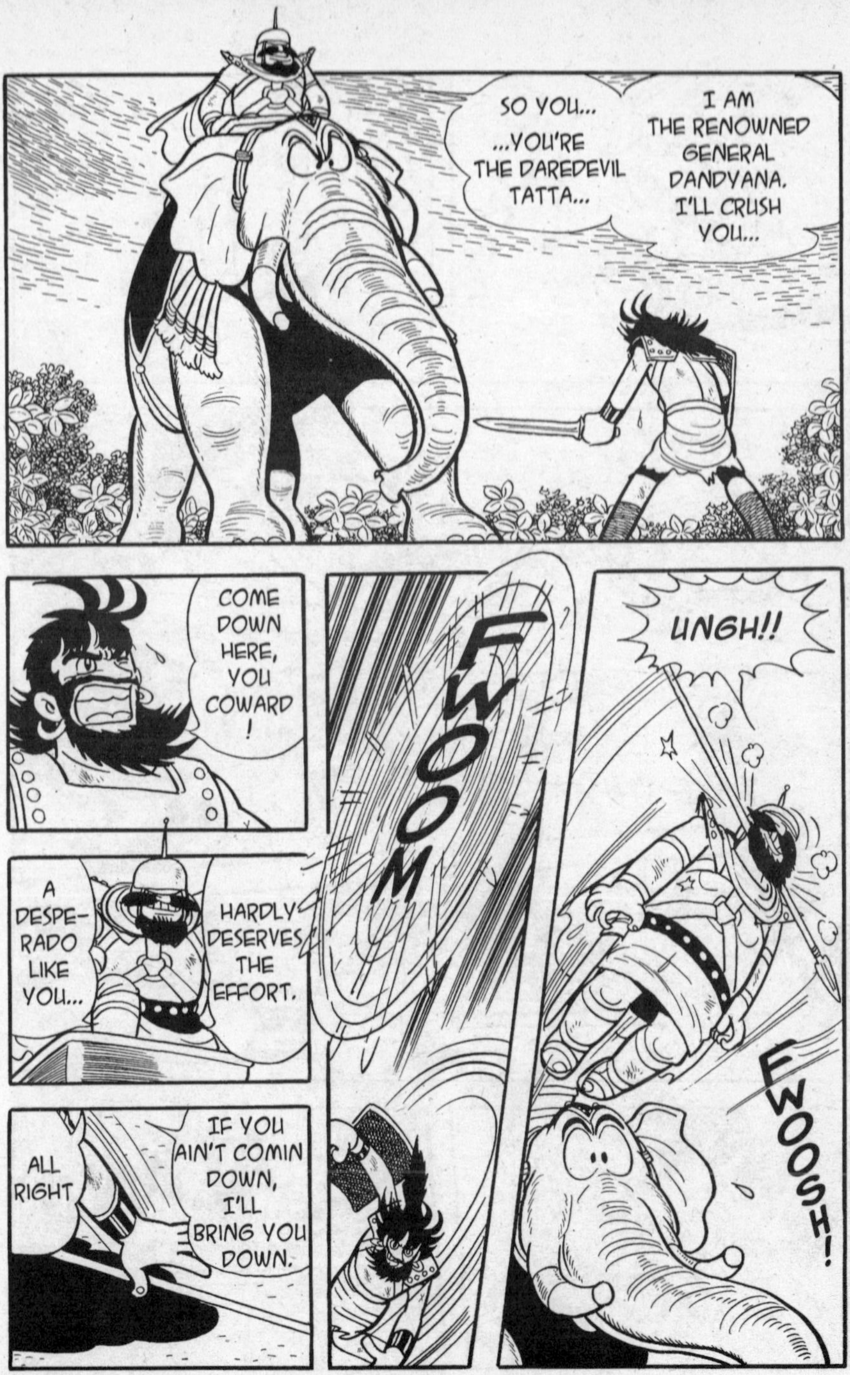
SO YOU... ...YOU'RE THE DAREDEVIL TATTA...
I AM THE RENOWNED GENERAL DANDYANA. I'LL CRUSH YOU...
COME DOWN HERE, YOU COWARD!
A DESPE-RADO LIKE YOU...
HARDLY DESERVES THE EFFORT.
ALL RIGHT
IF YOU AIN'T COMIN DOWN, I'LL BRING YOU DOWN.
FWOOOM
UNGH!!
FWOOSH!

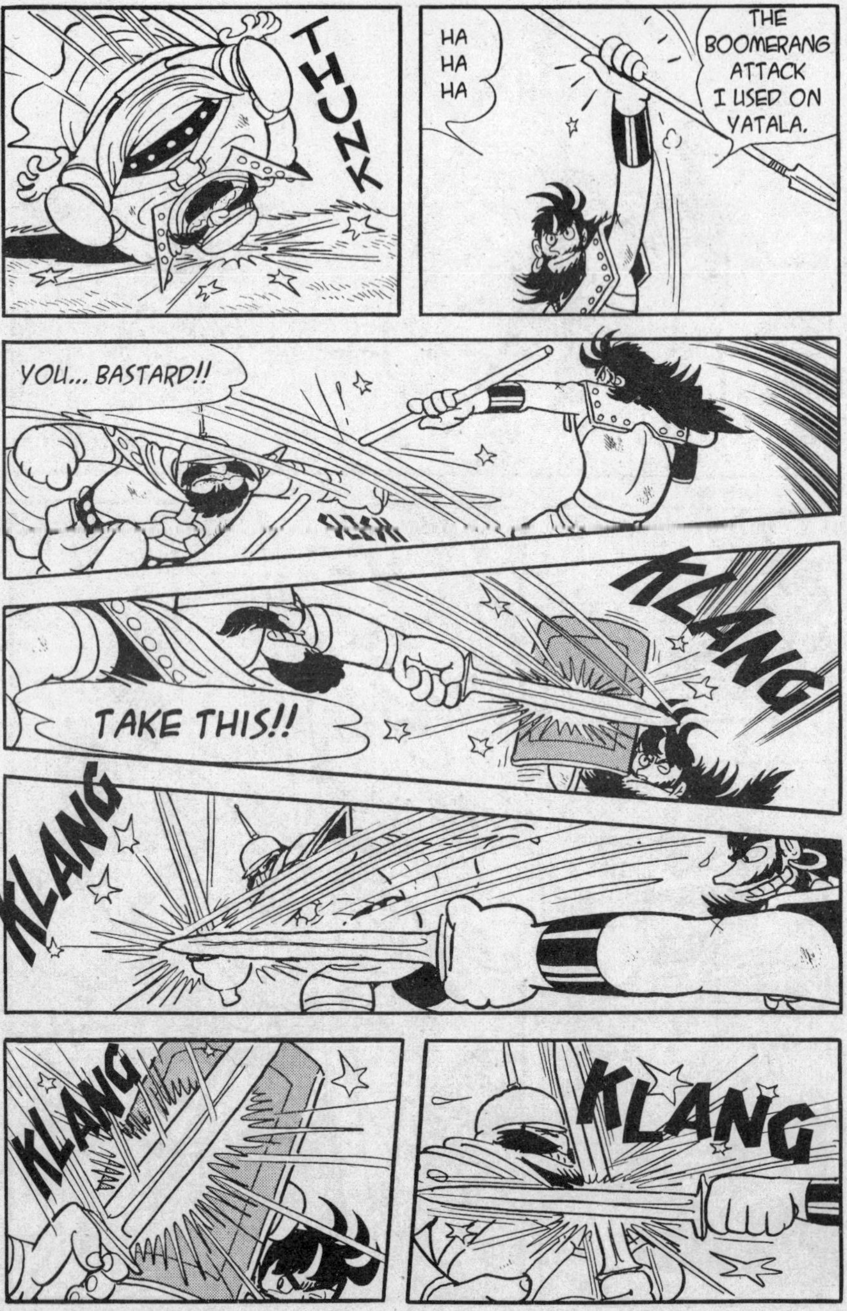
THUNK
HA HA HA
THE BOOMERANG ATTACK I USED ON YATALA.
YOU... BASTARD!!
KLANG
TAKE THIS!!
KLANG
KLANG
KLANG

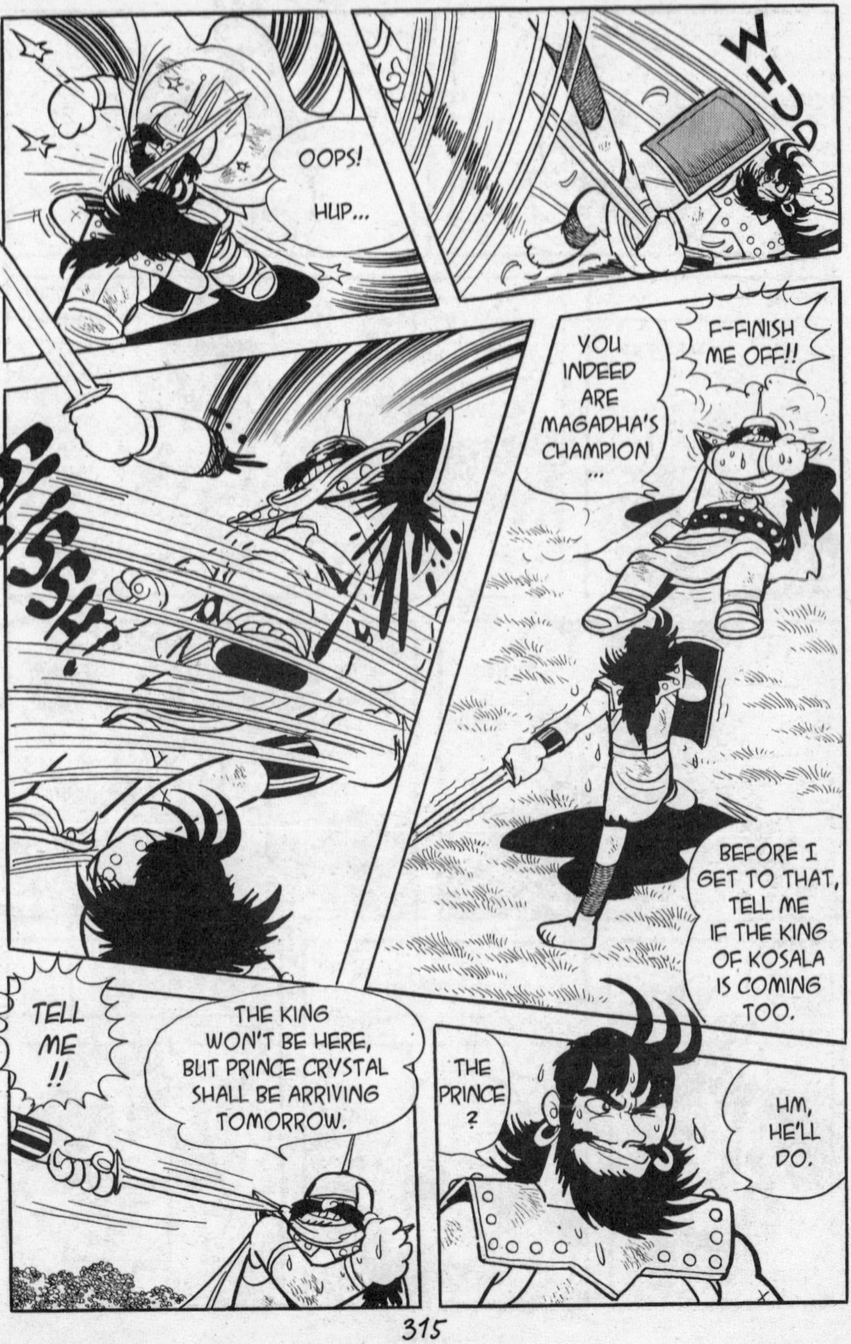
OOPS!
HUP...
WHUD
SLISSH!!
YOU INDEED ARE MAGADHA'S CHAMPION ...
F-FINISH ME OFF!!
BEFORE I GET TO THAT, TELL ME IF THE KING OF KOSALA IS COMING TOO.
TELL ME !!
THE KING WON'T BE HERE, BUT PRINCE CRYSTAL SHALL BE ARRIVING TOMORROW.
THE PRINCE ?
HM, HE'LL DO.

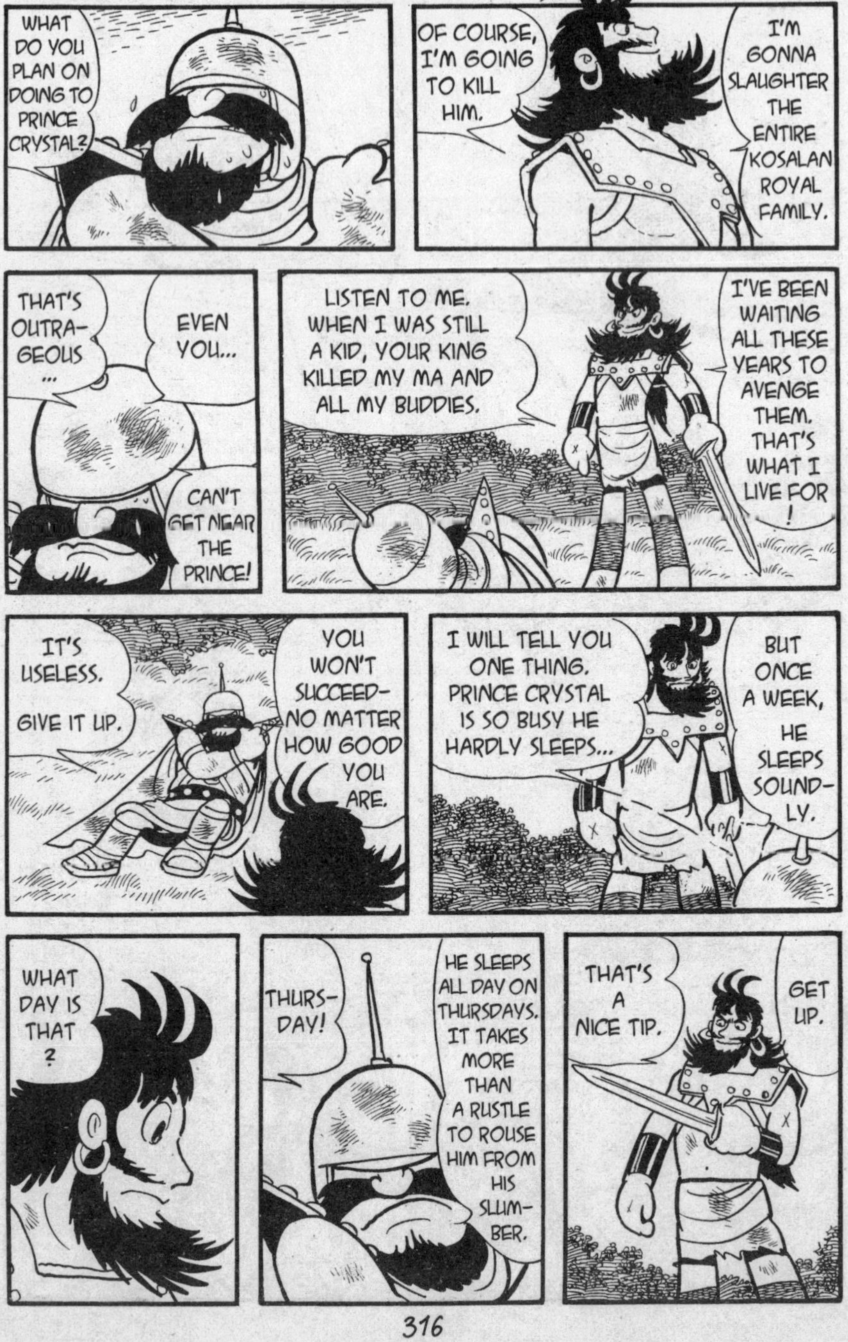
WHAT DO YOU PLAN ON DOING TO PRINCE CRYSTAL?
OF COURSE, I'M GOING TO KILL HIM.
I'M GONNA SLAUGHTER THE ENTIRE KOSALAN ROYAL FAMILY.
THAT'S OUTRAGEOUS ...
EVEN YOU...
CAN'T GET NEAR THE PRINCE!
LISTEN TO ME. WHEN I WAS STILL A KID, YOUR KING KILLED MY MA AND ALL MY BUDDIES.
I'VE BEEN WAITING ALL THESE YEARS TO AVENGE THEM. THAT'S WHAT I LIVE FOR!
IT'S USELESS.
GIVE IT UP.
YOU WON'T SUCCEED-NO MATTER HOW GOOD YOU ARE.
I WILL TELL YOU ONE THING. PRINCE CRYSTAL IS SO BUSY HE HARDLY SLEEPS...
BUT ONCE A WEEK,
HE SLEEPS SOUND-LY.
WHAT DAY IS THAT?
THURS-DAY!
HE SLEEPS ALL DAY ON THURSDAYS. IT TAKES MORE THAN A RUSTLE TO ROUSE HIM FROM HIS SLUM-BER.
THAT'S A NICE TIP.
GET UP.

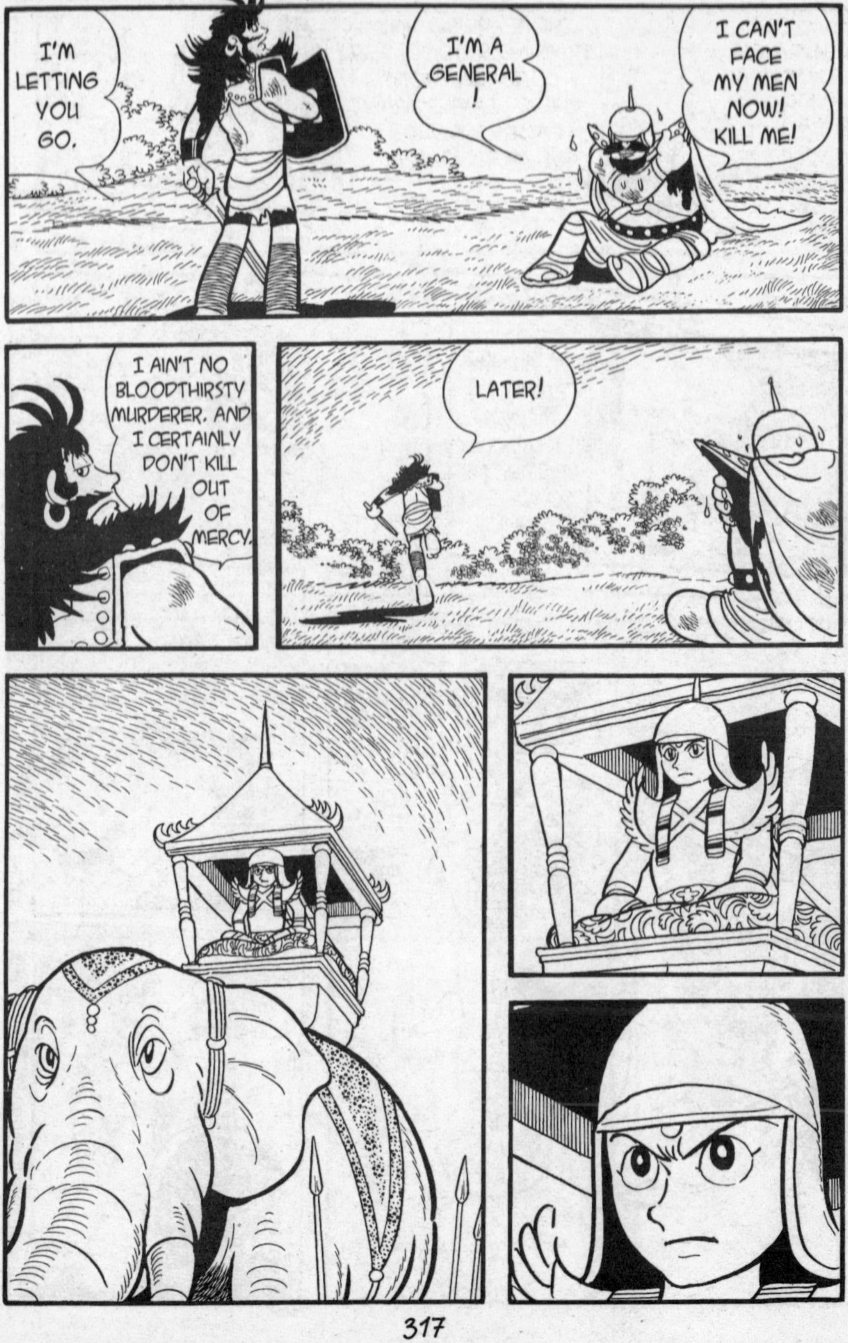
I'M LETTING YOU GO.
I'M A GENERAL!
I CAN'T FACE MY MEN NOW! KILL ME!
I AIN'T NO BLOODTHIRSTY MURDERER. AND I CERTAINLY DON'T KILL OUT OF MERCY.
LATER!

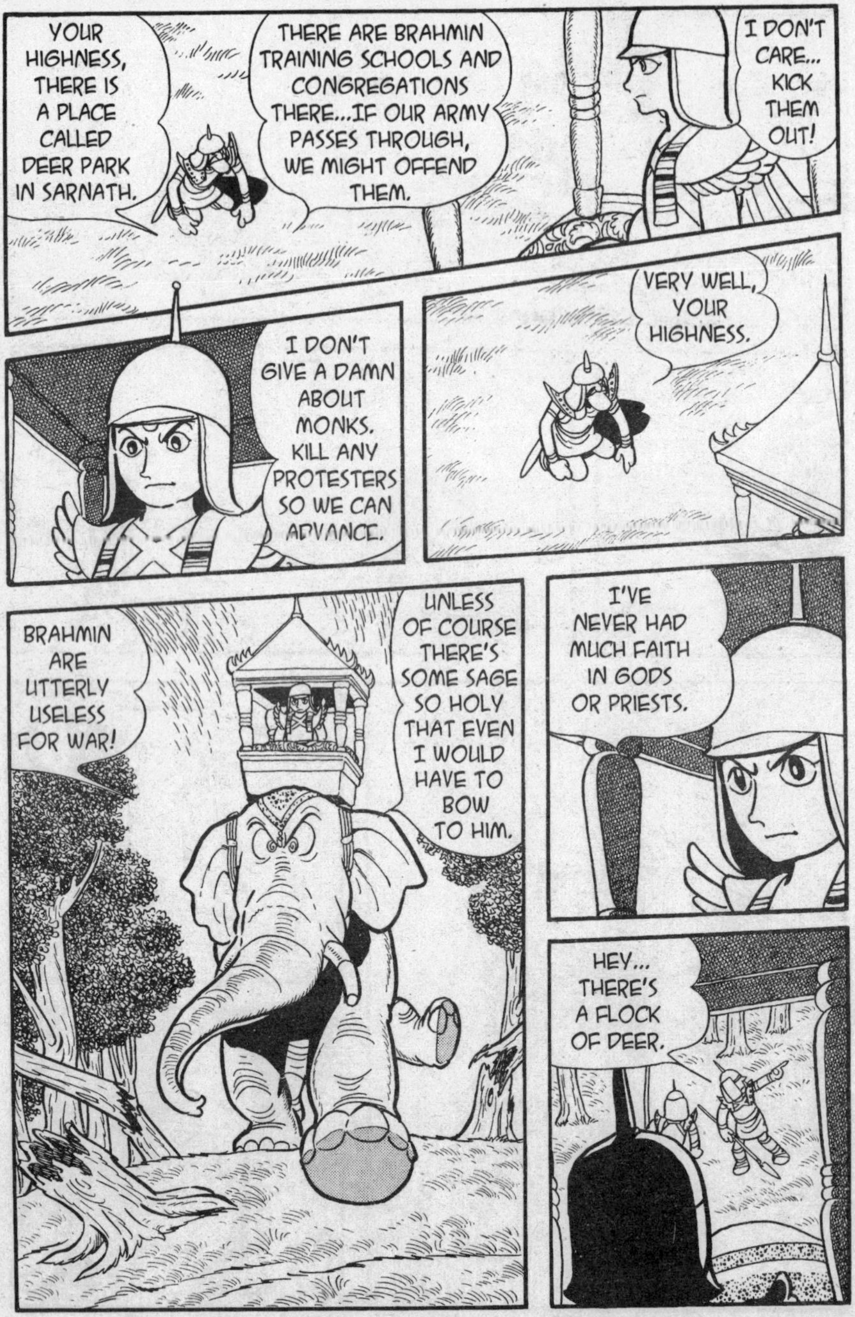
YOUR HIGHNESS, THERE IS A PLACE CALLED DEER PARK IN SARNATH.
THERE ARE BRAHMIN TRAINING SCHOOLS AND CONGREGATIONS THERE...IF OUR ARMY PASSES THROUGH, WE MIGHT OFFEND THEM.
I DON'T CARE... KICK THEM OUT!
I DON'T GIVE A DAMN ABOUT MONKS. KILL ANY PROTESTERS SO WE CAN ADVANCE.
VERY WELL, YOUR HIGHNESS.
BRAHMIN ARE UTTERLY USELESS FOR WAR!
UNLESS OF COURSE THERE'S SOME SAGE SO HOLY THAT EVEN I WOULD HAVE TO BOW TO HIM.
I'VE NEVER HAD MUCH FAITH IN GODS OR PRIESTS.
HEY... THERE'S A FLOCK OF DEER.

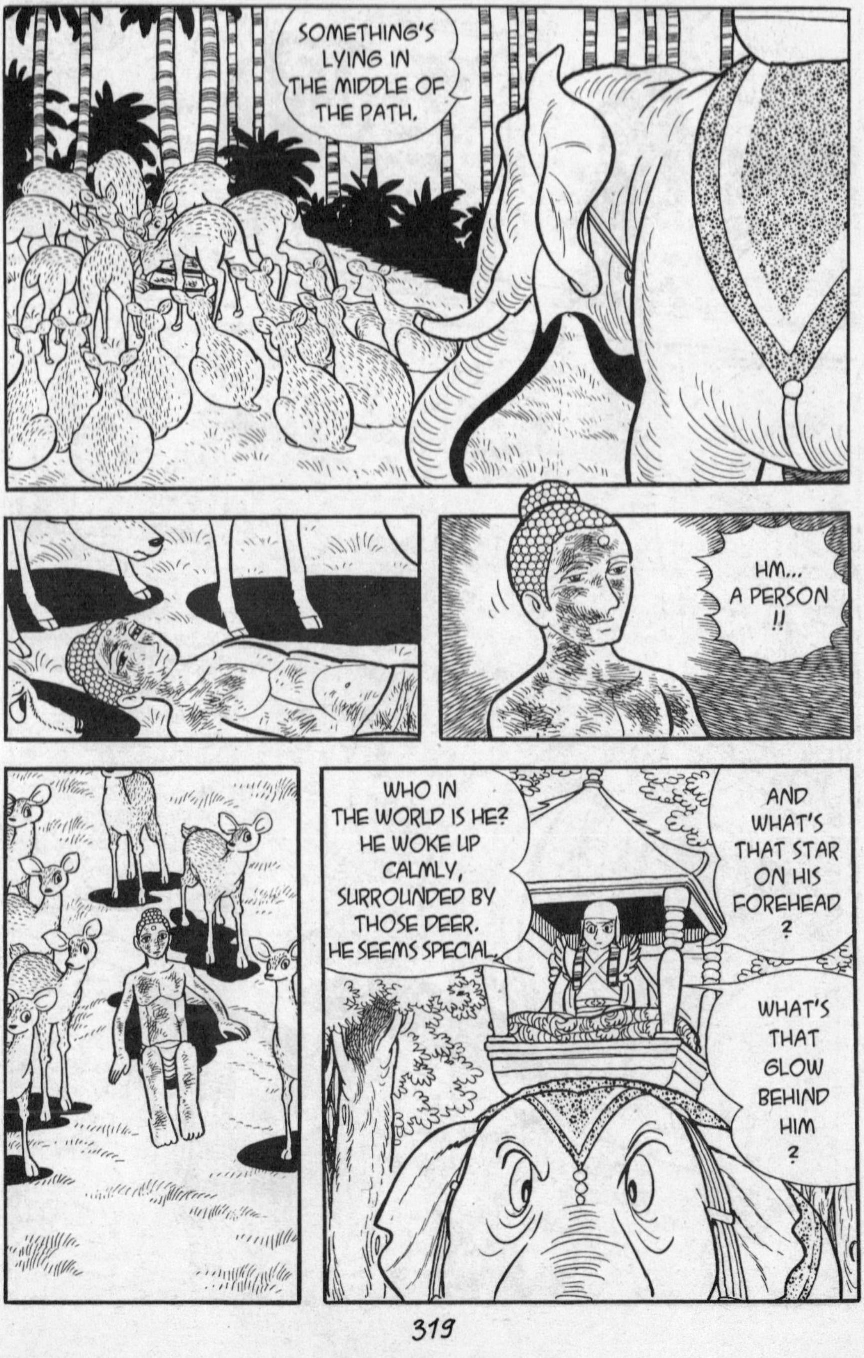
SOMETHING'S LYING IN THE MIDDLE OF THE PATH.
HM... A PERSON !!
WHO IN THE WORLD IS HE? HE WOKE UP CALMLY, SURROUNDED BY THOSE DEER. HE SEEMS SPECIAL.
AND WHAT'S THAT STAR ON HIS FOREHEAD ?
WHAT'S THAT GLOW BEHIND HIM ?

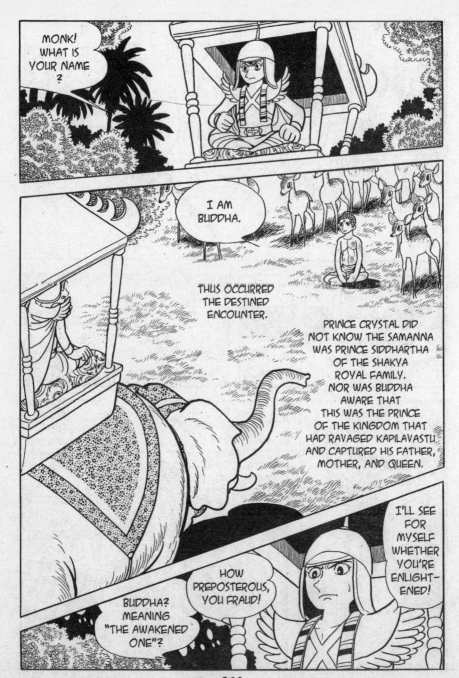

MONK! WHAT IS YOUR NAME?

I AM BUDDHA.

THUS OCCURRED THE DESTINED ENCOUNTER.

PRINCE CRYSTAL DID NOT KNOW THE SAMANNA WAS PRINCE SIDDHARTHA OF THE SHAKYA ROYAL FAMILY. NOR WAS BUDDHA AWARE THAT THIS WAS THE PRINCE OF THE KINGDOM THAT HAD RAVAGED KAPILAVASTU, AND CAPTURED HIS FATHER, MOTHER, AND QUEEN.

I'LL SEE FOR MYSELF WHETHER YOU'RE ENLIGHTENED!

HOW PREPOSTEROUS, YOU FRAUD!

BUDDHA? MEANING "THE AWAKENED ONE"?

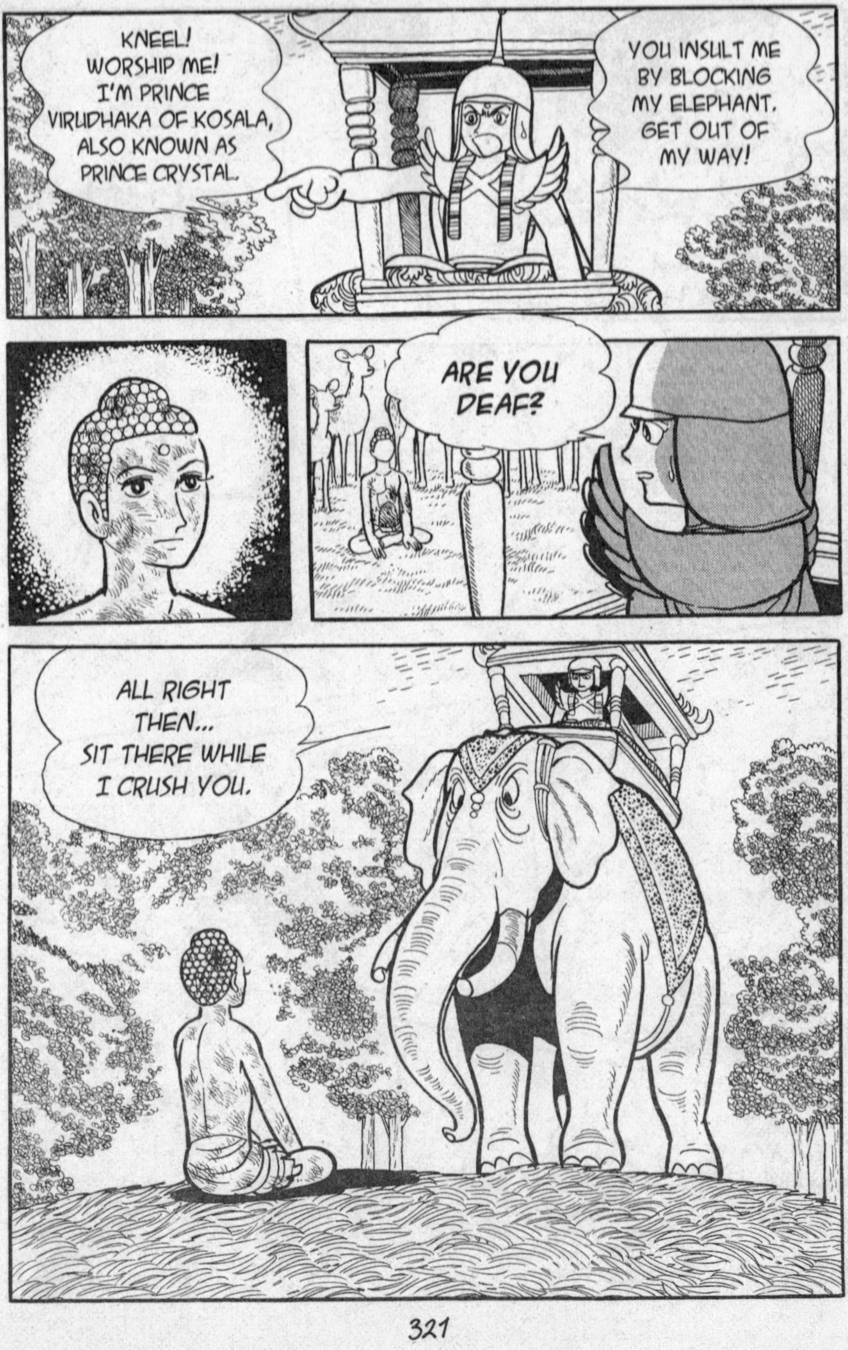
KNEEL! WORSHIP ME! I'M PRINCE VIRUDHAKA OF KOSALA, ALSO KNOWN AS PRINCE CRYSTAL.
YOU INSULT ME BY BLOCKING MY ELEPHANT. GET OUT OF MY WAY!
ARE YOU DEAF?
ALL RIGHT THEN... SIT THERE WHILE I CRUSH YOU.

HEY!
ORDER THE ELEPHANT TO STOMP ON HIM!
HUH ?
Y-YES
SIR.
YES
GO, MOVE!
CRUSH THAT MONK OVER THERE.
POOF
PFF
OOF
COME ON, GET MOVING, YOU SLOWPOKE.

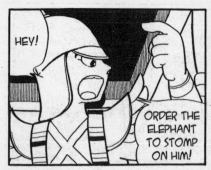

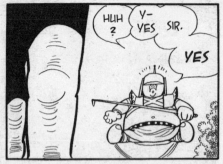

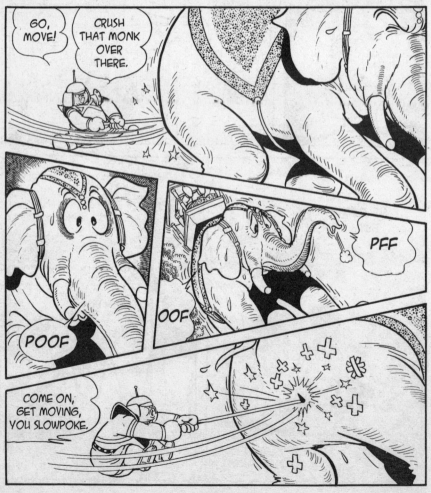

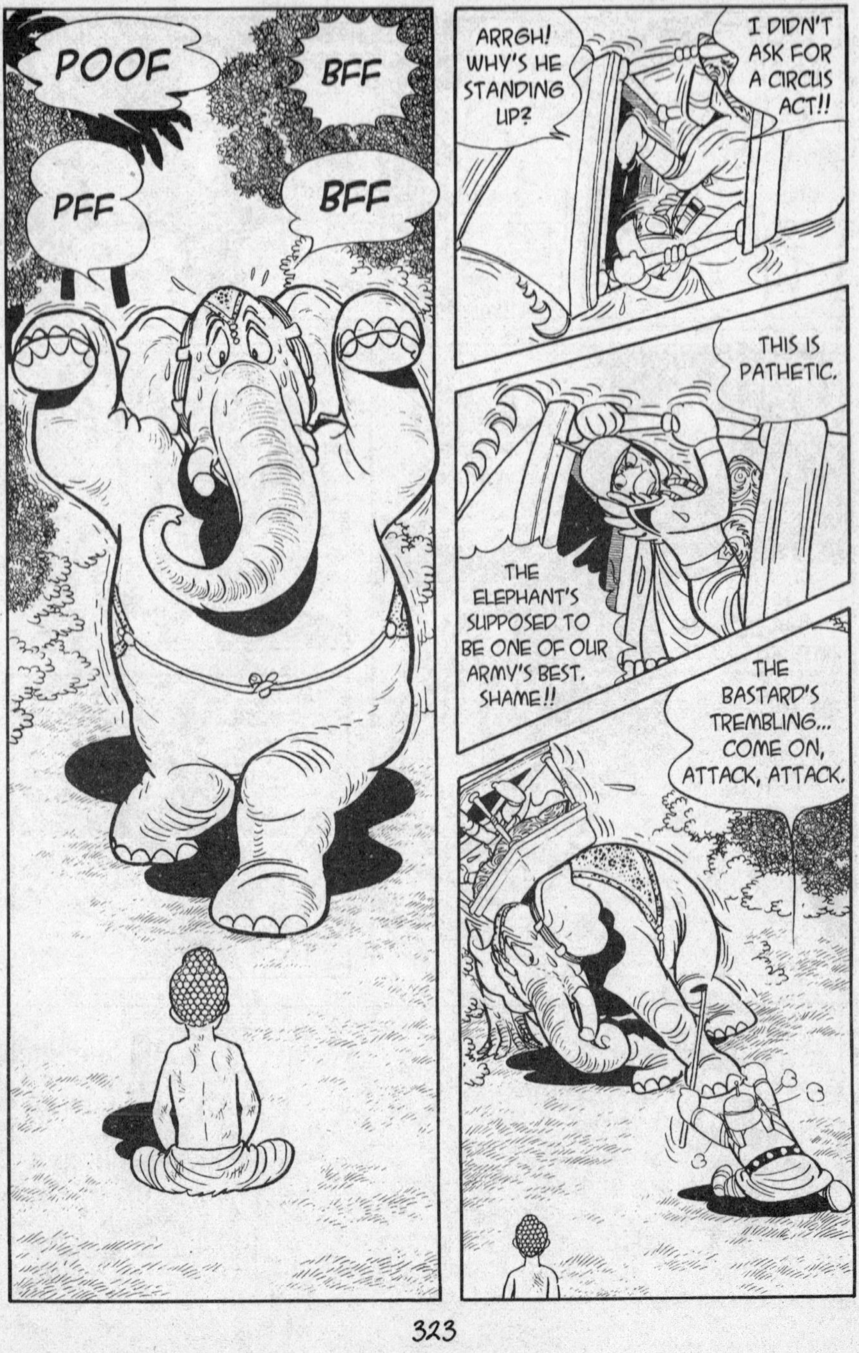
POOF
BFF
PFF
BFF
ARRGH! WHY'S HE STANDING UP?
I DIDN'T ASK FOR A CIRCUS ACT!!
THIS IS PATHETIC.
THE ELEPHANT'S SUPPOSED TO BE ONE OF OUR ARMY'S BEST. SHAME!!
THE BASTARD'S TREMBLING... COME ON, ATTACK, ATTACK.

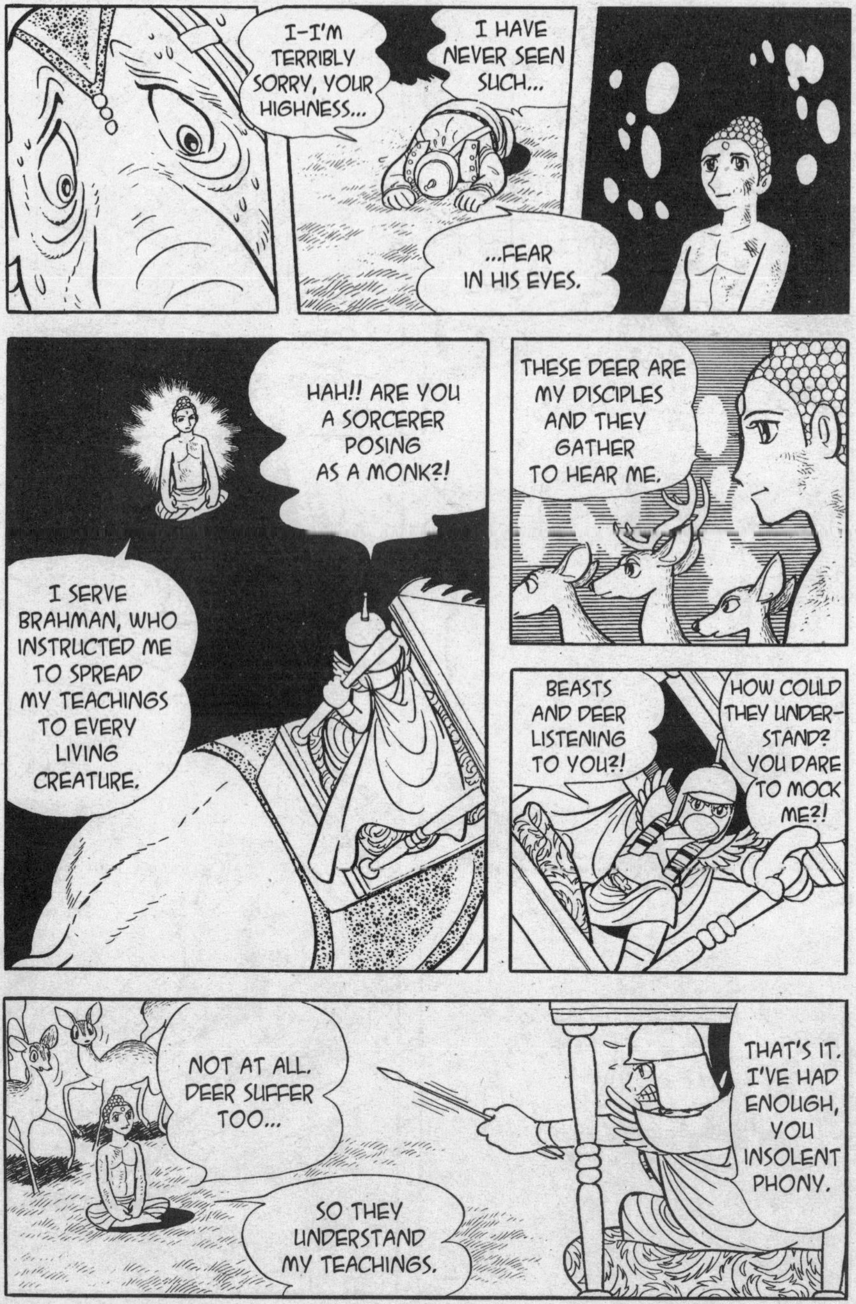
I-I'M TERRIBLY SORRY, YOUR HIGHNESS...
I HAVE NEVER SEEN SUCH...
...FEAR IN HIS EYES.
HAH!! ARE YOU A SORCERER POSING AS A MONK?!
I SERVE BRAHMAN, WHO INSTRUCTED ME TO SPREAD MY TEACHINGS TO EVERY LIVING CREATURE.
THESE DEER ARE MY DISCIPLES AND THEY GATHER TO HEAR ME.
BEASTS AND DEER LISTENING TO YOU?!
HOW COULD THEY UNDER-STAND? YOU DARE TO MOCK ME?!
NOT AT ALL. DEER SUFFER TOO...
SO THEY UNDERSTAND MY TEACHINGS.
THAT'S IT. I'VE HAD ENOUGH, YOU INSOLENT PHONY.

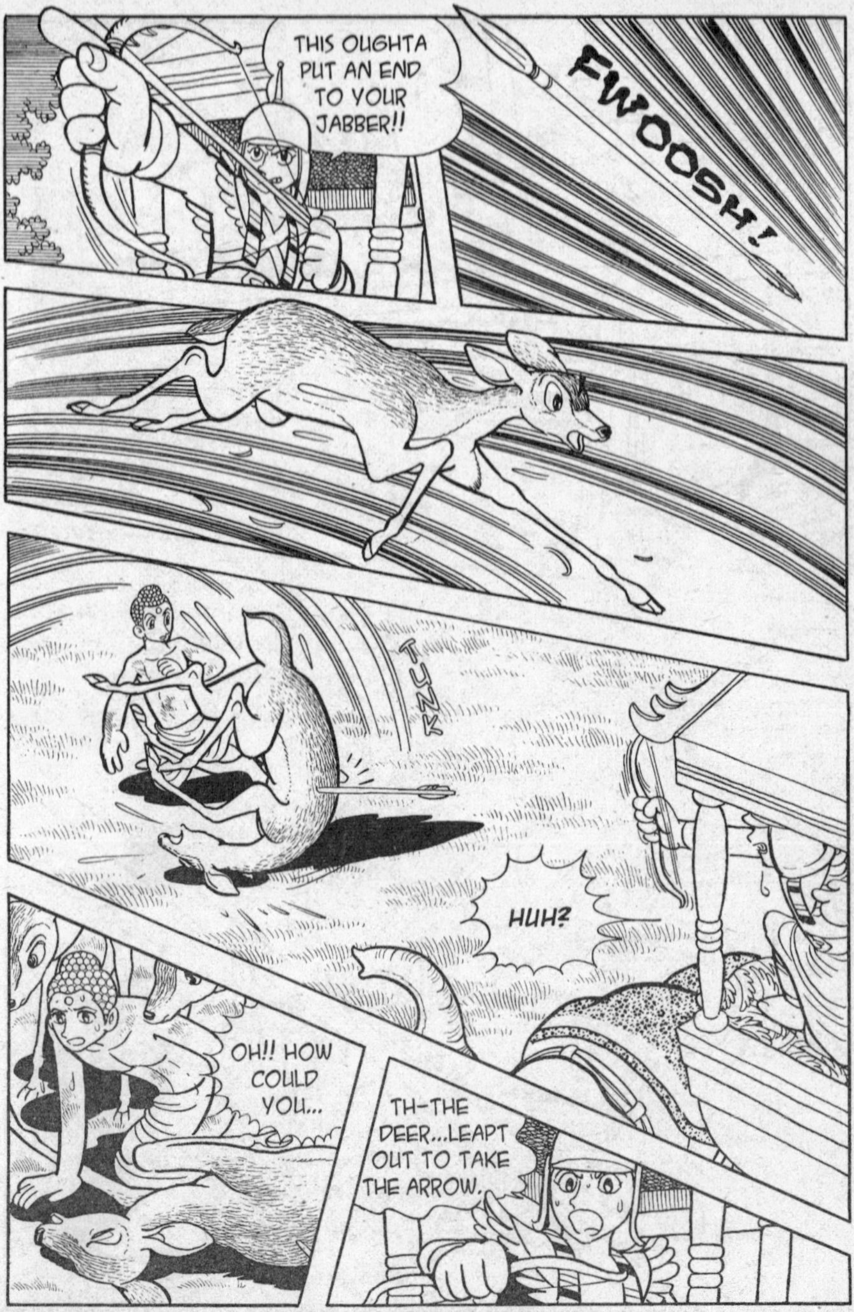

THIS OUGHTA PUT AN END TO YOUR JABBER!!
FWOOSH!
TUNK
HUH?
OH!! HOW COULD YOU...
TH-THE DEER...LEAPT OUT TO TAKE THE ARROW.

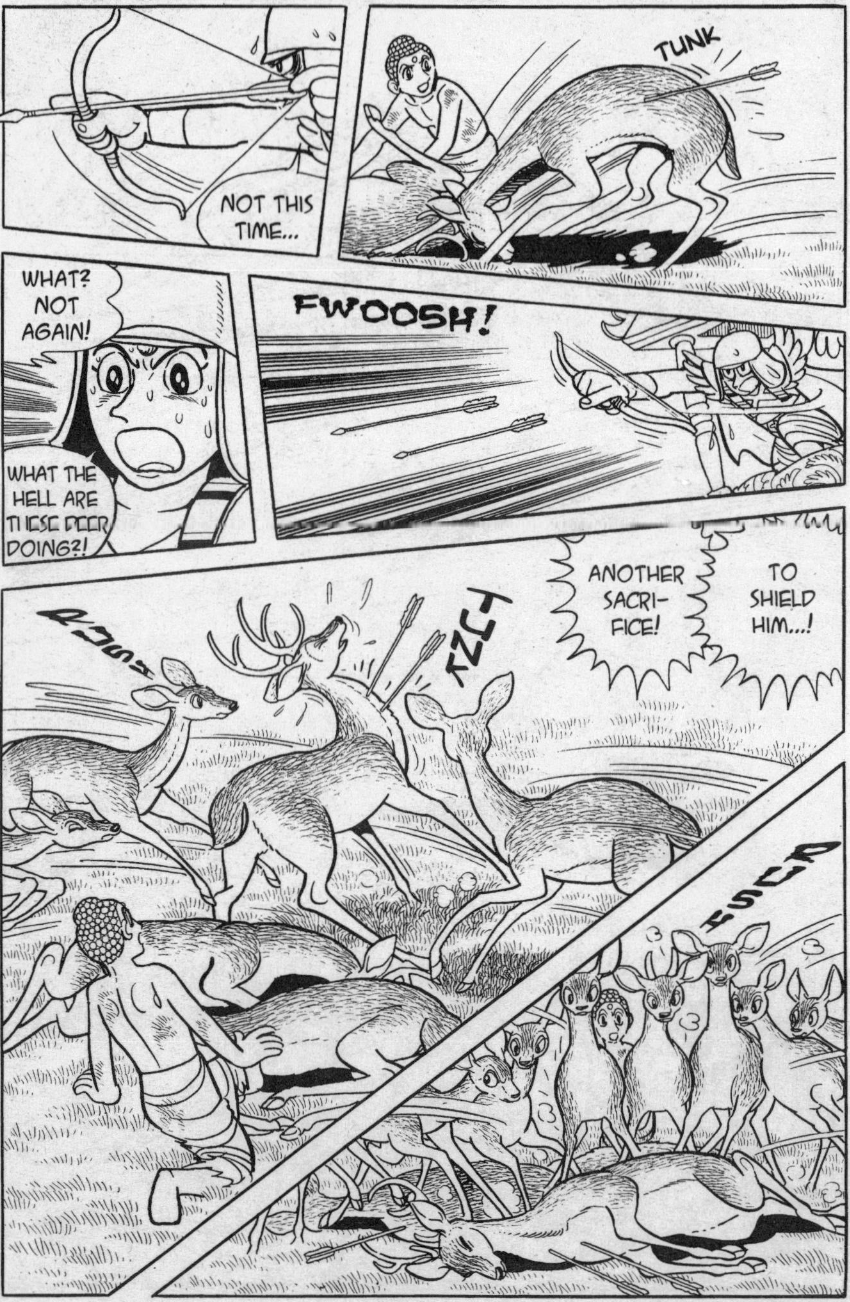
NOT THIS TIME...
TUNK
WHAT? NOT AGAIN!
WHAT THE HELL ARE THESE DEER DOING?!
FWOOSH!
ANOTHER SACRIFICE!
TO SHIELD HIM...!

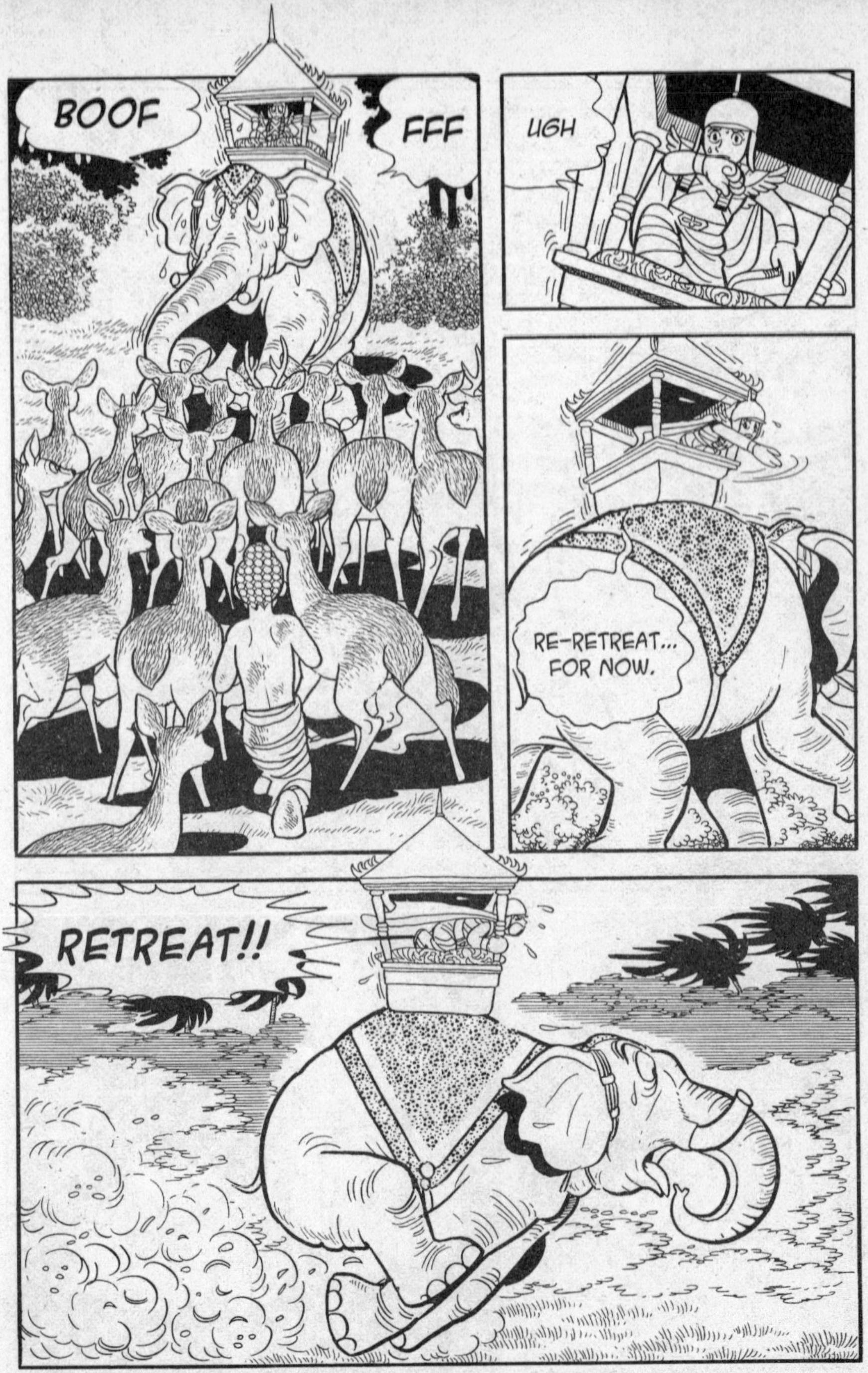
BOOF
FFF
UGH
RE-RETREAT... FOR NOW.
RETREAT!!

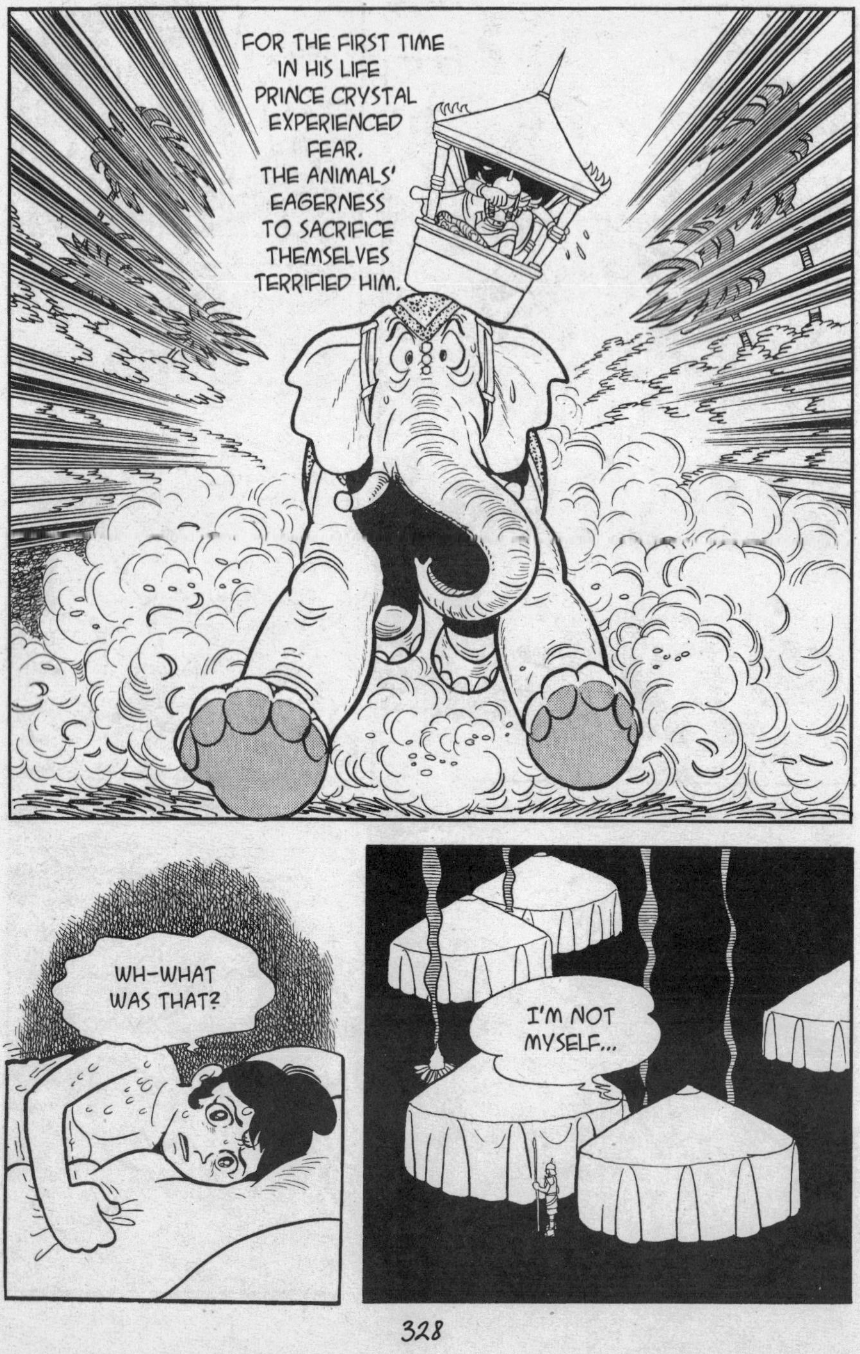
FOR THE FIRST TIME IN HIS LIFE PRINCE CRYSTAL EXPERIENCED FEAR. THE ANIMALS' EAGERNESS TO SACRIFICE THEMSELVES TERRIFIED HIM.
WH-WHAT WAS THAT?
I'M NOT MYSELF...

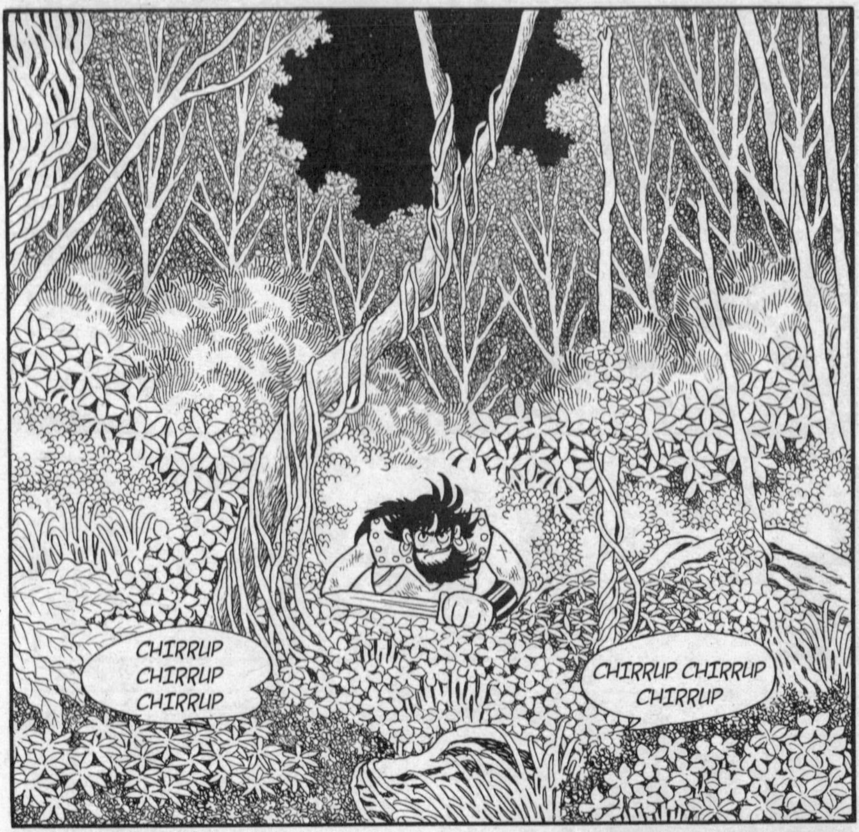
CHIRRUP
CHIRRUP
CHIRRUP
CHIRRUP CHIRRUP
CHIRRUP
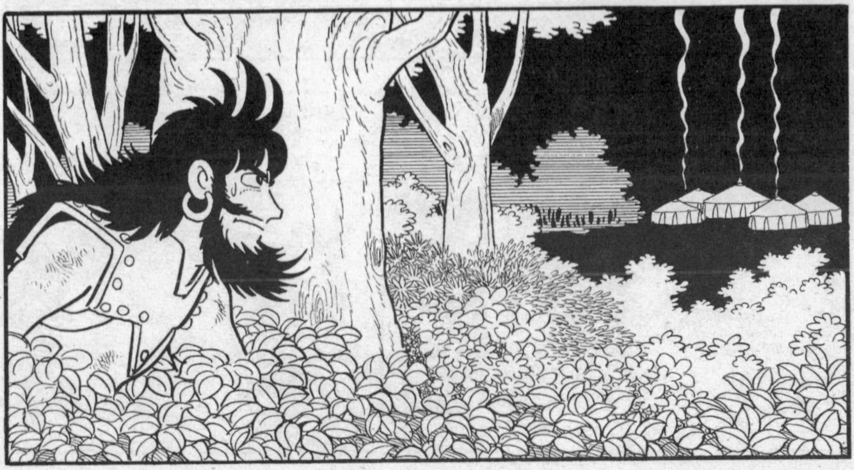

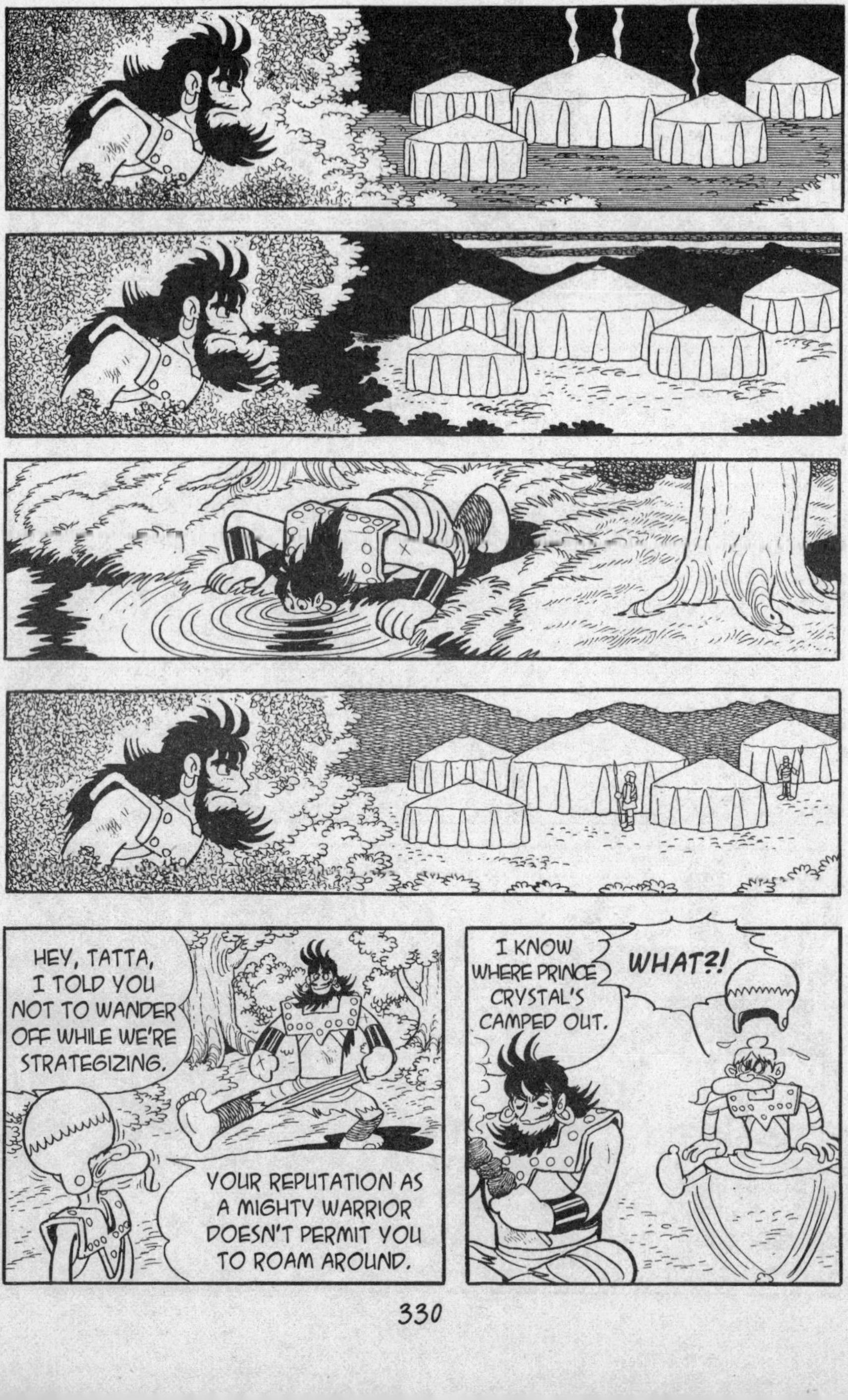
HEY, TATTA, I TOLD YOU NOT TO WANDER OFF WHILE WE'RE STRATEGIZING.
YOUR REPUTATION AS A MIGHTY WARRIOR DOESN'T PERMIT YOU TO ROAM AROUND.
I KNOW WHERE PRINCE CRYSTAL'S CAMPED OUT.
WHAT?!

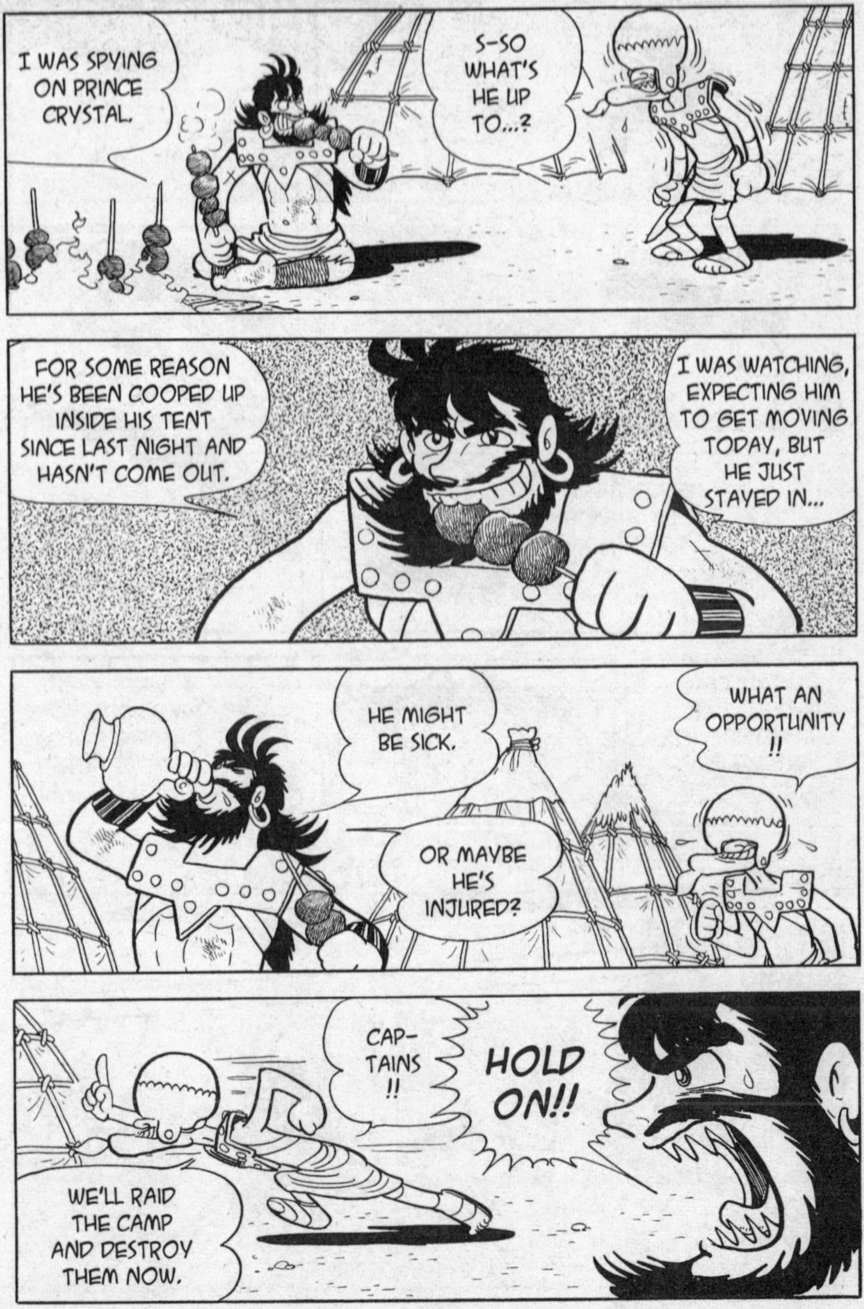
I WAS SPYING ON PRINCE CRYSTAL.
S-SO WHAT'S HE UP TO...?
FOR SOME REASON HE'S BEEN COOPED UP INSIDE HIS TENT SINCE LAST NIGHT AND HASN'T COME OUT.
I WAS WATCHING, EXPECTING HIM TO GET MOVING TODAY, BUT HE JUST STAYED IN...
HE MIGHT BE SICK.
OR MAYBE HE'S INJURED?
WHAT AN OPPORTUNITY !!
CAP-TAINS !!
WE'LL RAID THE CAMP AND DESTROY THEM NOW.
HOLD ON!!

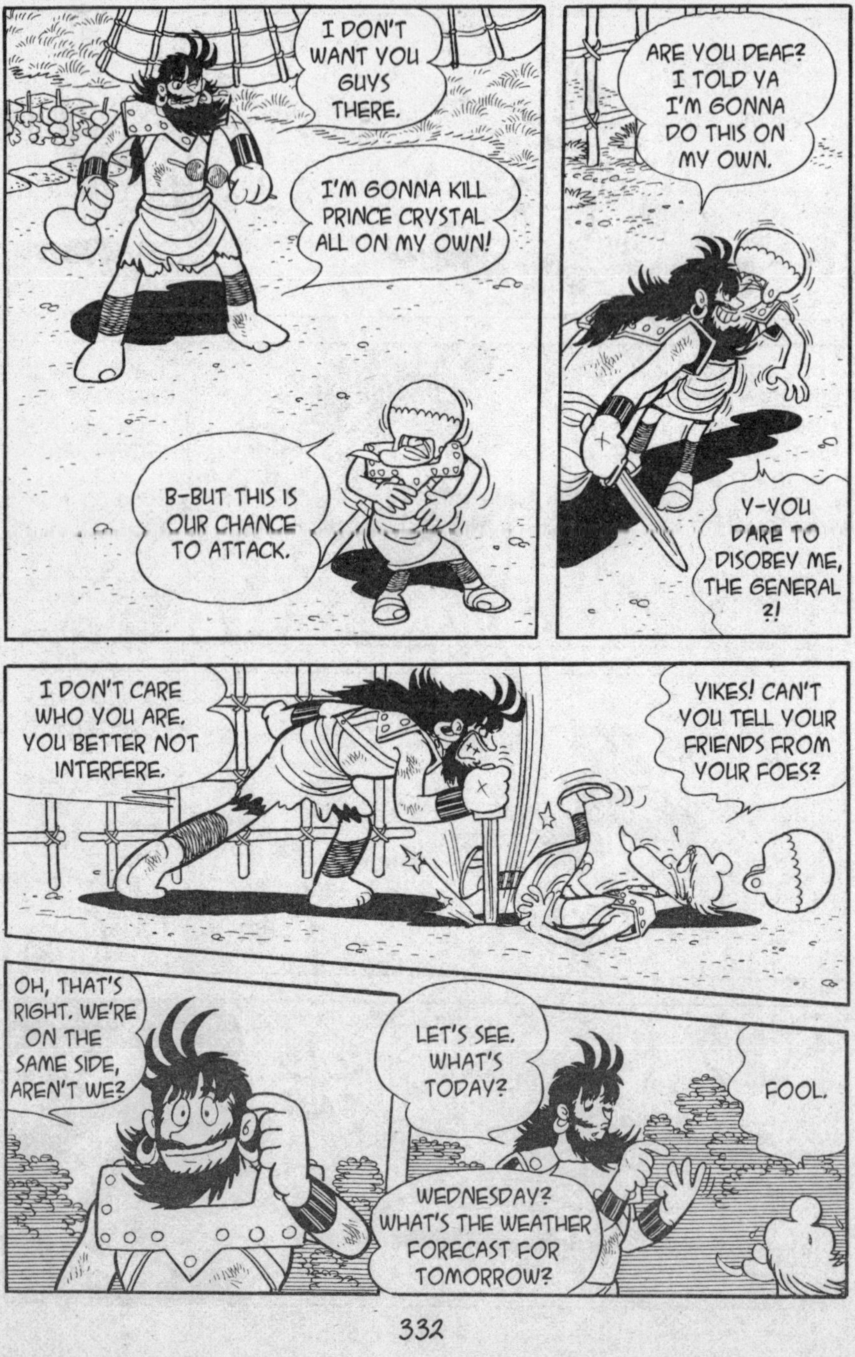
I DON'T WANT YOU GUYS THERE.
I'M GONNA KILL PRINCE CRYSTAL ALL ON MY OWN!
B-BUT THIS IS OUR CHANCE TO ATTACK.
ARE YOU DEAF? I TOLD YA I'M GONNA DO THIS ON MY OWN.
Y-YOU DARE TO DISOBEY ME, THE GENERAL?!
I DON'T CARE WHO YOU ARE. YOU BETTER NOT INTERFERE.
YIKES! CAN'T YOU TELL YOUR FRIENDS FROM YOUR FOES?
OH, THAT'S RIGHT. WE'RE ON THE SAME SIDE, AREN'T WE?
LET'S SEE. WHAT'S TODAY?
WEDNESDAY? WHAT'S THE WEATHER FORECAST FOR TOMORROW?
FOOL.

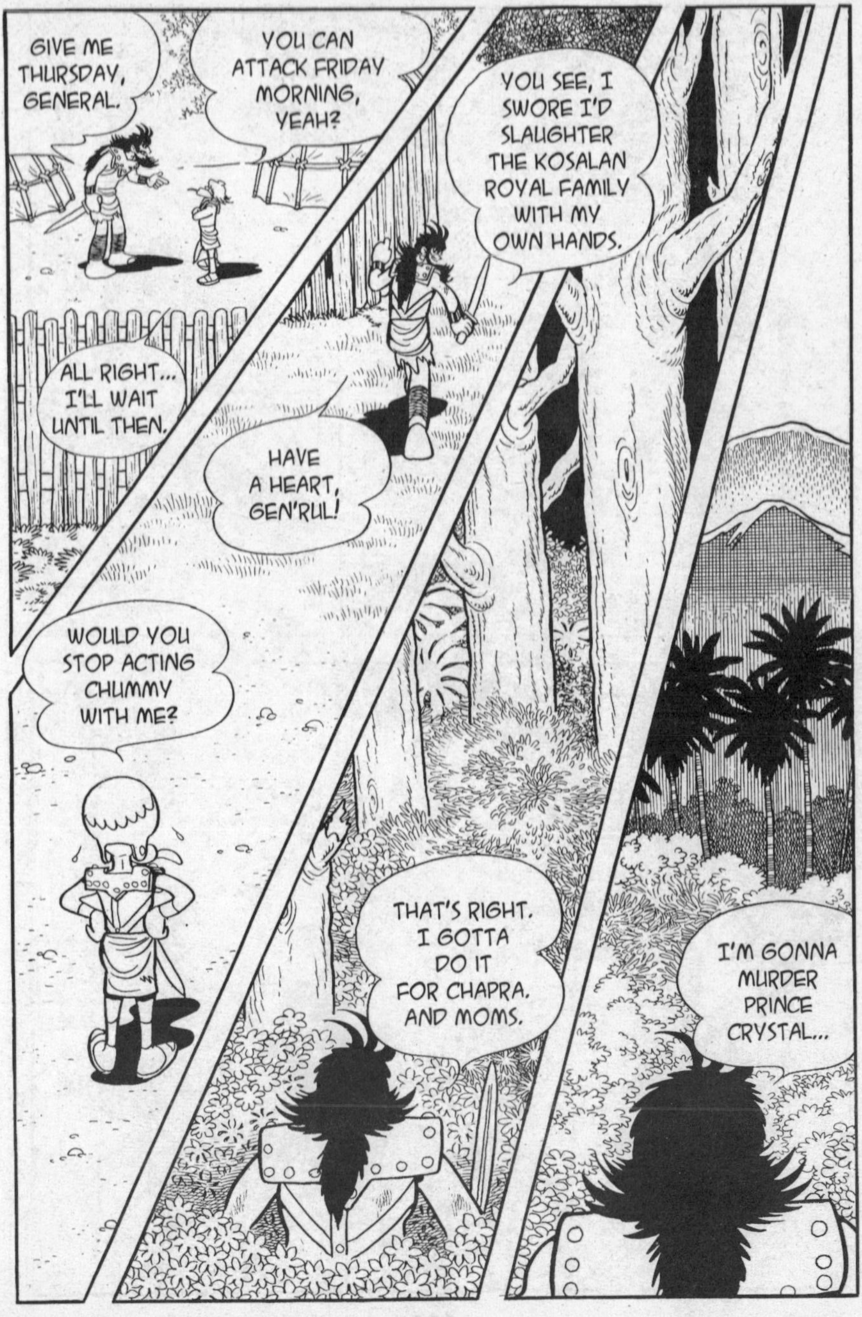
GIVE ME THURSDAY, GENERAL.
YOU CAN ATTACK FRIDAY MORNING, YEAH?
ALL RIGHT... I'LL WAIT UNTIL THEN.
HAVE A HEART, GEN'RUL!
WOULD YOU STOP ACTING CHUMMY WITH ME?
YOU SEE, I SWORE I'D SLAUGHTER THE KOSALAN ROYAL FAMILY WITH MY OWN HANDS.
THAT'S RIGHT. I GOTTA DO IT FOR CHAPRA. AND MOMS.
I'M GONNA MURDER PRINCE CRYSTAL...

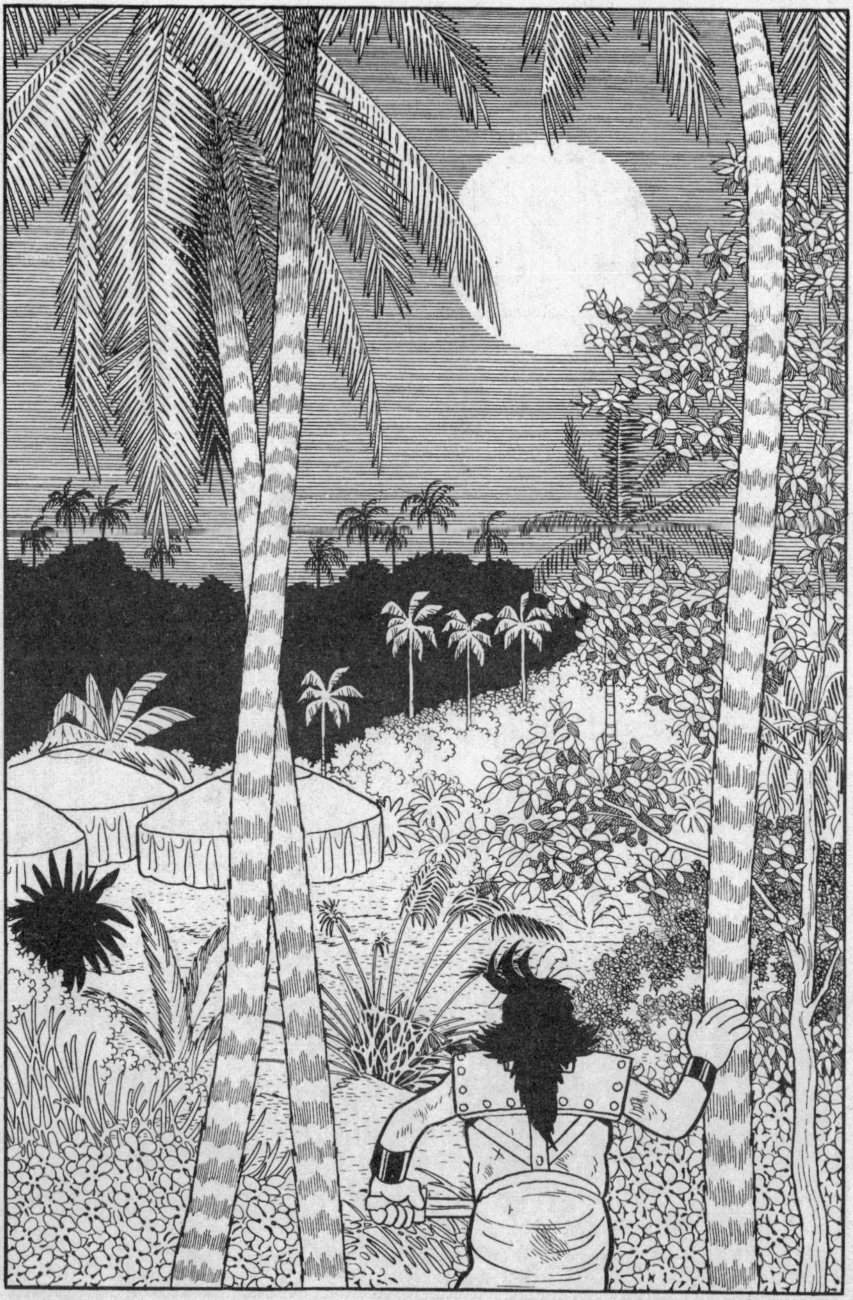

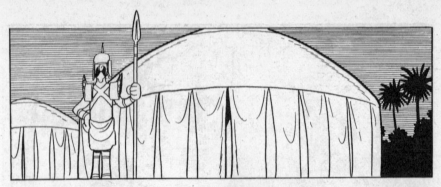

P-PRINCE!!

SHH

BE QUI-ET.

I'M GOING OUT...

DON'T TELL THE CAPTAINS.

OH, OH, IN THAT CASE...

LET ME ACCOMPANY YOU.

I'M FINE ALONE.

IT'S SOMETHING PERSONAL.

KLOP KLOP KLOP

BUT THE CAPTAINS ARE CONCERNED YOU FELT UNWELL ALL DAY YESTERDAY, SO...UH...OH?

HE'S GONE.

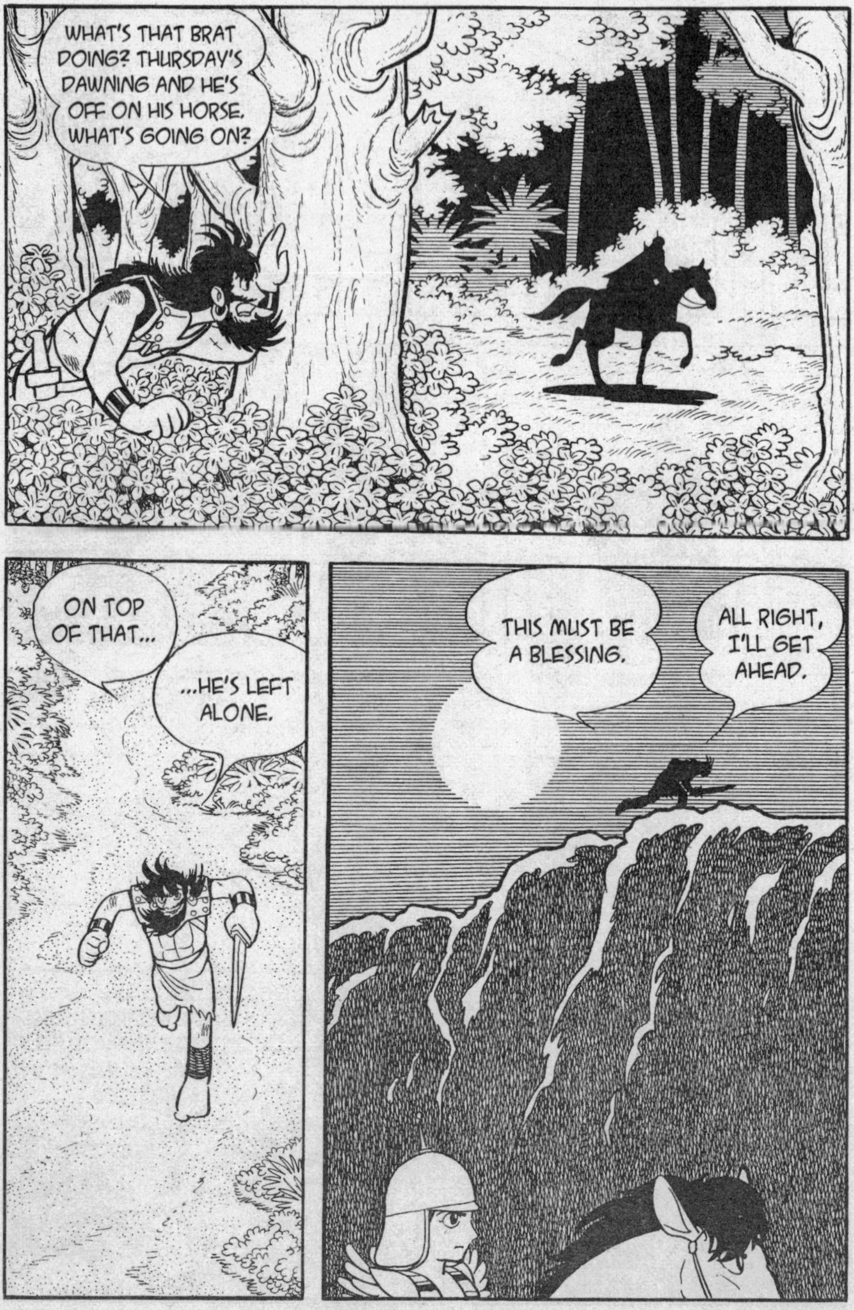
WHAT'S THAT BRAT DOING? THURSDAY'S DAWNING AND HE'S OFF ON HIS HORSE. WHAT'S GOING ON?
ON TOP OF THAT...
...HE'S LEFT ALONE.
THIS MUST BE A BLESSING.
ALL RIGHT, I'LL GET AHEAD.

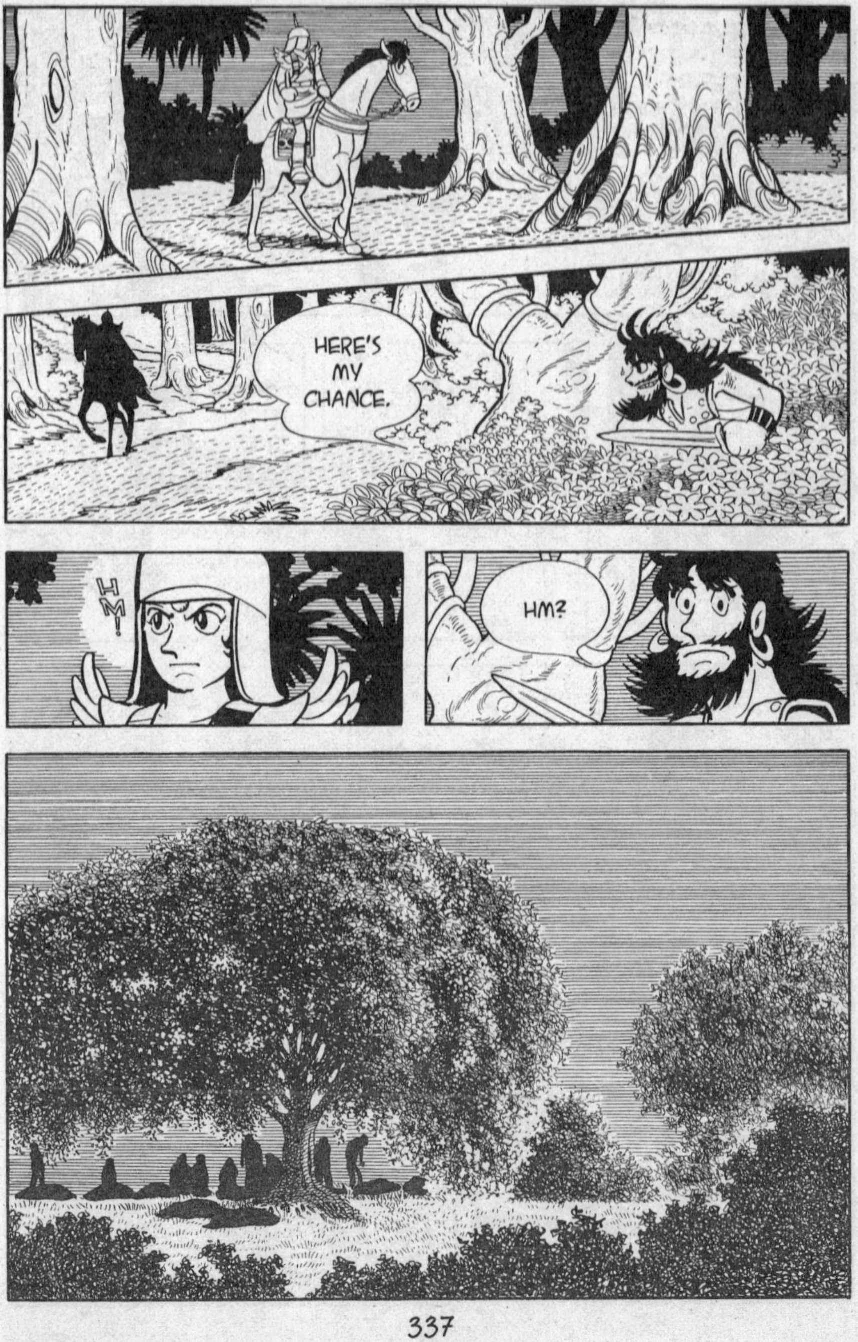
HERE'S MY CHANCE.
HM!
HM?

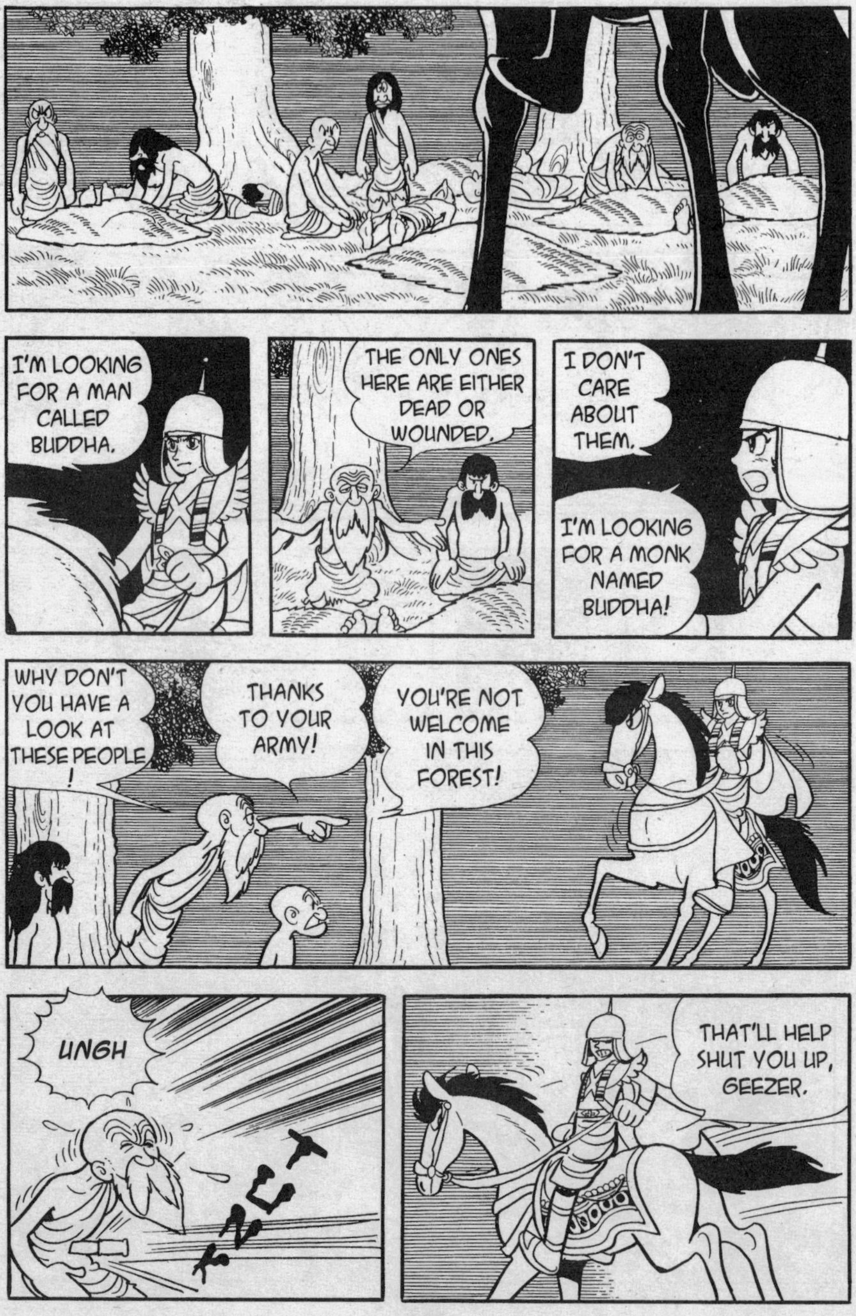
I'M LOOKING FOR A MAN CALLED BUDDHA.
THE ONLY ONES HERE ARE EITHER DEAD OR WOUNDED.
I DON'T CARE ABOUT THEM.
I'M LOOKING FOR A MONK NAMED BUDDHA!
WHY DON'T YOU HAVE A LOOK AT THESE PEOPLE!
THANKS TO YOUR ARMY!
YOU'RE NOT WELCOME IN THIS FOREST!
UNGH
KZUT
THAT'LL HELP SHUT YOU UP, GEEZER.

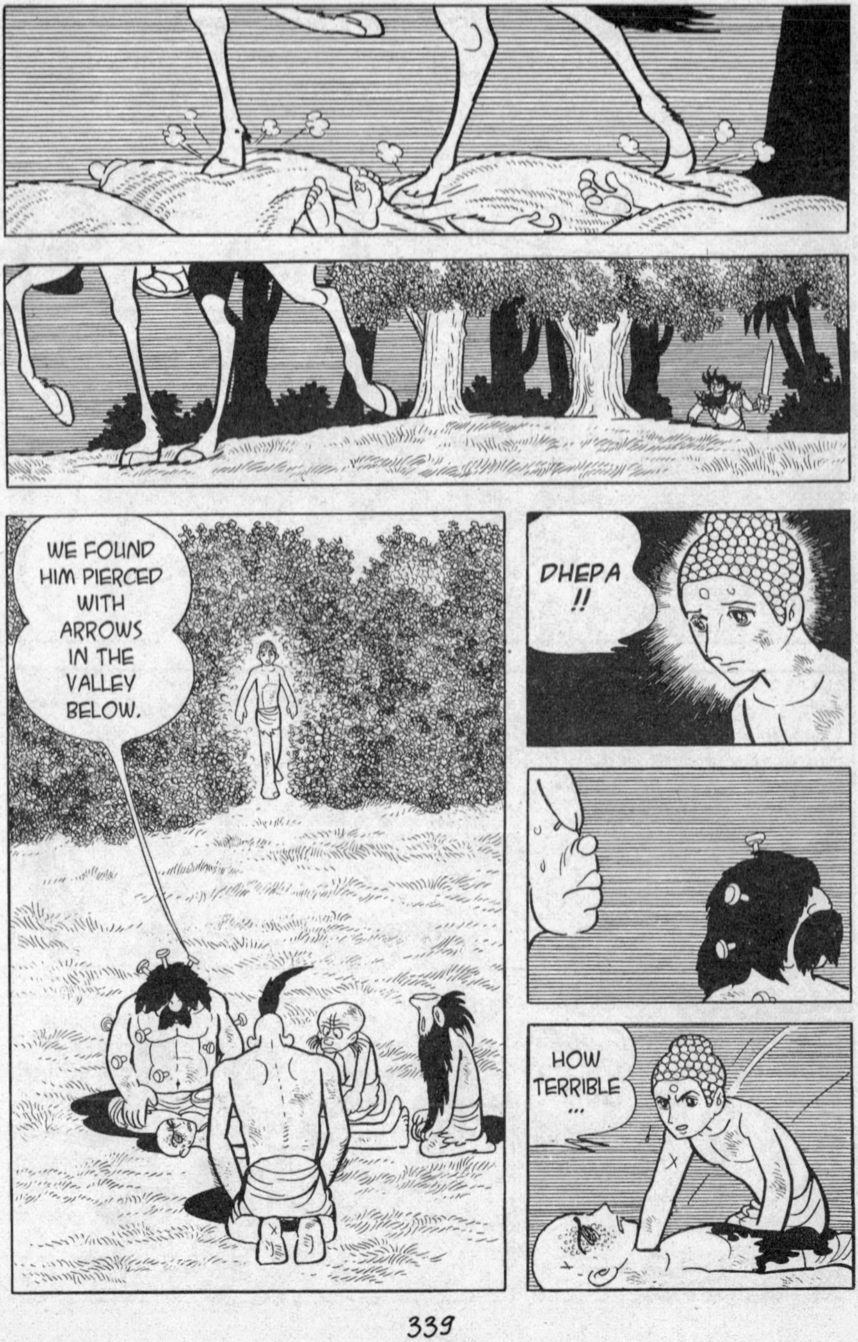
WE FOUND HIM PIERCED WITH ARROWS IN THE VALLEY BELOW.
DHEPA !!
HOW TERRIBLE ...

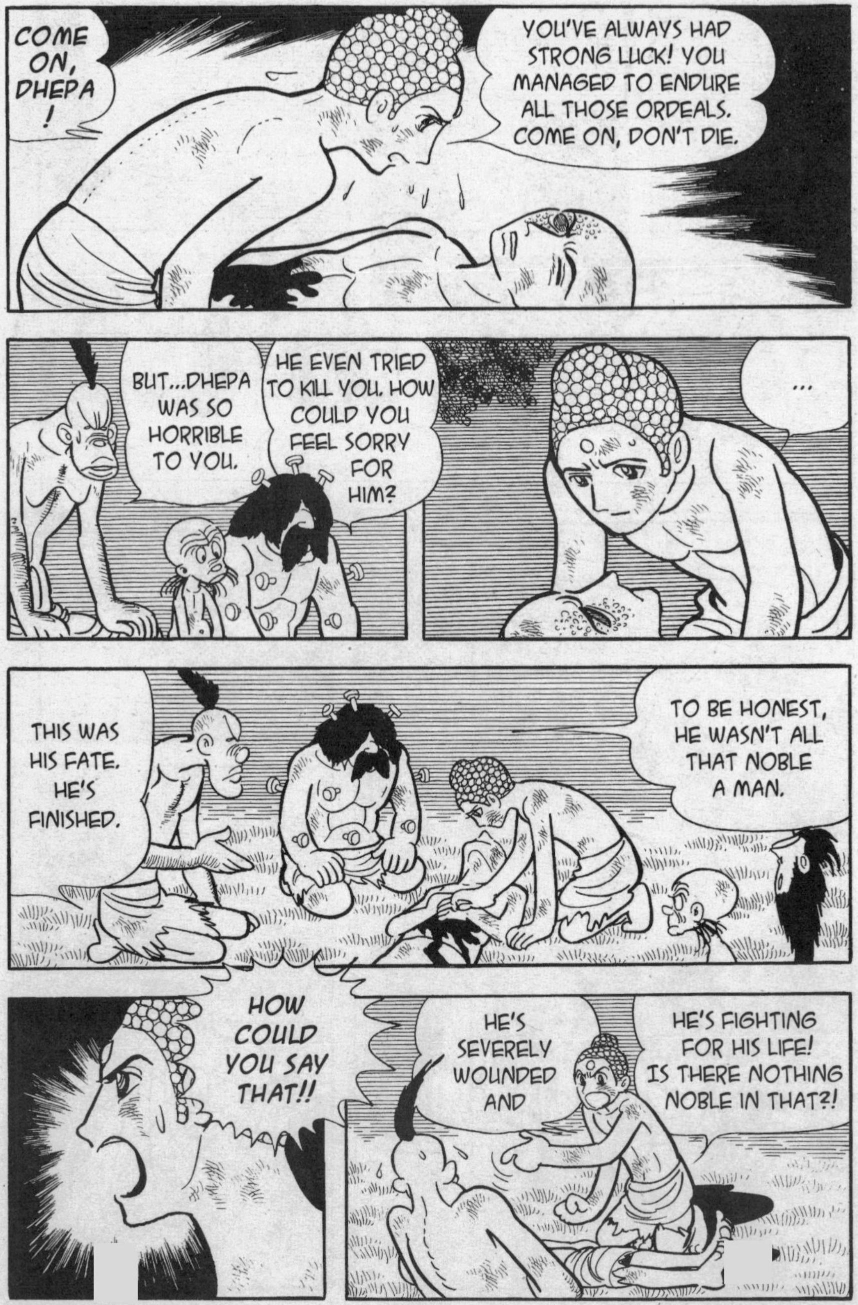
COME ON, DHEPA!
YOU'VE ALWAYS HAD STRONG LUCK! YOU MANAGED TO ENDURE ALL THOSE ORDEALS. COME ON, DON'T DIE.
BUT...DHEPA WAS SO HORRIBLE TO YOU.
HE EVEN TRIED TO KILL YOU. HOW COULD YOU FEEL SORRY FOR HIM?
...
THIS WAS HIS FATE. HE'S FINISHED.
TO BE HONEST, HE WASN'T ALL THAT NOBLE A MAN.
HOW COULD YOU SAY THAT!!
HE'S SEVERELY WOUNDED AND
HE'S FIGHTING FOR HIS LIFE! IS THERE NOTHING NOBLE IN THAT?!

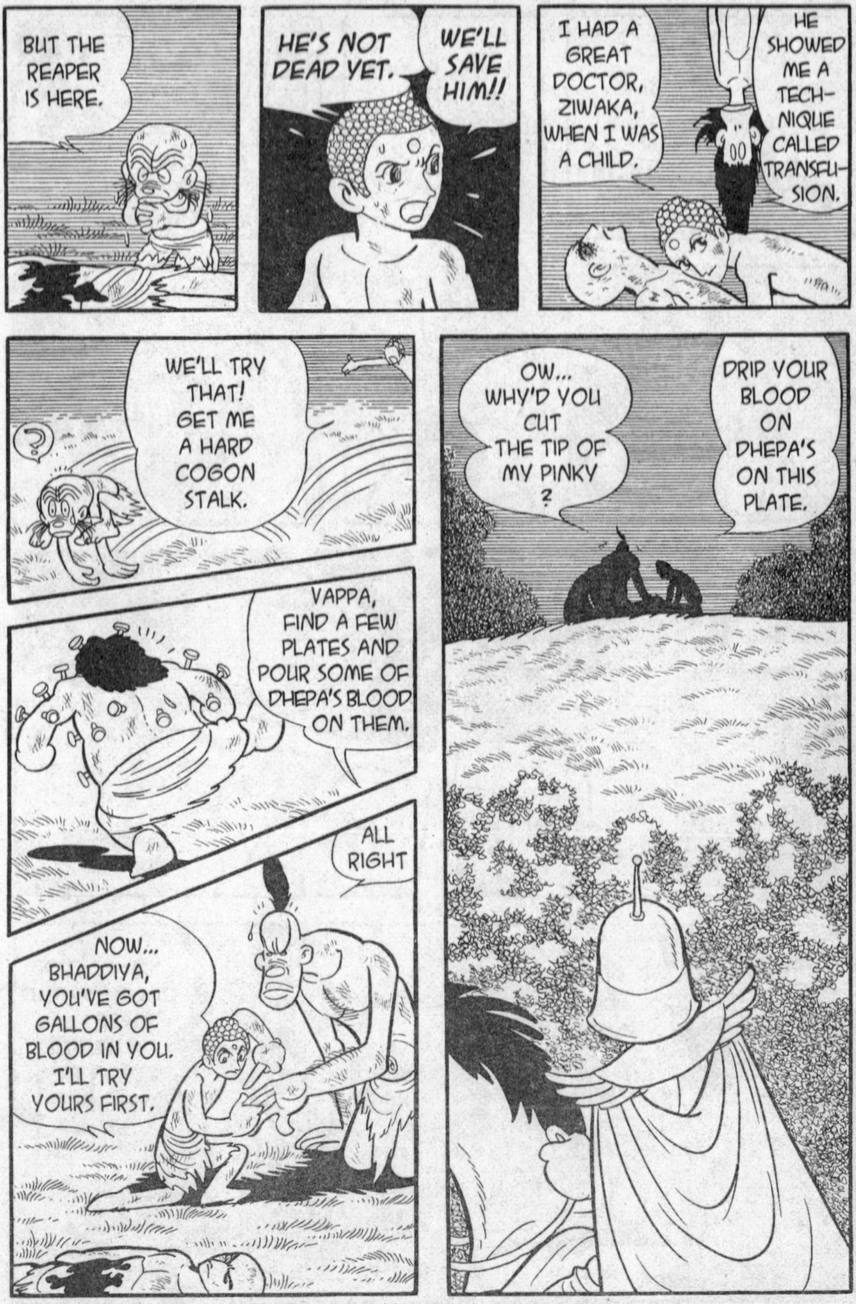
BUT THE REAPER IS HERE.
HE'S NOT DEAD YET.
WE'LL SAVE HIM!!
I HAD A GREAT DOCTOR, ZIWAKA, WHEN I WAS A CHILD.
HE SHOWED ME A TECHNIQUE CALLED TRANSFUSION.
WE'LL TRY THAT! GET ME A HARD COGON STALK.
?
VAPPA, FIND A FEW PLATES AND POUR SOME OF DHEPA'S BLOOD ON THEM.
ALL RIGHT
NOW... BHADDIYA, YOU'VE GOT GALLONS OF BLOOD IN YOU. I'LL TRY YOURS FIRST.
OW... WHY'D YOU CUT THE TIP OF MY PINKY ?
DRIP YOUR BLOOD ON DHEPA'S ON THIS PLATE.

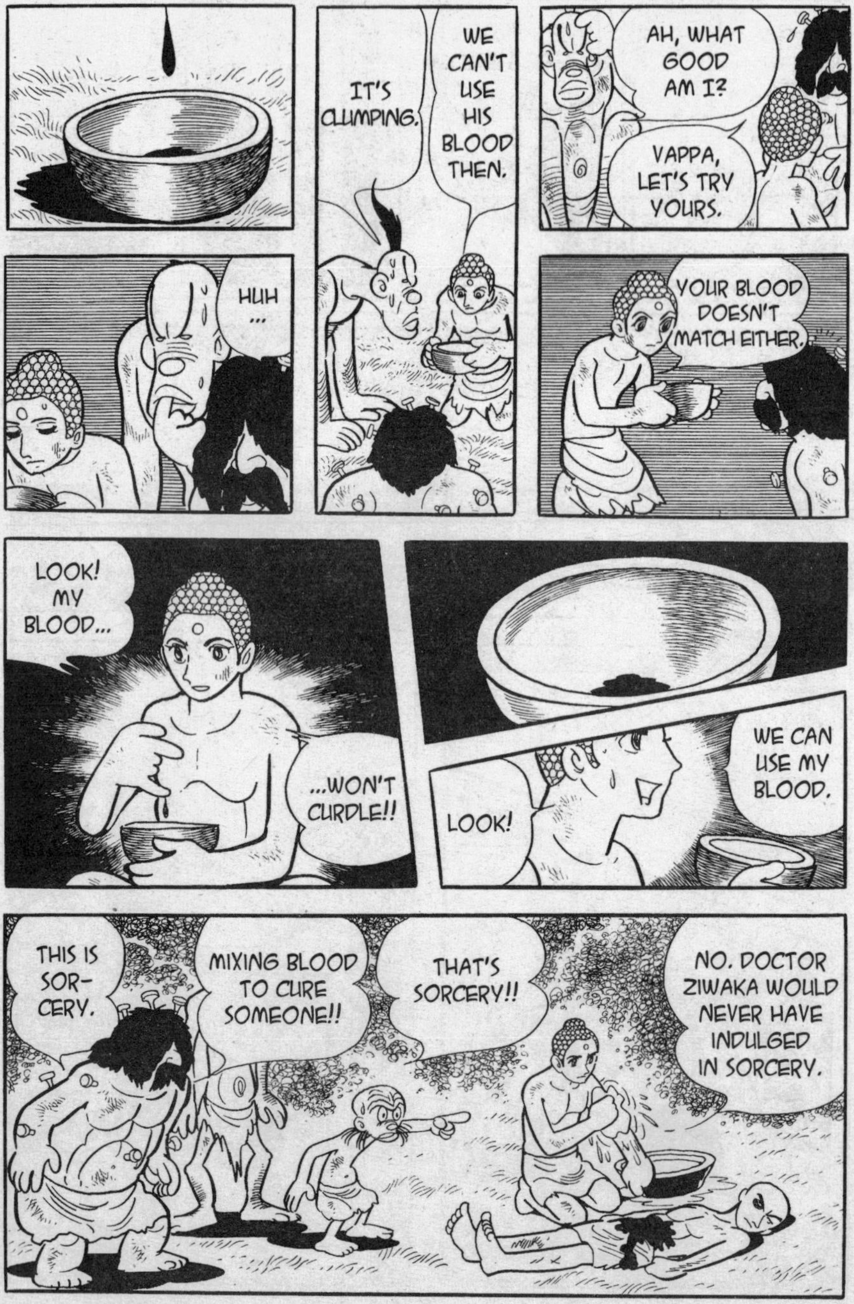
IT'S CLUMPING.
WE CAN'T USE HIS BLOOD THEN.
AH, WHAT GOOD AM I?
VAPPA, LET'S TRY YOURS.
HUH ...
YOUR BLOOD DOESN'T MATCH EITHER.
LOOK! MY BLOOD...
...WON'T CURDLE!!
LOOK!
WE CAN USE MY BLOOD.
THIS IS SOR-CERY.
MIXING BLOOD TO CURE SOMEONE!!
THAT'S SORCERY!!
NO. DOCTOR ZIWAKA WOULD NEVER HAVE INDULGED IN SORCERY.

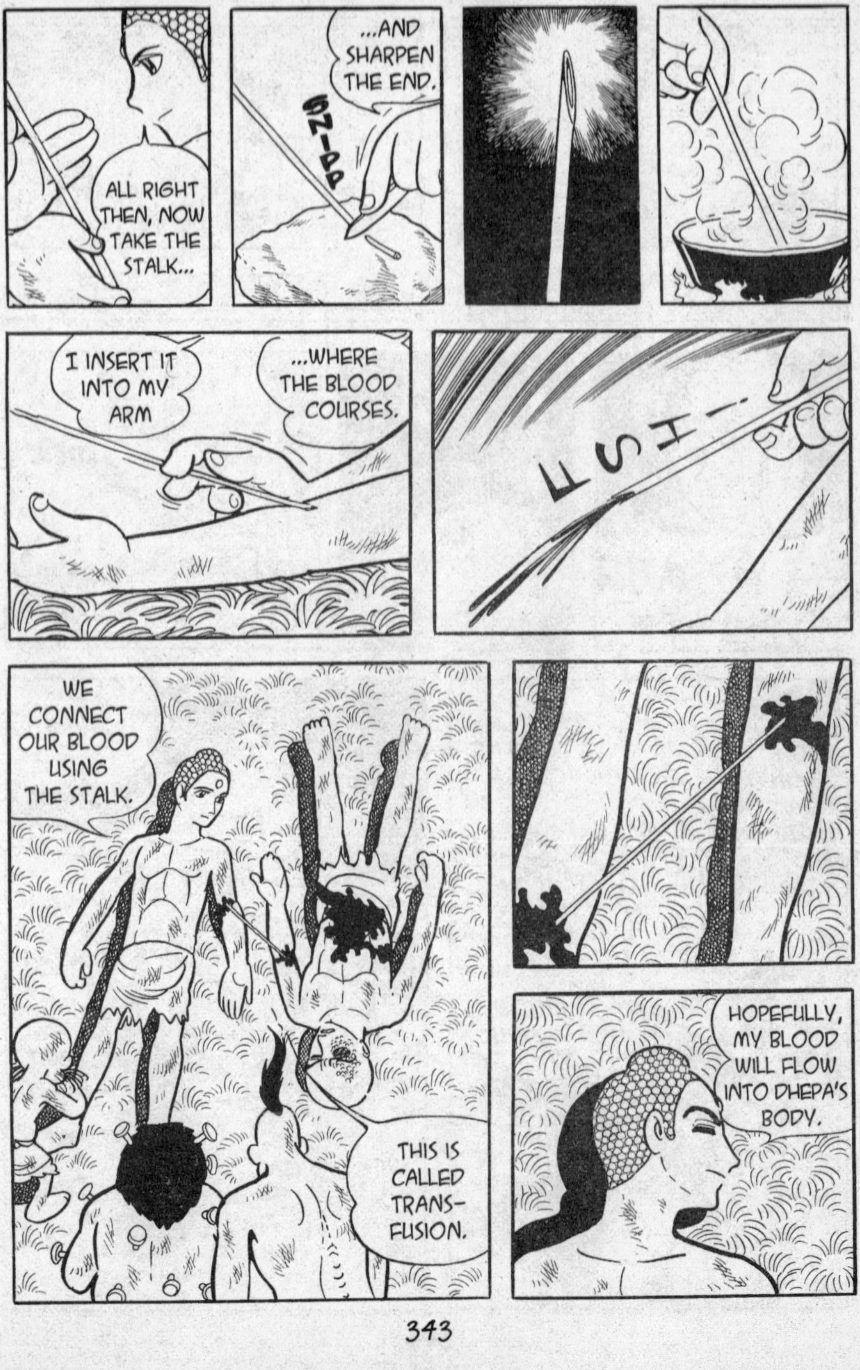
ALL RIGHT THEN, NOW TAKE THE STALK...
...AND SHARPEN THE END.
SNIPP
I INSERT IT INTO MY ARM
...WHERE THE BLOOD COURSES.
FSH
WE CONNECT OUR BLOOD USING THE STALK.
THIS IS CALLED TRANS-FUSION.
HOPEFULLY, MY BLOOD WILL FLOW INTO DHEPA'S BODY.

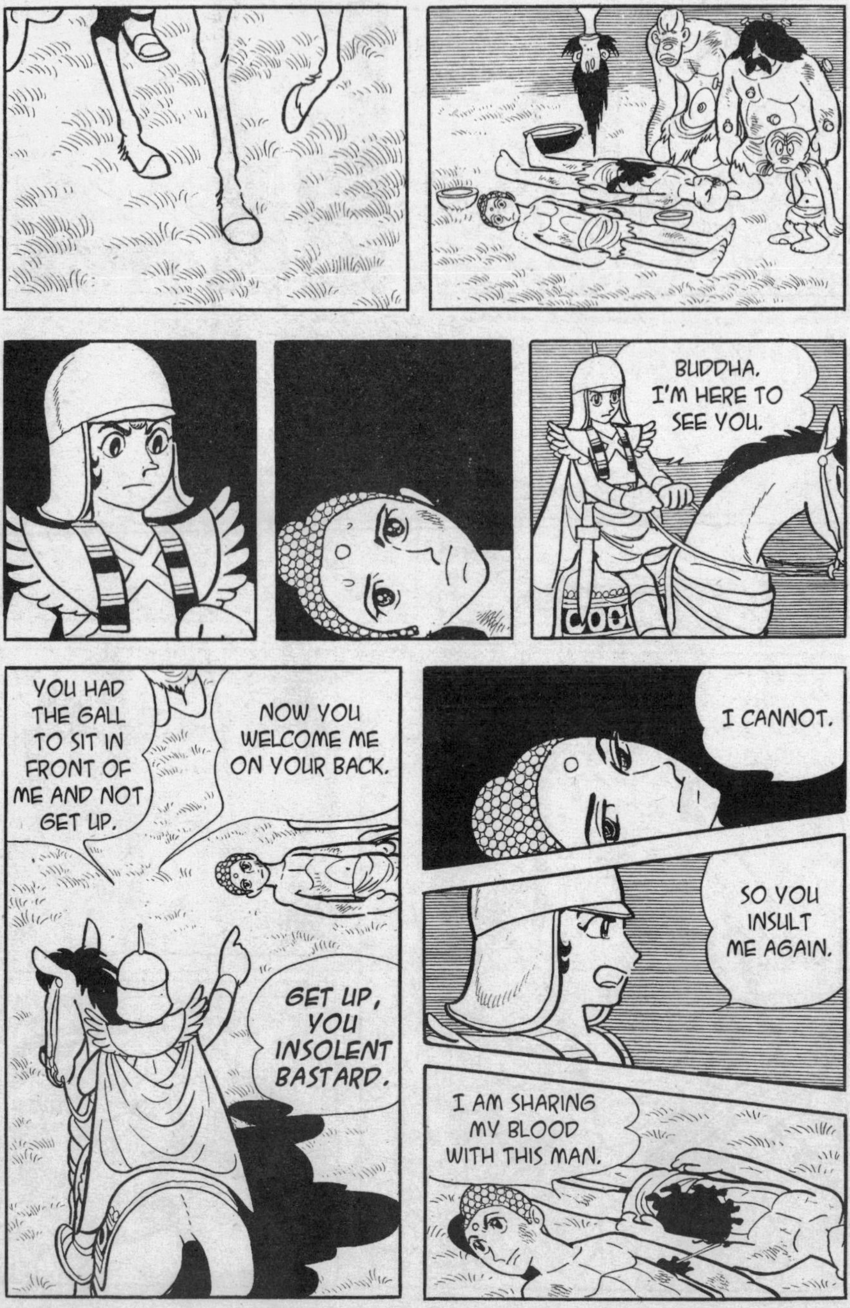
BUDDHA. I'M HERE TO SEE YOU.
YOU HAD THE GALL TO SIT IN FRONT OF ME AND NOT GET UP.
NOW YOU WELCOME ME ON YOUR BACK.
GET UP, YOU INSOLENT BASTARD.
I CANNOT.
SO YOU INSULT ME AGAIN.
I AM SHARING MY BLOOD WITH THIS MAN.

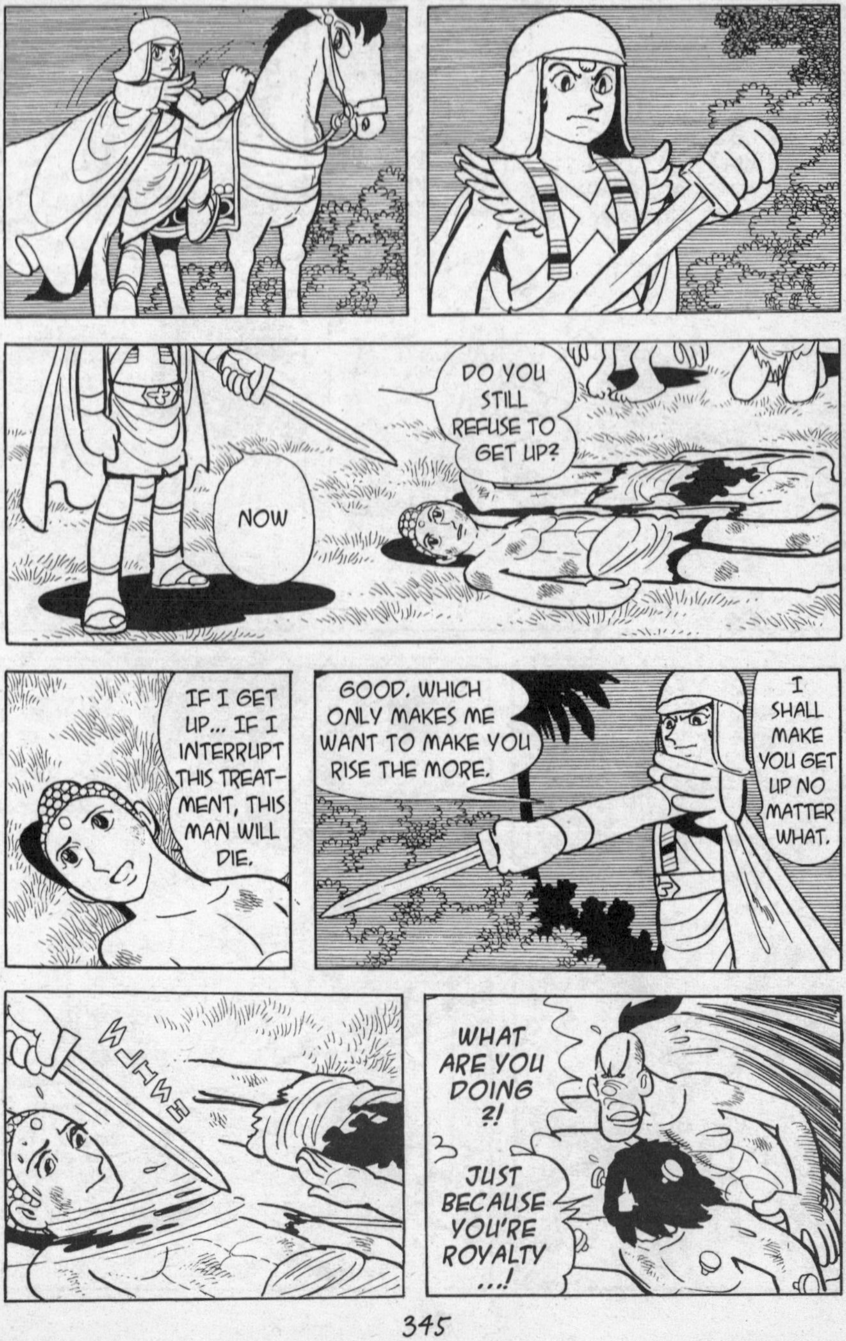
DO YOU STILL REFUSE TO GET UP?
NOW
IF I GET UP... IF I INTERRUPT THIS TREATMENT, THIS MAN WILL DIE.
GOOD. WHICH ONLY MAKES ME WANT TO MAKE YOU RISE THE MORE.
I SHALL MAKE YOU GET UP NO MATTER WHAT.
SWIP
WHAT ARE YOU DOING ?!
JUST BECAUSE YOU'RE ROYALTY ...!

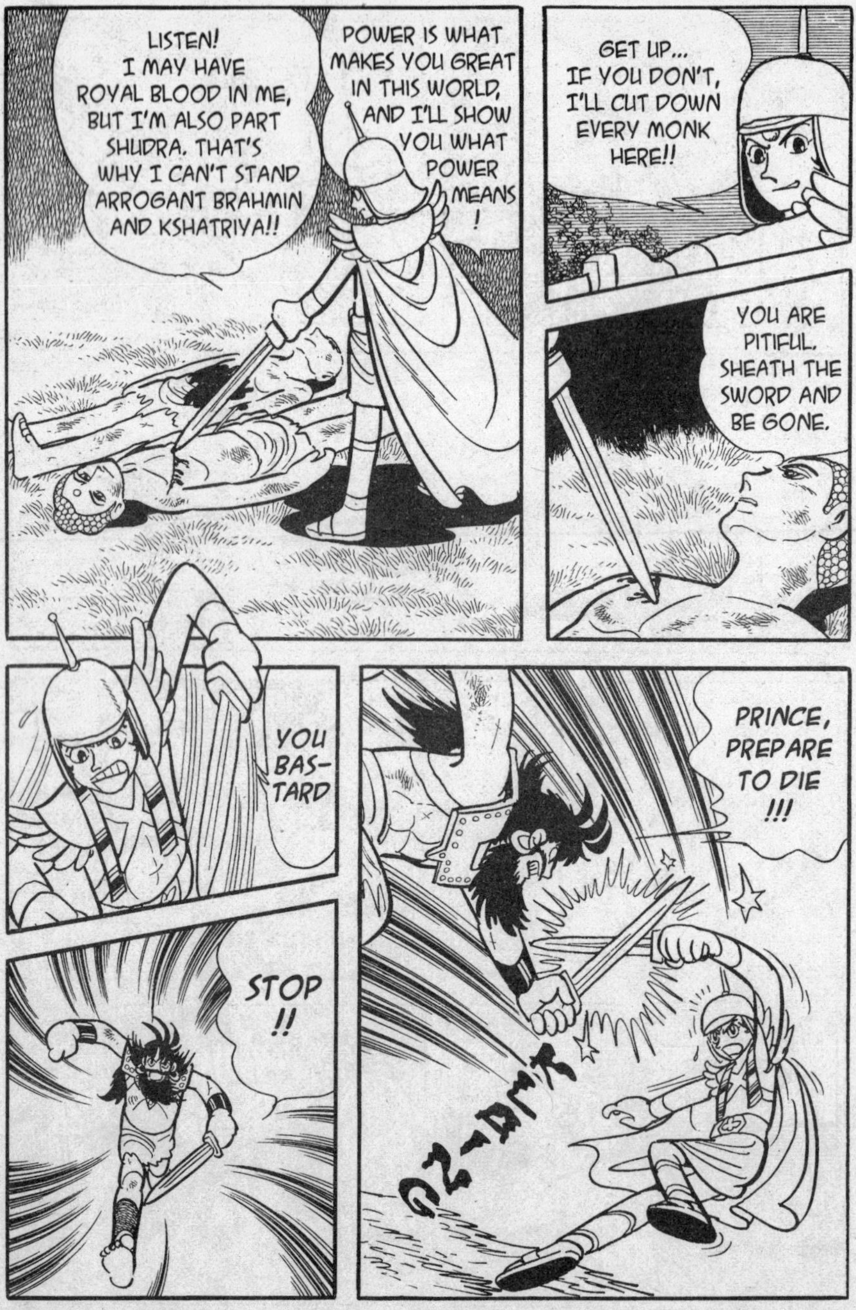

LISTEN! I MAY HAVE ROYAL BLOOD IN ME, BUT I'M ALSO PART SHUDRA. THAT'S WHY I CAN'T STAND ARROGANT BRAHMIN AND KSHATRIYA!!
POWER IS WHAT MAKES YOU GREAT IN THIS WORLD, AND I'LL SHOW YOU WHAT POWER MEANS!
GET UP... IF YOU DON'T, I'LL CUT DOWN EVERY MONK HERE!!
YOU ARE PITIFUL. SHEATH THE SWORD AND BE GONE.
YOU BAS-TARD
STOP!!
PRINCE, PREPARE TO DIE!!!

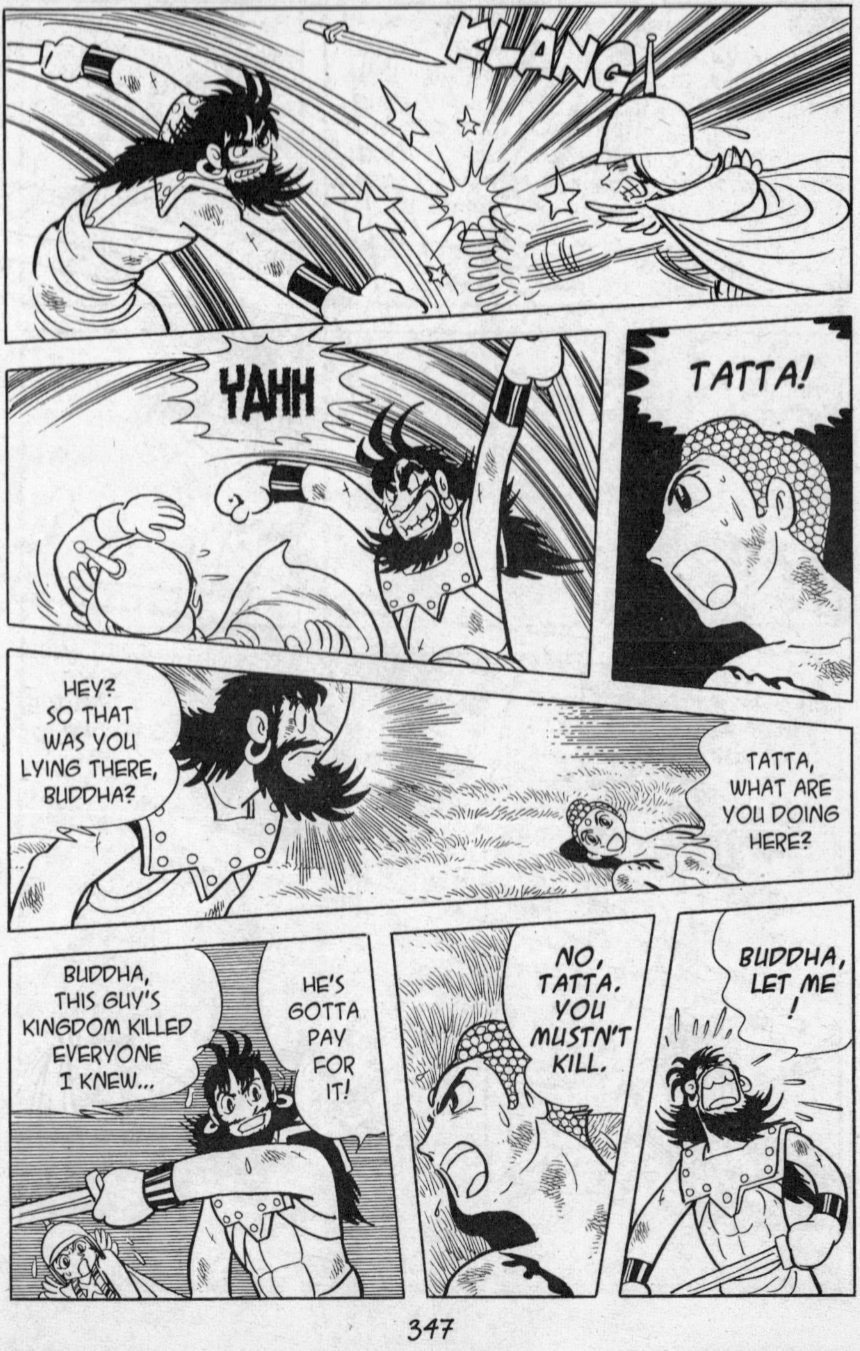
KLANG
YAHH
TATTA!
HEY? SO THAT WAS YOU LYING THERE, BUDDHA?
TATTA, WHAT ARE YOU DOING HERE?
BUDDHA, THIS GUY'S KINGDOM KILLED EVERYONE I KNEW...
HE'S GOTTA PAY FOR IT!
NO, TATTA. YOU MUSTN'T KILL.
BUDDHA, LET ME!

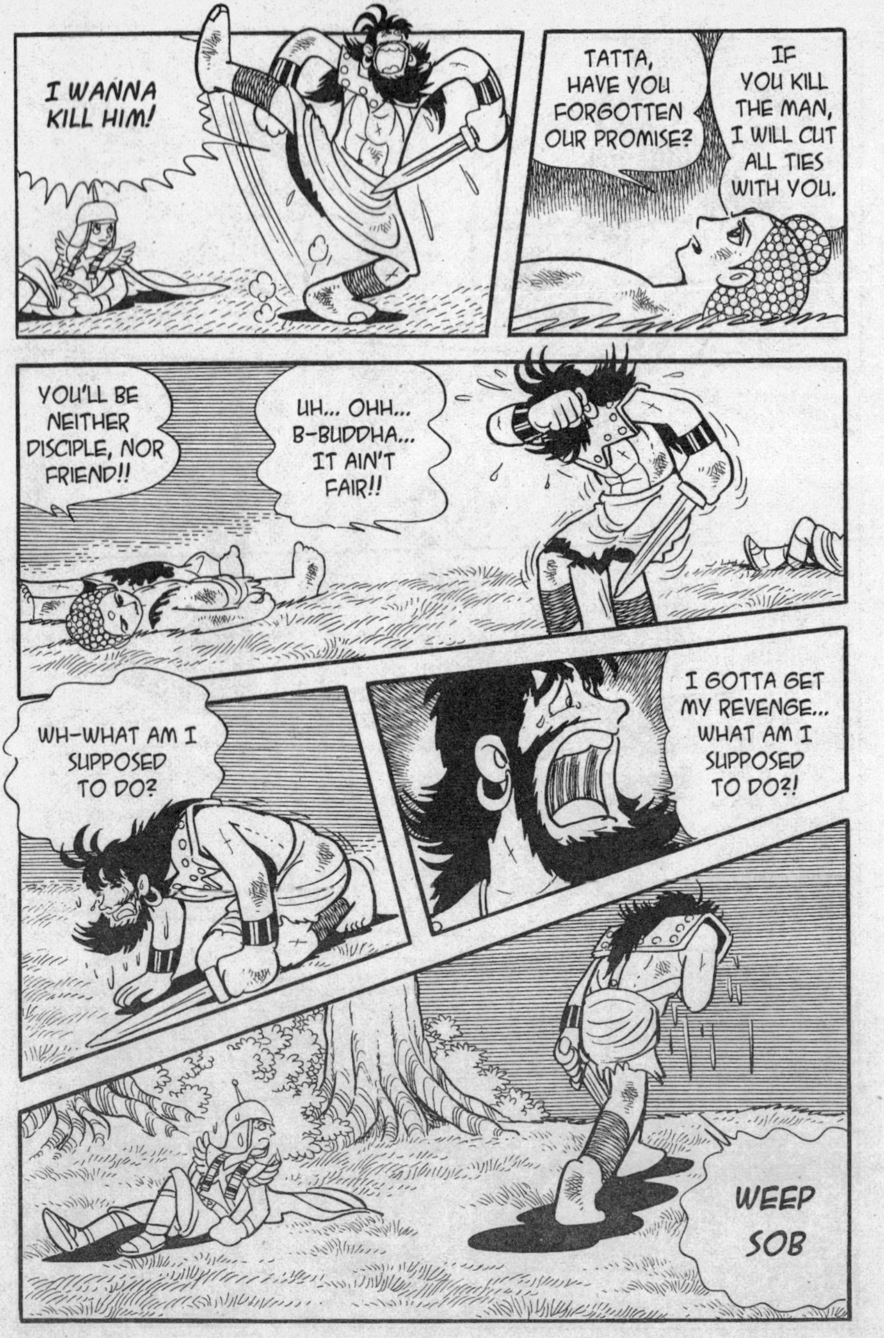
I WANNA KILL HIM!
TATTA, HAVE YOU FORGOTTEN OUR PROMISE?
IF YOU KILL THE MAN, I WILL CUT ALL TIES WITH YOU.
YOU'LL BE NEITHER DISCIPLE, NOR FRIEND!!
UH... OHH... B-BUDDHA... IT AIN'T FAIR!!
WH-WHAT AM I SUPPOSED TO DO?
I GOTTA GET MY REVENGE... WHAT AM I SUPPOSED TO DO?!
WEEP
SOB

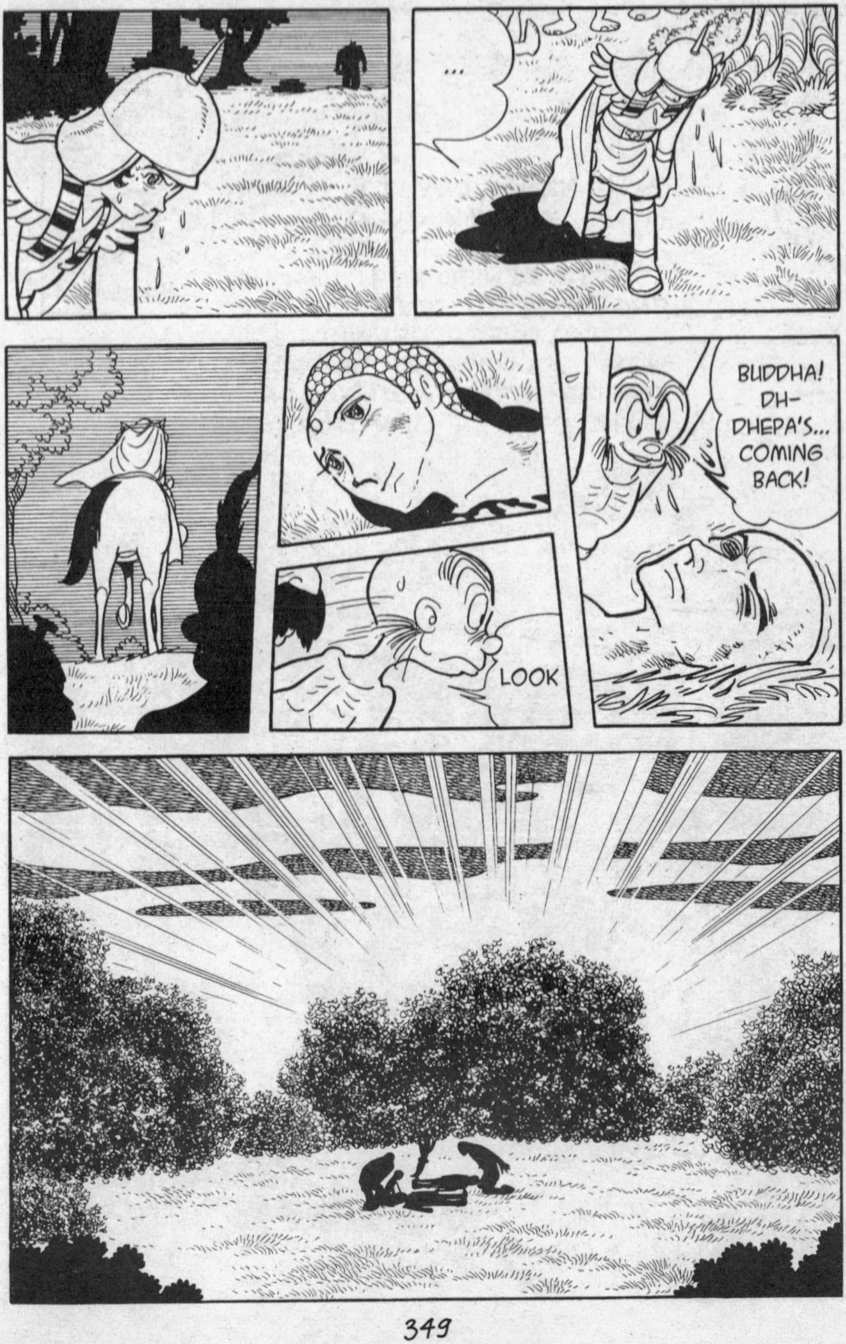
...
BUDDHA! DH-DHEPA'S... COMING BACK!
LOOK

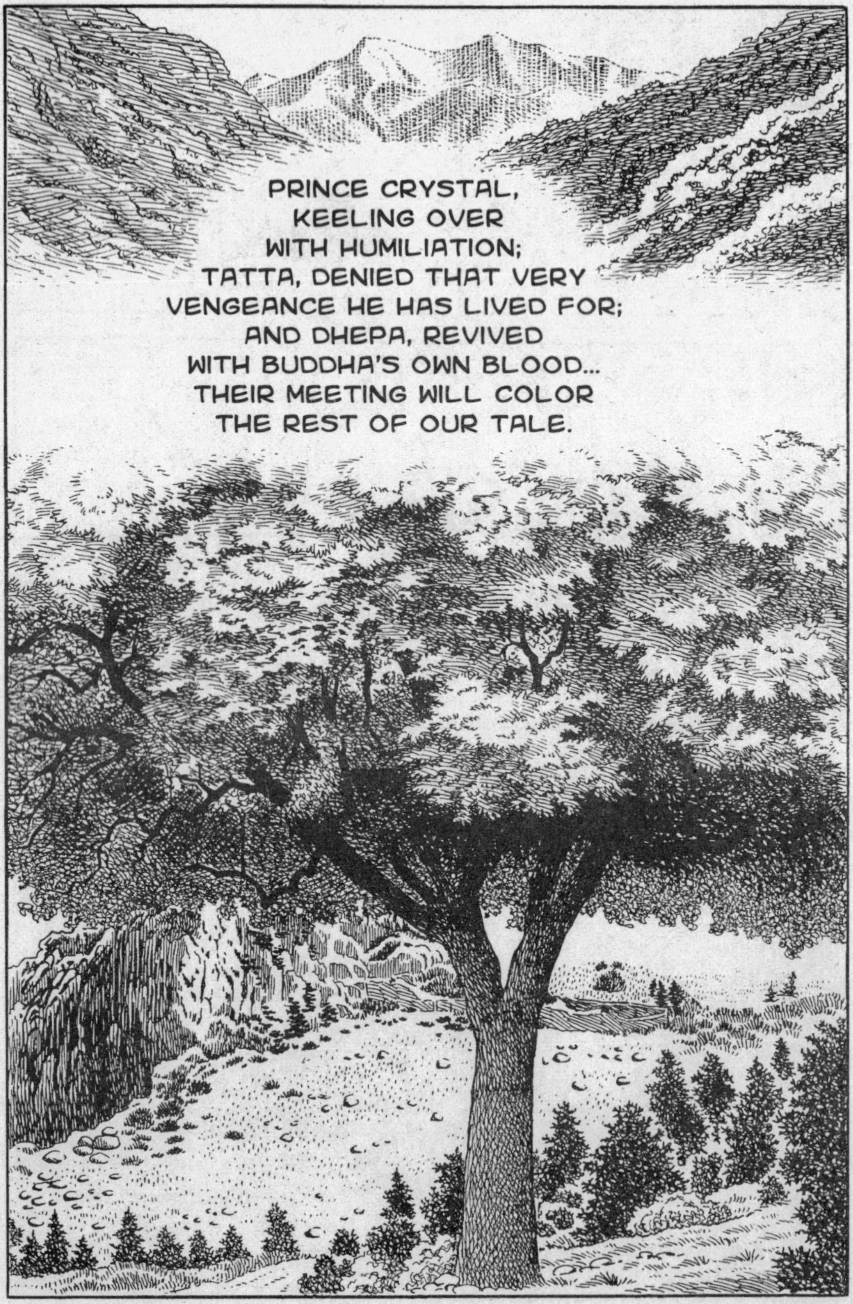
PRINCE CRYSTAL, KEELING OVER WITH HUMILIATION; TATTA, DENIED THAT VERY VENGEANCE HE HAS LIVED FOR; AND DHEPA, REVIVED WITH BUDDHA'S OWN BLOOD... THEIR MEETING WILL COLOR THE REST OF OUR TALE.

TO BE CONTINUED...

ENJOYED THIS BOOK? WHY NOT TRY OTHER BUDDHA TITLES BY OSAMU TEZUKA – AT 10% OFF! FREE POSTAGE AND PACKING IN THE UK.

☐ **Kapilavastu** 0 00 722451 6   £10.00
☐ **The Four Encounters** 0 00 722452 4   £10.00
☐ **Devatta** 0 00 722453 2   £10.00
☐ **The Forest of Uruvela** 0 00 722454 0   £10.00
☐ **Deer Park** 0 00 722455 9   £10.00   Total cost _____
☐ **Ananda** 0 00 722456 7   £10.00   10% discount _____
☐ **Prince Ajatasattu** 0 00 722457 5   £10.00
☐ **Jetavana** 0 00 722458 3   £10.00   Final total _____

To purchase by Visa/Mastercard/Switch simply call
08707 871724 or fax on 08707 871725

To pay by cheque, send a copy of this form with a cheque made payable to 'HarperCollins Publishers' to: Mail Order Dept. (Ref: BOB4), HarperCollins Publishers, Westerhill Road, Bishopbriggs, G64 2QT, making sure to include your full name, postal address and phone number.

From time to time HarperCollins may wish to use your personal data to send you details of other HarperCollins publications and offers. If you wish to receive information on other HarperCollins publications and offers please tick this box ☐

Do not send cash or currency. Prices correct at time of press. Prices and availability are subject to change without notice. Delivery overseas and to Ireland incurs a £2 per book postage and packing charge.